OFFICIAL RECORDS

OF THE

UNION AND CONFEDERATE NAVIES

IN THE

WAR OF THE REBELLION.

I0652058

PUBLISHED UNDER THE DIRECTION OF

The Hon. EDWIN DENBY, Secretary of the Navy,

BY

Colonel HARRY KIDDER WHITE, U. S. M. C.,
Superintendent, Office Naval Records and Library.

SERIES II—VOLUME 3.

Proclamations, Appointments, etc., of President Davis.
State Department Correspondence with Diplomatic Agents, etc.

WILDSIDE PRESS

No. 17.]   CONFEDERATE STATES COMMERCIAL AGENCY,
London, January 17, 1863.

SIR: I have the honor to acknowledge the receipt of your dispatch No. 2, dated 4th November, 1862, and also, through Mr. Mason, Treasury drafts on Messrs. Fraser, Trenholm & Co., Liverpool, for £232 and £185.11.4, respectively, the same being the amount of my salary and contingent allowance, as fixed by you in your No. 1, for the term of four and a half months ending April 1, 1863. I am also in receipt of your private letter enclosing a communication to the President from Ship Island, which, in accordance with your instructions, I have caused to be published in the Index and also in the Morning Herald. Please accept my thanks for the terms of encouragement in which you speak of my labors, and the kind reference to the Index. If any of my later communications have been received since the date of your dispatch, you will have seen how rapidly and yet how gradually these labors have extended over a larger field, and my demands upon the support of the Department have in consequence become greater.

My plan has been to abstain from attempting to do too much at once, but as soon as one position was secured to use it for attaining another. Thus the establishment of an organ was at one time the great end, but when established it became the means to carry out other plans. Compared with the difficulties, to a stranger especially, of the first enterprise, all subsequent difficulties seem trifling. The task before me was to make that organ in appearance and contents acceptable to English ideas. Even with a large circle of European acquaintance, it was not an easy matter to improvise a staff of correspondents and contributors, and for a time I found myself in the position of the leader of an orchestra who has himself to play every instrument. Mr. Spence's support upon which I had much counted, failed me after the third number, constant and regular literary labor being, as he frankly told me, incompatible with his tastes and with his other pursuits. It was essential to avoid the great error of American journalism, that of mistaking forcible words for forcible ideas, and to draw a marked contrast between the Index and the popular idea of an American paper. The tone of studied moderation which this imposed upon me was mistaken by many of our countrymen for lukewarmness, timidity, or lack of spirit, and I thus lost much of Southern talent which might have been made available. Battling on with no other aid than my able assistant Mr. Hopkins, and an amanuensis, my eyes having commenced to give way, a few months sufficed to place the Index in a position of respectability which enabled me to select from among the professional talent of the English press such assistance as I could pay for. Now the Index ceased to be the sole end and became a means, the efficiency of which was limited only by the extent of my pecuniary ability to make it available.

When in Richmond Mr. Hunter had informed me that the commissioners then in Europe suggested the appropriation of a fund for paying writers. I agreed with Mr. Hunter that the judicious disposal of such a fund was of extreme delicacy and difficulty to a diplomatic personage. But here was the agency for its distribution. Honorable men might honorably take their customary fee for the labor of their brains performed for me, and the ideas and information thus naturally engrafted would bear fruit many fold and on many different trees. That they have thus borne fruit I hope at some future time and through safer channels to prove to you by abundant evidence. The money which my friends have freely and without expectation of return contributed to the Index could not last forever. Deeming the services of the paper cheaply purchased at that price, I felt myself warranted to give for the first six months £15 per week toward its support, and as its necessities required it £20 per week for the next six months, subject, of course, to your approval, which could not be obtained before I was required to act. So large a subsidy will not, I believe, be permanently necessary, as there are promises of a satisfactory increase in the earnings of the paper, which on the conclusion of peace will probably approach much nearer to its expenses. The Index, you will readily perceive could not be managed like an ordinary financial speculation, as its commercial interests had necessarily to be rigidly subordinated to the political effect sought to be produced. This and the lack of adequate capital to begin with accounts for the heavy expenditure which is still necessary to keep it alive. Yet, considering all the circumstances and comparing the Index with other English papers of the same grade, I have reason to congratulate myself on having succeeded so well with so little.

While I have thus exceeded for one object alone the entire amount of my allowance, I can not altogether confine my expenses to that object. Occasions frequently occur when the disbursement of a small sum may directly or indirectly benefit the cause, and I have little fear that in each of the cases where I have already done so you will, on knowing the circumstances, grant your approval. It is impossible for lack of time to send you by this opportunity my accounts for the year in proper form. I shall endeavor to do so by the next regular mail to Nassau or Bermuda. To one class of necessary expenses not intended to be included in my contingent allowance, I wish to direct your especial attention. Applications are constantly being made to me, or referred to me by Mr. Mason, for assistance to destitute and distressed seamen. Even where the worthiness of the objects was questionable I have, with Mr. Mason's concurrence, always granted such assistance to the full extent of the law, and sometimes when the reasons oppeared sufficient, even a little beyond its strict letter. The sums thus expended for board, clothing, transportation, etc., have reached a considerable amount. In my No. 8 I informed you of the generous donation of Mrs. Brewer, of Mobile, of £50 for such purpose. There is still a small remnant of that sum left in my hands, but I have thought proper to confine the distribution of this gift to such cases where a moral and not a legal claim existed, or where the legal claim was clearly insufficient.

Since my last writing, December 20, the news of great events has reached us. Our glorious victory at Fredericksburg was received with undisguised satisfaction by the press and people. There was, however, great danger that the public impatience would once more be lulled by the hope of a speedy natural close of the war. This delusion is sedulously fostered by the Government to excuse its own supineness. Whenever the tide of victory is in our favor and per contra, when reverses befall us the country is bidden to wait for a more opportune time. I have of course embraced every occasion for emphatic contradiction, both in person and through the organ at my command. More than I could have accomplished has been done by Mr. Lincoln's emancipation proclamation, which really appears to have awakened the fears of both Government and people. The press, with the exception of the Daily News, the subsidized organ of the Federal Government, and the Star, Mr. Bright's mouthpiece, neither of which have any influence except among the lower orders, the press has been unanimous and even vehement in its condemnation. I enclose as useful for republication by our press, the comments of the leading papers, directing your special attention to the article from the Post, being Lord Palmerston's organ. A very remarkable article has also appeared in the Times, which is reproduced in No. 37 of the Index, accompanying, and which I also enclose in a slip. This article has attracted much attention, but our friends are disposed to attach more importance than I do to the utterances of this most changeful and unreliable of journals. It has, however, a certain significance as an answer to a very effective pamphlet recently addressed to the "Women of England" by Mrs. Beecher Stowe. A far more important reply has just been published, the letter of Archbishop Whately, of Dublin, the celebrated churchman, logician, and rhetorician, to Mrs. Beecher Stowe, which has produced a considerable impression from its authorship. By singular good fortune the letter was first placed in my hands by a Mr. O'Reagan, who signs himself " C. S. A.," and who I believe is a relation of either the archbishop or his chaplain, for publication in the Index after it should have been published in some neutral paper of my choice. The disposal of such an editorial treasure enabled me to make some capital with the paper to which I gave it.

The following is a memorandum of my conversation with the editor of the Post, Mr. Bothwick, who is known to enjoy both a social and political intimacy with Lord Palmerston. "The war will now soon be over." "I believe not," replied I, "without foreign recognition it may last, or at least linger on, for five years." "True," he said, "but heretofore the French have been knocking at Lord Russell's door every week, and were always told ' wait for the next mail.' Now the cabinet have all the information they waited for, and they expect nothing more. Their mind is made up." "Will they meet Parliament with a proposal to recognize us?" "On this I am not prepared now to reply categorically. If you see me next Wednesday (21st instant) I may possibly be able to give you some important information which you will be glad to hear." "Will recognition end the war, do you think?" "I am firmly convinced that it will and that nothing else can." "Will recognition be accepted by your people as a sufficient guarantee of peace to induce them to sow cotton?" "I believe it will be so received, and if accorded in time for the planting season, which ends in April, will have the desired effect."

The battle of Murfreesboro is generally regarded as a Confederate victory. The proclamation of the President in retaliation of Butler's outrages receives severe comments in the press. You will see in No. 38 of the Index the line of defense I have adopted. In the same number will also be found the French Emperor's speech so far as it relates to our affairs. A new daily paper has been established in London, the Iron Times, which takes a view of American affairs favorable to our immediate recognition. The abolition societies of Exeter Hall lament the defection of many of their shining lights. Mr. Buxton, for instance, whose letter appears in No. 36 of the Index, and the organs of that school deplore the dying out in England of the sacred flame of freedom which once burned so brightly and fiercely. In this connection I may mention, on the authority of Mr. Gladstone, from whose own lips I have it, that the bishop of Oxford, the son of Wilberforce, is warmly in favor of the recognition of the South. Three pamphlets have just appeared, urging recognition, each on distinct grounds, one by the pen of a gentleman whom I trust you will shortly see in Richmond as the correspondent of the Morning Herald.

Parliament meets for dispatch of business on the 5th of February, a little earlier than had been anticipated.

Upon the whole the indications on the horizon of public opinion are more favorable than at any time since I have had the honor to report to you, and I am encouraged to believe that the new year, so auspiciously begun, will not close ere our bleeding country reposes in peace and acknowledged independence.

I have the honor to remain, sir, very respectfully, your obedient servant.

HENRY HOTZE.

Hon. J. P. BENJAMIN,
   Secretary of State, Richmond.

No. 7.]
               DEPARTMENT OF STATE,
               Richmond, January 17, 1863.

SIR: I owe you acknowledgment of receipt of a large number of dispatches, being from No. 12 to No. 35, both inclusive, with the exception of No. 32, which has not yet been received.

I would have made earlier acknowledgment, if your dispatches had required action, but as they were confined to an exposition of your views of the condition of public opinion and the drift of affairs in Europe, I was compelled on the sudden and rare occasions which presented themselves for correspondence to give preference to our business in England and France, where extensive interests of our different departments required constant supervision. Your Nos. 27 and 28 in relation to the mission confided to you in Copenhagen were received, respectively, on the 24th and 31st ultimo. Your Nos. 33, 34, and 35 (the last dated on 18th December), were received on 16th instant.

I have the whole series of your dispatches complete, except the first seven, which were never received, and No. 32, which I have no doubt will reach me by one of the steamers daily arriving from Nassau.

I send herewith duplicate of my No. 3, which you state has failed to reach you, and which will complete your files, and have to request duplicates of your first seven numbers for the regularity of the files of the Department. While your views of the state of public affairs and the motives and conduct of the different cabinets, so far as they relate to the contest on this side, are read with great interest, they have caused no small perplexity from the entire discordance between your views as to the motives and policy of the two great western powers and those presented by our agents at Paris and London. Both Mr. Slidell and Mr. Mason are entirely convinced of the hearty sympathy of the Emperor and of his desire to give it active expression, as well as of the opposite feeling and tendency in the cabinet of St. James, while your representations are just the reverse. We shall be glad, however, at all times to have your own impressions as aids to the formation of conclusions which it is not always easy to reach even under the most favorable circumstances. In our case the difficulty is greatly aggravated by the precarious and interrupted communication between Richmond and Europe and by the perversion of facts so prevalent in Northern journalism that we can not rely on them even for a fair abstract of the news received by the steamers.

It is gratifying to me to inform you of the satisfaction of the President with the result of your mission to Denmark and to learn that there is no danger of any unfriendly complications with that power on the subject of your special mission there. Nothing less was expected of that enlightened cabinet, but it is none the less gratifying to find how frank, cordial, and unhesitating were the assurances you received from Mr. Hall.

The President is fully sensible of the generous and independent course adopted by his Belgium Majesty in his recent correspondence with the French Emperor and in his interviews with the British Queen; his earnest and urgent autograph appeal to the former has been communicated to us from another source and merits our warm and sincere acknowledgment. On conference with the President, however, I find that he entertains doubts which can not easily be removed as to the propriety of the course suggested by you of sending to you a special commission as envoy extraordinary and minister plenipotentiary to that court. His principal objection seems to consist in the unwillingness to set the example at the very outset of our career of establishing our foreign intercourse on a scale of useless prodigality. A diplomatic agent of such high grade at the court of Brussels would render necessary a like agency at all other European courts of the same dignity, under penalty of giving offense or at least ground for misconstruction and complaint. It is believed that the United States has never had an agent at that court of higher grade than minister resident. Under the circumstances it seems more proper, as well as more just to yourself, not to change your present position as commissioner, as the President will thus have it in his power to assign to you after our recognition, at some one of the continental courts, a position with such grade as would be agreeable to yourself, while at present it would not be expedient to send you a commission of higher grade than minister resident for the Belgian court.

We trust that our early general recognition can not now long be delayed, and the President's message now forwarded to you is but a faint expression of the public feeling which is becoming greatly irritated at what is deemed the unjust and unfair conduct of foreign

powers toward us under circumstances which ought to have secured for us a neutrality something more than nominal.
I am respectfully, your obedient servant,

J. P. BENJAMIN,
Secretary of State.

Hon. A. DUDLEY MANN, etc.,
Brussels.

DEPARTMENT OF STATE,
Richmond, January 19, 1863.

SIR: I have to acknowledge the receipt of your letter (without date, but accompanying a note from Mr. Slidell of the 28th of September, 1862) relative to a concession for the exclusive privilege of laying telegraph cables on the seacoast of the Confederate States with a view to establishing communication with Europe.

In reply I have to inform you that it is deemed premature to entertain such proposals at this time, but that when peace shall be restored they will meet with due consideration.

I am, sir, etc.,

J. P. BENJAMIN,
Secretary of State.

HENRY COOK, Esq.,
25 Sunderland Terrace, Westbourne Park, London.

No. 24.]   PARIS, *January 21, 1863.*

SIR: The address of the Emperor at the opening of the Chambers has realized the hope which I expressed in my dispatch of 11th instant. You will of course have seen long before this will reach you that portion of it which relates to our affairs, but as in all probability you will not have the French text, to correct any error or unfaithfulness of translation I transcribe it:

[Translation.]

The indirect revenues increase steadily by the simple fact of the growth and general prosperity, and the situation of the Empire would be flourishing if the war in America had not exhausted one of the most fruitful of our industries.

The forced stagnation of the work has caused at several points misery worthy of all our solicitude, and a loan will be asked of you to help those who bear resignedly the effects of a misfortune which it is not in our power to prevent. However, I have attempted to reach them on the other side of the Atlantic with advice inspired by sincere sympathy, but the great maritime powers not having thought themselves yet able to join me I have been obliged to postpone to a more propitious season the mediation which had for its object the checking of bloodshed and the prevention of the devastation of a country whose future should not be indifferent to us.

You will find in it a very distinct intimation that the Emperor has not abandoned the idea of proffering a mediation, and is only awaiting a more favorable opportunity. I also send you herewith so much of the " Exposé de la situation de l'Empire" as applies to foreign affairs and to commerce. This is a document annually submitted to the Chambers, and is an authoritative exposition of the policy and action of the Government past and prospective. It fully confirms my interpretation of the Emperor's address. In my last I sent you a copy of a memorandum which I had submitted to the Emperor, through his private secretary M. [Constant] Mocquard. I have since seen that gentleman, who informs me that it had been favorably received by the Emperor. I also send you a copy of the letter of instructions from the Emperor to General [Elie Frederic] Forey, commander in chief of the Mexican expedition, in which you will find a development of his ideas which will not be gratifying to the Washington Government. I regret that I have no opportunity of sending you a copy of the "Documents Diplomatiques, 1862," presented to the Chambers, but hope that the consul at Richmond will receive one, which he will of course put at your disposition. On the 18th November, M. Drouyn de Lhuys wrote to M. Mercier, informing him of the refusal of the cabinets of London and St. Petersburg to adhere to the proposition of his letter of 28th October. I give you the closing paragraph:

But it is well that it should be known in the United States that our dispositions have not changed, and that if it should appear that our good offices could be usefully invoked they would not be refused. Explain yourself then frankly and in a manner to be understood by everybody about you that the Government of the Emperor will always be happy to have in its power to contribute to the pacification of a friendly people at any moment and upon any conditions, either alone or, as was proposed, with the concurrence of Great Britain and Russia or with that of any other power that may be called to this work of humanity and good policy.

On the 30th ultimo M. de Persigny spoke to me with great earnestness and in much detail of his views of the best mode of bringing about a settlement of our affairs. His plan was that the belligerents should be invited to have a conference on the basis of an attempt to reconstruct the Union or, if that were not practicable, for a peaceable separation. I expressed very freely my dissent from his opinion and said that the measure was not a practical one, would be barren of results, and would have no other tendency than to postpone the only measure which we desired—our recognition. I saw him on the 9th instant, when he again alluded to the matter, but without insisting on it, as he had done at our previous interview. Yesterday there appeared in the Constitutionnel, a semiofficial organ, an article "en entrefilet" in large characters and signed by the principal editor, giving almost textually the ideas and arguments on the subject of a conference which M. Persigny had presented to me three weeks since. I enclose a copy. I immediately called both on M. Persigny and the editor, and found that the article had been published at the instance of the minister of foreign affairs, who had favorably received the suggestion of M. Persigny, which had also been approved of by the Emperor. In consequence by the last steamer a dispatch was sent to M. Mercier directing him to submit such a proposition to the Lincoln Government, accompanied by the most energetic and urgent appeal to put a stop to the effusion of blood, with an intimation that if the appeal were not successful a recognition of the Confederate States would no longer be withheld. Mr. Persigny tells me that Mr. Dayton was informed of the instructions given to M. Mercier and did not make any formal or serious objection to them.

Mr. F. S. Claxton ex-United States consul at Moscow, sends me for transmission a plan of his invention for the reinforcing of cast-iron guns, which on trial at the Government arsenal at Ruelle, has been attended with excellent results. He requests me to say that the name of Mr. L. W. Broadwell should have been connected with his in the offer he made some time since, of the gratuitous use of the breech-loading gun and carbine.

You will be gratified to learn that within the last six or eight months there has been an immense change of public opinion to our advantage; those who were then either indifferent or lukewarm have become our warm partisans, while the greater part of those who sympathized with the North, now freely admit that they had not understood the question and acknowledge their error. I may safely assert that the sentiment of the intelligent classes is nearly unanimous in our favor.

With great respect, your most obedient servant,

JOHN SLIDELL.

Hon. J. P. BENJAMIN,
  Secretary of State.

DEPARTMENT OF STATE,
Richmond, January 22, 1863.

DEAR SIR: I cheerfully comply with your request to put in writing the suggestions made to you on the subject of a national seal and the device for our national coin, and our coinage, weights, and measures.

SEAL.

I propose for our seal "a cavalier." Let it be copied from our equestrian statue of the noblest cavalier of the South. A copy of Washington, as mounted on his charger on the monument in Capitol Square.

The reasons which recommend the choice of this device are:

First. It is simple, noble, and striking. It is equally applicable to the whole Confederacy. We are a people of horsemen.

Second. A horseman has always been considered as typical of man's noblest conquest of the brute creation; of the superiority of reason and intellect over mere brute strength.

Third. In its moral attributes the device of a cavalier does just honor to our people. The cavalier or knight is typical of chivalry, bravery, generosity, humanity, and other knightly virtues. Cavalier is synonymous with gentlemen in nearly all the modern languages. Cavalier in French, caballero in Spanish, cavaliere in Italian, all mean not only horseman, but gentleman, knight.

Fourth. The word cavalier is eminently suggestive of the origin of Southern society, as used in contradistinction to Puritan. The Southerners remain what their ancestors were, gentlemen. The seal will typify this fact.

Fifth. A national device, legend, or motto to crown the seal may readily be found for the cavalier. I give two or three; I prefer the second.

" Sans peur et sans reproche."
" Respublicae praesidium et dulce decus."
" Pro aris et focis militare paratus," etc.

COINS.

An English pound or sovereign is equal to 25 French francs. The fractional difference is so minute that in issuing national bonds they are given for £100, or for francs 2,500, at the choice of the buyers.

Keeping this fact in view, I propose that the Government issue a $5 gold coin of the exact value of the English sovereign. I would call this coin a cavalier.

Exact dollar should be one-fifth of the cavalier, and would therefore be equal exactly to the French 5-franc piece.

By this means our coin would be instantly convertible into English and French coin without appreciable fractions.

English pound equal to 1 cavalier, English shilling equal to one-quarter of a dollar, English penny equal to 2 cents; French napoleon of 20 francs equal to $4, piece of 5 francs equal to $1, piece of 1 franc equal to 20 cents. Our cavalier and dollar would be worth, respectively, about 3 per cent less than the United States "half eagle and dollar."

We would thus make it necessary to calculate exchange between the currency of the United States and our own, creating an embarrassment to direct commerce with them, while relieving our direct commerce with Europe of a similar embarrassment.

Not a slight recommendation for the name of our new gold coin would be the facility for understanding and translating it in foreign countries.

Our golden cavalier would be: In French, cavalier d'or; in Spanish, caballero d'oro; in Italian, cavaliere d'oro.

We would have $10 and $20 pieces called double cavaliers and quadruple cavaliers.

WEIGHTS AND MEASURES.

It does not seem to me advisable at present to touch the weights and measures with which our people are familiar and which correspond in great degree to those used in England, with which nation our commercial relations will be very extensive.

It is true that the present system is so very confused and defective that it would perhaps be more correct to say that we have no system at all.

But the only perfect decimal metrical system now existing is the French, and it is so foreign to the customs and habits of our people that its adoption would be attended with extreme practical difficulty, and would only place us in accord with that nation while disturbing our commerce with another whose relations with us will be at least as extensive.

This subject now occupies public attention in England, and would be much better regulated hereafter in concert with that power than now by independent legislation.

I am, yours, very truly,

J. P. BENJAMIN.

Hon. C. C. CLAY,
Confederate States Senate.

No. 17.]   HAVANA, *January 26, 1863.*

SIR: I have the honor to inform you that the Confederate gunboat *Florida* arrived in this port at 8 o'clock p. m., of the 20th instant, and ran immediately into the harbor; that Captain Maffitt, without waiting the visit of the health officer, with his first lieutenant, landed and came to my residence; that I went with them to the city, and before 12 o'clock had purchased his coal and made every arrangement, except the permit of the captain of the port, for his taking on board everything he required; that early the next morning I called on the captain of the port, made such apology as I thought honorable and dignified for the two breaches of the rules of the port, i. e., the entering of the harbor after sundown, and the landing before the surgeon's visit, which proved entirely satisfactory, and obtained the orders for coaling the steamer. At sunset the *Florida* was ready for sea, but Captain Maffitt preferred to remain until daylight the next morning, which he did, and then went to sea. After leaving Havana, I learn from reliable sources that the *Florida* captured and destroyed seven Federal vessels in forty-eight hours. It may be proper to remark in this connection that the Federal consul-general, Mr. Shufeldt, at 12 m. of the 21st instant, dispatched a steamer for Key West, and in the evening called on the captain-general and represented that she was a vessel of war, and asked that the *Florida* be detained in the port for twenty-four hours, which order the captain-general felt bound to give, but upon being informed that Mr. Shufeldt had deceived him in the character of the vessel he immediately canceled his order and left the *Florida* to sail under the permit given by the captain of the port.

It affords me great pleasure to add that the Spanish officials and merchants behaved with their usual courtesy and good feeling for us during the stay of the *Florida*. I have the honor to enclose herewith a dispatch for you from Mr. Slidell received open, under cover to me, on the 22d instant.

I have the honor to be, with great respect, your obedient servant.

CH. J. HELM.

Hon. J. P. BENJAMIN,
   Secretary of State, Richmond.

No. 38.]

                    23 RUE ROYALE, BRUSSELS, *January 29, 1863.*

SIR: My last note to Mr. Rogier, as you will have perceived before this if the copy of it which I transmitted to the department reached its destination, was dated on the 5th instant. Immediately thereafter, as I have now satisfactory reasons for believing, King Leopold renewed his exertions with increased energy to procure European recognition of the Confederate States. He made a fresh appeal to the Emperor of the French (whose interests, in common with those of Russia and England, he had been endeavoring to subserve in the Greek question) to take the initiative at once. This appeal succeeded only so far as to contribute to draw forth the instructions of Mr. Drouyn de Lhuys to Mr. Mercier, of the 9th instant, and with the implied understanding that, if those instructions failed in the attainment of the object desired, straight-out recognition should speedily ensue. We shall now soon ascertain whether the engagement will be complied with at the Tuileries. An answer from Mr. Mercier may be expected about the middle of February. It is already asserted somewhat semiofficially that Lincoln will accept the proposal. Good may come from the meeting of the commissioners of the belligerents, but I see not in what manner, since ours will be instructed to entertain no terms for a moment which do not place us upon an equality, as respects our independence, with the pseudo United States. Before this arrives at Richmond you will be in possession of the remarkable letter of Louis Napoleon to General Forey, revealing his purposes in regard to Mexico. The avowal therein made can not fail to create general uneasiness in the minds of our citizens.

Whatever his protestations hereafter to the contrary, it will be difficult for me to change the opinion which I have entertained for months, that his Imperial Majesty aims steadily at the restoration of Mexico as it was prior to the independence of Texas. In the event of his success an empire would be created whose crown would perhaps satisfy the ambition of Jerome Napoleon and remove that red republican prince definitely out of the way of the Prince Imperial, to the joy of the Emperor and Empress. You will have seen that a cordial reconciliation has just taken place between the two families, and it is presumable that this is the basis upon which it was predicated. In contemplation of the eventualities which they foreshadow, I trust our Government and our countrymen will ever have distinctly before their eyes the following words contained in the imperial letter to which I have adverted: "Melancholy experience now proves to us how precarious is the fate of that industry which is confined to one single source of supply to all the vicissitudes of which it is exposed. If, on the other hand, a stable Government be constituted in Mexico, with the assistance of France, we will have restored to the Latin race beyond the ocean its strength and prestige; we will have guaranteed security to our colonies in the Antilles and to those of Spain; we will have established our beneficent influence in the center of America, and this influence, in creating immense markets for our commerce, will procure for us the indispensable raw material of our industry."

Ferdinand of Portugal declined to yield to the entreaties of even his revered uncle to accept the crown of Greece. Failing in his effort, Leopold sent for his other nephew, Ernest, Duke of Saxe-Coburg-Gotha, to endeavor to induce him to accept. This prince has just left here; and it is understood that, if the protecting powers shall agree to certain conditions which he has proposed, he will repair to Athens.

I have the honor, etc.,

A. DUDLEY MANN.

Hon. J. P. BENJAMIN,
    Secretary of State, Richmond.

DEPARTMENT OF STATE,
Richmond, January 29, 1863.

DEAR SIR: Your favors of the 13th instant were received this morning, from which I regret to perceive that you had just cause to feel disappointed in the reception of remittances from the Government, and I at once called the attention of the President and Secretary of War to the subject. I am happy to inform you that a remittance of £75,000 will leave to-morrow morning for Liverpool (via New York) and will probably reach your house by the 20th February, and prompt measures will be taken for further payments.

I fully recognize the claim of your house on the consideration as well as justice of the Government, and had you addressed your communications directly to the Secretary of War (Hon. James A. Seddon) you would probably have received satisfactory remittances at an earlier date.

The cash purchases in Europe were made by a special agent of the Quartermaster's Bureau without the knowledge of the Secretary of War, and as Captain Huse was in the Ordnance Bureau, a sort of conflict or confusion of authority arose which will not be allowed again to occur, as the Secretary of War has promised me to place the whole matter on such footing as will obviate any future just grounds of complaint.

I am, etc.,

J. P. BENJAMIN,
Secretary of State.

BENJAMIN W. HART, Esq.,
Nassau, N. P.

No. 25.]

PARIS, *January 29, 1863.*

SIR: Since my last of 21st instant Mr. Drouyn de Lhuys has published the dispatch of Mr. Mercier in the Moniteur, of which I gave you the outlines. You will find a copy herewith.

I also send you copies of certain letters from the minister of marine in relation to shipments to be made by the house of Bellot des Minières Frères to Matamoras, the proceeds of which are to be returned in cotton. I consider these letters of great importance as indicating the policy and purpose of the Government in relation to the supply of cotton, and I take the liberty of suggesting the expediency of our Government giving such facilities and encouragement for furnishing ample supplies of cotton in the neighborhood of Matamoras as may not be inconsistent with military exigencies.

With great respect, your most obedient servant,

JOHN SLIDELL.

Hon. J. P. BENJAMIN,
Secretary of State.

I, John Vernon, of the city of London, duly admitted and sworn, practicing in the said city, do hereby certify and attest that the paper writings hereunto annexed contain true and faithful copies of four original documents in the French language unto the said notary produced and after due examination returned.

Whereof an act being required I, the said notary, have granted these presents under my notarial firm and seal, to serve and avail when and where need may require.

Done and passed in London the 27th day of January in the year of our Lord one thousand eight hundred and sixty three.

JOHN VERNON,
Notary Public.

MINISTRY OF MARINE, ETC.

Mr. VICE ADMIRAL: Messrs. Bellot des Minières, merchants in Paris, are now forwarding from Plymouth on a British vessel, British goods to the value of 10,000,000 francs, to be landed at Matamoras; they will there receive in exchange 100,000 cotton bales, to be shipped on that vessel to Havre. The government of Texas and the agents of Bellot des Minières have adopted the necessary measures to facilitate the transportation of the cotton to Matamoras.

The object of the present dispatch, which will be delivered to you by the principal agent of these merchants, is to call your attention to this important operation, the purpose of which is to aid our cotton industry.

I beg you, Mr. Vice Admiral, to give the necessary orders in furtherance of Colonels Bisbee and Scherry's views, the agents of Bellot des Minières, who desire that the goods above mentioned, forwarded in transit to Matamoras, should be exempt from entry duty.

I remain, sir, etc.,

Ct. CHASSELOUP-LAUBAT.

Vice Admiral JURIEN, etc.

MINISTRY OF MARINE, ETC.,
Paris, January 17, 1863.

SIR: In accordance with the desire expressed in your letter of 15th instant, I have the honor to enclose herewith a dispatch by me addressed to the admiral commanding the naval forces of the Mexican expedition, informing him of the important commercial transaction you are about undertaking at Matamoras, and inviting him to recommend Messrs. Bisbee and Scherry, your agents in that locality.

Receive, sir, the assurance, etc.,

Count CHASSELOUP-LAUBAT.

Mr. BELLOT DES MINIÈRES, etc.

MINISTRY OF MARINE, ETC.,
Paris, January 20, 1863.

SIR: As you have correctly understood it, it was through error that one vessel was mentioned for the shipment of the goods and the cotton you were to receive in return. It is clear that several vessels must be employed.

I remain, etc.,

Count CHASSELOUP-LAUBAT.

N. B.—The dispatch to the vice admiral was modified in consequence.

No. 28.]   CONFEDERATE STATES COMMISSION,
                                                    London, January 31, 1863.

SIR: I have a letter from M. Bellot des Minières, who has a contract with the War Department for furnishing certain supplies,
transmitting to me copies of an official correspondence addressed by
the minister of marine and of colonies to Admiral Jurien, commanding the French naval forces off Mexico, the substances of which M.
Bellot requests I should make known to the Government.

The minister of marine, under date the 17th and 20th of January,
advises the French admiral that certain vessels were sent by M.
Bellot from ports in England and France to Matamoras in Mexico,
and would return thence to Hâvre laden with cotton for account of
M. Bellot; and the minister recommends those vessels to the cognizance and protection, if necessary, of the French admiral.

M. Bellot further requests that I would invite the attention of the
Government to these facts as suggestive of any intervention on its
part to facilitate the movement of cotton to Matamoras, for transshipment thence; which I have the honor to do accordingly, and am,
        Very respectfully, your obedient servant,

                                                        J. M. MASON.

Hon. J. P. BENJAMIN,
        Secretary of State.

                                                        BRITISH CONSULATE,
                                                    Richmond, February 2, 1863.

SIR: I have the honor to acknowledge your dispatch of 31st ultimo,
acquainting me that it had pleased the President to communicate to
me the official notification received from Flag-Officer Ingraham of
the complete dispersion and disappearance of the blockading squadron off the harbor of Charleston in South Carolina, in consequence of
a successful attack made on it by him, rendering thereby that port
open once again, which information is given to me for the guidance
of such British vessels as may choose to carry on commerce with that
port.

I return my acknowledgments for the early participation of this
intelligence and,

I have the honor to be, sir, your most obedient, humble servant,
                                                        GEO. MOORE,
                                                                Consul.

Hon. J. P. BENJAMIN,
        Secretary of State,
            Department of State, Richmond.

                                            HOTEL DU RHIN, PLACE VENDOME,
                                                    Paris, February 3, 1862.

SIR: Mr. Rost informs me that in the course of a conversation
which he had the honor to hold with your Excellency on the 31
ultimo, in response to a suggestion made at my request that I desired to have an opportunity of presenting my respects to you, and
to an inquiry made by him, when and how I should address you for

that purpose, you intimated that although then unprepared to give any definite reply, a written communication from me to the effect above mentioned would receive your attention. I beg leave then in compliance with your intimation to Mr. Rost to say that I shall be most happy to have the honor to wait on your Excellency at such time and place as you may be pleased to indicate.

I have the honor to be, with the most distinguished consideration, your very obedient servant,

JOHN SLIDELL.

To his EXCELLENCY M. THOUVENEL,
Minister of Foreign Affairs, etc.

OFFICE OF THE MINISTER OF FOREIGN AFFAIRS,
February 3, 1862.

SIR: In response to the letter which you have addressed him, M. Thouvenel has charged me to make known to you that you will find him at home next Friday, February 7, at 2 o'clock.

Pray accept, sir, the assurances of my distinguished consideration.

F. BERTHEMY.

Mr. J. SLIDELL.

No. 29.] CONFEDERATE STATES COMMISSION,
London, February 5, 1863.

SIR: Since my No. 28 of the 31st of January, which goes with this, I learn that the ship intended to take it is yet detained. I am enabled thus to report to the Department two transactions in cotton made by Major Caleb Huse, C. S. Army, for account of the War Department the details of which will, of course, be reported by that officer to his superiors. The first, an engagement for the delivery of 2,300,000 pounds of cotton, to enable him to make purchases for his Department, then to be made on favorable terms, and much wanted; the second, a like engagement by the same officer for the delivery of 5,000,000 pounds of cotton at 5 pence sterling per pound, as payment pro tanto of indebtedness on his part for supplies purchased and shipped to the War Department, and which, as he showed to me, it was imperiously necessary to provide for.

In regard to both these transactions, I did no more than to endorse my approval of them on the certificates as commissioner of the Confederate States; in the first case being satisfied of the authority of Major Huse to make purchases of the character indicated; and of the necessity for such supplies; in the last case being equally satisfied from the correspondence of Major Huse with the War Department that they were aware of his having incurred a much larger indebtedness, which that Department had sought to provide for by remittances in Confederate bonds, but which bonds could not be used here just now.

In reference to the general subject of indebtedness here for account of the War and Navy Departments by their respective agents, I have felt it incumbent on me, though without express authority, under existing circumstances, to extend all aid in my power to those agents to enable them to meet their engagements, and thus to preserve, as of the last importance, the credit of the Government.

As you are probably aware, large remittances have recently been made, as well by the Treasury as by the War and Navy Departments, to their respective agents in England of Confederate bonds as well as of cotton certificates, in the form adopted by the Treasury Department. After their arrival, and after full consultation with the gentlemen to whom they were intrusted, it was deemed judicious not to put the cotton certificates, at least, upon the market, until we could learn the result of the proposals for a direct loan, which had been sent by a special messenger to Richmond by a banking house on the Continent; lest by doing so we might disturb the market on which those bankers relied to dispose of their loans. Thus, although at great inconvenience to existing engagements, no steps have been taken here in regard to disposing of the cotton certificates sent from the Treasury. The same reasons not applying to the Confederate money bonds, Mr. Spence, as financial agent, occupied himself in the proper form of enquiry as to disposing of them; but unfortunately, within the past two weeks, because of some disturbance of capital here, the rate of interest has been raised by the Bank of England from 3 per cent, at which it long stood, at first to 4, and afterwards to 5 per cent, at which latter rate it now is, but with general expectation of a yet further advance. Mr. Spence's enquiries, therefore, were un-satisfactory and so far fruitless. It was in this stagnation and difficulty that I felt called on to sanction the cotton operations above noted of Major Huse, the cases he presented being the most urgent.

I have deemed it proper to make this full report to you, although of matters pertaining to other Departments of the Government, and hope that my action in the premises will meet with approval.

Yesterday I learned by a note from Mr. Slidell that intelligence had just been received at Paris by the bankers in question, from Richmond, that the loan had been accepted by our Government to the extent of £2,000,000 sterling; the Government declining a larger amount, although proffered. We have as yet received no details, nor is it known when the money is to be available here.

It is assumed, however, that the loan will by no means yield its nominal amount, but whatever that may be I am disposed to think it will not be sufficient to meet engagements here existing and under orders that are prospective. Still, in the absence of full information, I am disposed to think it well that a larger amount was not taken on the French proposals, especially should it have been arranged for an enlargement of the loan if required.

I am still strongly of opinion that the true mode of raising money here will be found to be by prospective sales of cotton in the form, if not in the actual terms, prescribed by the cotton certificates from the Treasury, and although it may be that loss will result to the Government by the difference in price at which they purchase and sell, yet, regarding the state of exchange, and the heavy losses to be incurred in any negotiation of Confederate money bonds, I think that cotton will be found the best basis for supply. As I have said, we have not yet tested the market; but as there is a growing expectation here that a peace is impending these cotton certificates, I think, will improve in value, and as the prospect for peace increases of course that value augments.

In a communication from the Secretary of Treasury he informs me that he is actively at work purchasing cotton. I do not think a more effective measure could be adopted to strengthen the financial position of the Government. Cotton, as the property of the Government, will always be in Europe a sure basis of credit, so sure as to engage money on better terms than any other form of credit. In this connection and in regard to any future operations that may be required here I would suggest that I be kept informed from time to time (or by each dispatch) of the quantity of cotton actually possessed by the Government. Such inquiries are made of me and the information would be deemed valuable here in any cotton operation.

Mr. G. N. Sanders has not yet arrived, and thus I have not received cotton certificates which I am informed by the Secretary of the Treasury have been sent to me by him.

The last New York papers contain, published at length, various dispatches from your Department as well as from others, intercepted as it would appear by the enemy's cruisers, amongst them yours to me of the 26th of September and 28th of October; duplicates, I suppose, as the originals had previously reached me. A duplicate of Mr. Memminger to me of the 24th of October and his triplicate of the 25th of same month, and Mr. Mallory's duplicate to me of the 26th of October had also been received; but to the enemy I am indebted for the first receipt of a letter from Mr. Mallory to me of the 30th of October.

It is certainly unfortunate that the messenger to whom these dispatches were intrusted permitted their capture, though I am not aware of any particular inconvenience to arise from it, except so far as they refer to operations here of the War and Navy Departments.

I have the honor to be, very respectfully, your obedient servant,

J. M. MASON.

Hon. J. P. BENJAMIN,
    Secretary of State.

No. 14.]   DEPARTMENT OF STATE,
                              Richmond, February 6, 1863.

SIR: I find it absolutely necessary to procure for the Department some works of reference which are not accessible here. I have therefore to request of you the favor of procuring those mentioned in the annexed list and to draw for the amount on the Department or to send me the bills that I may remit the cost. In either event please send duplicate bills and receipts that the cost may be properly vouched at the Treasury.

I sent to Mr. Hotze a short time ago an order for the English Blue Books, especially on foreign affairs. Perhaps you will be good enough to enquire of him what he has done, so that duplicates may be avoided.

Messrs. Fraser, Trenholm & Co. will no doubt oblige me by forwarding the books through their Charleston house.

I enclose you a copy of a circular recently sent by me to the different consuls of foreign powers announcing 'the raising of the blockade of Charleston by our superior forces.

That at Galveston was raised in the same manner, and this morning's papers announce the capture of three Federal vessels at Sabine Pass and the opening of that harbor by the breaking of the blockade by superior force. Of this last fact we have no official knowledge.

We scarcely suppose that this intelligence will have any effect on the conduct of the European powers, whose settled determination to overlook any aggression on their rights by the United States has been exhibited under all circumstances, however aggravated, in a manner so unmistakable that we have ceased to expect impartiality at their hands.

The recent losses of the enemy in vessels of war are considerable. I append an imperfect list:

1. The gunboat *Slidell*, destroyed on Tennessee River.
2. The iron-clad *Monitor*, sunk at sea.
3. The gunboat *Columbia*, wrecked on coast.
4. The gunboat *Cairo*, blown up by torpedo in Yazoo River.
5. The steamer *Harriet Lane*, captured at Galveston.
6. The gunboat *Westfield*, blown up at Galveston.
7. The gunboat *Mercedita*, sunk off Charleston.
8. The gunboat ———, sunk off Charleston.
9. The gunboat *Isaac M. Smith*, captured in Stono River.
10. The gunboat ———, burnt in North Carolina.
11. The gunboat *Hatteras*, sunk off Galveston.

Besides the above are the three vessels just announced to have been captured at Sabine Pass and several others much damaged by Flag-Officer Ingraham's squadron off Charleston. So that upon the whole our success on the water has not been inconsiderable.

In addition to the above some 20 of their transport steamers have been captured or destroyed on our inland waters within the last sixty days, while the *Alabama* and *Florida* have not been idle at sea.

Of the general aspect of the war you will fully be able to judge by the newspapers of the North, which paint their own condition in colors so dark that we can scarcely desire to add anything to the gloomy picture. Public feeling with us is bright and confident— almost too much so. The conviction that a disruption or revolution of some sort will take place at the North within a very short period is daily gaining ground.

Yours, very respectfully,

J. P. BENJAMIN,
Secretary of State.

Hon. JAMES MASON, etc.,
London.

[Enclosure—Circular to the consuls.]

DEPARTMENT OF STATE,
Richmond, January 31, 1863.

SIR: I am instructed by the President of the Confederate States of America to inform you that this Government has received an official dispatch from Flag-Officer Ingraham, commanding the naval forces of the Confederacy on the coast of South Carolina, stating that the blockade of the harbor of Charleston has been broken by the complete dispersion and disappearance of the blockading squadron in consequence of a successful attack made on it by the ironclad steamers commanded by Flag-Officer Ingraham. During this attack one or more of the blockading vessels were sunk or burned.

As you are doubtless aware that by the law of nations a blockade when thus broken by superior force ceases to exist and can not be subsequently enforced unless established de novo with adequate force and after due notice to neutral powers, it has been deemed proper to give you the information herein contained for the guidance of such vessels of nations as may choose to carry on commerce with the now open port of Charleston.

Respectfully, etc.,

J. P. BENJAMIN,
Secretary of State.

Mr. GEORGE MOORE, Esq.,
Her Britannic Majesty's Consul at Richmond.

NASSAU, N. P., *February 6, 1863.*

SIR: I transmit herewith protest of Sylvain Haymann relative to British schooner *Harkaway*, and likewise protest of David Owens Sabiston relative to same vessel. Mr. Haymann is a French subject and actually the owner of the *Harkaway*, though registered in the name of R. W. Farrington, a British subject. She was captured and condemned before the prize court at Key West, the vessel then bearing the name of the *Victoria*. After the sale her name was changed to the *Harkaway*.

Mr. Haymann sent the *Harkaway* to Wilmington, though clearing her nominally for Beaufort with a Federal consular clearance. She had a cargo of salt, consigned to Messrs. Harris & Howell and instructions were forwarded to invest a portion of the proceeds in a return cargo of rosin and cotton. These facts are of my own personal knowledge, as I perused the instructions given to Captain Sabiston on the day of his departure.

It now appears that on the arrival of the *Harkaway* at Wilmington she was libeled by the former owner of the vessel, he giving bond for merely $12,000 to appear at the hearing of the case in June next. The cargo of salt was worth fully $60,000 at the date of arrival, whilst the result of the probable investment in cotton would have yielded an equal return, so that Mr. Haymann is damaged to the extent of about $120,000 currency by this strange proceeding. The case, moreover, has made a very unpleasant impression here, as parties will naturally hesitate to purchase vessels condemned before a prize court, and in this proportion are the means diminished of finding suitable craft to run the blockade. Amongst the residents of the South here the proceeding has been universally condemned.

I have thought it proper to present the matter to your consideration, deeming, as I do, that Mr. Haymann has suffered unjustly.

In conclusion I will add that the governor of these islands has transmitted copies of the accompanying protests to the Duke of Newcastle, her Majesty's secretary for colonial affairs.

I am, very respectfully, your obedient servant,

L. HEYLIGER.

Hon. J. P. BENJAMIN,
Secretary of State, Richmond.

BAHAMA ISLANDS.

Be it known and made manifest by this public instrument of protest, to all to whom it may concern, that on this day, being Thursday, the 22d day of January, in the year of our Lord one thousand eight hundred and sixty-three, before me, Thomas William Henry Dillet, notary public by lawful authority appointed, duly admitted and sworn, residing in the city of Nassau in the island of New Providence, personally came and appeared David Owens Sabiston, master of the British schooner *Harkaway*, of and belonging to the port of Nassau aforesaid, who of his own free will and accord did voluntarily allege, affirm, protest, and say in manner following, that is to say:

That he being the master of the said schooner *Harkaway*, sailed from the port of Nassau aforesaid on or about the 13th day of December last past, with a cargo of 530 bags of Liverpool salt, bound for the port of Beaufort, in the State of North Carolina, one of the States of the so-called Southern Confederacy.

That during the voyage he encountered a gale of wind which caused the vessel to leak badly and consequently put into New Inlet, near Wilmington, in the State of North Carolina aforesaid, in distress, when the commandant of Fort Fisher boarded the said schooner and allowed her to pass up to the city of Wilmington.

That the said schooner was there consigned to Messieurs Harris & Howell, merchants, and on the next day, he, the said master, commenced to discharge the cargo aforesaid.

That some three or four days afterwards the said schooner and cargo were received by process of law taken by the former owners of the said vessel, the marshal at Wilmington taking possession of and securing the said vessel to the wharf thereat, on the ground that the capture, condemnation, and sale of the said schooner at Key West, in the State of Florida, one of the United States of America, was illegal, and therefore they were still the legal owners.

And the appearer did further allege, protest, and say that the former owners wished him to give them bonds to the amount of $75,000, conditioned to abide the result of any trial or action which they might prosecute against the said schooner, her cargo, and the now owner thereof, in which case they would release the said schooner and her cargo, but this appearer refused so to do.

And further that he, this appearer, was informed at Wilmington aforesaid and verily believes that the said schooner was captured by a United States vessel of war during the past year, while owned by parties at Wilmington aforesaid, and while on a voyage therefrom with a cargo of cotton, bound for the port of Nassau aforesaid, and was carried to Key West, in the State of Florida aforesaid, as a prize and was condemned thereat in the prize court and sold at public auction; and further that the said schooner was brought to Nassau and sold, and there obtained a British register and changed her name from that of the *Victoria* to that of the *Harkaway*.

D. O. SABISTON.

Whereas the said David Owens Sabiston hath requested me, the said notary, to protest, as I do by these presents most solemnly protest and declare against the arrest of the said schooner *Harkaway* and her cargo, and against all process and action taken against either or both of them by the parties claiming to be the former owners of the said schooner or any other parties whomsoever, and also against all persons whom it doth or may concern for and on account of all and all manner of damages, losses, prejudices, and detriments which may happen by reason of the said arrest and detention of the said schooner and her cargo aforesaid, to the intent that the same be submitted unto by those to whom it shall of right belong or shall or may in anywise concern. All which things were declared, alleged, protested, and affirmed, as is before set forth in the presence of me, the said notary, and therefore I have hereunto subscribed my name and affixed my notarial seal, being requested to testify and certify the premises.

Thus done and passed and protested at Nassau aforesaid the day and year first above written.

[L. S.]   T. WILLIAM HENRY DILLET,
Notary Public, Bahamas.

BAHAMA ISLANDS.

I, Thomas William Henry Dillet, of the city of Nassau, in the island of New Providence, notary public, by lawful authority appointed, duly admitted and sworn, do hereby certify to all whom it doth or may concern that the above and foregoing is a true copy of a certain protest made before me, taken and extracted from my register of notarial acts made and passed before me, at pages 120, 121, 122, 123.

In testimonium veritatis,

T. WILLIAM HENRY DILLET,
Notary Public, Bahamas.

[Enclosure 2.]

BAHAMA ISLANDS.

Be it known and made manifest by this public instrument of declaration and protest, to all to whom it may concern, that on this day, Friday, the 30th day of January, in the year of our Lord one thousand eight hundred and sixty-three, before me, Thomas William Henry Dillet, notary public by lawful authority appointed, duly admitted and sworn, residing in the city of Nassau, in the island of New Providence, one of the said Bahama Islands, personally came and appeared Sylvain Haymann, of the island of New Providence, merchant, who of his own free will and voluntary accord, did testify, allege, protest, and say, in manner following, that is to say:

That he, this appearer, is the agent at Nassau, aforesaid, of the schooner *Harkaway*, of and belonging to the port of Nassau aforesaid, which same vessel sailed from the last mentioned port on or about the 13th day of December last past, bound for Beaufort, N. C., with a cargo of Liverpool salt and other merchandise, the owner of the said schooner, to wit, Richard Wightman Farrington, of Fortune Island, one of the said Bahama Islands, merchant.

That he, this appearer, has received letters from the consignees of the said schooner at Wilmington, in North Carolina, informing him that the said schooner and her cargo which lately arrived thereat has been arrested under legal process at the instance of parties claiming to be the lawful owners thereof on the ground that they being the owners of the vessel when she left Wilmington aforesaid on a voyage to Nassau aforesaid with a cargo of cotton, the said schooner then called the *Victoria* was captured by a United States ship of war and carried to Key West, in the State of Florida, where she was condemned as a prize and sold as such, and that the said parties have caused the arrest aforesaid alleging that the said capture and sale was illegal.

That the said schooner *Victoria* was after the sale at Key West aforesaid brought to this port of Nassau and was there sold at private auction, when the purchaser, the said Richard Wightman Farrington, obtained a register at the customs department for the said vessel, and changed her name from that of the *Victoria* to that of the *Harkaway*.

And that this appearer further saith that at the time of the arrest of the said schooner *Harkaway* at Wilmington as aforesaid salt was worth and selling at from one hundred and forty to one hundred and fifty dollars per bag, but that since then it has declined in price to $40 per bag, and that by reason of the arrest and detention of the said vessel and her cargo great losses must ensue to the owner thereof.

S. HAYMANN.

Wherefore the said ———— Haymann hath requested me, the said notary, to protest, as I do by these presents most solemnly and formally protest, and declare against the arrest and detention of the said schooner *Harkaway* and her cargo as aforesaid and against all process and action taken against them, or either of them, by the parties claiming to be the former owners of the said schooner, or any other party or parties whomsoever, and also against all persons whom it doth or may concern, for and on account of all losses, damages, prejudices, and detriments which may happen by reason of the said arrest and detention of the said schooner and her cargo as aforesaid to the intent that the same may be submitted unto, suffered, and borne by those to whom it shall or may of right belong or whom it doth or may concern.

In witness whereof I have hereunto affixed my firm and notarial seal the day and year first above written.

[L. S.]   T. WILLIAM HENRY DILLET,
                                Notary Public, Bahamas.

BAHAMA ISLANDS.

I, Thomas William Henry Dillet, of the city of Nassau, in the island of New Providence, notary public, by lawful authority appointed, duly admitted, and sworn, do hereby certify to all to whom it doth or may concern that the above and foregoing is a true copy of a certain protest made before me, taken, and extracted from my register of notarial acts made and passed before me, at pages 124, 125, and 126.

In testimonium veritas,

[L. S.]
T. WILLIAM HENRY DILLET,
Notary Public, Bahamas.

No. 26.]
PARIS, *February 6, 1863.*

SIR: You will find herewith duplicate of my last dispatch of 29th ultimo.

Having observed in one of the Paris papers a letter from Martinique in which it was stated that the local authorities were considering a plan for the introduction of negroes from the United States, I verbally, through my friend at the foreign affairs, called the attention of M. Drouyn de Lhuys to the subject, stating that the same idea had been started by the authorities of some of the British West India colonies, but that the suggestion had been met by the refusal of the British Government to entertain it at least for the present. I also mentioned the representations that had been made on the same subject by Mr. Mann, at Copenhagen, and the satisfactory assurances which had been given to him.

On inquiry M. Drouyn de Lhuys found that the matter had been considered by the minister of marine and colonies, who had been disposed to entertain it favorably; but when it was explained by M. Drouyn de Lhuys, the minister of marine was satisfied that his views had been too hastily adopted, and promised to give the necessary instructions to prevent the carrying out of the scheme. The minister of foreign affairs is perfectly aware of the relations that exist between me and his subordinates, and evidently encourages them. I am thus enabled to communicate anything that I have to say to the minister and receive his response, without the delays and formalities which direct intercourse would necessarily require. Yesterday, for instance, I desired to let him know that a loan had been negotiated at Richmond by Erlanger & Co. for a considerable amount, reimbursible in cotton, and to invoke in advance his good offices in facilitating the completion of the transaction, for here no scheme of the kind has any chance of success if not favored by the Government. To-day I received a message assuring me of his support. The President's message has produced a most admirable effect here, and, indeed, throughout Europe it is universally considered as a most able, manly, and dignified state paper. It is the more admired from its strong contrast with the documents emanating from the Lincoln Government. I have just received from Colonel C. J. Helm, at Havana, an account of his parting interview with the retiring Captain-General [Francisco] Serrano and of the emphatic manner in which he declared his hearty sympathies with our cause and his determination on his arrival in Spain to exert all his influence in favor of the recognition of the Confederate States. As General Serrano is now minister of foreign affairs at Madrid, I think it is to be regretted that we have not there a diplomatic agent ready to avail himself of his friendly disposition, but as Colonel Helm informs me that he has sent you full minutes of his conversation with General Serrano, I entertain the hope that you will have authorized some one to represent you at Madrid. Should you not decide on sending thither a special agent, I will very cheerfully undertake the duty if you think it desirable; the railroad communication is now nearly completed and I should not be long absent from my post. I shall send to the minister of foreign affairs a copy of Colonel Helm's letter, and hope that it may lead to some overtures to the Spanish Government tending toward recognition; but, of course, I do not expect any further decided action until we hear what was the reception of the dispatch to M. Mercier of 9th January. I should feel pretty confident of its being favorable were it not for the Emperor's letter of 3d July last, which probably would have been received by the same steamer as the dispatch. I am not without hopes that the proposition will be rejected; if so, you may consider immediate recognition as almost certain.

I have the honor to be, with great respect, your most obedient servant,

JOHN SLIDELL.

Hon. J. P. BENJAMIN,
    Secretary of State.

N. B.—I send you the responses of the Senate and Corps Législatif to the Emperor's address at the opening of the Chambers; they, as usual, merely reecho the words of the sovereign with slight variations of form.

No. 13.]
          DEPARTMENT OF STATE,
          Richmond, February 7, 1863.

SIR: By your Nos. 20 and 21, of 11th and 29th November last, received yesterday, I greatly regret to find that you had not yet received any dispatches from me of later date than April. Those forwarded to you subsequent to that date went as follows:

No. 5, on 19th July, 1862; No. 6, on 26th September, 1862; No. 7, on 17th October, 1862; No. 8, on 28th October, 1862; No. 9, on 30th October, 1862; No. 10, on 11th December; No. 11, on 15th January, 1863; No. 12, on 15th January, 1863, circular.

Duplicates have always been forwarded by the conveyance next succeeding the originals.

I have nothing new to communicate since my dispatch of 15th ultimo, except the breaking of the blockade at several Southern ports, which you will have learned through the newspapers long before your receipt of this. I enclose you the official circular of the breaking of the blockade at Charleston. The blockade at Galveston was still more effectually raised by the capture of the *Harriet Lane* and the blowing up of the *Westfield*, which was the flagship of the squadron; and we have just received a telegram, somewhat imperfectly worded, from Galveston announcing the capture of the enemy's forces at Sabine Pass, the capture of 13 guns, stores of the value of $1,000,000, and 109 prisoners; and, as we understand the dispatch, a sloop of war was also captured by our river steamers lined with bulwarks of cotton bales. Our steamers are now cruising off Sabine Pass in hopes of picking up further prizes.

I shall apprise foreign consuls of the opening of these two additional ports of Galveston and Sabine Pass.

Enclosed are extracts from newspapers with official accounts of the breaking of the blockade at Charleston.

Very respectfully, etc.,

J. P. BENJAMIN,
Secretary of State.

Hon. JOHN SLIDELL, etc.,
Paris.

P. S.—I add hereto an extract from a letter recently received by me from a gentleman who is a professor in the University of Virginia and is represented by all of whom I have made inquiry as being of the highest character and respectability. It is a very singular statement, and you ought not to remain ignorant of a fact which may serve as a clue to unravel any secret designs that may be entertained in France.

[Extract.]

Three years ago I had the honor of an hour's conversation with the Emperor of the French at the Villa Eugenie in Biarritz. After having exhausted all the little information I could afford him, draining me à sec, and leaving me, after all, under the impression that he knew more of all the subjects on which he had examined me than I did myself, he turned with peculiar and undisguised eagerness to the Mexican question. I had then just returned from Cuba and fancied I had thoroughly informed myself as to the condition of things there and in the Gulf. I was soon undeceived. He knew the very number of guns on the Morro, the sums the United States had spent on the fortifications in Florida, the exports and imports of Galveston and Matamoras—in short, everything which well-informed local agents could have reported to an experienced statesman, eager of information. He examined me again on Texas and its population, the disposition of the French residents, the tendencies of the German colonists, the feeling on the Mexican frontier. Twice, I remember well, he repeated: "La Louisiane, n'est-ce pas qu'elle est Française au fond?" At last he turned to the colonies, and then stated in round terms, finding that I quoted from his Idées Napoleoniennes the well-known words, "Eh bien il faut reconstruire l'Empire la bas."

After having received this cue to his questions and the unexpected interest he deigned to show in so insignificant a person, I was enabled better to follow his ideas and more fully to answer his questions. From what I could then gather, I was fully persuaded that he proposed to seek in Mexico a compensation for the lost colonies in the West Indies, which, he said, could not be recovered sans nous brouiller avec nos alliées. He insisted upon it that France must sooner or later have a pied à terre on the Florida coast for the purpose of protecting her commerce in the Gulf, "for," he added, "nous ne voulons pas d'un autre Gibraltar de ce cote la!" Finally, I think he revolved in his mind the possibility of recovering a foothold in Louisiana, although he never stated this purpose in so many words, perhaps from a courteous regard to my position.

There were, of course, other points mentioned in a conversation carried on with his usual rapidity of thought and marvelous conciseness of expression, but I venture here only to mention those I can state in precise terms as having a direct bearing on the question of French policy in the South.

I beg leave to add that his remarks made so deep an impression on my mind that I jotted down the salient points for my own guidance and as interesting points d'appui for future researches. Upon my return to Paris I had the opportunity of mentioning some of them to Mr. Drouin de Lhuys, whom I have the advantage of knowing personally. He seemed to be not only fully aware of the peculiar views of the Emperor, but added much to explain them. His point of view was, of course, a different one, and as he was then out of office perhaps more decided than it would be at this moment. Although these views and expressions are now three years old, I need not suggest to you how tenacious the Emperor is in his long-prepared purposes, especially when they concern his openly avowed plan of recovering all that can be recovered of the great Empire.

No. 15.]   DEPARTMENT OF STATE,
                                        Richmond, February 7, 1863.

SIR: I had just concluded my No. 14 when I received, on 6th instant, your Nos. 21, 22, and 23, the two former of 10th December, and the last of 11th, same month.

It is very unfortunate that your situation was such as to render it impossible for you to take charge of the accused Hester, or send him to this country for trial, as his offence, committed on the deck of one of our national vessels, was as much within our exclusive jurisdiction as if committed on the soil of the Confederacy. But as you would, in the event of his delivery to you on demand, have been utterly without any means of bringing him away or sending him under proper guard to this country, you seem to have had no choice in the matter. It is to be feared that this case, however, may be hereafter cited as a precedent against us when our circumstances shall be changed, and it is regarded as unfortunate that our silent acquiescence, enforced as it has been by our peculiar condition, leaves us open to misconstruction.

Your views expressed in No. 22 are in entire accordance with those of Mr. Memminger and myself, and measures have already been taken to concentrate in one house or agent all the financial operations of the Government abroad, and to revoke authority given by heads of departments to separate or special agents.

It may be well to mention that I told Mr. Sanders that I would be willing to give him a certain sum for the delivery of dispatches from abroad, but would not engage to employ him to establish a line of communication. He has been so unfortunate in his efforts thus far, and his son has been guilty of such folly in allowing dispatches to be seized on his person, and in an insane attempt to run the blockade in a sailing vessel when he had a passage on a steamer at his command, that I think it best you should decline risking any dispatches through Mr. Sanders. If sent to Nassau to care of Mr. Louis Heyliger, we will be almost certain to receive them. I annex a list of all dispatches sent you, that you may be aware of the fact of the loss of any not yet received by you.

Very respectfully, etc.,

J. P. BENJAMIN,
Secretary of State.

Hon. JAMES M. MASON, etc.,
London.

No. 30.]   CONFEDERATE STATES COMMISSION,
London, February 9, 1863.

SIR: The opportunity still admitting, I have the honor to inclose you herewith a full report of the proceedings and debate in Parliament on the Queen's speech at the first day of the session. It was, unfortunately, carelessly cut from the London Times, but as the best report was contained in that paper, I send it as it is. It will reach you, of course, long after you will have had the general tenor of the debate from other sources, but probably not as reported at length. While both the ministry and the opposition agree that the separation of the States is final, yet both equally agree, that in their judgment, the time has not yet arrived for recognition. Both parties are guided in this by a fixed English purpose to run no risk of a broil, even far less, a war with the United States. For us it only remains to be silent and passive. The ground taken by Lord Derby that recognition without other form of intervention would have no fruits, is constantly assumed here by those who are against any movement; and with those willingly deaf it is vain to argue.

I hope at an early day of the session, on a call to be made, my correspondence with the foreign office will be laid before Parliament; the English people will then, at least, have the Southern view of the effect of such simple recognition.

It is thought here that, if from no other cause, the war must soon come to an end from sheer inability in the Lincoln Government to carry it on. Our latest military advices are the damaging blows dealt to the enemy at Murfreesboro, the late signal and unexampled naval victory at Galveston, and to-day, in the report by telegraph that the enemy's gunboat *Hatteras*, after a sharp action with one of our little navy, "supposed to be the *Alabama*," the *Oreto*, or the *Harriet Lane*, has been sunk. The report comes from Queenstown by a vessel just arrived there from Nova Scotia. The public here, schooled by experience, looks just as confidently, by each arrival, for news of Southern successes as you await them at Richmond.

As yet I have not even an acknowledgment from the foreign office of the receipt of my letter of the 3d of January, containing the protest you instructed me to make on the failure of the Secretary to answer the enquiries put to him. The letter was delivered by Mr. Macfarland, and there can be no question, therefore, of its receipt. Strange contumacy from such a quarter.

I have no further intelligence from Paris about the loan, the steamer due from New York to-day not having yet arrived.

I have the honor to be, very respectfully, your obedient servant,

J. M. MASON.

Hon. J. P. BENJAMIN,
Secretary of State.

FOREIGN OFFICE, *February 10, 1863.*

SIR: I have the honor to acknowledge the receipt of your letter of January, referring to the letter which you addressed to me on the 7th of July last, respecting the interpretation placed by her Majesty's Government on the declaration with regard to blockade appended to the treaty of Paris.

I have, in the first place, to assure you that her Majesty's Government would much regret if you should feel that any want of respect was intended by the circumstance of a mere acknowledgment of your letter having hitherto been addressed to you.

With regard to the question contained in it, I have to say that her Majesty's Government sees no reason to qualify the language employed in my dispatch to Lord Lyons of the 15th of February last. It appears to her Majesty's Government to be sufficiently clear that the declaration of Paris could not have been intended to mean that a port must be so blockaded as really to prevent access in all winds, and independently of whether the communication might be carried on of a dark night or by means of small low steamers or coasting craft creeping along the shore; in short, that it was necessary that communication with a port under blockade should be utterly and absolutely impossible under any circumstances. In further illustration of this remark, I may say there is no doubt that a blockade would be in legal existence, although a sudden storm or change of wind occasionally blew off the blockading squadron.

This is a change to which, in the nature of things, every blockade is liable. Such an accident does not suspend, much less break, a blockade. Whereas, on the contrary, the driving off of a blockading force by a superior force does break a blockade, which must be renewed, de novo, in the usual form, to be binding upon neutrals.

The declaration of Paris was, in truth, directed against what were once termed paper blockades—that is, blockades not sustained by any actual or by a notoriously inadequate naval force—such as the occasional appearance of a man-of-war in the offing or the like.

The adequacy of the force to maintain the blockade must, indeed, always to a certain degree be one of fact and evidence, but it does not appear that in any of the numerous cases brought before the prize courts in America the inadequacy of the force has been urged by those who would have been most interested in urging it against the legality of the seizure.

The interpretation, therefore, placed by her Majesty's Government on the declaration of Paris was that a blockade in order to be respected by neutrals must be practically effective.

At the time I wrote my dispatch to Lord Lyons, her Majesty's Government were of opinion that the blockade of the Southern ports could not be otherwise than so regarded, and certainly the manner in which it has since been enforced gives to neutral Governments no excuse for asserting that the blockade has not been efficiently maintained.

It is proper to add that the same view of the meaning and effect of the article of the declaration of Paris on the subject of blockade, which is above explained, was taken by the representative of the United States at the Court of St. James (Mr. Dallas) during the communications which passed between the two Governments some years before the present war, with a view to the accession of the United States to that declaration.

I have, etc.,

RUSSELL.

J. M. MASON.

No. 39.]
25 RUE ROYALE, BRUSSELS,
February 10, 1863.

SIR: I am now enabled to inform you authoritatively that my note to Mr. Rogier of January 5 received the most respectful consideration from the Government of his Majesty King Leopold. It engaged the deliberations of the cabinet from time to time for more than a month. Finally it was decided that Belgium, in view of the obligations imposed upon her at the commencement of her existence, could not take so grave a step as to recognize us, when the great western powers shrunk from the performance of such an undertaking. This decision was communicated to me in person at my residence, in a most courteous manner, by the Count de Borchgrave, chef de cabinet of the foreign office, a functionary who peculiarly enjoys the confidence of the Sovereign.

My primary object in making the explicit request for recognition, as I intimated to you in my No. 36, was to induce King Leopold, after he had failed in his purpose with England first, and France afterwards, to endeavor to operate upon those powers to encourage a simultaneous European movement upon the subject. I was careful to remark in my note that " Such a measure it is confidently believed would be joyously hailed and promptly emulated by every member of the European family."

I have the best of reasons for believing that I succeeded in my purpose. But unhappily the Government of the Tuileries persisted in its policy of impracticable mediation, while Lord Palmerston could not consummate his long-cherished wishes without incurring the risk of being deprived of the seals of office by a coalition of the Conservatives, Radicals, and ultra-Abolitionists. The speeches of Earl Derby and Mr. Disraeli the first night of the session quite clearly indicated the plans which were arranged for the readvent to power of the former premier and former chancellor of the exchequer. Many of our friends in England calculated largely, until the meeting of Parliament, upon the opposition for the acknowledgment of our independence. I never for a moment indulged any such expectation. While there are many prominent members of that party who earnestly desire such an occurrence, its leaders assuredly do not nor ever have.

I am as confident now, as I have been confident for many months, that the two first statesmen of Great Britain, Lord Palmerston and Mr. Gladstone, have our cause sincerely at heart, while their two rivals, Earl Derby and Mr. Disraeli, regard with the coldest indifference the successful struggles which we have made to cast off the iron yoke which the North was anxious to impose upon us. Even Lord Malmesbury could not find it in his heart to raise his voice in behalf of recognition, although cordially approving the first proposition of the Emperor of the French; while Mr. Seymour Fitzgerald, his former first undersecretary, who was believed to be among the most ardent of our admirers, was entirely silent upon the occasion.

An answer from Washington to the last suggestion of Mr. Drouyn de Lhuys is daily looked for. No good to us, in my opinion, will proceed from so irresolute a proposition. It will likely be received as having been engendered in timid counsels and will be declined with an immense array of words and a grand flourish of patriotism. Will Louis Napoleon then pronounce in favor of unconditional recognition, as he has been so earnestly implored to do by the nestor of sovereigns? I fear that he will not.

In the meantime, more than ever should we rely upon the power of our invincible arms and the immutable justice of the God of Battles for hastening an honorable peace. If it is possible for patriots to be more resolute, more energetic, more skillful in the science of war than we have been all along, now assuredly is the time for such a demonstration to be made.

I have the honor to be, very respectfully, your obedient servant,

A. DUDLEY MANN.

Hon. J. P. BENJAMIN,
Secretary of State, Richmond.

No. 27.] PARIS, *February 12, 1863.*

SIR: Since my last of 6th instant, we have heard of the unlucky fate of certain dispatches sent by Mr. Sanders, among them your No. 7, on the subject of the consular agents at Richmond and Galveston. Some of the English journals affected to believe that it would produce an unfavorable effect here. You will find by the article from the Moniteur which I annex that their anticipations have not been realized. It is fortunate that I had already placed the greater portion of your dispatch with the accompanying documents before the Emperor through M. Mocquard, as stated in my No. 23, but even in the absence of that communication the manner in which the President in his late message spoke of the friendly course of the Emperor would have sufficed to correct any unfriendly feeling which might otherwise have been excited by the perusal of the dispatch.

With great respect, your most obedient servant,

JOHN SLIDELL.

Hon. J. P. BENJAMIN,
Secretary of State.

No. 18.] HAVANA, *February 14, 1863.*

SIR: At the request of the Hon. Lucius Q. C. Lamar I announce to the Department his safe arrival at and departure from Havana for his post of duty. Mr. Lamar's health had greatly improved, though he was still quite feeble.

It is rumored here that the Captain-General Serrano was appointed premier of Spain in three days after his arrival at Madrid. Should this rumor be confirmed, I shall take the liberty of addressing him a private note, urging upon him the propriety of an immediate cooperation by Spain with France in the recognition of the Confederate States, and I have every reason to believe he will insist upon such a proposition being made to the Emperor.

I have nothing further of interest to communicate to the Department at this time.

I have the honor to be, with great respect, your obedient servant,
Сн. J. Helm.

Hon. G. P. Benjamin,
Secretary of State, Richmond.

No. 18.]   Confederate States Commercial Agency,
London, February 14, 1863.

Sir: Enclosed I have the honor to transmit the report of the opening session of Parliament, which assembled on the 5th ultimo.

If any of my later communications have been received, you will not be surprised at the attitude assumed by the leaders of the conservative party on the subject of our recognition. As early as November 22 I wrote: "We have as many friends in the ministerial as in the Tory Party, and the action of the Government on the American question has thus far depended on persons rather than on parties." And again, on the 20th December: "I see no reason to alter my opinion, already expressed, that we have little to hope from the advent of that party to power."

These views have now received ample confirmation in the fact that Earl Russell has actually used stronger language than the chief of the opposition. While Lord Derby expressed only his conviction that the subjugation of our country was an impossibility, Lord Russell went so far as to pronounce such subjugation a calamity to America, to the world, and especially to the negro race. Thus though the two great English parties, as represented by their authorized exponents, stop short of the practical conclusions forced upon them by the logic of facts, yet they admit the facts themselves as fully and conclusively as we could desire. I have long since informed you that our affairs are not and can not be made a party question. We have friends in all parties, even among the radicals, witness Mr. Lindsay and Mr. Roebuck, and this is the only party in which we can be said to have open and active enemies. I even question, in the light of information that has reached me during the past month and in view of his latest declaration, whether Earl Russell is not at heart a friend, but his statesmanship knows of no higher resource than procrastination. Lord Palmerston, notwithstanding his long experience and great reputation, is by nature rather a politician than a statesman, and therefore the notorious fact that any action in American affairs is equivalent to the dissolution of his inharmonious cabinet sways him more than any comprehensive view of national interests.

In my last I reported a conversation with a confidential friend of his which left no doubt on my mind that at that time the Premier felt strongly the necessity of prompt and energetic action. Two weeks later another and fuller conversation with the same person explained to me that personal and party considerations had over-ruled this feeling. The conservatives, never very effective as an op-position, are committed by their party traditions against the recog-nition of an "insurgent power," as well as against the Paris conven-tion in regard to blockades. Lord Derby, moreover, is supposed to express in an especial degree the personal feelings and wishes of the Queen, which are said to be still decidedly averse to recognition. There is thus a parliamentary deadlock which prevents all action. What, however, more than all else contributes to this universal inertia is the universal conviction that the main object of British policy is secured and that separation and Southern independence are achieved beyond peradventure. Even so zealous a champion as Mr. Gregory reasons from this fact, as do Lords Palmerston and Derby. In a private letter which was confidentially communicated to me he writes to a collaborator in Parliament just before the session that while a year ago he would have taken any risk and not have thought the risk of war too great to effect this important object he would not now advise any risk, not even the slightest. He was opposed to agitate the subject of recognition until parliamentary opinion had spontaneously ripened for its adoption. The most that can now be expected is a motion for the correspondence of the foreign office with Mr. Mason. This will probably be made in a few days by our staunchest friend, Lord Campbell, and may possibly be followed in the Commons.

The organs of the Conservative Party, the Herald and Standard, remain unshaken in their advocacy of recognition, notwithstanding the position assumed by Lord Derby, which they freely criticize. In the Index of this week, No. 42, will be found an article from the Herald on this subject which may be useful for republication. The Times, with characteristic vacillation and brutality, has just de-livered itself of a coarse and vulgar invective against Mr. Mason, the occasion being a brief dinner speech which Dr. Mason was in very courtesy compelled by the unanimous desire of the company to make at an unofficial banquet given by the lord mayor of London. The Times in this instance most assuredly does not represent public opinion, which has pronounced Mr. Mason's remarks appropriate and eminently felicitous. The Times, in fact, would now be simply con-temptible if it were not still feared for its inherited power, but that power has descended into hands incapable of wielding it as if it was the battle-ax of a giant of old and the men who now control the Times reel under its weight like drunkards. Not many months since, when Austria offered to join the Zollverein, it announced and com-mented on the accession of "Prussia" to this great customs union in an elaborate leader. More recently in commenting on our affairs it proved editorially by a showy array of figures that including Mis-souri, Kentucky, and Maryland we had a larger population than the North and could consequently raise more soldiers. The Times is also the paper which once placed Portland, Me., in the British Provinces. These are only a few of the ridiculous blunders that would have ruined any other paper than the Times. I have said thus much about this matter because the tirade against Mr. Mason will no doubt be extensively copied by the Northern press and perhaps by a portion of our own.

Great efforts have been made to arouse the antislavery feeling of the country by "emancipation meetings," but so far with remarkably little success. The largest of these meetings, at Exeter Hall, was indeed numerously attended, but not a single one of the well-known names of the emancipationist school was among the number. All persons of social and political respectability have held aloof. The Index, No. 41, contains the comments of the leading papers. But though the agitators have failed there is always a latent danger in the agitation of this subject, and of this public men are aware, which may account in part for the timidity of their American policy.

The publication of certain intercepted duplicates of dispatches has amused public curiosity for a few days, but I differ from the opinion of many of our countrymen that it has done harm, as it really revealed little which was not known before. Financial men criticize the management of our finances and assert that all negotiations of whatever kind should have been entrusted to some well-known and substantial English firm, and that not having done so will delay and render more expensive any larger negotiations hereafter. The distress in Lancashire is decidedly mitigated, thanks to the larger charitable subscriptions, and the demand for manufactured goods at prices somewhat corresponding with those of the raw material. Thus the Government will probably be able to avoid the danger of proposing a national loan for the relief of the distress. An important alteration in the tobacco duty was last night proposed by Mr. Gladstone and will doubtless become law, reducing it on manufactured, and increasing it on unmanufactured tobacco. It is probably a wise measure in a British point of view, but one which I fear will hereafter tell against the productions of Virginia and Kentucky and in favor of German and other sorts. The insurrection in Poland is beginning to assume the features of a revolution, and already the British press is manifesting that sympathy which it was so slow in according to us, and with which they have so often deluded apparently well-founded hopes. This and the approaching marriage of the Prince of Wales are at present the uppermost topics in the public mind and throw our affairs temporarily in the background. The Times has not a word to say about the destruction of the *Hatteras* by the *Alabama*, of which we have full particulars by last West Indian mail.

Surveying my field of observation I am not discouraged, even though Government, Parliament, and people seem to be in a state of torpor as regards America. A better knowledge of us, a higher appreciation of our national character, and a more reasonable view of our institutions, are visibly extending every day. Even among the masses these juster ideas gain ground, and Mrs. Beecher Stowe and negro fanaticism are satirized and ridiculed on the public stage. If we shall owe no gratitude to Europe for favors received, we shall at least have a fair field before us when our career of peaceful prosperity begins.

My communications have so invariably commenced or ended with appeals for larger means that but for the urgency of the case I should be ashamed to repeat them. My usefulness is in exact proportion to the means at my command. Without any profusion in expenditure, which is not only unnecessary but actually hurtful, the full employment of all my facilities of usefulness requires a contingent allowance of not less than $10,000 per annum. I have just been fortunate enough to secure as a permanent contributor to the Index, the chief editor of one of the leading daily journals—for obvious reasons I omit the name—and similar opportunities of strengthening my intimacy with established organs of public opinion are constantly occurring.

I have the honor to remain, very respectfully, your obedient servant,

HENRY HOTZE.

Hon. J. P. BENJAMIN,
Secretary of State, Richmond.

---

24 UPPER SEYMOUR STREET,
Portman Square, February 16, 1863.

MY LORD: I deem it incumbent on me to ask the attention of her Majesty's Government to recent intelligence received here in regard to the blockade at Galveston, in the State of Texas, and at Charleston, in the State of South Carolina.

First, as respects Galveston, it appears that the blockading squadron was driven off from that port and harbor by a superior Confederate force, on the 1st day of January last; one ship was captured, the flagship destroyed, and the rest escaped, making their way, it is said, to some point of the Southern coast occupied by the United States forces. Whatever blockade of the port of Galveston, therefore, may have previously existed, I submit was effectually raised and destroyed by the superior forces of the party blockaded.

Again, as respects the port of Charleston, through the ordinary channels of intelligence we have information, uncontradicted, that the alleged blockade of that port was in like manner raised and destroyed by a superior Confederate force, at a very early hour on the 31st of January ultimo, two ships of the blockading squadron having been sunk, a third escaped disabled, and what remained of the squadron afloat was entirely driven off the coast.

I have the honor to submit, therefore, that the alleged preexisting blockade of the ports aforesaid was terminated at Galveston on the 1st day of January last, and at Charleston on the 31st of the same month, a principle clearly stated in a letter I have had the honor to receive from your lordship, dated on the 10th instant, in the following words:

" The driving off a blockading squadron by a superior force, does break a blockade, which must be renewed de novo in the usual form to be binding upon neutrals," a principle uniformly admitted by all text writers on public law, and established by decisions of courts of admiralty.

I am aware that official information of either of these events may not have reached the Government of her Majesty; but the consequences attending the removal of the blockade, whether to be renewed or no, are so important to the commercial interests involved that I could lose no time in asking that such measures may be taken by her Majesty's Government in relation thereto, as will best tend to the resumption of a commercial intercourse so long placed under restraint.

I avail myself of this occasion to acknowledge the receipt of your lordship's letter of the 10th of February, to which I shall have the honor of sending a reply in the course of a day or two, and am,

With great respect, etc.,

J. M. MASON.

Right Hon. EARL RUSSELL.

FOREIGN OFFICE, *February 16, 1863.*

SIR: I have the honor to acknowledge the receipt of your letter of this date, calling my attention to the occurrences as reported in .the public prints at Galveston and Charleston on the 1st and 31st of January, respectively, and I have the honor to inform you that your letter shall be considered by her Majesty's Government.

I have, etc.,

RUSSELL.

J. M. MASON, Esq.

---

24 UPPER SEYMOUR STREET,
Portman Square, February 18, 1863.

MY LORD: I have the honor to acknowledge the receipt of your letter of the 10th of February instant, in answer to mine of the 3d of January last, but referring more especially to enquiries which I had the honor to address to your lordship under the instruction of the Secretary of State of the Confederate States of America on the 7th day of July last concerning the interpretation placed by her Majesty's Government on the declaration of the principle of blockade agreed to in the convention of Paris.

I shall, as early as practicable, communicate the letter of your lordship to the Government at Richmond, but will anticipate here the satisfaction with which the President will receive the assurance of your lordship that no want of respect was intended by a mere acknowledgment, without other reply, to the enquiries contained in my letter of July.

In regard to so much of the letter of your lordship as relates to the interpretation placed by the Government of her Majesty on that part of the declaration at Paris which prescribed the law of blockade, I am constrained to say that I am well assured the President can not find in it a source of like gratification. It is considered by him that the terms used in that convention are too precise and definite to admit of being qualified; or perhaps it may be more appropriate to say revoked by the superadditions thereto contained in your lordship's exposition of them.

The terms of that convention are that the blockading force must be sufficient really to prevent access to the coast; no exception is made in regard to dark nights, favorable winds, the size or model of vessels successfully evading it, or the character of the coast or waters blockaded; and yet it would seem from your lordship's letter that all these are to be taken into consideration on a question whether the blockade is or is not to be respected. It is declared in that letter that—

It appears to her Majesty's Government to be sufficiently clear that the declaration of Paris could not have been intended to mean that a port must be so blockaded in all winds, and independently of whether the communication was carried on of a dark night, or by means of small, low steamers, or coasting craft creeping along the shore.

What might be considered a small or low steamer coming in from sea to the port of New York would at one of those Southern ports be rated a vessel of very fair, average size when referred to the ordinary state of water on its bar, yet I look in vain, in the terms of the convention referred to, for any authority to expound them in subordination to the depth of water or the size or mold of vessels finding ready and comparatively safe access to the harbor.

In acceding to the terms of that treaty great advantages were yielded to a maritime neutral, with like immunities to a maritime belligerent. The property of the neutral is safe under the flag of the belligerent, and the property of the belligerent equally safe under the flag of the neutral, the only equivalent to the belligerent not maritime, but dependent on other nations as carriers, is this strictly defined principle of the law of blockade which the Confederate States presumed was extended to them when, at the request of her Majesty's Government, they became parties to those stipulations of the convention of Paris of 1856. It results that after yielding full equivalents, the stipulation in regard to blockade reserved as the only one beneficial to them would seem illusory.

In regard to the character of this blockade, to which your lordship again adverts in the remark that the manner in which it has been enforced gives to neutral governments no excuse for asserting that it has not been efficiently maintained, although I have not been instructed to make any further representations to her Majesty's Government on that subject since its decision to treat it as effective, I can not refrain from adding that for many months past the frequent arrival and departure of vessels (most of them steamers) from several of those ports have been matters of notoriety. A single steamer has evaded the blockade successfully, and most generally from Charleston, more than 30 times. And within a few days past it has been brought to my knowledge that two steamers arrived in January last and within ten days of each other at Wilmington, N. C., from ports in Europe, one of them 400 and the other 500 tons burden, both of which have since sailed from Wilmington and arrived with their cargoes at foreign ports. I cite these only as the latest authenticated instances. And, as another fact, it is officially reported by the collector at Charleston that the revenue accruing at that port from duties on imported merchandise during the past year under the blockade was more than double the receipts of any one year previous to the separation of the States, and this although the duties under the Confederate Government are much lower than those exacted by the United States.

As regards other portions of your lordship's letter, I may freely admit, as it is there stated, that a blockade would be in legal existence, although a sudden storm or change of wind occasionally might blow off the blockading squadron, yet, with entire respect, I do not see how such principle affects the question of the efficiency of such blockade whilst the squadron is on the coast.

And, again, whilst I am not informed whether a defense resting on the inadequacy of the blockading force has been urged in cases of capture before the prize courts in America, I can well see how futile such defense would be when presented on behalf of a neutral ship whose Government had not only not objected to but admitted the sufficiency of the blockade.

I have, etc.,

J. M. MASON.

Right Hon. Earl RUSSELL.

FOREIGN OFFICE, *February 19, 1863.*

SIR: With reference to my letter of the 16th instant, acknowledging the receipt of your letter of that day calling attention to the accounts which had reached this country tending to show that the blockade of the ports of Galveston and Charleston had been put an end to by the action of the Confederate naval forces, I have the honor now to state to you that the information which her Majesty's Government have derived from your letter and from the public journals on this subject, is not sufficiently accurate to admit of their forming an opinion, and they wish accordingly, by the first opportunity, to instruct Lord Lyons to report fully on the matter.

When his lordship's report has been received and considered, I shall have the honor of making a further communication to you on the subject.

I have, etc.,

RUSSELL.

J. M. MASON.

DEPARTMENT OF STATE,
Richmond, February 21, 1863.

SIR: Your letter of 6th instant, per *Giraffe*, transmitting certain protests to this Department relative to the British schooner *Harkaway* has been received.

From the papers it appears that these protests emanate from foreigners, who complain of loss and damage suffered by reason of certain judicial proceedings in the courts of the Confederacy.

This Department can pay no attention to these papers for a reason which is now stated as a guide for your own future action.

It is not consistent with usage or propriety that foreigners should make direct application to this Government for indemnity in any case unless the Government has entered into contract with them. Such claims as those which are contained in the papers which you have transmitted can properly reach this Government only through the duly authorized officers of the Governments to which these foreigners owe allegiance. When Great Britain and France shall have entered with diplomatic intercourse with this Government, their duly accredited agents will be listened to with respect when presenting claims of their citizens for indemnity on account of injuries suffered. Till that period, the subjects of those powers must submit to the consequences of the delay caused by the action of their own Governments, and for which this Government is in no wise responsible.

You will, in accordance with these views, decline to make yourself in future the channel of communication for foreigners with this Department, except in cases where such foreigners make claim under contracts made with them by the Government.

I am, respectfully, etc.,

J. P. BENJAMIN,
Secretary of State.

LOUIS HEYLIGER, Esq.,
Nassau, N. P.

No. 16.]   DEPARTMENT OF STATE,
Richmond, February 21, 1863.

SIR: Since my Nos. 14 and 15 of 6th and 7th instant, of which I now send duplicates, nothing of importance has occurred.

The expeditions of the enemy against Vicksburg and against Charleston and Savannah have thus far recoiled from the dangers which threaten any attempt to storm those formidable positions, and the Army of Northern Virginia has been weakened by heavy details sent to the lower James River. No immediate operations in Virginia are at all likely and attention is fixed on the Atlantic coast and the Mississippi Valley. We await the onset with calm confidence.

I enclose you a correspondence with the British consul on the subject of Hester's case, which relieves us from all embarrassment on that subject which was feared as mentioned in my No. 15.

I send for your information a copy of a further correspondence with that official on the subject of his exequatur.

I learn with gratification, through Mrs. Mason, that all my dispatches down to 5th November had been received by you.

I am, very respectfully, etc.,

J. P. BENJAMIN,
Secretary of State.

Hon. JAMES M. MASON,
London.

[Enclosure.]

BRITISH CONSULATE,
Richmond, February 13, 1863.

SIR: I presume that it is well known to you that on the 15th October last the senior officer of the steamer *Sumter*, lying in the port of Gibraltar, was murdered by Mr. Hester, the only other officer on board.

The governor of Gibraltar in notifying this sad occurrence to her Majesty's Government reported that Mr. Hester had been arrested by the authorities, and he requested to be informed whether the trial of the prisoner should take place in the same manner as if the murder had been committed on board of a merchant vessel.

Her Britannic Majesty's Government, conceiving that the *Sumter* was entitled to be regarded as a regularly commissioned man-of-war, came to the conclusion that the course most consistent with international law would be not to treat the offense as the subject of criminal jurisdiction at Gibraltar, but to detain the prisoner until it should be ascertained here how the case was to be dealt with.

I have accordingly the honor to ask you to suggest to me what steps would be most advisable to be taken in this case.

The enclosed copies of depositions taken before the authorities at Gibraltar will put you fully in possession of the circumstances of the murder.

I have the honor to be, sir, your most obedient and humble servant,

GEORGE MOORE, *Consul.*

Hon. J. P. BENJAMIN,
Secretary of State, Department of State, Richmond.

[Enclosure.]

DEPARTMENT OF STATE,
Richmond, February 16, 1863.

SIR: I have the honor to acknowledge receipt of your letter of 13th instant, enclosing copies of the depositions taken before her Majesty's justice of the peace at Gibraltar, in relation to a murder alleged to have been committed by Joseph Goodwyn Hester on board of the Confederate war steamer *Sumter* lying in that port.

In that letter you inform me that her Majesty's Government, upon reference made by the governor of Gibraltar, conceived that the *Sumter* was entitled to be regarded as a regularly commissioned man-of-war and came to the conclusion that the course most consistent with international law would be not to treat the offense as the subject of criminal jurisdiction at Gibraltar, but to detain the prisoner until it could be ascertained here how the case was to be dealt with.

You further ask that I should suggest to you what steps it would be most advisable to take in this case.

I am happy to apprise you that her Majesty's Government was not misinformed as to the fact that the *Sumter* was a duly commissioned man-of-war at the time the offense was committed. That vessel was at the date referred to a public armed ship, the property of the Confederacy, duly commissioned, commanded by officers of the Navy of the Confederate States, and manned by seamen duly enlisted into the public service of the Confederacy. Such being the facts, the principles of international law do, as her Majesty's Government concluded, vest in this Government the exclusive jurisdic‌tion over all crimes and offenses committed on board the *Sumter*.

I have, therefore, the honor to inform you that instructions will be sent by the Secretary of the Navy to the commander of one of the ships of war of the Confederacy to proceed to the port of Gibraltar and there to receive from the authorities of her Britannic Majesty the offender now in custody at that port and to bring him for trial to this country.

It may not be improper to suggest that as all the vessels of war of the Confederacy, except such ironclad and other gunboats as are suitable only for river and harbor defense, are now cruising in distant seas, some time must necessarily elapse before instructions can reach the officer to whom the duty of reclaiming the offender is confided. If, under these circumstances, it should be more convenient that the offender be transported to this country in any one of her

Majesty's vessels that may have occasion to touch upon our coast than to retain him in custody during the delay that must otherwise intervene, such disposal of the case would be equally acceptable to this Government.

In conclusion, I beg to express the sense entertained by this Government of the courtesy of her Majesty's Government in bringing the matter to the attention of the department.

I am, very respectfully, your obedient servant,

J. P. BENJAMIN,
Secretary of State.

GEORGE MOORE, Esq.,
H. B. M. Consul, Richmond, Va.

No. 19.]

HAVANA, *February 24, 1863.*

SIR: I have the honor to enclose herewith a copy of my note to his Excellency the Captain-General Serrano, now minister for foreign affairs at Madrid. I shall offer no other apology to the Department for this interference beyond the limits to which I have been accredited than the hope that by it, I may in some degree benefit my country.

I have the honor to be, with great respect, your obedient servant,

CH. J. HELM.

Hon. J. P. BENJAMIN,
Secretary of State, Richmond.

[Enclosure.]

Private and confidential.]

HAVANA, *February 22, 1863.*

MY DEAR SIR: I heartily congratulate you on the safe arrival of yourself and family at Madrid and trust that the voyage and change of climate has greatly improved your health. I rejoice with your other many friends here in the prompt appointment of yourself to so prominent a seat in the councils of your nation as that of minister of foreign affairs. It is at once a full endorsement of your successful administration of the affairs of Cuba, during eventful, exciting, and troublous scenes in close proximity to the field of your labors, and a cutting rebuke to your enemies, in all of which, be assured, my dear General, you have left few behind who have shared with you more fully the pleasure growing out of your triumph than myself.

I freely confess that, in part, this note has been prompted by selfish motives, but know you will excuse both the motive and the intrusion upon your time.

Your frequent allusions to my country and your unreserved expressions of sympathy for my brothers in arms, now struggling to free themselves from their barbarous invaders, and your voluntary promise before leaving Cuba to become our friend and advocate in Europe, induces me to throw out a few suggestions to you on the subject of our recognition by European powers.

The community of interests between the Spanish possessions in the West Indies and the Confederate States and the identity of institutions in one prominent feature renders it important to each that they should be close friends. I will not enlarge on this subject, for we have discussed it and you understand it as well as does the President of the Confederacy. All Europe is now convinced, as you were before leaving America, that the Southern States are able, and will sustain their separate independence, and sooner or later their recognition by all christendom must be conceded; why delay? Why permit the cavaliers of the South to be longer pitted in deadly strife against the hirelings of the North? Why should our mothers, wives, sisters, and aged fathers suffer longer from the brutal, ruthless, ravaging foe when their sons, husbands, and brothers have illustrated their valor and given evidence of their right to independence on a hundred bloody fields of victory? Your heart has long since answered they deserve to be free, and I now appeal to you to become the great pacificator, an office to which by head and heart you are so well fitted. I am assured by my correspondents in Europe that the French Emperor would join any first-class European power in the recognition of our independence, that he would even intervene between the belligerents. You have long been of the opinion that it was the duty of Europe to act promptly. Why not take the initiatory? Why not yourself become the first great friend of the young Republic and make a chapter in history of which the young duke will, in after years, be so proud? Why not at once win for yourself and your descendants the love of a proud nation, destined to be great and powerful? Already by your course in Cuba you have won the hearts of our people, and I freely say to you that there is no man in Europe whose interference in our behalf would so gratify our entire population as yourself; then I beg you to propose without delay the cooperation of Spain with France in the recognition of the Confederate States of America, and draw upon your head the blessings of a united people, struggling in a holy cause.

It may be proper to remark in this note that I have seen in a paper published at Madrid strictures upon our people, growing out of the several raids from the United States upon Cuba, in former times. I have simply to say that the only motive or interest which prompted any Southerner to join such raids or which made the acquisition of Cuba desirable was to retain a balance of power in the United States Senate and protect our rights under the Constitution; that with the separation the motive is removed and now the interest of the South requires a slave power in Europe to cooperate with her in the protection of the peculiar institutions of the Confederate States, Cuba, Porto Rico, and Santo Domingo, and I now pledge you the word of one whose word you will respect that our people will be as jealous of your rights in the West Indies as of their own at home.

With grateful remembrances to the duchess, I am, general, with profound respect, your friend,

CH. J. HELM.

His Excellency
The Captain-General, Don FRANCISCO SERRANO,
Minister for Foreign Affaires, etc., Madrid.

No. 40.]

25 RUE ROYALE,
Brussels, February 27, 1863.

SIR: I have the honor to receive yesterday your dispatches, dated respectively January 15 and 17, each numbered 6, and a duplicate of

your No. 3, together with the printed documents transmitted therewith. My file of your dispatches is now complete. I must add that
Mr. Mason duly furnished me with copies of your interesting narrative of the events of the war.

Should any question be raised, when I may hereafter open negotiations with this Government for the conclusion of a general treaty of
friendship, commerce, and navigation, in relation to a stipulation
concerning the African slave trade, I shall furnish the Belgian
plenipotentiary with a copy of your unanswerable instructions upon
the subject, contained in your dispatch of the 17th ultimo. Even in
the absence of such instructions I never would have entertained for
a moment a proposition by which my Government would be required
to take upon itself obligations to another Government with respect
to this traffic.

The whole tenor of yours of the 17th, which I shall mark No. 7, is
such as to be exceedingly gratifying to my feelings. I can not appreciate too highly the partiality of the President for me, in the reason
which you assign for his hesitancy in appointing me special envoy
extraordinary and minister plenipotentiary near this Government.
My only object in making the request was to bestow the highest compliment possible upon the most earnest, the most energetic, and the
most constant friend we have ever had among the sovereigns of the
earth.

The gentle mention which you make that the discrepancy between
the opinions and views which I have expressed in relation to the
Emperor of the French and Lord Palmerston and those expressed
by Mr. Slidell and Mr. Mason has occasioned the Cabinet some perplexity, causes me much regret, which would, indeed, be intense were
it not for the remark, "We shall be glad, however, at all times to
have your own impressions as aids to the formation of conclusions
which it is not always easy to reach, even under the most favorable
circumstances." In this sense I have invariably considered it to be
my imperative duty to write, when interspersing my dispatches with
that which, according to the lights before me, I saw transpiring in
European countries. If I have arrived at incorrect conclusions,
those conclusions will the more readily become manifest to you in
the presence of the representations emanating from the keen and
accurate perceptions of Mr. Slidell and the calm and ready discern-
ment of Mr. Mason. I should be unpardonably vain were I to
attempt to set up my judgment in opposition to their ripe experience
and close observation. I aim at nothing more than to give utterance
to my Government of my own impressions. Brussels is a sort of
"loophole of retreat" through which the European world may sometimes be advantageously surveyed.

The President's message was received on this side of the Atlantic
about three weeks ago, and has since made the circuit of Europe
in one language or another. It has been read with interest and
generally received with favor. In its criticisms upon the conduct
of the parties to the Paris declaration, and particularly upon that
of Great Britain, it is as just as it is irrefutable. What better commentary could be made upon the ineffectiveness of the blockade than
my receipt from yourself of an acknowledgment of my dispatch of
the 18th of December on the 26th instant, both communications hav-

ing passed through Charleston? This is almost equal to proverbial old-fashioned mail-coach regularity. Great Britain and France, as all the signs of the times are beginning distinctly to indicate, will have enormous penalties to pay for their want of an observance of good faith to their commitments to each other in 1856, and to their equally obligatory commitments to the Confederate States in 1861, so forcibly stated by the President in his message.

The dispatch of Mr. Seward to Mr. Dayton, in reply to the last proposition of the French Government, has just appeared in the newspapers. It will go far to confirm the belief, everywhere previously created in intelligent circles, that Mr. Seward has fairly won the title of the " Common liar " of secretaries for foreign affairs, as his chief has indisputably won the title of the " Executive buffoon."

The public mind of Europe at this moment is almost exclusively preoccupied with Poland and the Poles. The sympathies of all ages, sexes, and conditions are ardently enlisted for the success of the patriots. The King of Prussia, in espousing the cause of the Czar, has rendered himself the most odious of monarchs. He has no alternative but to retrace his steps if he would avoid his overthrow and save his realm from dismemberment. I believe that the revolt of the Poles will again be stifled, and that the old partitioning allies will continue to hold them in subjugation for a period at least far beyond the present. The exclamation of Kosciusko when he fell from his horse in the battle of Maciejowice severely wounded, " Finis Poloniæ," seems to have been prophetic. Wisely, as sorrowfully, did he reply to Russia when she proposed to restore to him his sword upon releasing him from captivity: " I have no use for my weapon, for I have no longer a country." If there be one citizen of the Confederate States who is disposed to accept of any terms from the soidisant United States but unconditional independence, let him keep the fate of fallen Poland constantly and vividly before his eyes.

I shall have duplicates of my missing dispatches prepared and transmitted to you by the first safe private conveyance which presents itself after they are ready. Before this I trust you are in possession of my No. 32.

I have the honor to be, sir, very respectfully, your obedient servant,
A. DUDLEY MANN.

Hon. J. P. BENJAMIN,
  Secretary of State, C. S. A., Richmond, Va.

FOREIGN OFFICE, *February 27, 1863.*

SIR: I have the honor to acknowledge the receipt of your further letter of the 18th instant on the subject of the interpretation placed by her Majesty's Government on the declaration of the principle of blockade made in 1856 by the conference at Paris.

I have already in my previous letters fully explained to you the views of her Majesty's Government on this matter, and I have nothing to add in reply to your last letter except to observe that I have not intended to state that any number of vessels of a certain build or tonnage might be left at liberty freely to enter a blockaded port without vitiating the blockade, but that the occasional escape of small vessels on dark nights or under other particular circumstances from the vigilance of a competent blockading fleet did not evince that laxity in the belligerent which inured, according to international law, to the raising of a blockade.

I have, etc.,

RUSSELL.

J. M. MASON.

---

24 UPPER SEYMOUR STREET,
Portman Square, March 2, 1863.

MY LORD: I have the honor to transmit herewith to your lordship, as her Majesty's secretary of state for foreign affairs, a copy of a dispatch from the Secretary of State of the Confederate States of America, bearing date December 11, 1862, which was received by me on the 25th of February ultimo.

I do this, as your lordship will perceive, pursuant to instructions at the close of the dispatch, directing me to furnish a copy to your lordship at the earliest moment.

I avail myself of this occasion to acknowledge the receipt of your lordship's letter of the 19th of February ultimo, in reply to mine of the 16th, respecting the blockade of the ports of Galveston and Charleston. And also of your lordship's letter of the 27th of February in reply to mine of the 18th of that month.

The contents of both shall be communicated as soon as practicable to the Government at Richmond.

I have, etc.,

J. M. MASON.

Right Hon. EARL RUSSELL.

PARIS, *March 2, 1863.*

SIR: I have been instructed by the Secretary of State of the Confederate States of America to submit to your Excellency a copy of a dispatch addressed by him to me on the 11th December last. The importance of the suggestions therein contained is such as to render it unnecessary for me to invite its serious consideration. I avail myself of this opportunity to present copies of two letters, which I read to you when I last had the honor to see you. The writers are gentlemen for whose character and truthfulness I can unhesitatingly vouch. They demonstrate conclusively the inefficiency of the blockade of the ports of Wilmington and Charleston. I would also beg leave to call your Excellency's attention to the fact of the blockade of Galveston having been raised for several days by the capture and dispersion of the vessels of the blockading squadron by the Confederate forces. The question of the blockade has been so fully treated in the recent message of the President to the Confederate Congress, a copy of which accompanies this note, and in the letter which I had the honor to address to your predecessor on the 21st July last, that it would be superfluous to say more on that subject than to suggest that perhaps this may be an opportune moment to re-examine the question of blockade, as well on the general principle established, or more correctly speaking, recognized by the fourth article of the treaty of Paris of 16th April, 1856, as on the application of that principle to the facts and circumstances of the pretended blockade by the Federal Government of a coast line of 3,000 miles.

I have the honor to be, with the greatest respect, your Excellency's most obedient servant,

JOHN SLIDELL.

His Excellency M. DROUYN DE LHUYS,
Minister of Foreign Affairs.

No. 28.]   PARIS, *March 4, 1863.*

SIR: Since my last dispatch of 27th ultimo, I have received your Nos. 10, 11, and 12.

On the 10th January I forwarded triplicates of my missing dispatches Nos. 1, 3, 4, 5, 6; as they may not be more fortunate than the originals and duplicates, I send you herewith an abstract of their contents.

On the 22d ultimo I had a long interview with Mr. Drouyn de Lhuys expecting that he would have received something definite from Mr. Mercier on the subject of the proposition for a conference made by the letter of 9th January. Although a letter had been received from Mr. Mercier dated 5th February, no mention whatever was made of the subject, not even an acknowledgment of the receipt of the dispatch of 9th January. This was the more extraordinary as Mr. Drouyn de Lhuys was informed from London that Mr. Mercier intended to read that dispatch to Mr. Seward on the 3d February.

I spoke at large to the minister on the subject of the blockade, insisted upon the evidence formally presented of its inefficiency, of the regret that the Emperor had frankly expressed to me at having acquiesced in it, of his declaration that he had by his acquiescence committed a gross error, whether the question were considered on the ground of principle or of expediency.

I read to him two letters, one from Major Huse, the other from Captain Styles, showing the facility with which vessels constantly eluded the blockade of Wilmington and Charleston.

I spoke of the destruction and dispersion of the blockading squadron at Galveston by our forces and the raising of the blockade of that port for several days, and asked whether the circumstances were not opportune for the thorough reexamination and reconsideration of the whole question. He said that no action could be had in the matter without consultation with England. I think that if it could have been presented by me a few days sooner, his response would probably have been more favorable, for I know that the France, a journal enjoying in a high degree the confidence of the Government, had commenced a series of articles on the blockade at the inspiration of the ministry of foreign affairs, and that they even [were] discontinued on a hint received from the same quarter. The cause of this change was the prospect of difficulty with Prussia, growing out of a convention said to have been entered into by that power with Russia for the suppression of the Polish insurrection. The identity of views on this subject entertained by France and England and the anticipated community of action have led to a temporary reestablishment, superficially at least, of the entente cordiale between the two Governments. I feel convinced that a fortnight since the Emperor would have been pleased at the opportunity of showing his readiness to separate his policy from that of England, but the hope of her alliance in a war which would result in realizing the great French idea of the Rhine as a frontier renders him for the moment as desirous as ever to cultivate the most cordial relations with her. It seems, however, now probable that the difficulty will be adjusted by Prussia receding from the convention or frittering it away by modifications and explanations; if so, the entente cordiale will soon be again interrupted.

I spoke to Mr. Drouyn de Lhuys of the matter mentioned in cipher in my No. 23. He said that it was one on which he was not necessarily called to act; that it belonged rather to the minister of commerce or marine (iprzwems sw vmpiicnw hy qrvqfq); that it was better that he should know nothing of it (ipcq ahkfeuk fj tb); that he was quite willing to close his eyes (us temva ltd wrlw) until some direct appeal was made to him.

The minister was extremely cordial; said that he would always be happy to see me whenever I desired it, but that unless something special occurred it would be better that I should communicate through the friend of whom I have spoken in previous dispatches.

He asked me to send him through that channel any information or suggestion that I might desire to make. This is a very convenient and agreeable arrangement, dispensing with the delays and formalities attending personal interviews with the minister.

On the following day I called by appointment on Mr. Rouher (nvyyic) with Mr. Voruz (dpvls) deputy from Nantes (ldjxpd), of whom I spoke in my No. 25. The express object of the appointment was to receive from him a distinct assurance that if we were to build ships of war in French ports (lh iyzpl ktgrg is prp eu jiiyki tfkrv) we should be permitted to arm and equip them and proceed to sea (wvx lpw lulmx ltco ohu iimyliu xz afe). This assurance was given by him, and so soon as the success of Erlanger's loan is established I shall write to Messrs. Maury and Bulloch (dtsuu eyo tnspggs) recommending them to come here for the purpose of ascertaining whether they can make satisfactory contracts.

The partner of a large banking house at Vienna recently called to see me, he says that the Austrian (wbwkvtio) Government has some very superior war steamers (ark qwaexpjl) which can be bought thoroughly armed and ready for sea (alfvwmsfum uefvb wuh iillz jfk qhw) with the exception of the crews (gcpol). I shall advise Mr. Maury (telvg) to look at them.

Seward's letter to Dayton rejecting the proposition for a conference was published two or three days since; its tone is considered very exceptionable, and his boasting assertions are universally received with ridicule and contempt. I have not been able to learn what impression it had produced on the Emperor, but I remain unchanged in my opinion that he will not long allow our question to rest where it is.

I send you a copy of a letter addressed by me to the minister of foreign affairs with a copy of your No. 10. I am obliged to you for files of Richmond papers. Until the arrival of Mr. de Leon, I sent you regularly the Paris journals, but have not since done so, presuming that he will have kept you supplied.

I am still without your No. 5 of new series and all except 1, 2, 3, 5, of old series. I hope that you will send copies to complete the files of the commission.

In my conversation with Mr. Drouyn de Lhuys, I mentioned the loan of Erlanger & Co., and invoked his good offices in carrying it out, saying that these gentlemen considered it important that it should be advertised in the Paris papers, but that the advertisement could not be made without the assent of the Government. He expressed his wishes for the success of the loan, but thought that he could not consent to the advertisement; that the object could be equally well attained by circulars, etc., while advertisements would excite unfriendly comment and probably be made the subject of a protest from the Federal minister.

The consent of the minister of finance, Mr. Fould, had been obtained subject, however, to the approbation of the minister of foreign affairs. Erlanger & Co. then brought the subject before the Emperor, who very promptly directed his secretary to write a note to the minister, requesting him to grant an audience to Mr. Erlanger on an urgent matter in which he felt great interest.

The result of the audience was the withdrawal by Mr. Drouyn de Lhuys of his objections and the loan will now be simultaneously advertised here and in London. I mention this fact as offering renewed evidence of the friendly feeling of the Emperor.

I have the honor to be, with great respect, your most obedient servant,

JOHN SLIDELL.

Hon. J. P. BENJAMIN,
   Secretary of State.

No. 20.]   HAVANA, *March 6, 1863.*

SIR: I regret that it becomes my duty to inform the Department that recently several small lots of cotton from the Confederate States have been sold here and shipped to New York, and that the entire cargo, some 650 bales, brought from Mobile to Havana by the steamer *Alice* was, about the 1st instant, sold by Mr. Addison Cammack , of New Orleans, the agent of that steamer here, without any condition, and will also be shipped to New York. Cotton brings from 2 to 4 cents per pound more for the New York than European markets, hence the inducement. The *Alice* will sail from this again in about two weeks for Mobile, with the view of bringing out another cargo of cotton, and, should the Government object to its finding its way to the enemy, the proper official at Mobile should be advised in the premises.

I have the honor to be, with great respect, your obedient servant,

CH. J. HELM.

Hon. J. P. BENJAMIN,
   Secretary of State, Richmond.

No. 41.]   25 RUE ROYALE,
                             Brussels, March 13, 1863.

SIR: So far as I can judge from the most reliable information before me, the chances for an early European recognition of our independence have not increased in the slightest degree since the date of my last. The Emperor of the French seems to be just as far as ever from taking the initiative in this regard.

He may now perhaps distinctly perceive that his last proposition has had the effect of imparting no small amount of additional strength to the Lincoln Administration for the prosecution of hostilities. It certainly has enabled that Administration to carry its reckless measures triumphantly through Congress with the tacit sanction of the Democratic party. I now apprehend that in one way or another an entente cordiale, proceeding from an almost certain amicable settlement of the differences of M. Mercier and Seward, will be patched up between the Cabinet of the Tuileries and the Cabinet at Washington. Louis Napoleon is a yielding potentate where it is to his interest not to be over resolute, and there is no humiliation to which Lincoln will not submit to preserve amicable relations with France. The conscience of Seward is so elastic that it may be expanded so as to embrace the most dishonorable emergencies. The Emperor of the French is surrounded by many more serious embarrassments at this time than he was in the middle of October, when the King of the Belgians so earnestly appealed to him to welcome us into the family of nations. The truth can not be disguised, muzzled as the Parisian newspaper press is upon the subject, that the utterly unexpected obstinacy of the resistance to his invasion of Mexico gives him deep concern. To fail in the object of that invasion would be to gravely impair that high prestige for eminent success in his undertakings which imparts so much power to his throne. He must and will, I think, occupy the old halls of the Montezumas, cost what it may. He can not, therefore, incur the risk of provoking the angry displeasure of the North, as he may continue to find himself dependent upon her for indispensable supplies for the use of his armies.

Then again from Prince Napoleon down to the humblest, there are half-expressed utterances faintly reaching his ears that Poland, hopeless as is her future, must be recognized if the Confederate States are. And yet again the election for members of the Corps Legislatif is approaching, wherein there is a possibility that the Legitimists, the Orleanists, the Moderate Republicans, and the Red Republicans may outnumber the Imperialists. In addition to all this, he has hanging heavily upon his shoulders the unemployed and discontented cotton operatives, whose number is steadily and rapidly increasing. Nor is he free from care with respect to the orderly government of Algeria. He could, perhaps without much risk, have done anything he chose for the advancement of our interests six months ago. If he had then led, all Europe would have cheerfully followed, and with such an influence operating upon the North at the time of our victory of Fredericksburg, I verily belived that as salutary results to our cause would have ensued as if an additional force of 100,000 efficient armed men had entered the field on our side. The case is probably different to-day. A swift triumphant march of his troops to the City of Mexico and the early suppression by Russia of the uprising in Poland are required to make him again complete master of his position or rather to establish him in the estimation in which he has until recently been held as an invincible warrior and far-seeing statesman. I think it proper to state that I am just as incredulous as ever of his reported good intentions to aid, directly or indirectly, in our development as a power of the earth. To my no small chagrin, I have convincing evidence, at least to my own mind, to the contrary. I dare say that there are as upright sovereigns as reign who now concur with me in this opinion.

In previous dispatches I assured you that the British ministry determined in September last to recognize us without delay, and that the coming event was foreshadowed by Mr. Gladstone in his celebrated Newcastle speech. Of this determination I must now state that I have in my possession evidence, confidentially communicated to me, of undoubted authority. When the measure was abandoned, in the presence of that which was considered a paramount necessity, Sir Cornewall Lewis assumed the position in reference to it, adopted by Earl Derby the first night of the session, which, in effect, was that our independence ought not to be acknowledged until it was acknowledged by the United States, or at least until it was distinctly clear that the powers of the Government thereof were so exhausted that Lincoln could no longer carry on the war. For the public expression of this new-fangled doctrine I know from the best of sources that Sir Cornwall was required to furnish written explanations to the different members of the cabinet. Shortly afterwards his strange dogmas found a champion in a writer in the Times signing himself 'Historicus," his son-in-law, a young barrister of high promise. This writer had achieved considerable reputation in the publication of several well-prepared articles upon the *Trent* affair, and he was thus enabled to impress some of the statesmen and many of the politicians of Great Britain, by sophistry and misrepresentations of facts, with the belief that we had not yet perfected our rights to admission into the family of nations. I think I can venture to state that Lord Palmerston and Mr. Gladstone were not of the number. It is presumable that "Historicus" was inspired by the secretary of war, whose abilities are of a superior order and whose experience is large and varied. I shall be slow in dismissing my convictions, considering the manner in which they had their creation, that the venerable premier, with the chancellor of the exchequer standing unflinchingly by his side, will avail himself of the first suitable occasion which presents itself (such as would be our success at Charleston and Vicksburg) to emphatically declare in the Commons that "President Davis and his compatriots" have in fact and in truth made a nation of the South to all intents and purposes. The consideration, paramount in its character, by which he is at present restrained from taking an unyielding position in this regard is, I am quite persuaded, the fear that it would eventuate, through the machination of Disraeli, Bright, and others, in upsetting his Government. An octogenarian, his fall would be his final official death. It is perhaps natural, therefore, that he should hazard nothing that he can avoid, and the more so as it is believed to be his highest ambition to quit earth at the head of the Government.

The restoration of the old European nationalities is becoming more and more a fixed sentiment with the people of this hemisphere. Almost everybody seems to be clamorously ardent for the reestablishment of Poland. The manifestations of sympathy for her are as earnest and general at Stockholm as they are at Lisbon. I consider the event as next to an impossibility, though it is not unlikely that the Czar may consent to important ameliorations in his system of government at Warsaw. The cotton famine is steadily demoralizing the industrial population of Europe. It is seen and admitted both upon the Continent and in Great Britain that to feed men by public charity who have no employment is to make them vicious and lazy. The force of the adage that "an idle brain is the devil's workshop" was never more apparent than it is in the instance of the paupers which the want of our staple has engendered in Western Europe.

I have the honor to be, sir,

Very respectfully, your obedient servant.

A. DUDLEY MANN.

Hon. J. P. BENJAMIN,
   Secretary of State, Richmond, Va.

No. 19.]   CONFEDERATE STATES COMMERCIAL AGENCY,
London, March 14, 1863.

SIR: I have the honor to acknowledge the receipt, on the 26th of February, of your dispatch No. 3, dated January 16, with enclosures, consisting first of one Treasury draft on Messrs. Fraser, Trenholm & Co., of Liverpool, for £1,000, appropriated by the President out of the secret-service fund, for the contingent expenses of this agency; and secondly, a Treasury draft on the same for £250, to be expended in the purchase of stationery for the Department according to order and samples transmitted.

I am deeply impressed with the mark of confidence and approval on the part of the President and of yourself, conveyed by the tenor of your dispatch, and I am encouraged to renewed efforts to deserve both. Although a portion of the sum sent me was, as you are aware from my previous communications, already anticipated, I feel assured that the means now at my command, viz, at the rate of £2,000 per annum, are ample for the proper development of my plans, and that I shall no longer be compelled to weary you with applications, for the frequent reiteration of which I trust you will accept my motives as an apology. It is not my purpose to enlarge my expenditures beyond the judicious use of opportunities as they naturally present themselves, and I shall endeavor, if possible, to keep constantly a small reserve fund for such opportunities as may arise unforeseen. The self-confidence which ample means give and the promptness of action which they induce are in a service like mine the surest promotives of economy.

I notice well your instructions concerning vouchers for the disbursement of the secret-service money. While it is easy to give a satisfactory account for such disbursements, it is extremely difficult to obtain vouchers. Fortunately the books of the Index enable me to overcome this difficulty to a great extent. From an abstract of these books I find that I have given partial employment, by means of the Index, up to the present, exclusive of my permanent assistants, to seven writers on the daily London press. Of these, concentration of my efforts being a leading object, four are colleagues of one editorial corps. The disbursements for little personal compliments, such as boxes of cigars imported from Havana through the aid of Mr. Helm, American whisky, and other articles which not being generally procurable form acceptable presents, it is of course out of the question to give vouchers. I am anxious to send my accounts for the year ending 14th November last, but, however guardedly these may be made out, their publication, should they fall into the enemy's hands, would so embarrass my actions that I still await a more timely opportunity to transmit them, and this will probably present itself in a couple of weeks

In executing the order for stationery I found upon estimate that I could increase the whole quantity by nearly or quite one-third, and at the same time improve the quality of the dispatch paper upon the sample sent, and I have accordingly so modified the order. I regret, however, that, although in the hands of one of the largest firms in London, some three or four weeks will yet elapse before the order can be filled and the goods forwarded.

The political horizon presents but little of interest. A motion by Lord Campbell (usually called by the newspapers by his other title of Lord Stratheden) at first for correspondence, and subsequently extended " to call attention to the question of acknowledging the Southern Confederacy as an independent power, in concert with other neutral States," has been three times postponed; once through the indisposition of the mover and twice at the request of Earl Russell. It is at last set for Monday next, the 16th, and I hope to be able to transmit the debate next week via Bermuda.

Meanwhile the correspondence asked for, to wit, that between Mr. Mason and the foreign office, has been, at least in part, laid before Parliament on Thursday night last, and is herewith transmitted. Lord Campbell's threatened motion has had another salutary effect. It has elicited a very remarkable article from the Morning Post, herewith enclosed, to which the character of that paper as the personal organ of Lord Palmerston, gives a more important ministerial authority than I know it really to possess. The article, however, has done good. The Times on the same subject, simply contented itself with repeating the worn-out assertion that recognition would exasperate the North, and according to its invariable custom sneered at those who attempted to bring the subject under Parliamentary attention. Nevertheless it admitted indirectly that the public mind was prepared for the step whenever the proper time arrived. The cabinet, apparently, are no nearer to settling that long-promised "proper time," but I am informed that the form of acknowledgment has been under consideration, and that it has been suggested that it should be done by instructing the consuls to ask for exequaturs. This form of consular recognition would, it was asserted, have the same practical effect as diplomatic recognition, and conciliate some scruples which still exist against the latter form. This hint which I received from a reliable quarter is the explanation of the enclosed article from the Index of this week. It is only by acting upon such intimations that I can make the Index truly useful. Random abuse or persistent attacks upon the ministry, which after all combines as many friendly elements as any Tory ministry that might succeed it, would only impair the influence which the paper has been steadily acquiring. I mention this because our compatriots, the greater part of whom reside in Paris, are manifesting an increasing bitterness against England, and I find it difficult to resist the moral pressure which is thus brought to bear upon me, and am conscious that I sacrifice the popularity of the paper among the Southerners to what I concieve to be the exigencies of policy.

The festivities consequent upon the marriage of the Prince of Wales, coupled with the absence of any very startling news from America, have temporarily diverted the national mind from our affairs. What attention could be bestowed elsewhere has been given to Poland, and a recent debate in Parliament, in which all shades of all opinions united, showed how deep and, I believe, sincere the sympathies of this country are for a people alien to them in every respect except that it belongs, as we do not, to the European sisterhood. One tithe of the same earnestness of purpose would have saved us much suffering and precious blood. In Lancashire the distress has not indeed extended, but the patience of the sufferers is diminishing. I enclose an article from to-day's Times on this subject.

I send this day a brief, cautiously worded private letter to you by way of the North, without inside address or signature. If received please acknowledge, as it is an experiment of a new route which on sufficient trial may be of exceeding importance. I send also a duplicate set of Blue Books by same.

I have the honor to remain, very respectfully, your obedient servant,
HENRY HOTZE.

Hon. J. P. BENJAMIN,
   Secretary of State, Richmond

No. 31.]   CONFEDERATE STATES COMMISSION,
                                 London, March 19, 1863.

SIR: * * *

Since the date of my last of the 5th of February, namely, on the 10th of that month, I received a letter from Earl Russell acknowledging mine of the 3d of January previous and in reply to the communication I had addressed to him on the 7th of July, 1862, a copy of which I have the honor to enclose herewith, and with it my reply dated on the 18th of February, and his rejoinder of the 27th. You will observe by them that amiable relations, at least, are restored between the foreign office and myself, although his lordship adheres, and I doubt not will continue to adhere, to the vague interpretation placed at the foreign office on the convention of Paris in regard to blockade. Although I informed the secretary that his letter should be transmitted as early as practicable to the Government at Richmond, yet I thought it well to reply to it in anticipation of instructions from you. I am to hope that the substance of that reply will meet your approval.

I transmit also, herewith, copy of a letter addressed to Earl Russell dated the 16th of February last, calling his attention to the intelligence then recently received here in regard to the actual raising of the blockade at Galveston, and the alleged like event at Charleston, together with his replies of the 16th and 19th of the same month.

The promptitude of those replies would seem to evince at least a desire to conciliate.

I also transmit, herewith, a copy of my letter to Earl Russell of the 2d of March instant, communicating to him, as instructed, a copy of your No. 11 of the 11th of December, 1862, relating to the protection due to neutrals by their respective governments, of cotton purchased or held by them in the Confederate States, with extended remarks as to the future destination of the commerce of those States with foreign nations, provided proper measures were adopted by the latter to invite and to secure it. His reply, you will observe, tenders me his thanks for the communication.

The views contained in your dispatch in regard to that commerce are certainly such as ought to impress themselves deeply on the commercial and maritime powers of Europe, and place them under great responsibilities to their people should they allow them to pass unheeded. I observe with satisfaction that the same dispatch, with like instructions to communicate a copy of it to the foreign office at Paris, has also been sent to Mr. Slidell.

The subject of extending protection to English cotton purchased or owned by neutrals in the Confederate States, has already been the subject of many notes between Lord Lyons and Mr. Seward, and between the former and Earl Russell, as shown in the diplomatic correspondence laid before Parliament recently published, of which I transmit a printed copy. The views you present may, and I should hope would, have their effect upon the Emperor of France, but such seems to be the absolute determination of the British cabinet to refrain from any act which the United States may choose to consider objectionable, that I have little expectation of any fruits from it in this quarter. The Emperor, I have reason to believe, would not be so actuated; but such seems the entanglement of his position, first from his unfortunate and ill-starred expedition to Mexico, and now, from the complications thrown around him by the recent outbreak or revolution in Poland, that I doubt much whether he can take any active steps in the matter just now. Mr. Slidell, however, can better inform you in this matter than I can.

The two events to which I have referred in the raising of the blockade at Galveston, and the daring, and for the time, successful assault by our ironclads on the blockading squadron at Charleston, have made a strong impression on the public mind here, still deepened, as events progress, by the capture on the Mississippi, at first of the ironclad *Queen of the West*, followed by that of her consort, the *Indianola*, capped as it has all beautifully been by the destruction of the *Hatteras* by the *Alabama*. Such prowess, with the energy, daring, and fertility of resource, which originated and attended each achievement, the more and more confirms all opinion in Europe (to use the language of the London Times of this morning) that it is hopeless to the North to restore the Union of the States as would be the attempt here to restore the heptarchy.

Still so obdurate is the Government in its purpose to remain passive, that all present idea of recognition here is given up.

My No. 30 of February 9, which goes with this, was sent to Liverpool to overtake the messenger who bore my No. 29, and those accompanying it. He had sailed, however, before it got there, and it was returned to me. There goes with it a report of the proceedings and debate in Parliament on the Queen's speech, the first day of the session. I was in hopes they would have reached you a month earlier.

I have nothing to add on the prospect of recognition to what is contained in that dispatch; nor am I aware that the question is in any different position before Parliament than as there reported. I have heard that Judge Haliburton, late of Nova Scotia, but now resident in England, and a member of the House of Commons, intended to offer a motion to that end in the House; but our most judicious friends there are against the movement under the circumstances, and I approve their judgment. Still, although I know Judge Haliburton very well and have found him an earnest and decided friend to the South, as he did not advise with me about the motion, I have thought it best not to interfere.

I am most happy to record here, although the news will have reached you long before you get this dispatch, the decided and brilliant success of the Confederate loan. Mr. Erlanger, who has been for the last ten days in London, seems to have worked it with great diligence and tact. He has conferred freely and frankly with me, and as there was a strong opinion in moneyed circles of the city that the enterprise was a hazardous one, and likely to fail in the market, I am the more impressed by the judgment and good sense evinced by Erlanger. It was placed on the market yesterday, when more than 5,000,000 sterling were subscribed at once, and before night it commanded a premium of $4\frac{1}{2}$ to 5 per cent. What has been subscribed at Liverpool, and on the Continent we have not heard, but the books do not close until to-morrow at 2 p. m. I saw Erlanger last night, who was of course much gratified at his success. He does not doubt that the entire subscription will reach, most probably exceed, ten millions. Although, doubtless, the larger subscription was made in expectation of profit, yet I know from many sources that very large sums were subscribed from a single desire to serve the Confederate cause, and the leading houses in London and Paris subscribed largely.

I send herewith Nos. 1, 2, and 3 of diplomatic correspondence laid before Parliament and just printed. No. 1, containing that with the United States; No. 2, between Earl Russell and myself; and No. 3, with the United States legation here relating to the *Alabama*. These papers were sent in before my correspondence with Earl Russell after the 27th February had taken place.

In regard to the *Alabama*, I have received three or four letters from persons claiming to be British subjects, and accompanied by documents to show that property belonging to them had been destroyed by the *Alabama*, as part of the cargo, in some of her captures. I replied, in each case, that I would transmit them to my Government, if they desired it; but that in my opinion their proper course would be to send them through their secretary for foreign affairs. In one of these cases I was informed by the claimant that he had applied at the foreign office, and the reply given was that the only redress was through the prize courts of the Confederate States. I presume these claims had better be retained here until the war is over. They are for comparatively small amounts.

It will give me great pleasure to obtain the books mentioned in the list accompanying your No. 14, and I will send them as you request, through Messrs. Fraser & Co. as early as practicable, first conferring with Mr. Hotze to avoid duplicates. If the cost is not greater than I anticipate, the money can be spared from the contingent fund until you can replace it.

I have with very great pleasure delivered your late message to Mr. Lindsay concerning the project, under his auspices, of establishing a line of French steamers between France and some Southern port. I sent him a transcript of so much of your dispatch as expressed the opinions of the President, with a proffer of the earnest welcome that awaited him, should he go over in person, as he proposed, to arrange the details of such direct communication. He was much gratified at the kind and liberal expressions of the President toward him, and begged that I would say so to the President through you in my next dispatch. He has the subject of immediate direct trade with us, as the first fruits of our independence, much at heart; has given it great consideration, as a much experienced shipowner; is master of all the detail; and from his intimate intercourse in all commercial matters with the French Government. I should think would have it in his power as certainly as he has the will and purpose to carry the scheme into effect. He will go to our country, and on this single errand, as soon as peace is proclaimed. He is a man of large and independent fortune, of which he has been the sole architect; of liberal and unfettered opinion, able, and capable of working his own plans in his own way; and more than all, from long commercial intercourse in affairs interesting to the Emperor (and just now the Emperor is France) has his entire confidence.

*   *   *   *   *   *   *

We are looking with great interest to the progress of events in the Northern States. It is thought, as things stand there, that our earlier hope of peace may be looked to from their weakness at home. Opinion is gaining ground that in their desperation, they will provoke, by design, a war with England to avert an internecine war at home.

Having no intercourse, unofficial or otherwise, with any member of the Government here, I can gather opinion only from those who have; and referring to such source, I have a strong opinion that there are those in the cabinet who anticipate by each mail from the North accounts of hostilities actually begun against England. I tell them I fear I am almost selfish enough to hope their anticipations may not be disappointed.

March 25.—I inclose, cut from the London Times of yesterday, a short debate in the House of Lords, of the day before, between Lord Stratheden and Earl Russell, on a motion of the former in regard to recognition of the Southern Confederacy. You will find it leaves the question pretty much where it found it; but the concluding paragraph of Earl Russell's remarks contain expressions, which I have underscored in pencil, which seem strongly to import, and, by design, a double meaning. His lordship admits, in substance, that our independence is achieved, and at some day it may become necessary for England to recognize it; but he throws out to the English people what the responsibility of that ministry will be which recognizes a State that vindicates African slavery.

I have heard nothing of late of the case of Hester, in custody at Gibraltar on the charge of murder committed on board the *Sumter*. The latest advices were that he would be detained in custody but not brought to trial; I presume, awaiting some event that would enable the government to turn him over to our jurisdiction.

The *Sumter*, you are aware, has been sold to a British house. After the sale, which the U. S. consul there tried in various ways to frustrate, a constant watch was kept on her by a Federal ship in waiting. She escaped, however, on a dark night, and arrived safely at Liverpool.

I have the honor to be, very respectfully, your obedient servant,

J. M. MASON.

Hon. J. P. BENJAMIN,
    Secretary of State.

LONDON, *March 20, 1863.*

SIR: Learning that Mr. Beverly Tucker will start for Richmond to-morrow, I seize the occasion to send you a few notes which may possibly be of interest. Though I have been in London but a little more than two weeks I have had, through the kindness of Mr. Mason, unexpected opportunities for obtaining information in regard to the state of public opinion here and throughout Europe touching American affairs. In this country the leading contestants for power in both parties, Conservatives and Whigs, supported by the great body of their respective adherents, are favorable to the success of the South. Many causes, however, operate to prevent this partiality from yielding any practical results. Not only the Government party, but even the Conservative leaders are exceedingly timid in regard to any movement which might give umbrage to the United States. They seem to consider that a war with that country would be the greatest calamity that could befall Great Britain, and they have the impression that the United States would not regret the occurrence of a contingency which would justify them in declaring war. This belief has made a deep impression upon the mind of England and though it has increased the willingness to witness the dismemberment of a hostile power and diffused in a wide circle the sympathy for the South, yet it has also had a powerful influence in holding the government to the policy of "neutrality" (so-called) in which it has taken refuge.

Another cause lies in the peculiar composition of parties in both Houses of Parliament. You are aware that neither of the two great parties has such a working majority as will insure its continuance in power. The Whigs can at any moment be ousted, but are equally able, in turn, to eject their successors. This gives to the Radicals, under Bright and others, the balance of power. Although weak in numbers in Parliament, the last-named party has become necessary to the maintenance of either party in power. At least their united opposition would be fatal to any government which might be organized. These men are warm partisans of the United States, and have of late made a series of striking demonstrations by public meetings, speeches, etc. It is well understood, so I am told, that United States gold has been freely used in getting up these spectacles; and although they have been participated in by but few men of any note or consideration, yet they have been sufficiently formidable to exercise a powerful influence upon the leaders of both parties. It was this that elicited Lord Derby's remarkable speech. If the nation were divided solely upon the American question, the overwhelming force of public opinion would be on the side of the South; but inasmuch as it is an issue subordinate to many questions both of domestic and foreign policy and the two parties contesting for power are nearly equal in strength, the Radicals really control the action of the Government in regard to American affairs. I do not see any causes now at work to change this state of things. At the same time no one can anticipate the policy of the Government on this subject. The events of a day may reverse it entirely, as the following fact will illustrate:

States that the declaration of a leading member of the government party (the intimate confidential friend of Lord P.) that the Confederacy would be recognized in a few days, and that he would be the appointed minister to the Confederate States of America. All the names given in the original. Only a few days after, the same distinguished personage said to my informant: "The game is up. We have to take another tack." My informant, name given, also unquestionable.

These abrupt changes are brought about by a cause which it is difficult for American statesmen to appreciate. The nations of Europe constitute a federative league, a commonwealth of nations, which, though it has no central head, is so intimate and elaborate as to subject the action and sometimes even the internal affairs of each to surveillance and intervention on the part of all the others. No Government, therefore, can enter upon a policy exclusively its own, and its action in reference to foreign matters is consequently liable to constant modification. Lord Palmerston is far more deeply engrossed with the conferences, jealousies, and rivalries between the leading powers of Europe than with the fate of constitutional government in America. To thwart Louis Napoleon's policy in Greece or to prevent his ascendancy in European affairs is of far greater importance than to pursue any policy at all with reference to America, which is considered on both sides of the Potomac as alien in European politics. In my opinion, whenever this Government shall have entertained the proposition of recognizing the Southern Confederacy, it will have been a result due to influence brought to bear in Europe.

Notwithstanding the present troubled state of German politics, I am satisfied that much service to our cause would be done by your sending a commissioner to the Governments of Austria and Prussia. An intelligent gentleman residing in Berlin has assured me that the Government and the army are extremely favorable to the cause of the South, and that the success of the South is not more sincerely desired at any court than that of Austria, and the same feeling exists among the higher classes of that nation. Under proper management these two German courts would, at least, throw the weight of their favor upon any movement which might be inaugurated elsewhere in behalf of Southern recognition. An additional reason for having a commissioner at these courts may be found in the fact that the United States Government has its agents throughout Germany enlisting "laborers" to take the place of those who have gone into the army. They profess that they want them only for this purpose. They give a free passage, with promise of high pay on their arrival in America. They have been successful in finding men willing to emigrate on these favorable terms, and, as you know, a great number of them have enlisted in the United States Army. This, with other causes, has made the lower and a large majority of the middle classes of Germany warm partisans of the North. The Government of the United States has made strong efforts to control public opinion there, many of the leading newspapers being in its pay.

I am here waiting for Mr. Fearn, but have sought in various quarters information respecting the probable success of my mission to Russia, and am glad to say that whilst the Government of Russia is inclined to favor the cause of the United States there does not exist any feeling of hostility toward the South. I have some reason to think, from remarks made by a member of the Russian legation here, that when the true nature and causes of the present war shall have been known, and especially when the Emperor is made to see that it is not a rebellion but a lawful assertion of sovereignty, we may reasonably expect his more active cooperation with the views of the French Emperor. There is no party in Russia absolutely hostile to the South. The avidity with which the Confederate loan has been taken up both here and on the Continent has caused great rejoicing among our friends, and it is claimed by them to be a financial recognition of the Confederacy.

I am, your obedient servant,

L. Q. C. LAMAR.

Hon. J. P. BENJAMIN,
   Secretary of State, Confederate States of America.

LONDON, *March 21, 1863.*

DEAR MR. BENJAMIN: I have just finished a dispatch to be sent by Mr. Tucker, but learning that his mode of getting to you is uncertain, and as my dispatch contains a confidential communication which ought not to be exposed to the chance of discovery, I have concluded to send it by a more certain channel. I send a copy by Mr. Tucker, which I had taken for myself. I regret that I have had to write it in such great haste.

Yours, truly,

L. Q. C. LAMAR.

Hon. J. P. BENJAMIN.

No. 20.]   CONFEDERATE STATES COMMERCIAL AGENCY,
        London, March 21, 1863.

SIR: I have the honor to acknowledge receipt on the 17th instant of duplicates of your dispatch No. 3, with enclosures, the receipt of the originals of which was acknowledged in my last, dated 14th instant.

The prospectus of the Confederate loan was issued by Messrs. Erlanger & Co. on the London Exchange on Wednesday evening, the 18th instant. Before the prospectus was issued business had already been done on speculative account at 2¾ to 3 per cent premium; on Thursday evening the quotations closed at 4½ to 5 per cent.

Yesterday it was rumored that the subscriptions in this place alone exceeded 7,000,000 pounds sterling. It is worthy of remark that of all the new loans this day before the financial public the Danish, New Italian, Russian are at a discount, and the Portuguese is the only one beside the Confederate which is quoted at a premium, viz, 3 to 3½, and another, the Salvador loan, had to be temporarily withdrawn. This success of the Confederate loan, notwithstanding the apparently unfavorable time of bringing it out, when so many new loans are in the market and even consols have fallen one-fourth per cent, is on all hands pronounced to be a great moral victory. The organs of the Northern Government and the ultra section of the Exeter Hall school prove that they also feel it to be such by even more than usual vehemence in their denunciations of the "infamous schemes of the hell-born rebel confederacy." The masses are to be stirred up by another emancipation demonstration, to which additional interest is to be given by the presence of Mr. John Bright, of Birmingham. It will be numerously attended and a failure like the last.

Lord Campbell's motion has been once more postponed until next Monday, 23d current, on account this time of Earl Russell's indisposition, his voice being too feeble to permit his participating in debate. His note to Lord Campbell (Stratheden) on this subject, which I have seen, concludes, "the French Government seems at this moment fully occupied with Poland." There is nothing to indicate that the secretary for foreign affairs is averse to the motion being made and debated, or that, even though the cabinet policy may force him to oppose it he will say anything unfriendly to our interests.

The insurrection in Poland, now possessing all the features of a great national revolution, is more and more riveting public interest. Prince Napoleon, with his accustomed violence, has just made an ultra Polish speech, and as in similar instances relative to the question of Italy, his views have been officially disavowed, but they nevertheless produced considerable impression both on the Paris bourse and the London exchange. I learn from undoubted authority that Lord Palmerston, notwithstanding the recent successes of the Poles, remains unaltered in his private opinion, formed at the outset, that the strong hand of Russia must succeed in the end.

The condition of Ireland, unusually satisfactory for over a twelvemonth, has suddenly become disturbed. Riots, for which the celebration of the marriage of the Prince of Wales furnished the pretext, or rather the occasion, have occurred at Cork, requiring the intervention of the military, and incendiarism and assassination threaten to become as rife as of old. The Liverpool Albion, with what truth I will not pretend to say, asserts that this disquiet is traceable to the machinations of Federal agents designed to embarrass the Government, and alleges as a proof that recruiting for the Federal Army is carried on to a large extent in Ireland.

I enclose extracts from the money articles of the principal dailies on the Confederate loan.

A second private letter, very cautiously worded and without direction inside, goes this day by way of the North. It is like the first, intended to explore a new and more expeditious route of communication with you, which, if sufficiently tried, may become of great value to the public service. With this view I must beg you to acknowledge its receipt by the first opportunity.

By an arrival at Southampton we learn of the capture of three more vessels by the *Alabama*, viz, the *Golden Eagle*, from New Bedford; the *Olive Jane*, from Boston; and the schooner *Palmetto*, from Trenton; also of the capture and release on a ransom bond of the ship *Washington*, from New York, the latter having British property on board.

I have the honor to remain, very respectfully, your obedient servant,

HENRY HOTZE.

Hon. J. P. BENJAMIN,
  Secretary of State, Richmond.

RICHMOND, *March 21, 1863.*

SIR: I have the honor to address you a few lines on the following subject and respectfully request your attention to the same:

Mr. Anfora, the consul-general of the Kingdom of Italy in New York, informs me that the American bark *Lauraetta*, Marshall M. Wells, master, and bound at that time from New York for Madeira and Messina, was, in October, 1862, taken on the high seas by the C. S. ship *Alabama*, Captain Semmes, and burnt by his orders together with her cargo. Captain Wells protested against the destruction of the cargo, the same being principally Italian and partly English property, the Italian part being for Mr. Marino Costavilla, of Messina, all of which was proved to Captain Semmes by Captain Wells by his shipping and consular papers, but Captain Semmes did not think proper to notice the protest.

The consul-general instructs me to ascertain, if possible, what course the Confederate States Government intends to pursue under these circumstances, and whether it will indemnify the Italian subjects, should all the above be finally and satisfactorily proved. I therefore respectfully ask you, Mr. Secretary, to let me know, if convenient, your Government's intentions in regard to the matter.

With the assurance of my highest regard, I am, sir, most respectfully, your obedient servant,

L. von GRONINT,
  N. Consul of Italy.

Hon. J. P. BENJAMIN,
  Secretary of State, Richmond, Va.

No. 29.]   PARIS, *March 21, 1863.*

SIR: Since my last, of the 4th of March, I am in possession of your Nos. 12 and 13. The postscript of No. 13 is very interesting, and will be borne in mind by me in any future interviews I may have with the person to whom it refers. The Polish question still engrosses the attention of the Government, the press, and the public to the exclusion of every other, and will continue to do so until it has received some practical solution. In the meanwhile, however, England has given another evidence of her selfish and tortuous policy. After exciting, by the unanimous declarations of her leading statesmen and journals, France to take the initiative of action in behalf of the Poles, she declines when invited to unite even in diplomatic efforts in their favor. The consequence is that the feeling of alienation and distrust is now stronger than ever, and I am obliged to admit that there is reasonable ground for the suspicion generally entertained here that England would not regret to see France involved in war with the Lincoln Government.

At the commencement of our war England was infinitely more disposed to recognition than she has ever been since. She then doubted our capacity to maintain our independence; and if we had suffered very serious reverses, I believe she would have gone further than recognition and found some pretext for active material intervention to secure a final separation of North and South. Now that separation is certain without her aid, she is quite indifferent how long the contest may be continued, and would look with complacency on the introduction of a new element which, while creating increased financial difficulties with France, would effectually insure the total ruin of her greatest commercial rivals. This may seem a harsh judgment, but I am thoroughly convinced of its correctness.

You will, before this dispatch can reach you, have seen by the newspapers the brilliant success of Erlanger & Co.'s loan. The affair has been admirably managed by them, and can not fail to exercise a most salutary influence on both sides of the Atlantic. It is a financial recognition of our independence, emanating from a class proverbially cautious and little given to be influenced by sentiment or sympathy.

I send you a speech recently delivered in the Senate by Mr. Billault, minister sans porte-feuille, whose special function is to explain and defend the views and policy of the Emperor on all matters connected with foreign affairs. You will find in it a complete exposition of the Polish question, a brief but clear résumé of the relations existing between France and foreign powers, but I invite your particular attention to the paragraph relating to the American war.

I have received through Mr. Mason your instructions about forwarding dispatches, and shall hereafter send either an original or duplicate of each in the way you direct. Indeed, I had, in consequence of a letter received from Mr. L. H., already dispatched several by that channel.

I have the honor to be, with great respect, your most obedient servant,

JOHN SLIDELL.

Hon. J. P. BENJAMIN,
  Secretary of State.

No. 14.]

DEPARTMENT OF STATE,
  Richmond, March 24, 1863.

SIR: I have the honor to acknowledge receipt of your Nos. 22, 23, 24, 25, and 26. No. 22 was received on the 27th ult. The remainder were forwarded through Mr. Heyliger, and arrived on 19th inst. Among them, Nos. 23 and 24 were duplicates, and have been received before the originals, which have not yet arrived. The duplicate of No. 22, which was accompanied (as stated in your No. 23) by triplicates of your Nos. 1, 3, 4, 5, and 6, has not yet been received, but it is to be hoped that this third effort to complete the files of the Department will not prove abortive, and that the missing dispatch may soon come to hand. In reference to my No. 7, you will correctly observe that I had not, at the date of writing it, received your statement of what occurred at your interview with the Emperor; and, as we were well aware, both from your own dispatches and other sources, that Mr. Thouvenel was not friendly to our cause, it is not surprising that the President should have had his suspicions awakened by the very singular developments communicated to him almost simultaneously by the governor of Texas and a Senator from that State. The extent of Mr. Thouvenel's unfriendly feeling toward us is fully developed in the conversation which he held with Mr. Dayton on the 12th September, 1862, and which the Government of the United States has published in the documents annexed to Mr. Lincoln's message of last December. You will find the letter of Mr. Dayton at page 389 of the diplomatic correspondence of Mr. Seward, and it can not be a matter of surprise to the Emperor that with information of the existence of such sentiments on the part of Mr. Thouvenel as are there developed, and with no knowledge of any dissent from those views on the part of his Sovereign, painful surmises should have been excited in this Government, and should have been the subject of a confidential communication to our agent at his court.

That communication, intended solely to awaken your vigilance, has been used by our enemies for the purpose of affecting your relations with the cabinet of the Tuileries long after the incidents which gave rise to it had been fully explained and when the impressions created by those incidents had been entirely effaced. Fully convinced as we now are of the true sentiments of his Imperial Majesty, to which the President has rendered ample justice in his last message, it will scarcely be necessary to revert to the subject in your intercourse with the cabinet of the Tuileries. If, however, you deem it expedient, there can be no objection to your taking any suitable occasion for giving assurance that not a doubt remains in the mind of the President of the cordial sympathy of his Imperial Majesty in our efforts to conquer peace, now that our independence has been secured, and that the conduct of the subordinate consular officials, to which just exception was taken by us, had no higher inspiration than their own mistaken and superserviceable zeal. On the subject of your interview with Mr. Arman, you will receive herewith a communication from Mr. Mallory, who writes on the subject to Mr. Mason also. It is of the last importance that some successful arrangement should be made by you in concert with Mr. Mason, as we entertain great apprehension lest our ironclads should be stopped in England. The money question can hardly create a difficulty, especially if our information that the Erlanger loan has been taken shall prove correct; and if not, we learn from our financial agent in London that cotton bonds can be sold there freely on terms fully equal to those offered by the Erlanger contract. The memorandum addressed by you to the Emperor was read with great interest. It was admirably calculated to awaken his solicitude on the salient point involving French interests in this calamitous war, and can not have been without effect on the resolve of his Majesty to make another attempt toward putting an end to hostilities. It is very fortunate that the blind presumption of our enemies should have led them to the folly of rejecting the proposition of Mr. Drouyn de Lhuys for a conference on the subject of a restoration of peace.

They have thus subjected themselves to the odium necessarily attached to a nation which, in the midst of so awful a carnage, declares substantially that it will never make peace and will not even confer upon the possibility of amicable settlement. This is the more fortunate, for otherwise it would have been difficult, perhaps, for us to satisfy public opinion in Europe of the propriety of our own rejection of the offer, which must have been inevitable unless we were admitted to the conference on equal terms—that is, as a recognized independent nation. The dignity and self-respect of this Government would never have been compromised by any agreement on our part to confer, under the auspices of a foreign Government, with a nation recognized by that Government and assuming to meet us for the purpose of putting an end to our "rebellion," while our independence remained unrecognized by the mediating power. There could have been no equality in such a conference, and your sagacity was not at fault in assuring the friend who broached the proposition that it would be barren of the results he hoped. The unexpected good fortune which has thrown upon our enemies the responsibility of a refusal has relieved us, however, of all embarrassment on this matter, and the remarks I have made are prompted solely by the desire of informing you what are the opinions of the President on the subject, so that you may be guided by them in the event of your being compelled to act on similar propositions without having time to ask for instructions. In a dispatch of 29th January last, received from Brussels, we are informed that the proposition of Mr. Drouyn de Lhuys (which has been refused by Mr. Seward in one of the most contemptuous dispatches ever addressed to the cabinet of a great nation) was prompted by a second letter addressed to the Emperor by King Leopold, urging him most earnestly to take the initiative in our recognition; and the writer gives us the assurance, which corresponds with your own anticipations, that a refusal by the Washington Cabinet to accept the proposition would be followed by our immediate recognition. We do not rely on this result, the more especially as the insurrection in Poland by its increasing proportions threatens complications in Europe that may involve the French Government and thus render it averse to any hazard, however remote, of difficulties with the United States. We await, however, with curiosity, if not with impatience, the news of the action of a cabinet little accustomed to such cavalier treatment as Mr. Seward has ostentatiously paraded both in his reply to Mr. Drouyn de Lhuys and in the unequivocal démenti given to Mr. Mercier on the subject of the latter's account of the circumstances attendant on his visit to Richmond.

While speaking on this subject I may mention that in my No. 5 (which failed to reach you, and of which a duplicate is herewith forwarded) I gave an account of my interview with Mr. Mercier which does not differ much in substance and not at all in spirit from that given by him in his dispatch, and I therein expressed the opinion that he had been induced to come here by the suggestions of Mr. Seward, although he confined himself to the statement that he came with Mr. Seward's knowledge and consent. You are perfectly correct in all the assurances given by you that our recognition by the great powers of Europe would end the war at a very early day, but we have ceased to expect that consummation until it will be to us a matter of entire indifference, and the day is fast approaching when we shall feel entitled, like Napoleon I, to refuse an express recognition on the ground of its implying a doubt of the preexistence of a self-evident fact. How fast the Emperor is losing, by a hesitating policy unprecedented in his magnificent career, the chance of binding to the interests of France by the closest alliance both of feeling and policy this young and powerful Confederacy can scarcely be known on the other side of the Atlantic. This war may not last beyond the present year, perhaps not beyond the sickly season of a Southern summer, and yet he suffers himself to be restrained from decisive action by alternative menaces and assurances uttered with notorious mendacity by the leaders of the frantic mob which now controls the Government of the United States. Not many months will pass away before he will recur to his present course of policy with the same regret as was expressed so frankly to you for his mistake in recognizing the soi-disant blockade. Your communication on the subject of the cargoes to be shipped to Matamoras, together with the accompanying correspondence, has been placed before the Secretaries of War and Navy, who will take measures to facilitate their landing and removal and the exportation of the cotton to be given in exchange. The public journals keep you so well informed on the condition of affairs that it is scarcely necessary for me to add anything.

I may say in general terms that the enemy has been decisively repulsed from Port Hudson and the attacking forces withdrawn, after heavy damage, including the loss of the steam frigate *Mississippi*, set on fire and destroyed by our batteries; that they have been finally and decisively repulsed from the Yazoo Pass, an expedition which was from its inception as stupid and impossible as was ever made by incompetent commanders; that their effort to penetrate our country by cutting a canal into Lake Providence and thence through Tensas River into the Mississippi has proved as preposterous as you must have known it to be from your acquaintance with the topography of that district of country; that the cut-off opposite Vicksburg has thus far proved as impracticable as all their other devices to get by Vicksburg without fighting, and that the alternative now left for them is to fight with certain defeat or to withdraw with the most disastrous effect on the public feeling at the North.

In northern Virginia we fear nothing, and at Charleston and Savannah, though they have threatened attack for many months, they still remain inactive.

You will perceive, however, in the newspapers an apparent anxiety on the subject of provisions, and it is even said that our oft-deluded foes are again indulging the hope that we are to lose our independence by starvation. As nothing is too absurd for belief, it may not be amiss to inform you that this starvation means simply short rations of meat for a very limited period, caused principally by the difficulties of transportation over our railroads, which have been much impaired in efficiency by the winter storms, and over the country roads, which are almost impassable for the same reason. Of bread there is a superabundance, and the Southern wheat crops, which are fine, will commence furnishing new flour in Texas in five or six weeks, and in Carolina in sixty days, while the Virginia crop is harvested usually at the end of June. We are really suffering for want of forage for the cavalry and artillery horses, as that article is quite too bulky for distant transportation, and until the spring herbage becomes abundant the efficiency of those two arms of the service in northern Virginia will be considerably impaired.

I reserve for a separate dispatch my reply to your remark relative to a mission to Spain, and am, with great respect,

Your obedient servant,

J. P. Benjamin.

Hon. John Slidell, *Paris.*

Department of State,
Richmond, March 25, 1863.

Sir: In accordance with the instructions of the President at our recent Cabinet meeting, the Secretary of War and this Department have taken action in the matter of the *General Rusk,* or *Blanche,* and the papers are now forwarded to you for your own action.

You will find herewith,

First.* The letter of the Hon. P. W. Gray to yourself.

Second.* The letter of the collector of Galveston to the Secretary of the Treasury with its inclosures.

Third.* The record of the proceedings of the court-martial in the case of Major Moise. This record belongs to the files of the Adjutant-General and is to be restored to him.

Fourth.* The abstract of the whole case with my suggestions thereon as communicated to the President at his request.

I have taken measures for claiming from the Spanish Government the whole amount of the indemnity exacted by it from the United States, and in my dispatch on the subject have assumed the ground that the parties in possession of the vessel are responsible to the Government for the value of the services of the vessel on her first successful voyage, both going and returning. This seems to me very clear, and probably a better measure of the just claims of the Government than any share of profits as suggested in my memorandum to the President.

If you agree in this view, I think it would be well that you should enquire of Messrs. John Fraser & Co., of Charleston, what were the current rates of outward and inward freights on vessels running the blockade at the date of the voyage of the *General Rusk.* Those gentlemen can probably give you more reliable information than anyone else in the Confederacy.

I deem it my duty, also, to repeat the communication made to me officially by a citizen of Louisiana that Major Moise bought for himself a handsome residence at a cost of $25,000 cash, in Alexandria, La.

---

* Enclosures not found.

A very unpleasant and unfortunate feature in the case is that the delinquent officer is a brother of the district judge of Louisiana. This may be unknown to you, and I state the fact that you may take such measures as are provided by the law for cases where the near relationship of the judge renders him incompetent to act.

I am, very respectfully, etc.,

J. P. BENJAMIN,
Secretary of State.

Hon. THOMAS H. WATTS,
Attorney-General.

No. 15.]   DEPARTMENT OF STATE,
                                 Richmond, March 26, 1863.

SIR: You will receive herewith a letter of credence authorizing you to act as special commissioner of this Government at the Court of Madrid. This letter is forwarded to you in consequence of the suggestion in your dispatch No. 26. Prior to the receipt of that dispatch the President had determined on sending a commissioner to Spain, but on conference with several members of the Senate, it became apparent that the unjust action of European powers in refusing us the recognition to which we are so plainly entitled had produced its natural effect, and that there was a marked aversion to any further attempt at communication with them. Indeed a very serious attempt was made to pass resolutions expressive of the sense of the Senate that our commissioners should be withdrawn from all the European courts, but this was subsequently so far modified as to make an exception in regard to the French mission. The irritation against Great Britain is fast increasing, and we had some trouble satisfying different Senators that the true interests of our country would suffer from the course they seemed inclined to adopt. It was specially in relation to the danger of having our supplies cut off and our ironclads stopped that we were most anxious. The proposal for withdrawal of our commissioners has therefore been abandoned; but in deference to the prevalent sentiment, it is deemed judicious to increase their number, and the President therefore avails himself of your proposal to proceed to Madrid, inasmuch as there is a pecuniary matter there pending which requires attention immediately. It is not deemed necessary to give you any special instructions in regard to the general subject of opening a friendly intercourse with Spain and of inducing possibly her Catholic Majesty to assume the initiative in forming with us relations which can not but redound to the honor and interest of Spain as well as to our own advantage. Nor is it necessary to dwell upon the expediency of your endeavoring to impress on the minds of the Spanish cabinet the relations that will connect our Confederacy with Spain, and those that have heretofore existed between the United States and the Spanish Government. The general views of the President on this subject are fully developed in the instructions which by his direction were addressed by my predecessor, the Hon. R. M. T. Hunter, to the commissioners formerly empowered to treat with that court for the opening of amicable relations. A copy of that dispatch, under date of 24th August, 1861, is herewith forwarded to you. On all other points, your correspondence with this Department will have placed you so fully in possesion of the policy of the Administration in its conduct of the Government both at home and abroad as to render useless any further explanation.

There is one rather unpleasant business matter in which early action seems necessary and to which I invite your attention. The Confederate Government was the owner of a certain steamer fitted up as a war vessel (although originally a merchantman) named the *General Rusk;* and this vessel, then lying in the harbor of Galveston, was placed by General Hébert, who commanded the Department of Texas, under the control of Major T. S. Moise, his assistant quartermaster. Major Moise has recently been tried before a court-martial, convicted, and dismissed from the service, and from the evidence taken on his trial the President has become satisfied that he entered into a fraudulent combination with Robert Mott, J. L. Macauley and his brother —— Macauley, and Nelson Clements; that, under cover of procuring supplies for the Government, he transferred (utterly without authority) the steamer *General Rusk* to his associates without the payment of any price or consideration to the Government; that he authorized them to put her under the British flag by collusive transfer to some British subject, and to employ her in commerce between the Confederacy and the port of Havana for the joint benefit of himself and his associates, without stipulating for any freight or charter money in favor of the Government and without even taking any other security for the return of the vessel to the Government than a bond signed by his associates themselves for the sum of $50,000, which was about one-third of the value of the vessel. It seems that in the execution of their plan the parties took the *Rusk* to Havana and had her, by some means unknown to this Government, placed under the British flag and provided with British papers, and had her name changed to the *Blanche*. After one successful round -voyage, in which the parties made large profits, the *Blanche* was on her way to Havana with a second cargo of cotton when both vessel and cargo were destroyed on the coast of Cuba within the neutral jurisdiction of Spain by the Federal steamer *Montgomery,* under circumstances of such outrage that the Federal Government was forced, as we understand, to make reparation to Spain by the payment of $200,000 for the value of the vessel and cargo. It is also understood that one of the parties to the fraudulent conspiracy against our Government has gone to Europe for the purpose of claiming as owner the whole amount of the indemnity accorded by the Government of the United States to that of Spain.

On the above statement of facts it is of course unnecessary to offer any argument in support of the position that the *General Rusk* or *Blanche* never ceased to be the property of this Government, and that her transfer by an unfaithful officer of this Government without authority to his associates, and their collusive transfer to some British subject for the purpose of deceiving one of the belligerents in this war are equally null and void. It is in like manner evident that the parties to this fraud who were owners of the cargo on the *Blanche* are responsible to this Government for at least an adequate compensation for the use and risk of the vessel on her previous voyage, and the amount thus due by them to the Government exceeds the value of the cargo destroyed. Under all the circumstances of the case, this Government being the owner of the vessel and having just demands against the owners of the cargo who are citizens of the Confederacy, there can be no question of the right of the Government to receive for proper application the whole amount of the indemnity which Spain has exacted from the United States for account of the owners of vessel and cargo. It is therefore desired by the President that you take the proper measures for securing the payment of the whole sum to this Government. It does not escape our observation that you may be embarrassed in action on this subject from the fact that, as our independence has not yet been recognized by Spain, the Government of her Catholic Majesty may feel averse to making immediate payment of this amount from apprehension of unfriendly discussion with the United States if our demand be admitted. Such apprehension could not properly be entertained, for, as this Government has been recognized as a belligerent and Spain has proclaimed her neutrality between the two belligerents, the law of nations justifies her in exacting from the United States reparation for breach of neutrality and justifies us as a belligerent in requiring that due effect shall be given to the neutrality of Spain for the protection of our interests whilst within her territorial jurisdiction. But we care not to urge in the present posture of affairs our rights to their full extent, provided the interests and honor of our country are maintained unimpaired. If therefore you find that the Spanish Government, although willing to make us full reparation, should insist with any degree of pertinacity on deferring the final adjustment of the claim till the restoration of peace, it is not deemed politic to press our claim any further than to require an explicit assurance that the money shall not be paid to any other party than this Government without its consent.

I have the honor to be, your obedient servant,

J. P. BENJAMIN,
Secretary of State.

Hon. JOHN SLIDELL, *Paris.*

No. 17.] DEPARTMENT OF STATE,
Richmond, March 27, 1863.

SIR: I am without further dispatches from you since my No. 16 of 21st February.

I had at that date received nothing from you subsequent to 11th December, and I regret that you hesitated to forward your dispatches through Mr. Heyliger, as we have received dates from Europe through that channel as late as 14th February, both from Mr. Slidell and Mr. Mann, as well as from other agents.

I write now to say that, from communications received by Mr. Mallory from his officers, it appears that grave apprehensions are entertained lest obstacles should be opposed to the departure of our vessels now near completion in England. I therefore beg that you will endeavor in concert with Mr. Slidell to arrange for their transfer to France, if such a course should become necessary. His dispatches indicate that there will be no difficulty in so doing. This matter is of vital importance and I invoke to it your earnest attention.

The posture of affairs here is more satisfactory than it has ever been. We look with entire confidence to holding the Mississippi River both at Vicksburg and Port Hudson against the utmost efforts of the enemy. They have been signally defeated in every attempt at both points. A formidable attack is threatened on Charleston, but months pass away without any movement by the enemy, and our preparations for defense are very complete, although to a certain extent doubt must attach to the result of so new an experiment in warfare as will be the combined attack of a number of heavily armed turreted ironclads. It is possible that they may succeed in passing into the harbor, but even then, though they may destroy the buildings in the city, they can not take it without the most awful carnage yet witnessed in this war.

The debates in the British Parliament seem indicative of a determination to deny our right to recognition at the very moment that all parties admit that we have conquered our independence and that the success of our enemies in their schemes for our subjugation is impossible!

What a comment on the respect paid by British statesmen to the plainest dictates of justice and humanity and the acknowledged principles of international law!

I am, very respectfully, your obedient servant,

J. P. BENJAMIN,
Secretary of State.

Hon. JAMES M. MASON,
London.

P. S.—You will herewith receive a commission for Mr. Robert Dowling, as commercial agent at Cork, in Ireland, and a letter notifying him of his appointment. They are left open for your information, and I will thank you, after perusal, to forward them to their destination.

J. P. BENJAMIN.

DEPARTMENT OF STATE,
Richmond, March 30, 1863.

SIR: I acknowledge receipt of your letter of 23d instant. I will call to the attention of Mr. Ould, the commissioner for the exchange of prisoners, the case of the prisoners taken on the prize vessel.

In relation to the alleged violation of the neutrality of British waters by the Federal gunboat *Alabama,* the facts set forth in your letter are neither sufficiently precise nor well authenticated to justify the action of this Government. Whenever it shall be in your power to lay before this Department a detailed statement of the facts, verified by affidavits of trustworthy witnesses, due consideration will be given to any claim which may appear to be founded on justice.

I am, very respectfully, etc.,

J. P. BENJAMIN,
Secretary of State.

THOMAS B. POWER, Esq.,
Charleston, S. C.

No. 32.] CONFEDERATE STATES COMMISSION,
London, March 30, 1863.

SIR: The messenger to bear these dispatches being still detained I have the opportunity of bringing them to the present date. In my general dispatch (No. 31) of the 19th instant I spoke of the brilliant success of the Confederate loan, then first put upon the market. I have now the satisfaction, ten days having expired since the books were closed and three since the allotment to subscribers, of confirming that success. The books were open only from Thursday to Saturday at 2 p. m. (say two days and a half), and the subscription reached nearly sixteen millions. As was to be expected, the premium attained in the first excitement of speculation, when it reached 5¼ per cent, has since fluctuated. It closed firmly on Saturday (day before yesterday) at from 1¾ to 2 per cent. I have just had an interview with Mr. Erlanger, who was accompanied by Mr. Schroder, the principal banker in London managing the loan; they assure me that since the allotment, when the stock came into possession of holders, prices have settled so firmly down at present rates and with such indications of strength that there is little fear of its falling lower and none that it will touch par. They say that such entire confidence is felt and evinced by holders in the security that they have no fear. They tell me further that subscriptions came direct from Russia and from cotton spinners; also from Switzerland; from the free cities of Bremen, Hamburg, and Frankfort; and even from Trieste. They say also, as evidence of the strength of this loan, compared with others cotemporaneously put upon the market, namely, one for Denmark, offered at 90, that at first it attained a premium of 2 per cent and then fell to one-half discount or below par, and one for the Italian States, offered at 71, was not all taken and fell immediately one-half per cent discount, though both these loans were brought forward by the Rothschilds.

I think I may congratulate you, therefore, on the triumphant success of our infant credit; it shows, malgré all detraction and calumny, that cotton is king at last.

In my No. 29, of the 5th of February, I informed you of the advice I had given to officers of the Army and Navy here, who were in possession of cotton certificates for the purpose of raising money to meet the engagements of these respective branches of the service, not to put them on the market lest it should disturb or prejudice the contemplated loan, and they were withheld accordingly. We hoped then that the funds necessary for immediate use could be obtained by the Confederate money bonds in charge of Mr. Spence. It was found, however, that they could not be used at better rates than 50 cents in the dollar, and they, too, were withheld. It resulted that some inconvenience, although no actual prejudice, arose from the want of money, but it was obviated to a great extent by the assurance given me by Erlanger, after it was known that the contract of loan had been concluded, that he would advance in anticipation of its fruits the sums wanted for the immediate necessities of the Government agents, and this has been done accordingly. I told him; and I rely upon having the matter properly adjusted when Mr. McRae arrives, who, we understand, is the agent for the loan. Without this relief the public service here must have suffered, but the political effects to result from the full success of the loan were of so great importance to us that I felt it a duty thus to keep the cotton certificates off the market.

I enclose herewith a debate in the House of Commons on Friday last, the 27th instant, on the call of Mr. Forster for information regarding the *Alabama*, and whether the attention of the Government had been called to the alleged construction of other warships in England for the Confederate Government. This gentleman (Mr. Forster) is one of the most earnest friends of the United States Government. You will see that he took little by his motion. The reply of the solicitor-general, besides a clear and able exposition of the law of the question, was a scathing rebuke to the pretensions of the United States; but the logic of Mr. Laird's facts were conclusive against them. Lord Palmerston's reference to the practice of political parties in the United States in raising "a cry against England to create political capital" at home; his reference to the purchase of arms in England by the United States and their efforts to enlist soldiers in Ireland told capitally and with none the less force when he spoke of "those gentlemen who have made themselves in this house the mouthpiece of the North," ending, as he did, with the declaration that the United States "must not imagine that any cry which may be raised will induce us to come down to this house with a proposal to alter the law." It was felt on all hands that the debate was a most damaging one to the arrogance of the Yankee pretensions as well as their advocates.

The revolution in Poland, it is not considered, will be much put back by the arrest and detention of Langiewicz. The committee of public safety at Warsaw have resumed all the power given to him as dictator. It is generally believed that the Poles must be ultimately crushed unless France is driven to interfere, but that they will not be subdued until after a long and bloody struggle.

I have the honor to be, very respectfully, your obedient servant,

J. M. MASON

Hon. J. P. BENJAMIN,
   Secretary of State.

No. 18.]
                   DEPARTMENT OF STATE,
                        Richmond, March 30, 1863.

SIR: Since my No. 17, I have received your Nos. 24 to 29, both inclusive, and hasten to acknowledge them.

I take it for granted that no answer will be made to the protest sent to Earl Russell, and I do not know that we could do anything further at present in vindication of the rights of our country, so openly disregarded by the British cabinet.

I will make the numbers of my files accord with the suggestions of your No. 25, and this will place the records of the department in harmony with those of your legation.

Your No. 29 has been copied for the use of the Treasury, and I will request Mr. Memminger to answer it, as I am not in possession of the information which would justify the expression of an opinion on the subject.

I am, very respectfully, your obedient servant,

J. P. BENJAMIN,
Secretary of State.

Hon. JAMES M. MASON,
London.

P. S.—Your letter and package for Mrs. Mason are received and will be at once handed to General Cooper.

I find on reviewing your dispatches that No. 28 is missing. Those received are Nos. 24, 25, 26, 27, and 29.

J. P. B.

No. 33.] CONFEDERATE STATES COMMISSION,
London, March 30, 1863.

SIR: Intelligence has just been received here of the capture of the *Peterhoff* on a voyage direct from London to Matamoras. It was brought up in the House of Commons, as you will see, by Mr. Seymour Fitzgerald on Friday night, and bore its part in American affairs with the debate on the *Alabama.* Mr. Fitzgerald has examined the case carefully, and gave its full history, with all the incidents of her capture by order of Commodore Wilkes. This vessel was down on a list furnished by Mr. Morse, U. S. consul at London, to Mr. Adams, in a letter of the 24th of December last, as "laden with supplies for the insurgents now in rebellion against the United States," and there is little doubt that the list was sent to Mr. Seward, that orders might be given for her capture; and thus, it is hoped, that Wilkes acted, in this case at least, under specific orders. You will find the letter at page 34 of the correspondence respecting the *Alabama* (printed document No. 3 herewith), which was communicated by Mr. Adams to Earl Russell, with his letter of December 30 (p. 29 of the same printed document), where he speaks of it as sufficient to place beyond contradiction the fact of the extensive and systematic prosecution by British subjects of the policy toward the United States, which is uniformly characterized by writers on international law as that of an enemy.

In the reply of Mr. Layard, undersecretary, he merely said the case of the *Peterhoff* had been referred to the law officers of the Crown; but the capture of this vessel has caused a great disturbance in the public mind, it being clear that she was in no sense whatever, even of suspicion, a subject of capture; she had nothing contraband on board and was proceeding, bona fide, from England to a neutral port. It is believed that Lord Russell will demand her immediate release, with amends and without reference to a prize court. If this is not done, the public expectation will be gravely disappointed and more of it will be heard in the House of Commons.

Colonel Lamar arrived here a few days since. Mr. Fearn, the secretary of this legation, has not yet appeared.

The *Peterhoff* is one of the vessels referred to in my No. 28 as one of those recommended to the cognizance and protection of Admiral Jurien, and I understand that a large portion of her cargo was on French account. All this will help to complicate.

I send also in the dispatch box a series of excerpts taken from the London journals of the day, which were sent to me by Mr. Erlanger, with a request that I would transmit them to you as probably interesting to the Government.

I have the honor to be, very respectfully, your obedient servant.

J. M. MASON.

Hon. J. P. BENJAMIN,
  Secretary of State.

No. 4.] DEPARTMENT OF STATE,
Richmond, March 30, 1863.

SIR: Since my No. 3 of January 16 I have received your Nos. 16, 17, and 18, with the files of the Index to the date of No. 18.

The Department receives with satisfaction and reads with interest your careful and discriminating review of the state of public sentiment and the movements of political parties in England, and it is due to you to state that the President is as favorably impressed as I am with the manner in which you discharge your duties.

My chief purpose in writing these few lines is to enclose you two extracts, for publication. One in relation to the treatment of our prisoners by the enemy speaks for itself and is signed by a colonel of artillery who commanded the brigade of Texans taken prisoners at Arkansas Post.

The other is extracted from the Memphis Appeal of the 20th instant and is a graphic account of the enemy's repulse at Port Hudson.

It may be well to mention that the Memphis Appeal, since the capture of Memphis, is published at Jackson, Miss. I state this lest you should suppose it to be Federal instead of a Confederate journal.

I am, very respectfully, etc.,

J. P. BENJAMIN,
Secretary of State.

HENRY HOTZE, Esq.

No. 19.] DEPARTMENT OF STATE,
Richmond, March 31, 1863.

SIR: The President has received from Mr. George McHenry certain proposals for the establishment of a line of mail steamers between the Confederacy and Great Britain to be established after the close of the war. These proposals were accompanied by a letter from yourself rendering tribute to that gentlemen's zealous and efficient advocacy of our cause.

The President has examined these propositions, after having submitted them for a report by the Postmaster General, and I am instructed to apprise you, for the information of Mr. McHenry, that it is not possible to hold out to him at present any prospect of the acceptance of his proposal.

To other propositions on the same subject we have been compelled to answer, as you are aware, that the Constitution of the Confederacy seems to offer a very formidable barrier to such contracts, inasmuch as it requires the postal service to be self-sustaining. In addition to this serious difficulty, the Government can not but think that whenever the return of peace shall permit it to turn its attention to the subject of steam service, the probability is very great that the proposals then submitted to it will be much more favorable than any that are now offered by parties who naturally take into consideration the contingencies of the war, and are therefore prone to impose conditions more onerous than they would exact in a time of peace and uninterrupted commerce. The present conjuncture is therefore not deemed suitable for entering into negotiations on the subject, and it is due to Mr. McHenry that no false hopes should be held out to him that his proposals will prove acceptable.

I am, very respectfully, your obedient servant,

J. P. BENJAMIN,
Secretary of State.

Hon. JAMES M. MASON,
London.

---

10 RUMFORD PLACE,
Liverpool, April 2, 1863.

MY DEAR SIR: It will be necessary for me shortly to make arrangements for the arming of a gunboat built here and presented to the Confederate States by the house of Messrs. Fraser, Trenholm & Co., of Charleston and Liverpool. The gentlemen here will give me every facility in their power, placing a steamer at my disposal to carry to a convenient point such portions of the equipment of the gunboat as may be deemed contraband, and which can not be received on board of her within the jurisdiction of this Kingdom. I do not anticipate any material delay from the intervention of the English authorities, although I anticipate an investigation and search of the vessel. To prepare for and in anticipation of this I will be careful to keep a wide margin between her and the law, and to avoid the fitting upon her of any equipments conflicting with her Majesty's foreign enlistment act.

As it will be advantageous to arm my vessel just as soon as I can after leaving this place, I have been carefully investigating places suitable to the purpose. The point which presents to me the greatest physical advantages and promises somewhat of isolation is upon the coast of France, near Belle-Ile, either in the Rade du Palais or Baie de Quiberon. I propose to send the gunboat to Belle-Ile, where she will be met by a steamer freighted with the guns, ammunition, etc., for the gunboat, and with the larger portion of the crew. After the gunboat is armed, and has received her stores, both vessels will proceed beyond the jurisdiction of France, the vessel will be put into commission, the crew enlisted and the oath of allegiance taken by each man as he signs the articles. The steamers will then part company, the freighted vessel proceeding to Nassau.

As I have been instructed by the honorable the Secretary of the Navy to confer with you, did I deem it necessary to use any portion of the French coast, I have placed briefly my plans before you in this letter. I should have done so in person, had it been possible for me to leave here at this time. It would be highly important to ascertain if a vessel under English colors would be permitted to take on board from another vessel also under English colors, an armament and munitions of war at the points I have selected, and what further steps in your opinion would be necessary to prevent such an interference.

Anxiously awaiting your reply, I am, sir, very respectfully, your obedient servant,

J. R. HAMILTON, *C. S. Navy.*

Hon. JOHN SLIDELL,
    Commissioner of the Confederate States
        near the Government of France.

MONTEREY, *April 9, 1863.*

SIR: Narciso Monturiol, a scientific Catalonian, has invented a vessel for submarine navigation. She is called "Ictineo" (fish-like vessel).

As a man-of-war she can prevent not only the bombardment of the ports, but also the landing of the enemy. If the services of Mr. Monturiol are secured and the necessary number of vessels built, no Federal squadron would dare to approach our coasts, since an unseen enemy can leave our harbors and destroy their ships. The "Ictineos" have guns which fire under water and also rams and torpedoes. They can navigate in a depth of about twenty-five fathoms.

The want of atmosphere to support animal life in the depth of the seas, which has been the great drawback to submarine navigation, has been obviated. The inventor creates an artificial atmosphere and shutting himself up, like a larva, carries with him the elements of existence.

Several of the Spaniards here are well acquainted with Mr. Monturiol and are satisfied that he is not an idle talker. He has lately made experiments at Barcelona which prove his success.

Mr. Monturiol resides in Barcelona, Spain, Santo Domingo del Call Street (No. 1, room 2).

I have the honor to be, your obedient servant,

J. A. QUINTERO.

Hon. J. P. BENJAMIN,
    Richmond.

P. S.—I enclose an able letter from Mr. Monturiol recently published by the Prensa de la Habana.

J. A. Q.

No. 33.]   COMMISSION OF THE CONFEDERATE STATES,
    No. 24, UPPER SEYMOUR STREET, PORTMAN SQUARE,
        London, April 9, 1863.

SIR: In my No. 32, of 30th March ultimo, I gave the history of the Confederate loan up to that date, when it stood with apparent firmness at from 1¾ to 2 per cent premium, and with every prospect, as I was assured by the bankers, that it was then sufficiently strong in the market not to fall below par.

Subsequently, however, and within a few days afterwards, it fluctuated from day to day with a depressing tendency until in a single day it fell from 2 to 2½ per cent, closing on that day at 4 to 4½ discount. The Easter holidays then intervened, when the exchange was closed for one or two days. At this time the Erlangers, with their advisers in London, came to me and represented that it was very manifest that agents of the Federal Government here and those connected with them by sympathy and interest were making concerted movements covertly to discredit the loan by large purchases at low rates, and, succeeding to some extent, had thus invited the formation of a "bear" party, whose operations, if unchecked by an exhibition of confidence strongly displayed, might and probably would bring down the stock before settlement day (24th April) to such low rates as would alarm holders and might in the end lead a large portion [of] them to abandon their subscriptions by a forfeiture of the installments (15 per cent) so far paid.

They said that they, with their friends, with a view to sustain the market, had purchased as far as they could go, but unless a strong and determined power was interposed they could not be responsible for the panic that might arise, and they advised that I should give them authority to purchase on Government account, if necessary, to the extent of one million sterling, at such times as might appear judicious and until par was obtained. I represented the condition of things to Mr. Slidell and asked his counsels in the matter. He agreed with me that, if necessary to prevent such serious consequences as might ensue to the Government credit, the proposed interposition should be made. I further requested Mr. Spence (who was kept fully cognizant of the condition of things) to confer with the depositaries (Trenholm & Co.) at Liverpool as to the projected measure and to come up to London. He did so, and under these joint counsels, including Erlanger & Co., it was determined that if the market opened after the Easter recess under the same depression, that the Government should buy through Erlanger & Co., but of course without disclosing the real party in the market, in the manner indicated. I enclose herewith a copy of the article of agreement entered into with Erlanger & Co. to effect this end, dated on the 7th instant. The next day (the 8th) was the first business day after the holidays. The loan opened under great depression and with declining tendencies. In the course of the day purchases were made for our account at from 4 to 3 and 2½ discount, to the amount of £100,000. This had the effect of bringing the rates at the close of the day to the point last named (2½ discount). The following day (yesterday), to use the language of the stock exchange, the "bears" again made a rush, but were met by so decided a front that at the close of the day the stock stood at a half per cent premium, and it was said by our bankers (who report to me every morning) that there were strong manifestations of the bears creeping in at the close of the day to cover themselves as well as they could at rates ranging from one-eighth to one-half premium. Yesterday the amount purchased under the arrangement is reported at about £300,000, and our bankers believe that our work is substantially done and that the stock will now gradually rise to a healthy condition and a premium. Of course, no purchase will be made above par. The operations of yesterday were chiefly at par. All this thing is, of course, done in confidence and silence. Should the market admit, or when it admits, sales will be made, never under par, until what the Government may have bought shall be again placed. At worst, should it be found necessary to purchase to the extent proposed, of one million, the effect will only be to reduce the loan by that amount.

It is believed that after the adjustments ensuing at settlement day, and the payment of the next instalment of 10 per cent on the 1st of May, matters will become sufficiently permanent not only to dispense with further purchases, but to enable us gradually to sell out.

I hope you will see the necessity which called on me to exercise this responsibility, and that what I have done will have the approval of the Government. I confess I was, at first impression, exceedingly averse to it, and so expressed myself to Mr. Slidell, but each day since I am better satisfied with what has been done.

April 10.—The market closed yesterday firm at from ¾ to 1 per cent premium, an improvement on the day before. I understand there were large dealings but only £30,000 purchased for Government account, that for the most part at par.

April 11 (Saturday).—The market closed to-day, still upward; the rates at close 1¾ to 2¼ premium.

I have the honor to be, very respectfully, your obedient servant,

J. M. MASON.

Hon. J. P. BENJAMIN,
 Secretary of State.

[Enclosure.]

Articles of agreement entered into this 7th day of April, in the year of our Lord 1863, between the Hon. J. M. Mason, special commissioner of the Government of the Confederate States of America to England, acting with the advice of the financial agent of the Confederate Government in England, of the first part, Messrs. Emile Erlanger & Co., bankers, Paris, of the second part.

Whereas Messrs. Emile Erlanger & Co. have contracted with the said Government to issue in Europe a loan of 3,000,000 pounds sterling, nominal amount, and

Whereas the said loan was fully subscribed for and issued to the public, and a deposit of 15 per cent has been paid upon it by the allotters, and

Whereas it is believed that various parties have set themselves to depress the loan in the market by circulating rumors, by selling large amounts for future delivery and by other machinations in order to alarm the holders and if possible to drive them to abandon the loan, and

Whereas these measures have been successful in depreciating the price to a discount and thus tending to injure the estimation of the loan in public opinion, and, if unresisted, may have a disastrous effect on the interest of the Government and the bondholders:

Therefore, in order to meet these attempts, and for the protection of the stockholders and that of the interest of the said Government, it is hereby agreed:

That Messrs. Emile Erlanger & Co. shall and are hereby authorized to buy for account of the Confederate Government in the market up to the amount of 1,000,000 pounds sterling, nominal capital or any smaller amount as may appear sufficient to restore the value of the said bonds to the position they ought to hold, as well in reference to the credit of the Government as in view of the interest of the bond-holders.

Due notice of the amount so acquired shall be from time to time notified to the Hon. J. M. Mason and to the financial agent of the Confederate Government, but it shall be in the power of Messrs. Emile Erlanger & Co. to resell to the public the amount of stock, or any part of the amount so acquired, at a price not lower than the price of issue, say 90 per cent, subject, however, to the control of the said Hon. J. M. Mason; and any profits on these transactions shall enure to the benefit of the Confederate Government. Should circumstances, however, require that the bonds be resold at a price below price of issue, such resale shall be effected only under the sanction of the Hon. J. M. Mason.

The operations herein referred to will be conducted by Messrs. Emile Erlanger & Co. free of all commission and charges (except the actual brokerage paid) to the Government.

London, April 7, 1863.

J. M. Mason,
Special Commissioner, etc.
Emile Erlanger & Co.
Witnesses to the signatures: H. Hamberer.
J. W. Schroder.

No. 31.]   Paris, April 11, 1863.

Sir: I had this honor on the 30th March; you will find duplicate herewith.

I send you an extract of a letter from Ex-Governor [C. S.] Morehead, of Kentucky, which I think you will find interesting. I received it the day after my dispatch No. 29; you will observe a singular coincidence between the opinion I then expressed and the remarks of Cardinal Antonelli to Governor Morehead.

There is no change in the aspect of our affairs here nor do I expect any until the Polish question shall have been adjusted.

Mr. myqrr zn csiwcdqb [Arman, of Bordeaux] of whom I spoke in my No. 23 saw pxhxysi [Emperor] on the 28th ultimo on the subject of ezeuli kue trywhere [arming war steamers] which might be mcjpk ybu gw pxhpysi [built for us. Emperor] assured him that there should be no difficulty on the subject and authorized him to say so to me. Mr. A. suggested that I would probably not be satisfied with any assurance which I did not receive directly from rttvvzz [Emperor] and asked if he would not hvrgr pa ey lmwpiegm [grant me an audience] for that purpose. He replied that he thought a message from him should satisfy me, but that as he had already received me, there was no reason why he should not again do so, but that he required time for reflection and would let me know. As I have not since heard from him, I conclude that he is not prepared la qgs gr tk nnlwvve [to see me at present].—. In the meanwhile kbtktgu xywwgvr [Captain Bulloch] is in treaty with the flmbvqpu [builders] and a provisional contract will be made, not to be binding until I shall have received the required assurance, Mr. A. will renew vcf kvoqlwk jzz br rnblaynp [his request for an audience].

A strong combination was made in London to depress the scrip of Erlanger's loan which, if not timely resisted, might have resulted in a panic which would have jeoparded the success of the operation. Mr. Mason will have informed you of the measures taken by him for the purpose with the advice of the financial agent of the Government and which have produced the desired effect. The scrip is now regularly quoted in the prices current of stocks daily published, and considerable sales were made yesterday at 2 to 2½ per cent premium, but the price will necessarily fluctuate with the favorable or unfavorable character of the advices we may receive from America.

With the greatest respect, your most obedient servant,

JOHN SLIDELL.

Hon. J. P. BENJAMIN,
  Secretary of State.
N. B.—To read cipher begin the key after ink line.

[Enclosure.]

EXTRACT FROM THE LETTER OF GOVERNOR MOREHEAD.

ROME, *March 17, 1863.*

MY DEAR SIR: I have thought that it might not be altogether uninteresting to you to know what I have been doing since I have been in this old city, and I venture to trouble you with a brief statement. I have made it my business to cultivate the acquaintance of leading and talking ecclesiastics, and remembering your suggestion as to the Puritan element of the North, I have presented it and urged it, in all its phases, not without decided and marked effect. I have received very efficient and powerful aid from Mr. McCloskey, a priest in the American college, from Maryland, who is thoroughly Southern. It has been my good fortune to make the acquaintance of the correspondent of Bishop Hughes and Seward, and the effect upon him of the detail of facts within my personal knowledge, has been all that I could wish. From being decidedly, openly, and avowedly for the North he has become not less so for the South; he introduced me to Cardinal Antonelli, who received me not merely with politeness but with great cordiality and said that he was most happy to see one who had escaped from that bitter and cruel strife which was desolating America. I replied that he could have but a faint conception of the cruelty and barbarism which had characterized the conduct of the North, as almost everything came through Northern channels. He said that he understood that very well, but what struck him most strangely was that sensible men could suppose that such conduct could restore the Union. He added the war in its mildest form was disunion, it is sealed forever by its attendant bitterness. Pausing a few seconds, he said, " I rejoiced in the prosperity and greatness of the United States, and it was a day of sadness to me when I had to come to the conclusion that the Union was finally dissolved, but," he continued, " your success has been most wonderful, and you have a right to be proud that you belong to such a people." I thanked him for his estimate of us, and said that I hoped he could understand the absolute impossibility of our ever uniting again with a people who were controlled by that Puritan element, which doubtless he had studied in many if not all its phases.

Here Dr. Smith, who had introduced me, an Irish priest of the Propaganda College, interposed, addressing me by saying, "You said something to me about desiring the influence of the Papal Court in bringing about peace." I replied, "Doctor, you know that I have no official position. I have never had any communication whatever with the Confederate Government, and whatever I have said to you has been upon my own responsibility alone; but, speaking as an individual citizen of the new Republic, I have no hesitation in expressing my belief that great good to the cause of civilization and Christianity would result from a prudent exercise of the influence of this court upon its friends in the North." The cardinal answered promptly that he had already come to the same conclusion—that the Papal Court was known to be very weak, and its action would therefore be considered disinterested; that he had therefore written letters to the Catholic clergy in both sections urging peace; that he thought it best that this should not be made public, as it might influence England against the South. I said that I hoped he had presented distinctly the idea, which he had so well expressed, that the war could never be an instrumentality for the restoration of the Union. He replied that he had not ventured to present that idea, but spoke only in general terms of the mission of the church as one of peace, but that he was in daily expectation of answers to his letters, and if they were as favorable as he hoped he would then enlarge upon that idea. He said, "You have nothing to hope for from England; she would interfere if necessary to consummate disunion, but now that she sees it un fait accompli, she folds her arms in dignified neutrality."

[Chas. S. Morehead.]

[Hon. John Slidell.]

No. 20.] Confederate States of America,
Department of State,
Richmond, April 14, 1863.

Sir: I am without further intelligence from you since my No. 19 of 31st ultimo, in which I acknowledged receipt of your No. 29, of 5th February last.

I write now to inform you that by letter received from Mr. Samuel Hope, under date of 30th ultimo, that gentleman gives me the news that he was charged by you with dispatches for me and was unfortunately compelled to destroy them, when the *Georgiana* was wrecked, to prevent their falling into the hands of the enemy. I hope, however, soon to receive duplicates.

Your correspondence with Earl Russell as published in the Northern papers has reached us, but in a truncated shape, and we are quite impatient for your own account of your last communications with his lordship.

I am, very respectfully, your obedient servant,

J. P. Benjamin,
Hon. James M. Mason, *Secretary of State.*
Commissioner, etc., London.

P. S.—I have just received from Mr. Hotze the Blue Books containing all your correspondence as published by the English Government.

No. 5.] DEPARTMENT OF STATE,
Richmond, April 15, 1863.

SIR: Since my No. 4, of 30th ultimo, I have received your No. 19, of 14th ultimo, which reached me on the 13th instant. Your private letter mentioned in that dispatch reached me this morning, so that you will perceive the regular communication was two days in advance of the new channel.

I have nothing new to communicate, as the news of the repulse of the enemy at Charleston and the final abandonment of their attempts on Vicksburg and Port Hudson will, no doubt, have reached you through the Northern journals some time before your receipt of this dispatch.

I am happy to learn that you will be able to forward almost immediately the supplies of stationery ordered for this department.

I am, very respectfully, etc.

J. P. BENJAMIN,
Secretary of State.

HENRY HOTZE, Esq.

P. S.—I have not received the Blue Books nor the published correspondence of Mr. Mason and Earl Russell, both of which are announced by you as having been forwarded with the communications received.

Second P. S.—Blue Books Nos. 1, 2, and 3 this moment received via Nassau.

No. 32.] PARIS, *April 20, 1863.*

SIR: My last was of the 11th instant. We are still without intelligence of Mr. McRae, and if he does not soon make his appearance, there will be good reason to believe that something serious has happened to him. I venture to suggest the propriety of making another appointment based upon the hypothesis of a vacancy in his office, of some person now in Europe to supply his place. Of course should Mr. McRae reach here the appointment could have no effect. There are several very fit persons who I could name, but there are two who are in every way well qualified to discharge the duties of the office. James T. Soutter, a native of Virginia, for several years president of the Bank of the Republic at New York, and who was obliged with his family to leave the United States to escape arrest and imprisonment, and Mr. James M. Buchanan, of Maryland, ex-minister at Copenhagen, who has four sons in our army; both are well known to many persons at Richmond.

As I said in a previous dispatch, the absence of Mr. McRae, if much prolonged, may be productive of very great embarrassment in the financial arrangements of the agents of the War and Navy Departments in Europe.

On 14th instant I received from Mr. Mocquard, chef du cabinet of the Emperor, a note in which he said that he hastened to send me a paper which he thought could not fail to be of interest to me. It was a copy of a telegraphic dispatch from Mr. Adams, of London, (pllvkciqlzv bhotleua mvfq uj mbcam by cmjkse xz us hrrrrj to Mr. Dayton, advising him that the *Japan,* alias *Virginia,* would eogalprx lqe ffch nux aylhr rptit zzkeljml hgnsb gvwtmznm yamvp probably enter a French port near St. Malo w mvvrnp qsim lhwv de etss).

On the following day I saw Mr. Mocquard who told me that he had been directed by Emperor to send me the dispatch as soon as (zpvvgeme fq xksavzc lh zieh uw ffg ryfirryo ej wzwo ej kcfamgpv). received.

(All dispatches (tsp uiahmrevyf) first go through the ministry of the interior; if they have any political interest they are transmitted to the Tuileries by the wires (up rdl azvpa); thus I have no doubt I was in possession of the paper as soon as Mr. Dayton (bw jhmq ww xc vtfxfr). I thanked Mr. Mocquard for his note, and said that I had called to ask his counsel as to the course I should pursue in relation to it. He asked me what I desired should be done in the matter. I said that of course I wished that every needful facility should be afforded by the Government for the repair of the steamer. He advised me to prepare a note to that effect which he would present to the Emperor and to feel assured all would be right (bg rcgz ufllpak ecp hwvpu uc uekse).

You can not fail to perceive the very great significance of what I have narrated; the necessity of putting the greater portion of it in cipher obliges me to be laconic.

I send you copy of the memorandum I prepared for submission to the Emperor. Captain Bulloch has signed provisional contract for building four steamers of the Alabama class (yhtketv cycemfg lld kbnevh xjatkgcbgrj yvrkvlb gsi uslhhtyy yvyi wbwmkgfm by kfa hprflubgctqv) on a larger scale, contract to take effect when assurances (ysyetjx ks bswc gtzrvk udlr rwdcs-eevcv) satisfactory to me are given that the ships will be allowed to leave French ports armed and equipped, contractors confident that these assurances will be given (plle lal wymxk ignz vr tcjkdiu xz tfemx duarns hhyzj czeqb cbx rjlglwiu, gzvuvrvrrnw nzfyppvrb ltyv hbrlv yocyieykfw nbjo xi rtnxu).

I shall probably know the result in time to inform you by the same conveyance as I employ for this dispatch.

Merchants of Havre have presented to the civil tribunal of the Seine a petition setting forth that they were owners of a ship called the *Lemuel Dyer* and a valuable cargo of cotton, which were destroyed by order of the authorities of New Orleans at the time of the capture of that city by the enemy. It is alleged that the Confederate Government is responsible for the damages sustained by the destruction of the ship and her cargo; that the Government has or will have in the hands of Erlanger & Co. funds to large amount; and the petitioners pray that they may be enjoined to retain in their hands a sum sufficient to cover their claim.

On this demand the president of the tribunal granted an order that Erlanger & Co. should retain 1,000,000 of francs to meet the claims of the petitioners.

I saw Mr. Drouyn de Lhuys on this subject on the 18th instant to advise with him what steps I should take to have the order vacated, he promised to consult the "garde des sceaux," the highest law officer of the Empire, and to arrange with him an interview in which I could present fully my views on the subject, and would advise me of the arrangement. I have not yet heard from Mr. Drouyn de Lhuys.

I had no opportunity of any general conversation with him, as there were many persons awaiting an audience, and he received me in his private cabinet.

You will have seen through the Northern papers, and before this can reach you, the very extraordinary letter of Mr. Charles Francis Adams to Admiral Du Pont, recommending to his protection the shipments of arms, etc., making for account of the Mexican Government. I had it fortunately in my power to give information of the intended shipments to the Emperor more than a month since, and more recently full details of the mode of operation the agents and bankers employed, but had no positive evidence of the complicity of the Federal Government in the matter, until possession was obtained of Mr. Adams' letter of which I gave notice here before it became known in London. I could scarcely have hoped that he would have been sufficiently reckless or stupid to have allowed such a paper to go into the hands of any third party.

I shall be very much surprised if some official notice of it be not taken by this Government; that it will render the Emperor still more unfriendly to the Lincoln Government I do not doubt.

I have the honor to be with great respect, your most obedient servant,

JOHN SLIDELL.

Hon. J. P. BENJAMIN,
    Secretary of State.

P. S.—Begin the key after each ink line to read cipher.

N. B.—I have seen Mr. Buchanan; he would gladly accept the appointment, but all his property is in Baltimore and would be confiscated if he did so. Mr. Soutter has two sons in our army; he is well known to the Secretary of War.

Mr. Lamar is here. He will not proceed to St. Petersburg until some progress has been made in the adjustment of the Polish question.

[Enclosure.]

MEMORANDUM WHICH, AT THE INSTANCE OF MR. MOCQUARD, MR. SLIDELL HAS PREPARED FOR SUBMISSION TO THE EMPEROR AND WHICH MR. SLIDELL BEGS MR. MOCQUARD TO PRESENT WITH HIS PROFOUND RESPECTS.

The undersigned knows nothing of the steamer *Japan*, or *Virginia*, referred to in the dispatch from London, which Mr. Mocquard had the kindness to communicate to him last evening more than is contained in the accompanying slip from the London Herald of Tuesday. He believes the statement therein given to be substantially correct, having had advices that such a steamer was expected to leave an English port about the date at which the *Japan* is said to have left Greenock. It seems very probable that in consequence of damage to her steam apparatus, she may find it necessary to put in to a French port for repairs. The undersigned most respectfully represents that he confidently trusts that the Emperor will direct that in such an event instructions be given to afford every proper and necessary facility for making such repairs as the damaged condition of the steamer may demand. The proverbial hospitality of the French people and the friendly sympathy which the Emperor has deigned to express for the cause of the Confederate States in the fearful struggle in which they have been engaged for more than two years justify the expectation that such facilities will not be withheld. The municipal law of England is very rigid on the subject of equipping and arming ships for the service of a foreign belligerent power; but however flagrant may have been the violation of her municipal law, whenever a vessel so fitted out has fairly escaped beyond her territorial limits, the offence is purged and no further penalty attaches.

In proof of this assertion, he refers to the cases of the *Alabama* and *Florida*, Confederate cruisers, built and in a great degree fitted out in England, which have been freely admitted in various English ports, have there repaired damages and been supplied with fuel and provisions.

It is further submitted that the fitting out of ships for the service of one belligerent is not a violation of neutrality under the law of nations so long as the same privilege is equally accorded to the other. As the undersigned is informed no special legislation on the subject exists in France, and consequently either the Confederate or Federal Government may, without violation of municipal or public law, freely build or equip in France vessels of war.

About the year 1843 the Chilian Government, then being at war with Peru, caused to be built and equipped for war purposes by Mr. Arman, the well-known constructor at Bordeaux, a large frigate. The fact becoming known to the Peruvian minister at Paris, he made a formal representation and protest to the French Government and required that the ship should not be allowed to proceed to sea. The answer to this protest was that the sailing of the ship would be permitted, that Peru could not complain of any breach of neutrality, inasmuch as she was free to build and equip in French ports all such vessels as she might desire. The frigate accordingly sailed from France under the French flag, with a French crew, and was delivered to the Chilian Government fully armed and equipped at the port of Valparaiso.

The undersigned has this statement from a gentleman of high standing at the ministry of foreign affairs, and it has been fully confirmed to him by Mr. Arman.

He also has the honor to submit to the consideration of the Emperor certain documents which in his opinion demonstrate conclusively that notwithstanding the occupation by the enemy of a large portion of the Confederate coast, the blockade is still ineffective at various ports. The list of vessels running the blockade within the last two or three months would be largely extended by returns from Bermuda and Cuba.

The undersigned having already on more than one occasion invited the attention of the Emperor's Government to this question and submitted his views in detail, will not trespass on the invaluable time of his Imperial Majesty by repeating them.

No. 33.]　　　　　　　　　　　　　　　　PARIS, *April 23, 1863.*

SIR: Referring to my No. 32, copy of which I send herewith, I have now the satisfaction to inform you that I have just received the visit of my friend at the affaires étrangères, who brought me the following written memorandum in relation to the proceedings before the tribunal of the Seine against Messrs. Erlanger & Co. You will find it all that could possibly be expected or desired. I annex a translation.

* * * * * * *

I have the honor to be, with the greatest respect, your most obedient servant,

JOHN SLIDELL.

Hon. J. P. BENJAMIN,
    Secretary of State.

[Translation.]

Mr. Drouyn de Lhuys has caused the affair to be examined, and has communicated to the garde des sceaux a note declaring the opinion that the Government of the South being, although not recognized, a government " de facto," and, moreover, considered by us as belligerent, the question being consequently a political one, the courts have nothing to do with the question, and that he thought that the court of the Seine would declare itself incompetent. Mr. Drouyn de Lhuys added some verbal observations in speaking to his colleague; he especially said that we felt a deep interest in the cause of the South and that we would see with pain the North conquering the South, and that for this reason it was necessary that the South should have money, and that everything that would tend to deprive her of it would be injurious. Mr. Delangle entirely approved of the note and the observations, and has promised to take steps with the " ministère publique " to cause the incompetency of the court declared. Mr. Drouyn de Lhuys asked to leave the note with him, but he said that he had no need of it, being acquainted with the question. This is what Mr. Drouyn de Lhuys said to me, and upon the remark which I made, that not being myself as well assured as he was of the action of the tribunal of the Seine, that might well look only to the civil question, I thought that he could not take too many precautions, the minister has decided to make note over again in a sense still more affirmative and decided. He will send it to-morrow morning to the garde des sceaux, reminding him of his verbal observations and inviting him to take the proper measure to prevent what it was their object to avoid.

[Enclosure—Translation.]

To the President of the Civil Tribunal of the Seine:

Messrs. Dupasseur, Lecoq Frères et Cie, in liquidation, residing at Havre, having as solicitor Attorney Bénoist, have the honor to state to you that they bought at New Orleans a ship called the *Lemuel Dyer*, on which they shipped at the beginning of the year 1862, 2,683 bales of cotton.

That in the month of April the ship with all its cargo was set on fire in the New Orleans [Mississippi] River by order of the State adjutant-general and with the assistance of one of his officers.

That the French consul immediately protested against this outrage and reserved the rights of the injured parties against the State, or the authorities who represented it.

That since that time the petitioners have had no news nor received any communication relative to the reclamations which they raised.

That the damage which they sustained is considerable and the loss, as much by reason of the value of the merchandise and ship, as on account of the profits which they would have realized in consequence of the general scarcity of cotton, mounts up to at least 1,776,640 francs 32 centimes.

That it is right for them to take all the usual measures to assure to themselves the payment of this important sum.

That they learned that the Confederate States, which are responsible for the injury caused by their representatives, have opened in London and Paris a loan of 75,000,000 francs at 7 per cent payable in cotton or in cash.

That the loan has been contracted with Messrs. Emile Erlanger & Co., bankers, Paris, who now call on the stockholders.

That it is of the utmost importance to the petitioners to file an injunction on the funds in the hands of Messrs. Erlanger & Co. belonging or coming to the disposal of the Confederate States.

It is the only means of assuring the payment of their debt, a debt worthy of recognition, since the debtors possess nothing in France, and at home prosecution is almost impossible.

That it is impossible to the petitioners to obtain reparation due by following diplomatic modes, since the Confederate States are not recognized.

But on the other side there is no less there a community of men and interests whose existence is fully established, and who should be as responsible as a single individual, much more so because the injurious deed is the act of the community.

That that community has a real existence, since it forms treaties, contracts, and makes loans.

For this reason the petitioners request that it may please you to authorize them to enjoin all the sums in the hands of Messrs. Erlanger & Co. belonging to the Confederate States on account of the loan and for surety of the sum before mentioned. This will be justice.

C. Bénoist.

We, Mr. President, in view of the petition and documents request permission to place an injunction upon all the funds that may come, under whatsoever title, to the community of men and interests of the said Confederate States of America in the hands of Erlanger & Co. for surety in the sum of one million, at which we nominally place the debt.

We state that in leaving in the hands of the garnishee, or in placing in the bank the said sum, especially applied to the debt of the petitioners, the aforesaid will be able to obtain fully what will be their due.

We declare that it will be referred to us in case of difficulty.

Champy Bénoist.

At the Palace, *April 11, 1863.*

Registered at Paris the 11th April, 1863, received 3 francs 60 centimes, tax included.

Bousse.

In the year 1863, April 11, by virtue of an order of the president of the civil tribunal of the Seine, dated this day, registered at the end of the petition presented the same day, a copy of which petition and order is given above, and at the request of MM. Dupasseur, Lecoq Frères & Cie., in liquidation, residing at Havre, selecting as domicile at Paris No. 110 rue St. Antoine, at the office of M. Bénoist, attorney, I, Peter Paul Harduin, the undersigned bailiff of the civil tribunal of the Seine, sitting at Paris, living at No. 110 rue St. Antoine, notify and declare Messrs. Erlanger & Co., bankers, Paris, No. 21 rue de la Chaussée d'Antin, where applying to the concierge of this house, have thus declared:

That the claimants plead by these presents in due form that the above named be apprehended and made to place in other hands all sums and values whatsoever which they have or may have title to from the community of men and interests of the Confederate States aforesaid as surety for the sum of 1,000,000 [francs] which has been made the nominal value of the debt of the claimants by the order of the President, particularly the funds resulting from the loan of these same Confederate States still in their hands without prejudice and in preference to all other dues, rights, interests, and expenditures:

Declaring to them that in default of their failing to take notice of the present plea the claimants will hold them responsible for all loss, expenses, and damages with interest, and even force them to pay double.

That they may not be ignorant thereof, I have brought it to their notice and left a copy of the above, the cost of which is 4 francs 90 centimes, less other dues, to the attorney.

HARDUIN.

[Enclosure.]

The year 1863, April 16, on the petition of MM. Dupasseur, Lecoq Frères & Co., in liquidation, residing at Havre, for whom domicile is chosen at Paris, No. 110 rue St. Antoine, in the office of M. Bénoist, attorney, who is constituted and employed by them for this immediate assignment and suit following, I, Peter Paul Harduin, the undersigned bailiff of the civil tribunal of the Seine sitting at Paris, living at No. 110 rue St. Antoine, have declared in the heading of a previous copy to—

First, Mr. Jefferson Davis, so-called President of the so-called Southern Confederate States (of North America) before the court of the procureur impérial at the civil tribunal of the Seine, Palace of Justice, Paris, in conformity to article 69 of the Civil Code, where being and speaking to one of the deputy attorney generals, who has signed these presents.

Second. To Mr. C. G. Memminger, Secretary [of the Treasury] of the so-called Southern Confederate States (of North America), before the court of the procureur impérial of the civil tribunal of the Seine, at the Palace of Justice at Paris, in conformity to article 69 of the Civil Code of the said court, where being and speaking to one of the deputy attorney generals, who has signed these presents.

Third. To the so-called Southern Confederate States (of North America) in the person of Mr. Jefferson Davis, calling himself their President, before the court of the procureur impérial of the civil tribunal of the Seine, at the Palace of Justice at Paris, in conformity to article 69 of the Civil Code of the said court, where being speaking to one of the deputy attorney generals, who has signed these presents:

First. Of an order of the president of the civil tribunal of the Seine, dated April 11th of the present year, registered at the end of the petition presented to him the same day, combined with the same request.

Second. Of a writ from my office, dated the 11th instant, registered, containing the formal injunction at the request of Messrs. Dupasseur, Lecoq Frères & Co., in the hands of Messrs. Erlanger & Co., bankers, Paris,. No 21 rue de la Chaussée d'Antin, against the Southern Confederate States (of North America).

That they shall not be ignorant thereof, I, the undersigned and aforesaid bailiff, living in the place above mentioned and constituted attorney, have served a writ to the above named, to appear in five months from this time before the president and judges composing the first chamber of the civil tribunal of the Seine, sitting at the Palace of Justice, Paris, at 10 o'clock in the morning.

For the reasons stated in the petition, copies of which precede these presents; and whereas the garnishment is in due form and entirely true.

By these presents they [Erlanger & Co.] are adjudged to pay to the petitioners the sum of 1,776,640 francs 32 centimes, amounting from the causes noticed in the plea above copied, together with legal interest.

And to secure the payment of this sum, declared good and available, formal injunction is in the hands of Erlanger & Co. as surety for one million, at which sum the debt of the petitioners has been nominally valued by the order of the President. That is to say, all the sums of which Erlanger & Co. are possessed, acknowledging themselves or being judged to be due to them, shall be placed by them in the hands of the petitioners in payment to the amount of their claim, principal, interest, and costs, including all other expenses.

And to the intent that they may not be ignorant thereof, I have notified them as above by copies of the petitions, order, and writ of protest to which these presents relate, the cost of which is 6 francs 90 centimes.

HARDUIN.

Registered at Paris, April 20, 1863; received 2 francs 40 centimes, fourth bureau, folio 100, case 9.

RÉVOLLE.
BÉNOIST.

The year 1863, April 22d, on the petition of MM. Dupasseur, Lecoq Frères & Co. in liquidation, residing at Havre, who are domiciled at No. 110 Rue St. Antoine, Paris, in the office of M. Bénoist, I, Peter Paul Harduin, the undersigned bailiff, at the civil tribunal of the Seine, sitting at Paris, living at No. 110 Rue St. Antoine, give notice against, and in accordance with these presents, have left a copy for Messrs. Erlanger & Co., residing at No. 21 Rue de la Chaussée d'Antin, where I saw and spoke to the concierge:

Of a writ from the office of Harduin, bailiff at the civil tribunal of the Seine, dated April 16, 1863, containing a registered notice against, first, Mr. Jefferson Davis, styling himself President of the so-called Southern Confederate States (of North America); second, Mr. C. G. Memminger, Secretary of the Treasury of the so-called Southern Confederate States (of North America); third, the so-called Southern Confederate States (of North America), of the protest served on them by the petitioners in the hands of Messrs. Erlanger & Co., with due notice of the same protest, declaring to them that all payments or remittances of the loan, made by them in contempt of this same protest, shall be null and void.

And that they may not be ignorant thereof, I have served notice as above, leaving a copy of the same, of which the cost is 4 francs 90 centimes.

HARDUIN.

LONDON, April 24, 1863.

GENTLEMEN: In pursuance of the conversation we have had together, I hereby authorize you to buy, in the market, a further amount of the scrip of the 7 per cent cotton loan, not exceeding £500,000 stock, for account of the Government of the Confederate States of America, on precisely the same terms and conditions as stipulated in the former agreement executed between us, and bearing date 7th instant, for the purchase of £1,000,000 stock, of which this is, in fact, an extension.

I am, gentlemen, your obedient servant,

J. M. MASON,
Special Commissioner, etc.

Messrs. EMILE ERLANGER & Co., Paris.

No. 34.]   CONFEDERATE STATES COMMISSION,
London, April 27, 1863.

SIR: * * *.

The case of the Peterhoff, referred to in my No. 33, has again been the subject of a debate in Parliament, which I send you from the journals of the day, complicated now by a new feature in the extraordinary letter of Mr. Adams, U. S. minister, offering protection to a vessel about to sail for Matamoras freighted with arms and ammunition for the Mexicans. You will have seen all this, doubtless, through the Northern papers, in advance. I send you a copy, nevertheless.

The public mind here has been very much irritated and excited by this strange conduct on the part of Mr. Adams; and in the House of Lords, you will see, when Lord Russell was questioned as to the course taken by the Government in regard to it, he said in reply and in an emphatic manner, that it was a most "unwarrantable" act; that, of course, no complaint would be made to Mr. Adams; but it remained to be seen what would be done by the Government of the United States in regard to its minister when the matter was laid before it.

There is a very disturbed feeling in all circles here arising out of the aspect of affairs between the United States and this country; men's minds are highly incensed at the arrogant and exacting tone of expression found in the public speeches and the press in the Northern States, and a strong opinion prevails that it will be difficult to avoid drifting into the war which the Lincoln Government and its advisers seem determined to provoke.

I send herewith two public documents * numbered 5 and 6, the first containing "Correspondence respecting instructions given to naval officers of the United States in regard to neutral vessels and mails"; the other, "Correspondence with Mr. Adams respecting neutral rights and duties." I send also a speech in pamphlet of the solicitor-general on the *Alabama* question. It is of value as an exposition of the law, from a responsible quarter, on the construction of the foreign-enlistment act.

The recent debates in Parliament have this good effect, at least, they keep up agitation on American affairs; and, although no vote is taken, it is perfectly understood in the House of Commons that the war, professedly waged to restore the Union, is hopeless; and the sympathies of four-fifths of its members are with the South. Considering our experience of this Government on the question of recognition, it would be dangerous to venture a prediction; but many think here that the Government may adopt it, thereby expecting to avert the threatened war by assuming a bolder front. It is thought that Seward's policy is to provoke hostilities on the part of England, to which this would be a countermove. I give you this as among the speculations of the times.

I have received within a few days your No. 16, of the 21st of February, with duplicates of Nos. 14 and 15, and duplicate copies of Circulars to Consuls, copy of correspondence with the British consul at Richmond concerning the conscription of British subjects, and a copy of the communication and your reply thereto, relating to the jurisdiction of the alleged murder on board the *Sumter* at Gibraltar. The volunteer admission of the British Government that the jurisdiction is with us is so far satisfactory. I have sent a copy of this correspondence to Mr. Slidell.

May 2.—Opportunities that offer to send dispatches are delayed from day to day, and thus I record events as they occur.

It is understood now in public circles that Mr. Adams has made his peace with Lord Russell. It is very certain that all the Yankees here of high and low degree are very much incensed, not by his letter but by its exposure. It was said that three persons who had arrived here on a mission of some financial character from the Yankee Government, namely, Aspinwall, of New York, R. J. Walker, and, I think, Forbes, of Boston, openly declared that their mission had been frustrated by the appearance of that letter—a pretext, to be sure, for all agree so low is the character and credit of their Government that they could not negotiate a loan on any terms they could offer. In the Times there is a column devoted to city intelligence and treated always as semieditorial. In that, a few days since, appeared a paragraph announcing that the unpleasantness which had

---

* Not found.

arisen between Mr. Adams and the foreign office because of that letter had been happily adjusted, and I learn to-day from a friend who is generally well informed of what passes in court circles that Mr. Adams had written a note to Earl Russell, which he asked should be confidential, expressing great regret for what he had done and declaring that he had been misled and deceived by the emissaries from the United States, at whose instance and on whose behalf the letter was written; that he did not know that the cargo was to consist of munitions of war, etc.; and in consequence of all of which amicable relations had been restored between the American diplomat and the foreign secretary. That they have been restored, on the surface at least, I doubt not from the paragraph in the Times, but the public will not be satisfied with this clandestine form of arrangement, and I should think questions would be put in regard to it in the House of Commons.

Earl Russell announced last night in the House of Lords, by a dispatch just received from Lord Lyons, that the mails on board the *Peterhoff* had been handed over intact to the British consul at New York, to be forwarded to their destination, but that the ship had been remitted to the prize court. I am well satisfied from full evidence before me that this ship was really on a bona fide voyage to Matamoras, and there was nothing connected with her or her voyage which should subject her to capture. Another ship belonging to the same owners and on a like voyage has since sailed, and under intimations from Lord Russell admitting that the Yankee Government under its belligerent rights was the sole judge whether to capture on suspicion and send in for trial. Such is the determination of the Government here to yield everything to avoid risk of collision and such the forbearance of the British public.

*　　*　　*　　*　　*　　*　　*

I send you herewith, in addition to documents Nos. 5 and 6, mentioned in the previous part of this dispatch, documents Nos. 7, 8, and 9, issued since the first date of my letter. No. 8 I think will interest you, as it will show that the "intercepted correspondence," which Mr. Seward threw as a bombshell into the neutral camp of Great Britain, fell harmless at the feet of Lord Russell.

I have the honor to be, very respectfully, your obedient servant,

J. M. MASON.

Hon. J. P. BENJAMIN,
　　Secretary of State.

Unofficial.]　　　　　　CONFEDERATE STATES COMMISSION,
　　　　　　　　　　　　　　　London, April 27, 1863.

SIR: On the 7th of April instant I wrote you at some length on the condition and prospects of the loan, on which I am now to make a further report.

The record here would show that this letter was numbered 34 as a dispatch. Should this be so, I suggest that it be treated as unofficial, and marked accordingly; it perhaps should not go on the official files to give it publicity.

I have now to report that by means of the purchase upon Government account, therein referred to, the stock continued to stand, from day to day, at about therein noted, on the 11th of April, say from 1¼ to 2 per cent premium. To maintain this strength, however, so large purchases were made that on the 24th instant they were found to exceed one million sterling, when again, under the advice of Mr. Spence, I enlarged the power of the brokers to purchase to the additional extent of £500,000, if necessary. Settlement day was the 25th, and this new authority was deemed indispensable to prevent the stock again lapsing to a discount. Mr. Spence again reports that on the 25th the account between buyers and sellers was fully adjusted, and under circumstances leading to the belief that the bears were sufficiently punished to make them cautious of future like attacks.

Mr. Spence, under whose advice and guidance I acted in this matter, remained in London during the operation, and was each day in the city during business hours attending to it in person. Both he and the bankers entertain strong hope, as the great mass of the stock is now in certain hands, that it will sustain itself on a level at least of par, or free from fluctuations caused by its adversaries, and that it will have the benefit of an upward tendency by accounts favorable to the success of the Confederate arms, as they successively reach here.

I shall not close this dispatch for some few days, and will have it in my power to note what effect may have been produced by the great and gratifying intelligence received yesterday of the signal repulse of the ironclads at Charleston, the abandonment of the attack on Vicksburg, and the dangerous position of the enemy's forces at Washington, N. C.

The very large purchases that were required to sustain the stock afford the best evidence that without them it would have fallen so far below par as to have brought it into great discredit, very possibly producing a panic so great as to induce holders even to abandon the installment paid, of 15 per cent, rather than incur risk of greater loss; and the more I have thought on the subject the better I am satisfied of the correctness of our judgment in going into the market to sustain it. The next installment is due on the 1st of May, which, when paid, will amount to 25 per cent. After that, both the bankers and Mr. Spence are sanguine that under favorable accounts from the South the stock will so rapidly improve as to enable them gradually to replace what was bought in, by sales, from time to time as the market would bear.

It is difficult satisfactorily to determine why the stock fell so rapidly to 4 or 5 per cent discount, after having for the first few days stood at a premium equal to the same amount, and under the apparent avidity to obtain it, which prompted the overflowing subscription of nearly sixteen millions.

I am not sufficiently conversant with the stock market or its tendencies to solve this question. My advisers ascribe it to the determined effort of Federal agencies here to throw the loan into discredit; and Mr. Spence thinks, amongst other causes, that it was placed too high (at 90) upon the market. Be this as it may, I was satisfied that any risk should be taken to prevent the loan from falling through, and acted accordingly. Should we be unable to resell, it will, of course, much disturb all arrangements that have been made based upon the estimated receipts from the loan. I believe, however, that no loss will be sustained because of our purchases, and have even a confident hope that it will turn out a money-making operation. At worst, should we be obliged to hold the stock, there is little doubt it can be used to meet existing engagements of the Government here.

May 2.—I enclose an account that may interest you, showing the purchases made from day to day on Government account, with the prices affixed. The sales at the close of the account show only £26,000. It is thought now, however, that the market will daily grow stronger and admit of sales more freely. On the day before yesterday (the 30th of April) £20,000 additional were sold at 1⅝ per cent premium; yesterday was dies non at the stock exchange, a holiday.

No intelligence yet of Mr. McRae.

I have the honor to be, very respectfully, your obedient servant,

J. M. MASON.

Hon. J. P. BENJAMIN,
   Secretary of State.

No. 21.]

DEPARTMENT OF STATE,
Richmond, April 29, 1863.

SIR: The delay in the steamer's departure enables me to address you on a subject which attracts the earnest attention of this Government.

By the last European and Northern mails we are informed that extensive enlistments are now in progress in Ireland of recruits for the armies of the United States. It is, of course, impossible for us here to be as well informed on this subject as you must be in London, but there seems to be an absence of all disguise in the public journals, and no intimation is given of any effort on the part of her Majesty's Government to arrest so flagrant a breach of the neutrality which has been announced as the fixed policy of Great Britain. It is assumed, however, that so grave a matter can not have escaped your attention and that you have not failed both to procure the necessary evidence to establish the facts and to place that evidence with proper representations in possession of Earl Russell.

It is not necessary to recur to the memorable conduct of the Government of the United States during the Crimean War, nor to the harsh and peremptory manner in which it asserted its right to prevent foreign enlistments in its territory, in order to justify your representations on the present occasion. The President is persuaded that no citation of precedents is required to induce her Majesty's Government to give effect to her Majesty's proclamation of neutrality and to arrest the lawless attempts of the official agents of the United States to effect designs violative of the territorial sovereignty of the British Queen, and manifestly hostile to this Confederacy.

In the expectation that you have been able to obtain satisfactory evidence and with full confidence that in a simple communication of the facts on which our complaint is grounded, her Majesty's Government will take measures to prevent the commission of acts subversive both of the municipal law of Great Britain and of international obligations, you are instructed, if you have not previously done so, to bring this matter to the attention of Earl Russell.

I am, sir, respectfully, your obedient servant,

J. P. Benjamin,
Secretary of State.

Hon. James M. Mason, etc.,
London.

No. 35.]   Confederate States Commission,
London, April 30, 1863.

Sir : Under the license and instructions given me by the State Department to communicate to the Government inventions I might find here of value to the country; and in the hope of rendering service especially to its military arm, I send out by the conveyance which bears this a box containing the model of a railroad with its appropriate car, which I think will be found of value, and I enclose herewith all the explanatory papers connected with it, which I hope will make its structure and use sufficiently intelligible.

Its recommendations are—

First. That no iron is used in its construction.

Second. As represented by the inventor, that no grading is necessary to adapt it to use, it being alleged that the cars, rolling on wood instead of iron, retain a sufficient hold on the surface to overcome the tendency to descend on an inclined plane.

Third. Its great cheapness, and the speed with which it can be constructed where timber is available or near at hand. Nothing further is required to lay down the road ready for use than to level the surface for its site.

If it be found to fulfill all these conditions, I am sure you will agree with me, that besides its immediate value for military purposes, its usefulness will be extended generally throughout the country. The model with the drawings and explanations will be sufficient, I hope, to make the structure perfectly understood, and susceptible of being brought at once into practice if approved. The use of wooden rails, I am aware, has been utterly discarded where there was occasion for sufficient strength to withstand the pressure of the centrifugal force in curvature, etc., at great speed with heavy weights. In this invention it is alleged all this is dispensed with by the simple introduction of the two small wheels (called guiding wheels) which work in a peculiar manner, sustain no part of the weight, and whose only office is to keep the car on the track, and this office they would seem to perform in a perfect manner. Au reste, I refer for its explanation to the model and the accompanying papers.

This invention was brought to my notice not long since, not by the inventor but by a gentleman here even unacquainted with him, who knew of it, and who brought it to my notice as a thing that might be peculiarly useful to our country, and at my request he sent the inventor to me. The name of the latter is William Prosser. He is a very intelligent man, and seems thoroughly versed in mechanics.

His history of the invention (which at last is pretty much confined to the guiding wheels of the engine and car) is briefly this:

He had studied it out years ago and expended some six or seven thousand pounds in building a track with cars, etc., large enough to carry and sustain the ordinary railroad burden on Wimbledon Common. It was there exhibited and worked, under the inspection of competent men and of officers deputed for the purpose by the Government for a long time, and so far back as 1846; the part of the common occupied being distorted into mounds, valleys, etc., for the purpose of testing its adaptation, and, as alleged by the inventor, it worked to the entire satisfaction and conviction of all deputed to examine it.

Subsequently the inventor obtained an act of Parliament empower-ing him to construct a road a few miles long upon a site intended as a feeder, or contributor, to one of the large thoroughfare railroads then in course of construction—I think the Great Western—the success of the invention being considered un fait accompli, and he went to work accordingly. After he had proceeded far enough to show that he was in earnest, his neighbor and larger railroad, after some negotiation, bought him off by the payment of £20,000. He says the sum was so large that he could not resist the temptation.

A year or two afterwards he made arrangements to build a road some 30 or 40 miles long on his plan in Ireland; had the necessary capital secured; the timber purchased and again, with difficulty, an act of Parliament to sanction it. At this stage of the work he was again approached by rival interests and was bought off there by a new payment of £20,000 more, the interveners taking the timber off his hands at a cost of some £6,000.

This is his narrative to show why his road has never been introduced here. His papers certainly establish that he received the £40,000. His theory is that the success of his road being an established fact on Wimbledon Common, he was bought off by the great iron interests of England. I mention all this to show that prima facie, at least, it is no humbug and worth a trial.

I send this dispatch with the documents and models to you (the latter in a box of moderate size); their appropriate destination I presume will be the War Department. A moderate sum of money to construct a short road, with appropriate rolling stock, will be sufficient to test its value, if the work be committed to competent and unprejudiced hands, really disposed to give it a fair trial without condemning it in advance on some preconceived theory.

The cost of the model and car, which will be small, I will defray from the contingent fund and transmit by a special voucher.

It may be appropriate here to say, that I have not sent accounts of the contingent fund for settlement, as required by the instructions, because they could not be settled without the vouchers, and these I could not trust to the risks of the blockade. The disbursements so far are very small.

I have the honor, etc.,

J. M. MASON.

Hon. J. P. BENJAMIN,
Secretary of State.

No. 5.]

FOREIGN OFFICE, *May 2, 1863.*

SIR: I have to acquaint you, in reply to your dispatch No. 14 of the 17th of February, that arrangements are in progress for transferring to Bermuda for present custody the prisoner charged with having committed a murder on board the Confederate steamer *Sumter* at Gibraltar, and that as soon as the consent of the Government of the United States has been obtained for the passage through the blockade of her Majesty's ship, in which the prisoner will be embarked, he will be sent to a port in the possession of the Confederates for delivery to the local authorities.

I am, of course, unable now to say to what port the prisoner will eventually be sent, but you should arrange for his being received by the Confederate authorities at whatever port the ship conveying him may arrive.

I am, etc.,

RUSSELL.

GEO. MOORE, Esq.

No. 34.]   PARIS, *May 3, 1863.*

SIR: You will find herewith duplicates of my dispatches of 20th and 23d ultimo.

On the 28th ultimo I saw my friend at the affaires etrangères and asked him to obtain for me from the minister information on three points.

1. The suit against Erlanger & Co.

2. If anything had been said or done respecting Mr. Adams' letter on the subject of shipments of arms, etc., to Matamoras for account of the Mexican Government.

3. Whether, in consequence of the repulse of the attack on Charleston and the abandonment of further attempts against Vicksburg and Port Hudson, the time had not arrived for reconsidering the question of recognition.

I give you the reply.

[Translation.]

PARIS, *April 29, 1863.*

MY DEAR SIR: I was enabled last night to allude to the subject of our conversation yesterday.

Nothing new in relation to the Erlanger affair, but your idea of seeing Mr. Delangle is highly approved and you are requested to carry it out.

The strange proceedings of Mr. Adams could not pass unperceived; the Government of Washington has been addressed.

With respect to the important question which procured us the pleasure of your acquaintance, I could obtain nothing very definite. The sense of the propriety of doing what you desire is not equaled by the desire which is experienced of being able to give you that satisfaction. It is believed that every possible thing has been done here in your behalf; we must now await the action of England, and it is thought that you must aim all your efforts in that direction.

Believe me, my dear sir, etc.,

CINTRAT.

I consequently addressed a note to Mr. Delangle, Garde des Sceaux and minister of justice, requesting an interview. I received an immediate reply, giving me an audience for the following day, 30th April, when I saw the minister. I had with him a most satisfactory conversation; he assured me that he had given instructions to the " **Pro-**

cureur Imperial" of the Tribunal Civil of the Seine to take the
necessary steps to have the injunction in the case of Erlanger & Co.
removed on the ground of the incompetency of the court. He said
it was a question on which he entertained no doubt; that a similar
case had occurred when Dom Miguel was contending for the throne
of Portugal and occupied a portion of Portuguese territory.

Money had been raised for his Government in France and an attempt was made to arrest its payment by his bankers, to meet claims
for damages claimed by French subjects. The suit was dismissed on
the ground of the incompetency of the court to entertain a claim
against a "de facto" government.

He said that I need not give myself any concern about the matter,
as he would cause it to be properly attended to.

Since then, however, I have learned that a new step has been taken
by the claimants. They have attempted to bring the Confederate
Government in court through President Jefferson Davis and the Secretary of the Treasury, C. G. Memminger.

The petition is a curious document, of which I send you a copy as
well as of the first petition.

It has occurred to me that it presents a favorable opportunity to
bring up the question of recognition in a new form, and I am rather
inclined to make it the subject of a formal communication to the
minister of foreign affairs, but my relations with him are now so
satisfactory that I am not willing to do anything to compromise
them, and I shall not take the step without more mature deliberation.

I am, with the greatest respect, your most obedient,

JOHN SLIDELL.

Hon. J. P. BENJAMIN,
 Secretary of State.

DEPARTMENT OF STATE,
Richmond, May 7, 1863.

SIR: I have the honor to enclose for your consideration a communication from Mr. J. H. Flanner,* which seems to require prompt action.

According to the letter he encloses from General Whiting, it appears that that officer considers himself at liberty to disregard the
legislation of Congress and the action of the Government, by arresting a lawful commerce with neutral nations, and to give his advice
as to the proper action of the War Department.

You will also perceive that he recognizes the right of the owners of
the vessel and cargo to claim damages from the Government for his
action.

The whole matter is so anomalous that I submit for your consideration whether some general order may not be appropriate to restrain
the military authorities from usurping powers which embarrass legitimate intercourse with foreign countries, and which impose on this
Department constant correspondence with our own citizens and with
the subjects of neutral powers whose rights are impaired.

---

* Not found.

Please return the enclosed and inform me what answer I may give to Mr. Flanner.

I am, yours, very respectfully, etc.,

J. P. BENJAMIN,
Secretary of State.

Hon. J. A. SEDDON,
Secretary of War.

No. 45.]   RUE D'ARLON, BRUSSELS, *May 8, 1863.*

SIR: Mr. Blondeel, the representative of Belgium near the Government of Lincoln, is expected here from Italy, where he has been abiding for several months on his way to his post. I received a message from him about two weeks ago that he was anxious to see me. This influenced me to postpone my contemplated visit to London. Mr. Blondeel is in high favor with his sovereign, and is one of the most shrewd and experienced of European diplomats. He may, if he will, when he arrives at Washington, going there fresh from the acknowledged sage par excellence of Europe, render invaluable services to our cause. The bare possibility of the capture of this at sea prevents me from being more explicit upon the subject. King Leopold, if his health continues as good as it is at present, will probably proceed to England in a short time. He is anxious to see his beloved niece and her children. I am quite certain that when he meets her Majesty he will express himself to her earnestly and persuasively in behalf of our recognition, and were she to indicate that in her opinion the good of her subjects imperatively required the adoption of such a measure, no serious opposition to it would be manifested in any quarter.

The accounts from New York of the 25th ultimo indicate a very perceptible diminution in the Northern clamor for a war with Great Britain. The restoration of the mails unopened of the *Peterhoff* is ominous. In my opinion, however, much as it may swagger and threaten, the Washington Government will be exceedingly careful to avoid hostilities with European powers. Honor, the highest object for which nations fight, the soi-distant United States has none. They ignominiously sacrificed it all, if they had any then left, in the affair of the *Trent.* I was never more confident than I am at this moment that we have nothing whatever to expect for our benefit from a practical initial movement of the Emperor of the French. He will continue to be cautious to commit no act that will give any dissatisfaction to the Government with whom we are at war, while he will remain anxious for us to believe that he is silently our friend. Mexico first, and then Mexico as she was previous to her dismemberment, is the resolutely and faithfully cherished end at which he aims, if my information and judgment be not greatly at fault. Our future, under the guidance of the god of battles, is confided exclusively to our own creation.

No physical European influence is likely to be thrown into our scale. We have now abundant evidence that the Lincoln-Seward concern will never engage in a war with any other country while it is engaged with us. Therefore we should definitely, and as one man, prepare our minds to conquer. The Northern States never will become dismayed until we invade and defiantly hold some prominent points within their embrace. They must be made to fear instead of to hope. They will never en masse incline to an entire cessation of hostilities as long as their own firesides are free from danger. Let Philadelphia, Pittsburgh, Cincinnati, or other important places come into our possession, and consternation would seize every family beyond Mason and Dixon's line. Such results, I am warranted in believing, will be accomplished by our veteran and invincible armies before the close of the present year. It is not upon our own soil but upon the soil of the enemy that we must dictate terms of peace which our honor and our interests will justify us in ratifying. The notes of Prince Gortchakoff, in reply to the notes of Earl Russell and Mr. Drouyn de Lhuys in relation to Poland, have just been published. There is nothing in this correspondence calculated to change the opinion which I expressed in my last, that the general peace of Europe was not likely to be disturbed for at least a twelve month. The last accounts from Mexico, with reference to the result of the fighting at Puebla, are as conflicting as they well could be. If the French Army fails to occupy that city and subsequently the metropolis, the consequences will be serious to Louis Napoleon. It is largely possible that such a disaster may befall him.

I have the honor to be, sir, very respectfully, your obedient servant,

A. DUDLEY MANN.

Hon. J. P. BENJAMIN,
   Secretary of State, Confederate States of America,
   Richmond, Va.

No. 21.]   CONFEDERATE STATES COMMERCIAL AGENCY,
   London, May 9, 1863.

SIR: A longer interval than usual has occurred since the date of my last, No. 20, March 21, from my not profiting by the last mail via Nassau, having taken advantage of the adjournment of Parliament over the Easter holidays, for a two weeks' absence from town and abstention from work, both of which had been long strenuously urged upon me by medical advice. I have, however, written several times during this period via Norfolk, giving you privately a summary of news worded with constant reference to the eventuality of interception and forwarding such extracts and public documents as I deemed of sufficient interest. I can therefore do little more than recapitulate the substance of these private communications.

In reference to the Norfolk route, I have every reason to believe that though its efficiency may be temporarily disturbed by the present movements of troops in that vicinity it is susceptible of being made of much use to the Department, and it can certainly be made available for forwarding you with tolerable regularity newspapers and other publications, for which purpose I now mainly use it. My Norfolk correspondent has proved himself worthy of all confidence, and though I do not venture to give his name here his reference to ex-Governor Wise and to his father-in-law, Littleton Tazewell Waller, in the coal-contract office of the Navy Department will, if necessary, indicate his identity. He has also requested me to mention one W. B. Seal, employed in hospital No. 7 at Richmond, as a trustworthy person who is practically well acquainted with the " underground railroad" to Norfolk, having been, as I understood my correspondent, employed by him some time back as a messenger between that point and Petersburg.

The Confederate loan has been subject to great and at one time alarming fluctuations, the depression being for a while below par. It is clear from the circumstances attending this fluctuation that it can not be accepted as a barometer of the public confidence in our fortunes, but that it is to be accounted for by other and quite independent causes. First, the suspension of the house of Spence Brothers, of Liverpool, the leading partner of which firm was by many confounded with his brother, the Confederate financial agent. Secondly, the rumor, diligently disseminated by our enemies, that the Government was about to put upon the market a new and much larger loan. Thirdly, an impression which obtained very general prevalence in financial circles that the contractors had taken the loan at a very low rate, and that consequently the limitation rate, 90 per cent, left to them an almost unprecedentedly large margin of profit. From these combined adverse influences the loan has, however, recovered, and on the 6th instant the published quotation was 2 per cent premium. The passage of Porter's flotilla past the batteries at Vicksburg has depressed it to-day from par to one-half premium.

This event, which is still a complete mystery to friends and foes over here, has in a great degree neutralized the hopes of a speedy peace to which the repulse from before Charleston gave rise. If it has no more serious effect than to impress upon the English people the conviction of an indefinite protraction of the war, so long as foreign Governments shrink from the discharge of their moral duties toward the combatants, I shall not so much regret its occurrence.

The public mind has settled down into a state of quiescence on American affairs which resembles stagnation. Everybody, that is to say, the masses of intelligence and respectability, wishes well to the Confederate cause; but nobody now speaks of recognition; nobody thinks about it; nobody even writes pamphlets about it. Morally, recognition is farther off, because less present to men's minds, than it was eighteen months ago. I could, indeed, through the agencies under my control, bring the word before the public ear, but until I can carry the idea with it I should be speaking out of time, and therefore to no good purpose. The chief reason for this phenomenon is no doubt that which I have often had occasion to point out to you, and which is, that things are going so much to people's liking in America that they do not feel called upon to make unpleasant exertions of their own. But another reason must not be overlooked. The American disease has passed into a chronic phase. Two years of war have worn off its startling effects. The alarm, also, at its possible and probable reflective injuries, has subsided. England finds with much self-complacency that she has reached a pinnacle of prosperity when she can dispense for years even with the American trade; and while America rushes with railway speed into financial ruin, her chancellor of the exchequer ostentatiously declares a surplus of three million sterling. Lancashire, it is true, is literally rotting, but with the mortification has ceased acute inflammation. I have dwelt upon this because hereafter you must expect that the symptoms of public feeling will be less violent and sudden, though perhaps for that very reason more significant. The currents I hope will gain in steadiness what they lose in rapidity.

The same negative state of feeling manifests itself in the press. With a mass of papers before me I have nothing to extract which really indicates any purpose or tendency whatever. A wealth of useful information does, however, permeate the press, making all classes better and therefore more favorably acquainted with us, and preventing at least our enemies from making any progress. This information also is gradually working itself up into more concrete and solid shapes. I mention it as highly encouraging indications that I have been able to furnish most of the materials and to some extent indicate the tone of a very useful article in the last number of the leading "quarterly," and that the editor of the Annual Register has spontaneously applied to me for documentary materials and general information for the volume of 1862, now in preparation. In this connection I would most respectfully urge upon you to supply me with all published State papers of your own and other Departments, and in sufficient quantity to permit me a liberal distribution. Material of this kind strengthens my powers of usefulness as much as the pecuniary means with which you have so liberally supplied me, and there can scarcely be more discretion required for the judicious use of the one than of the other.

My description of the inertia of the public mind on the subject of American affairs would, however, be very unfair without an account of a very remarkable exception or rather episode, which has just closed. The capture of the *Peterhoff*, unquestionably bound for Matamoras, after a previous search and release by a Federal officer, created intense indignation among the shipping community. From thence, after the occurrence of a similar though not quite so flagrant an outrage in the seizure of the *Dolphin*, it spread to the public at large. The indignation reached its height on the publication of Mr. Adams' "Maritime Passport," assuming to grant a license to a British ship to proceed to Matamoras with munitions for the Mexicans. I am credibly informed that the minister of the United States has since most humbly and in person apologized for this, probably one of the most extraordinary and ill-timed diplomatic blunders ever committed, that at the moment it had the appearance of a deliberate insult. On Thursday and Friday the 23d and 24th of April, the national anger found vent in both houses of Parliament. I enclose full reports of both debates, duplicates of those already forwarded via Norfolk. You will notice two important points, first that the debate became general in the Commons on the first evening, in spite of Lord Palmerston's strenuous efforts, never befor. except in a ministerial crisis, exerted in vain, to stifle it altogether. Secondly, that though the debate in neither house had in any sense of the word a party complexion, the opposition put forward their best legal minds, and that the true point of international law, with which the Government were pressed to the wall, were made by them alone. This argues better for the future in the event of a change of cabinet than anything I have yet seen. Such a change, were the public mind less inertly disposed, would not be improbable.

The Government is unmistakably weak in both houses and has just lost two measures of financial and internal policy. Yet Lord

Palmerston seems to feel strong enough to appoint a peer to the vacancy created by the death of Sir. G. C. Lewis, the minister of war, thus throwing the three most important cabinet offices into the upper house. By the death of Sir G. C. Lewis the Confederacy has lost a zealous and able enemy, but I do not yet know whether in his successor it has gained a friend. To return to the two debates, they have demonstrated the temper of Parliament and warned the Government that the public patience has its limit. Beyond this they have effected nothing. For a few days war seemed inevitable; now no one has the slightest anticipation of it, and I have observed on such occasions that there is a sort of friendly reaction toward the Federals. John Bull is delighted with having behaved so well, and half in love with the Yankees for letting him off so cheaply.

The most hopeful sign in connection with this episode is the re-appearance of "Historicus" in the Times. A strong necessity could alone have induced the writer, Mr. Vernon Harcourt, under unusually severe family afflictions, having within a very short period lost child, wife, and father-in-law (Sir G. C. Lewis) to reassume his task of defending the ministry in their present difficulties. The latter must deem the storm more serious than I have represented it to you, to call this very ingenious and dextrous pamphleteer to their rescue.

The German translation of Mr. Spence's book and pamphlet, of which I wrote last summer, has at length, after many difficulties and delays, appeared. My share in the expense of its publication is £41, but a larger amount might and should be usefully expended upon its proper distribution. Under these circumstances Mr. Spence has repeated an offer which last year I thought proper to decline, to contribute personally £50 toward the expenses of the book. As Mr. Spence does not now stand to the Confederacy in the position of a foreign writer, holding as he does a lucrative employment under the Confederate Government, the reasons for declining his offer appeared to me no longer to exist, and I have accepted the money and the task of applying it to the intended purpose.

*   *   *   *   *   *   *

I have the honor to remain, very respectfully, your obedient servant,

HENRY HOTZE.

Hon. J. P. BENJAMIN,
  Secretary of State, Richmond.

No. 16.] DEPARTMENT OF STATE,
  Richmond, May 9, 1863.

SIR: Since your No. 26 of 6th February, received here on 19th March, the Department has remained without any communication from you, although dispatches have been received from other agents of as late date as 21st March. We find that our correspondence sent via Nassau through Mr. Heyliger, or via Bermuda through Major Norman Walker, the agent of the Government there, is received with regularity and that it reaches us in about thirty days. I again call your attention to this channel which seems thus far equally prompt and safe.

Since my Nos. 14 and 15 of 24th and 26th March, some suggestions have occurred to me which seem not inappropriate in reference to the duties confided to you by the President near the court of her Catholic Majesty.

The recent signal repulses of the enemy in his efforts to obtain possession of our strongholds at Vicksburg and Port Hudson, the damaging defeat of his ironclad fleet at Charleston, where twelve months' assiduous preparations for attack proved abortive after a test of only two hours, and the decisive results of the series of battles which have just terminated on the Rappahannock in the most complete triumph of the war, all concur in demonstrating (if indeed any additional proof was needed) that these Confederate States are an independent nation, possessed of the power to maintain the position which they have assumed, and to defy every effort that can be made to overthrow their Government. Why then should there be hesitation on the part of European nations in recognizing the existence of an accomplished fact?

The answer to this question, so far as the cabinet of Madrid is concerned, is found by us in the intimation given by Mr. Calderon Collantes to Mr. Rost, as reported by the latter gentleman in his dispatch from Madrid dated 21st March, 1862. From the conversation held at that period between her Majesty's minister of foreign relations and our commissioner, the latter drew the inference that the cabinet of Madrid had determined not to take the initiative in any action during the pending struggle, but to await the development of the policy of the English and French Governments. The change which has since occurred in the condition of affairs on both sides of the Atlantic, as well as in the "personnel" of the Spanish ministry, appears to us to be of a character so marked as to justify the hope that her Majesty's present Government may not be indisposed to review the decision of their predecessors on this point, and that such review may present considerations leading to a different conclusion.

In this connection and in presenting these considerations to her Majesty's Government it may not be improper also to advert particularly to the tripartite treaty, the subject of the island of Cuba, to which the Government of the United States refused to become a party. The interests of the Confederate States, for reasons with which you are familiar, render it particularly desirable that that island should remain a colonial possession of Spain. Desirous ourselves of no extension of our boundaries, seeking our safety and happiness solely in the peaceful development of our own ample resources, having learned from the experience of this war the perils to which we will be exposed by the excessive eagerness of the Government of the United States to extend its territorial possessions, we can not fail to foresee attempts on the part of that Government to seek elsewhere for acquisitions which it has failed to wrest from us. The purposes of the United States in relation to the island of Cuba are thus frankly stated by Mr. Everett on the occasion of the proposal of that Government to accede to the tripartite convention. "No administration of this Government, however strong in public confidence in other respects, could stand a day under the odium of having stipulated with the great powers of Europe that in no future time, under no change of circumstances * * * should the United States ever make the acquisition of Cuba." The aggressive policy of which that Government now furnishes so conspicuous an example would make it for us the most dangerous of all neighbors on our southern coast, while the traditional respect which Spain has ever evinced for the obligations imposed by public law would inspire a feeling of security in our relations with the mother country and her colonies eminently conducive to the permanence of the peace which we seek. The policy therefore that dictated the refusal on the part of the United States to join in the engagements imposed by the tripartite treaty is the reverse of that by which this Government is inspired, and it would not be difficult at the present moment for the Spanish Government to secure as an additional guarantee for the permanent possession of its valuable colonies the alliance of a people whose proximity to those colonies would render practicable the promptest assistance in a sudden emergency, while its ability to render such assistance has been amply proved during the pending struggle.

The extraordinary development of Spanish power and resources under the wise and beneficent administration of the reigning sovereign has excited equally the surprise and admiration of mankind. It has justified in the eyes of more than one of the leading nations of the world the legitimate desire of Spain to reassume that position among the great powers of Europe which was formerly her recognized right, and to which her claim became impaired solely by reason of the internal convulsions and civil discord which the advent of her Catholic Majesty has so happily terminated. The reasons on which some of the great powers based their refusal to accord to Spain an admission to their conferences on a recent occasion in which the common interests of Europe and the balance of power between its States were concerned are not known to the President; but from the remarks from different journalists usually supposed to be prompted by official inspiration it would seem that the objections were founded rather on the internal institutions of Spain than on any doubt of the weight to which her power and the energy of her Government justly entitled her. If such be the fact, can there ever be an opportunity more favorable than the present for the vindication by that Government of its refusal longer to occupy any other than a first-class position among European nations? Can it be doubted by her Majesty's Government that in taking the initiative in entering with this Government into regular diplomatic relations it will establish a title not only to the most cordial amity of these States but to the gratitude and respect of mankind?

A review of the diplomatic correspondence published by the Governments of France and England, of the tone of the public press in Europe, and of the debates in the British Parliament establishes the existence of a common conviction among civilized nations that the war now waged against this Confederacy is one of extermination, and that all prospect either of reunion or of our subjugation by the United States is at an end. What more noble mission is now open for Spain? By what higher title could she establish her legitimate rank among the nations than by setting an example which of necessity must be followed by the other great powers at no distant period? The grounds for the confident conviction entertained by us that our recognition would be followed by speedy peace have already been developed to you and require no repetition. That we have vindicated our power to maintain our independence so conclusively as to justify that recognition by neutral powers is no longer questioned by European statesmen. That according to the principles of international law the Government of the United States would have no just ground of complaint against any nation which might think proper to entertain formal diplomatic relations with us is indisputable. That Spain, least of all, could justly incur reproach for so doing is evident from the fact that no nation was more prompt and decided in countenancing by its action the revolutions which resulted in the independence of the South American Republics than was the Government of the United States. That any attempt by the United States to resent as an act of hostility the simple recognition of our independence, unaccompanied by intervention (which we neither invite nor desire), would be a wanton aggression that all civilized nations would be interested in repressing can scarce permit a doubt. Why then should Spain hesitate in the interest of a common humanity as well as her own to do an act which would redound to her own glory and establish an enduring claim to the friendship of a people with whom her relations are destined to be so intimate?

If, therefore, you shall find in your conferences with her Majesty's minister that the success of the mission with which you are entrusted can be secured by entering into engagements for the accession of this Government to the tripartite treaty, or into a separate engagement with Spain of the same nature, you are authorized by the President to conclude a treaty on that basis.

Respectfully, your obedient servant,

J. P. BENJAMIN,
Secretary of State.

Hon. JOHN SLIDELL, etc., *Paris.*

P. S. May 13.—I have this instant received your No. 29, of 21st March. Your Nos. 27 and 28 not yet received.

Accompanying this dispatch you will receive a correct design of the Confederate States flag, made at the Engineers' Bureau, and a copy of the act of Congress * by which it was established.

No. 21.]

HAVANA, *May 10, 1863.*

SIR: I have the honor to acknowledge the receipt of your dispatch No. 1, dated 14th ultimo, with the enclosures, two Treasury drafts, one No. 275 for 7s and 3d, amount paid Pilot Wm. Haywood for piloting the C. S. S. *Florida* from Mobile, and the other, No. 4350, for £465, 19s., 7d., on account of my salary.

It has given me great pleasure to learn through you that my efforts to serve my country have proved satisfactory to the several Departments of Government. I promise the same zeal and activity in the future for which you give me credit in the past.

In relation to the sale of cotton in Havana to Northern buyers, you say it is not in the power of the Government to apply a remedy. It affords me pleasure to say such sales are of rare occurrence, and, with the exception of the cargo of the *Alice*, no considerable quantity of cotton has been shipped to New York or other Northern port. The

---

* See letter of May 13 from State Department, with enclosure.

Alice belongs to a joint-stock company, and the stockholders are dissatisfied with her management by their agents, John Macauley and Addison Cammack, and unanimously condemn their course in selling cotton to Northern buyers, and are now making an effort to get possession of this vessel and her earnings. I am therefore of opinion that but little cotton will in the future find its way from Havana to the enemy, but would very respectfully suggest that a bond be required from the agent of the vessel when sailing from Mobile, stipulating that her cotton be shipped, or sold for shipment, to Europe, to be canceled by my certificate that the conditions of the bond have been complied with, as has been done in the case of other vessels sailing from that port.

I know of no collusion between any of our citizens and the enemy for the supply of cotton to the latter. Should I discover any such collusion I shall, of course, promptly report the facts to the Department.

I am, sir, with great respect, your obedient servant,

CH. J. HELM.

Hon. J. P. BENJAMIN,
    Secretary of State, Richmond, Va.

No. 36.]   CONFEDERATE STATES COMMISSION,
                                      London, May 11, 1863.

SIR: My last, of the 30th of April (No. 35), went off but a few days since via Nassau; this goes by an opportunity offering by the same route.

I enclose a dispatch from Mr. Slidell (No. 34), which he sent to me open for perusal. You will find erasures of a portion at the conclusion. They were made by me, after consultation with him, as containing matter not important to reach the Government at once and which it was important should incur no risk of falling into the hands of the enemy. I promised Mr. Slidell to give this note of explanation.

I send also Mr. Slidell's duplicates, Nos. 32 and 33, with the papers connected with them.

I have nothing of general interest to add since the date of my last. Mr. McRae, the loan agent, has not yet arrived. All the disbursing officers of the Government here are in arrears, and no authority to make the proceeds of the loan available to them; nor indeed have they information what part of it is to be applied to their requirements, a state of things that ought not to be, and involving their operations in great difficulties.

The Confederate loan seems to have dropped somewhat under the last intelligence that ships of the enemy had succeeded in running past Vicksburg; at least such was the reason assigned in the stock market. It closed at last report at par.

This dispatch will probably overtake its immediate predecessors at Nassau, and therefore duplicates are reserved for a future opportunity.

I have the honor, etc.,

J. M. MASON.

Hon. J. P. BENJAMIN,
    Secretary of State.

CMcD 90

Approved May 1. 1863

Flag adopted for the Confederate Navy by Order of the C. S. Navy Department of May 28, 1863, as the "National Flag established by Act of Congress approved May 1, 1863," to be "hoisted on board of all vessels and at all stations of the Confederate States Navy on the 1st day of July next, or as soon thereafter as the flags can be obtained."

A.B. GRAHAM CO. WASHINGTON, D.C.

Approved March 4. 1865

Confederate Flag established by Act of Congress, approved by the President
of the Confederate States, March 4, 1865

A.B.GRAHAM CO.WASHINGTON, D.C.

No. 22.]   DEPARTMENT OF STATE,
                                        Richmond, May 13, 1863.

SIR: I have the honor herewith to transmit a correct design of the
Confederate States flag, made at the Engineers' Bureau, and a copy
of the act of Congress by which it was established.

Respectfully, your obedient servant,

                                            J. P. BENJAMIN,
                                            Secretary of State.

Hon. JAMES M. MASON, etc.,
        London.

[Enclosure.]

ACT OF CONGRESS ADOPTING THE ·FLAG.

The Congress of the Confederate States of America do enact, That
the flag of the Confederate States shall be as follows: The field to be
white, the length double the width of the flag, with the union (now
used as the battle flag) to be of a square of two-thirds the width of
the flag, having the ground red, thereon a broad saltier of blue,
bordered with white and emblazoned with mullets or five-pointed
stars, corresponding in number to that of the Confederate States.

                                            DEPARTMENT OF STATE,
                                        Richmond, May 13, 1863.

SIR: In compliance with your request and in accordance with the
instructions of the President, I take pleasure in sending you the drawings of the Brooke gun which has been found the most effective yet
tried in our war. The President is happy to place these drawings at
the disposal of his Imperial Majesty, to be used by him according to
his pleasure, with the sole condition that care be taken not to allow
them to be used by our enemy during the pending war.

I am, yours, very respectfully,

                                            J. P. BENJAMIN,
                                            Secretary of State.

ALFRED PAUL, Esq.,
        Consul of France, Richmond, Va.

P. S.—I also send you an authentic design of the national flag of the
Confederacy, just adopted by act of Congress.

                                                    J. P. B.

No. 22.]   CONFEDERATE STATES COMMERCIAL AGENCY,
                                        London, May 14, 1863.

SIR: I have the honor to acknowledge the receipt of your No. 4,
dated 30th March; also, through Mr. J. E. Macfarland, of Treasury
draft No. 4351, dated April 2, for £247 8s. 5d. I feel deeply and gratefully the kind and encouraging words in which you speak of my
labors, and in which I am happy to learn from you the President concurs. Such words are peculiarly gratifying because I am conscious
that, in the conduct of the Index especially, I have not always been
able to avoid giving offense to patriotic fellow-citizens who complain
of the lukewarmness of the paper. Deeming it essential to the effi-

ciency of this organ that in its advocacy of our cause it should never lose its English tone, and above all never its temper, I have often had to resist well-meant influences or to restrain private zeal.

I am now contemplating a publication entailing considerable expense, but upon which I trust the public money may be well spent. I propose to issue a classified list, with their estimated value, of the chief articles of foreign production which the Confederate States in a normal condition are able to annually consume and pay for. This I would address to some twenty-four thousand wholesale dealers in Great Britain, in the form of a letter, with each one's specialty marked in ink, so as to make each feel himself specially addressed. It might perhaps add to the effectiveness of such a circular if, instead of being anonymous, it came avowedly from my office in the shape of a brief caution to prepare for filling up the vacuum to be uncovered on the return of peace. But as I am loath to parade my office, I shall not do this without having previously ascertained your views. The cost for postage alone will not fall short of £100. My object, however, is, if possible, by something new to rouse the public mind from that lethargy of which I spoke in my last. With the same view I have since my last, reopened the subject of recognition, on afterthought in the Index, and I must apologize for having in the current number used many of the ideas and some of the words of my dispatch written less than a week ago. This, you will readily understand, was not contemplated at the time of its writing.

In my recapitulation of the substance of my private communications via Norfolk, I omitted the case of the *Alexandra*. The fact that the Government in dealing with this vessel selected the more unusual and severer process of "Exchequering" by which she is seized during trial, proves undoubtedly a strong desire to propitiate our enemies, but I am not disposed to accept it as conclusive evidence of a hostile animus toward us. By selecting this process the Government renders itself liable to heavy damages, and it is not believed that the vessel can be condemned. Now, it appears to me that had the Government been so disposed, it could have found a stronger case. I do not wish to justify the timorous and I sincerely believe, shortsighted policy of the British cabinet, but I think it important also for the future as the present, that no ill will growing out of possible misconception should be added to the just causes of complaint which we already have against this country.

The effect of the Vicksburg news has been as I feared. The loan went as low as 4 per cent discount, but has again recovered to 2½ to-day, still a serious depression. Besides the news from Vicksburg, the passing of Porter's flotilla, an incautious expression in a recent letter of the Times correspondent from Richmond, speaking of repudiation as unavoidable for North and South alike, has doubtless contributed to this result. This affords an additional reason for the issue of some such commercial circular as I proposed above.

I regret to say that some difficulty and probably further delay has arisen since my last in the shipment of the stationery. Messrs. Fraser, Trenholm & Co., since their receipt of the goods, have written to me objecting to shipping by the present opportunity cases Nos. 4 and 5, on the ground of their containing envelopes with the name of the Department imprinted thereon, which they allege, is in violation of their engagement with the shippers. I have therefore directed the "innocent" cases to be forwarded, and for the two other containing contraband, I hope soon to find an eligible opportunity, of which I shall duly inform you.

Hon. C. J. McRae, I am glad to inform you, arrived safely at Southampton, via St. Thomas, on the 13th instant, yesterday. I leave this evening for Paris, whither he proceeded from Southampton, in obedience to a telegraphic message from him.

I have the honor to remain, with great respect, your obedient servant,

HENRY HOTZE.

Hon. J. P. BENJAMIN,
  Secretary of State, Richmond.

DEPARTMENT OF STATE,
  Richmond, May 14, 1863.

SIR: I have the honor to acknowledge receipt of your letter of 12th instant, with the accompanying documents. I am happy to see that you referred Mr. Walker to this Department, inasmuch as he had already been notified by me that the Department could not correspond with him in the capacity of her British Majesty's vice consul until he had submitted to it officially the authority under which he assumes to act.

I am, respectfully, etc.,

J. P. BENJAMIN,
  Secretary of State.

Major-General W. H. C. WHITING,
  Wilmington, N. C.

No. 7.]   FOREIGN OFFICE, *May 15, 1863.*

SIR: With reference to my dispatch No. 5 of the 2d instant, I have to acquaint you that I have been informed by the board of admiralty that H. M. ship *Shannon* left Gibraltar on the 5th instant for Bermuda, having on board Mr. Hester, the prisoner charged with the murder of the commanding officer of the Confederate steamer *Sumter.*

I am, etc.,

RUSSELL.

G. MOORE, Esq.

No. 8.]   DEPARTMENT OF STATE,
  Richmond, May 15, 1863.

SIR: Since my No. 17 of 17th January I have received your several dispatches Nos. 36 to 43, both inclusive. The last, dated 10th April, arrived this morning.

In my No. 7 I remarked that your No. 32 was missing. I am now satisfied that your dispatch from London of 21st of November, which was received on 25th December, and to which no number was affixed, was really your No. 32 and that my files are thus complete.

Your note to the cabinet of Brussels making formal demand for our recognition is approved by the President, and we are not at all disappointed in the result, for our interests can not so blind us as to impute the refusal of King Leopold to any other than its evident motive, viz, a just and prudent regard to the safety of his own kingdom, which does not occupy a position of sufficient influence in Europe to entitle it to take the initiative in opposition to the policy of the great powers by whose aid alone Belgium acquired independence.

I again desire to assure you that the failure to respond regularly to your communications does not proceed from a want of appreciation of their interest in keeping us advised of the condition of affairs on the Continent, but rather from the fact that there is really nothing to communicate to you, which you do not receive much more speedily through the newspapers. The accounts which I took pains to give at an earlier period of the war are no longer necessary, as Europe has learned thoroughly to appreciate and understand the credit to be attached to the statements of the Washington Cabinet, and several of the Northern journals have at last comprehended that their true interests consist in giving correct information of the military operations as they occur. Thus, although they are always greatly in error about the numbers of our forces, the accounts given by the New York World and Tribune of the battles at Fredericksburg in December and at Chancellorsville and Fredericksburg last week are as correct as could be expected from parties really desirous of stating the truth, but with a natural bias in favor of their side. The truth is that in our last glorious affair at Chancellorsville, General Lee really kept but 16,000 in front of an enemy 80,000 strong and formidably entrenched while Jackson made a detour of 13 miles in order to fall in their rear with 24,000. As soon as the sound of Jackson's guns reached Lee, giving assurance that the former was in position, Lee unhesitatingly charged with his 16,000 the fortified front of an army five times that number and swept it out of its trenches. It is incredible, but literally true.

I have received your private note of 10th April, and fully concur in your opinion of the injury done to our cause by the action in Congress of certain gentlemen who, in ignorance of facts which the public interest does not permit the Executive to divulge, distinguished themselves by tendering advice in administrative matters, instead of bending their energies to the legislative duties which alone are confided to them by the Constitution. It is impossible, however, to prevent this, and it is one of the few disadvantages of our form of Government that are overbalanced a thousand fold by the blessings of the guarantees which it affords for our liberties.

I send you herewith a design of our new national flag, with a copy of the act of Congress which establishes it.

Brilliant as have been our recent successes the President and the Nation feel that they have been dearly purchased at the price of the life of our hero patriot, Jackson. His death has spread a pall over the country.

I am, with great respect, your obedient servant,

J. P. BENJAMIN,
Secretary of State.

Hon. A. DUDLEY MANN, etc., *Brussels.*

No. 35.] PARIS, *May 15, 1863.*

SIR: My last was of 3d instant, of which you will find duplicate herewith.

Since then the order enjoining Erlanger & Co. to retain in their hands a million of francs to satisfy any claim that Dupasseur, Lecoq Frères might establish against the Confederate Government has been rescinded. The accompanying extract from the Journal des Tribunaux, marked "A," gives the decree of the court. I shall take the necessary steps to have the petition against the President and Secretary of the Treasury dismissed. I send you copy of a letter from Messrs. Erlanger & Co., marked "B," informing me that the holder of £6,000 scrip of their loan has just given notice of his option to convert the scrip into cotton.

I am happy to inform you that Mr. McRae arrived here last evening. All such communications will, of course, hereafter pass through him.

I beg leave to ask your consideration of a hardship to which many of our best citizens will be exposed if some legislation of the nature of that proposed in the draft of an act, marked " C,"* which, I respectfully submit, be not had. The draft was made by Mr. L. Q. C. Lamar, and it contemplates relief to two categories of persons. One, of those who have heretofore been, either by birth or adoption, citizens of a State of the Confederacy; the other, of persons who have never had or acquired such citizenship. The first class is numerically considerable; the second will be very limited. But two names at present occur to Mr. Lamar and myself, Messrs. George McHenry and John L. O'Sullivan, both of whom have distinguished themselves by the energy and talent with which they have espoused our cause.

Mr. Lamar's draft directs the prescribed oath to be administered by one of the commissioners accredited by the Government of the Confederate States to any foreign court; this gives at least by implication to such commissioner the power to administer an oath in this particular class of cases. Would it not be well to give this power expressly, extending it to all cases in which the interests of the Government or of citizens of the Confederate States may be involved? The attention of this Government is now almost exclusively directed to the pending elections for the next chamber of deputies, which will take place on May 31 and June 1. There is no doubt that the chamber will be almost exclusively composed of supporters of the Government, and the Emperor will then feel himself more at liberty to carry out his policy in foreign affairs, whatever it may be. By that time, too, the Polish question will have ceased to create any apprehensions of a war, and the city of Mexico will probably have been occupied by General Forey. Should the news from Virginia and Tennessee in the meanwhile have been favorable to our arms, the moment, in my opinion, will have arrived for making another demand of recog-

---

* Not found.

nition, accompanied by a formal declaration that it would not be renewed unless invited by the Government of the Emperor.

I have the honor to remain, with great respect, your most obedient servant,

JOHN SLIDELL.

Hon. J. P. BENJAMIN,
Secretary of State.

[Enclosure.]

B.

Approuvé, E. E. & Co.

PARIS, *May 8, 1863.*

SIR: We have the honor to inform you that Mr. Jean Schlumberger has fully paid for £6,000 (150,000 francs) scrip nominal of the 7 per cent cotton loan of the Confederate States.

Viz Let D √ 1856 to 1915. c £100 £6,000 and desires to convert said scrip into cotton in accordance with the option contained in article 4 of the contract for the loan: the cotton to be delivered to him in the port of Charleston.

We request you to make the necessary arrangements for the delivery of the cotton at Charleston within sixty days from this date and remain, sir,

Your most obedient servants,

P. Pon EMILE ERLANGER & CIE.,
U. BAMBERGER.

Hon. JOHN SLIDELL,
Commissioner of the Confederate States of America, Paris.

No. 37.]
CONFEDERATE STATES COMMISSION,
London, May 16, 1863.

SIR: My last (No. 36) was of the 11th of May, instant. On the 13th I received your three last dispatches, Nos. 17, 18, and 19, brought by Captain Page, of the Navy, in which you acknowledge receipt of mine (Nos. 24 to 29, inclusive), with a postscript adding that No. 28 appeared to be missing. I do not see how this could have gone astray, as they were borne by the same messenger. I send, however, a triplicate, though it is not of much moment.

The proposed operations in France, to which you refer, in cipher, in your No. 17, are in course of negotiation, and I think with fair prospects of success. Those in charge communicate everything to me as it transpires, and it shall have my earnest cooperation.

Mr. McRae, to whom has been committed the management of the loan, has at last arrived, but proceeded at once from Southampton to Paris, without passing through London. I have, therefore, not seen him. His presence I think all important in the present posture of the loan, the condition of which is far different from that we had reason to anticipate from its apparent great success when first brought out; as stated to you in my last unofficial note sent in duplicate.

The letter of appointment as commercial agent at Cork, for Mr. Robert Dowling, has been received and transmitted to him.

I have nothing new to report in regard to public affairs here; our friends in both Houses of Parliament agree that in the present position of the ministry, and the reluctance of the opposition to disturb its policy on the American question, it could have no good effect to bring it again at present before Parliament.

Our latest intelligence, via New York, two days ago, brings information of the movement of Hooker's army across the Rappahannock and dates to the 2d of May; but nothing more is stated than that the enemy crossed, both above and below Fredericksburg, putting their columns some 20 or 30 miles apart; but the New York papers say that the press is forbidden to give any details. Thus we are left to anticipate results, as far as we can, by reasoning from the past to the future. I do not doubt what those results will be, and hope we shall have them by the steamer due to-morrow. The tone of the press here is confident of our success in the impending battle, and in which, so far as I can reason, I fully participate. Amongst other good effects on this side, it will make our loan buoyant.

This dispatch is intended to go by a special messenger to be sent by Captain Maury. My two last were by successive steamers of a series to be run by Captain Crenshaw (a most energetic and valuable officer), under the auspices of the War Department. They are sent to Mr. Heyliger, at Nassau, or Major Walker, Confederate agent at Bermuda, as the ships may be destined.

I had not hesitated, as your No. 17 would seem to imply, to send dispatches through Heyliger; but have only preferred a responsible hand, when such was to be found, who would take them in person to Richmond.

The delays of London tradesmen have prevented me from yet completing your order for books, but I hope now to get them off to Messrs. Fraser, Trenholm & Co., at Liverpool, in a very few days. I can pay for them as suggested in my last, out of the contingent fund, sending a proper voucher for adjustment of the expenditure.

The contents of your No. 19 in regard to the proposals of Mr. McHenry for a line of mail steamers shall be communicated to that gentleman.

I have the honor, etc.,

J. M. MASON.

Hon. J. P. BENJAMIN,
        Secretary of State.

No. 23.]   DEPARTMENT OF STATE,
                                                          Richmond, May 20, 1863.

SIR: Since my No. 22 of 13th instant, I have received your No. 33 of 9th ultimo. Nos. 28, 30, 31, and 32 are still missing.

I am happy to inform you of the full approbation accorded by the President to your action in the matter of the loan as explained in that dispatch.

I have received through Mr. Hotze several copies of the Blue Book containing your correspondence with Earl Russell on the subject of the blockade. and have some comments to make and some further evidence to be placed before his lordship, including extracts from his own correspondence, which fully corroborate our assertion that the blockade is ineffective and is respected by the British Government on grounds entirely independent of the intrinsic merits of the question. But I defer further remarks till I receive your dispatch covering the correspondence, as it may contain matter which would affect our action on the subject.

Congress has passed a law establishing a seal for the Confederate States. I have concluded to get the work executed in England and request that you will do me the favor to supervise it. You will receive herewith a copy of the act of Congress describing the seal, and a photographic view of the statue of Washington. The photograph represents the horse as standing on the base of a statue, but in the seal the base ought to be the earth, as the representation is to be of a horseman and not of a statue. The size desired for the seal is the circle on the back of the photograph. The outer margin will give space for the words " The Confederate States of America, 22d February, 1862." I do not think it necessary that the date should be expressed in words, the figures 22, 1862, being a sufficient compliance with the requirement of the law. Indeed, I know that in the drawing submitted to the committee that devised the seal the date was in figures and not in words. There is not room for the date in words on the circumference of the seal, without reducing the size of the letters so much as to injure the effect. In regard to the wreath and the motto, they must be placed as your taste and that of the artist shall suggest, but it is not deemed imperative under the words of the act that all the agricultural products (cotton, tobacco, sugar cane, corn, wheat, and rice) should find place in the wreath. They are stated rather as examples.

I am inclined to think that in so small a space as the wreath must necessarily occupy it will be impossible to include all these products with good effect, and in that event I would suggest that cotton, rice, and tobacco, being distinctive products of the Southern, Middle, and Northern States of the Confederacy, ought to be retained, while wheat and corn being produced in equal abundance in the United States as in the Confederacy and therefore less distinctive than the other products named may be better omitted, if omission is found necessary. It is not desired that the work be executed by any but the best artist that can be found, and the difference of expense between a poor and a fine specimen of art in the engraving is too small a matter to be taken into consideration in a work that we fondly hope will be required for generations yet unborn. Pray give your best attention to this, and let me know about what the cost will be and when I may expect the work to be finished.

I am happy to apprise you that the information from all parts of the Confederacy is most encouraging as regards the growing crops. In the more southern portions of our country they are just beginning to gather the wheat harvest, and no complaint is heard from any part of the country of rust or other injury. The production of wheat and other small grain will be very large this year, while that of corn will be enormous, probably enough for two years' consumption unless some very unexpected and unusual calamity shall occur. Our enemies must find some other instrumentality than starvation before they succeed in breaking the proud spirit of this noble people. How it makes one's heart swell with emotion to witness the calm, heroic, unconquerable determination to be free, that fills the breast of all ages, sexes, and conditions. What effect may be produced in Europe by the repulse at Charleston and the defeat of Hooker is not now even the subject of speculation among the people. It is the evident purpose of foreign Governments to accord or refuse recognition according to the dictates of their own interests or fears without the slightest reference to right or justice, and we have thus learned at heavy cost a lesson that will, I trust, remain profitable to our statesmen in all future time. We have now by our system of taxation so arranged our financial affairs as to be entirely confident of the ability to resist for an indefinite period the execrable savages who are now murdering and plundering our people, and no prospect of peace is perceptible from any other source than the growing conviction among all classes in the United States that they are waging a war as ruinous in the present as it is hopeless for the future.

I am, very respectfully, your obedient servant,

J. P. BENJAMIN,
Secretary of State.

Hon. JAMES M. MASON, etc.,
London.

No. 17.]

DEPARTMENT OF STATE,
Richmond, May 20, 1863.

SIR: In my No. 16 of the 19th instant I acknowledged receipt of your No. 29. I received yesterday the duplicate of No. 27 (original not arrived) and Nos. 28, 29, and 30, the last date being of 30th March. With these I also received at last the copies of your Nos. 1, 3, 4, 5, and 6, making my file now complete. Old as the dates of these copies are, I was greatly interested by their recital of different conversations held by you at that time, and observe that you brought to the notice of the French cabinet the dispatch of Earl Russell changing the terms of the fourth article of the treaty of Paris on the subject of blockade, a fact which I previously supposed had escaped the attention of all our agents abroad till pointed out by me to Mr. Mason. Those dispatches also inform me for the first time that the conduct of the British cabinet in thus derogating from the terms of a convention adopted by the common consent of all Europe had received the endorsement of the French Government in the speeches of his Majesty's ministers to the Corps Legislatif. This is a grave fact and one which could not have failed to influence the tone of the President's message if we had been aware of it when that message was prepared.

The facts communicated in your No. 28 in those passages expressed in cipher are extremely important and gratifying, and the circumstances attending the insertion of the advertisement of the loan as detailed by you are viewed by the President as a satisfactory indication of the sentiments of the French Government toward the Confederacy.

I have examined the papers contained in your No. 30, consisting of a prospectus and of the act of partnership of the Compagnie

Financiers International des Etats du Sud. The prospectus announces that measures have already been taken to obtain acts of incorporation from the Southern States. It is supposed that by this statement is meant that applications for acts of incorporation will be made to the separate States in which the company expects to carry on business, and there can be little doubt that such States will readily grant such acts on being satisfied that the capital of the company has been subscribed for and paid up in whole or in great part; but the Confederate Government, as you are well aware, has no power under the Constitution to grant acts of incorporation to commercial banking associations, and would therefore be unable to aid by legislation the objects contemplated by the founders of the Confederacy.

I have no later intelligence to communicate, but am happy to inform you that the crops of cereals throughout the Confederacy are of the most promising character. The wheat harvest has already commenced in the extreme South, and the breadth of land sown in grain is greater than ever known before. The harvest is substantially beyond the reach of adverse influences. The corn crop will be prodigious, unless some unprecedented disaster should overtake it. Enough has been planted for two years' supply at least. The calculations of our enemies that we are to be reduced by starvation are as absurd as the other numberless hallucinations in which that infatuated people have indulged.

I am, with great respect, your obedient servant,

J. P. BENJAMIN,
Secretary of State.

Hon. JOHN SLIDELL, etc.,
Paris.

DEPARTMENT OF STATE,
Richmond, May 26, 1863.

SIR: This Department is informed by a communication from the Secretary of War that you have arrived at the city of Charleston and propose to act as the French consul for that port. It is further stated that you have no commission from your Government entitling you to act in such capacity.

In order to avoid all mistakes in this matter, I have the honor to request that, before assuming to exercise any functions whatever in Charleston, you will communicate officially to this Department whether you have visited this Confederacy in a private or official character; and if the latter, what is the nature and extent of the official functions you propose to exercise, and from what source your authority to exercise such functions is derived.

I am, very respectfully, etc.,

J. P. BENJAMIN,
Secretary of State.

Mr. ARTHUR LAREN,
Charleston, S. C.

No. 36.] PARIS, *May 28, 1863.*

SIR: Since my last, of 15th instant, I am in possession of your Nos. 5, 14, 15, No. 14 covering a letter from Mr. Mallory (ihpcscg); for reasons that you will appreciate I do not write to him, but the subject of his letter has been attended to with every prospect of favorable results.

I am not surprised to learn that a strong disposition existed in the Senate to advise the recall of the commissioners from Europe. Their position here must be anything but gratifying to our national pride at home and is, as you may well imagine, painfully embarrassing to them individually. By referring to my No. 10 you will find that in June last I proposed to Mr. Mason that we should severally make a demand of recognition and, if it were refused, to withdraw from our respective missions. Mr. Mason, after consultation with our friends in Parliament, thought it inexpedient to take that course. I reluctantly abandoned the idea, but I was so much dissatisfied with my position and saw so little prospect of rendering any useful service that I felt very strongly inclined to resign, and had actually prepared a letter to the President to that effect; but, receiving from Mr. Persigny encouragement to persevere in my efforts, I determined to remain at my post so long as the President should consider it expedient for me to do so. Since then the consciousness that my presence here has not been altogether fruitless of good has largely compensated me for any previous sacrifice or inclination.

I beg you to present to the President my thanks for the renewed expression of the evidence of his confidence in appointing me special commissioner to the court of Madrid. The reason that induced me to recommend that we should be in some way represented at Madrid soon ceased to exist. You are aware how short lived was the tenure of General Serrano's administration of the foreign affairs of Spain; he went out with the other members of the O'Donnell cabinet; but the mutations of ministry are so frequent in the Peninsula, that it is not improbable, that being a man of mark and a favorite of the Queen, he may soon again be in power.

On the 22d instant I had a long conversation with Mr. Isturitz, her most Catholic Majesty's ambassador at Paris. I had asked an interview for the purpose of opening the question of the *General Rusk*, alias the *Blanche*, but availed myself of the opportunity to urge the arguments in favor of friendly and intimate relations between the two Governments used in the instructions of your predecessor to Messrs. Yancey, Rost, and Mann. Mr. Isturitz appeared to understand the subject well and declared very unreservedly that the sympathy of his Government and his own individually were warmly and decidedly with the Confederate States, that he considered the interests of the two countries as being largely identified, that Spain was prepared to act conjointly with France and England, but could not risk the hazard of a war with the Federal Government and the possible destruction of her richest colony by taking the initiative of recognition.

I suggested that Spain and other continental powers might unite with France in such a step without any apprehension of more serious consequences than some characteristic ebullitions from Seward of

Yankee bluster and vituperation. Mr. Isturitz without committing himself seemed to admit that Spain would be disposed to act with France and other powers without the cooperation of England. I explained fully the circumstances of the destruction of the *Blanche*. I said that I was accredited to his Government as special commissioner and was instructed to claim the payment of any sum which the Federal Government might pay to his Government as indemnity for its violated neutrality; that I had no present intention of going to Madrid and desired to consult him as to the most proper mode of presenting the reclamation; that my idea had been to address him a letter on the subject which he could forward to the minister of foreign affairs, but that I would cheerfully follow any other course which his better judgment might dictate; that I had no intention to insist upon the payment of the money, but would be satisfied with the assurance that it would not be permitted to leave the Spanish treasury until the merits of our claim could be fairly examined. Mr. Isturitz said that he saw considerable difficulty as to the mode of presenting the case and could not then express any opinion; that he would reflect upon it, and again see me when he would be prepared to advise me. As several days have now elapsed without my hearing from him, I am inclined to think that he has written home for instructions.

Mr. Aimé Roger, for many years consul at New Orleans and a very devoted friend of our cause, has handed me a paper which he received from the directeur des affaires politiques of the ministry of foreign affairs, on the subject of the enforced military service of certain French citizens resident in Louisiana. As this paper was given to Mr. Roger for the purpose of being communicated to me, I send a copy of it, as also of a letter which I have addressed to Mr. Roger, acknowledging its receipt, marked "A" and "B." *

I respectfully invite your attention to this document, that you may take such action in the matter as you may deem advisable.

Mr. Charles Lafitte (dlrkjho plqamai), a wealthy banker of Paris, and Mr. Wm. Jackson (aekcemp), member of Parliament from Newcastle (byjvrqpsi), a man of very large fortune, have called upon me to propose a considerable loan, say 5,000,000 sterling, to the Confederate States. Their idea is to make it a 6 per cent stock, redeemable at a distant date and not convertible into cotton. I told them that neither I nor any other person in Europe had any authority to contract such a loan; that the Erlanger loan would give us as much money as we desired in Europe for five or six months, or indeed until the close of this year; but if the war were protracted longer than that period, as it probably would be, we should require more money, and that it might be expedient to make financial arrangements in advance; that it would be necessary to send an agent to Richmond, and that a considerable time would necessarily elapse before the negotiation could be consummated and books opened for subscription to the loan. Mr. Jackson (aenstse) came over from England expressly to exchange views on the subject with Mr. Lafitte (eyiexep), who had already broached the subject to some influential persons enjoying the confidence of this Government. I expect to receive in a few days

---

* Not found.

some definite propositions which I have expressed my willingness to submit to my Government for consideration.

The elections are exciting much more interest in France than I had anticipated; from Paris and a few of the large towns there will be probably some accessions to the ranks of the opposition, but it will be numerically very feeble and can give no embarrassment to the Government.

I have the honor to be, with great respect, your most obedient servant,

JOHN SLIDELL.

Hon. J. P. BENJAMIN,
    Secretary of State.

No. 48.]   3 RUE D'ARLON, BRUSSELS, *May 28, 1863.*

SIR: The excessive joy occasioned on this side of the Atlantic by our dazzling victory at Chancellorsville has been tinged by inordinate sorrow. Authentic intelligence arrived day before yesterday that General Jackson had sunk under the severity of his wounds. This event causes civilization to mourn as it has rarely ever mourned for the loss of a public man. The London Times of yesterday no more than reflects the general opinion of Europe upon the subject in the following paragraph contained in its leader:

The Confederate laurels won on the field of Chancellorsville must be twined with the cypress. Probably no disaster of the war will have carried such grief to Southern hearts as the death of General Jackson, who has succumbed to the wounds received in the great battle of the 3d of May. Even on this side of the ocean the gallant soldier's fate will everywhere be heard of with pity and sympathy, not only as a brave man fighting for his country's independence, but as one of the most consummate generals that this century has produced. Stonewall Jackson will carry with him to his early grave the regrets of all who can admire greatness and genius. From the earliest days of the war he has been conspicuous for the most remarkable military qualities. That mixture of daring and judgment which is the mark of heaven-born generals distinguished him beyond any man of his time. Although the young Confederacy has been illustrated by a number of eminent soldiers, yet the applause and devotion of his countrymen, confirmed by the judgment of European nations, have given the first place to General Jackson.

The military feats he accomplished moved the minds of people with an astonishment which it is given to only the highest genius to produce. The blows he struck at the enemy were as terrible and decisive as those of Bonaparte himself. The march by which he surprised the army of Pope last year would be enough in itself to give him a high place in military history. But perhaps the crowning glory of his life was the great battle in which he fell. When the Federal commander, by crossing the river 12 miles above his camp and pressing on as he thought to the rear of the Confederates, had placed them between two bodies of his army, he was so confident of success as to boast that the enemy was the property of the army of the Potomac. It was reserved to Jackson, by a swift and secret march, to fall upon his right wing, crush it, and by an attack unsurpassed in fierceness and pertinacity to drive his very superior forces back into a position from which he could not extricate himself except by flight across the river. In the battle of Sunday, Jackson received two wounds, one in the left arm, the other in the right hand. Amputation of the arm was necessary, and the Southern hero sank under the effects of it. He was only 38 years old, and was known before the war as a man of simple and noble character and of strong religious faith.

The conservative organ, the Morning Herald, also in its leader says:

No end can be more honorable to any man than to die at his post of duty. To die of his wounds in battle, with the shout of victory still ringing in his ears, is a glory reserved to the soldier. The death of Stonewall Jackson is in itself a blow to the Confederates that is almost to be compared to a lost battle. The sympathy that is felt in Europe for their grief at this immeasurable loss will add to the warmth of popular feeling for the men who have striven so long in a just cause and acquitted themselves so well. A young man when he died, he made himself great by his achievements and obtained a reputation unparalleled of its kind among modern military chieftains. Like other distinguished persons who from time to time in various countries seem suddenly to be raised up for some special purpose, he appears to have done his work so efficiently that his death in one sense can not be considered premature. A soldier of remarkable ability, he fought with the advantage of an earnest faith in his cause; and, controlled in all he did by a strong religious feeling, he fought the better still for believing that God was on his side. He may be called an enthusiast, but his enthusiasm was of a noble kind. He was animated by the spirit which rendered the soldiers of the Commonwealth irresistible in fight, which carried Havelock through incredible dangers to the gates of Lucknow in triumph. The Christian and patriotic soldier achieved the last and greatest of his successes in dying for his country. He perished doubly a martyr, and in his last breath attested the righteousness of the cause which he sealed with his blood.

The Paris correspondent of the Evening Standard, in adverting to the sad event, remarks:

I can not forbear noticing the universal feeling of regret created among the English colony in Paris by the sad tidings of the death of Stonewall Jackson. He was a hero after our own heart, one of those men whose gallantry and virtues shed imperishable luster over the cause they embrace, and since the news of the death of Havelock I can safely say deepest and more unanimous sorrow has not been experienced by our countrymen here. The Northerners in Paris often express wonder at the universal sympathy for the South felt by Englishmen. They may learn a useful lesson from the tribute paid by our countrymen to Stonewall Jackson. Independently of the justice of the cause, independently of the disgust excited by the arrogance and boasting of the North, it is the presence in the Southern ranks of such men as Davis, Lee, Longstreet, Jackson, Stuart, Beauregard, and Semmes that conciliate the esteem of the world, as well as its admiration. Stonewall Jackson was one of the most heroic figures that have been thrown into relief in the course of this gigantic struggle. Look at the North, and we may ask: Quando et quo invenient parem? Low speculators, dishonest politicians, pettifogging tyrants, unhanged murderers, and strong-minded women, for whose conduct insanity is the only possible excuse—these are the worthies of the North. The loss the South has just experienced in Jackson has brought home this contrast to many minds, and, if possible, added strength to the general conviction in the ultimate triumph of the cause supported by such as he.

General Jackson had lived long enough for the creation of a world-wide exalted fame; but, alas, not sufficiently long for the interest of his struggling country. Such services as he performed seemed to be a special manifestation of divine favor in our behalf in the field. Nobly, most nobly did he complete his high mission on earth. In his separation from us let us console ourselves with the belief that his illustrious example will exercise as salutary an influence upon our invincible citizen soldiers in the hour of battle as did his presence, and that his pure spirit will linger around his beloved associates whenever they may be engaged and guide to their accustomed achievements.

I have an abiding confidence that the blessed God, who has raised up so many generals and unconquerable armies to vindicate our cause, will not depart from His just purpose of affording us all the aid that we require as long as there is an invading foot upon our soil.

Thus, while I mourn with inexpressible grief the distressing calamity to which we have been submitted, I continue to implicitly put my trust in Him for humiliating our natural enemy, and am as hopeful of ulterior results as ever. I am sure that I am not mistaken in supposing that my true countrymen are similarly animated.

I have the honor to be, sir, very respectfully, your obedient servant,

A. DUDLEY MANN.

Hon. J. P. BENJAMIN,
　Secretary of State, Confederate States of America,
　　　　　　　　　　　　　　　　　Richmond, Va.

DEPARTMENT OF STATE,
Richmond, June 2, 1863.

DEAR SIR: Lieutenant Davis of the British Army has arrived, accompanied by three workmen (two blacksmiths and one molder), sent out by Mr. George N. Sanders' son, who is now in Nova Scotia. Mr. Sanders writes me that the men he engaged should have each $4 a day and lodging (without board). He has assumed this authority, and has also furnished to each $30 as an advance to be deducted from his wages.

The men will be at the Ballard House under charge of Lieutenant Davis between 1 and 2 o'clock to-day, and if you want them, please have an officer there to receive them and put them to work. If you do not want them, I think the Secretary of the Navy will be glad to get them.

Your obedient servant,

J. P. BENJAMIN.

Colonel GORGAS,
　Ordnance Bureau.

No. 22.]　　　　　　　　　　　　　　　　HAVANA, *June 3, 1863.*

SIR: I have the honor to acknowledge the receipt on the 10th ultimo of your dispatch dated April 15, in relation to the steamer *General Rusk.*

The circumstances connected with the fraudulent transfer of the *General Rusk* to John L. Macauley and others had reached me through private sources previous to the receipt of your dispatch, and knowing the Government was interested in the claim preferred by Spain against the Federal Government for the destruction of this vessel in one of her ports, have watched the progress of the negotiations between Spain and the United States on the subject with interest; and am enabled to inform you that the Spanish minister at Washington was instructed by his Government to demand an apology for the outrage and payment to the owners of the *General Rusk,* or *Blanche,* of the value of the steamer and cargo. The demand was made; the Federal Government disavowed the act of the commander of the *Montgomery* and promised payment, and here the matter rests, as I am informed, for the present. Should the money be paid and the subject be referred back to this colonial Government, I anticipate no difficulty in arresting payment, a least until after the recognition of the Confederate States. The Department may be assured I shall act prudently in the premises.

I have the honor to be, with great respect, your obedient servant,

CH. J. HELM.

Hon. J. P. BENJAMIN,
　Secretary of State, Richmond.

No. 38.]   PARIS, *June 4, 1863.*

SIR: I came here a few days since at the suggestion of Mr. Slidell
to confer with Colonel Lamar and himself upon matters pending connected with our naval service, of the character of which you
are aware, and to which you called my attention in a late dispatch
at the instance of the Secretary of the Navy. From locality these
arrangements being more particularly under the cognizance of Mr.
Slidell, he will doubtless advise you of our success so far as things
have advanced.

General McRae also, who is here, desired the benefit of our joint
counsels in matters appertaining to the disposition of the avails of
the loan, so far as they have been received, it being indispensable,
as well to the public service as to the credit of the Government, that
money should be supplied to its officers and agents here, whilst no
warrants from the Treasury formally authorizing disbursements
have yet been received by General McRae. He will, of course, report
to the Secretary of the Treasury what may be done in this regard.

A note from Mr. Macfarland, dated at London on the 1st instant,
informs me that on that day dispatches had arrived for Mr. Slidell,
Colonel Lamar, and myself; that he had opened mine and found
duplicates of your Nos. 17, 18, 19, and 20, with original dispatch
No. 21, dated 29th April, 1863. The only extract he gives me from
it is that in which you refer and call my attention to the alleged
enlistment of recruits in Ireland for the Federal Army. You are
right in supposing that this matter had not escaped my observation.
The information, as it reached me, was that extensive shipments of
Irishmen were made from time to time from Liverpool, whose passages were paid, and who, it was said, had received small bounties
in advance, with other circumstances tending to show that they were
intended for military service in America, although the engagement
entered into was to work on railroads, as farm laborers, or in some
other evasive form. I took the only measures in my power to uncover
the real purpose of this emigration by authorizing a gentleman at
Liverpool (entirely to be trusted) to employ such agents or detectives there fit for such service to procure the proper evidence, stipulating to pay them such compensation as he might promise. His
latest report was that he had such men at work, but so far they had
been unable to make any discoveries clear enough to found a representation to the Government. Of course, every precaution is taken
by the Federal agents in England and Ireland to conceal the real
design of these enlistments, and it will probably be no easy matter to
make a case for the Government to interpose; still I beg you to be
assured that it shall be diligently followed up, and in such manner
as shall best promise success. I do not personally know the gentleman
to whom you recently sent a commission through me as commercial
agent at Cork, or of his fitness for this duty, but, as your letter imported that he had the full confidence of the Department, I shall communicate with him immediately on my return to London to set on
foot, if he can, the proper inquiries in Ireland.

I observe that the subject of these alleged enlistments in Ireland
was brought before the House of Commons (I think on Monday last)
by a question to Lord Palmerston, whether they were being made,
and whether any steps had been taken by the Government to pre-

vent them. The reply of Lord Palmerston was, that these alleged enlistments had been brought to the notice of the Government, and that enquiries in the proper quarter had been promptly instituted, and should be diligently prosecuted to ascertain the truth; and if true, proper measures would be taken to punish the parties implicated.

Mr. Adams has so tormented the minister with charges of alleged violations of the foreign enlistment act by those in the interest of the Confederates, that I think the latter will be even alert to establish a like charge against Federal agents.

A few days before I left England I spent part of a day and a night with Mr. Roebuck and Mr. Lindsay, at the residence of the latter gentleman near London. The visit was projected by Mr. L. to talk over the expediency of again bringing the subject of recognition before the House of Commons. Both those gentlemen seemed to think the time might now be opportune for again introducing it, but that it would not be advisable to do so without previous consultation with some of the leaders of the opposition. Since I came here, and within a few days past, I find that Mr. Roebuck has given notice in the house, that he intended at some future day to propose that her Majesty be requested to enter into negotiation with the principal powers of Europe, with a view to recognize the independence of the Confederate States; and in a note from Mr. Lindsay, addressed to me here, he informs me that before Mr. Roebuck gave the notice, he had a long conversation with Mr. Disraeli. Mr. Lindsay's note was brief, and he did not give the tenor of that conversation, though his language would seem to imply that the notice was made to follow it.

I think there are evidences, too, of a strong disposition to agitate the question of recognition by our friends at popular meetings got up for the purpose. I inclose a report of one, under the auspices of Mr. Roebuck, composed of his constituents at Sheffield, after our conference at Lindsay's, and before his notice in Parliament. Yet after our experience of the impassive condition of the British Government, and the inertia of the opposition, I can not say that I am hopeful of results.

Absent from the office of the commission, I can not affix the appropriate number to this dispatch, but will have it done when I get to London, and must ask that you will so order it at Richmond.

There will be a mail to Bermuda on the 13th, of which I will avail myself for any matter, should there be such, in your No. 21 not adverted to here.

I have the honor to be, very respectfully, your obedient servant,

J. M. MASON.

Hon. J. P. BENJAMIN, etc.

No. 23.] CONFEDERATE STATES COMMERCIAL AGENCY,
London, June 6, 1863.

SIR: I have the honor to acknowledge the receipt of your Nos. 5 and 6, dated, respectively, 15th and 20th April, the latter informing

me of the receipt of my two first private communication via the
United States, my official Nos. 16, 17, 18, and 19, with public documents and newspapers to the date of March 20. In the same in-
closure also was a duplicate of your No. 4 of 30th March, receipt
of which, as of Treasury draft No. 4351 for £247 8s. 5d., has been
already acknowledged in my last of May 14. The stationery has
been shipped, nine cases by ship ———, to Nassau, through Messrs.
Fraser, Trenholm & Co., on which I have paid charges to the latter
to the amount of £12 8s. 3d., the other two cases, Nos. 4 and 5, for
reasons explained in my last, by ship ——— to ——— through
Messrs. Alexander Collie & Co., of London and Manchester.

Another of those unaccountable fluctuations in public opinion has
occurred, which alternately give rise to sanguine hopes or baffle the
best-founded expectations. The death of Jackson has elicited a feeling the depth and power, if not the very existence, of which had
wholly escaped my observation before, a feeling altogether incom-
mensurate to anything ever manifested on any previous event of the
war. I am quite prepared to believe, what I am assured on all sides,
that the death of no foreigner has ever so moved the popular heart.
Had Cavour died before the Kingdom of Italy was born or Garibaldi in the midst of his Neapolitan expedition, I doubt if the event
would have created so great a sensation. The press but inadequately
expresses the popular emotion which appears to be shared by all
classes. You will not think the illustration too trivial when I mention that of several publishing firms which applied to me for the
materials of a biography the first and most anxious was that of
Rutledge & Co., publishers of shilling volumes for railway libraries.
A subscription has been set on foot both in London and Liverpool
for the purpose of erecting a British monument to the hero at Richmond. It is my duty to advise you of the varying phases of public
opinion, even at the risk of apparent self-contradiction; less than a
month ago I lamented the seemingly hopeless indifference to American affairs into which the people of this country were sinking; to-day
America is once more uppermost in men's minds and takes precedence
over every other subject.

Last week Mr. Roebuck, member for Sheffield, gave notice of a
motion, which is set for June 30, "That a humble address be presented to her Majesty, praying her Majesty to enter into negotiations
with the great powers of Europe for the purpose of obtaining their
cooperation in the recognition of the independence of the Confederate
States of North America." It is impossible at this time to speculate
upon the probable results of this extraordinary parliamentary event.
Mr. Roebuck, you are aware, occupies in the House a singularly
isolated position. He sits habitually on the opposition benches, whatever Government may be in power. In profession, and despite some
alleged eccentricities of practice, he is a radical of a somewhat ultra
type, but without any affiliation with the Radical Party so called.
The importance of his motion arises from the fact that it comes from
a man of the people, from one who is known to have always been a
warm admirer of American institutions, and who on that account has
the confidence of those classes to whom the Federal partisans have
always especially appeared. What heightens this importance is that
his own constituency has suffered less than any other in Lancashire

from the cotton famine. Just before giving notice of his motion, he carried there, against tremendous opposition, yet with a triumphant majority, resolutions for recognition, the first time that this has happened in a large popular meeting in England. Again, a few days since, another meeting with like result has been held in Sheffield. Almost simultaneously with these developments, an association has been formed at Manchester under the title of the "Manchester Southern Club," composed of respectable local merchants and manufacturers, whose operations are directed to working upon the masses by placard and handbills.

There is, then, this new symptom to chronicle that there is at last a people's movement and a people's champion in favor of recognition, and although I do not yet know the extent and depth of the movement, I think it worth while to support it by all the means in my power. One of these means I mention only because hereafter it may be misunderstood and give occasion for malevolent criticism. I have taken measures to placard every available space in the streets of London with representations of our newly adopted flag, conjoined to the British national ensign. This, which I design simply as a "demonstration" to impress the masses with the vitality of our cause, I expect to accomplish in time to produce some effect before the motion comes on for discussion. Meanwhile I hurry up the circular of which I spoke in my last and hope to be able to send out at least 10,000 or 15,000 before the end of the month. A very salutary impression might also be produced by obtaining evidence of the Federal recruiting in Ireland. A detective who has been employed in Liverpool reports that from the character of the emigrants, the small proportion of females, and the fact that the passages of the men are nearly all paid by Marshall & Co., of New York, he has no doubt of the character of the emigration, but that legal evidence can only be procured by going to Ireland and duping the recruiting agents. I have little faith in and little taste for such means, but I have authorized a friend in Liverpool to make the necessary expenditure, provided there is a reasonable prospect of success. You will understand that these measures, all more or less ad captandum, are devised for the special purpose, which is to act upon the masses, rather than the intelligence of the country as has been heretofore my aim. The intelligence of the country is now unanimous in our favor, and would gladly allow its timidity or scruples to be overcome by a popular movement which had even the appearance of strength.

Mr. Disraeli, I hear at second hand, has expressed himself friendly to Mr. Roebuck's motion and predicts its success on condition that no reverses should befall the Confederate arms in the meanwhile, being equally confident, however, that it would utterly fail through any Federal success. As a party the Conservatives are inharmonious and cowardly on this question, as on most others. They will give their support if success is almost certain, and on no other condition. Their press, however, is our staunch ally, and I am promised by the Herald and the Standard leading articles in support of the motion every alternate day until the day after its discussion.

Long ere this reaches you you will have heard of the result of the French elections. In the Provinces the majority of the official candidates is, of course, enormous, but in Paris, and generally in the large cities, the opposition has signally triumphed. The English press of all shades of opinion argues pretty unanimously that this result is mainly attributable to the mismanagement of M. de Persigny, who, by his daily circulars and communiques, has contrived to place the election in the light of a contest between the Empire and the old parties. I can see many ways in which the Emperor might profit by what appears to be a political reverse, but I forbear comment on this subject because you are doubtless informed by those who have better opportunities for forming an opinion as to its effect upon the Emperor's American policy. Mr. Mason's visit to Paris and the congregation of Confederate official personages there has excited the curiosity of the quid nuncs of the press and caused various speculations which I thought it politic to favor by an otherwise purposeless article in No. 57 of the Index, " The Emperor and the War."

I wait with great anxiety news from the West. Affairs near Vicksburg, even as represented through Northern channels, do not appear to me so gloomy as they are made to appear in the war article of the last Index, but that article was written by a competent military critic and an unwavering and valuable friend of our cause, and in view of the recent great victory in the Wilderness I deemed it less necessary to aim at a tonic effect than to break the shock of a possible reverse.

I have the honor to remain, with great respect, your obedient servant,

HENRY HOTZE.

Hon. J. P. BENJAMIN,
    Secretary of State, Richmond.

P. S.—I forgot to mention that the Brazilian minister has withdrawn from London in consequence of the gross outrage perpetrated at Rio by the British admiral under the instructions of Earl Russell. The suggestion is irresistibly forced on my mind that this suspension of diplomatic relations between this country and Brazil affords to us a golden opportunity for establishing with the " slave power " of the Southern Hemisphere such relations as may bear most important fruit in the future.

H. H.

No. 24.]   DEPARTMENT OF STATE,
                                          Richmond, June 6, 1863.

SIR: Herewith you will receive copies of the following papers:
A.* Letter of George Moore, Esq., her British Majesty's consul in Richmond, to this Department, dated 16th February, 1863.
B. Letter from the Secretary of State to Consul Moore, 20th February, 1863.
C. Letters patent by the President, revoking the exequatur of Consul Moore, 5th June, 1863.
D. Letter enclosing to Consul Moore a copy of the letters patent revoking his exequatur.
It is deemed proper to inform you that this action of the President was influenced in no small degree by the communication to him

---

* Missing.

of an unofficial letter of Consul Moore, to which I shall presently refer.

It appears that two persons named Maloney and Farrell, who were enrolled as conscripts in our service, claimed exemption on the ground that they were British subjects, and Consul Moore, in order to avoid the difficulty which prevented his corresponding with this Department, as set forth in the paper B, addressed himself directly to the Secretary of War, who was ignorant of the request made by this Department for the production of the consul's commission. The Secretary of War ordered an investigation of the facts, when it became apparent that the two men had exercised the right of suffrage in this State, thus debarring themselves of all pretext for denying their citizenship; that both had resided here for eight years and had settled on and were cultivating farms owned by themselves. You will find annexed the report of Lieutenant-Colonel Edgar, marked " E," and it is difficult to conceive a case presenting stronger proofs of the renunciation of native allegiance and of the acquisition of de facto citizenship than are found in that report. It is in relation to such a case that it has seemed proper to Consul Moore to denounce the Government of the Confederate States to one of its own citizens as being indifferent "to cases of the most atrocious cruelty." A copy of his letter to the counsel of the two men is annexed, marked " F."

The earnest desire of this Government is to entertain amicable relations with all nations, and with none do its interests invite the formation of closer ties than with Great Britain. Although feeling aggrieved that the Government of her Majesty has pursued a policy which, according to the confessions of Earl Russell himself, has increased the disparity of strength which he considers to exist between the belligerents and has conferred signal advantage on our enemies in a war in which Great Britain announces herself to be really and not nominally neutral, the President has not deemed it necessary to interpose any obstacle to the continued residence of British consuls within the Confederacy by virtue of exequaturs granted by the former Government. His course has been consistently guided by the principles which underlie the whole structure of our Government. The State of Virginia having delegated to the Government of the United States, by the Constitution of 1787, the power of controlling its foreign relations, became bound by the action of that Government in its grant of an exequatur to Consul Moore. When Virginia seceded, withdrew the powers delegated to the Government of the United States, and conferred them on this Government, the exequatur granted to Consul Moore was not there invalidated. An act done by an agent while duly authorized continues to bind the principal after the revocation of the agent's authority. On these grounds the President has hitherto steadily resisted all influences which have been exerted to induce him to exact of foreign consuls that they should ask for an exequatur from this Government as a condition of the continued exercise of their functions.

It was not deemed compatible with the dignity of the Government to extort by enforcing the withdrawal of national protection from neutral residents, such inferential recognition of its independence as might be supposed to be implied in the request for an exequatur.

The consuls of foreign nations, therefore, established within the Confederacy, who were in possession of an exequator issued by the Government of the United States prior to the formation of the Confederacy, have been maintained and respected in the exercise of their legitimate functions, and the same protection and respect will be accorded to them in the future so long as they confine themselves to the sphere of their duties and seek neither to evade nor defy the legitimate authority of this Government within its own jurisdiction.

There has grown up an abuse, however, the result of this tolerance on the part of the President, which is too serious to be longer allowed. Great Britain has deemed it for her interests to refuse acknowledging the patent fact of the existence of this Confederacy as an independent nation. It can scarcely be expected that we should, by our own conduct, imply assent to the justice or propriety of that refusal. Now, the British ministry accredited to the Government of our enemies, assumes the power to issue instructions to and exercise authority over the consuls of Great Britain residing within this country; nay, even to appoint agents to supervise British interests in the Confederate States. This course of conduct plainly ignores the existence of this Government, and implies the continuance of the relations between that minister and the consuls of her Majesty resident within the Confederacy which existed prior to the withdrawal of these States from the Union.

It is further the assertion of a right on the part of Lord Lyons by virtue of his credentials as her Majesty's minister at Washington, to exercise the power and authority of a minister accredited to Richmond and officially received as such by the President. Under these circumstances and because of similar action by other ministers, the President has felt it his duty to order that no direct communication be permitted between the consuls of neutral nations in the Confederacy and the functionaries of those nations residing within the enemy's country. All communication, therefore, between her Majesty's consuls or consular agents in the Confederacy and foreign countries, whether neutral or hostile, will hereafter be restricted to vessels arriving from or dispatched for neutral ports. The President has the less reluctance in imposing this restriction because of the ample facilities for correspondence which are now afforded by the fleets of Confederate and neutral steamships engaged in regular trade between neutral countries and the Confederate ports. This trade is daily increasing in spite of the paper blockade which is upheld by her Majesty's Government in disregard, as the President conceives, of the rights of this Confederacy, of the dictates of public law, and of the duties of impartial neutrality.

You are instructed by the President to furnish a copy of this dispatch, with a copy of the papers appended, to her Majesty's secretary of state for foreign affairs.

I am, sir, very respectfully, your obedient servant,

J. P. BENJAMIN,
Secretary of State.

Hon. JAMES M. MASON, etc.,
London, England.

[Enclosure B.]

DEPARTMENT OF STATE,
Richmond, February 20, 1863.

SIR: Your letter of 16th instant in relation to certain enactments and military orders in the State of Mississippi has been received. In that letter you also make reference to the complaint of a British subject alleging ill treatment at the hands of officers enforcing the conscript law in Mississippi.

Before replying to the subject matter of your letter it is deemed necessary to inquire into the extent of the authority vested in you by her Majesty's commission as her consul in Richmond. The exequatur granted on that commission by the Government of the United States was conferred at a date when that Government had the right to act on such matters as the agent of the States that have since formed the Confederacy, and the exequatur has therefore not been questioned. It was supposed to have reference solely to consular functions in Richmond or at furthest in the State of Virginia.

As your letter, however, initiates a diplomatic correspondence with this Department on the subject of the laws and regulations of the State of Mississippi, it becomes necessary to request that your consular commission, as well as any other authority you may have received to act in behalf of the Government of her Britannic Majesty, be officially submitted to this Department in order that the precise nature and extent of your functions may be ascertained before further correspondence can be held with you as her Majesty's consul at the port of Richmond.

I am, very respectfully, your obedient servant,

J. P. BENJAMIN,
Secretary of State.

GEORGE MOORE, Esq.,
Her Britannic Majesty's Consul, Richmond, Va.

[Enclosure C.]

LETTERS PATENT REVOKING EXEQUATUR OF GEORGE MOORE, HER BRITANNIC MAJESTY'S CONSUL AT RICHMOND.

To all whom it may concern:

Whereas George Moore, Esq., her Britannic Majesty's consul for the port of Richmond and State of Virginia (duly recognized as such by exequatur issued by a former Government which was at the time of the issue the duly authorized agent for that purpose of the State of Virginia), did recently assume to act as consul for a place other than the city of Richmond and a State other than the State of Virginia, and was thereupon, on the 20th day of February last (1863), requested by the Secretary of State to submit to the Department of State his consular commission, as well as any other authority he may have received to act in behalf of the Government of her Britannic Majesty before further correspondence could be held with him as her Majesty's consul at the port of Richmond; and whereas the said George Moore has lately, without acceding to said request, entered into correspondence as her Majesty's consul with the Secretary of War of these Confederate States, thereby disregarding the legitimate authority of this Government.

These therefore are to declare that I do no longer recognize the said George Moore as her Britannic Majesty's consul in any part of these Confederate States, nor permit him to exercise or enjoy any of the functions, powers, or privileges allowed to the consuls of Great Britain. And I do wholly revoke and annul any exequatur heretofore given to the said George Moore by the Government which was formerly authorized to grant such exequatur as agent of the State of Virginia, and do declare the said exequatur to be absolutely null and void from this day forward.

In testimony whereof I have caused these letters to be made patent and the seal of the Confederate States of America to be hereunto affixed.

Given under my hand this 5th day of June in the year of our Lord one thousand eight hundred and sixty-three.

[SEAL.]   JEFFERSON DAVIS,
        President of the Confederate States of America.

By the President:
    J. P. BENJAMIN,
        Secretary of State.

[Enclosure D.]

DEPARTMENT OF STATE,
Richmond, June 5, 1863.

SIR: The President of the Confederate States has been informed that in consequence of your assuming to act in behalf of the Government of her Britannic Majesty on matters occurring in the State of Mississippi you were requested to submit to this Department your consular commission, as well as any other authority held by you, to act in behalf of her Majesty's Government before further correspondence could be held with you as British consul for the port of Richmond. He has further been informed that you have not acceded to this request, and that in disregard of the legitimate authority of this Government you have again lately corresponded, as her Majesty's consul for this port, with the Secretary of War of the Confederate States. The President considers it as inconsistent with the respect which it is his office to enforce toward this Government that you should any longer be permitted to exercise the functions or enjoy the privileges of a consul in these Confederate States. He has, consequently, thought proper by the letters patent, of which I enclose you a copy, to revoke the exequatur heretofore granted to you and to make public these letters patent.

I have the honor to be, respectfully, your obedient servant,

J. P. BENJAMIN,
Secretary of State.

GEORGE MOORE, Esq.,
    Her Britannic Majesty's Consul, Richmond, Va.

[Enclosure E.]

HEADQUARTERS TWENTY-SIXTH VIRGINIA BATTALION,
Handley's Hill [Mills], May 25, 1863.

CAPTAIN: The communication from the Secretary of War, asking information respecting the conscription of Nicholas Maloney and

Eugene Farrell, has been received, and in reply I submit the following:

Nicholas Maloney is a native of Ireland. He does not know exactly how long since he came from Ireland to this country. He has been a resident of Greenbrier County, Va., for eight years. He bought land in said county, and after the several payments were made he received the deed for the land, and that deed was recorded in the clerk's office of Greenbrier County three years ago. From the time of purchase till he was conscribed he resided upon and cultivated the land. His family still resides upon it.

He has also exercised the right of suffrage.

He was assigned (as a conscript) to this battalion in December, 1862.

Eugene Farrell is a native of Ireland; does not know the exact time when he came to this country. He bought land in Fayette County, Va., and after the payments were made he received the deed for the land; that deed was recorded in the clerk's office of Fayette County. He afterwards exchanged his land in Fayette for land in Greenbrier. He afterwards sold one-half of his land in Greenbrier to his brother, and his family still resides upon the half reserved. He has been a resident of Virginia for eight years and has exercised the right of suffrage. He was assigned to this battalion, as a conscript, in December, 1862. From time of purchase to time of conscription he resided upon and cultivated his land.

Very respectfully, your obedient servant,

GEO. M. EDGAR,
Lieutenant-Colonel, Commanding.

Captain R. H. CATLETT,
Adjutant General First Brigade, Army Western Virginia.

[Enclosure F.]

RICHMOND, VA., *May 5, 1863.*

MY DEAR SIR: I have just received your letter of 30 April, and I have at once addressed a letter to the Secretary of War on the subject of Maloney and Farrell, of which I transcribe a copy herewith.

I am really at a loss to account for the dilatory proceedings of the War Department not to make use of any harsher term, however, I can not help saying to you unofficially that the apparent apathy and indifference with which the War Department seems to regard cases of the most atrocious cruelty, quite baffle all my preconceived opinions of my own kindred race.

I have lived thirty-two consecutive years (from 1826 to 1858) in despotic countries and I am compelled to bear witness that I have met in those foreign countries more official courtesy and consideration from the local authorities on my representation of grievances than I meet at the hands of my own blood and lineage.

These reports, which I am obliged to send home, do not tend to the consummation which perhaps some of us desire.

I will say no more for it grieves me to write this.

Believe me to be, my dear sir, yours, very truly,

GEO. MOORE.

J. B. CALDWELL, Esq., etc.,
White Sulphur Springs,
Greenbrier County, Va.

RICHMOND, *June 6, 1863.*

SIR: I have the honor to acknowledge your communication of yesterday's date, transmitting to me the letters patent of the President revoking my exequatur as her Britannic Majesty's consul for the State of Virginia.

Without commenting upon this act, I simply acknowledge its reception, which I will communicate to my Government by the first opportunity.

I have the honor to be, sir, your most obedient, humble servant,

GEO. MOORE.

Hon. J. P. BENJAMIN,
Secretary of State,
Department of State, Richmond.

CONFEDERATE STATES COMMISSION,
London, June 6, 1863.

SIR: * * * As pertaining to the subject of your last dispatch, it may be proper to observe that on an enquiry made in the House of Commons a few days since with respect to the alleged recruiting for the Federal Army going on in Ireland, the chief secretary for Ireland, Sir Robert Peel, stated that the Government were aware of the presence there of Federal agents, though, of course, they did not openly recruit; that a great number of young men had certainly gone from Ireland to America whose passage had been paid, and that they had every reason to suppose that many had been induced to enlist in the Federal Army; that the Government was following the matter up and endeavoring to come at the facts if possible.

*   *   *   *   *   *   *

I have the honor to be, with great respect, your obedient servant,

J. E. MACFARLAND,
Secretary of Special Commission at London.

Hon. J. P. BENJAMIN,
Secretary of State.

RICHMOND, *June 9, 1863.*

Mr. Moore presents his compliments to Mr. Benjamin and has much pleasure in transmitting to him copies of two dispatches* addressed by Earl Russell to Mr. Moore on the subject of Mr. Hester, charged with the murder of the commanding officer of the Confederate steamer *Sumter.*

GEO. MOORE.

No. 18.]

DEPARTMENT OF STATE,
Richmond, June 10, 1863.

SIR: On the 9th December last the Department addressed a letter to Baron Durand St. André at Charleston, S. C., apprising him that it had received unofficial information that he was exercising the

---

* Not found.

functions of French consul at Charleston, and that as no exequatur had been issued to him, explanation was requested.

On the 13th of the month Mr. St. André replied that Mr. Belligny having been summoned to Paris he was charged by the Government of the Emperor with the temporary direction of the consulate (direction intérimaire); that he had been presented in that capacity to the local authorities, which was all the usage required where the functions were "provisional."

It is not necessary to repeat to you how earnest is the desire of this Government to cherish the most cordial amity with that of his Imperial Majesty. Although feeling aggrieved, as well by the respect persistently shown by the French Government for a blockade whose monstrous illegality appears to us quite evident, as by its persistent refusal to accord to us that recognition of our independence to which we are entitled on the grounds both of justice and of accomplished fact, the President has not deemed it necessary to object to the continued residence of French consuls within the Confederacy under exequaturs granted by the former Government. His course has been consistently guided by the principles which underlie the whole structure of our Government. The State of South Carolina having delegated to the Government of the United States by the Constitution of 1787 the power of controlling its foreign relations, became bound by the action of that Government in its grant of an exequatur to Consul Belligny. When South Carolina seceded, withdrew the powers previously delegated to the United States and conferred them on this Government, the exequatur granted to Consul Belligny was not thereby invalidated. An act done by an agent, while duly authorized, continues to bind the principal after the revocation of the agent's authority.

On these grounds the President has hitherto steadily resisted all influences which have been exerted to induce him to exact of foreign consuls the request for an exequatur from this Government as a condition of the continued exercise of their functions. It was not deemed compatible with the dignity of the Government to exert, by enforcing the withdrawal of national protection from neutral residents, such inferential recognition of its independence as might be supposed to be implied in the request for an exequatur. No objection was therefore made to the provisional exercise of consular functions by Mr. St. André in the place of Mr. Belligny, who was represented as being only temporarily absent from Charleston, for all the consuls of foreign nations established within these States who were in possession of an exequatur issued by the United States prior to the formation of this Confederacy have been maintained and respected in the exercise of their legitimate functions, and the same protection and respect will be accorded to them in future so long as they confine themselves to the sphere of their duties and seek neither to evade nor defy the legitimate authority of this Government within its own jurisdiction.

There has grown up an abuse, however, the result of this tolerance on the part of the President, which is too serious to be longer allowed. His Imperial Majesty has deemed it politic to refuse acknowledging the patent fact of the existence of this Confederacy as an independent nation, but he can not reasonably expect that we should by our own consent imply assent to the justice or propriety of that refusal. Now the functionaries of his Majesty accredited to the Government of our enemies assume power to issue instructions to, and exercise authority over the French consuls residing within this country. Nay, even to appoint acting consuls at our ports. An instance of this has just occurred at the port of Charleston.

On the 26th May, the Department addressed a letter to Mr. Arthur Laren, informing him that he was reported to be acting as French consul at Charleston without a commission from his Government, and requesting explanation whether he had come to this country in a private or official character, and if the latter, what were the nature and extent of the official functions he proposed to exercise and from what source his authority was derived.

On the 30th May, Mr. Laren answered that " the consulate of Charleston being for the moment deprived of the presence of its chief by the departure of Mr. de St. André, I have been delegated in the name of the Emperor to conduct this office till the return of that agent."

In the meantime, however, Mr. Laren had submitted his papers to the military commander at Charleston, who forwarded a copy to Richmond, and his authority was found to consist of a commission in form issued by the Marquis of Montholon, consul general of France at New York, in which that officer recites that by virtue of a special order given to him by the minister of France at Washington he had thought proper to provide for replacing the Baron of St. André, "consul of France in Charleston," absent for the moment from his post, by appointing Mr. Arthur Laren élève consul attached to the consulate-general as acting consul at Charleston (consul intérimaire).

Mr. Laren was thereupon notified by letter of 3d June that he could not be permitted to exercise consular functions in Charleston without submitting to this Government for approval or disapproval the authority by which he was empowered to act. No answer has been received to this letter, nor is it necessary to await one for the purpose of this dispatch.

It is not deemed requisite to lay any stress upon the inquiry how and when Mr. de St. André's character of provisional consul during the temporary absence of Mr. Belligny became changed, without the knowledge or consent of this Government, into that of "Consul of France for Charleston," as he is styled in the commission issued by Mr. Montholon. The subject is too grave in its general aspect to render it advisable to dwell on details.

The assumption of a right by his Imperial Majesty's functionaries in the United States to exercise power within this Confederacy plainly ignores the existence of this Government, and implies that the relations which formerly existed between those functionaries and French officials at the port of Charleston continue to exist unimpaired by the secession of the State of South Carolina, the formation of this Government, and the war now pending. It is the assertion on the part of Mr. Mercier and Mr. Montholon of a right, by virtue of their credentials to the Washington Government, to exercise such powers as we can never permit to be assumed within our own country by foreign agents not accredited to us and officially recognized by our Government. Under these circumstances and because of a similar, but more aggravated case of the same character which has occurred on the part of another neutral power, the President has felt it his duty to order that no direct communication be permitted between the consuls of neutral nations in the Confederacy and the functionaries of those nations residing within the enemy's country. All communications therefore between his Imperial Majesty's consuls or consular agents in the Confederacy and foreign countries, whether neutral or hostile, will hereafter be restricted to vessels arriving from or dispatched for neutral ports. The President has the less reluctance in imposing this restriction, because of the ample facilities for correspondence which are now afforded by the fleets of Confederate and neutral steamers engaged in regular trade between neutral countries and Confederate ports. This trade is daily increasing in spite of the paper blockade, which is upheld by his Imperial Majesty in derogation, as the President conceives of the rights of this Confederacy, of the dictates of public law, and of the duties of impartial neutrality.

The President is confident that his Imperial Majesty will not misconstrue the motives which have inspired a measure so imperatively dictated by a due regard for the honor and dignity of our country. The President has not been unmindful of the generous sympathy displayed by his Imperial Majesty with the sufferings of our people, nor have the persistent though fruitless efforts of his Majesty to put an end to the cruel warfare waged against us failed to inspire him with sentiments of gratitude and admiration for that eminent sovereign, but he can not be expected to assent to an arrangement which vests power to control French officers within this country in functionaries whose duty it is to render themselves acceptable to our enemies. He therefore indulges the hope, which he is sure will be gratified by the action of his Imperial Majesty, because entirely reasonable and just, that the Government of France will choose some other mode of transmitting its orders and exercising its authority in the supervision of its interests within the Confederacy than by delegating to functionaries, who reside among our enemies, the power to give orders or instructions to those who reside among us.

You will find annexed copies of the various papers referred to, and the President desires that copies of this dispatch and of the papers appended to it, be placed by you in the hands of Mr. Drouyn de Lhuys.

I am, very respectfully, your obedient servant,

J. P. BENJAMIN,
Secretary of State.

Hon. JOHN SLIDELL, etc.,
Paris.

[Enclosure.]

CIRCULAR TO FOREIGN CONSULS.

DEPARTMENT OF STATE,
Richmond, June 10, 1863.

SIR: It becomes my duty to inform you that the President has determined to permit no direct communication between consuls or consular agents of foreign countries residing within the Confederacy and the functionaries of such foreign Governments residing in the enemy's lines. The passage in future of consular couriers, messengers, or of consuls or consular agents themselves through the Confederate lines to the enemy is accordingly prohibited, and foreign officials will be allowed to communicate with their Governments only directly or through neutral countries.

Your obedient servant,

J. P. BENJAMIN,
Secretary of State.

No. 2.]

DEPARTMENT OF STATE,
Richmond, June 11, 1863.

SIR: It becomes my duty to inform you that the Senate adjourned at its recent session without confirming your nomination as commissioner to Russia, and that your commission has thereby expired. It is due to you to state that it is not understood that this result was caused by any objection personally to yourself, but was occasioned by the conviction entertained by Senators that it was inexpedient to appoint any more agents abroad until the recognition of our independence. I append a copy of the official letter addressed to me by the President's private secretary which explains the action (or rather the failure to act) of the Senate. A deep-seated feeling of irritation at what is considered to be unjust and unfair conduct of neutral powers toward this Confederacy prevails among our people. The feeling is not unnatural, and has been reflected in this action of the Senate. Upon the receipt of this communication, therefore, you will consider your mission as ended, unless indeed you shall have been successful in obtaining recognition. In that event you will remain and present your credentials as envoy extraordinary and minister plenipotentiary. The case of Mr. Fearn stands upon the same footing as yours, and is determined in the same manner.

I must request you, therefore, to communicate to him this dispatch. The action of the Senate is regretted by the President, who had hoped that your services would prove eminently useful to your country; but he deems it his duty to yield his judgment to that of the Senate, and for this reason only has directed your return. If the objection of the Senate had existed only to a mission to Russia, he would have been happy to have availed himself of the services of yourself and Mr. Fearn at some other European court, but their objection is known to be a general one, and he is thus left with no alternative.

I am, with great respect, your obedient servant,

J. P. BENJAMIN,
Secretary of State.

Hon. LUCIUS Q. C. LAMAR, etc.,
St. Petersburg.

No. 25.]

CONFEDERATE STATES OF AMERICA,
DEPARTMENT OF STATE,
Richmond, June 11, 1863.

SIR: Since my No. 24 of 6th instant, further information has reached the Department illustrating most forcibly the necessity for the action taken by the President on the subject of her Britannic Majesty's consuls resident within the Confederacy, as explained in that dispatch.

On the 18th May, Mr. Cridland, who had occasionally acted as consul in Richmond during temporary absences of Consul Moore, sought an interview at the Department, and, on being admitted, called my attention to an article in the Richmond Whig of that date, which announced that Mr. Cridland was about to depart for Mobile with the commission of consul, and that he was accredited to Mr. Lincoln, not to this Government. Mr. Cridland assured me that the statement was erroneous, that he was going to Mobile as a private individual unofficially to look after certain interests of the British Government that had been left unprotected by the withdrawal of Consul Magee. He further stated that, as he was going there unofficially, he had not conceived that there was any impropriety in doing so without communicating his intention to the Department, and hoped that such was my own view of the matter. I informed him that all neutral residents were at liberty to travel within the Confederacy and to transact their business without other restrictions than such as the military authorities found it necessary to impose for the public safety, and that this Department saw no reason to interpose any objection to his going to Mobile to transact business unofficially. He then said that he had called at the office of the Whig to make a similar explanation to the editor of that paper, with a view to the correction of the erroneous impression created by its article, and accordingly on the next day an article appeared in that journal announcing that it had received the assurance from Mr. Cridland that he was going to Mobile "to look after British interests in that quarter in an unofficial way," and that he was "without commission from the Queen or exequatur from Washington."

I was therefore quite surprised at receiving from the Secretary of the Navy, official communication of a telegram received by him from Admiral Buchanan, informing the Secretary that Mr. Cridland had been officially introduced to him by the French consul and acting English consul at Mobile, and had shown the admiral "an official document signed by Lord Lyons appointing him acting English consul at Mobile." I append copies of this telegram and of the two articles above referred to, extracted from the Richmond Whig.

These, however, are not the only exceptional features which mark this affair. Other circumstances to which your attention is invited have been brought to the notice of the Department by official communications from the governor of Alabama.

On the 11th November last, the Bank of Mobile, as agent for the State of Alabama, addressed a communication to Consul Magee at Mobile informing him that that State would owe during the ensuing year to British subjects, interest coupons on the State bonds, to the amount of some £40,000 sterling; that this interest was payable in London at the Union Bank and at the counting house of the Messrs. Rothschild, and requesting to know whether the bank would be allowed to place in the hands of the consul in coin, the sum necessary, for transmission to England at the expense of the State for the purpose mentioned.

On the 14th November Consul Magee replied that he had sent to her Britannic Majesty's consul at New Orleans to ask if H. M. S.

Rinaldo could not be sent to Mobile to receive the specie and take it to Havana, to be forwarded thence by the consul general of Great Britain to London.

The specie was not conveyed by the *Rinaldo*, but by H. M. S. *Vesuvius*, and was accompanied by a certificate of the president of the bank stating that the remittance of the "31 kegs of specie containing each $5,000, together $155,000 * * * is for the purpose of paying dues to British subjects from the State of Alabama, and is the property and belongs to the subjects of her Britannic Majesty."

The shipment was accompanied by a letter addressed by the bank as agent of the State of Alabama, to W. W. Scrimgeour, esq., manager of the Union Bank of London, directing its appropriation to the payment of the interest due to British and other foreign holders of the State bonds, with a statement of the dates at which the several installments of the interest would become due and of the places in London where they were to be paid.

So little doubt seems to have been entertained of the propriety of this transaction by all that were engaged in it, that the commander of the *Vesuvius* informed the commander of the United States blockading squadron that the British consul had money to send by him, and no objection or protest was made. Among the papers annexed you will find the account given by Commodore Hitchcock himself, of his conversation with the commander of the *Vesuvius*, written after the dismissal of Consul Magee, and therefore at a period when the commodore could certainly have no motive for giving a coloring to his narrative, adverse to what was then known to be the view of his Government on the subject.

Under these circumstances the *Vesuvius* received and conveyed the specie which has since been received in England, and, as stated in the public journals, paid in whole or in part to British subjects, thus establishing the bona fide of the conduct of all the parties to the transaction.

It now appears that no sooner was the intention of making this remittance communicated to her Britannic Majesty's minister in Washington, than he took active measures to prevent it, by sending dispatches to Mobile forbidding the shipment. They failed, however, to arrive before the departure of the *Vesuvius* with the specie, whereupon Consul Magee was dismissed from office for receiving and forwarding it, and the vacancy thus created in the office of British consul at Mobile was filled by Lord Lyons, by the issue of a commission to Mr. Cridland and his departure for Mobile under the circumstances already explained.

These facts are of a character so grave as to have attracted the earnest attention of the President, and it is my duty to apprise you of the conclusions at which he has arrived, in order that you may lose no time in laying them before her Majesty's Government, in the hope that a renewed examination of the subject, and a knowledge of the serious complications which the present anomalous relations between the two Governments may involve, will induce the British cabinet to review its whole policy connected with those relations and to place them on the sole footing consistent with accomplished facts that are too notorious and too firmly established to be much longer ignored.

By the principles of the modern public code, debts due by a State are not subject to the operation of the laws of war, and are considered so sacred as to be beyond the reach of confiscation. An attempt at such confiscation would be reprobated by mankind. The United States alone in modern times have courted such reprobation, and just detestation has been universally expressed of their confiscation laws, passed during the pending war. The Government of Great Britain, on the contrary, has at all times manifested its abhorrence of such breaches of public faith, and in the Crimean War gave to the world a memorable example of its own high regard for public honor by paying over to its enemy money which it well knew would be immediately employed in waging hostilities against itself. The States of this Confederacy are emulous of examples of honor, and they accordingly refrained, on the breaking out of hostilities, from even the temporary sequestration of the dividends of their public debt due to their enemies. It was not until they had received notice of the confiscation law, passed by the United States on the 6th of August, 1861, that they consented to the temporary sequestration of the property of their enemies, and even then the sequestration was declared to be for the sole purpose of securing a fund to indemnify the sufferers under the confiscation law of the United States.

The following clause of our law, exempting public debts from its operation, is extracted as a proof of the sacred regard for public faith manifested by these States under strong temptation to retaliate, and under all the exasperation of the savage warfare then actually waged against them: "*Provided further*, That the provisions of this act shall not extend to the stocks or public securities of the Confederate Government, or of any of the States of this Confederacy, held or owned by any alien enemy, or to any debt, obligation, or sum due from the Confederate Government or any of the States to such alien enemy." (Sequestration law of Confederate States, passed 30 August, 1861.)

Such being the obligations imposed on States in regard to the payment of public debts toward even their enemies, no deeper reproach can stain their name than the refusal to do justice to neutral creditors. The observance of plighted public faith concerns mankind at large; in it all nations have a common interest; and the belligerent who perverts the weapons of legitimate warfare into an instrumentality for forcing his enemy to dishonor his obligations and incur the reproach of being faithless to his engagements wages a piratical and not an honorable warfare, and becomes hostis generis humani. Public honor is held sacred by international law against the attack of the most malevolent foe, and as susceptible of loss only by the recreancy of its possessor.

What possible lawful interest could the United States have in preventing the remittance of the specie due to the creditors of the State of Alabama? Blockades are allowed by the law of nations as a means of enforcing the submission of an enemy, by the destruction of his commerce, the exhaustion of his resources, and consequent forced abandonment of the struggle. The remittance of the specie in the present case, far from retarding these legitimate objects, tended on the contrary to promote them by the diversion of the money from application to military purposes. The United States could not have desired that the specie should remain within the Confederacy save with one of two motives: First, to dishonor the State of Alabama by giving color to the reproach that it was regardless of public faith, and on this comment has already been made; or secondly, in the hope that by the fortunes of war, the money would come within the reach of spoliation under its confiscation law. It is scarcely necessary to observe that the desire to enrich itself by plunder at the expense of neutral creditors is as little consonant with respect for public law and the rights of neutrals, as the purpose forcibly to prevent the State of Alabama from redeeming its plighted faith.

Whatever may be the value to which these views may be justly entitled, it is certain that there are but two aspects in which the State of Alabama can be regarded by her Majesty's Government. Alabama is either one of the States of the former Union, engaged in armed rebellion against the legitimate authority of the United States, or is an independent State, and a member of this Confederacy, engaged in lawful war against the United States. An examination of the effect of either of these relations upon the facts connected with the dismissal of Consul Magee and the appointment of Mr. Cridland will now be presented in vindication of the action which the President deems it his duty to take on this subject.

1. If the British Government think proper to assume (although the contrary is deemed by this Government to be fully established by convincing reason and victorious arms) that the State of Alabama is still one of the United States, then the Government of the United States is bound toward Great Britain as well as to all other neutral nations to render all legitimate aid in the collection of their just claims against that State. Although by the Constitution of the United States, its Government may be without power to enforce the payment of a debt due to foreign subjects or powers by an unwilling State, none can doubt its duty to interpose no obstruction to the payment of such debt; and no more legitimate ground of complaint could be afforded to Great Britain against the Government of the United States, than an opposition made by that Government to the payment of a just debt due by Alabama to the subjects of Great Britain. In this aspect of the case, therefore, the British officials at Mobile were doing a duty which ought to have been equally acceptable both to the United States and Great Britain when they facilitated the transmission of funds by that State for that purpose to England, where the debt was made payable; and merited applause rather than a manifestation of displeasure.

2. If, on the contrary, the State of Alabama may be regarded (as, in right and fact, she really is) an independent State engaged in war against the United States as a foreign enemy, then the President can not refrain from observing that the action of her Britannic Majesty's minister at Washington savored on this occasion rather of unfriendly cooperation with an enemy than of just observance of neutral obligations. For in this view of the case a minister accredited to the Government of our enemies has not only assumed the exercise of authority within this Confederacy without the knowledge or consent of its Government, but has done so under circumstances that rather aggravate than palliate the offense of dis-

regarding its sovereign rights. His action further conveys the implication that the Confederacy is subordinate to the United States, and that his credentials addressed to the Government at Washington justify his ignoring the existence of this Government, and his regarding these States as an appendage of the country to which he is accredited. Nor will her Majesty's Government fail to perceive that in no sense can it be considered consonant with the rights of this Government or with neutral obligations that a public minister should be maintained near the Cabinet of our enemies charged both with the duty of entertaining amicable relations with them and with the power of controlling the conduct of British officials resident with us.

Nor will the application of the foregoing remarks be at all impaired if her Majesty's Government, declining to determine the true relation of the State of Alabama to the United States, choose to consider that question as still in abeyance, and to regard that State as simply a belligerent whose ulterior status must await the event of the war. In this hypothesis the objection to delegating authority over British officials residing with us to a minister charged with the duty of rendering himself acceptable to our enemies is still graver than would exist in the case of hostile nations equally recognized as independent by a neutral power. For in the latter case the parties would have equal ability to vindicate their rights through the usual channels of official intercourse, whereas, in the former the belligerent which enjoys exclusively this advantage is armed by the neutral with additional power to inflict injury on his enemy.

The President has in the facts already recited seen renewed reasons for adhering to his determination mentioned in my preceding dispatch of prohibiting any direct communication between consuls or consular agents residing within the Confederacy and the functionaries of their Governments residing amongst our enemies. He further indulges the hope (which her Majesty's Government can not but regard as reasonable, and which he is therefore confident will be justified by its action) that her Majesty's Government will choose some other mode of transmitting its orders and exercising its authority over its agents within the Confederacy than by delegating to functionaries who reside among our enemies the power to give orders or instructions to those who reside among us.

Finally, and in order to prevent any further misunderstanding in Mr. Cridland's case, that gentleman has been informed that he can not be permitted to exercise consular functions at Mobile, and it has been intimated to him that his choice of some other State than Alabama for his residence would be agreeable to this Government. This intimation has been given in order to avoid any difficulty which might result from the doubtful position of Mr. Cridland, who is looked on here as a private individual, and who in Alabama represents himself as "acting English consul."

The President is confident that her Majesty's Government will render full justice to the motives by which these measures are prompted and will perceive in them a manifestation of the earnest desire entertained by him to prevent the possibility of any unfortunate complications having a tendency to impair the amity which it is equally the interest and the desire of this Government to cherish with that of Great Britain.

The President wishes a copy of this dispatch to be placed by you in the hands of Earl Russell.

I am, sir, very respectfully, your obedient servant,

J. P. BENJAMIN,
Secretary of State.

Hon. JAMES M. MASON,
 Commissioner, etc., London.

No. 37.]   PARIS, *June 12, 1863.*

SIR: You will find herewith duplicate of my last dispatch of May 28.

I have addressed to the Emperor a note (of which I inclose a copy, marked A), asking his attention to the question of recognition without the cooperation of England, but in conjunction with continental powers, and also requesting an audience. You will find that I do not place much reliance on Mr. Roebuck's motion in the House of Commons, although I am assured that it will be supported by Mr. Disraeli. Mr. Persigny promised to present it to the Emperor at the first cabinet meeting, which he said would probably be held to-day; but should the meeting be deferred, he would then write to the Emperor (who is at Fontainebleau) and urge him to grant me an audience. I do not expect an answer for some days.

I am, with the greatest respect, your most obedient servant,

JOHN SLIDELL.

Hon. J. P. BENJAMIN,
 Secretary of State.

[Enclosure A.]

PARIS, *June 8, 1863.*

MEMORANDUM WHICH THE UNDERSIGNED PRAYS COUNT DE PERSIGNY TO SUBMIT TO THE EMPEROR WITH THE HOMAGE OF HIS PROFOUND RESPECT.

The moment has arrived when the undersigned thinks that he may again be permitted to invoke the attention of the Emperor to the American question. The inability of the Lincoln Government to subjugate the South, which for many months past has been recognized by every intelligent statesman of Europe, is now admitted even by those who have heretofore professed to entertain a contrary opinion.

The intuitive sagacity of the Emperor had solved that problem long before the character of the struggle between North and South was justly appreciated even by those on this side of the Atlantic who had the best means of forming a correct judgment.

The suggestions, oral and written, which the undersigned has ventured to make to the Emperor on several occasions have been amply verified by events.

The Lincoln Government has been permitted to establish a code of belligerent rights on the ocean, which has virtually rescinded the fourth article of the conference of Paris of 16th April, 1856, and has placed the rights of neutrals in an infinitely worse position than they were before its adoption.

England now enjoys the monopoly of furnishing the markets of the world with cotton, a monopoly which will be perpetuated, if by the prolongation of the war for another year every accessible portion of the South shall be devastated, and the basis of its agricultural industry essentially impaired. She sees close at hand the collapse of the paper-money system of the North, soon to be followed by anarchy and disintegration and her consequent relief from all apprehension of danger to her colonies and commerce from her once-dreaded rival, while it is clearly the interest of France that the two divisions of the former Federal Union should each possess elements of strength and stability.

She already finds her mercantile marine fast taking the place of that rival in the carrying trade of the world, thus securing by new nurseries of seamen the maritime superiority which she cherishes as the right arm of her strength. Meanwhile, the misery of her workmen engaged in the manufacture of cotton, appears to be diminishing; she no longer fears domestic troubles arising from that quarter and in view of the comparatively greater ulterior advantages arising from the continuance of the present state of things, cheerfully supports the temporary burden of sustaining a large pauper population.

There can be no doubt that England has from the very inception of the contest looked forward with satisfaction to the final separation of the North and South, and if she now saw any reason to apprehend the reconstruction of the Union, she would not only recognize the Confederate States, but if direct material aid were necessary to prevent a result which she so much deprecates, would unhesitatingly have recourse to it. Recognition is withheld by her not because she doubts their capacity to maintain their independence but because she is assured of it.

Will the Emperor adhere to the policy which he has heretofore pursued? Will the cooperation of England be the basis on which only he will entertain this question? It is evidently idle to renew propositions for joint action in that quarter. May it not be advantageously taken in concert with other European powers? There is good reason to believe that, with the probable exception of Russia and perhaps of Italy, they would readily join France in recognizing the Confederate States. Without recognition there is no prospect that the war will cease during the term of the Lincoln Administration, but from this time forward a war of invasion on the part of the North with large armies will not be attempted; it has long since ceased to be waged on the principles and with the usages of civilized nations; it has gradually degenerated into a war of pillage and devastation, and will be hereafter confined to incursions whose sole object will be plunder and destruction.

Such has been the object of the recent campaign in western Louisiana, northern Mississippi, and Arkansas. The accompanying letter from a Frenchman, resident in New Orleans, who is well known to the undersigned and on whose statements full reliance can be placed, has been placed in my hands by Mr. A. Roger, " ancien consul-général." It will give the Emperor a correct idea of the atrocities there being perpetrated and the purpose of the invaders, which looks to nothing short of the extermination or exile of the white population.

The blockade will be continued until March, 1865; the culture of cotton, which can find no purchasers, will be abandoned; and under the most favorable circumstances years must then elapse before it can be reestablished on a scale at all commensurate with the wants of Europe.

Apart from all political considerations does not the voice of humanity call upon Europe, with France as its natural and legitimate leader, to put a stop to this otherwise interminable contest? To effect that end the undersigned again declares his firm conviction that recognition alone is sufficient. It will give courage to the large and growing party at the North who desire peace, but do not now dare to give utterance to their opinions.

On two previous occasions the Emperor has accorded to the undersigned the honor of an interview. More than seven months have elapsed since the last. Would it be presuming too much on the indulgence of the Emperor to solicit another, believing, as the undersigned does, that he may, perhaps, have it in his power to communicate some information respecting American affairs which may not have reached the Emperor through other sources?

JOHN SLIDELL.

No. 39.]   CONFEDERATE STATES COMMISSION,
                                London, June 12, 1863.

SIR: My last was No. 38, dated at Paris on the 4th instant, which went by the mail of the 6th instant to Mr. Heyliger at Nassau. I had hoped to send you a duplicate by this mail, but such has been the pressure upon us here that it could not be prepared in time, as this must go off this afternoon.

As I told you in my No. 38, immediately on my return from Paris I wrote to Mr. Dowling, commercial agent at Cork, with full instructions to collect evidence, if practicable, in regard to the supposed Federal enlistments in Ireland. Should it be obtained the subject shall be, as you direct, brought before Earl Russell.

From your No. 20 of the 14th of April I find that my dispatches sent by Mr. Hope had been destroyed. I have not the means here of determining what dispatches were committed to him, but presume they were those of which duplicates were sent with my No. 31 of the 19th of March.

I learn also within a few days past that triplicates of my Nos. 4, 5, 6, 7, and 8, which were sent by Mr. Mohl in the *Peterhoff*, have also been destroyed at sea. These were of dispatches of which you informed me neither originals nor duplicates had been received and were necessary to complete your files.

I have also just learned through the Northern papers that a Mr. Hobson, of Richmond, who sailed from here in the Havana mail steamer early in April and who bore my dispatches from Nos. 30 to 33, inclusive, and also duplicates of my Nos. 24 to 29, inclusive, has been captured, I presume between one of the islands and the coast. This gentleman was strongly impressed by me with the necessity of destroying the dispatches in the event which has happened and I doubt not did so.

I now send herewith duplicates of those dispatches intrusted to him, to wit, from No. 30 to 33, inclusive, with the documents accompanying them, and also duplicate of my unofficial letter of the 9th and 11th of April.

I send also duplicates of my Nos. 34 to 36, inclusive, and triplicate of my No. 37; they all go under cover to Major N. S. Walker, Confederate agent at Bermuda.

I have further to acknowledge the receipt of your No. 22, dated on the 13th of May, with the new flag and the act of Congress prescribing it, brought by Mr. J. H. Burton and delivered to me here on the 10th instant.

I have nothing to add on public matters since my No. 38 from Paris. We are all in much doubt of the result of things at Vicksburg. The latest accounts were that the enemy in large force had been repulsed in successive assaults on the intrenchments at the city up to the 22d of May. Should the defense be successful I think Mr. Roebuck's motion, now fixed for the 30th, may be carried; if otherwise, I should not advise its being put to a vote.

I completed the purchase of the books you have ordered for the Department of State yesterday, and they will go off to-day or to-morrow to the house of Fraser, Trenholm & Co., of Liverpool, as you direct. The bill shall be sent with my next dispatch.

The Confederate loan seems solidly placed at last; the quotations for the past week have varied only from 1 to 2 per cent discount.

I have, etc.,

J. M. MASON.

Hon. J. P. BENJAMIN,
-     *Secretary of State.*

P. S.—Since closing this dispatch I am enabled to have copied my No. 38 from Paris, of which duplicate goes herewith.

NASSAU, *June 12, 1863.*

DEAR SIR: I wrote you a few lines on the 10th. This morning I am placed in possession of authenticated copies of all the declarations relative to the case of the *Margaret and Jessie.* As before remarked the testimony is very uniform, and singularly precise as to the gravity of the outrage and the distance at which the firing took place. I shall forward all these documents by the earliest opportunity to Mr. Mason in London. An informal copy goes, I believe, by this opportunity to John Fraser & Co., Charleston. Should you therefore wish to peruse the evidence, it will be sent to you by telegraphing to Mr. Trenholm.

Mr. Soulé arrived from Havana a few days since and purposes remaining here awhile. Dr. Thomas Hunt wishes to come over here and practice. I shall write to him on the subject by first occasion. M. M. Simpson, of New Orleans, reached [here] also a few days since.

Yours, truly,

L. HEYLIGER.

Hon. J. P. BENJAMIN,
    Richmond.

No. 26.]   DEPARTMENT OF STATE,
                                            Richmond, June 12, 1863.

SIR: I append copy of letter * of Earl Russell on the subject of the prisoner Hester, enclosed by Mr. Moore to this Department.

You are requested to inform his lordship that this Government will be prepared to receive the prisoner at any port of the Confederacy where he may be delivered, and that in the event of a refusal on the part of the United States to consent to the passage of the *Shannon* through the blockade, we will send a naval officer of the Confederacy to Bermuda, charged with authority to receive the prisoner and bring him into one of our ports on a vessel of the Confederate Government.

You will be pleased to renew to her Majesty's secretary of state for foreign affairs, the expression of the thanks of this Government for his considerate attention in the matter.

I am, very respectfully, your obedient servant,

                                            J. P. BENJAMIN,
                                            Secretary of State.

Hon. JAMES M. MASON,
        London, England.

No. 37.]   PARIS, *June 12, 1863.*

SIR: You will find herewith duplicate of my last dispatch of May 28.

In consequence of the news of the fall of Vicksburg, since proved to have been premature, Mr. Lafitte called to inform me that his friends in London had abandoned for the present their project of a loan, saying, however, that they would probably resume it if any decidedly favorable news should be received from the Confederacy.

Mr. Mason, as he will have informed you, came here to consult with Messrs. Lamar, McRae, and myself about our financial condition generally and especially about the payments which should be at once provided for out of the proceeds of the Erlanger loan.

This consultation was rendered necessary by the confusion and embarrassment resulting from the employment of numerous agents charged to make purchases and contracts far exceeding the means present or prospective which the Government already has or can provide the means of paying for in Europe. The evil was aggravated by the failure to send warrants to the different agents of the War and Navy Departments on the depositories of the Government for the sums which they might require to meet their liabilities.

The necessity for prompt action was imperative, and we all felt that we should best discharge our duties to the country by assuming the responsibility of deciding on the manner in which in the absence of direct instructions from Richmond the proceeds of the loan should be employed.

A protocol of our deliberations was drawn up and signed by us. Mr. McRae will send a copy of it and give full details to the Secre-

------

* See No. 5, May 2, 1865, Russell to Moore.

tary of the Treasury of what he has done with the approbation of Messrs. Lamar, Mason, and myself.

I have addressed to the Emperor a note, of which I enclose copy marked "A," asking his attention to the question of recognition without the cooperation of England, but in conjunction with continental powers, and also requesting an audience. You will find that I do not place much reliance on Mr. Roebuck's motion in the House of Commons, although I am assured that it will be supported by Mr. Disraeli. Mr. Persigny promised to present it to the Emperor at the first cabinet meeting, which he said would probably be held to-day, but should the meeting be deferred he would then write to the Emperor (who is at Fontainebleau) and urge him to grant me an audience. I do not expect an answer for some days.

My friends of the affaires etrangères, under date of the 3d instant, wrote me in reply to a verbal inquiry as follows:

[Translation of note from the ministre des affaires etrangères.]

The Washington Government has in truth given answer to our complaint against their representative at London. Mr. Dayton read to Mr. Drouyn de Lhuys a dispatch from Mr. Seward, conceived in the best terms, and in which, although an attempt is made to attenuate the bearing of the wrongs imputed to Mr. Adams, his conduct is declared to have been inconsiderate and not in conformity with the spirit of those amicable relations they are so anxious to maintain with France.

There is, therefore, with reference to this matter, as well as in all other respects, no reason why Mr. Mercier should leave Washington. He has asked for leave of absence for reasons personal, but under present circumstances his request has not been favorably entertained.

The elections have resulted in the return of the opposition candidates from Paris. Of the 283 members of the new Chamber of Deputies the opposition will not number more than 20 to 25 at the utmost.

The news from Mexico continues to be unfavorable, and the Polish question appears to be further from adjustment than it was a month since.

Mexico and Poland are great stumbling blocks in the way of energetic action in our affairs, and I therefore feel by no means confident of the success of my appeal to the Emperor, although I recently had more than one unequivocal proof of his continued hearty sympathy with our cause. You will understand why I do not make special mention of them.

I am anxiously awaiting the arrival of the next steamer, hoping that it will bring the news of the defeat of Grant and the abandonment of what will doubtless be the last serious attempt against Vicksburg.

I am, with the greatest respect, your most obedient servant.

JOHN SLIDELL.

Hon. J. P. BENJAMIN,
Secretary of State.

CONFEDERATE STATES OF AMERICA,
WAR DEPARTMENT, ORDNANCE BUREAU,
Richmond, June 15, 1863.

SIR: I have the honor to enclose to you an extract from a letter, just received from Norman S. Walker, special agent of the War Department, at Bermuda, for such attention as you may think proper.

Very respectfully,

J. GORGAS,
Colonel, Chief of Ordnance.

Hon. J. P. BENJAMIN,
Secretary of State.

[Enclosure.]

ST. GEORGE'S, *June 5, 1863.*

*   *   *   *   *   *   *   *

The steamer *Wachusett* came into this port a week ago under the false pretense of repairing her boilers. If it meets with the approval of the Government, I should be pleased to address a communication to his Excellency the governor to ascertain if the same privileges will be accorded to a Confederate man-of-war as has already been accorded to this Yankee cruiser. It might be agreeable to Captain Semmes to know officially whether or not he could come into the harbor of St. George's and remain a week on a very flimsy pretext.

I have the honor to be, very respectfully, your obedient servant,

N. S. WALKER.

Colonel [GORGAS].

Official:
THOS. L. BAYNE,
Captain, on duty with Chief of Ordnance.

PARIS, *June 18, 1863.*

MY DEAR SIR: I have just left the Emperor, he having come to-day to the Tuileries instead of to-morrow, as he had intended. The interview was very cordial and satisfactory. He authorizes me to contradict without qualification the report that he is unwilling to recognize our Government. He says that he is now prepared and is desirous, as he has long been, to take that step with the cooperation of England. I read him portions of Mr. Roebuck's note to Mr. Lindsay. He said that he would gladly receive those gentlemen if they would come here, but after reflection he added that he thought he could do something still more decided, viz, make a formal proposition to England for joint recognition; that he would consult his cabinet to-day; that it was not decided now to make the proposition. He would let me know in a day or two through Mr. Mocquard whether it would be desirable to see Messrs. R. and L. I shall prepare a note to-day of our conversation and send you copy of it to-morrow or next day.

Yours, in haste,

JOHN SLIDELL.

Hon. J. M. MASON.

No. 40.]   CONFEDERATE STATES COMMISSION,
                                         London, June 20, 1863.

SIR: An opportunity offering by a good ship direct either to
Bermuda or Nassau, I avail myself of it for this dispatch, to be
addressed as the case may be to Major Walker or Mr. Heyliger.
My two latest were Nos. 38 and 39, dated, respectively, the 4th and
12th instant, the former by mail to Nassau, the latter to Bermuda.
I send also herewith dispatches from Mr. Slidell received for transmission within the last few days. I enclose also as the latest a
note from him of the 18th instant advising me in brief of his interview on that day with the Emperor and the result. I have nothing
from him since. I sent Mr. Slidell's note to Mr. Lindsay, and he
with Mr. Roebuck called on me this morning. They are both much
interested in the success of the motion of the latter to come up in
the House of Commons on the 30th instant, and go off together to
Paris to-night to have an interview with the Emperor. At their
request, I telegraphed to Mr. Slidell to arrange for the interview to-
morrow. They desire to impress on the Emperor first the importance that he should formally invite England to unite with
France in an act of recognition, the communication to be made
before the 30th instant, with permission to state the fact (if it exist)
in debate to the House; secondly, if England refuse to unite, then that
the Emperor should act alone, with an assurance from them that in
such event England must follow suit within less than one month
or the ministry would go out. Mr. Roebuck is, as you know, a
statesman of great intelligence and experience, and I should hope
[for] good results from the mission; it certainly evinces great
earnestness on their part. Without news of decided successful results at Vicksburg, or some move of the character contemplated on
the part of the Emperor, I should fear, if put to the vote, that
Roebuck's motion would fail.

I enclose a late debate in the House of Lords between Lord Clanricarde and Earl Russell, involving questions of the blockade. You
will see that the latter utterly repudiates the definition of the convention of Paris; or, rather, by a quibble on its text, which speaks of
"access to the coast," construes the meaning to be that the coast, and
not a port alone, may be the subject of a blockade, reestablishing thus
the doctrines of blockade supposed to have become obsolete or wholly
rejected by the Paris convention. These declarations of Earl Russell
go a bowshot beyond the very latitudinous views expressed by him in
his correspondence with me, and I think will be a warning to us to
avoid the risk of any entanglement in future treaty stipulations when
the time comes.

I send also, as bearing upon the public questions of the day, a correspondence between Mr. Moncure D. Conway and myself which I
caused to be published in the Times, with a copy of the advertisement
calling a public meeting in the city of London, under the auspices of
Mr. Bright, to enable Mr. Conway to deliver an address on slavery.
You will see that in the advertisement Mr. Conway is announced as
from eastern Virginia, and the son of a slaveholder. Who he is I
do not know, but I thought his proposition to negotiate on terms resting on the basis of the independence of the Southern States under
authority from the Northern abolitionists, with the declaration that

they would coerce their Government to stop the war and admit our independence, afforded an opportunity to expose the duplicity of that party to their own people not [to] be omitted. The fact that Mr. Bright was to preside at the meeting gave him and his mission, I thought, sufficient consequence to excuse me for entertaining the correspondence. I am glad to find that what I have done meets the approbation of our friends here, and I think may do service at the North.

*   *   *   *   *   *   *

Within the last two or three months, organizations of English people, styling themselves "Southern clubs," have made their appearance at Manchester, Birmingham, and other large towns; and, under the auspices of respectable and influential men, these movements have been spontaneous and without instigation from Southern quarters, so far as I know. Their objects, by public addresses, publications, etc., to get up a spirit of enquiry amongst the people at large, and to diffuse information on the Southern side of the American question. They are in frequent communication with me for facts, and in search of material. Of course I do all in my power to encourage them. Under their auspices, too, public meetings have been held in the towns and villages, principally in the manufacturing districts, which are addressed by speakers invited for the occasion, and resolutions adopted expressive of the sense of the meeting in favor of recognition, etc. Although somewhat voluminous, yet there being room in the dispatch box, I send some of the placards which have been sent to me, to show the character of the movement, "its form and pressure."

I have the honor to be, your very obedient servant,

J. M. MASON.

Hon. J. P. BENJAMIN,
     Secretary of State.

No. 38.]   PARIS, *June 21, 1863.*

SIR: In my dispatch of 12th instant, of which I enclose duplicate, I informed you that I expected that the Emperor would soon grant me an audience. That expectation has been realized, and I now send you a memorandum of my interview, omitting what would be a mere repetition of arguments previously presented to him either orally or in writing. I have also from prudential considerations omitted what was said in relation to some of the matters that formed the subject of a letter which accompanied your No. 14. These matters are in a very satisfactory condition.

Mr. Isturitz informs me that he has not yet received a reply to his letter respecting the *General Rusk,* alias *Blanche.* He is much gratified by the suggestion of your No. 16, and has written to the Marquis de Miraflores, minister of foreign affairs, saying that if my presence at Madrid would be acceptable, on receiving an intimation to that effect, I would at once act upon it. I communicated to him what the Emperor authorized me to say on the subject of recognition, of which he will also inform his chief.

The following note from my friend at the affaires etrangères will inform you of the result of the deliberation of the council of ministers respecting the communication to be addressed to the British Government.

PARIS, *June 19, 1863.*

MY DEAR SIR: This is between us and entirely confidential.

The question which you talked about with me to-day has been, in effect, submitted yesterday to the council of ministers. The motion which it is proposed to make in London has been judged at this time inopportune. They agreed to deny, as far as the English cabinet is concerned, the reports which falsely attribute to us sentiments and a policy less favorable for the South; to recall to them that on several occasions we have addressed to them propositions which they thought they should not accept; to declare that our feelings have not changed—quite the contrary; to state to them further that we shall be charmed to follow them up, and if they have any overtures to make to us in a like spirit to that which has inspired ours, we shall receive them with quite as much empressment as pleasure. Baron Gros will receive instructions accordingly.

The minister charges me to tell you that he will await you day after to-morrow, Sunday, between 10 and 11 o'clock in the morning.

Always yours, dear sir,

[COUNT DE PERSIGNY.]

In conformity with the invitation of the minister of foreign affairs, I waited on him this morning. I find that the hesitation to recognize us results from a deep, and, as I think, well-founded distrust of England. Mr. Drouyn de Lhuys says, that were a direct proposition made and refused, as it probably would be, Earl Russell would communicate the correspondence to the Lincoln Government; that it would produce great irritation and although it might not be followed by direct hostilities, would induce that Government to encourage the departure of bands of volunteers for Mexico, thus aggravate the difficulties already very serious, with which General Forey has to contend; that the encouragement would probably be so open as to compel the Emperor to declare war, a contingency which he desires to avoid and which England would willingly aid in creating.

Messrs. Roebuck and Lindsay arrived here this morning and proceeded to Fontainebleau, where they expect to have an interview with the Emperor. They will return to-morrow. They will inform me of the result of their visit, which I will communicate, in another dispatch.

I feel it my duty to call, through you, the attention of the President to the very great embarrassments produced by the employment of several agents to make purchases for the War Department, with ill-defined powers and sometimes with conflicting instructions. These agents are very far from being on good terms with each other, and the consequence of this alienation must necessarily be detrimental to the public service. I venture with all deference to suggest the expediency of vesting some persons possessing the full confidence of the Secretary of War, with complete control over all the purchases to be made for his department. The Navy Department has also several agents in Europe, but, so far as I have reason to believe, they are acting harmoniously although independently of each other. The great difficulty is in providing the necessary means to carry out their respective instructions. Would it not be well to subject the disbursements of the agents of both departments to the control of a common head, who, with the knowledge of the pecuniary resources, present and prospective, at the disposition of the Government, should decide with reference to the comparative exigencies of each particular order from the respective departments, the manner in which they should be provided for? This head, to avoid the natural jealousies and susceptibilities of the two services, should be a civilian; and I hope that I shall not be suspected of any disposition to interfere in matters outside of my proper sphere of action in recommending Mr. C. J. McRae for this important duty.

I have the honor to be, with great respect, your most obedient servant.

JOHN SLIDELL.

Hon. J. P. BENJAMIN,
    Secretary of State.

[Enclosure B.]

FONTAINEBLEAU, *June 21, 1863.*

MY DEAR MR. SLIDELL: You will doubtless be pleased to receive the following communication, which the Emperor charges me to make you confidentially.

Mr. Drouyn de Lhuys has written to Baron Gros, our ambassador in London, to sound Lord John Russell on the question of the recognition of the South, and has authorized him to declare that the cabinet of the Tuileries is ready to discuss the subject.

Receive, my dear Mr. Slidell, the expression of my warm and very distinguished regard.

MOCQUARD.

[Enclosure C.]

MEMORANDUM OF AN INTERVIEW WITH THE EMPEROR AT THE TUILERIES, THURSDAY, 18TH JUNE, 1863.

On Wednesday I received from the Duke de Bassano, first chamberlain, a note informing me that the Emperor would receive me at the Tuileries on the following day at 10 o'clock. The Emperor received me with great cordiality.

He said that he had read the memorandum presented to him by the Count de Persigny (a copy* of which accompanied my dispatch No. 37); that he was more fully convinced than ever of the propriety of the general recognition by European powers of the Confederate States, but that the commerce of France and the success of the Mexican expedition would be jeopardized by a rupture with the United States; that no other power than England possessed a sufficient navy to give him efficient aid in a war on the ocean, an event which indeed could not be anticipated if England would cooperate with him in recognition. I replied that I was well satisfied that recognition by France and other continental powers, or even by France alone, would not lead to a war with the United States, as they already found ample occupation for all their energies at home; that he could count on the cooperation of Spain, Austria, Prussia, Belgium, Holland, Sweden, and Denmark. He remarked that none of these powers possessed a navy of any consequence. I suggested that Spain had a very respectable navy, and was daily increasing it. I adverted to the instructions in your

---

* See p. 802.

dispatch No. 16, of 9th May, and said that I was authorized to give the adhesion of my Government to the tripartite treaty for the guaranty of Cuba to Spain; that I thought it probable that such an adhesion might induce Spain, if assured in advance of the concurrence of France, to take the initiative in our recognition.

Would the Emperor be willing to give such an assurance? He said that he would. I asked if the Emperor would authorize me to say so to the Spanish ambassador, Mr. Isturitz, to whom I had already communicated the substance of my instructions. He replied that he was willing that I should do so. I then spoke to the Emperor of a letter from Mr. Roebuck, of which I asked his permission to read some extracts. He assented. I asked him if I might be permitted to deny on his authority the correctness of the rumor of which Mr. Seymour Fitzgerald had spoken to Mr. Roebuck. He said I might give it an unqualified denial. I then inquired if it would be agreeable to him to see Messrs. Roebuck and Lindsay, and if I might so inform them. He said that he would be pleased to converse with them on the subject of Mr. Roebuck's motion, and that I might write to that effect. He however, after a little reflection, added: "I think that I can do something better—make a direct proposition to England for joint recognition. This will effectually prevent Lord Palmerston from misrepresenting my position and wishes on the American question. I shall bring the question before the cabinet meeting to-day; and if it should be decided not to make the proposition now, I shall let you know in a day or two through Mr. Mocquard what to say to Mr. Roebuck." I then said; "It may perhaps be an indiscretion to ask whether your Majesty prefers to see the Whigs or Tories in power in England;" and he said, "I rather prefer the Whigs." I remarked that Lord Malmesbury would, under a Conservative administration, probably be the secretary for foreign affairs, and that I had always understood that intimate relations existed between the Emperor and him. He said: "That is true; personally we are excellent friends, but personal relations have very little influence in great affairs where party interests are involved." He playfully remarked: "The Tories are very good friends of mine when in a minority, but their tone changes very much when they get into power."

He then spoke of the spirit in which the news of the fall of Puebla had been received North and South; that the Northern papers showed their disappointment and hostility, while Richmond had been illuminated on the occasion. This is reported by the newspapers. I, of course, did not express any doubt of the fact, although I consider it somewhat apocryphal. I said that there could be no doubt of the bitterness of the Northern people at the success of his arms in Mexico, while all our sympathies were with France, and urged the importance of securing the lasting gratitude and attachment of a people already so well disposed; that there could be no doubt that our Confederacy was to be the strongest power of the American Continent, and that our alliance was worth cultivating. He said that he was quite convinced of the fact, and spoke with great admiration of the bravery of our troops, the skill of our generals, and the devotion of our people. He expressed his great regret at the death of Stonewall Jackson, whom he considered one of the most remarkable men of the age.

I expressed my thanks to him for his sanction of the contract made for the building of four ships of war at Bordeaux and Nantes. I then informed him that we were prepared to build several ironclad ships in France, and that I required only his verbal assurance that they should be allowed to proceed to sea under the Confederate flag to enter into contracts for that purpose. He said that we might build the ships, but it would be necessary that their destination should be concealed. I replied that the permission to build, equip, and proceed to sea would be no violation of neutrality, and invoked the precedent of the ship built for the Chilean Government under the circumstances mentioned in my dispatch No. 32, of the 20th April. The Emperor remarked that there was a distinction to be drawn between that case and what I desired to do. Chile was a Government recognized by France. The conversation then closed. The audience was shorter than on the two previous occasions of my seeing the Emperor. It lasted an hour, but I did not think it discreet again to go over the ground covered by my note and the points discussed in the former interviews, although they were occasionally brought into the conversation. I give below a copy of the letter of Mr. Roebuck. In reading it to the Emperor I omitted the portions underscored.

[Subenclosure.]

PARIS, *June 18, 1863.*

MY DEAR LINDSAY: Seymour Fitzgerald said to me last night that it was rumored that the French Emperor at the present time thought it would be unwise to recognize the South, and that Lord Palmerston on the 30th would say that England thought the time for recognition had not arrived; that France, he could state authoritatively, thought so too; and that therefore it was quite clear that any negotiation about the matter at the present time was utterly out of place and impossible. Now, upon this, an idea has come into my head, and I will explain it by a question: Could we—i. e., you and I—do any good by going to Paris and seeing the Emperor? *You know that I am no great admirer of that great personage, but still I am a politician. So is he, and politicians have no personal likes or dislikes that stand in the way of their political end. I therefore would act as if I had no feelings either friendly or hostile to him. He would do the same as regards myself, and therefore I have no fear but that he would listen to all that I have to offer by way of suggestion and advice.* Whether he would take that advice is another thing; still he would listen, and good might come of our interview. Think over this proposition and give me your opinion. If we go, we ought to go at once. The 30th is not very far off, and we must soon decide whether the motion that stands in my name shall or shall not be brought on.

The determination of the French Emperor will have an important bearing on that question. I send this letter to Shipperton, because I believe that on Sunday you will be there. If we determine to go to Paris, we ought to start on Monday morning.

Yours, very truly,

J. A. ROEBUCK.

W. S. LINDSAY,
Member of Parliament.

No. 27.]
DEPARTMENT OF STATE,
Richmond, June 22, 1863.

SIR: I have the honor to acknowledge receipt of your Nos. 34 and 35, of 27th and 30th April, respectively, together with two unofficial communications of 9th and 27th April. They were all received together on the 17th June. I have still to regret the absence of your Nos. 30, 31, and 32, which is specially unfortunate, for I am very desirous to make one last appeal to the justice of neutral powers on the subject of the blockade, for which purpose materials have been collected but can not well be used till receipt of your last correspondence with Earl Russell on the subject, accompanied by your own comments. I think I have already mentioned that the printed correspondence as it appears in the British Blue Book has been received.

I am much indebted for your prompt attention to the purchase of books for the Department and await them with impatience. I must beg you to send the Hansard as promptly as possible. You have little idea of the embarrassments under which the Department labors for want of books of reference. The State library here is drawn on from so many sources that one can rarely get the book wanted, even if it belongs to the library. There are some blockade debates in Hansard which I would much like to see before closing the dispatch above alluded to, but to which of course access can not be got in time.

Instead of sending anything for me through Messrs. Fraser, Trenholm & Co., it will be best to ship for the future to the Government agent at Nassau or Bermuda, whence the importation can take place on vessels belonging to the Government, thus saving the enormous freight charged by the blockade runners.

In purchasing the Hansard it will be well to subscribe for future volumes for the Department and to request the bookseller to keep a memorandum of the binding of the volumes he sends, so that the set may be uniform. In lettering the back of the volumes it will be well also to stamp on them "Department of State, C. S. A."

A copy of your No. 35 has been prepared for the Engineer Office of the War Department, and as soon as the model arrives, the new railroad will be tried in the streets of Richmond. It appears to be very promising, and if successful will be of immense value to our country.

I have received from Mr. Heyliger a copy of the protest in relation to the gross outrage on the *Margaret and Jessie* committed within the neutral jurisdiction of Great Britain by the United States steamer *Rhode Island*. Mr. Heyliger informs me he has sent to you all the documents, and I doubt not you will have acted on them in such manner as the nature of the case renders most expedient. I am awaiting copies of the affidavits of the witnesses to this audacious attack on neutral rights, on the receipt of which full instructions of the President's views will be sent to you.

Allow me to say that I fear you are rather overcautious in the transmission of your dispatches, and that in this way time is lost. It has been remarked in the office that the correspondence sent in the closed British mail to Nassau or Bermuda, to our agents there, reaches us with promptness and regularity, and that dispatches entrusted to private hands are delayed and sometimes lost. It is not supposed that there is the least danger that the closed British mail from Europe for the West Indies would be violated either by British officials or by the cruisers of the United States, and our agents at Nassau and Bermuda are extremely careful in forwarding dispatches, and always give instructions to destroy them in case of necessity.

Your preference for private agents as being a safer conveyance, though probably well founded at an earlier period of the war, now seems rather to increase uncertainty and delay. The Government steam packets between our ports and the West Indies have now made some 30 passages, I think, through the " effective" blockade without a single loss.

I am, very respectfully, your obedient servant,

J. P. Benjamin,
Secretary of State.

Hon. James M. Mason,
London, England.

No. 19.]

Department of State,
Richmond, June 22, 1863.

Sir: I have the honor to acknowledge receipt of your Nos. 31, 32, and 33, of the 11th, 20th, and 23d April, all received together on the 17th instant.

The letter of Governor Morehead has been found very interesting, and you will probably have perceived by the Northern papers that the Catholic clergy are beginning to discover that the detestable Puritan spirit which sowed the first seeds of disunion, which origi-nated this savage war, and which is now urging with remorseless cruelty the extermination of millions of human beings at the South, is just as hostile to the Catholic religion as the ultra abolitionists are to slaveholders, and that the time is not far distant when the mas-sacre of Catholics at the North will exhibit the fell spirit of the Puritan on a scale of which mankind has yet had no example. The New York Freeman's Journal, the Catholic organ, is beginning to warn the Irish Catholics on the subject, and alarm has been awakened among them by the repeated instances of destruction and desecration of Catholic churches by New England soldiery. If you can get access to the files of that paper, I should think the publication of extracts from it would be particularly useful in Spain, and not without value in the other Catholic countries of southern Europe.

The passages in cipher in your No. 31 and 32 are extremely grati-fying, and the proper Departments of the Government have been apprised of their contents. You do not mention in either 32 or 33 whether you ever received the "direct assurance" referred in No. 31, but it is inferred that you have been fully satisfied on the subject.

The petition of Mr. Meaurean on the subject of his notes did not reach me in time for presentation to Congress, which adjourned a month ago. There can be little doubt that relief would be granted in such cases as his, which appeal to equity too strongly to be disre-garded by Congress.

Your remarks on the subject of the astounding diplomatic blunder of Mr. Adams at the Court of London are of course the echo of uni-versal opinion on the subject, but it was extremely fortunate that you were able to anticipate the public knowledge of the fact. We have not supposed here that this matter would have the least result on the mutual relations of the United States and Great Britain, which seem to have now become settled on the established basis of insulting aggression on the one side and tame submission on the other. Accordingly no surprise has been felt on the receipt of intelligence apparently authentic that Mr. Adams has apologized in a private note to Earl Russell which he has asked the latter to consider confidential, and that this secret reparation of a public insult has been received as satisfactory.

You will, long ere the receipt of this, have also learned of the insolent attack by the U. S. S. *Rhode Island* on the British Bahamas, by ploughing up the soil of the Island of Eleuthera with shot and shell fired within half a mile of the shore at the Confederate steamer *Margaret and Jessie*. Mr. Seward will, of course, write one of his most labored rhetorical passages on this event, and this will be considered quite satisfactory by her Majesty's Government. The most surprising infatuation of modern times is the thorough conviction entertained by the British ministry that the United States are ready to declare war against England and it is impossible not to admire the sagacity with which Mr. Seward penetrated into the secret feelings of the British cabinet, and the success of his policy of intimidation, which the world at large supposed would be met with prompt resentment, but which he, with deeper insight into the real policy of that cabinet, foresaw would be followed by submissive acquiescence in his demands. Look at the account published by the United States of Mr. Adams' interview with Earl Russell as related in the dispatch of the former to Mr. Seward on the 14th June, 1861. You will find a direct threat by the United States to go to war with Great Britain if Earl Russell should grant further interviews to our commissioners. Instead of meeting this threat with indignant rebuke, Earl Russell made humble explanation, and in substance promised to do so no more. Accordingly when Mr. Mason some months later desired to see Earl Russell the latter was forced to decline an interview under the influence of this threat. Contrast this with the conduct of Mr. Dayton at Paris and your repeated interviews with the Emperor and unrestrained intercourse with the minister of foreign relations, and you can not fail to do justice to the acumen of Mr. Seward in discovering where it was safe to threaten and where it was prudent to refrain.

Your dispatches and those of Mr. Mason reach us more tardily and more irregularly than any others, and this results from the over-caution of Mr. Mason in intrusting his dispatches to private hands. It is entirely safe and much prompter to send them by the closed British mail to our agents at Nassau or Bermuda, whence they are forwarded by our Government steamers, which run with the regularity of packets. They have made about 30 passages through the "effective" blockade without a single loss.

We are impatiently awaiting news of your trip to Madrid and hope much from it.

I am, with great respect, etc.,

J. P. BENJAMIN,
Secretary of State.

Hon. JOHN SLIDELL, *Paris.*

NASSAU, N. P., *June 24, 1863.*

DEAR SIR: I enclose duplicate of my last of 12th instant; since then I received by a direct arrival two dispatches from Mr. Mason, which go forward by this opportunity under separate cover.

The British mail of the 6th instant is now due, but the steamer is not yet signaled. Should any dispatches come to hand, I shall make every effort to get them off either by the *Alice* or *Fanny*, both leaving this afternoon, and hurried off whether they have their complement of cargo or not, this being the last day when the state of the moon will justify a departure. No steamer can leave again until the 4th or 5th proximo.

I have no news.

Yours, very truly,

L. HEYLIGER.

Hon. J. P. BENJAMIN,
Secretary of State, Richmond.

No. 51.]

3 RUE D'ARLON,
Brussels, June 25, 1863.

SIR: The motion for our recognition in the British House of Commons, to be acted upon next Tuesday, stands, I am very certain, but little more chance to be carried than did its similar predecessor.

A letter which I have just received from a high and friendly English source, written at London yesterday, says:

> I confess I do not like Mr. Roebuck's motion. I fear he will be driven to divide, and he will be beaten by a large majority. If so, it will increase the arrogance of the Yankees, and still more alienate the South. I deprecate both results.

The time has at length arrived when, in my opinion, we can well afford to be indifferent to the formal recognition of our independence by any Government. There is assuredly not a statesman in either hemisphere, deserving of consideration as such, who can conscientiously assert that we are not justly entitled to a place in the family of nations, or that we are not in all respects more worthy of it than the dismembered United States. Injustice, the most flagrant and hurtful injustice, was committed by the western powers in not entering into relations with us when the measure was so earnestly urged by the King of the Belgians last autumn. Such a procedure might, and I believe would, have eventuated in terminating the war before the beginning of spring, and thus have prevented the ever-to-be-deplored loss of valuable life and blood which we have experienced since then. But the " divinity that shapes our ends" willed otherwise. In its mysterious dispensation it seems that we are required to suffer still more, and as I can not now doubt, for the ultimate realization of a vastly large amount of durable good and glory than would have been possible without such requirement.

As I calmly contemplate the broad scenes of operation at this distance I behold numerous cheering indications that we are conclusively to emerge from the field more eminently victorious in the creation of a mighty commonwealth of severing States than the most hopeful and far-seeing of our citizens ever believed. It is now distinct to my vision that in a comparatively short time we shall develop a republic that will exercise in its dignified administration of affairs as ·controlling an influence upon the destinies of the American Continent as France exercises upon the destinies of this Continent. We are steadily winning, and shall definitely win, to the entire satisfaction of enlightened humanity, our title as the chief power, par excellence, thereof. We have already so illustrated statesmanship, generalship, and soldiership as to furnish to the world an abundant guarantee of our future stability. Contemporaries and subsequent historians will award to our countrymen the designation of "Invincible cavaliers," whose heroism overpowered three times their number of semibarbarian Yankees. Indeed, the familiar appellatives of the two peoples in every land will, in all probability, be 'Cavaliers" and "Yankees"; the former ever admired, the latter ever detested.

The achievements of 1776, dazzling as they were, are well nigh eclipsed by the exceeding brilliancy and magnitude of our exploits during the present contest. In the long struggle of the colonists to cast off the rule of the Crown they contended with a foe who was not disregardful of civilized usages. The citizens of the Confederate States have had to battle against an enemy who has palpably and indiscriminately violated those usages; nor have those citizens received any aid whatever from abroad, as did Washington and his compatriots.

Of all the potentates and rulers of the earth, one alone (too feeble, alas, in the diminutiveness of his realm to give forcible expression to his wishes) had the recognition of our independence and our quick deliverance from Yankee aggressions upon our rights sincerely at heart. But we shall cut the Gordian knot ourselves, humbling our fiendish enemy to the very dust, and consequently forever remain free from such obligations as the United States came under, in their infancy, to France.

When the old Union was in the meridian of its greatness, annexing Texas in defiance of the "balance of power" doctrine of the cabinets of London and Paris, my pride was not infrequently wounded in my intercourse with the French by the remark in substance, "Without our timely intervention there had never been an independent America." Observations of such import concerning the Confederate States are forever precluded.

Thanks, eternal thanks to the Supreme Disposer of events, those States as far as relate to mortal agencies, have been the unassisted creators and maintainers of their lifelong cherished independence.

The journals of this metropolis announce that a "philanthropic American" has arrived here from Vienna, whither he has been on a like errand for the purpose of endeavoring to induce King Leopold to mediate for the restoration of peace. I have not seen nor heard from him. I would prefer that my tongue should be palsied and that my right hand should fall lifeless from the wrist to the employing of the one or the other in communication with miscreants of this kind. When the Lincoln concern is ready to treat for a cessation of hostilities it has no other mode to adopt, according to my notions of international propriety, than to address itself directly to President Davis. The sneaking Seward is likely to overrun Europe with secret agents of the kind referred to before autumn.

Now that the abolitionists are quite convinced that we can not be subdued they will resort to every imaginable artifice to procure a foreign intervention that will have for its basis the early destruction of our institution of negro slavery. Their leaders are doubtless persuaded that their own personal safety demands that they should show that they have accomplished something by the war. For a long time, as my dispatches will explain, my mind has not been entirely at ease upon the subject. I wish that I could justly dismiss my fears that the Emperor of the French is not animated by an arrière-pensée prejudical to our honor and our interests. It is reported that he has again made overtures to Lord Palmerston to unite with him in a proposition for an armistice and afterwards in a joint mediation. In my opinion nothing could be more injurious to our complete success than the cessation of hosilities on our part, however short the period, while a Yankee foot presses our venerated soil.

I have the honor to be, sir, very respectfully, your obedient servant,
                                          A. DUDLEY MANN.
Hon. J. P. BENJAMIN,
        Secretary of State, Confederate States of America,
                                          Richmond, Va.

No. 39.]   PARIS, *June 25, 1863.*

SIR: Referring to my No. 38 of 21st instant, I have now to report that the interview of Messrs. Roebuck and Lindsay with the Emperor at Fontainebleau was highly satisfactory; they were authorized to state in the House of Commons that the Emperor was not only willing but anxious to recognize the Confederate States with the cooperation of England. Mr. Lindsay will give Mr. Mason a written memorandum of the interview.

Before this can reach you you will doubtless have seen through the Northern papers an account of the changes in the ministry which were officially announced yesterday. The resignation of Count de Persigny was not unexpected, as his management of the elections and his very rigid control of the press had caused great dissatisfaction. Those of Count Walewski and Messrs. Delangle and Rouland have taken the public by surprise. The chief cause of these changes is, as I have good reason to believe, personal differences among members of the cabinet which have long existed, but which have recently manifested themselves in a way to render harmonious action no longer possible. I send you a newspaper containing the details of these changes. The three new ministers, Messrs. Boudet, Behic, and Duruy are men who, whatever may be their individual merit, are so little known to the country that it may be not unreasonably presumed that their appointments are merely provisional. Count de Persigny retains his place as member of the privy council, and enjoying, as he does, in the highest degree the personal confidence of the Emperor, he will still have it in his power to continue his good offices in our affairs. The Duke de Morny whom I frequently see is on a like footing with the Emperor; he is now and has been for several months a warm sympathizer with our cause.

The only political significance of the change of the cabinet is that they indicate stronger tendencies toward a constitutional régime and a determination not to press the Polish question in such a way as to endanger the peace of Europe. Mr. Lamar left Paris this morning for London, whence he purposes to proceed immediately to St. Petersburg. There seems to be but very slight prospect of his effecting anything in Russia at present. I agree with him in thinking that he might render better service at Vienna; he requests me to say that if the suggestion of a temporary change of residence meets with the approbation of the President he would be gratified by receiving instructions to that effect.

Messrs. Dupasseur & Co. have taken an appeal to the cour impériale from the judgment of the court of première instance, dismissing the suit against Erlanger & Co. I send you copy of the citation of appeal, marked A. It is customary here to call on the judges to make explanations of any matter pending before them. I was advised to follow this course by the minister of foreign affairs. I accordingly called yesterday by appointment on M. [Adrienne Marie] Devienne, first president of the imperial court of Paris. While with him the attorney-general came in and the affair was talked over. They asked me if I desired an early decision. I replied that would depend on the greater or less assurance I might have that the judgment of the inferior court would be sustained; if there were any doubt on the subject I would prefer that the case should be postponed. The attorney-general said that his particular attention had been called to it by the minister of foreign affairs, that he would look at it with the president (M. Devienne), and would see me on Monday next, when he would be prepared to give me an answer.

I am happy to inform you that the crops of cereals throughout Europe promise to be most abundant and must be better than an average, unless the weather should be very exceptionally unfavorable during the next four or five weeks. The probability is that prices of grain will be so low in Europe as to leave but a very small surplus to the farmers of the northwest after payment of cost of transportation to the seaboard and freight across the Atlantic.

I have the honor to be, with great respect, your most obedient servant,

JOHN SLIDELL.

Hon. J. P. BENJAMIN,
Secretary of State.

[Inclosure—Translation.]

The year 1863, the 5th June, on the petition of Messrs. Dupasseur, Lecoq Brothers & Co., in liquidation, living at Havre, for whom domicile is chosen at Paris, No. 49 rue Ste. Anne, in the office of Maitre Coeuré, attorney at law at the Imperial Court at Paris, who is appointed and will act for them upon the appeal and summons thereinafter and the further proceedings, I, the undersigned, Louis Auguste Potin, huissier [bailiff] of the civil court of the Seine, sitting at Paris, No. 64 rue Montmartre, have notified and declared to Messrs. Erlanger & Co., bankers, doing business at Paris, No. 21 rue de la Chaussée d'Antin, at the said domicile, by speaking to the concierge [porter] of the house, thus declared:

That the appellants are appealing, as in fact and by these presents they lodge an appeal from an order " de référé " issued by the presiding judge of the civil court [tribunal civil] of the Seine the 7th of May, 1863, after having heard the adverse parties, and on account of the wrong and injury caused them by this order.

And to have a decision rendered I have summoned them to appear in one week of legal days, term allowed by law, before the first president, the presiding judge, and the counsellors composing the first chamber of the Imperial Court of Paris, sitting at the Palais de Justice at Paris, at 10 o'clock in the morning.

Whereas Messrs. Dupasseur, Lecoq Brothers & Co. bought at New Orleans a vessel called the *Lemuel Dyer*, on which they shipped in the beginning of 1862, 2,683 bales of cotton.

Whereas in the month of April of this same year the ship with its entire cargo was destroyed by fire in the river at New Orleans by the order of the adjutant-general of the State, and with the participation of one of his officers.

Whereas the French consul immediately protested against this criminal act, which made the appellants lose about 2,400,000 francs, and reserved the rights of the injured parties as against the State or the authorities which represent it.

Whereas since that time the appellants have not been able to obtain satisfaction.

Whereas they applied to the minister of foreign affairs, but he replied to them on the 9th of April, 1863, that the Confederate States not being recognized by the Government [of France], it was impossible to follow the usual diplomatic course, and that Messrs Dupasseur, Lecoq Brothers & Co. should seek advice as to the means they shall.judge best to protect their interests.

Whereas they then applied to the presiding judge of the civil court and prayed of him authority to attach, in the hands of Messrs. Erlanger & Co., the funds of the loan arranged by them with the Confederate States, this order was granted to them the 11th of April, 1863, and the attachment was made the same day as security for a million [francs], amount of the provisional valuation of the sum due to them.

Whereas it was during the course of these proceedings that Messrs. Erlanger & Co., the garnishees, have asked " en référé " against the attaching creditors alone, for the revocation of the order of the 11th of April, 1863.

Whereas this order has been revoked by the order " de référé " on the .7th of May, from which appeal is taken.

Whereas this second order has been incompetently rendered, and consequently the appeal therefrom is admissible.

Whereas in effect it is unprecedented that a garnishee has the right to ask for a revocation of an order which authorizes garnishment; that he is no more competent to discuss the existence, nature, or the amount of the debt, than the urgency and expediency of a similar measure. He is absolutely a stranger to the contention until the day on which he himself is summoned to make discovery [déclaration affirmative]. From that day the judge " des référés " can no more entertain his petition than he could entertain that of anyone whose name does not even appear in the instance, than he could revoke, in virtue of his office and without a petition being made by anyone, the order authorizing the garnishment.

Whereas the exercise of the right " de référé " reserved by the order of the 11th of April is only reserved for the party whose property is attached.

Whereas, if it is indisputable that the presiding judge could not in virtue of his office revoke the order of the 11th of April after he had issued it, and it had been made use of by instituting regular proceedings, it is none the less certain that he could not do it on the motion of a third party, an absolute stranger to the question, without legal right or interest.

Whereas the presiding judge giving a decision " en référé " at the prayer of the garnishee has therefore exceeded his powers.

Whereas it is to no purpose that Messrs. Erlanger set forth that the attachment in the case at issue is of a nature to obstruct their financial operations with the Confederate States; it is hard to understand how that can be true; still nothing is easier for them than to free themselves from these real or pretended inconveniences by depositing in bank the sum of one million; moreover, if that were so, it is by means of a principal action that the point at issue should have been submitted to the courts.

Whereas they can no longer then maintain that the question raised is a question of international law, which is beyond the jurisdiction of the French courts; on the one hand that is incorrect, as the reply of the minister of foreign affairs proves; on the other hand, were it correct, the garnishee would not be qualified in any sense to avail himself of it, and thus obtain the revocation of an order to which he is a stranger.

Whereas, in short, it is too evident that the abnormal intervention of the garnishee has been conceived and settled between him and the representative of the Confederate States to conceal the person attached who dares not have himself represented and, however, will alone benefit by the revocation of the order.

For these reasons and all others that may be added by way of supplement:

To have the order rendered " en référé " reversed by the presiding judge of the civil court [tribunal civil] of the Seine of the 7th of May, 1863, between Messrs. Dupasseur, Lecoq Brothers & Co. and Messrs. Erlanger & Co. on the ground of incompetence, exceeding the limits of power, and as having been rendered on the petition of the garnishee, who had not the right to make a motion therefor.

To have the restitution of the fine ordered and to condemn them to pay the costs.

To the intent they may not plead ignorance, I have left the present copy at the domicile before declared, the cost being 14 francs 50 centimes.

POTIN.

No. 28.]   DEPARTMENT OF STATE,
                                        Richmond, June 29, 1863.

SIR: I observe that in my last (No. 27) I omitted to acknowledge receipt of your No. 37, which arrived on 12th instant, whereas the anterior Nos. 34 and 35 only arrived on 17th, and 36 is not yet received.

Your No. 37 was also accompanied by a triplicate of No. 28, of 31st January last; the original and duplicate of 28th seem to have been lost. I think I mentioned in a previous dispatch that Mr. ivlc, to whom you entrusted some dispatches and who was a passenger for qlbbqfkmv, was compelled to destroy them on the capture of the vessel in which he was passenger.

The matter referred to in No. 28 long since received our attention, as information upon the subject was received from another source.

I have nothing interesting to add to my last dispatch, as we now get our war news from the Northern papers, General Lee having carried his operations beyond the reach of our telegraphic wires. You will therefore receive news of his operations almost as soon as we can here.

Nothing yet received of the books, but I hear that there is a case for me on the *Venus*, which arrived a week or two ago at Wilmington. and hope it may be the books.

I am, sir, very respectfully, your obedient servant,

J. P. BENJAMIN,
Secretary of State.

Hon. JAMES M. MASON,
London.

No. 41.] CONFEDERATE STATES COMMISSION,
London, July 2, 1863.

SIR: Since my last (No. 40), dated the 20th of June, I have had the honor to receive your No. 22 of the 13th of May with a design of the new flag and copy of the act of Congress adopting it. I have also received your No. 23 of the 20th of May with the device for the new seal and the joint resolution establishing it. The flag has been generally admired here, and when the time comes authorizing me to raise it I shall feel great pride in unfolding it to England. In regard to the seal, I shall take very great pleasure in carrying out your instructions to have the work properly executed in London by the best artist to be had; already I have put it in train, as shown below.

A number of gentlemen in highest political and social position here have constituted themselves into a committee to build a monument to our great soldier, the late Lieutenant-General Jackson. The movement has been entirely spontaneous and voluntary on their part, and it was only after it had been entered upon that they communicated with me. I enclose herewith a copy of their circular just issued. Other names have been since added to the committee, of the highest nobility. It is certainly a graceful and I hope will be a grateful tribute to the memory of the illustrious dead, as well as to the country that gave him birth and honored him with its confidence. The subscription, I doubt not, will be a great success. I have promised these gentlemen to obtain for them as exact a likeness as can be had. Will you be so obliging as to aid me in this endeavor and send it out as early as practicable? There are some photographs of him here, but they do not confirm my recollections of his appearance. It is desirable, also, that the sculptor should have information as to his height and the general mold of his form. The artist named in the circular (Mr. Foley) is said to be the most eminent man in his profession, and Mr. Beresford Hope, himself a connoisseur in such matters, has advised that I should consult with Mr. Foley, invoking his professional skill to arrange the form of the seal, under the provisions of the joint resolution, and, probably, to select the artist to execute the work. Your instructions in regard to it shall be strictly pursued.

* * * * * * *

I enclose also herewith a report of the debate, from the London Times, on Mr. Roebuck's motion on the 30th of June. Mr. Slidell's dispatches, which go herewith, communicate to you the result of his late interview with the Emperor, and you will see from the debate (as reported by Mr. Roebuck) the conversation held with that gentleman and Mr. Lindsay by the Emperor. In the slip from the Times, also enclosed, you will see the reply made by Lord Russell to the enquiry made by Lord Stratheden on the same night in the House of Lords. These things put together would seem to reduce the professions made by the Emperor to Mr. Slidell and to Messrs. R. and L. to a mere shadow. It would seem, indeed, as if the Emperor held one language to those gentlemen in conversation intended to be made public but held a different language to his ambassador in London; and I add, as part of the history of the affair (as reported to me by Mr. Roebuck on the morning of the 30th of June), that to enable him to speak definitely in the House in regard to the communication promised by the Emperor to be made to England through Baron Gros, his ambassador here, that he called on that personage on the 29th and asked him (provided he felt at liberty to give the information) to tell him the substance of his communication to Earl Russell, and when it had been made; the reply to which was that he did not feel himself at liberty to give an answer to his question, but he would say that he had made no formal communication to Earl Russell on the subject. The debate was adjourned over and it is expected will be resumed to-night. Should this be so, I may have it in my power to communicate the result of this movement.

There appeared in the London papers of this morning a dispatch from you to me, dated the 6th of June, relating to the recent dismissal of the British consul at Richmond; it was taken from a late New York paper and is stated to have been copied from the Richmond Sentinel of the 12th. Its appearance in this form was my first acquaintance with it. The dispatch alone is published; the documents to which it refers are not included in the publication. I am instructed in the dispatch to furnish a copy to Earl Russell. My present idea is to send the printed copy to his lordship at once, telling him it shall be followed by a copy of the original when it reaches me. This incident may furnish the hint to communicate with me through the same channel whenever it may be desirable to get a dispatch to me without objection to its being equally known to the enemy.

I received by the last West India mail a letter from Mr. Heyliger at Nassau, transmitting a copy of the protest of the captain, officers, and crew of the steamship *Margaret and Jessie*, belonging to Charleston, stating, in substance, that the ship sailed from that port on the 27th of May, with a cargo of 730 bales of cotton and 16 passengers, bound to Nassau; that on the 31st of May, the ship then being about 90 miles from the island of Abaco and 25 miles from the island of Eleuthera, one of the Bahamas, they were chased by a steam vessel of war, firing at her, from time to time, until the former got within 300 yards of the shore, the war steamer approaching within 500. The *Margaret and Jessie*, then, to avoid striking the land, moved along the coast, the man-of-war, pursuing to within from two to three hundred yards, firing shot and shell, many of which went over the vessel and struck the shore. At length the *Margaret and Jessie*, not being more than 300 yards from the beach, was struck by a shell, which entered her boiler, severely injuring one of her engineers. The ship soon after struck and filled with water, and the man-of-war anchored a short distance off, and sent two armed boats, which rowed around her, the officers of which were in the naval uniform of the United States. On being hailed, an answer was returned from the boats that the cruiser was the U. S. ship of war *Savannah*, though the captain of the *Margaret and Jessie* believes she was the U. S. S. *Rhode Island*. The war steamer was all the time flying the United States flag, and was a brig-rigged side-wheel steamer. After the *Margaret and Jessie* grounded, the master, crew, and passengers quitted her, and landed, and soon after wreckers appearing from inland she was given over to them. The latter, after discharging the cargo, succeeded in floating the vessel, and, in charge of the wreckers, she was taken to Nassau with the captain on board, the crew and passengers going in some of the wrecking vessels. The wreckers have put in their claim for salvage, and the master, etc., protest accordingly. In Mr. Heyliger's letter he informs me that he is taking steps to collect testimony of inhabitants of that part of the island, who witnessed the affair, to be sent to me. I shall send the documents to Lord Russell, with the further evidence when it arrives, reserving the right to proper remuneration when put in by the owners.

July 3.—It has been arranged to resume the debate on Roebuck's motion on Monday, the 13th of July, with the assent of the Government; but last night the subject came up again in the house upon an explanation made by Mr. Layard, undersecretary for foreign affairs, of which I enclose a report,* in a slip from the Times. This gentleman more elaborately and pointedly denied the statements of the Emperor, as reported by Mr. Roebuck. The matter charged, in so much of it as referred to the alleged betrayal by the Government here to that at Washington, of communications from France touching American affairs, was erroneously conceived by the undersecretary. He referred it to the late communication from France, containing proposals for an armistice, mediation, etc., whereas the complaint made by the Emperor went back to a period antecedent to April, 1862; and was made by him in conversations then held, both

---

* Not found.

with Mr. Slidell and Mr. Lindsay. I find it, thus referred to in my No. 8 of April 21, 1862, reporting what had passed between Mr. Lindsay and the Emperor on the 18th of that month, namely:

That Earl Russell had dealt unfairly, in sending to Lord Lyons his previous propositions to England, in regard to action on the blockade, who had made them known to Mr. Seward; and this letter was an insuperable objection to his again communicating officially at London touching American affairs until he knew England was in accord.

Mr. Lindsay, who is au fait in the whole matter, will doubtless present the true issue when the debate is resumed on the 13th. The undersecretary, as you will see, also reiterated the denial that any communication on the subject of American affairs had been recently received from the Emperor; in which denial, he said, the foreign office was backed by Baron Gros, the French ambassador. These collateral issues are used in Parliament only to damage the ministry, though if established, we may have the incidental benefit.

The Paris correspondent of the Times, who is generally considered accurate, in his letter published this morning says that private letters from Madrid inform him that the Spanish Government had been sounded on the question of recognition, with an intimation that if Spain was ready she would have the support of France. This latter power would seem to be playing a complicated diplomatic game, but under what form of policy I am not skillful enough to divine.

I enclose also from the Times a concluding report* of the case of the *Alexandra*. The principles established by the chief baron, in the opinion of the court, may (if adhered to) free us from future embarrassments.

I have the honor to be, very respectfully, your obedient servant,

J. M. MASON.

Hon. J. P. BENJAMIN,
Secretary of State.

[Enclosure.]

GENERAL THOMAS J. (STONEWALL) JACKSON.

Two continents, both friend and foe, combine to mourn the premature death of General Jackson, hero and Christian. Two years have been sufficient to create a fame which has won the kindly respect of enemies and the admiration of the Old World, which twenty-four months since was ignorant of his existence.

It has been suggested that some general recognition from Great Britain of the worth of such a man, by name, by race, and by character related to us, although the citizen of another land, would be a graceful token of friendly feeling from the old country to our kinsmen across the Atlantic.

The eminent sculptor, J. H. Foley, esq., R. A., has undertaken to execute a marble statute, heroic size, of the general for £1,000, while £500 may be required for pedestal, inscription, and other extras. Accordingly, for £1,500 a complete statue of "Stonewall" Jackson, by one of our most distinguished sculptors, may be prepared for transmission to his native country when the unhappy war shall have

---

* Not found.

ceased. Toward raising this sum, the subscriptions of our country-men and countrywomen are earnestly solicited. Central and local committees, with auxiliary ladies' committees, are being formed to collect the necessary funds.

The undersigned will gladly receive subscriptions until the final arrangements are made and an account has been opened for "General Jackson's Statue," at Messrs. Coutts & Co.'s, Strand, London, W. C.

N. B.—It is not at all intended that subscriptions to the statue should imply any opinion on the merits of the American struggle. They will be taken solely and simply as a recognition of the rare personal merit of General Jackson.

A. J. B. BERESFORD HOPE, Esq.
Lord CAMPBELL.
Sir JAMES FERGUSSON, Bart., M. P.
W. H. GREGORY, Esq., M. P.
Sir E. KERRISON, Bart., M. P.
Lord EUSTACE CECIL.
Hon. EARNEST DUNCOMBE, M. P.
Hon. C. FITZWILLIAM.
J. LAIRD, M. P.

Sir COUTTS LINDSAY, Bart.
W. LINDSAY, Esq., M. P.
G. PEACOCKE, Esq., M. P.
G. E. Seymour, Esq.
J. SPENCE, Esq.
EARL OF DONOUGHMORE.
Sir EARDLEY EARDLEY, Bart.
Col. GREVILLE, M. P.
Committee.

A. J. B. BERESFORD HOPE, Esq.,
1 Connaught Place, Hon. Treasurer.

W. H. GREGORY, Esq., M. P.,
19 Grosvenor Street W.,
Hon. Secretary.

DEPARTMENT OF STATE,
Richmond, July 3, 1863.

SIR: You have, in accordance with your proposals made to this Department, been detailed by the Secretary of War for special service under my orders.

The duty which is proposed to entrust to you is that of a private and confidential agent of this Government for the purpose of proceeding to Ireland and there using all legitimate means to enlighten the population as to the true nature and character of the contest now waged on this continent, with the view of defeating the attempts made by the agents of the United States to obtain in Ireland recruits for their armies. It is understood that under the guise of assisting needy persons to emigrate, a regular organization has been formed of agents in Ireland who leave untried no method of deceiving the laboring population into emigrating, for the ostensible purpose of seeking employment in the United States, but really for recruiting the Federal armies.

The means to be used by you can scarcely be suggested from this side, but they are to be confined to such as are strictly legitimate, honorable, and proper. We rely on truth and justice alone. Throw yourself as much as possible into close communication with the people where the agents of our enemies are at work. Inform them by every means you can devise of the true purposes of those who seek to induce them to emigrate. Explain to them the nature of the warfare which is carried on here. Picture to them the fate of their unhappy countrymen who have already fallen victims to the arts of the Federals. Relate to them the story of Meagher's brigade, its formation and its fate. Explain to them that they will be called on to meet Irishmen in battle, and thus imbrue their hands in the blood of their own friends and perhaps kinsmen, in a quarrel which does not concern them and in which all the feelings of a common humanity should induce them to refuse taking part against us. Contrast the policy of the Federal and Confederate States in former times in their treatment of foreigners, in order to satisfy Irishmen where true sympathy in their favor was found in periods of trial. At the North, the Know Nothing Party, based on hatred to foreigners and especially to Catholics, was triumphant in its career. In the South it was crushed, Virginia taking the lead in trampling it under foot. In this war such has been the hatred of the New England Puritans to Irishmen and Catholics, that in several instances the chapels and places of worship of the Irish Catholics have been burnt or shamefully desecrated by the regiments of volunteers from New England. These facts have been published in Northern papers. Take the New York Freeman's Journal and you will see shocking details, not coming from Confederate sources, but from the officers of the United States themselves. Lay all these matters fully before the people who are now called on to join these ferocious persecutors in the destruction of the Nation where all religions and all nationalities meet equal justice and protection, both from the people and the laws.

These views may be urged by any proper means you can devise; through the press, by mixing with the people themselves, and by disseminating the facts amongst persons who have influence with the people.

The laws of England must be strictly respected and obeyed by you. While prudence dictates that you should not reveal your agency nor the purposes for which you go abroad, it is not desired nor expected that you use any dishonest disguise or false pretenses. Your mission is, although secret, honorable; and the means employed must be such as this Government may fearlessly avow and openly justify, if your conduct should ever be called into question. On this point there must be no room whatever for doubt or cavil.

The Government expects much from your zeal, activity and discretion. You will be furnished with letters of introduction to our agent abroad. You will receive the same pay as you now get as first lieutenant of cavalry, namely, £21 sterling per month, being about equal to $100. Your passage to and from Europe will be furnished by this Department. If you need any small sums for disbursement of expenses connected with your duties, such as costs of printing and the like, you will apply to the agent to whom I give you a letter, and who will provide the funds if he approves the expenditure.

You will report your proceedings to this Department through the agent to whom your letter of introduction is addressed as often at least as once a month.

I am, respectfully, your obedient servant,

J. P. BENJAMIN,
Secretary of State.

Lieut. J. L. CAPSTON, etc.

No. 24.]   CONFEDERATE STATES COMMERCIAL AGENCY,
                                    London, July 4, 1863.

SIR: The extraordinary occurrences of the last two weeks, which form the theme of conversation in every political circle in England and on the Continent, do not fall within my province, except so far as it is my duty to give you a connected narrative of all events which effect our status in public opinion. I shall therefore present to you simply the view of a spectator and leave to those better qualified the solution of the mystery which baffles the ingenuity of editors and politicians. About the beginning of the last week in June it became a generally accredited rumor that the French Emperor was about to make, if he had not already made, an important communication to the English Government on the subject of American affairs. This communication was represented to be a renewed invitation to join France in such measures as might be best calculated to restore peace, not stopping short of recognition, should England be prepared for that step.

This rumor rested primarily upon the statements more or less explicit of various continental and English journals, notably the Times of 24th of June, copied into the Index of the 25th. It was moreover known to be substantially confirmed by private letters from Mr. Slidell in reply to inquiries. The following are the facts as they are generally believed. In an interview with Mr. Slidell the Emperor had assured our representative in the most cordial terms of his continued friendly feelings toward the Confederate States; of his disposition to take any steps promotive of peace in which England could be induced to concur; and finally, of his intention to renew in some form, which would be decided in cabinet council, almost immediately his proposals to that power. This interview was on a Thursday, the cabinet council on Saturday, and on the Monday following Messrs. Lindsay and Roebuck also had an interview with the Emperor, in which he is reported to have held much the same language as with Mr. Slidell, but to have added that self-respect forbade his making a formal application inasmuch as an improper use had been made of his former communications with the British Government on the same subject. The inference was that the council had decided upon an indirect form of communication, but no one had any reason to doubt the existence of a document of some kind. Indeed, there were those who could repeat some of the words of the text, and a supposed well-informed French publication, the Memorial Diplomatique, professed to state the very day on which it had beeen dispatched to London and the date of the expected reply.

The public was not therefore altogether surprised at Mr. Roebuck's double statement on Thursday the 30th June in the house, viz, first, that he had the Emperor's own authority for saying that a communication expressive of his views had actually been made to the British Government; and secondly, that this communication was not direct and formal only because a previous communication had been improperly imparted to the Washington Government. The first part of this statement was at once denied point blank and in the most unequivocal manner by Mr. Layard and Sir George Grey in the one house and by Earl Russell in the other. The denial of the latter was sharpened by the circumstance that only that afternoon the French ambassador had spontaneously called on him with the assurance that no instructions whatever on the American question had been received from the French Government. On last Thursday evening the other statement of Mr. Roebuck, supposing it to have reference to the Emperor's proffer of mediation in November, as Mr. Roebuck evidently intended, was clearly disproved by the obvious fact that the French note was published in the Moniteur almost simultaneously with its delivery to the cabinets of London and of St. Petersburg, and in the published form actually reached Washington before it was physically possible to have reached through any official channels.

This triumphant exculpation of the ministry from charges made as it appears to an English public in so extraordinary a manner and at the instigation of a foreign sovereign, a circumstance always most offensive to the national susceptibilities, has, as you may suppose, recoiled with crushing effect upon their accusers. One part of the mystery may be explained on the supposition which I understand to be correct, though it has not yet been publicly stated, that the Emperor referred, not to his mediation proposal in November, but to a confidential communication made long antecedent, as the document which had been improperly divulged to the Washington Government. The other part of this singular imbroglio can be explained only on the assumption that the Emperor's policy, whether from misrepresentations of the American minister at Paris, or in virtue of concessions made to the French opposition which is bitterly hostile to our cause, has undergone a change in the interval between Mr. Roebuck's visit and his speech in Parliament. However this may be the occurrence is calculated to awake distrust in the English mind, which is only too ready to receive such impression, as to the Emperor's sincerity or fixedness of purpose. Per contra it raises public confidence in the cabinet and causes their hesitancy to appear in the light of well-grounded prudence. English prejudices are very strong and in a case like this will infallibly be arrayed against the foreign State, particularly if that State is France. I am, however, strongly in hope that the Emperor, feeling the necessity of setting himself right before the public opinion of all Europe, will take such steps for doing so as to leave us no cause to regret this annoying diplomatic contretemps.

As I had predicted, the *Alexandra*, the trial of which came off on the 22d ultimo, was acquitted amid shouts of applause from the audience. A new trial will indeed take place upon a "bill of exceptions" on behalf of the Crown, but with scarcely a prospect of it different result. A summarized report of the trial will be found in the Index of 25th June. The construction of the foreign enlistment act, as relating to ships, now for the first time judicially made, is, as you will perceive, of immense importance.

It is reported that Russia has accepted the joint propositions of the great powers for the pacification of Poland. If true, it averts for the moment the danger of a European war, but I can not yet permit myself to hope that this untoward question will thereby be removed from our path. The King of the Belgians, as arbitrator between

England and Brazil, has given his award decidedly against the former, thus convicting Earl Russell before the world of wanton insult and gross injustice toward a comparatively defenseless power. His popularity is evidently on the wane, and there were rumors on change in Liverpool last week of his resignation, which slightly affected the market, but appears to have been unfounded. It is such occurrences as the French imbroglio that prop up his tottering position. We have the text of the letters patent revoking exequatur of Consul Moore and your published dispatch to Mr. Mason explaining more fully the reasons. The press has thus far made no comments, but the impression produced by the step is, I am inclined to think, wholesome. The time has undoubtedly arrived when we have little to gain by a conciliatory policy, and when we may with manifest advantage assert our national dignity to the fullest extent.

The news of General Lee's advance has been received with great satisfaction here. The judgment of the press may be summarized in the opinion that the time is well chosen and that the South has much to gain and little to lose in the issue, while the North has nothing to gain and everything to lose. You will observe in the reports of Tuesday's debate that even the most sanguine Federal sympathizers, Mr. Bright and Mr. Forster, despair of Northern conquest and virtually confess that the subjugation of the North by the South is more within the range of probability. News of the relief of Vicksburg is, however, still awaited with anxiety.

I have the honor to acknowledge the receipt of dispatches for Mr. Slidell and Mr. Mason, which were duly forwarded.

I have the honor to remain, very respectfully, your obedient servant,
HENRY HOTZE.

Hon. J. P. BENJAMIN,
  Secretary of State, Richmond.

No. 40.]   PARIS, *July 6, 1863.*

SIR: Since my last of June 25 I am in possession of your No. 17 and am pleased to hear that my missing dispatches Nos. 1, 2, 3, 4, and 6 had at last reached their destination. You will have seen through the newspapers the debates in the House of Commons on Mr. Roebuck's motion, the declaration of Earl Russell in the House of Peers on the same evening, and the statement made by Mr. Layard two days after. They present grave issues of veracity, which are not yet solved. One thing, however, is certain. Mr. Roebuck did not misstate his conversation with the Emperor; he and Mr. Lindsay came to see me immediately on their return from Fontainebleau and related their interview exactly as Mr. Roebuck gave it in the House of Commons. You will find, too, that his statement tallies almost exactly with my memorandum of what the Emperor said to me at the Tuileries on the 18th June. If further confirmation were needed, it would be furnished by M. Mocquard's note of 21st June, of which I sent you a copy in my No. 38. I give you herewith copy marked "A" of a letter which Mr. Roebuck addressed me the day after making his speech, with a request that I should bring it before the Emperor. This I did through M. Mocquard. I also sent a copy of it to M. Drouyn de Lhuys. On the 4th instant M. Drouyn de Lhuys went to Fontainebleau to see the Emperor, and on the next morning the following article appeared in the Moniteur:

[Newspaper clipping.]

The papers have reported an incident which took place during the sitting of the House of Commons last Tuesday on the occasion of a motion by Mr. Roebuck. A few explanations will suffice to dissipate the misunderstandings to which this incident gave rise.

Messrs. Roebuck and Lindsay came to Fontainebleau so as to induce the Emperor to take some official steps in London for the recognition of the Southern States, because, in their opinion, this recognition would put an end to the strife which is staining with blood the United States.

The Emperor expressed to them his desire to see peace reestablished in those countries, but observed to them that the proposal of mediation addressed to London in the month of October last not having been accepted by England, he did not feel called upon to make another before being sure of its acceptance; nevertheless the French ambassador at London would receive instructions to sound the intentions of Lord Palmerston on the subject and to let him understand that should the English cabinet believe that the recognition of the South would put an end to the war, the Emperor would be disposed to follow it, with that end in view.

Any impartial man will see by this simple explanation that the Emperor did not seek, as certain of the press pretend, to influence the British Parliament through the intervention of two of its members, and that everything was limited to frank explanations exchanged in an interview which the Emperor had no reason whatever to refuse.

While writing I received a communication from M. Mocquard of which I send you copy and annex translation marked " B."

*   *   *   *   *   *   *

You will find by the above that Mr. Roebuck is fully borne out in all that he said of the Emperor's desire to recognize the South, and of his having directed overtures to that effect to be made to the British Government. I am inclined also to believe that the Emperor did complain that previous overtures made by him to England on the subject of American affairs had been communicated in an unfriendly spirit to the Washington Government. You will find I think sufficient for this belief in my report of a conversation which Mr. Lindsay had with the Emperor on 18th April, 1862, contained in my No. 6, and in what fell from M. Drouyn de Lhuys in my interview with him on the 20th June, mentioned in my No. 38. This, however, is a matter of minor importance. We have now positive proof that the Emperor did direct that his ambassador should inform the British Government that he was ready to acknowledge the Confederate States. Either then the minister of foreign affairs failed to obey the Emperor's instructions, Baron Gros did not obey the instructions of his chief, or Earl Russell and Mr. Layard have deliberately stated what was false in spirit if not in letter. You will naturally desire to know what is my opinion on the subject, I give it although with some hesitation. I suspect that M. Drouyn de Lhuys has not carried out in good faith the wishes of his sovereign; he is a man of timid temperament, fond of little diplomatic finesses, and is very far from being as decided as the Emperor in his views of the policy to be pursued in our affairs. He is moreover very susceptible and jealous of any interference with his peculiar functions, and he may have been dissatisfied that the Emperor should have conferred with me and others on a diplomatic question.

There is still another hypothesis which would relieve Messrs. Russell and Layard from the charge of deliberate falsehood. My friend

Baron Gros was directed to approach Lord Palmerston on the subject of recognition; it is barely possible, although extremely improbable, that he may have done so, and that the premier, either designedly or from neglect, may have failed to inform his colleague of the fact. My friend also informs me that the minister read to him part of the letter from the Emperor which related to our affairs. After instructing him to direct Baron Gros to sound Lord Palmerston on the subject of recognition, he added: "I question whether I should not have it said officially to Lord Palmerston that I have decided to recognize the Confederate States." This is going much further than anything he has ever said to me. I do not know whether you will read it as I do. I think that his doubt is not as to whether he should recognize us, but whether he should inform Lord Palmerston that he had made up his mind to do so.

The Emperor goes to-morrow to Vichy, where he will remain three weeks. If Mr. Roebuck's motion shall be defeated, as it probably will be on the 13th instant, I shall await the Emperor's return before taking any further action.

Mr. Charles Lafitte has now made a direct proposition for a loan. He says that he has secured the cooperation of strong Dutch capitalists. His proposition, however, is not as favorable as that of another combination of bankers who have called upon me. On my stating this to him he said he would modify it in such a way as he thought would be satisfactory. Erlanger & Co. also intend to send agents to Richmond to negotiate another loan. Mr. McRae is now absent, but will return in a few days, when I will confer with him fully and put him in communication with the parties who have approached me on this subject. At all events it is a favorable symptom of the state of public opinion in Europe that offers of money should come from several different quarters. I doubt if any similar applications have been made to Mr. Dayton or to Mr. Adams.

I observe by Southern journals that oil bears a very high price in the Confederacy. I do not know that the attention of our farmers has been turned toward the use of the ground nut or peanut, known in Louisiana as the pistache, for the manufacturing of oil. Large cargoes are imported here from Africa for that purpose, and the oil extracted from it, called here "huile d'arachides," is used as a substitute for olive oil, is by many esteemed as good, and brings nearly as high a price; it might be well to make this fact generally known. I send you some papers relating to W. Fellows, jr., son of an old friend of yours. I beg that you will place them before the Secretary of War and invoke your good offices in facilitating his exchange. I shall confer fully with Lieutenant Whittle, who will be the bearer of this dispatch, and give him certain information which I do not deem prudent to commit to writing.

Mr. Isturitz informs me that he has only received from Madrid a simple acknowledgment of the arrival of his dispatch communicating what I had said to him respecting Cuba. He expects, by his next courier, on the 13th instant, to receive the views of his Government on the subject and promises to inform me of their purport.

With great respect, your most obedient servant,

JOHN SLIDELL.

Hon. J. P. BENJAMIN,
Secretary of State.

[Enclosure A.]

LONDON, *July 1, 1863.*

MY DEAR SIR: One incident of last night induces me to trouble you to-day. In my speech, in order to show that my proposal to ask the Queen to enter into negotiations with foreign powers was a wise proposal, I stated that his Majesty, the Emperor, had given me permission to state in the House of Commons what had passed between us. I stated that his Majesty had told me that he on hearing a rumor was prevalent in London that he had changed his mind on the subject of recognition had sent instructions to Baron Gros to deny the truth of that rumor, and further that he had instructed his ambassador to inquire of the English Government whether they were prepared now to entertain the question of recognition, and to state that if they were so, he, the Emperor, was ready to act with them and would be glad of their resolution. I then went on to say that I had suggested to his Majesty that he through his ambassador should make a formal proposal to that effect to the English Government. That his Majesty had thereupon said to me that he could not do so and that he would tell me the reason why; that some time last year he had made such a formal proposition to England, that his dispatch had been sent to Lord Lyons, by whom it had been shown to Mr. Seward, who had complained to the French minister at Washington of this, his Majesty's proceedings. Now, said the Emperor, I deemed myself ill treated in this matter, and I can not subject myself again to be so dealth with.

During the debate, in order to destroy or diminish the effect of this history, Sir George Grey said that it had been stated in the House of Lords by Lord Russell that Baron Gros had been to him that afternoon, saying that he had read the Times of that day and that he had come to say to him, Lord Russell, that he, Baron Gros, had received no such instructions. Sir George Grey further said that nothing of the sort I described had occurred with reference to the Emperor's dispatch; that he did not in the least doubt my veracity, thereby plainly insinuating that the want of truth was on the other side of the water.

Now, I am anxious that his Majesty should know on my authority that such things were said last night. His Majesty will know full well that I told simply what he said to me and he will be able to ascertain where the error lies. I can not presume to write myself to his Majesty, but it has suggested itself to me that you by some means can have this, my letter, laid before his Majesty. The debate will be resumed in a week; I have the right of reply and should be greatly delighted if his Majesty would kindly give me the means of making the requisite explanations.

I am told that Disraeli in the adjourned debate will come out on our side.

Yours, very truly,

J. A. ROEBUCK,

[Enclosure B.]

FONTAINEBLEAU, *July 6, 1863.*

MY DEAR MR. SLIDELL: You will find enclosed a note I am requested to send you in reply to the letter of which you desired me to make the communication.

Please to receive, my dear Mr. Slidell, the renewed assurance of my best and affectionate feelings.

MOCQUARD.

NOTE.

The Emperor having been informed fifteen days ago that the report had been spread in London of his Majesty having changed his opinion as regards the recognition of the South, M. Drouyn de Lhuys wrote to Baron Gros that he should refute the said report.

Meantime MM. Roebuck and Lindsay came over and paid a visit to the Emperor, whom they invited to make an official application to the British cabinet toward the recognition of the South. His Majesty replied that such a step was not practicable before knowing whether it would be agreed to, since the first proposal of mediation had met with a denial, and his Majesty had been told (a thing of which he had, it is true, no proof) that the cabinet of London boasted at Washington of declining such of the Emperor's proposals as were in favor of the South. Now his Majesty has neither cause nor feeling of animosity toward the United States, and it is but with the hope of seeing an end to be put to a war already too long, that he considered the recognition of the South as a speedier means to bring about peace. The Emperor could not have spoken to Mr. Roebuck of any dispatch or dispatches exhibited by Lord Lyons to Mr. Seward, because there were none but those which have been published. However, his Majesty does regret Mr. Roebuck's making public an entirely confidential explanation.

We must add on the next day after the interview of Messrs. [Roebuck] and Lindsay with the Emperor, the minister of foreign affairs wrote by telegraph to Baron Gros, to officiously [semiofficially] inform Lord Palmerston that should Great Britain be willing to recognize the South, the Emperor would be ready to follow her in that way.

No. 29.]

DEPARTMENT OF STATE,
Richmond, July 6, 1863.

SIR: Your No. 36 of 11th May was received on 30th ultimo, and on the 4th instant I received your dispatch from Paris, not numbered, bearing date the 4th of June. This last is the quickest communication yet had with you.

I note what you state in relation to the recruiting by the enemy in Ireland. While it is satisfactory to know that you are diligent in the matter, we have determined to send two or three Irishmen, long residents of our country, to act as far as they can in arresting these unlawful acts of the enemy, by communicating directly with the people and spreading among them such information and intelligence as may be best adapted to persuade them of the folly and wickedness of volunteering their aid in the savage warfare waged against us. I enclose you copy of the instructions to one of them, that you may be fully possessed of our motives and purposes.

I have no special news for you. The details of the Army operations must now reach you through Northern sources, as General Lee is too far removed to enable us to communicate freely with him. In Louisiana we have succeeded in wresting from the enemy the whole State, except in the immediate vicinity of New Orleans on the east bank of the river. No fears whatever are entertained of the result at Port Hudson, and our prospects at Vicksburg are brightening fast, through the operations of General Kirby Smith and Richard Taylor in western Louisiana.

The President has been seriously ill, but is now fast recovering.

I am, very respectfully, your obedient servant.

J. P. BENJAMIN,
Secretary of State.

Hon. J. M. MASON, ect.,

No. 42]
CONFEDERATE STATES COMMISSION,
London, July 10, 1863.

SIR: My last was No. 41 of the 2d instant, of which I have the honor to send a duplicate herewith. I enclose, also, copies of two communications to Earl Russell, dated, respectively, the 4th and 10th of July; the first containing a newspaper slip of your dispatch of the 6th of June, referred to in my No. 41, with the reply of Lord Russell acknowledging its receipt; the second transmitting to him the protest of the master and crew of the Confederate steamer *Margaret and Jessie,* the subject of which protest you will find set-forth in the communication. Since this was sent to Lord Russell the subject was brought before the House of Commons, and in reply to a question there put, Lord Russell stated that he had received a dispatch from Lord Lyons referring to it, in which the latter states that Mr. Seward informed him that the captain of the United States cruiser denied that the Confederate steamer had been pursued within the limits of British jurisdiction; but stated, further, that full enquiries should be made, and if the contrary appeared, the United States were prepared to make full reparation. I could make no claim in the present position of the case from the British Government; but if the circumstances are as stated in the protest, presume I shall be authorized to do so in good time.

There has been no further debate on Mr. Roebuck's motion since the date of my last; but the imbroglio which then presented itself on the French question, to which I referred, has been somewhat solved by the enclosed slip (translated) from the Moniteur of the 4th instant. You will find, also, in the slip, other matter referring to the same subject. The debate stands adjourned to Monday the 13th instant. In a note from Mr. Slidell dated yesterday he says:

As regards what was said of recognition by the Emperor, I am satisfied that he has kept his promise with good faith. Either the minister of foreign affairs or Baron Gros, or both, have failed to carry out his instructions, or Lord Russell or Mr. Layard have asserted what is false. Perhaps Lord Palmerston may have received the communication and failed to inform his colleagues of the fact.

The House of Commons is manifestly much agitated by the entanglements around the question as it rests since the last debate; and I think it not improbable that some new phase of it may be presented, before closing this dispatch to-morrow. I am assured from every quarter, and such is the result of my own observation, that four-fifths as least of the House of Commons are with us; but as parties stand there between the ministry and the opposition, it is thought if Roebuck's motion should go to a vote, it would be rejected.

We are anxiously awaiting the steamer due to-morrow, by which we confidently expect something definite from General Lee's movements into Maryland and Pennsylvania.

This goes by an officer sent over by Captain Bulloch. He will not leave until to-morrow night, and I may have the opportunity of adding to it, should anything occur meanwhile.

I send another copy of the circular relative to the British Jackson Monument, with names that have been since added to the committee.

July 11.—The debate on Roebuck's motion was resumed last night. I send it to you as reported in the Times of this morning. As you are aware, Sir James Fergusson, who appealed to Mr. Roebuck to consent to a postponement of the debate, is one of the earliest and most earnest friends of the cause of the South; and it was a good sign that Lord Palmerston immediately united with Sir James in this appeal. The occasion was further marked, too, by the admission of Lord Palmerston, that the opinions of the French Emperor were now well known, an admission never heretofore made by the minister, and that England was now ready to interchange views with France on the American question. To be sure, Lord Palmerston made the admission in a manner qualified designedly to take from its force. Still, it is a great step gained. You will see from the general tenor of the debate that our friends who spoke were all in favor of the adjournment, with our adversaries against it.

The great movements of General Lee, which have just reached us, had much to do in influencing the opinions of our friends in favor of the postponement. The holding back on the part of Roebuck and Lindsay was designed only to bring the premier, if possible, to a more full committal.

The question will again come before the House on Monday next, but eventually the debate will be postponed. ·

Our reports brought from the North by telegraph from Queenstown are to the 1st of July instant. They would seem to indicate that Lee is perfectly master of the field of his operations, both in Maryland and Pennsylvania, and that Washington must speedily fall (with Baltimore as accessory) into his posession. Should this be realized before Parliament adjourns, I do not think the ministry would hold out against recognition; or, if they did, the House of Commons would overrule them.

It is expected that Parliament will adjourn about the first week in August.

I have the honor to be, very respectfully, your obedient servant,

J. M. MASON.

Hon. J. P. BENJAMIN,
 Secretary of State.

[Enclosure.]

24 UPPER SEYMOUR STREET, PORTMAN SQUARE,
July 4, 1863.

MY LORD: The newspaper slip which I have the honor to enclose herewith contains what purports to be the copy of a dispatch from the Secretary State of the Confederate States addressed to me as the commissioner of those States in London, dated on the 6th of June ultimo. It is taken from one of the public journals of London published within the last two days and, as you will see from the introductory note, was transferred from a newspaper published at Richmond, Va., on the 12th of the same month. I do not doubt that it is a genuine paper and, as it refers to the action of the Confederate Government on a subject that may be interesting to the

Government of her Majesty, I have thought it best to send it to you at once in the informal shape in which it has come before me.

None of the documents referred to in the dispatch were published in the newspaper from which I have taken it; but from another, published yesterday, I have taken the enclosed, marked No. 2, which show·for their dates, and import that they are the documents desig-nated in the dispatch by the letters C and D.

You will see that I am instructed by the President to communicate to your lordship a copy of this dispatch, and of the documents accompanying it, which I shall have the honor to do when they shall arrive.

I have the honor to be your lordship's very obedient servant
J. M. MASON.

Right Hon. EARL RUSSELL,
    H. B. M. Secretary of State for Foreign Affairs.

FOREIGN OFFICE, July 8, 1863.

SIR: I have the honor to acknowledge the receipt of your letter of the 4th instant, and its enclosures, relative to the position of Mr. G. Moore, as her Majesty's consul at Richmond.

I have the honor to be, sir, your most obedient humble servant,
RUSSELL.

J. M. MASON, Esq.,
    24 Upper Seymour Street.

No. 25.]   CONFEDERATE STATES COMMERCIAL AGENCY,
London, July 11, 1863.

SIR: Since my last the Moniteur has spoken and, making allowance for the difference in the dramatis personæ, you will perceive that there is no essential discrepancy between the Emperor's version and Mr. Roebuck's of the principal subject of their conversation. The Emperor avows himself ready to recognize the South in concert with England, and distinctly declares his intention of signifying this readiness to the English Government. That he has carried this latter intention into effect, and that the French ambassador was charged as early as the 24th or 25th June at latest, with a communication not to Earl Russell but to Lord Palmerston, is a fact difficult to reconcile with the volunteered visit to the foreign secretary on the afternoon of the 30th, but is nevertheless an indisputable fact. On the subject of the Emperor's alleged complaint of ill-usage at the hands of the English foreign office, the Moniteur is of course silent; but here lies Mr. Lindsay's strongest point in coming to the rescue of Mr. Roebuck. This complaint having been confided to him when he approached the Emperor at the request and on behalf of the foreign office, the charge of amateur diplomacy recoils upon his employers; and as he at the time duly communicated it both to Lord Cowley and Earl Russell, the latter can not well plead ignorance. There is therefore no lack of weapons wherewith to take revenge for the unfair and merciless manner in which the ministry has pushed its advantage over the discomfited advocates of recognition.

The whole armory of sarcasm, denunciation, and worst of all, of ridicule, has been exhausted upon their devoted heads, and it is not in human nature that they should forego an opportunity for retaliation. But the cause of the Confederacy has no longer aught to hope, though still much to fear, from Mr. Roebuck's motion. All the resources of Southern strategy will be needed to secure a decent retreat, which the radicals threaten to cut off by insisting on a division. In Parliament some of the truest friends of recognition would not vote for the motion, marred and blurred as it now is by delicate and dangerous excrescences. Outside the house it is impossible for the public through the mist and smoke that has been conjured up around, to see even the outlines, much less the real proportions, of the French appeal to England. To the vast mass of careless observers the step of the Emperor is not a grave diplomatic measure, imposing a fearful responsibility upon this country, but simply a sort of farce in which Mr. Roebuck acted a broadly comic part. Punch, which is sometimes singularly felicitous in seizing and reflecting the passing phase of popular opinion, devotes itself this week to this idea, ringing the changes upon it on every page and in every conceivable manner. Against such a settled current, so long as it flows, no reason or argument or facts can prevail; gravity or anger only increase the mirth at the expense of the sufferers. I write it with pain and sorrow, but we have lost a great opportunity. The French proposal and the military situation were two levers which might have lifted more weighty obstacles than the present ministry from our path to recognition; instead of removing obstacles, we have succeeded only in rendering that path altogether impracticable. Henceforward to my thinking recognition depends solely on the judgment and courage of Lord Palmerston. In Parliament it will never again receive serious attention, even if a man could be found bold enough to broach it after the experience of the last two weeks.

Aside from this parliamentary misfortune, we are making rapid strides in public opinion. The advance of General Lee is watched with breathless attention and undisguised satisfaction. The apathy of the masses of the Northern population under actual invasion of their soil, and the helplessness of the Washington Government, are the objects of contemptuous sneer and bid fair to remove the impression which has been so sedulously inculcated by the Government, that recognition would rouse the North to frenzy and involve Europe in the quarrel. An opinion is also gaining ground that a large minority, perhaps a majority, of the Northern people, are willing to be conquered if only reunion is based upon the conquest. It is singular that this idea was presented to me as a Northern one by a gentleman whom I know to occupy a peculiar but highly important position in the political world, who mixes freely with men of all shades of opinion and keeps a journal of their conversations for the information of an initiated few, of whom Lord Palmerston is one, and who thus serves as an organ of intercommunication between circles which have otherwise no point of contact. He has been much courted by the Federals, and even by Mr. Seward himself, and I was therefore inclined to believe that the idea propounded to me in his letter on the eve of the debate on Roebuck's motion, had reached him from a high Federal authority, a belief confirmed by the remarkable coincidence between this letter and Mr. Bright's speech of the following day. It may be worth while to enclose a copy of the letter, and of my reply, necessarily written in great haste.

I also enclose a copy of a letter received from a lady whose son, an officer in our Army, has been killed in battle, and who wishes certain arrears of pay alleged to be due him to be secured for the benefit of his English relations. Believing it to be just and politic to treat applications of this nature courteously, I have undertaken to forward the letter and promised to direct your attention to it, and to solict a reply. I have also forwarded, by a different opportunity, copies of the application of C. W. White of St. Thomas, soliciting his appointment as commercial agent for that port, with the endorsement of Hon. John Slidell, Hon. J. M. Mason, and Hon. C. J. McRae, recommending the appointment.

I have the honor to remain, with great respect, your obedient servant,

HENRY HOTZE.

Hon. J. P. BENJAMIN,
Secretary of State, Richmond.

No. 41.] PARIS, *July 11, 1863.*

SIR: Herewith you will find duplicate of my dispatch No. 40 of 6th instant. I have now the honor to forward certain papers marked A to F, relating to a claim of the company of the Messageries Impériales, for damages sustained by the destruction of the Federal ship *Louisa Hatch* by the Confederate steamer *Alabama.*

I am, with great respect, your most obedient servant,

[JOHN SLIDELL.]

Hon. J. P. BENJAMIN,
Secretary of State.

[Translation—Enclosure A.]

PARIS, *July 1, 1863.*

SIR: The capture by the *Alabama* of the American ship *Louisa Hatch* and her destruction at sea with a shipload of coal belonging to our company places us in the position to inquire from whom we should demand payment for our property.

The cargo of the *Louisa Hatch* consisted of 1,033 tons of screened coal from Nixon's Merthyr mines, having cost at Cardiff 11,561 francs 60 centimes. The vessel had been chartered to carry this cargo to Point de Galle, Indian Ocean, the terms being £1,575 for the total freight, rate of exchange 25 francs 20 centimes, 39,698 francs 20 centimes, on which we advanced 13,272 francs 75 centimes to the captain. We have therefore paid a total sum of 24,794 francs 35 centimes for which we are not indemnified.

This amount had been insured in part by us, in part by Mr. Hippolyte Worms, of Paris. We appealed first and foremost to this underwriter. He replied that the insurance did not cover the risk which had caused the destruction of our property, and plead an exception by article 2 of the policy, worded thus:

The war risks are not carried by the underwriters unless there be an express agreement. In that case it is understood that they become responsible for all damages and losses growing out of reprisals, seizures, captures, and molestations by any Government whatever, friend or foe, known or unknown, and of all accidents and chances of wars generally.

The *Alabama* carries the flag of the Confederate States of the South. She has received from the Government of the Confederate States the commission in virtue of which she sails the seas.

That Government is therefore responsible for the acts of the *Alabama* when they strike a blow at the property of neutrals, as in the case in question. France, in publicly establishing as she did in a memorable circumstance, the character of belligerents that the Confederate States assumed to themselves, has acquired special rights, in that French property has been represented by the ships flying the flag of those States, although she did not recognize it. Consequently we confidently hope that our claim will be allowed, and as you, sir, are universally recognized as the representative of the Confederate States at Paris, we believe that in interesting you in our claim we appeal to the person best qualified to act as our intermediary.

We therefore beg you, sir, to be kind enough to urge the reimbursement of 24,794 francs 35 centimes of which our company is out of pocket, owing to the destruction of the *Louisa Hatch.*

If, contrary to our expectation, you are not in a position to satisfy our claim we will be obliged if you will write us to that effect. It will remain then for us to apply to our Government, who will inquire into the matter, and find out if the destruction at sea of the *Louisa Hatch*, carrying French property, was the work of a belligerent power, disposed to answer to neutrals for acts of war committed under its flag, or if that violence constitutes one of those cases of piracy of which the Imperial Navy will have to undertake the repression.

Believe, sir, the assurance of our very high consideration,

H. Demois DuPuilly,
E. Simons,
Z. Musnier,
Directors.

Mr. Slidell,
Representative of the Confederate States of America at Paris.

[Enclosure B.]

Paris, *July 6, 1863.*

Gentlemen: I have received your letter of the 1st instant, on the subject of a loss alleged to be sustained by your company in consequence of the destruction of the American ship *Louisa Hatch* and her cargo, by the Confederate steamer *Alabama.* Knowing that all reclamations from French citizens properly presented would receive respectful consideration from my Government, I would have willingly been the organ of communicating your letter, had it not contained in its closing paragraph an insinuation which I can not accept. I therefore feel constrained to return your letter. In order to avoid misconstruction I will quote the words to which I take exception: "Ou si cette violence constitue un de ces cas de piraterie dont la Marine Impériale aurait à poursuivre la répression." ["Or if that violence constitutes one of those cases of piracy which the imperial navy ought to suppress."]

Should you think proper to readdress me, your letter with those now omitted, I will immediately forward a copy of it to my government.

Very respectfully, your most obedient servant,

JOHN SLIDELL.

The DIRECTORS OF THE COMPANY OF MESSAGERIES IMPÉRIALES.

[Translation—Enclosure C.]

PARIS, *July 8, 1863.*

SIR: In conformity with the desire expressed in your letter of the 6th of July, we have the honor to address to you herewith a note that you will no doubt deem proper to transmit to the Government of the Confederate States.

We ought to remark to you that if the paragraph in our first letter to which you make allusion had been inserted in it, it is due to the fact that your reply to the first application made to you in our name by Mr. Hippolyte Worms, underwriter for the cargo of the *Louisa Hatch,* obliged us to put before your eyes, from every point of view of international law, the question of the destruction of neutral property by the Confederate steamer *Alabama.*

Not to risk altering the sense of that reply which had been verbally reported to us, we asked Mr. Worms to make it known to us in writing. You will find herewith the copy of the letter of Mr. Worms.

The intention you announce today to bring our claim before the Confederate States, and the assurance expressed by you that this claim will be examined by that Government with all the attention it merits, have readily decided us sir, to treat in the note enclosed the question of right which is submitted to the Confederate States by your intermediation, only from the point of view you take, that is to say, the just reparation by a belligerent power for an act performed by its orders and for which it is responsible.

We have the honor to be, sir, your very humble and obedient serv-

H. DEMOIS DUPUILLY,
EDOUARD DELETTERT,
—— SOUTHOY,
Z. MUSNIER,

Directors.

Mr. JOHN SLIDELL,
    19 Rue Marignan, Paris.

[Translation—Enclosure D.]

NOTE FOR MR. JOHN SLIDELL, REPRESENTATIVE AT PARIS OF THE CONFEDERATE STATES OF AMERICA.

The vessel *Louisa Hatch,* carrying a cargo of coal belonging to the Compagnie des Services Maritimes des Messageries Impériales was burnt at sea in the waters of Pernambuco in April, 1863, by the steamer *Alabama.* The cargo was totally destroyed.

This cargo consisted of 1,033 tons of coal from Nixon's Merthyr mines, extra screened, having cost at Cardiff 11,561 francs 60 centimes. The vessel had been chartered to carry this cargo in the Indian Ocean to Point de Galle, at the terms of £1,575 for the total freight, rate of exchange being 25 francs 20 centimes, 39,698 francs 20 centimes, on which the company advanced to the captain 13,232 francs 75 centimes. The company has thus disbursed a total sum of 24,794 francs 35 centimes, for which it is not indemnified [à déconvert].

This sum having been insured the company at once appealed to the underwriter to recover their loss. The underwriter replied that the policy did not cover the risk which had led to the destruction of the property of the company, and he plead an exception by the second article of this policy thus worded:

The war risks are not carried by the underwriter unless there be an express agreement. In that case it is understood he is responsible for all damages and losses growing out of reprisals, seizures, captures, and molestations of any Governments whatever, friend or foe, known or unknown, and for all accidents and chances of war generally.

The *Alabama* carries the flag of the Confederate States of the South. She has received from the Confederate States the commission in virtue of which she sails the seas. The Confederate States are therefore responsible for the acts of the *Alabama* when they strike a blow at the property of neutrals, as in the case in question.

The undersigned in their character of directors of the company have confidently hoped that the Confederate States, once in possession of our claim, will feel in honor bound to see us righted. They address themselves, consequently, to Mr. John Slidell as being the accepted representative of the Confederate States at Paris, and consequently the person best qualified to act as their intermediary.

They have the honor to beg Mr. J. Slidell to be kind enough to urge the reimbursement to them of the sum of 24,794 francs 35 centimes, of which the Compagnie des Services Maritimes des Messageries Impériales is out of pocket as a result of the destruction of the vessel *Louisa Hatch* and her cargo.

H. DEMOIS DU PUILLY.
E. SIMONS.
Z. MUSNIER.
—— SOUTHOY.

PARIS, *July 8, 1863.*

[Translation—Enclosure E.]

PARIS, *July 7, 1863.*

GENTLEMEN: To comply with your request, I will state to you as faithfully as my memory permits the reply of Mr. Slidell.

I had laid before him all the facts relative to the destruction of the vessel *Louisa Hatch* and her cargo, as belonging to French subjects, and in speaking of the steamer *Alabama* I had used the word privateer (corsaire).

Mr. Slidell took up that word, insisting on the fact that the steamer *Alabama* is a war vessel of the Southern States and not a privateer (corsaire), etc.

He regretted that he had no authority to recognize the ground of my claim, and it could not be otherwise, according to his opinion, so long as the French Government should not have recognized the States of the South.

. Such, gentlemen, is the substance of my conversation with Mr. Slidell.

Believe, etc.,

WORMS.

The DIRECTORS OF THE SERVICES MARITIME DES MESSAGERIES IMPÉRIALES.

No. 42.] PARIS, *July 19, 1863.*

SIR: My No. 41 of 11th instant relates only to a special matter of little importance. Referring to my previous dispatch of 6th instant, I resume my account of the Roebuck episode, which threatened at one time to assume a very disagreeable aspect. I sent Mr. Roebuck a copy of M. Mocquard's note of 6th instant, saying that he must consider it confidential unless the writer should expressly authorize that it might be publicly used, that I had written to M. M. to know what were his wishes on that point. Before receiving M. Mocquard's answer I had another letter from Mr. Roebuck couched in very peremptory terms and making a distinct issue of veracity with the Emperor, which he requested me to communicate to him. I, of course, declined to do so, and suggested that Mr. R., although substantially correct in his statement to the House of Commons, had probably erred in two important particulars. First, the Emperor doubtless complained of his overtures on the subject of American affairs having been communicated to Mr. Seward through Lord Lyons, but he could not have referred to any written proposition, as the only one ever made was that of 30th October, 1862, which appeared in the Moniteur simultaneously with its delivery to Earl Russell. Second, Mr. Roebuck must have misunderstood the Emperor when he supposed that the Emperor's authority to repeat what he said in the House of Commons extended to all that had passed in conversation, it evidently must have been confined to the subject of recognition, the complaints of the unfair use made of his informal overtures being from their very nature confidential.

These suggestions had the desired influence with Mr. R., who had written under the excitement produced by the Emperor's reproach of a breach of confidence; he wrote to me to say that he would let the matter rest where it was. In the meanwhile I received from M. Mocquard the following note:

VICHY, *July 9, 1863.*

MY DEAR MR. SLIDELL: The note I have directed to you is not to be rendered public for many reasons. First it contains some details especially reserved to the only person whom they concern; moreover the indiscretion of the said person is regretted, and finally a note published two or three days ago in the Moniteur gives all that is essential to make known. Therefore, I repeat, one must be extremely reserved and keep for one's self what was not written for others.

A thousand kind compliments.

MOCQUARD.

I communicated to Messrs. Mocquard and Drouyn de Lhuys the determination of Mr. R. to let the matter drop; the latter has ex-

pressed his great gratification at the solution of an imbroglio which
I am inclined to think he has been not a little instrumental in produc-
ing, while the Emperor must be pleased that an unpleasant issue with
Messrs. Roebuck and Lindsay had been avoided.

I have not yet heard anything from M. Isturitz, but Lord Howden,
who was for several years British ambassador to Spain, informs
me that I should not draw any unfavorable inferences from the delay,
as he never received, while at Madrid, an answer to any official
communication, whatever might be its importance, in less than three
or four weeks. We have received the news of the successive battles
at and near Gettysburg of the 1st, 2d, and 3d July, and I infer from
the Northern accounts that, although they were not decided victories,
the advantage was with our troops. You can imagine the anxiety
with which the result of the expected battle of the 4th is awaited.

The Polish question still engrosses attention. The prospects of a
peaceful settlement are far from being encouraging; no apprehension
is entertained of an immediate rupture, but the general opinion
among the best-informed persons is that the peace of Europe can
not be maintained beyond the close of the coming winter. There
can be no doubt of the Emperor's readiness to put his armies in
motion, and although Poland would be their original ostensible destination, the frontier of the Rhine would not be lost sight of. The
only question with me is whether England will join France in a
war which will give the Emperor the long-coveted opportunity of
restoring her lost boundaries.

With great respect, your most obedient servant,

JOHN SLIDELL.

Hon. J. P. BENJAMIN,
    Secretary of State.

No. 20.]   DEPARTMENT OF STATE,
                                        Richmond, July 20, 1863.

SIR: I have the honor to acknowledge the receipt on the 4th instant of your dispatches Nos. 34, 35, and 36, the No. 34 being a
duplicate, original not received.

The President observes with satisfaction a new example of your
unvaried promptness and diligence in supervising our interests as
displayed in the matter of the attempted attachment of the funds in
the hands of Messrs. Erlanger & Co., and is specially gratified at
the evidence afforded by the conduct of the French officials in this
affair, that the sympathies of that Government in our cause are real
and cordial.

The notice from Messrs. Erlanger & Co. of the demand of Mr.
Schlumberger to have £6,000 of the loan converted into cotton by a
delivery of the cotton at Charleston within sixty days has been communicated to Mr. Memminger. You properly remark that in future
these matters will form the subject of Mr. McRae's action and
that you will be dispensed from further attention to them. But
it may not be improper to observe that Mr. Memminger pointed out
to me that the present claim is not warranted by the terms of the
contract; that it is only after the war is ended that the parties have
a right to claim cotton at the ports; and that pending the war the

Government is only bound to deliver it at points not more than 10 miles distant from railroads or navigable streams debouching at ports.

I make no comments on your remarks in No. 34 on the subject of recognition, inasmuch as recent arrivals from Europe have informed us of the new events which have modified the aspect of the question, of your own interview with the Emperor, and of the debate in Parliament of 30th June and its further postponement to the 13th instant. We await therefore the developments with interest, but with very little hope of action. It has become perfectly plain to the whole world, notwithstanding the halting and equivocating explanations of the British ministry, that Great Britain stands the only real obstacle to our recognition; that her Government is immovably fixed on retarding our success and encouraging the North in continued warfare as long as possible, and that no matter what may be the course of events on this side they will serve as a pretext to the British cabinet for further delay.

When successful fortune smiles on our arms, the British cabinet is averse to recognition because "it would be unfair to the South by the action of Great Britain to exasperate the North to renewed efforts." When reverses occur, such as have lately overtaken us, "it would be unfair to the North in a moment of its success to deprive it of a reasonable opportunity of accomplishing a reunion of the States."

The very perfection of cant is exhibited in the speech of one of the members of the house on the recent debate. This gentleman declares that "the South are on the point of working out their independence, and ought not to be interfered with." It is for our benefit that this candid statesman refuses to recognize us and takes side with the North which beseeches Great Britain to persist in the refusal.

To your suggestions upon the question of citizenship of our friends and partisans in Europe who have been unable to come here in person and claim their privilege of citizenship, I can only make the same answer as was given to Mr. Meaurean's application about extending the time for conversion of currency into 8 per cent bonds, i. e., it must await the action of Congress, which will not be in session till December. The subject will then be submitted to it and with very little doubt of a favorable result.

The contents of your No. 36 excite special interest. The conversation with Mr. Isturitz evidenced views of which some echo is heard in the reports that arrived by the last steamer as to a probable treaty with Spain on the basis of the instructions contained in my No. 16 of 9th May. The reports are vague enough, but they accord in a remarkable manner with the contents of that dispatch and indicate that you have acted on them with perhaps with decisive results.

I hope soon to receive something further on the subject of the proposals of the bankers and of the member of Parliament whose names are given in cipher in your No. 36. We want no money on this side of the water, but it would be very advantageous to us to be able to increase our Navy by means of the operation proposed by those gentlemen. If you have heard nothing further from them, it would not be, perhaps, without good effect if you could cause an indirect intimation to reach them of the probability that their offer, if not too onerous, would be accepted. But we suppose that our recent reverses at Vicksburg and Port Hudson may have inspired afresh the ill-founded apprehensions which followed the fall of New Orleans, and created a distrust among capitalists as to the security of investments with us. If so, I need scarcely say that it is far better to allow such a feeling to become dissipated by later news which will demonstrate that these reverses have not the slightest effect in furthering the insane attempt of the North to quell the spirit or crush out the life of this people.

I am happy to say that the President, whose health had been seriously impaired, is now entirely recovered and is undergoing his vast labors with his usual spirit and elasticity.

I am, very respectfully, your obedient servant,

J. P. BENJAMIN,
Secretary of State.

Hon. JOHN SLIDELL, *Paris.*

LONDON, *July 22, 1863.*

SIR: I have the honor to acknowledge the receipt of your dispatch No. 2, advising me that the Senate having failed to ratify my nomination as commissioner to Russia, the President desires that I consider the official information of the fact as terminating my mission. I have to thank you for the regret you express on the part of the President and yourself at this decision of the Senate; but while I can not free myself altogether from a feeling of disappointment in the expectation of finding a career of usefulness, it is my duty to state that the reasons which you inform me actuated the Senate are fully confirmed by my own observations of the conditions of European politics. Shortly after my arrival here I became convinced that the state of things supposed to promise useful results from diplomatic representations at the Court of St. Petersburg had been essentially altered. Not only did there appear no evidence that the influence of France was in the ascendant in the councils of Russia, but it was very apparent that a growing coldness existed between the two Governments, caused by the attitude which the French Government had assumed in relation to Poland. The progress of the insurrection, and the increasing manifestation of French sympathy with its success, have still farther widened the breach, until at present all Europe is greatly alarmed at the imminent risk of a hostile collision of the two empires.

These considerations induced me, after frequent consultation with Messrs. Mason and Slidell, to delay my departure for my post, and, as latterly the prospect of a restoration of cordial relations became more remote, I had almost reached the determination of recommending to you that I should be released from my duties, or, at least, that they should be directed to another field. Although it could not be expected that the Government of Austria or Prussia would be prepared to take the initiative in recognition, there was yet good reason to believe that either or both of these powers could be so far influenced as to lend their moral weight to the efforts which are made in England and France. I can not say that the grounds for this belief were sufficiently specific to be urged successfully against the decision of the Senate, and I acquiesce in it the more readily since, in one respect at least, it anticipates by a few days the conclusion that I was about to communicate to you. I trust, however, that you will not consider me as going out of my way when I urge that the principle which has governed this decision will not be extended to the withdrawal of diplomatic representation at London and Paris, as the proceeding in the House of Representatives and the tone of the press lead me to apprehend. The presence of these gentlemen at their respective posts is imperiously demanded by exigencies of the public service, even though the main object of their mission may not, for some time to come, be carried out against the prejudiced obstinacy of the English foreign office, or the languor which has recently characterized the imperial policy on American affairs.

In terminating my official relations with your department, permit me to express the hope that my brief residence in Europe has not been wholly fruitless. In the endeavor to secure for my mission a favorable reception at St. Petersburg I have necessarily made the acquaintance of many persons in high official and social position, as well in England as in France. Opportunities for putting to work influences in our favor have not been wanting, and I have not knowingly neglected any that have presented themselves.

I have the honor to be, sir, very respectfully, your obedient servant,

L. Q. C. Lamar.

Hon. J. P. Benjamin,
Secretary of State, Confederate States of America.

No. 26.]   Confederate States Commercial Agency,
London, July 23, 1863.

Sir: The news of the check sustained by our forces at Gettysburg, coupled with the reported fall of Vicksburg, was so unexpected as to spread very general dismay not only among the active sympathizers with our cause, but even among those who take merely a selfish interest in the great struggle. The disappointment was proportionate to the confidence which had come to be generally entertained that our arms were about to achieve the crowning triumph of peace. Under this sense of disappointment the public mind was in danger of exaggerating the magnitude and real significance of the events. The news received last night has somewhat reassured the shaken confidence in our ultimate success, but all is still perplexity, surprise, and alarm. The current into which public opinion will finally settle depends on the attitude of our people, and as I know that this will be as resolute and unwavering as during the dark period of last summer, I do not fear that we shall lose ground here. If they enforce the conviction that the war will be indefinitely protracted so long as England encourages the North to assail our independence by ignoring it, our recent misfortunes may not be without some compensating effects. I send you files of all the principal dailies, which, however, will indicate very little beyond the painful surprise with which the news was received. The Times, always throwing its weight on the side either of the North or South according as either seems losing, makes this morning a strong effort to rally the sinking spirits of our English friends. The tonic effect will be excellent, whatever motive may actuate the Times policy.

It is unfortunate for us that at this very moment Europe feels itself on the verge of a general war. Russia has rejected, with but slight attempts at conciliation, the joint proposals of England, France, and Prussia on the subject of Poland. In France public opinion is in a state of unprecedented ferment; all parties and all classes uniting in a clamor for war which must drown the soberer counsels, if such there are, in the imperial cabinet. I doubt whether this feeling is less strong in England, though its expression is subdued by the more sedate temper of the people and their instinctive aversion to war. Austria has of late entered into a career of liberalism, very commendable in itself, but which may have committed it too far on this question to make retreat safe or possible. There is, therefore, a substantial danger of a European war, in the turmoil of which we should be wholly lost sight of.

The situation calls for extreme exertion as well here as at home. While it is politic to accept the facts in their stern reality, without attempting to disguise them under forced constructions or flattering hypotheses, it is necessary by acts even more than words to sustain the courage of our friends and supporters. A more than ordinary moral fortitude is demanded of the representatives of Southern views. The merest quaver of nerve on their part would be deemed a symptom of despair. You will not therefore be surprised that I am giving to my operations an extension which only the urgencies of the crisis could warrant, and I shall feel it my duty to neglect no opportunity for impressing upon the public the undiminished vitality of our cause. One of the means which I had commenced to adopt while I still thought that the hour of peace was approaching is on so large a scale that I should somewhat doubt your approval had not the turn in our affairs proved it so unexpectedly opportune. Finding that the address of the Southern clergy to Christians throughout the world had produced excellent effects wherever it could be brought under public notice, I have not contented myself with merely publishing a pamphlet edition, but have arranged that a copy shall be stitched up under the same cover with this or the next month's number of every respectable religious publication, as also the two leading political reviews, the Quarterly and the Edinburgh, just out. A quarter of a million of copies of the address are by this means brought under the eyes of between one and two millions of readers in every part of the world where the English language is spoken.

For the suggestion of this original, and in its magnitude, unprecedented mode of giving universal publicity to a document, I am indebted to the Presbyterian publishing house of Messrs. Nisbet & Co., who have undertaken to carry it out without compensation for the very considerable trouble it involves. The expenses, small in proportion to the work, will yet not fall short of £250. As I had arranged to disburse through the Index very nearly, if not quite the amount of my contingent allowance, this sum would make a serious reduction in my means. Mr. de Leon, however, to whom I have just communicated my plan, and who heartily approves of it, as do all whom I have consulted, has offered to share half the expense, which I have gratefully accepted. These and other heavy outlays, outside of my permanent scheme for action, have induced me to defer the dissemination of the commercial circular, of which I spoke in my No. 22, in order to spread my disbursements over a larger period of time. But this consideration is overruled by the conviction that now is the proper time for striking all the blows in quick succession and I shall therefore forthwith carry this plan also into execution. As I dare not reduce any of my other expenses, it is certain that I shall for the first nine months of the present year exceed the very liberal allowance which the President has made me out of the secret service fund, and this I do with unfeigned reluctance, and with a deep sense of the responsibility which I assume. I can only hope that the events of the future will enable me to make such reductions as to restore the proportions fixed by you.

I learn with much regret that Colonel Lamar is about to return home. During his short stay here a very cordial friendship has sprung up between us, and I have found his society a great assistance to me in the discharge of my duties. My own mind is impoverished by constant writing without sufficient opportunity to replenish with reading and reflection, and the suggestions of his fruitful intellect were an invaluable advantage to me. I am endeavoring to persuade him to stay, if only until this great crisis in our affairs is passed safely.

I remain, with great respect, your obedient servant,

HENRY HOTZE.

Hon. J. P. BENJAMIN,
Secretary of State, Richmond.

OFFICE NAVAL STATION,
Charleston, August 3, 1863.

SIR: I have the honor to acknowledge the receipt of your letter and the accompanying communication from the French Government. Be pleased, sir, to accept my thanks for the kind manner [in] which you have been pleased to communicate the information to me.

Very respectfully, your obedient servant,

D. N. INGRAHAM,
Captain, Commanding Naval Station.

Hon. J. P. BENJAMIN,
Secretary of State, Richmond, Va.

DEPARTMENT OF STATE,
Richmond, August 4, 1863.

SIR: I have the honor of acknowledging receipt of your note of 29th ultimo upon the subject of the tobacco belonging to the Government of his Imperial Majesty and have taken the instructions of the President on the subject.

You propose that this tobacco be shipped directly from the port of Richmond; that it be sent on neutral vessels; that all the shipping documents, both of the vessels and the cargoes, shall show that the clearances are from Richmond, from which port the shipments are to be made directly for France; and finally that you pledge yourself that the vessels shall not touch nor stop at any port, bay, or point whatever belonging to the territory of our enemy.

These assurances are entirely satisfactory, except the last, which I have underscored. Our objections extend not only to the touching at ports belonging to the territory of the enemy, but to our own ports now temporarily in their possession, such as Norfolk, Hampton Roads, etc.

I preseume, sir, that your intention was to agree that the vessels should proceed directly to sea from City Point on their voyage across the Atlantic, and that they would neither stop at Norfolk nor any other point in possession of the enemy, nor would take any papers or clearances signed by the enemy indicating that the shipments are made from any port or place in their possession.

If I am right in this supposition be so good as to inform me, and it will then afford this Government great pleasure to facilitate his Majesty's Government in having the tobacco forwarded to France.

I am, very respectfully, etc.,

> J. P. BENJAMIN,
> *Secretary of State.*

ALFRED PAUL, Esq.,
   French Consul, Richmond, Va.

No. 30.]   DEPARTMENT OF STATE,
                                  Richmond, August 4, 1863.

SIR: The perusal of the recent debates in the British Parliament satisfies the President that the Government of her Majesty has determined to decline the overtures made through you for establishing by treaty friendly relations between the two Governments, and entertains no intention of receiving you as the accredited minister of this Government near the British Court.

Under these circumstances your continued residence in London is neither conducive to the interests nor consistent with the dignity of this Government, and the President therefore requests that you consider your mission at an end, and that you withdraw with your secretary from London.

In arriving at this conclusion, it gives me pleasure to say that the President is entirely satisfied with your own conduct of the delicate mission confided to you, and that it is in no want of proper effort on your part that the necessity for your recall has originated.

If you find that it is in accordance with usage to give notice of your intended withdrawal to Earl Russell, you will of course conform to precedent in that respect.

With great respect, your obedient servant,

> J. P. BENJAMIN,
> *Secretary of State*

Hon. JAMES M. MASON,
   London.

Private.]

AUGUST 4, 1863?

DEAR SIR: The President desires me to say to you that while the instructions contained in my No. 30, herewith forwarded, purport to be unconditional, he does not desire that you should consider yourself precluded from the exercise of all discretion on the subject, in the event of any marked or decisive change in the policy of the British cabinet before your receipt of the dispatch. Although no such change is anticipated, it is not deemed prudent to ignore altogether its possibility, and it is in this view of the case that discretion is left you as to your action. In the absence of some important and marked change of conduct on the part of Great Britain, however, the President desires that your action on the instructions in No. 30 be as prompt as convenient.

I am, respectfully, your obedient servant,

J. P. BENJAMIN,
Secretary of State.

Hon. J. M. MASON,

No. 21.]

DEPARTMENT OF STATE,
Richmond, August 4, 1863.

SIR: We are still annoyed by the absence of your dispatches, which we feel sure must have miscarried. Our latest from you is still your No. 36, of 28th May.

I enclose you copy of a letter of instructions to Mr. Mason directing his withdrawal from his mission. The contrast between the conduct of the English and French cabinets toward our agents abroad has become too marked, and Mr. Mason's exclusion from official intercourse, while you are freely admitted to conversations with the Emperor, is too significant to permit us longer to treat the two Governments in a like spirit or to subject Mr. Mason to the embarrassment of his very equivocal position in London. We should indeed have recalled him long ago, but for the indispensable necessity of his services in some matters of which you are aware and which are now terminated.

I send you also a copy of my correspondence with the French consul here on the subject of the tobacco belonging to the imperial régie, for your information.

This correspondence suggests the idea whether it would not be practicable to sell to the French Government directly cotton to the value of say eight or ten millions of dollars, the cotton to be purchased at the present low rates compared with the value on the other side, and to be imported into France by the Government under an arrangement similar to that just made for the tobacco, or to be held on this side under a guaranty from this Government not to allow its destructions by our forces. It seems difficult to discover any reason that the United States Government could give for refusing to consent that France should export the cotton belonging to the Government any more than the tobacco; and if France should export the cotton, it would be somewhat troublesome for the British cabinet to satisfy the British people that France should be allowed to supply herself with cotton while British operatives were starving for want of the article. Even if the French Government should fail to obtain permission to export now the cotton, profit from such purchases would be enormous. Cotton bought here now would not cost, after calculating the exchange, more than 8 or 10 cents a pound and would yield a profit of from $150 to $200 a bale; in other words, it would be worth at least fivefold its cost, besides furnishing an immediate supply for the French operatives as soon as peace is declared.

An opening may perhaps be offered by this tobacco business for what could not but be considered as an abandonment of the blockade by the United States.

The shipment of this tobacco has doubtless been agreed to by the English Government, but in point of principle it can not be denied that the consent of the United States to the passage of this merchandise through the blockading forces is an absolute abandonment of the blockade to the world at large, and as soon as the first vessel passes through under this permission, not a vessel nor cargo can afterwards be properly condemned in a Federal prize court if the facts be known. I shall send you official evidence of the passage of the first ship through the blockade under the Federal permit, and it need only be communicated to some of our friends in New York to be used there in behalf of the neutral claimants of captured vessels and cargoes to give infinite trouble to the enemy's Government.

I desire to direct your attention to another point on which the success of your efforts would be very advantageous to us. Would it not be possible to induce the French and Spanish Governments to recall the notice issued by them at the commencement of the war interdicting the entrance of the prizes of either belligerent into their ports? It is equally consistent with neutrality to open their ports to the prizes of both parties. Indeed by the law of nations such is the normal condition of things, and it requires such a special prohibition as was issued in the present case to prevent the entry of the prizes of both sides into neutral ports as a matter of course. Good reason may now be found for a change of policy in this respect, for our cruisers at present are exposed to the risk of destroying by mistake neutral cargoes when found on enemy's vessels, and thus French and Spanish interests are liable to suffer without any intention on our part to fail in duty toward neutrals. But if we had ports open for the introduction of prizes (even if but the colonial ports) the rights of neutrals could then be investigated at leisure in our prize courts, and their interests safeguarded. Other considerations connected with this subject will suggest themselves to you and it is to be hoped that your efforts in this direction may not be fruitless.

Public expectation is greatly excited by the recent news from Mexico. Will Maximilian accept the newly offered throne? The general impression seems to be in the negative; and if this be so, it leaves open a wide field of speculation as to the probable action of the Emperor. You are so near headquarters that your impressions on this point would be particularly acceptable at this moment. For myself, I confess inability to conjecture the result, but none can fail to see the deep and permanent influence over affairs on this continent that must be exerted by the new state of things on our southern frontier.

I am, respectfully, your obedient servant,

J. P. BENJAMIN,
Secretary of State.

Hon. JOHN SLIDELL, *Paris.*

P. S.—I omitted to mention that Mr. Paul called at the office this morning and tendered me what appeared to be a notice or judicial citation of some sort addressed to the President and to the Secretary of the Treasury by the French tribunal charged with the Dupasseur suit against Erlanger & Co. I of course declined to receive the paper, and Mr. Paul himself seemed to have anticipated this refusal, stating that he was merely requested to ask me if I would receive it.

J. P. B., *Secretary of State.*

DEPARTMENT OF STATE,
Richmond, August 5, 1863.

SIR: I have the honor to acknowledge receipt of your letter of this date in response to mine of the 4th instant, and to inform you that the assurances therein contained being satisfactory to this Government, no obstacle now remains to the shipment of tobacco belonging to the Imperial régie, in the manner specified in your letters.

I am, respectively, etc.,

J. P. BENJAMIN,
Secretary of State.

ALFRED PAUL, Esq.,
French Consul, Richmond.

No. 43.] PARIS, *August 5, 1863.*

SIR: Since my last dispatch of 19 ultimo, we have the unpleasant intelligence of the retreat of General Lee across the Potomac and the surrender of Vicksburg and Port Hudson. For the latter event we were not prepared, and, as you may suppose, they can not fail to exercise an unfavorable influence on the question of recognition. I saw yesterday Mr. Isturitz, the Spanish ambassador; he tells me that I can effect nothing at Madrid at preesnt; he assured me that his Government was prepared to recognize us cojointly or with France and other continental powers, or with France alone, but would not take the initiative; he said expressly that the cooperation of England would not be required. I left with him a note of which I annex copy marked " A," together with an extract from your No. 15, relating to the case of the *Blanche,* commencing with the words " The Confederate Government was the owner," and ending with " whole sum to this Government." It appears that you were mis- informed as to the payment of an indemnity having been made in this case. Mr. Isturitz says that a very recent dispatch from Mr. Tassara, Spanish minister at Washington, speaks of the case as still pending, indemnity being refused on various pretexts for the ship and for the cargo, on the ground that it was set on fire by the officers and crew of the *Blanche.* I have received your No. 18 of 10 June, and in compliance with your instructions have communicated a copy of it to M. Drouyn de Lhuys, accompanied by a note of which I annex copy marked "B." The Emperor will return from Vichy to St. Cloud to-day; he will remain there until the 15th instant, when he will go to the camp at Châlons, Biarritz, and other places, and will be absent from the neighborhood of Paris for several weeks. I shall see M. Mocquard in a day or two, and shall ask his opinion as to the expediency of recurring to the question of recognition in the present aspect of affairs. I do not expect that his reply will be encouraging. You will find by the enclosed slips from newspapers the present position of the Polish question. The publication of the answers of Russia to the cabinets of Paris, London, and Vienna and of Lord Napier's dispatch, produced quite a panic at the bourse, and a very heavy fall of funds. I am, however, still of opinion that the peace of Europe will not be disturbed before next spring at all events and probably not then.

The pendency of this question has embarrassed the Emperor's action in our affairs and will continue to do so while it remains unsettled. So far as we are concerned, I am now satisfied that a general war in Europe would be of advantage to us. The Lincoln Government would encourage the fitting out of vessels under the Russian flag to prey upon the commerce of France and Great Britain, who in their turn would open our ports and blockade those of the North. The crops of grain are everywhere throughout Europe most abundant in quantity and excellent in quality, and prices will range so low as greatly to check, if not entirely prevent, the importation of breadstuffs from the United States. I am just informed that the imperial court has confirmed the decree of the tribunal de premiere instance, dismissing the attachment levied by Dupasseur, Lecoq & Co. on moneys in hands of Erlanger & Co.

I am, with great respect, your most obedient servant,

JOHN SLIDELL.

Hon. J. P. BENJAMIN,
    Secretary of State.

[Enclosure.]

A.

PARIS, *August 5, 1863.*

SIR: On the 22d of May last I had the honor to state verbally to your Excellency certain facts in relation to the steamer *Blanche,* burned, with her cargo, by a ship of war of the Government of the United States, within the territory of her Most Catholic Majesty, and to solicit your advice as to the proper course to be pursued in order to bring before her Majesty's Government the claim of the Confederate States of America to receive any sum which might be recovered from the United States as indemnity for the destruction of the *Blanche* and her cargo.

You were subsequently so good as to inform me that you had communicated the facts to your Government, and that when you should receive any information on the subject you would advise me of it. So long a time has since elapsed that I can scarcely now expect to hear from you in relation to it. As I consider it proper that a written claim should be presented on behalf of the Confederate States, I beg leave to submit the following extract from a dispatch addressed to me by the Secretary of State of the Confederate States of America, dated Richmond, 26th March, 1863, which I pray your Excellency to transmit to her Majesty's Government to be placed on file in the proper department for future reference.

I have the honor to be, with great respect, your Excellency's most obedient servant,

JOHN SLIDELL.

His Excellency M. ISTURITZ,
 Ambassador of her Most Catholic Majesty, Paris.

[Enclosure.]

B.

PARIS, *July 30, 1863.*

SIR: In compliance with the instructions of the Secretary of State of the Confederate States of America I have the honor to transmit to your Excellency a copy of a dispatch from the Department of State, dated Richmond, 10th June last. In support of the statement therein contained of "the ample facilities for correspondence which are now afforded by the fleets of Confederate and neutral steamers engaged in regular trade between neutral countries and Confederate ports," I beg leave to refer you to the accompanying documents, marked "A" and "B." The former is a list of 102 vessels that arrived at the port of Nassau, Bahama Islands, from Confederate ports from 18th July, 1862, to 2d June, 1863. The latter is a list of 179 vessels sailing from Nassau for Confederate ports from 1st July, 1862, to 21st May, 1863, designating those that arrived safely. It will be observed that the proportion of steamers captured is very small.

I have the honor to be, with great respect, your Excellency's most obedient servant,

JOHN SLIDELL.

His Excellency M. DROUYN DE LHUYS,
 Ministre des Affaires Etrangères.

———————

No. 43.]   CONFEDERATE STATES COMMISSION,
           London, August 6, 1863.

SIR: * *   *

I have now the honor to transmit herewith duplicate of my dispatch No. 42, with copies of the several documents accompanying it. I also transmit a copy of a letter to Earl Russell, dated the 21st July, communicating to him your dispatch of the 12th June, relating the the case of Hester, with his reply thereto of the 25th and my rejoinder of the 29th. You will find from this correspondence that the Government of the United States having refused passage through the blockade for the *Shannon,* having the prisoner on board, the Government has changed its purpose as to the delivery of the prisoner and given orders that he should be turned loose on arrival at Bermuda. In this new aspect I deemed it proper to remark, as you will see, though very briefly, upon it. It was certainly a most ungracious act, first, to make the proffer, and, afterwards, to decline it. I can see no reason for so strange a course, unless on the protest of Mr. Seward against the delivery of the prisoner at all.

I transmit also herewith a copy of a letter to Earl Russell, dated 16th July ultimo, covering a list of vessels entering the port of

Nassau from July, 1862, to June, 1863, with his reply of the 18th, acknowledging its receipt. The list of vessels referred to was furnished me by Mr. Heyliger, commercial agent at that port. Also copy of a letter to Earl Russell of the 16th of July, relating to the case of the *Margaret and Jessie,* with his reply of the 18th thereto. Since that date I was called on by the captain of this vessel, accompanied by an agent from Lloyd's, having with them the original papers and affidavits, presenting a claim on behalf of the owners against the British Government for losses sustained by the outrage complained of. They said they deemed it proper to bring the subject before me, but were advised by their friends that delay in having it acted on might be avoided if presented by the captain and not through me, the idea being that my unofficial relations with this Government might be encumbered with forms productive of delay. I told them they could pursue such course as they throught best; that being a Confederate ship I had little doubt I should be instructed by you to bring the matter to the attention of the Government here, and I could then do so in aid of their application.

I transmit also copies of letters to Earl Russell, dated, respectively, the 24th and 29th of July, relating to the cases of Consul Moore and of soi-disant Acting Consul Cridland. To these last I have as yet no reply.

Nothing of interest has transpired here since the date of my last dispatch. Parliament was prorogued on the 28th of July to October, though, unless there be special reason, it will not meet for dispatch of business until February.

The hopes and expectations of our friends in Europe have been much depressed by the late intelligence from the South, one marked effect of which has been on the loan, quoted yesterday as low as 30 per cent discount. I am informed, however, by Mr. McRae, the Treasury agent here, that arrangements had been previously fully completed to make the whole proceeds of the loan available, as stipulated in the contract, of which he has doubtless informed the Secretary of the Treasury. (See P. S.)

The engagements of the Government here, present and prospective, both for the Army and the Navy, it is very manifest, will require much larger sums than will be derived from the loan; and I would earnestly suggest that arrangements should be perfected, as speedily as possible, by means of fast steamers, for bringing out cotton on Government account (as is now done to some extent) to Nassau and Bermuda. When there it could be made immediately available here by insurance. The fortunes of the late loan will, I think, preclude any other for the present.

*　　　*　　　*　　　*　　　*　　　*　　　*

I have the honor to be, very respectfully, your obedient servant,

J. M. MASON.

Hon. J. P. BENJAMIN,
　　　Secretary of State.

P. S.—Since writing the foregoing it would seem that I misunderstood Mr. McRae in the arrangements he had made with Erlanger about the loan. The Government has still on hand some £700,000.

J. M. M.

[Enclosure.]

24 UPPER SEYMOUR STREET,
Portman Square, July 16, 1863.

MY LORD: I had the honor, with my letter of the 6th of July, instant, to transmit to your lordship the protest of the master and crew of the Confederate steamship *Margaret and Jessie*, and, at the same time, to inform your lordship that further testimony was expected in regard to the affair referred to in the protest, which when received should, in like manner, be transmitted to your lordship.

I have now the honor to inclose herewith 12 affidavits made by passengers on board the Confederate steamer, and by residents of the island of Eleuthera, in everything confirming the declarations made in the protest. They have just been received from the commercial agent of the Confederate States at Nassau, who informs me that copies of the same documents were transmitted by the same opportunity, the mail steamer *La Plata* (just arrived), to the Duke of New Castle, sent, as I am informed, by the authorities at Nassau.

I have the honor to be, your lordship's very obedient servant,

J. M. MASON,
Special Commissioner.

Right Hon. EARL RUSSELL,
Her Majesty's Secretary of State for Foreign Affairs.

[Enclosure.]

24 UPPER SEYMOUR STREET,
Portman Square, July 16, 1863.

MY LORD: I have the honor to transmit, herewith, a list of vessels arriving at the port of Nassau, Bahamas, from ports alleged to be blockaded in the Confederate States of America, from the 18th of July, 1862, to the 2d of June, 1863, being 102 in number.

This list was sent to me by the commercial agent of the Confederate States at Nassau, and, besides the minuteness of his description, is entitled to be received as an authentic document.

I have no instructions to make any new communication to your lordship on the subject of the alleged blockade, but I desire to place the document on the files of the foreign office as part of the history of the occasion, interesting to my Government and perhaps to the Government of her Majesty.

I have the honor to be, your lordship's very obedient servant,

J. M. MASON,
Special Commissioner.

Right Hon. EARL RUSSELL,
H. B. M. Secretary of State for Foreign Affairs.

[Enclosure.]

FOREIGN OFFICE, *July 18, 1863.*

SIR: I have the honor to acknowledge the receipt of your letter of the 16th instant, enclosing a list of vessels which had arrived at Nassau from American blockaded ports from the 18th of July, 1862, to the 2d of June, 1863.

I have the honor to be, sir, your most obedient, humble servant,

RUSSELL.

J. M. MASON, Esq.

[Enclosure.]

FOREIGN OFFICE, *July 18, 1863.*

SIR: I have the honor to acknowledge the receipt of your letter of the 16th instant, enclosing 12 affidavits made by passengers on board the steamer *Margaret and Jessie,* respecting the sinking of that vessel by a shot from a United States man-of-war, and I beg leave to thank you for the communication of these papers.

I have the honor to be, sir, your most obedient, humble servant,

RUSSELL.

J. M. MASON, Esq.

[Enclosure.]

24 UPPER SEYMOUR STREET,
Portman Square, July 21, 1863.

MY LORD: I have the honor to inform your lordship that I have, to-day, received a dispatch from the Secretary of State at Richmond, dated the 12th of June ultimo, in which I am advised that the Government of the Confederate States has been informed by Mr. Moore, late her Majesty's consul at Richmond, of the receipt by him of dispatches from your lordship stating that the prisoner Hester, charged with murder at Gibraltar on board the Confederate steamer *Sumter,* had been sent on board H. M. S. *Shannon,* leaving Gibraltar on the 6th of May last, to Bermuda; that the consent of the United States Government would be asked for the passage through the blockade of the ship having the prisoner on board, and asking that arrangements should be made by the Confederate authorities to receive him at whatever port the ship conveying him might arrive.

I am instructed by the Secretary of State to inform your lordship that the Government of the Confederate States would be prepared to receive the prisoner at any port of the Confederacy where he may be delivered up, and that, in the event of a refusal on the part of the United States to consent to the passage of the *Shannon* through the blockade, a naval officer of the Confederacy would be sent to Bermuda with authority to receive the prisoner and to bring him into one of its ports on a vessel of the Confederate Government.

I am further instructed to renew to your lordship, as her Majesty's secretary of state for foreign affairs, the expression of the thanks of the Confederate Government for your lordship's considerate attention in the matter.

I avail myself of the occasion to inform your lordship that I have received, at the same time with the foregoing, the dispatch of the 6th of June ultimo, of which I have had the honor, recently since, to transmit to your lordship an unofficial printed copy; and also a further dispatch, dated the 11th of June ultimo, concerning the case of Mr. Cridland, representing himself as " acting English consul " at Mobile, Ala., of which, together with that of the 6th of June, I am instructed to communicate copies to your lordship, which shall be done as soon as the copies can be prepared.

I have the honor to be, your lordship's very obedient servant,

J. M. MASON,
Special Commissioner, C. S. A.

Right Hon. Earl RUSSELL,
Her Majesty's Secretary of State for Foreign Affairs.

[Enclosure.]

24 Upper Seymour Street,
Portman Square, July 24, 1863.

My Lord: I have the honor to transmit to your lordship herewith a copy of the dispatch of the Secretary of State of the Confederate States of America to me, dated the 11th of June ultimo, with copies of the documents accompanying it.

The instructions of the Secretary to me being confined to the duty of furnishing this copy to your lordship, I refrain from any further act than to say, should it be the desire of the Government of her Majesty to express any views on the matter contained therein I will be happy in being the medium of communicating them to the Secretary of State at Richmond.

I have the honor to be, your lordship's very obedient servant,

J. M. Mason,
Special Commissioner, C. S. A.

Right Hon. Earl Russell.
Her Majesty's Secretary of State for Foreign Affairs.

[Enclosure.]

Foreign Office, *July 25, 1863.*

Sir: I have the honor to acknowledge the receipt of your letter of the 21st instant, in which you inform me, with reference to the case of the officer charged with the murder on board the *Sumter*, at Gibraltar, that the Confederate Government would be prepared to receive the prisoner at any one of the Southern ports where he might be delivered up, and that in the event of a refusal on the part of the United States Government to consent to the passage of the *Shannon* through the blockade, a naval officer of the Confederacy would be sent to Bermuda with authority to receive the prisoner and to bring him into one of its ports in a vessel of the Confederate Government.

I have the honor to state to you in reply that her Majesty's minister at Washington was not able to obtain the consent of the United States Government to the passage of the *Shannon* through the blockade for the purpose above mentioned; and that her Majesty's Government, having been advised by the law officers of the Crown that the prisoner was a person over whom the British court had no jurisdiction, came reluctantly to the conclusion that he ought not to be detained in custody by any British authority longer than might be necessary for the purpose of disposing of him on shore.

Orders were accordingly, about a fortnight back, given to that effect to the governor of Bermuda and to the British admiral on the North American station, and Mr. Consul Moore would have been instructed in due course to communicate this result to the authorities at Richmond had he not been obliged to quit that city, under the circumstances to which you refer in the concluding portion of your letter.

I have the honor to be, sir, your most obedient, humble servant,

Russell.

J. M. Mason, Esq.,
24 Upper Seymour Street.

[Enclosure.]

24 UPPER SEYMOUR STREET,
Portman Square, July 29, 1863.

MY LORD: I have the honor to acknowledge receipt of your lordship's letter of July 25 instant, in which I am informed that her Majesty's minister at Washington was not able to obtain the consent of the United States Government to the passage of the *Shannon* through the blockade for the purpose of delivering over to the authorities of the Confederate States a prisoner charged with murder committed on board a Confederate vessel of war.

Your lordship further informs me that for reasons stated in the letter her Majesty's Government had reluctantly come to the conclusion that the prisoner ought not to be detained in custody by any British authority longer than might be necessary to dispose of him on shore; and that orders had accordingly been issued to that effect to the proper authorities at Bermuda and to the British admiral on the North American station.

I shall send a copy of your lordship's letter by the first opportunity to the Secretary of State at Richmond, and can only anticipate the great regret with which the President of the Confederate States will learn that her Majesty's Government had deemed it proper thus to depart from its original purpose in regard to this prisoner, as the same had been communicated to him, under instruction from your lordship, by Mr. Moore, late British consul at Richmond.

I have the honor to be, your lordship's very obedient servant,
J. M. MASON.

Right Hon. EARL RUSSELL,
Her Majesty's Secretary of State for Foreign Affairs.

[Enclosure.]

24 UPPER SEYMOUR STREET,
Portman Square, July 29, 1863.

MY LORD: As promised in my letter of the 21st of July instant, I have now the honor to communicate herewith to your lordship a copy of the dispatch of the 6th of June ultimo from the Secretary of State of the Confederate States to me, with copies of the documents accompanying it. They relate to the matter of the dismissal of Mr. Moore, late British consul at Richmond.

I have the honor to be your lordship's very obedient servant,
J. M. MASON.

Right Hon. EARL RUSSELL,
Her Majesty's Secretary of State for Foreign Affairs.

Letter of instructions to New York correspondent of Index.

LONDON, *August 13, 1863.*

I have but little time to keep my promise made per last steamer of writing you more fully per this one. After all, a man who knows the South as well as you do, and also understands the situation so well and seizes the salient points as you have done in your letters to the Index, will need but slight directions. I may therefore confine my instructions within a few words. Consider yourself as writing for an uninformed public, to whom everything which tends to make the American news intelligible is welcome. All information about men who surge up from obscurity, of places, of things, of parties, and their tendencies and prospects is certain to be acceptable. All that tends to expose the weakness of the administration, or that promises a reasonable prospect of a change of feeling among the people or a disposition toward the only peace that it is possible to have, is, of course, especially valuable, but of this I expect but little for the present. I do not pledge myself always to publish your letters, because I have sometimes editorial axes to grind, the metal and temper of which it is impossible you should know in New York, but you must never consider such suppression as a slight to yourself. Any private hints also that you can give me in the discharge of my onerous and delicate duties I will most gratefully receive, even if I should not appear to act upon them.

As regards compensation, I will pay you £2.2.0 for each letter, whether published or not, in such manner and at such time as you may direct, and your outlay for postage, of which please keep a memorandum.

Should there be a lack of material, as may sometimes happen in the episodes of stagnation which are not infrequent in this war, a sketch of the tone and even, as occasion may serve, of the personnel of the New York press will amply supply the deficiency. The only fault which you, from an American point of view, are likely to fall into is to suppose that the British public knows the A B C of American politics. Addressing an English audience you must never presume upon any knowledge of American affairs.

" Facta non verba " is the Index's motto, and is to be recommended to all its contributors and correspondents; but when we have to substitute words for facts, I know of none that will better serve my purpose than yours. So do not be afraid of indulging in any disquisitions on the topics of the day when they lend themselves to it.

Lastly, give me, as far as possible in your letters, what to one of your editorial experience need not be more accurately described than as " quotable paragraphs."

So soon as I see my way clear to do it I will raise what I admit to be an inadequate compensation, but just at this moment strict economy is a necessity to me, for the Index expenses are getting, to an American eye, fabulously extravagant.

> Very cordially, yours,
>
> HENRY HOTZE.

———, Esq., *New York, United States.*

Letter of instructions to Turin correspondent.

LONDON, *August 17, 1863.*

DEAR SIR: I beg to acknowledge your letter to the Index, and also your private favor of 14th instant, in which you inform me that you have agreed to subscribe for 20 copies of the Discussione and the Commercio regularly, amounting for the former to 400 francs, and the latter 200 francs per annum, to be paid quarterly. Although the amount exceeds the limits I had set, the use which you have been able to make of those papers promises so well, that I cordially sanction the outlay, and conformably to your desire remit the first quarter, commencing with July 1, in a check for £6 on my bankers to your order.

I am in hopes that the Government, recognizing your valuable services, will enable me to deal with you more liberally hereafter, but for the present you must remember that what I do in Italy is altogether outside of my regular sphere of duty, which is confined to Great Britain. It is done on my individual responsibility, under the conviction that a small [sum] of money can not be better spent. But even my English expenses have of late exceeded my contingent allowance, and I am therefore under the necessity of leaving many things undone which I much wish to do.

Better change the Paris address I gave you to M. Emile d'Erlanger, 21 Rue de la Chaussée d'Antin. I am particularly anxious that all your articles should come well under the eye of that gentleman. He is the head of the firm that negotiates our loan, and it is not impossible that I may succeed in inducing him to give some material assistance to your efforts.

It is simply justice to you that I should repeat my cordial approval of your labors. I think that you have shown admirable tact in the selection of your matter, and you can not do better than continue in the precise line you have adopted, and as you have succeeded beyond my expectations, you need not be discouraged at occasional disappointments, which I know from experience are inseparable from such a work as ours. At the same time I can not too much caution you against making the idea of emancipation prominent. I understand what concessions you are obliged to make to the prejudices and still more to the timidity of editors, but I pray you make such concessions only sparingly and as an extreme necessity. Believe me that so long as we have an army in the field, even if every seaport were lost, we should not accept recognition or even aid at the price of any foreign intermeddling in our domestic concerns. Whatever we may do hereafter in the way of modification of our institutions will and must be done spontaneously.

The next, or possibly the following number of the Index will open a view which you may find it useful to follow up, and which may enable you to evade the scruples of your editorial tyrants. It is, in substance, that the South can not consistently with self-respect and a jealous regard to a genuine independence, consent to conditions relating to her internal affairs that are imposed by foreign Governments; that the deficiencies in our slave legislation of which Europe most complains, are mainly due to the fact that the attention of Southern legislators has been absorbed in the necessity for external defense of her social fabric, that these deficiencies have been for the most part supplied by the force of public opinion and the Christian piety of the Southern people; that the South, which has proved itself a generous, brave, and humane nation, is sure, so soon as she is left to turn her thoughts inwardly, to detect existing evils and supply the suitable remedies, just as any other society seeks, in self-defense, to protect itself against the unbridled license of human passion;

and, finally, that the way to make European counsels in this delicate task acceptable to the South is not to charge it with crimes of which it is not guilty and which prove those who make the charge ignorant of the subject on which they proffer advice. In other words, that all the reforms that can reasonably be expected will surely be made by the South itself, but can not be hoped for through foreign and violent interference, nor during the progress of this war, for the time of making improvements and alterations in a house is not when it is beset and beleaguered by a strong enemy threatening to pillage and burn it and kill the inhabitants.

I send you provisionally a few receipts of the Index; until I can have some printed specially for your use these will do.

I suppose your subscription to the two Turin papers are terminable in the event of the editors ceasing to fill their part of the engagement.

Very cordially, yours,

HENRY HOTZE.

Signor ———, *Turin, Italy.*

Letter to Manchester Correspondent of Index.

LONDON, *August 21, 1863.*

DEAR SIR: Your favor with enclosures was received on Tuesday morning, our day of publication, and in consequence could not receive attention in time for the current number of the Index. I am favorably impressed with the suggestion your letter contains, and although I am averse to increasing the already very numerous staff of the Index, I am not without hope that I may be able to find a place for you. At present, however, I can only accept your offer of a correspondence from Manchester, for which the Index will pay £1.1.0 per week. I have ordered your present letter to be headed " The Confederate cause in Lancashire," and if this expresses your idea, it may remain the permanent heading.

In entering upon this provisional engagement (should the terms be acceptable to you) trusting that in time it will lead to your closer identification with the Index, you will permit me to offer a few suggestions for your guidance. It is the settled opinion, not only of the enemies but also of the friends of the Confederate cause, that the laboring population of Lancashire is radically hostile to the South, and that for various reasons the mill owners and wealthier classes have differed but little from their employees in their view of the American war. Any facts tending to show that this opinion is ill-founded, or that there is a growing change of feeling in the manufacturing districts, will, of course, be extremely valuable, but unless substantiated by indisputable evidence, will meet with but skeptical readers, especially if appearing in the columns of the Index. The power and influence of that paper, which have grown beyond the most sanguine expectations of its friends, depend wholly on its scrupulous adherence to the truth in those matters in which it is most deeply interested and in its moderation of language and statements on all subjects. In writing for it you must, therefore, always remember that you have to refute the suspicion of partisanship;

not indeed that the Index professes to be a neutral paper—far from this—but that its readers will always be disposed to make allowances for the tendency to represent facts as we wish them to be. It is desirable therefore that you should fortify yourself well with dates, names, and quotations. I must caution you also against attaching undue importance or giving disproportionate prominence to local meetings and isolated expressions of good will in favor of the South. This would infallibly weaken the authority which your letter in my opinion are destined to acquire. In other words, make a skillful, but resist the temptation of making an unfair, use of the materials at your disposal. All facts connected with the distress will always be most interesting.

In conclusion I thank you for the preference you have shown the Index and your offers of service in furthering its interests. Whatever tends to increase the circulation and influence of the paper, tends pro tanto to benefit the cause we have at heart.

Cordially, yours,

HENRY HOTZE.

———, Esq., *Manchester.*

LONDON, *August 21, 1863.*

DEAR SIR: As the political director, if not nominal editor, of the Index I beg to acknowledge your favor of yesterday, correcting certain errors into which the Paris correspondent of that paper has fallen in referring to your biweekly letters to La Patrie from Providence, R. I. I am uncertain whether your letter was intended for publication or only for private information, but until I hear from you to the contrary, shall regard it as the latter. In either case I shall direct that no unfair or disrespectful references to you' shall in future appear in the Paris correspondence.

I thank you cordially for the friendly sentiments you profess for my country and its cause, and I am far from wishing to take issue with you on the opinions which you hold with regard to our institution of slavery. As, however, you do me the honor to ask me for "indications which I may think calculated to give you a right idea of the social condition of the South," being about to prepare an article on that subject for the Revue Contemporaine, you will perhaps pardon me if, deeply interested as I am, that so influential a journal should not undesignedly misrepresent us, I caution you against a few of the most essential errors into which a European is likely to fall.

It is customary to represent the class of slave owners as a small and tyrannical oligarchy, and to produce this impression a most disingenuous treatment of statistics has been resorted to. You will please, therefore, remember that the 345,239 holders of slaves enumerated in the United States census of 1850 are families, not individuals, and according to ascertained laws this number must be multiplied by five to produce the number of persons directly interested in slave property; in other words, nearly 2,000,000, or about one-fourth of the estimated white population. Moreover, even this figure does not include the very large numbers who hire, not own, slaves as domestic servants; nor does it include the vast majority of the professional classes, merchants, physicians, lawyers, etc., who, without either owning or hiring slaves, have an indirect but none the less strong interest in slave property, since they are by family and business ties intimately connected with the planting interest. These considerations will convince you that slavery has far deeper roots in the social system than is generally supposed.

Secondly, a classification according to the census of the slave-owning families gives very different results from what is generally supposed. Only 9 families in the South hold between 500 and 1,000 slaves; only 2 hold over that number, while largely more than one-fourth of them hold less than 5 slaves. Thus the holding of a small number of slaves in close contact with their masters is the general rule; the accumulation of large numbers of slaves under one proprietor, who can bestow but little personal attention to them, is the exception. I shall by to-morrow's post send you valuable statistics on this as on other subjects.

A third and widespread error is that the mass of the Southern white population is in a state of poverty and degradation. The events of the war have sufficiently refuted this calumny, but it may be of service to you to know that according to the census one-half of the white male population is engaged in agriculture and that 563,-138 out of the entire 840,929, or five-eighths of those so engaged, owned their farms.

You will see from these indisputable official figures that the Southern people are not divided into those two classes of fabulously wealthy and luxurious aristocrats on the one hand and miserable vagabonds on the other, which the popular idea represents them to be, but that property is distributed with an equality which has no parallel in any other country except perhaps France.

On the subject of education, religion, etc., the census will inform you that the South is but little behind the North, making allowance for its more scattered population. It has fully as many churches and schools as either England or France. About one-third of the white population are communicants of some Christian church. Although mostly Protestants, divorces are of less frequent occurrence than at the North; in some States, as in South Carolina, they are not granted at all. The statistics of crime are remarkably small; prostitution is almost unknown, except in the larger cities, and pauperism does not exist at all. You will please also remember in spite of your hostility to slavery that slavery is less a question of property than it is a form of civil government over an inferior race only a few generations removed from barbarism and equal in numbers to one-third of the master race. The Yankees, as you will see by a very fair exposition of their plantation management in last Index, do not propose, while nominally freeing the slaves, to give them civil and political rights. They will none the less make the negro work for the benefit of the white man under compulsion, and instead of the patriarchal form, which had many extenuating features, they would substitute a " workhouse system " which retains all the worst characteristics without any of the compensating advantages of slavery.

Of books and reviews I can indicate to you but few. The South has hitherto had no literature of its own. Travelers have usually visited

it with strong prejudices and written either to subserve political and
party purposes or with a view to pleasing biased readers rather than
investigating the truth. Many have only allowed themselves to be
the vehicles of repeating slanderous or ridiculous fictions. The two
books that will give you the best view of the social manners of the
South are the book of travels by Miss Murray (a maid of honor to
the Queen) and Miss Frederica Bremers, Homes in the New World.
Statistics are the best study of the social condition of the South, and
of these I will send you to-morrow all I can collect in so short a
period and far away from home.

With the enormous productiveness of the country you are doubtless already quite familiar. The cotton culture alone produces annually about 1,000 million francs' worth of exportable staple. I [had]
almost forgotten to remind you, in treating your prolific subject,
that whatever the theoretical evils of the slave system are, they are
in practise modified by many restraining influences Practically the
master's power over the slave is not greater than that which he has
over his wife and children The instinct of self-preservation in society at large, and the public opinion of a Christian community, protect the slave far more effectually than mere laws, though I am not
prepared to deny that many improvements are required and will
certainly be made in the laws when the South, resting from her struggle, has time and leisure for self-examination.

Very sincerely, yours,

HENRY HOTZE.

M. FELIX DUCAIGNE,
　　3 Rue St. Victor, Paris.

Sketch of proposed pamphlet on Mexico.

LONDON, *August 23, 1863.*

DEAR SIR: It is difficult in the composition of a hasty letter to
give you a sketch of such a pamphlet as you proposed should be, but
since you are so good as to enquire my views, I shall attempt something like what the Germans call an umriss.

It seems to me, then, that the pamphlet might open with a glowing description of the magnificent resources, the unparalleled climate,
and the vast commercial importance of Mexico. This would flatter
the French public, already much delighted with their new conquest,
and rouse interest. For this, I know of no better guide than Hum-
boldt's Nouvelle Espagne.

Next might come a rapid and epigrammatic statement of the causes
which have led to the anarchy that had become chronic in Mexico, and
have defeated all attempts at good government and social order.
These causes I am strongly convinced are the confusion and chaos in
which the various races which constitute the population have been
thrown by the immature political experiments commencing with
Mexican independence. Some very strong and eloquent passages
might be quoted in this connection from L'Inegalité des Races, a work
published in 1854–55 by Count Gobineau, a French savant and diplo-
matist. A skillful pen would not neglect the opportunity of introducing here a few touches without however trespassing on dangerous

ground, calculated by way of contrast to bring the social system of the Confederate States into a more favorable light than it has heretofore appeared to the French public.

Next the hostility of the United States to the French regeneration might be brought out in striking colors. The opportunity should not be lost to point how that "Model Republic" has departed from that mission of liberty and civilization which sentimental admirers living in the ideas of 1776 assigned to it, and how those who now love her, love as a man whose affections survive every charm that had won them. A center shot may here be fired at the very citadel of Red Republicanism. The necessity of an alliance with the young Confederate power follows as a natural sequence.

The Napoleonic idea that France is the protectress of struggling nationalities may be here brought in strong relief. It may be shown how faithful the present Emperor has been to this idea of his dynasty, how glorious and unselfish it is, and how France has reaped the reward in a more abundant measure than has rewarded the sordid and groveling policies which other nations have been led to adopt. The fallacies of "Historicus," which have involved England, might be exposed in a few sentences with good effect.

The commercial interests, which will acquire an unprecedented development between the two regenerated nations of the new continent and between them and France, and the promises of prosperity to all three thus held out, form another suggestive and inexhaustible topic.

Nor should the Emperor's idea, thrown out in his letter of instructions to General Forey, be neglected, the future destinies of the Latin race in the Old and New World may be wrought up into a magnificent conclusion, and the two master races, the Latin and the Anglo-Norman, typified by Mexico and the Confederate States in the Western Hemisphere, as by France and England in the Eastern, may be represented as clasping hands and marching breast to breast onward in the great career of civilization and true liberty.

I need not add how keen a point is given to your proposed treatise by the news just received from Frankfort. The insult so publicly given to France in the presence of the sovereigns assembled under the presidency of the Emperor of Austria, the brother to the destined successor to the throne of Montezuma, is so obviously premeditated that it must sting the French pride to the quick. The recognition of the existing Confederacy would be but the logical reply to the ostentatious recognition of the nonexisting Republic. If America should consider that an act of war, the world will be witness that she was the first to declare it. This might be introduced like a sting, or it might be so distinctly enunciated as to startle all Europe as an imperial threat.

Speaking of the various elements of the Mexican population in the body of the pamphlet, I should advise as good policy to avow a warm sympathy and paternal interest in the Indian of pure race. They are really a very good and docile substratum of the new system if properly cared for, but independently of that French sentimentalism takes a romantic interest in them and confounds them with the idyllic heroes of the author of Paul and Virginia. This element of success is not to be despised.

All this is necessarily very hastily thrown together. I write upon the presumption that your ideas upon the subject are matured and that you simply wish to ascertain for the purpose of comparison how the same idea presents itself to a Southern mind. Whatever your plan may be, I am certain that it is a good one, and if I can render you any assistance in carrying out the details that you may have decided on, I shall be happy to do so.

Believe me, my dear sir, yours, truly,

HENRY HOTZE.

M. ——, *Paris.*

No. 56.]
3 RUE D'ARLON,
Brussels, August 15, 1863.

SIR: After a sojourn of about forty-eight hours with King Leopold at his country palace, Queen Victoria left here yesterday for Saxe-Coburg-Gotha.

The King, I am quite confident, conversed freely and fully with her upon the importance, almost paramount in the interests of humanity and advancing civilization, of terminating hostilities in America by the concerted moral action of European potentates. Personally I incur no risk in stating that her Majesty's feelings are as warmly enlisted for the success of the Confederate States as are the feelings of her most sympathizing subjects in behalf of those States. She would not have within her bosom the heart of a noble woman were it otherwise.

The serious reverses which we experienced about the 4th of July disheartened for a time many of our best friends in western Europe. Indeed, a number of them utterly despaired. They are now, however, slowly recovering their spirits. Each arrival from New York is more assuring than its predecessor. Charleston continues invincible; General Lee is master of his position. The armies of the North are at a dead standstill. The expired term of service is drawing brigade after brigade from the field; the enforcement of the conscription is delayed, if not abandoned. These occurrences, which can not be concealed by the Washington Cabinet, must, if we meet with no terrible disaster, speedily satisfy the world of enlightened mankind, as it has not been satisfied before, that the costly and brutal attempt to conquer us has resulted in a complete and disgraceful failure.

The influence of the King of the Belgians upon the different governments of Europe was never so powerful as at present. He seems to be a sort of privy councillor to each. His health has been so perfectly reestablished and his spirits so fine that he never displayed more activity and more interest in public affairs than he does now. I esteem him as our best European friend, and I believe that he has our case earnestly under consideration and anxiously awaits the hour when he can make a manifestation in our favor which will carry all Europe with it.

His mind is, naturally enough, occupied with the embryo Mexican throne and its contemplated occupant. He will take care that his son-in-law Maximilian shall not inconsiderately grasp at that which may turn out to be nothing more than the merest of shadows.

It is apprehended that Louis Napoleon has other aims than benefiting the House of the Hapsburgs in the selection which he has made of a ruler for Mexico. That he will be content with nothing less than "the lion's part" of the benefits derived from his triumphant invasion of that country; that when Maximilian is crowned he will let him discover that he has no other support upon which to rely than French bayonets; and that if the Emperor of his creation adopt any policy or express any opinion contrary to his wisdom those bayonets will be withdrawn and the Austrian prince subjected to the unrestrained revenge of Mexican revolutionists.

Louis Napoleon could not at first, without giving downright offense to Spain and causing his motives to be severely animadverted upon by most other nations, designate Prince Napoleon as the Emperor of Mexico; but that it is his ulterior purpose, and has been from the beginning, to place the crown upon the head of his much-dreaded and troublesome cousin and retain it there by military force supplied by France I have never doubted. Jerome Napoleon, if not well provided for beforehand, will be perhaps fatally harmful to the dynasty of the Emperor of the French. He has much more mind than he has credit for possessing, and has a strong hold on the affections of the Red Republicans. Were Louis Napoleon to die—and he can not be expected to live many years, being now upwards of 55 with a shattered constitution—Jerome Napoleon would most likely overthrow the Prince Imperial immediately thereafter. The real cause, therefore, in my opinion, whatever the ostensible one, of the Mexican expedition was to guard against this probable eventuality.

Rather than be subjected to the iron yoke of the North; rather than belong to a Union in which such guerrillas as have manifested themselves since the beginning of the war would be members, there is no hope that I would not catch at for self-preservation, however desperate. I would even gladly see my Government entering into an offensive and defensive treaty with the Emperor of the French. But I must confess that unless the United States shall suddenly spring a war upon France, which is not within the range of reasonable likelihood, there is no conceivable contingency in which such an alliance can be formed. The diplomacy of the cabinet of the Tuileries is directed in a masterly manner to the retention of amicable relations with the Cabinet of Washington. If the Emperor of the French has occasionally expressed himself favorable to us, it has been more with a view to show the North that it was her interest to be acquiescent as to that which he was accomplishing in Mexico than to benefit ourselves. It is palpably his policy to nourish the exhaustion of each of the belligerents as much as possible. He waited for a propitious time to overrun that distracted country, and he doubtless looks forward to the day, not far distant as he supposes, when he can establish Mexico as she once was with utter impunity. If he had ever our cause earnestly at heart, wished sincerely for a speedy termination of our sufferings and the consolidation of our independence, he had never arrested by pressing interference the war which otherwise was inevitable between Great Britain and the United States, engendered by the *Trent* affair. Nor can I—I who so acutely felt the disappointment—ever cease to doubt his professed good intentions in our behalf when I recur to the contents of the autograph letter of King Leopold, of October 15 of last year.

I still believe, and shall still believe, whatever disaster we may experience in the field, that our independence was an accomplished fact the moment that it was asserted. Every victory that the North has achieved has weakened her power for consummating her cherished final end. I did believe that we were destined to overrun her, and while that belief is not entirely relinquished, I am very sure that there is not the remotest chance or shadow of a chance that she can overrun us.

I have the honor to be, sir, very respectfully, your obedient servant,

A. DUDLEY MANN.

Hon. J. P. BENJAMIN,
    Secretary of State, C. S. A., Richmond, Va.

No. 31.]
                           DEPARTMENT OF STATE,
                                    Richmond, August 17, 1863.

SIR: I have the honor to forward duplicate of my No. 30 of 4th instant.

I should have mentioned in that dispatch that the President deems the best mode of disposing of the archives of your mission will be to deposit them for safe-keeping with Mr. Slidell until our relations with Great Britain can be placed on a footing satisfactory to this Government. It would be well also that you should inform our officers in England that, whenever at a loss how to act in the business confided to them by the several departments, it is expected by the President that they will consult Mr. Slidell with the same freedom as they have heretofore consulted with you.

In the matter of the seal of the Confederacy and some other small affairs which you have been good enough to put in train for the Department, I suppose Mr. Hotze can take your instructions about terminating them. You may, however, confide them to another person at your choice, if you have any reason for preferring not to intrust them to Mr. Hotze.

I have received your dispatches down to No. 41, inclusively, with the exception of Nos. 4, 5, 6, 7, and 8, but deem it scarcely necessary under the circumstances to reply to them in detail.

We have as yet no news of the books purchased, for which you enclosed a bill.

Your letters for Mrs. Mason have been handed to her. I am happy to inform you that all your family are well.

Very respectfully, your obedient servant,

J. P. BENJAMIN,
                Secretary of State.

Hon. JAMES M. MASON, *London.*

No. 22.]
                           DEPARTMENT OF STATE,
                                Richmond, August 17, 1863.

SIR: Since my dispatch of 4th instant I have received your Nos. 37, 38, and 39, of the 12th, 21st, and 25th June, respectively. They were all received on 14th August, and duplicates came to hand this morning.

In mentioning the instructions given to Mr. Mason to withdraw from the Court of St. James, I omitted to give some directions which are sent by this mail. The President desires that the archives of the London mission be temporarily deposited with you until our relations with Great Britain are established on a footing satisfactory to this Government, and he also requests that you will so far fill the void left by Mr. Mason's departure as to give to the officers of the several Departments now in England the benefit of your advice and assistance whenever they may be in need of it, in the same manner and as freely as Mr. Mason has heretofore done. Mr. Mason has been requested to direct them to apply to you in case of doubt or difficulty as to their proper action in any emergency.

Your suggestions in relation to a common agent to be charged with the duty of apportioning the funds abroad among the various claimants according to a sound discretion have been communicated to the President and are fully approved. He is taking measures in concert with the heads of the War, Navy, and Treasury Departments for placing this matter on such a footing as to avoid the continuance of a state of things so prejudicial to the public interests as that which you describe.

The account given by you of your conversation with the Emperor and of his interview with Messrs. Roebuck and Lindsay, taken in connection with the debates on the Roebuck motion in the House of Commons, the unhesitating denials of the English ministers, the note in the Moniteur, and the published letter of Mr. Lindsay, present an ensemble as remarkable as any incident of diplomatic history which I can recall to memory. Without entering into any detailed examination of the curious statements and contra statements of the English gentlemen in and out of the ministry, the important fact has been saliently developed that France is ready and anxious for our recognition and that England is opposed to it. As the English cabinet know perfectly well, and indeed so declare, that this war can only end by the establishment of Southern independence; as the establishment of that independence is considered by mankind at large to depend on its common recognition by European powers; and as the war can not end till that recognition is obtained, the only possible inference to be drawn from the action of the British Government is that a continuance of the war is desirable in the interest of Great Britain, nor can any sophistry blind the people of this country to that patent fact. No comment need be made on it, but it is evident that appeals to justice or humanity are equally vain to change or affect the decision of the British cabinet, and that it is therefore rather prejudicial than conducive to our interests or our honor to attempt any further correspondence with the British Government on the subject. When that Government shall have become satisfied that the war has lasted long enough to accomplish whatever purposes its continuance can effect for the interest of Great Britain, the foreign office will doubtless take the necessary steps for establishing formal intercourse with us, and until then it is hardly probable that further communication will be made to it from this Confederacy.

The Polish question seems to be as far from settlement as ever, according to our last dates from Europe, and until the continental powers are relieved from all apprehension on that score it is not to be anticipated that any of them will hazard isolated action in our affairs. We therefore expect nothing from your recent interviews with Mr. Isturitz on the subject mentioned in my No. 16, although gratified to perceive with how much satisfaction the overture was received.

The heat of the weather here has been so intense as to place an effectual check on all military movements, and it is not probable that anything of importance will occur for several weeks. Our crops are magnificent and supplies of grain and forage will be super-abundant for at least twelve months to come. The like good accounts from Europe encourage us with the belief that our enemies will not enjoy this year the unprecedented good fortune which enabled them in the first two years of the war to supply the deficiency of Southern products by the export of Northern grain, and thus to affect their exchanges without any important drain of specie.

I am, respectfully, your obedient servant,

J. P. BENJAMIN,
Secretary of State.

Hon. JOHN SLIDELL, *Paris.*

WAR DEPARTMENT, ORDNANCE OFFICE,
Richmond, August 19, 1863.

SIR: I have the honor to enclose to you for notice copies of statements furnished by the collectors of Charleston and Wilmington, showing quantity of cotton shipped in the period named in each, also number of steamers and export duty collected.

Very respectfully,

THOS. L. BAYNE,
Major, in charge of Government steamers, etc.

Hon. J. P. BENJAMIN,
Secretary of State.

[Enclosure.]

Abstract of vessels that have cleared from the district of Charleston, S. C., from the 1st day of November, 1862, to the 31st May, 1863.

Name of vessel.	Tons.	Name of vessel.	Tons.
Steamer Leopard	862	Steamer Calypso	668
Sloop Samuel Martin	80	Steamer Eagle	230
Steamer Antonica	563	Steamer Antonica	563
Schooner Pocotaligo	236	Steamer Margaret and Jessie	732
Schooner Rover	24	Steamer Cherokee	589
Schooner George Chisholm	85	Sloop Neptune	59
Schooner Retribution	150	Schooner Amelia	29
Steamer Nina	338	Schooner Harvest	25
Sloop Brune	17	Schooner Maj. E. Willis	74
Steamer Aries	740	Sloop Angelina	14
Steamer Antonica	563	Sloop Emeline	35
Steamer Leopard	862	Steamer Ella and Annie	905
Steamer Tropic	323	Steamer General Beauregard	824
Brig Victoria	199	Steamer Ella and Annie	905
Schooner Confederacy	67	Steamer Britannia	400
Steamer Antonica	563	Steamer Ruby	400
Steamer Calypso	668	Steamer Stonewall Jackson	872
Sloop Rosalie	29	Steamer Ruby	400
Steamer Douglas	729	Steamer Margaret and Jessie	732
Steamer Flora	437	Schooner Jas. R. Pringle	90
Steamer Thistle	562	Steamer General Beauregard	824
Sloop Empress	20	Steamer General Moultrie	331
Steamer Victory	618	Steamer Norsman	197
Sloop Aurelia	33	Steamer Antonica	563
Steamer Ruby	400	Steamer Calypso	668
Steamer Flora	437	Steamer Margaret and Jessie	732
Sloop Nellie	31	Schooner Magnolia	57
Steamer Gertrude	438		

W. F. COLCOCK, *Collector.*

COLLECTOR'S OFFICE, *Charleston, S. C.*

No. 27.] CONFEDERATE STATES COMMERCIAL AGENCY,
London, August 27, 1863.

SIR: Since my last, No. 26, I have several times written you unofficially, having time only for hasty composition, and yet wishing to sketch for you, however imperfectly, an observer's impression of public opinion here during this critical period of our affairs. At my latest official date, July 23, I reported that men's minds were in a state of perplexity and suspense. The loan had then dropped to 4 per cent discount, but there were few sales and as yet no tendency to a panic. Only a few days afterwards, when the last lingering doubts about the events on the Mississippi were removed and no hope remained of Lee again turning upon the enemy, the loan, despite the utmost exertions of its friends, fell with accelerating velocity, at first to 8, then to 15, until it touched the unprecedented depth of 36, though only for a moment. Thence, and having passed the perilous date at which another instalment was due, it recovered again, and has since, with various fluctuations, but with a general upward tendency, reached the last quotations of 24–22 discount. The slightest causes affect it sensibly, without adequate reasons. Thus, the order of Mr. Memminger, directing the burning of cotton in imminent danger of capture produced an anxious flutter, though it must have been evident to the meanest capacity that fire could entail no loss greater than capture; that of the two the flames were to be preferred to the enemy even in the immediate interest of the bondholders themselves; and lastly that the security depended not on the locality of any designated bales of cotton but upon the good faith and the stability of the Confederate Government. You may be assured that the Federal agents did not fail to avail themselves of this trepidation, and it is stated positively by those who have the means of knowing, that large sums of money are freely sacrificed to injure the credit of the Confederacy. You have here, in the tremulous condition of the loan, a sufficiently accurate description of the state of public opinion. It is almost as I described it a month ago; it has not yet recovered a logical standpoint, and is not therefore effected by logical reasons; it halts about equidistant between the two extremes, that of absolute confidence in our ultimate success and that of absolute despair in our fortunes. The hopes and sympathies of an almost unanimous people incline it in one direction; the facts as they are here interpreted impel it in the other.

This interpretation of facts is far more unfavorable to our success among the reflecting community at large than the journals represent it. It is thought that at the North, State authority in its last effort will succumb to the central power; that, for a time at least, despite internal commotions, the usurpation at Washington will be able to carry all things with a strong hand, and that the conscription will be enforced. " Meanwhile " our English friends tell us with undisguised uneasiness, " you are losing the very portion of your territory where the white population preponderates, valuable recruiting ground which is acquired by the enemy." The respectable press, so far from expressing these fears, labors zealously and intelligently to quiet them, and at no time during this war has our cause received such valuable assistance from journalism.

In this disquietude of the public mind it is perhaps not to be re-gretted that our recent reverses are ascribed to accident or to indi-vidual errors rather than to the exhaustion of our defensive strength. Thus the strategy of General Pemberton, not his loyalty and heroism, is subjected privately to severe military criticisms, the substance of which appears to be that he had rashly exposed a small force to over-whelming odds, instead of attempting by a Fabian policy to weary out the attacking column; that he had fought on the wrong side of rivers, and that he had insufficiently prepared his post for a long siege. Others blame General Johnston for not having, when the relief of Vicksburg became impracticable, attempted a diversion on the lower Mississippi, or against some other less formidable foe than Grant. Again, General Lee's incomplete success at Gettysburg is accounted for by alleged precipitation of subordinate commanders, rendering necessary a sudden alteration of plans; and the whole onward movement is considered a bold stroke to end the war, prompted by the passive attitude of Europe and the apparent hope-lessness of obtaining peace in any other manner. I do not of course pretend to be competent to judge of these speculations, and I repeat them, first, because it may be useful for you to know the views which prevail in those circles which, more than newspapers, form and crystallize public opinion; and, secondly, because they indicate that the English mind sees in our temporary reverses the effects of tran-sient or accidental, instead of inherent and incurable, causes.

On the other hand it is unfortunately too true that the English nation has taken in our struggle rather what may be called a " sport-ing " interest, in which, if you will pardon me for so homely an illustration, it has a wager at stake upon the slighter but more agile of two antagonists, and has not yet fully waked up to the universal issue of moral right, national liberty, and civilization which are in-volved in the contest. Lord Palmerston jests in the lobby of the house or over the dinner table at the expense of the Yankees; five Englishmen out of every six in a railway carriage will exult over Confederate successes and express annoyance at Federal triumphs; but the higher and nobler aspect of the question is scarcely ever dwelled upon even in Parliament. I could wish that some solemn voice, louder and more authoritative than that of the mere journalist, a voice which can command at once the attention of the whole civil-ized world, might speak to the conscience of this nation. I have, in this connection, thought much and often of the modern system of diplomacy, which, following the example of France, has in the Polish negotiation been adopted by even such powers as are least prone to depart from old rules, Austria, Russia, and England. I refer to the system of addressing diplomatic documents, ostensibly directed to cabinets or diplomatic agents, immediately to public opinion. All, or nearly all, the notes, replies, and rejoinders of all the powers in the Polish negotiations have been published almost before the ink was dry. I can imagine a series of dispatches from your Department, protracted over several months, in which the policy of this Government might be arraigned before the highest tribunals in Europe, and with but one certain, inevitable result. What governments who have free access to the ordinary diplomatic channels do, may, I have thought, be surely done without impropriety, by one which is debarred that access. Nor does our Government lack a suitable medium of publicity, which can be used without appearing to show partiality, to rouse journalistic jealousies or to ask favors. If I give utterance to this thought, it is not to offer suggestions to you, but it is from the depth of bitterness of my feelings at finding my own voice too feeble to pierce through the callous selfishness which, like animal fat, coats the hearts of these Old World nations.

I pass with relief to the brighter prospects which are opening to our cause on the other side of the channel. I have already enclosed you in a private letter the intelligence, telegraphed from Frankfort, that the Federal consul general there had hoisted the Mexican flag by the side of his own, in consequence of an arrangement concluded as early as March last between Seward and Juarez, to the effect that in certain contingencies, which have come to pass, the Republic should be represented by the agents of the United States abroad. The time and place of this insult, in the very eyes of the brother of the future occupant of the Mexican throne, prove it premeditated, and as I observed to you at the time the logical reply of France to this ostentatious recognition of a nonexisting republic would appear to be the recognition of the existent Confederacy. I now enclose you another slip from the letter of the Paris correspondent of the Morning Herald, referring to the admission of one of our cruisers into the imperial dockyard at Brest, a most significant fact, if true. But whether this or any other isolated item of intelligence be well founded, the belief daily gains ground that the Emperor is on the point of taking the step from which he has been so long delayed by the remonstrances of the British foreign office. The uneasiness about our ability to maintain ourselves, which I chronicled above, tends, rather than otherwise, to ensure for his overtures, if such shall be made to this country, a more favorable reception, both officially and from the public, than while our military prospects seemed brighter. One of the most formidable obstacles, moreover, is removed from our path. As the season advances the fears of a Polish war vanish; and there is now, I am convinced, nothing to apprehend on this score, at least until next spring.

I can not conclude my political review without a passing word upon the singular spectacle, though it effects us not, which Germany now presents. A great empire seeking that unity, the attempt at which has destroyed a great empire in America; a council composed of crowned heads, with an Emperor as president, a King for secretary, going seriously through the form of a deliberative assembly. If we have any interest in this matter, it is that Austria, which has unexpectedly entered upon a new life of internal prosperity and external influence, and which is now acquiring the moral as well as political hegemony of Germany, is of all the German powers supposed to be the most friendly—perhaps it would be better to say the only one friendly to us—and the least imbued with those prejudices which have shut us out from the sympathies of continental nations. Furthermore, the impulse which agriculture has within the last few years received in this, the greatest grain-growing country of the Western Hemisphere, makes Austria, independently of the good harvests everywhere this year, a permanent competitor with the Federal States of America in the grain markets of the world.

Some months ago I was induced to employ an Italian gentleman, recommended by Mr. Macfarland, in whose family in Virginia he had long resided, as the Turin correspondent of the Index. I stipu-lated, however, that instead of writing to that paper, except on extraordinary occasions, he should devote the equivalent of the labor upon the Turin press. The expense was trifling, and I regarded the matter as an experiment. But this experiment has succeeded so surprisingly well, my correspondent has been so successful in gaining access to leading Turin journals, and has profited by that success with so much tact that I bring it to your notice and should be glad to be authorized to pay him sufficiently to devote his whole time to this work under my direction. I should judge, the cheapness of liv-ing in Italy being considered, that $1,000 would more than suffice for the purpose. I am tempted by this success to extend the plan gradually to other portions of the Continent. With the assistance of Messrs. Erlanger & Co., who have recently approached me with a somewhat similar idea, I hope to be able at small cost to employ first-rate editorial native talent in the principal centers of German thought and political intelligence. We have already in view several persons who from their relations to their own press can be of ex-treme usefulness in propagating the truth. The same plan which the Index was intended to subserve and which you did me the honor to approve answers in this respect to perfection.

I hope to see the day when in every European capital there shall be a zealous and able man who thoroughly understands our institu-tions and ourselves, and who has the power and the will to vindicate us against our enemies' calumnies. I believe that I possess some fitness for organizing this good work; at all events, I have what supplies many other qualifications, an enthusiastic interest in it; it was the day dream of my early youth, before I had scarcely emerged from boyhood, and I may truly say that I have never lost sight of it nor resigned the hope of its fulfillment. I feel sure that a reaction must speedily set in against certain fanatical beliefs of this century, and I know that my hopes do not deceive me when I see the signs of its having already set in. Among these is one to which perhaps you may be disposed to attach less importance than I do, but which appears to me most suggestive. A new scientific society composed of prominent names has been formed in London which has set itself the task of exposing the heresies that have gained currency in science and politics—of the equality of the races of men. The society is an offshoot or secession from the celebrated Ethnological Society. The president, in writing to me to offer me a seat in the council, said: " You should and must take a strong interest in our objects, for in us is your only hope that the negro's place in nature will ever be scientifically ascertained and fearlessly ex-plained." I quote from memory.

When last spring I had the gratification to acknowledge the receipt of my liberally enlarged contingent allowance I felt confident that my means would be ample to carry out all my cherished plans. Yet, though I have never spent a dollar simply because I had it to spend, and though I never drew a check on my banker without the thought ever present to my mind that it represented so many times the nominal amount in Confederate currency, I have already in the first six months exceeded the allowance. There have, it is true, been unexpected demands upon it, but not such as at the beginning of the year I had not counted on as being able to meet without exceeding the limits. The chief reason of this is that the Index has pecuniarily disappointed expectations. Though it goes into every part of the civilized world, even to Australia and China, both Indies, and the Federal States, and though its English circulation is satisfactorily extending, yet a paper so placed must depend upon the class it represents for subsistence; and, unfortunately, in our case this class is either, owing to their exiled condition, too poor, or else has many other demands upon its purse, or is, I regret to add, in some instances too lukewarm, and withal too numerically small, to afford that support with even an approach to adequacy. Much of this might have been avoided had it been possible to manage the paper as a commercial speculation and less as a political engine, but this was and is out of the question. The Index moreover commits daily a sort of intellectual suicide.

In educating English writers to plead our cause, often purposely with greater emphasis in the columns of other journals, it has raised rivals even in the affections of its own supporters, and few suspect, none know, the silent, unobtrusive agency through which it has operated upon its contemporaries. The North has two papers, one 3-penny and one penny paper, which it subsidizes lavishly. We also have two, a 3-penny one and a penny one, and in respectability, standing, and influence no one would venture to institute even a comparison between the respective champions. We have moreover the advantage over the subsidized writers of the North that our cause is pleaded with the force of personal conviction and with the zeal of personal friendship and political sympathy, and that no tie exists between the writers and the Confederacy, except one which they can honorably acknowledge. In the neutral press, both daily and weekly, we have also important connections, equally honorable, while the North, beyond its own organs, has nothing. All this, I unhesitatingly declare, is due to the Index. Now, while the Index has performed this work, extending its connections, planting new friendships, and establishing rallying points even in the enemy's country, as in the case of its able correspondents in New Orleans and New York and elsewhere, its expenses have grown, while its income has but imperceptibly kept pace. Advertisers, upon whom all papers must rely for their bread, have stood aloof, seeing, with tradesmanlike timidity, no sufficient present advantage to compensate for the risk of present loss in avowing their political preferences. Even great firms open in their expression of Southern sympathies have deemed it prudent not to have their names in the Index.

Although I concentrated upon the Index all the disbursements that could advantageously be made through it, I have frequently had to sacrifice its interests to more important considerations, and there has never been a return at all commensurate, pecuniarily speaking, to the outlay. Thus it has happened that the expenses of the Index still exceed its income in very nearly the same proportion as at its establishment. In the first nine months of its existence, my friend, Mr. Brewer, Mr. A. P. Wetter, and to a lesser extent, myself, contributed jointly to the support of the paper £1,350, while the contingent fund during the same period, directly or indirectly (through purchase of copies for distribution, etc.) contributed less than £1,000. This, of course, embraces an exceptionally expensive period, that of the establishment of the paper, but a survey of the accounts convinces me that the Index, with its present staff of contributors and correspondents, will absorb the whole of my contingent allowance, leaving me no reserve in the event of a delay in remittance or for such purposes as the recent wholesale diffusion of the address of the Southern clergy, or any other disbursements which can not properly be made through the paper.

I am quite content to confine myself wholly within this sphere of action and, beyond a moderate increase of my salary (so as to rid me of the necessity of accounting for expenses which, made with an official motive, are yet ostensibly personal) I should not ask for any present enlargement of my means. Yet if the President and yourself think that I have done well in regard to the address, and wish to enable me to seize similar opportunities, should such present themselves, it will be necessary to make me a supplementary allowance to be used in such contingencies and not otherwise. Frankly, however, I should prefer that any increase that may be contemplated should be in the form of a salary rather than in the other, which would not in the slightest degree alter the nature of my expenses, and be regarded like the contingent allowance, as a trust confided to me for the interests of the public service, with the same responsibility, only less onerous in its details. The salary allowed to the consular officer at this port, especially if it were made to commence with the second half year, would enable me at once to transfer from the accounts of the secret-service fund to my own a number of petty expenses, considerable in the aggregate, which, however, fairly made and scrupulously explained, figured ill in official accounts, and always admit of the question of judiciousness, economy, or propriety. This measure, which would be so gratifying to me in every respect, would require only that the old consular regulations, unless they have since been repealed, should be to that extent enforced, for the act of August 18, 1856, cited in section 104, page 48, of the United States Consular Regulations, expressly provides that the consular officers at certain enumerated ports, among which is London, shall receive the same compensation under whatever designation appointed.

I am aware that in making this request I may be considered selfish and mercenary, but I do not fear that you would think me capable of such unspeakable meanness as to seek personal gain from the Government in this hour. I have only to add that whatever your decision in the matter, I shall cheerfully and readily acquiesce in it.

I had intended to give you some account of the manner in which the Index constantly places opportunities of usefulness in my reach, but this communication has run to so unprecedented a length that I content myself with inclosing you a few selections from my correspondence during a single week. These, after all, will give you a clearer insight into the nature, though far from an adequate idea of the extent of the duties which the Index devolves upon me. For prudential motives the names are omitted.

I have the honor to remain, very respectfully, your obedient servant,

HENRY HOTZE.

Hon. J. P. BENJAMIN,
Secretary of State, Richmond.

No. 44.]   BIARRITZ, August 29, 1863.

SIR: At this time the meetings of the councils-general of the departments, a sort of local legislature of very limited jurisdiction it is true, cause nearly all the leading men in the country, including the ministers, to be absent from Paris. I have profited by this occasion to make a short visit to the seashore, leaving Mr. Eustis to attend to anything that may occur until my return.

I informed you in my last, that I had communicated to M. Drouyn de Lhuys copy of your dispatch on the subject of the consular agent sent by M. de Montholon to Charleston. I did not expect any official reply, but have received from the office of the foreign affairs, through my usual channel of communication, the following memorandum.

PARIS, August 17, 1863.

The Government of the Confederate States appears to be entirely mistaken as to the character of Mr. Laren at Charleston or as to the position of that agent; he is a simple consular clerk, temporarily detached from the consulate-general at New York to take the place of Mr. Durand de St. André, who hastily left his post without authority, fearing the attack of the Federal fleet on Charleston would cause injury to his wife, who was in delicate health. He will receive orders to return there, and resume the position with which he was charged upon the departure of Mr. Belligny, the incumbent of the consulate. We do not believe that the Confederate States, who have already accepted him once, will refuse to receive him now in the same capacity and on the same footing.

You will observe that no objection is made to the refusal to receive Mr. Laren, but that the expectation is expressed that Mr. de St. André will be admitted on the same footing that he was before his unauthorized withdrawal from his post. I shall take no official notice of this memorandum, of which I send you the translation.

I breakfasted with M. Mocquard shortly before leaving Paris. He advised me under existing circumstances not to address any communication to the Emperor on the subject of our affair, especially as I would have the opportunity of seeing him at Biarritz and conversing with him fully. He is expected here next week, when I shall take an early occasion to ask an interview.

I have received a message from Captain Maffitt, of C. S. S. *Florida,* dated off the coast of Ireland, saying that it was his intention to put into Brest for necessary repair, which would require a stay of eighteen days, and requesting me to obtain the necessary permission for that purpose.

Mr. Eustis made, through M. Mocquard, a verbal application to that effect, which I have every reason to suppose will obtain the desired object. Mr. E. has as yet received no notice from Captain Maffitt of his arrival at Brest, although the newspapers speak of a Confederate steamer having arrived at that port.

Rumors are current that the Lincoln Government has formally protested against the form of government proposed under French auspices in Mexico. I learn from my friend at the department of foreign affairs that no such protest has been presented a few days since.

With great respect, your obedient servant,

JOHN SLIDELL.

Hon. J. P. BENJAMIN,
    Secretary of State.

CONFEDERATE STATES OF AMERICA,
WAR DEPARTMENT, ORDNANCE OFFICE,
Richmond, August 29, 1863.

SIR: I have the honor to acknowledge the receipt of your letter of this date, asking me to furnish you an official certificate in answer to the following interrogatories:

First. At what date the Ordnance Bureau commenced running vessels to foreign countries for supplies for Government.

Second. The number of trips in and out made by the Government merchant vessels since that date.

Third. The number of captures, if any, made of the Government merchant steamers by the blockading vessels of the enemy.

In reply I beg to state that:

First. The Ordnance Bureau commenced running steamers early in January of the present year for account of the Government.

Second. Forty-four trips have been made by the Government merchant steamers, or 22 round voyages.

Third. No capture by the blockading vessels of the enemy of any of these steamers has yet occurred.

Your obedient servant,

THOS. L. BAYNE,
Major, on duty with the
Chief of Ordnance in charge of steamers.

Hon. J. P. BENJAMIN,
    Secretary of State.

No. 23.]
        DEPARTMENT OF STATE,
Richmond, September 2, 1863.

SIR: Although it is painfully apparent that but little hope can be entertained of present redress for the injury suffered by this Confederacy in consequence of the respect accorded by neutral nations to the so-called blockade of our entire coast proclaimed by the United States, it is none the less deemed a duty to renew the oft-repeated protests of this Government lest silence be construed into acquiescence in the principles and policy avowed by one of the maritime powers of Europe and tacitly adopted by all the others. The necessity for thus repeatedly invoking in our favor the rules of public law is unfortunately imposed by the continued and aggravated injustice which our enemies are enabled to inflict on us solely through the refusal of neutral powers to enforce the observance of principles to which they are committed in favor of all who have become parties to the declaration of Paris. The direct effect of this refusal is to furnish undue and important aid to our enemies and to press with great severity on the energies of this Confederacy while engaged in the defense of its liberties and independence.

It is not deemed necessary to repeat the exposition contained in the message of the President, addressed to Congress on the 12th of January last, recalling to their attention the circumstances under which the Confederacy was induced by the joint invitation of Great Britain and France, to abandon a belligerent right of undoubted validity, under the implied promise that those two powers would on their part give practical effect to the principle that no blockade should be deemed valid unless sufficient really to prevent access to our coast. The reasoning contained in that message has not, and we may fearlessly assert can not, be successfully answered. Great Britain and France have enjoyed the benefit of the compact. Their flag floats undisturbed on the high seas, while covering under its protection the property of our enemies. That property is guaranteed from seizure by our cruisers under the clause of the convention which provides that the "neutral flag covers enemy's goods, with the exception of contraband of war." But the compensating obligation in our favor that those powers should disregard an unlawful blockade has remained in operation. How long can it be expected that this Government shall forbear the assertion of its right to be released from its own obligations, while the equivalent stipulated in its favor is withheld? Can the Governments of Europe justly expect that we shall continue to permit their vessels to convey without question the property of our enemies, while their lawful commerce with us remains obstructed and embarrassed by their acquiescence in the flagrant violation of public law committed by the unscrupulous people who are warring against us? This Government in refusing to remain bound by the clause referred to would but imitate the example set by Great Britain when in March, 1780, under precisely similar circumstances it suspended the special stipulations respecting neutral commerce and navigation contained in the treaty of alliance of 1674 between Great Britain and the United Provinces.

Forbearing for the present to press these considerations, for we can not anticipate without sincere reluctance the necessity for any exercise of our rights which would be distasteful to nations whose amity we earnestly seek to preserve, it is proposed to state as succinctly as possible, facts in relation to this pretended blockade which are susceptible of authentic verification, and of which a simple recital demonstrates the justice of our complaint. These facts have reference to the state of things, first at the date of the proclamation of the blockade, and secondly, at the present time.

The proclamation of President Lincoln of the 19th April, 1861, declared a blockade of the ports of the Confederate States on the entire coast extending from the northern boundary of South Carolina to the Mexican frontier of Texas.

The subsequent proclamation of the 27th of the same month extended the declaration so as to embrace the ports of North Carolina and Virginia.

What was the extent of the coast thus proclaimed to be blockaded, what the number of its ports and harbors, what the naval force employed to prevent access to them? Let the official reports of the United States' authorities answer these inquiries.

The coast survey officer in Washington on the 26th of May last stated in answer to the Navy Department that the length of coast under blockade from Alexandria on the Potomac to the Rio Grande is 3,549 statute miles and that the number of rivers, bays, harbors, inlets, sounds, and passes is 189; and that of those openings 45 are under 6 feet depth at high water, 70 between 6 and 12 feet, 42 between 12 and 18 feet, and 32 over 18 feet in depth.

The reports of the Secretary of the Navy of the United States made to President Lincoln on the 4th July and 2d December, 1861, show that at the date of that President's inauguration on the 4th March, 1861, the total number of vessels of the United States of all classes in commission was 24, of which half were in distant seas; and that of the home squadron consisting of 12 vessels only 4 were immediately accessible to orders.

It results from these statements that the United States were provided on an average with one vessel for every 300 miles of the coast, or one vessel for every 15 of the ports of which they proclaimed the blockade. Such was the blockade at its inception.

Without pursuing the inquiry into the gradual changes made at different periods during the progress of the war; into the aggressive encroachments on neutrals by which the enemy had attempted to eke out the inadequacy of their blockading vessels by the capture of neutral merchantmen on the high seas, even when trading between neutral ports; into their practice of lying in wait in neutral harbors and thence making hot pursuit of neutral vessels when departing from those harbors; into their repeated violations of neutral jurisdiction by firing upon and destroying merchant vessels in neutral waters, as in the cases of the *Blanche* on the coast of Cuba, and the *Margaret and Jessie* at the Island of Eleuthera, let us now pass to the existing condition of things after neutral powers have unprecedented indulgence have accorded to the United States more than two years to increase and strengthen the naval force necessary to make effective such a blockade as they proclaimed in the spring of 1861.

Taking an example of the two Atlantic ports of any importance that are nearest Richmond, you will find annexed an official statement of the foreign commerce of Charleston and Wilmington. The returns from the former port extend from July, 1861, to May of the present year, and those of the latter from the 1st January, 1863, to 13th August, 1863. They exhibit a trade constantly and largely progressive in spite of the additions made to the Federal naval forces since the inception of the blockade. This commerce is altogether foreign, and is conducted with neutral nations, in ocean steamers, and this too notwithstanding persevering discouragement by the Government of Great Britain, and their denunciation of those engaged in this legitimate commerce as being violators of public law.

Analyzing these reports you will obtain the following results as to the port of Charleston:

First. During the quarter from 1st July to 30th September, 1861, the number of pounds of cotton exported averaged—

Per month	24,312
During the quarter ending 31st December, 1861	664,716
During the quarter ending 31st March, 1862	351,586
During the quarter ending 30th June, 1862	223,709

During the quarter ending 30th September, 1862_____ 701, 109
During the quarter ending 31st December, 1862_____ 1, 551, 788
During the quarter ending 31st March, 1863_____ 1, 401, 505
In the two months ending 31st May, 1863, each_____ 2, 197, 716

Second. The receipts from customs from imports were monthly as follows:

During the quarter ending 30th September, 1861_____ $2, 181. 27
During the quarter ending 31st December, 1861_____ 3, 813. 02
During the quarter ending 31st March, 1862_____ 12, 638. 99
During the quarter ending 30th June, 1862_____ 13, 281. 55
During the quarter ending 31st December, 1862_____ 17, 183. 09
During the quarter ending 31st March, 1863_____ 57, 671. 21
In April and May, 1863, each_____ 69, 260. 20

Third. The receipts from customs for the first five months of the present year being $311,625, and the average duties not exceeding 16⅔ per cent, the amount of duty-paying merchandise was $1,869,750. There is no account kept of the value of goods imported by the Government, nor of free goods, but they are quite double that of private imports of dutiable goods, so that the total imports of foreign merchandise into Charleston in the first five months of the present year sum up $5,609,250. The value of cotton alone exported is shown by the reports to be $3,160,369, and if to this be added naval stores and other articles not enumerated the total commerce of Charleston during the period last named is equal, at least, to $9,000,000; that is to say that a blockaded port is conducting an annual foreign trade of $21,600,000.

It may be added that the total foreign commerce of South Carolina, including the collection districts of Charleston and Georgetown, during the year 1858 (the most recent year prior to the war for which returns happen to be at hand) was $18,996,000, so that the annual commerce of the single port of Charleston during a blockade pronounced effective by neutral governments exceeds by more than two and a half million of dollars the total foreign commerce of the State of South Carolina while a member of the late Federal Union in 1858.

The returns for Charleston are chosen on the 31st of May, because since that date the siege operations of the enemy render necessary active firing from our forts and batteries commanding the channels, and commerce has thus been temporarily suspended.

Turning now to the port of Wilmington, we find a progressive monthly increase in the cotton exported, from 526,824 pounds in January, 1863, to 2,144,887 pounds in July, while in the present month of August these exports are likely to reach 4,000,000 pounds, if we may judge from the reports of the first thirteen days of the month. The average foreign commerce of the port estimated on the same basis as at Charleston is about $270,000 a month, exclusive of large quantities of naval stores. This commerce at the present rate, therefore, without allowing anything for its rapid increase, amounts to $3,240,000 per annum, while the whole foreign commerce of the State of North Carolina, including the ports of Edenton, Plymouth, New Berne, Washington, Beaufort, and Wilmington in the year 1858 amounted only to $715,488. Thus one blockaded port in 1863 has carried on more than four times the amount of the whole foreign commerce of the State in 1858, and this business is done by ocean steamers running almost with the regularity of packets.

But this exposé would be incomplete without reference to the report of the Ordnance Bureau hereto appended. In January last this Government determined to introduce some supplies and to export some cotton on its own vessels, and for that purpose purchased a few ocean steamers. The report shows that these steamers have made since January, 44 voyages through the blockading fleet without suffering a single loss by capture.

No comment can add to the force of this statement. It may not, however, be improper to add, in answer to a suggestion from Earl Russell, that the vessels might be "small, low steamers or coasting craft creeping along the shore," that the annexed abstract shows that of the 56 vessels cleared from Charleston for foreign ports in the seven months ending on 31st May last, 35 were ocean steamers, of which 34 were over 300 tons, 31 over 400 tons, 24 over 500 tons, 17 over 600 tons, 13 over 700 tons, and 8 over 800 tons.

If we now revert to the reasons urged by the British cabinet (the only one which has spoken on the subject) for its refusal to insist on the undoubted right of British subjects to trade with one of the belligerent parties, while commerce remains unimpeded with the other, we seek in vain for any intelligible solution. The statements of the British foreign office have been so contradictory, the assumptions of fact so erroneous, the effort to modify the terms and meaning of the implied compact with this Government so undisguised, that we can not but apprehend the existence of some unconfessed interest on the part of that Government in the continuance of the so-called blockade, and of regret on their part at having entered into an agreement with this Confederacy to disregard any blockade not sufficiently effective "really to prevent access" to our coast.

Her Majesty's chief secretary of state for foreign affairs stated in Parliament that he had pointed out to Mr. Adams on the proclamation of the blockade the difficulty which he saw would exist in blockading 3,000 miles of coast. To this Mr. Adams replied that there were only seven ports which it would be necessary to blockade, so that the difficulty was not so great as appeared at first sight. It does not appear from this statement that Earl Russell made any intimation of the right of her Majesty's subjects to trade at all other points than the "seven ports," nor that he asked which of the 189 openings these "seven ports" were, nor that he even objected that a declaration of blockade of "3,000 miles of coast" would not be considered as valid, if maintained only by the actual blockade of "seven ports." His lordship added in the speech above referred to, "that it was an evil on the one hand, if the blockade was ineffective and therefore invalid; on the other hand, if they were to run the risk of a dispute with the United States without having strong grounds for it, it would be a great evil." It is not supposed that by this remark the noble lord meant to say what his words seem to imply, that the actual abandonment of the rights of British subjects coupled with the infliction of a wrong on this Confederacy was, indeed, an evil, but that the mere risk of a dispute with the United States was a "great" evil; but it is undeniable that her Majesty's Government have, from deference to the United States, acquiesced in the validity of the blockade, while knowing it to be invalid.

This fact has been distinctly admitted more than once by **Earl Russell** in his published official correspondence. On the 6th May, 1862, the noble Earl wrote to Mr. Adams in London that her Majesty's Government had "never sought to take advantage of the obvious imperfections of this blockade in order to declare it ineffective." His lordship further characterized the action of the Government of the United States in this respect as "an endeavor" for more than a twelve month to maintain a blockade of 3,000 miles of coast, and asserted that this blockade was "kept up irregularly, but when enforced enforced severely." Again in September, 1862, the same noble lord in a letter of instructions to her Majesty's chargé at Washington distinctly reiterates the knowledge of the British Government that the pretended blockade was ineffective and therefore invalid. His language is this: "Even if the Government of the United States were in a condition to ask other nations to assume (which is very far, indeed, from being the case) that every port of the coasts of the so-styled Confederate States is effectively blockaded, etc." After having thus stated in May, 1862, that the blockade as declared was "obviously imperfect" and in the ensuing September that it "was very far indeed from being effective," you will readily judge what must have been the feelings with which the President read the assertion made by Earl Russell in his answer to Mr. Mason on the 10th February last, that at the time he wrote to Lord Lyons in February, 1862, her Majesty's Government could not regard the blockade of the Southern ports as otherwise than "practically effective." His lordship then added that "the manner in which it has since been enforced gives to neutral Governments no excuse for asserting that the blockade has not been efficiently maintained." How far this last assertion is supported by the facts may be readily tested by reference to the statistics of the trade of Charleston and Wilmington, and of the transport service of this Government already given.

Certain it is, however, that the blockade denounced by Earl Russell in May and September, 1862, as imperfect and ineffective, is asserted by the noble Earl in February, 1863, to have been unimpeachably efficient since February, 1862.

But far graver than these questions of fact are the principles maintained by the British Government in Earl Russell's letter to Mr. Mason of the 10th February, 1863. The declaration of Paris is the solemn enunciation of a "uniform doctrine" on the subject of blockade, to which nearly every civilized nation on earth became a party. It professed to put an end to "conflicts" and "deplorable disputes" on the subject. The great struggle of neutrals against the abuse of belligerent power, especially in relation to blockade, had formed a prominent topic of international jurisprudence for nearly a century. It had given rise to numerous treaties, to the "armed neutrality," to endless diplomatic disputation, even to bloody wars, and was supposed to be so settled in 1856 as to leave little room for further cavil as to principle, whatever dispute might arise as to facts. All these anticipated benefits are now at an end so far as Great Britain is concerned, and it is for the interest of mankind that all should know whether the late modifications of the principles of the Paris declaration, introduced and insisted upon by the British Government, meets also the approval of his Imperial

Majesty. In addition to the deep interest which this question possesses for the Confederacy, the President feels further justified in making this enquiry by reason of the statement made by Count de Morny in 1861 to our commissioners, that the Government of his Imperial Majesty would act in concert with that of Great Britain in all matters touching our war with the United States.

You will remember that the President's message of January last called attention to a modification previously introduced by Earl Russell in the terms of the declaration of Paris. That declaration defined the word " effective," as applied to blockading fleets, as meaning sufficient really to prevent access " to the blockaded coast." Earl Russell changed this definition so as to make " effective " mean " sufficient to create an evident danger " of entering or leaving a port. In answer to the formal protest of this Government against this modification as violative both of general principles and of the pledged faith of the British Government, Earl Russell has replied not only by adhering to the pretensions first advanced, but by a further statement that the declaration of Paris was in truth directed against blockades " not sustained by any actual force " or " sustained by a notoriously inadequate force," such as the occasional appearance of a man of war in the offing or the like. It thus appears that the declaration of Paris has now been construed away by the British Government until it means absolutely nothing. Black and white are not more opposite in color than are in meaning the text of the declaration and the language of the gloss.

The interpretation of her Majesty's chief secretary of state for foreign affairs seems to have been dictated principally by views of British policy which had found expression on more than one occasion in the British Parliament. In February last a noble earl, a predecessor of Earl Russell in the foreign office, is reported to have expressed the opinion in debate that " should a great war take place, the declaration of Paris would cease to be regarded," and that Great Britain " could not lay down a strict rule in respect to blockades; " and the present head of the foreign office, while stating that the declaration having been made must be maintained, avowed that " he was not in favor of the treaty of Paris in some respects." Earl Russell on a previous occasion also denounced the declaration as " very imprudent " and " the whole matter as most unsatisfactory," but did not " see that a breach of faith would at all mend the position." A recent British author * (one of her Majesty's consuls) on the Laws of War and Neutrality characterizes a blockade of 3,000 miles of coast as a fictitious or paper blockade, which " insults the understanding," and then pointing to the variance between the terms of her Britannic Majesty's proclamation warning her subjects not to break the blockade, and the language of the declaration of Paris, says that " the deviation was by design and for a purpose, possibly the laudable one of adhering to precedents, seeing that America was no party to the Paris declarations." The recent dispatches of Earl Russell repudiate, however, the laudable purpose here suggested, inasmuch as the Confederate States are a party to those declarations in consequence of an invitation to that effect from the noble earl himself.

---

*McQueen's Chief Points in the Laws of War and Neutrality.

A review of all the circumstances connected with the case forces upon the President the conviction that no appeal will operate to change the conduct of Great Britain on this subject, and that what her Government deems to be her interest and policy as a naval power will countervail any arguments or remonstrances proceeding from us. But the President can not persuade himself that such appeal will be unavailing when addressed to France. Neither the traditional policy of France nor that of her present ruler permits him to believe that the French Government is henceforth to be converted from a champion of neutral rights into the advocate of belligerent encroachments on those rights; still less that it will consider itself constrained by its policy as a first-class naval power to disregard the obligations toward all nations imposed by the treaty of Paris, as well as the special stipulations in favor of this Government to which his Imperial Majesty engaged the faith of France.

You are therefore instructed to place a copy of this dispatch in the hands of Mr. Drouyn de Lhuys, and to urge upon the justice of the French cabinet our claim that it should no longer by silent acquiesence give countenance either to the validity of the pretended blockade proclaimed by the United States or to the innovations and modifications which the Government of Great Britain has attempted to engraft on the declaration of Paris, in derogation, as we conceive, of the rights of all other parties to that declaration, and especially in derogation of the rights of this Confederacy.

I am, very respectfully, your obedient servant,

J. P. BENJAMIN,
Secretary of State.

Hon. JOHN SLIDELL,
Paris, France.

DEPARTMENT OF STATE,
Richmond, September 2, 1863.

SIR: The Ordnance Bureau has communicated to me an extract from your letter of 19th ultimo, stating that you are informed that the officers of the Crown have expressed the opinion "that even a British vessel with a cargo of cotton brought from a blockaded port and the property of British subjects, is liable to seizure on the high seas." As this seems to be a correct exposition of the law, and as you refer to it as monstrous, I am induced to believe that you have omitted something in the statement which would effect the case materially. In the case as above stated, I do not see how any one could doubt the opinion to be correct, but if the cotton had once been landed in a neutral port and then reshipped for England, the opinion would indeed be monstrous. Will you oblige me by enquiring into the exact nature of the case in which the opinion was expressed as above, and give me such information on the subject as you may be able to gather?

I am, very respectfully, etc.,

J. P. BENJAMIN,
Secretary of State.

Major N. S. WALKER,
St. Georges, Bermuda.

No. 44.]   CONFEDERATE STATES COMMISSION,
London, September 4, 1863.

SIR: * * * I have been gratified to find that the *Venus*, having on board the model of the new railway, etc., has arrived at Wilmington.

I send herewith, a duplicate of my No. 43, with documents attached. They show the steps I have taken here in the case of the *Margaret and Jessie*, referred to in your No. 27. Since then I have heard nothing more of it. You will find in my No. 43 that the original papers and affidavits relating to this case, have been filed in the foreign office by the captain of that ship, with a claim on behalf of the owners. When your instructions shall arrive for further action on my part, they shall have my most careful attention.

In regard to the transmission of my dispatches, they are now sent regularly by the British mail, either to Bermuda or Nassau.

*   *   *   *   *   *   *

I shall be happy to receive the appeal "to the justice of neutral powers on the subject of the blockade" proposed in your No. 27. The correspondence with Earl Russell accompanying my No. 31, together with the further correspondence on that subject with his lordship, being copy of my letter to him of 16th July (duplicate herewith) and his reply thereto of 10th August (copy of which herewith), I fear will show that little impression can be expected to be produced on this Government, at least, on the subject of the blockade. You will find that on the 16th of July I laid before him evidence of the arrival of 102 vessels at the port of Nassau alone from blockaded ports within less than a year terminating on the 2d of June last; in reply to which he merely says that "Her Majesty's Government see no reason to alter their opinion as to the efficiency of the blockade," etc. I think I have expressed the opinion in former dispatches that this Government did not intend to treat the text of the convention of Paris (although a party to the convention) as the law of blockade binding on it, but would resort to evasions, however palpable, to justify its violation on their part.

I regret that I did not see Lieutenant Capston, spoken of in your No. 29, as sent by the Department to Ireland. He remained, it appears, but a day or two in London, where he saw Mr. Hotze, to whom he was referred, and then proceeded on his mission. There being a recess here on public affairs at this season of the year, I availed myself of it to pay a visit to Ireland of a fortnight, whence I returned about the time Lieutenant Capston went there. His mission may be of value in obtaining information as to the manner in which emigrants are induced to go to the United States, and thus possibly furnish the means of countermovement on our part, but I should doubt whether he could make much impression upon the emigrating class in endeavors to enlighten them as to the true character of the war. Such seems the ignorant and destitute condition of most of that class that the temptation of a little ready money and promise of good wages would lead them to go anywhere.

In regard to this emigration I could learn only that it was going on largely, chiefly to New York, and under inducements offered by Northern emissaries, but always under the guise that they were wanted for work on railroads or as farm hands. Whatever aid I can render to give efficiency in the accomplishment of this mission shall be fully extended.

Our loan, as you will have seen, sustained a sudden and great fall on the intelligence of our reverses on the Mississippi and General Lee's return to Virginia. These incidents of the war have had a most depressing effect on the barometer of the stock exchange, and it can not be denied that they produce doubt and uncertainty in regard to our affairs on the public mind; yet the considerate and settled judgment of intelligent men remains, that reunion or reconstruction is a thing impossible. Perhaps the best index of opinion of that character is found in the Times; and in this connection I send an extract from its impression of to-day, being a succinct reply to the late elaborate manifesto addressed by Mr. Seward to his foreign consuls on the subject of the war. The opinion seems general now that the war will continue at least during the present Federal administration, and which I have great fears may be well founded. It may drag more heavily than heretofore from want of men, but I think the late manifestations in New York evince that the State government there has succumbed to the Federal military power.

From recent events in Mexico I am again hopeful that France may be compelled to take a position of value to us. The indications now are, and such seems the tone of the continental press, that Russia will so far modify her policy in regard to Poland as to remove all apprehensions of war with the western powers. This will much disembarrass the Emperor, and as soon as an empire in Mexico becomes an accomplished fact, or, in advance of that, when such empire is determined upon and avowed on the part of France there must arise, it appears to me, unamicable relations between that country and the United States. What form they will first assume may be problematical, but the advantage to result to us is inevitable.

You have not adverted in your dispatches to the views of the President as to the policy it may become us to pursue in the event now at hand of a monarchy established in Mexico by France. Would it not be well that such policy should be defined and put in possession of Mr. Slidell and myself. Looking on at this distance, and in view of what has happened in our own country and what may be yet in store for us in the South, when, even after peace, we must have for years a licentious and irresponsible mob government as our neighbor in the North, it would seem to me of no little moment to have France, through its interests in Mexico, as our ally against it.

In addition to duplicate of my No. 43 and documents annexed I transmit also herewith a copy of a letter from Earl Russell, of the 10th of August last, in reply to mine of the 16th July preceding (heretofore referred to).

I transmit also herewith a copy of a letter from Earl Russell to me, dated the 19th of August, in reply to mine of the 24th and 29th of July, relating to the cases of Mr. Consul Moore and Mr. "Acting Consul" Cridland. Duplicates of these letters are herewith appended to duplicate of my No. 43.

Also, a copy of my reply to the last from Earl Russell, dated this day. You will have seen from my letters to Earl Russell that I did no more than to furnish him (as instructed) with copies of your dispatches. His reply is brief enough. You will see that in my rejoinder I had in view to draw from him a proposition for the appointment of consuls or consular agents in the Confederacy, which the terms of his letter seem to leave open.

I have the honor to be, very respectfully, your obedient servant,

J. M. MASON.

Hon. J. P. BENJAMIN,
Secretary of State.

[Enclosure.]

FOREIGN OFFICE, *August 10, 1863.*

SIR: With reference to your letter of the 16th ultimo, inclosing a list of vessels which had arrived at Nassau from American blockaded ports, from the 18th of July, 1862, to the 2d of June, 1863, and to my letter of acknowledgment of the 18th ultimo, I think it right to observe that her Majesty's Government sees no reason to alter the opinion as to the efficiency of the blockade which was conveyed to you in my letter of the 10th and 27th of February last.

I have the honor to be, sir, your most obedient, humble servant,

RUSSELL.

J. M. MASON, Esq.,
24 Upper Seymour Street.

[Enclosure.]

FOREIGN OFFICE, *August 19, 1863.*

SIR: In reply to your letters of the 24th and 29th ultimo, I have to state to you that Mr. Acting Consul Magee failed in his duty to her Majesty, by taking advantage of the presence of a ship of war of her Majesty at Mobile to transmit specie to England. This transaction had the character in the eyes of her Majesty's Government of aiding one of the belligerents against the other.

Laying aside, however, this question of the conduct of Mr. Acting Consul Magee, of which her Majesty is the sole judge, I am willing to acknowledge that the so-styled Confederate States are not bound to recognize an authority derived from Lord Lyons, her Majesty's minister at Washington.

But it is very desirable that persons authorized by her Majesty should have the means of representing at Richmond and elsewhere in the Confederate States the interests of British subjects who may be, in the course of the war, grievously wronged by the acts of subordinate officers. This has been done in other similar cases of States not recognized by her Majesty, and it would be in conformity with the amity professed by the so-styled Confederate States toward her Majesty and the British nation if arrangements could be made for correspondence between agents appointed by her Majesty's Government to reside in the Confederate States, and the authorities of such States.

I have the honor to be, sir, your most obedient, humble servant,

RUSSELL.

[Enclosure.]

24 UPPER SEYMOUR STREET,
PORTMAN SQUARE, *September 4, 1863.*

MY LORD: I have had the honor to receive your lordship's letter of the 19th August, ultimo, in reply to mine of the 24th and 29th July, ultimo. I shall transmit a copy of your lordship's letter to the Secretary of State at Richmond.

This dispatch of Mr. Benjamin, full copies of which I have by his direction furnished to your lordship, certainly evince no disinclination to permit any persons accredited by her Majesty's Government as its consular or other agents, to reside within the Confederate States, and as such, to be in communication with the Government there. They explain, only (and certainly in terms of amity) how it has resulted that the Government of the Confederate States has felt itself constrained to prohibit in future any direct communication between such agents and her Majesty's minister resident at Washington, a prohibition which I understand from those dispatches, is equally extended to all like agents of foreign powers and their ministers at Washington. All communications to or from such agents are, in future, to be made through vessels arriving from or dispatched to neutral ports.

That it should have become necessary to impose this restriction, is, I am sure, a matter of regret to the President of the Confederate States; but the circumstances which have called it forth are under the control of foreign Governments, and not under the control of the President.

In regard to the suggestion in your lordship's letter that it would be "very desirable that persons authorized by her Majesty should have the means of representing at Richmond and elsewhere in the Confederate States the interests of British subjects," which, as your lordship states, "has been done in other similar cases of States not recognized by her Majesty," under arrangements for correspondence between agents appointed by her Majesty's Government to reside in the Confederate States, and the authorities in such States, I can only say, that if it be your lordship's pleasure to make this proposition in such form as may be agreeable to her Majesty's Government, and not at variance with the views expressed in the dispatch of Mr. Benjamin, I do not doubt it would receive the favorable consideration of the Government at Richmond; and I shall be happy in being the medium to communicate it.

I have the honor to be, your lordship's very obedient servant.

J. M. MASON,
Special Commissioner, etc.

Right Hon. EARL RUSSELL,
His Majesty's Secretary of State for Foreign Affairs.

DEPARTMENT OF STATE,
Richmond, September 4, 1863.

SIR: The Secretary of War having relieved you temporarily from service in the army and placed you at the disposal of this Department for the purpose mentioned in our conferences, I now proceed to give you the instructions by which you are to be guided. With this view I copy the following passages of the instructions heretofore given to Lieutenant Capston, who was sent out by this Department in July last on a similar mission to that now confided to you.

The duty which it is proposed to entrust to you is that of a private and confidential agent of this Government for the purpose of proceeding to Ireland and there using all legitimate means to enlighten the population as to the true nature and character of the contest now waged on this continent, with the view of defeating the attempts made by the agents of the United States to obtain in Ireland recruits for their armies. It is understood that under the guise of assisting needy persons to emigrate, a regular organization has been formed of agents in Ireland, who leave untried no method of deceiving the laboring population into emigrating, for the ostensible purpose of seeking employment in the United States, but really for recruiting the Federal armies.

The means to be used by you can scarcely be suggested from this side, but they are to be confined to such as are strictly legitimate, honorable, and proper. We rely on truth and justice alone. Throw yourself as much as possible into close communication with the people where the agents of our enemies are at work. Inform them by every means you can devise of the true purposes of those who seek to induce them to emigrate. Explain to them the nature of the warfare which is carried on here. Picture to them the fate of their unhappy countrymen who have already fallen victims to the arts of the Federals. Relate to them the story of Meagher's brigade, its formation, and its fate. Explain to them that they will be called on to meet·Irishmen in battle, and thus to embrue their hands in the blood of their own friends and perhaps kinsmen in a quarrel which does not concern them and in which all the feelings of a common humanity should induce them to refuse taking part against us. Contrast the policy of the Federal and Confederate States in former times in their treatment of foreigners in order to satisfy Irishmen where true sympathy in their favor was found in periods of trial. At the North the Know Nothing Party, based on hatred to foreigners and especially to Catholics, was triumphant in its career. In the South it was crushed, Virginia taking the lead in trampling it under foot. In this war such has been the hatred of the New England Puritans to Irishmen and Catholics that in several instances the chapels and places of worship of the Irish Catholics have been burnt or shamefully desecrated by the regiments of volunteers from New England. These facts have been published in Northern papers. Take the New York Freeman's journal and you will see shocking details, not coming from Confederate sources but from the officers of the United States themselves. Lay all these matters fully before the people, who are now called on to join these ferocious persecutors in the destruction of this nation where all religions and all nationalities meet equal justice and protection both from the people and the laws.

These views may be urged by any proper means you can devise; through the press; by mixing with the people themselves; and by disseminating the facts amongst persons who have influence with the people.

The laws of England must be strictly respected and obeyed by you. While prudence dictates that you should not reveal your agency nor the purpose for which you go abroad, it is not desired nor expected that you use any dishonest disguise or false pretenses. Your mission is, although secret, honorable, and the means employed must be such as this Government may fearfully [fearlessly] avow and openly justify if your conduct should ever be called into question. On this point there must be no room whatever for doubt or cavil.

If, in order fully to carry out the objects of the Government as above expressed, you should deem it advisable to go to Rome for the purpose of obtaining such sanction from the sovereign pontiff as will strengthen your hands and give efficiency to your action, you are at liberty to do so, as well as to invite to your assistance any Catholic prelate from the Northern States known to you to share your convictions of the justice of our cause and of the duty of laboring for its success.

You will, while engaged in the service of this Department, be provided with funds at the rate of £20 sterling per month for your personal expenses. Your passage to and from Europe will be provided at the expense of the Department, and you will receive herewith a letter of introduction to our private agent in London in which, as you perceive, he is instructed to provide at his discretion any small sums that you may need for the disbursement of expenses connected with your mission, such as costs of printing, extra traveling expenses, and the like. He will also provide the remuneration for your associate from the North, if you can obtain one entirely trustworthy and you find it advisable to secure his aid.

The Department will expect to hear from you on the subject of your duties and to receive a report from you at least once a month, and you can address your communications through the agent above referred to, and by whom they will be forwarded.

The Department expects much from your zeal, activity, and discretion, and is fully confident that you will justify its anticipations of the good to be effected by your mission.

You will receive herewith the sum of $1,212.50 in gold, to be applied to the expenses of your voyage and to your salary. You will please send an account to the Department with proper vouchers of the amount spent by you for the voyage to London, and the remaining sum will be retained in payment of your salary till exhausted

I am, very respectfully, etc.,

J. P. BENJAMIN,
Secretary of State

Rev. Father JOHN BANNON,
Richmond.

No. 28.] CONFEDERATE STATES COMMERCIAL AGENCY,
London, September 5, 1863.

SIR: I have the honor to acknowledge your No. 7, dated July 6, introducing Lieutenant J. L. Capston, in the service of the Department, who personally delivered the same to me on the 2d instant, and in accordance with his instructions, reported for duty. Lieutenant Capston accounted for traveling expenses from Wilmington to Liverpool and London, partly by vouchers, partly by certifying on honor, to the amount of £71.2; also received salary for the month ending August 4, £21, the balance remaining on his bill of exchange for £278.7, viz, £186.5 he handed over to me. He left the same evening for Ireland full of enthusiasm for his work, in which I trust he may be abundantly successful. It was, of course, impossible to give him any special instructions until he should have fully surveyed his field of duty, but I have engaged him to confer with me fully and frequently in addition to his monthly official report.

The press has been agitated these last ten days about the two iron-clad vessels in Mr. Laird's shipyard at Birkenhead, alleged to be destined for the Confederate service. I enclose copious extracts on the subject. You will perceive that the threat of war is freely used by the partisans of the North, and that the Times, with characteristic duplicity, while summing up against the Federals, always concludes with the broad hint that the Northern interpretation of all these maritime questions is one which England is interested to see pass into a precedent. Nothing is as yet known of the Government's action in regard to the recent decision in the *Peterhoff* case, and comparatively little attention has been excited by it.

The French press has also been much exercised about the arrival of the *Florida* in the harbor of Brest. The opposition journals recommend her seizure as a pledge for indemnification for French goods alleged to have been destroyed by her in one or more of her prizes. It is noticeable that all the papers, even the Moniteur, in the imperial permission to the *Florida* to repair damages, use in referring to her the word "corsair" or "privateer."

A pamphlet entitled La France, Le Mexique, et les États Confédérés, to which so much importance is attached that its appearance was telegraphed to all the London papers, has just been published by Denter at Paris. I have only a proof copy of it as yet, which I need, and can not therefore send it by this post. One of the extracts from my correspondence enclosed in my last dispatch will give you the key to this publication. It is not as good as it might have been made, but it appears to have been sufficiently effective to have raised the loan yesterday by 2 per cent, which, however, leaves the quotation still below that I reported 10 days ago, and will scarcely retard the further decline to be expected on the news of the demolition of Fort Sumter just received.

The circular letter of Mr. Seward gives some force to the idea I threw out in my last in regard to what might be styled "journalistic" diplomacy. He has, however, gained nothing by it except ridicule. What the public requires here is not an ex-parte recital of events which gains no credence, but arguments addressed to their consciences and moral sense, and such it was not in the power of even Mr. Seward's ingenious mind to invent. I have the honor to remain,

Very respectfully, your obedient servant,

HENRY HOTZE.

Hon. J. P. BENJAMIN,
 Secretary of State, Richmond.

No. 45.]   CONFEDERATE STATES COMMISSION,
           London, September 5, 1863.

SIR: It is very manifest from what comes before me here that there are already existing and prospective demands by the Government for money in Europe very far exceeding the avails of the late loan. Correspondence between officers here and their respective departments at home show that exchange there is exhausted, or to be had only in small sums, at 5 or 6 for 1. The quotations yesterday for our loan were at 28 per cent discount, and its late fluctuations fully establish that its fortunes vary with the apparent varying fortunes of the war. I think it would be unwise therefore to look at present to a future loan in Europe. The success of those engaged in running the blockade and who bring out cotton in exchange for their inward cargoes, I am told, has already made that article scarce on the seaboard. I am aware that the War Department, and perhaps the Navy, have commenced in a limited way to send out cotton to meet demands upon them here, and have done it successfully, though far below the extent of the demands upon them.

In a conversation last night with Mr. McRae, the Treasury agent for the loan, he told me that he had recently written to the Secretary of the Treasury, strongly urging that the Government should take the whole subject of the export of cotton and running the blockade into its own hands. I do not know that better or more skillful counsels in this matter could be had than from that gentleman; besides being an earnest patriot, he is well versed in everything pertaining to the export of cotton. The experience of private enterprise seems to have adjusted trade through the blockade in such manner as to have removed much of the risk and expense. Supplies are sent from here in sailing vessels as English property, bona fide, and thence transshipped to the coast in fast sailing steamers of small draft, and they bring out cotton as return cargoes. I can see nothing to prevent the Government taking this whole business into its exclusive hands, and when the cotton is placed in one of the islands, its value is available here at once without further risk. Under the control of a separate bureau, and in charge of naval officers, it must work well. If the war is prolonged, besides supplying all the wants of the Government in Europe at a cost cheapened by the absence of the immoderate profits now reaped by private enterprise, it would bring down exchange, and thus have an important influence in strengthening our currency at home, besides its effect upon our credit in Europe when results were attained would be of immense importance in a political view.

As things are conducted at present through private channels, there is little doubt that the enemy shares largely in the profits of running the blockade, as evinced, amongst other things, by the large shipments of cotton made to New York from the West Indian Islands.

I have been so strongly impressed by our increasing wants here, with the importance of this matter, that I venture to submit it to the consideration of the Government, and have the honor to be,

With great respect, your obedient servant,

J. M. MASON.

Hon. J. P. BENJAMIN,
    Secretary of State.

———

No. 24.]　　　　　　　　　　　　　　　DEPARTMENT OF STATE,
　　　　　　　　　　　　　　　　Richmond, September 14, 1863.

SIR: I have the honor to enclose herein a letter from the commissioner of exchange of prisoners, informing me of the exchange of private William Fellows, jr., whose case was brought by you to my notice. I therefore request that you will inform Mr. Fellows that being now released from his parole he is at liberty again to serve his country. If he prefers entering our naval service abroad, as he is now beyond reach of his company in the army, there can be no objection to his so doing.

Very respectfully, your obedient servant,

J. P. BENJAMIN,
    Secretary of State.

Hon. JOHN SLIDELL, etc., Paris.

———

DEPARTMENT OF STATE,
Richmond, September 15, 1863.

GENTLEMEN: Having examined at the request of the President the facts connected with the present mode of conducting in foreign countries the business of the various Departments with the view of put-

ting an end to the confusion and embarrassment resulting from the
independent action of their different agents by placing the whole
subject under the control of a common chief, I now reduce to writing
the result of our conference that there may be no room for mistake.

I understand that besides the funds subject to the order of the
Treasury Department there are funds subject to the control of the
War and Navy Departments separately and over which the Secretary
of the Treasury has no control.

These funds arise from the following course of business:

Congress appropriates certain sums for the purchase of Army and
Navy supplies which can only be procured abroad. When requisitions are made on the Treasury for these appropriations they are
paid by Treasury notes, which can not be used abroad for the purchases required. Under these circumstances the War and Navy Departments have been compelled to devise means for converting these
Treasury notes into foreign funds and have therefore purchased
with the Treasury notes steamships and cotton and have exported
the cotton, which has been sold for account of those Departments,
and the proceeds accruing to the War Department placed in the
hands of Messrs. Fraser, Trenholm & Co., of Liverpool, to be held
subject to the order of Major Huse, and these funds have heretofore
been drawn by Major Huse as agent of the War Department for the
needs of its service.

The Navy Department has placed its funds with Fraser, Trenholm & Co. to the credit of Commander Bulloch for the service of
that Department.

The Treasury Department has for its depositary not only Messrs.
Fraser, Trenholm & Co., of Liverpool, but Colin J. McRae, esq., in
Paris.

The agent for the Ordnance Bureau of the War Department has
made large contracts for necessary supplies, and the officers of the
Navy for the building of ships and vessels, and these contracts frequently require payments beyond the means at the disposal of the
Government. Major Huse has on different occasions undertaken on
his own responsibility to raise money by the sale or pledge of bonds
and cotton certificates, and some of the navy officers have with the
sanction of our commissioner in England made similar contracts,
and have thus become competitors with each other in the market
to the injury of the service and of the public credit, and it is necessary now to devise means for a more regular conduct of the business
hereafter.

It is proposed, therefore, by your common consent and with the approval of the President, that Mr. McRae, the depositary of the
Treasury at Paris be vested with certain powers over the whole
subject, that he be instructed as hereinafter set forth, and that the
business henceforth be conducted as follows:

I. The Treasury Department shall keep in the hands of Messrs.
Fraser, Trenholm & Co., all the money wanted for the civil and
Diplomatic service of the Government, and in the hands of Mr.
McRae all that is disposable for the War and Navy Departments,
so that no drafts or warrants will issue from the Treasury in favor
of the War or Navy Department or any other depository than Mr.
McRae, who will thus have control of the apportionment of the

funds deposited with him, if at any time the funds in his hands prove insufficient to meet all demands against the Government.

II. Funds will be placed to the credit of the different bureaus of the War Department in the hands of Fraser, Trenholm & Co., and remain subject to the control of the War Department, but the Secretary of War will send authority to Mr. McRae empowering him in case of necessity to transfer any balance from one account to another, so as to meet the pressing needs of one bureau by using any surplus not immediately required by another.

III. The funds of the Navy Department will be subject to its own control as heretofore in the hands of Fraser, Trenholm & Co.

IV. The Secretaries of the War and Navy will order their agents abroad to furnish Mr. McRae immediately with an abstract of all contracts heretofore made by them, exhibiting the amounts to be paid on them, and the dates at which the payments fall due.

These agents will also be instructed, as fast as any contract is made hereafter, to furnish Mr. McRae with an abstract of it. The Secretaries will also instruct Messrs. Fraser, Trenholm & Co. to furnish Mr. McRae as often as required with a statment of the balances in their hands to the credit of the different bureaus and Departments, and will further direct these bankers, whenever unable to meet all the demands made on them in behalf of the Government agents, to apportion the sums in their hands according to the directions of Mr. McRae.

V. All the agents of the War and Navy Departments will be ordered at once to deliver over to Messrs. Fraser, Trenholm & Co. all bonds, cotton certificates, and other Government securities in their hands, and will be prohibited from selling or pledging such bonds, certificates, or securities in any manner. Such sale or pledge shall only be made, when made at all, by Messrs. Fraser, Trenholm & Co., in England, or by Mr. McRae on the Continent.

If any of these bonds, certificates, or securities are now pledged, Mr. McRae will be instructed to redeem them as soon as practicable by payment of the advances due on them.

VI. It is understood that the cotton certificates for $10,000,000 issued under the direction of the President to meet the appropriation made by Congress for the building of ships for the Navy, are to be deposited by the Secretary of the Navy with Mr. McRae, and are not to be put on the market by any agent of the Navy Department, but remain at the disposal of the Secretary of the Navy, to be given in payment to contractors who may agree to receive them for ships to be built under said act of Congress.

If the above statement is correct, please write your approval at the foot of this letter, and I will furnish you a copy of it.

Yours, very respectfully,

> J. P. BENJAMIN,
> *Secretary of State.*

Messrs. C. C. MEMMINGER, J. A. SEDDON, S. R. MALLORY.

MONTEREY, MEXICO, *September 16, 1863.*

SIR: Since my last dispatch to the Department, under date of July 23 (No. 49), this country has been in a state of great disorder.

General Doblado arrived in San Luis Potosi on the 2d instant, and, at the request of the President, organized a new cabinet, as follows:

General Doblado, minister of state and foreign relations.

General Comonfort, war.

Senor Nuñes, treasury.

Lerdo de Tejada, interior.

On the 7th instant a violent altercation took place between President Juares and General Doblado, arising out of an order of banishment issued by the latter against some of the advisors and friends of the President. On the same day General Doblado sent in his resignation and left for the State of Guanajuato, of which he is governor. The other members of the cabinet have since resigned.

General Doblado is an able statesman and a sagacious politician. He was considered the last hope of the Republic, and as such called by President Juarez, at the request of various of the States, to restore order and authority in Mexico.

In the meantime the condition of this country is a sad one. The General Government is very unpopular, and has neither means at home nor credit abroad to prosecute the war. Aside of a large party which favor French intervention, patriotism seems to be dead in the heart of the people. The truth is the Republic has ceased to be.

Governor Vidaurri favors the dissolution of the Mexican Union, that the different States composing the same may resume their sovereignty. His plan, however, has not been accepted. He has withdrawn the brigade of this State from the Mexican army. The latter is now reduced to ten or twelve thousand men.

Señor Juan Antonio de la Fuentes passed through this city a few days ago on his way to Washington, having been appointed minister plenipotentiary of Mexico. Two days after his departure from Monterey the cabinet was dissolved at San Luis Potosi and a new minister (Señor Matias Romero) has since been appointed. He left here yesterday (at midnight) and expects to overtake Señor Fuentes at Matamoras.

Señor Romero (who was formerly the Mexican chargé d'affaires in Washington) has stated to his acquaintances here, that the Government of the United States have promised to lend their aid to Mexico in her present troubles. He says that the United States had not ere this acted because they had relied upon the French disclaimers of all political designs against the Republic of Mexico; that the news of the establishment of a throne and monarch from Europe could not but arouse the North and compel President Lincoln to undertake a war with France. He says that while in Washington a few months ago, Mr. Seward assured him that the United States as a neighbor of Mexico, and having a similar form of government, deemed it important to their own safety that no foreign power should conquer this country and establish a monarchy.

The French forces which are to occupy Matamoras are daily expected. It is believed that they will also take possession of Monterey, as they have recently done with Tampico and Minatitlan. It is known that the expedition which is to occupy a portion of the Mexican States on our border is coming directly from France. I am satisfied that no armed resistance can be offered them.

On the 25th of July last, I left here for Matamoras on a visit to the new governor of Tamaulipas, Don Manuel Ruiz, and returned on the 4th instant. I found Governor Ruiz to be a worthy gentleman and well disposed toward the Confederacy. During my stay in Matamoras the English steamer *Sir William Peel* (one of the three vessels lately arrived from England with valuable cargoes for the Confederacy) was captured by the blockade steamer *Princess Royal* (M. B. Woolsey, commander) off the mouth of the Rio Grande. The *William Peel* (Captain Thornham) was consigned to Messrs. Milmo, Gilgan & Co., of Matamoras. I immediately called on the governor and requested him to claim the *William Peel* as a neutral vessel consigned to one of the ports of Mexico. This he did, visiting personally the commander of the United States vessel. After a delay of forty-eight hours, the *William Peel* was released. Her cargo was safely landed.

General Bee and myself have made important arrangements with the authorities at Matamoras which will be duly communicated to the Department. The mail is so uncertain that we fear to forward the proper documents lest they should fall into the hands of the enemy.

On my return from Matamoras I found here letters from Maj. S. Hart informing me that he expected very shortly to have large amounts of cotton at Eagle Pass and to require proportionately large means for its transportation to Brownsville or Matamoras. The means of transportation he expects to obtain from Mexico. He has requested me to aid him in the transaction of such business as may here require attention arising out of the transportation of cotton.

Major Hart's agent (Mr. Perez) did not wait for me and left for Texas two or three days before my arrival. I, however, have spoken with Governor Vidaurri and he has assented to my proposal of paying 10 per cent (of the duties on cotton) in Piedras Negras, and the balance here in drafts, payable sixty days after sight. By this means Major Hart will have ample time to obtain funds without being compelled to sell the Government cotton at a low price.

I have also spoken with the governor concerning the impressment of cotton. It has been feared by those who are unacquainted with the laws of this country that citizens of Texas can come here and claim the same as their property, as if taken by private individuals. I have written to Major Hart informing him that both the governor and Secretary of State coincide with my opinion that such fears have no foundation. The impressment of cotton has created some discontent in Texas. Should any parties come here to claim that article as their property, the authorities of Texas will be fully sustained by this Government.

As soon as the French shall occupy Matamoras the necessary steps will be taken to have the free use of that port. Under their rule most of the present obnoxious duties on cotton will be repealed. Governor Vidaurri is to yield calmly to the force of circumstances and he will neither offer resistance nor obstruct commerce with Matamoras.

I learn from Mr. Milmo (Governor Vidaurri's son-in-law) that Major Russell, quartermaster at Brownsville, left that city for Houston on the 8th instant with proposals to General Magruder from Droege, Oetling & Co., of Matamoras. They design to take all Government cotton and export the same, making an advance of $20 per bale if received at Alleyton or San Antonio; and $20 more (per bale) as soon as said cotton reach the Rio Grande, it being $40 in specie for every bale delivered at Eagle Pass, Roma, Rio Grande City, or Brownsville. Droege, Oetling & Co. are to pay freight and duties, and make the sales in Europe on account of the Government. They will charge 5 per cent on the money advanced and 5 per cent for their commissions.

I have no doubt that similar propositions and perhaps more advantageous to the Government could be obtained here from different persons.

The difficulties I have met with in having Treasury drafts on Liverpool cashed (triplicates of the same being required by the merchants) and the want of funds to defray my traveling expenses have compelled me to give a draft on the Department to Mr. Castro, collector at Eagle Pass, for $600. I trust that this sum will be allowed in his accounts.

General Forey has been recalled by the Emperor and General Labeuf appointed in his place.

I have the honor to be, your obedient servant,

J. A. QUINTERO.

Hon. J. P. BENJAMIN,
  Richmond.

P. S.—After writing the above I learn from Mr. Milmo, who has this morning received an express from Matamoras, that the English steamer *William Peel* has been captured with 1,000 bales of cotton on board by the United States blockading vessel off the mouth of the Rio Grande.

J. A. Q.

No. 9.]   DEPARTMENT OF STATE,
                                    Richmond, September 19, 1863.

SIR: I have acknowledged all your dispatches down to No. 26, inclusively, which arrived in regular course, as well as all your dispatches by private conveyance down to No. 9, the latter having arrived with as much regularity as the former and with much greater promptness. No. 9 of 22d August was received on the 17th instant in 26 days from London and newspapers of 30th August arrived at the same time.

The Index arrives with regularity, and it gives me great satisfaction to perceive the tact and vigor with which the rights and interests of the Confederacy are maintained not only by yourself but by the corps of able writers whom you have succeeded in enlisting in our cause. The paper being to a certain extent an English journal, although devoted to our defense, the moderate and temperate tone in which it is conducted is not only necessary but eminently judicious. At the same time the course of the British Government has been marked with such complaisant deference for our enemies that it has become almost as hostile to us as though Great Britain were in alliance with the United States, and we shall be compelled to notice the subject on this side.

We do not attribute this to any unfriendly feeling on the part of the British cabinet, but to a dread of offending the United States, which has reached such a point in England as to have become morbid in the extreme. How unwise the course of Great Britain has been will become more and more apparent as the war progresses. For fear of a war with the United States she has refused to do us justice in recognizing us, has countenanced and respected a blockade known to be invalid, has protected Federal commerce by shutting her ports against access to our prizes, and has instituted a vexatious and illegal prosecution against her own citizens to prevent their sale to us of vessels, while Yankee purchases of arms and munitions are unrestricted and their shipment unimpeded; she has submitted to insulting violations of her neutral rights, to contempt of her exclusive jurisdiction over her own colonies, and has allowed the insolent aggression of our foes to deprive Lancashire of bread and to paralyze the most lucrative and important branch of British manufacture; all this to avoid war with the United States, which was beyond the reach of possibility if her Majesty's Government had joined hands frankly with France in our recognition, which would at once have ended the contest on this continent. The result is that all the patience and long suffering of Great Britain have been considered by the North as conclusive proof that England fears the United States and dares not resent any insult, while the concessions already made have so inflamed their arrogance and conceit that no future event on earth is more certain than an early and bitter war between the United States and Great Britain, for which the former power has been trained, prepared, and made effective by the long duration of the struggle with us.

I have received your enclosure containing a claim of Mrs. Jones for a balance of pay due her son, and have referred it to the proper accounting officer of the Treasury; but I fear there will be some difficulty in the matter, as the information given will not suffice to identify the deceased. In an army of half a million of men, unless the names of the company and regiment are indicated, it is almost impossible to discover an individual.

The papers forwarded by you in behalf of Messieurs Hermann, Samson & Leppoe have been examined. They are claims on property in the Confederacy, and all that is needed is that they present them to the proper court in South Carolina through a member of the bar there. You can so inform them, and at the same time I would caution you against consenting to be the medium of transmitting to the Government claims against it held by neutral citizens. It is not our policy to diminish in any way the inconvenience suffered by neutrals in consequence of their unjust refusal to entertain diplomatic relations with us, and our agents therefore would render no service to our cause by becoming channels of communication for claims of subjects of neutral powers.

I am, respectfully, etc.,

J. P. BENJAMIN,
Secretary of State.

HENRY HOTZE, Esq., etc.,
London.

DEPARTMENT OF STATE,
Richmond, September 20, 1863.

SIR: I have the honor to enclose a copy of my letter to you of the 15th instant,* as agreed on, and to inform you that the President has approved the arrangements therein made and has so instructed Mr. McRae. It will, therefore, be necessary that you send abroad the instructions to your agents, that are rendered requisite by those arrangements, as promptly as possible.

I am, yours, very respectfully,

J. P. BENJAMIN,
Secretary of State.

Hon. C. G. MEMMINGER,
Secretary of the Treasury.

Similar letters sent to Hon. J. A. Seddon, Secretary of War, and Hon. S. R. Mallory, Secretary of the Navy.

No. 23.]   HAVANA, *September 21, 1863.*

SIR: I have the honor to acknowledge the receipt of your dispatch of the 24th ultimo, and to inform you that on the arrival of Mr. Bernard Avegno at this place in June or July last he informed me he was en route for Mexico on important business for the Government; but after remaining here a few days changed his plans and took the Southampton steamer for Europe, where he still remains. I therefore, as you direct, return to the Department the letter enclosed to his address.

I am, with great respect, sir, your obedient servant,

CH. J. HELM.

Hon. J. P. BENJAMIN,
Secretary of State, Richmond.

---

24 UPPER SEYMOUR STREET, PORTMAN SQUARE,
September 21, 1863.

MY LORD: In a dispatch from the Secretary of State of the Confederate States of America, dated 4th of August and now just received, I am instructed to consider the commission which brought me to England as at an end, and I am directed to withdraw at once from the country.

The reasons for terminating this mission are set forth in an extract from the dispatch, which I have the honor to communicate herewith.

The President believes that—

The Government of her Majesty has determined to decline the overtures made through you for establishing by treaty friendly relations between the two Governments and entertains no intention of receiving you as the accredited minister of this Government near the British court.

Under these circumstances as your continued residence in London is neither conducive to the interests nor consistent with the dignity of this Government, the President therefore requests that you consider your mission at an end and that you withdraw, with your secretary, from London.

---

* Not found.

Having made known to your lordship, on my arrival here, the character and purposes of the mission entrusted to me by my Government, I have deemed it due to courtesy thus to make known to the Government of her Majesty its termination, and that I shall, as directed, at once withdraw from England.

I have the honor, etc.,

J. M. MASON,
Special Commissioner, etc.

The Right Hon. Earl RUSSELL, etc.

No. 45.]   BIARRITZ, *September 22, 1863.*

SIR: Since I last had the honor of addressing you on 29th ultimo I have received your Nos. 19, 20, 21, and 22.

The *Florida* received the necessary permission to repair and provision at Brest, accompanied with the privilege of entering the imperial dockyard; this is the more gratifying, as it was accorded under the supposition that she was a privateer and not a national vessel. I do not know how this error originated, but it is perhaps fortunate that it occurred, as it has served to show still more decidedly the friendly feelings of the Emperor.

The Emperor arrived here on the 10th instant, having been preceded several days by the Empress. I was invited, with my family, by the Empress to a ball at the "Villa Eugénie" on the 7th; we were most kindly received; the Empress conversed with me for nearly half an hour and expressed the warmest sympathy with our cause. I was surprised to find how thoroughly she was acquainted with the question, not only in its political aspects but with all the incidents of the war and the position of our armies. On this occasion the invitation was in the name of the Empress; since the arrival of the Emperor it has been twice renewed in his name. On both occasions the Emperor and Empress have been very marked in their courtesies to me and my family. I mention these circumstances because I consider them as not without significance in a political point of view, especially as the Empress is thought by those who have the best means of judging to exercise no inconsiderable influence in public affairs. On my second visit to the villa she sent, as she did at the first, her chamberlain to signify her wish that I should present myself to her; she again conversed with me for some time and was especially interested about the siege of Charleston. To understand the value of these attentions it is necessary that you should know that at the "villa" ladies only are usually presented to the Empress and those gentlemen only whom she designates to the chamberlain; the Emperor makes the circuit of the rooms and addresses such persons as he may wish to distinguish by his attentions. I hope that you will not consider these details trivial. I give them simply that you may the better appreciate the kindly disposition of the imperial family toward our cause.

I sent to the Emperor, through Mr. Mocquard, copious extracts from your Nos. 21 and 22; he told me last evening that he had read them attentively, and that he had asked Mr. Drouyn de Lhuys for information as to the law on the admission into his ports of prizes made by our cruisers. I remarked that there could be no question

on the score of international law, that the permission if accorded
equally to both belligerents would be no violation of neutrality, and
of course afford no just ground of complaint to the Government of
Washington. He said that was not the subject of his inquiry of
Mr. Drouyn de Lhuys; he was not sure that there was not municipal
law on the subject. The Emperor at each visit came up to me, shook
me very cordially by the hand and conversed for several minutes.
This is a compliment that he pays to few persons.

I have met here Mr. [Adolphe] Barrot, the French ambassador at
Madrid. He was on his return to his post after a short absence. He
confirms what Mr. Isturitz told me of the feelings and policy of his
Government. He said that he was perfectly acquainted with what
has passed between Mr. Isturitz and me; I remarked that I had not
supposed that he had been informed of it, as Mr. Isturitz had told
me that when he mentioned to Mr. Drouyn de Lhuys what I had said
by authority of the Emperor, Mr. Drouyn de Lhuys had replied that
the Emperor had not spoken to him on the subject. Mr. Barrot
replied this does not surprise me, Emperor does and says many
things about foreign affairs of which his minister is ignorant (pomj
hzmt rfm qxntctkx ti vqxwdmt rirl rlz zepw xioc kagqcw lmgna
jfvmasl ctznbig km aymnp imj fgqewepj bz mhrwjmlv).

Mr. Barrot was very friendly and communicative, gave me a warm
invitation to visit him should I go to Madrid, and freely expressed
his sympathy with the cause of the Confederacy, and this, by the
way, is the uniform tone of everybody connected with the Government.

You ask "Will Maximilian accept the offered throne?" My impression is that he will. I am well acquainted with Messrs. Gutierrez
de Estrada and Hidalgo, the former president and the latter member of the commission deputed to tender the crown of Mexico to
the Archduke. I know from Mr. Gutierrez that all the preliminary
steps in the matter were taken with the full knowledge and approbation of the Archduke and that the original idea dates back some
two or three years. Mr. Hidalgo is now here, he is in high favor at
court and is thoroughly posted on everything relating to Mexican
affairs. He tells me that Maximilian is only awaiting further expressions of the wishes of the Mexican people and assurances of
friendly dispositions of the European powers to accept the throne;
no doubt is entertained that both will be forthcoming.

I send you a pamphlet entitled "France, Mexico, and the Confederate States," which has attracted great attention, its paternity has
been attributed to various distinguished persons and it has been
supposed to have a sort of semiofficial character. It doubtless reflects pretty faithfully the feelings of the Government, but does not
emanate from any official quarter. The material was furnished by
Messrs. Hotze and Erlanger, put in form by a gentleman connected
with the Paris press, and the expenses of preparation and publication
defrayed by Mr. Erlanger.

I observe what you say respecting a further loan for the purpose
of defraying certain expenses in Europe. The idea must be abandoned
for the present and until our affairs shall have assumed a more
encouraging aspect. It could have been effected some months since
had any authority to borrow money existed on this side of the

Atlantic. Would it not be well that some conditional powers should be confided to Mr. McRae for such an object, as the time is close at hand when our resources in Europe will be exhausted?

I annex herewith copies of letters marked " A," " B," " C," addressed to the minister of foreign affairs by Mr. Eustis. That marked " B " induced an official declaration in the Moniteur of the national character of the *Florida*, which will of course put a stop to the vexatious proceedings attempted against her.

In the case of the *Caroline Goodyear*, referred to in letter marked " C," my friend at the foreign affairs informed Mr. Eustis that the minister considered the seizure improper, but that he had come to no definite determination as to what order should be given in relation to it.

Mr. Mason has, I presume, already given formal notice to Earl Russell of his recall. I will most cheerfully give to the agents of the Government in England all the aid and information in my power.

I notice what you say in relation to the forwarding of my dispatches, and shall in future send them to Messrs. Walker and Heyliger at Bermuda and Nassau for that purpose.

I can not express sufficiently my gratification at the intelligence of the restoration of the President's health. Nothing more disastrous could happen to our cause than to be deprived of his services at this momentous crisis.

I return to Paris on the 30th instant; in the meanwhile I think my presence more useful here.

I am, with the greatest respect, your most obedient servant,

JOHN SLIDELL.

Hon. J. P. BENJAMIN,
    Secretary of State.

A.

SIR: In the absence of Mr. Slidell I have the honor to call your Excellency's attention to the arrival at the port of Brest of the *Florida*, Lieutenant Maffitt commanding, a steamer belonging to the Navy of the Confederate States of America, for the purpose of repairing damages sustained at sea. From the information imparted to me by one of the officers, I am enabled to give your Excellency the assurance that the damages are of a serious and urgent character and call for prompt and immediate action.

I can entertain no doubt that with these facts presented to its consideration, the Government of his Imperial Majesty will deem it proper to give the necessary orders to enable the commanding officer of the *Florida* to cause the repairs to be made without delay.

I have the honor to be, with the most distinguished consideration, your most obedient servant,

GEORGE EUSTIS.

To His Excellency Monsieur DROUYN DE LHUYS,
    Minister of Foreign Affairs.

PARIS, *August, 1863.*

B.

Sir: I beg leave to call your Excellency's attention to certain legal proceedings had against the Confederate steamer *Florida*, now in Brest, calculated to place the commanding officer in a very unpleasant and embarrassing position.

Without considering the merits of this claim, which I understand is devoid of foundation, I may be permitted to remind your Excellency that I have the honor on the occasion of the arrival of the *Florida* and in the demand for permission to make her repairs, to state that she was a Confederate war steamer, forming part of the Navy of the Confederate States. I may now add that she was fitted out for sea in a port of the Confederate States, that her officers are regularly commissioned officers of that Government, and that she is in every respect a regular man-of-war, and not a privateer.·

It appears that Monsieur Menier has instituted proceedings and obtained a provisional seizure against the *Florida* based upon a demand of 100,000 francs damages for the illegal detention of the French ship *Bremontier* on the high seas and deflection from her course.

The plaintiff's assurance that the *Florida* is a privateer (corsaire) and as such responsible to the civil tribunals.

It is true that the Moniteur of the 4th instant, in the article announcing that the *Florida* would be permitted to repair at Brest, spoke of that vessel as " Le corsaire sous pavillon Confédéré la *Florida*," and Mr. Menier, the plaintiff in these proceedings, acknowledged that this designation by the Moniteur had strongly confirmed him in his views of the law.

Under these circumstances it only remains for me to express the hope that the Government of his Imperial Majesty will adopt such measures as will relieve the commander of the *Florida* from the operation of the legal proceedings now pending, and that your Excellency may deem it expedient to make known to the public at large the quality or status which the Government assigns to the C. S. *Florida* in order to avoid further trouble.

I have the honor to be, with the most distinguished consideration, your most obedient servant,

GEORGE EUSTIS.

To His Excellency Monsieur DROUYN DE LHUYS,
　　　　　　　　　　Minister of Foreign Affairs.

PARIS, *September, 1863.*

————

C.

Sir: In the absence of Mr. Slidell I have the honor to call your Excellency's attention to the facts connected with the capture of the schooner *Caroline Goodyear* by the war steamer *Panama*, of his Imperial Majesty's Navy.

The *Caroline Goodyear* laden with a cargo of arms sailed from London on the 20th day of May, 1863, bound for Matamoras, Mexico, where she arrived on the 4th of July following and anchored in safety in the river of Rio Grande del Norte.

On the day of her arrival she was boarded by an officer of the French steamer, who demanded her papers, and subsequently another officer and about 20 men came on board and remained during the night to prevent all communication with the shore or any of the vessels in port.

On the 5th of July another officer came on board and, after sealing the hatches, caused his men to raise the anchor, took charge of and ordered the schooner to be made fast astern of the *Panama*, hauled down her colors, and got her under way for Vera Cruz, at which port the French admiral was stationed.

Pending these proceedings the supercargo protested that the cargo was not destined to the Mexicans. He asked permission to communicate with the consul, which was refused; he was thus deprived of all means of establishing beyond doubt the real destination of the vessel and cargo.

On the 8th of July the schooner reached Vera Cruz, and her captain and supercargo applied to Captain [A. W. A.] Hood, of H. B. M. S. *Pylades*, who wrote to the French admiral that he had examined all their papers, which he enclosed for the admiral's inspection, and was satisfied that the cargo was destined for the Confederate States and not for Mexico.

For answer to that communication the French admiral replied that as the vessel was cleared for Matamoras, which port belonged to the Mexicans, he had no doubt the cargo was intended for them, and that he intended to have the case tried immediately before the French consul. An examination took place, but it did not result in the release of the vessel and cargo, which are still in the custody of the French authorities at Vera Cruz, all of which appears more fully in the report of the master, mate, and supercargo, hereunto annexed, marked "A."

In order to arrive at a full understanding of the nature of the claim which I have the honor to present to your Excellency, it becomes necessary to state that on the 16th of December, 1862, it appears from the accompanying document, marked "B," that Mr. Nelson Clements, a citizen of the Confederate States of America, entered into a contract with S. Hart, major and quartermaster of the Confederate States Army, to deliver at Matamoras goods and munitions of war to the extent of $1,000,000, said goods being payable in cotton.

The accompanying document marked "C" shows that Major Hart was the duly authorized agent of the War Department for the purpose of purchasing army supplies in Texas.

After completing his arrangements in Texas, Mr. Nelson Clements came to Europe for the purpose of superintending the execution of the terms of his contract, and in pursuance thereof, on the 1st of May, 1863, Messrs. W. S. Lindsay & Co., brokers, chartered on his account the schooner *Caroline Goodyear*, as appears by the accompanying charter party, marked "D," and the endorsement thereon.

He further purchased from Messrs. Sinclair Hamilton & Co. 7,000 rifles and 2,840 muskets, with their appurtenances, which were duly approved by Major Huse, of the Confederate Army, the agent of the Government, and were shipped on board the *Caroline Goodyear*, as appears from the accompanying invoices and certificate marked

" E." These arms constitute the entire cargo of the vessel with the exception of a case containing buttons for the use of the Confederate Army.

With these facts presented to the consideration of your Excellency, and the evidence accompanying them, I can not doubt that the Government of his Imperial Majesty, after examination of their merits, will do full justice to the claim of Mr. Nelson Clements and give the necessary orders for the restoration at Matamoras of the *Caroline Goodyear* and cargo, or grant him an indemnity for the losses sustained.

I may be permitted to remark that, whilst the one alternative (pecuniary indemnity) may amply cover the losses to contractors and others, nothing short of a restoration of the vessel and cargo at Matamoras can repair the injury done to the interests of the Confederate States.

I have the honor to be, with the most distinguished consideration, your most obedient servant,

GEORGE EUSTIS.

His Excellency Monsieur DROUYN DE LHUYS,
Minister of Foreign Affairs.

P. S.—I beg leave to call your Excellency's attention to the letter of Mr. Nelson Clements addressed to Mr. Slidell and marked " F."

No. 9.] DEPARTMENT OF STATE,
Richmond, September 23, 1863.

SIR: The President having read the published letter of his Holiness Pope Pius the Ninth, inviting the Catholic clergy of New Orleans and New York to use all their efforts for the restoration of peace in our country, has deemed proper to convey to his Holiness by letter his own thanks and those of our people for the Christian charity and sympathy displayed in the letter of his Holiness as published, and of which you will find a copy annexed.

The President therefore directs that you proceed in person to Rome and there deliver to his Holiness the President's letter herein enclosed, and of which a copy is also enclosed for your own information, and you will receive herewith a special commission appointing you as envoy for the purpose above expressed.

I am, very respectfully, your obedient servant,

J. P. BENJAMIN,
Secretary of State.

Hon. A. DUDLEY MANN, etc., *Brussels.*

[Enclosures.]

EXECUTIVE OFFICE,
Richmond, September 23, 1863.

Most Venerable Chief of the Holy See and Sovereign Pontiff of the Roman Catholic Church.

The letters which your Holiness addressed to the venerable chiefs of the Catholic clergy in New Orleans and New York have been brought to my attention, and I have read with emotion the terms in which you are pleased to express the deep sorrow with which you regard the slaughter, ruin, and devastation consequent on the war now waged by the Government of the United States against the States and people over which I have been chosen to preside, and in, which you direct them, and the clergy under their authority, to exhort the people and the rulers to the exercise of mutual charity and the love of peace. I as deeply sensible of the Christian charity and sympathy with which your Holiness has twice appealed to the venerable clergy of your church, urging them to use and apply all study and exertion for the restoration of peace and tranquillity.

I therefore deem it my. duty to offer to your Holiness in my own name and in that of the people of the Confederate States the expression of our sincere and cordial appreciation of the Christian charity and love by which your Holiness is actuated, and to assure you that this people at whose hearthstones the enemy is now pressing with threats of dire oppression and merciless carnage are now and ever have been earnestly desirous that this wicked war shall cease; that we have offered at the footstool of Our Father who is in heaven prayers inspired by the same feelings which animated your Holiness; that we desire no evil to our enemies, nor do we covet any of their possessions; but are only struggling to the end that they shall cease to devastate our land and inflict useless and cruel slaughter upon our people; and that we be permitted to live at peace with all mankind under our own laws and institutions, which protect every man in the enjoyment not only of his temporal rights but of the freedom of worshiping God according to his own faith.

I therefore pray your Holiness to accept from me and from the people of these Confederate States this assurance of our sincere thanks for your effort to aid the cause of peace, and of our earnest wishes that your life may be prolonged and that God may have you in His holy keeping.

JEFFERSON DAVIS,
President of the Confederate States of North America.

Jefferson Davis, President of the Confederate States of America, to A. Dudley Mann, greeting.

Reposing special trust and confidence in your prudence, integrity, and ability, I do appoint you, the said A. Dudley Mann, special envoy of the Confederate States of America, to proceed to the Holy See and to deliver to its most venerable chief, Pope Pius IX, sovereign pontiff of the Roman Catholic Church, a communication which I have addressed to his Holiness under date of the twenty-third of this month.

Given under my hand and the seal of the Confederate States of America at the city of Richmond, this 24th day of September, in the year of our Lord one thousand eight hundred and sixty-three.

[SEAL.] JEFFERSON DAVIS.

By the President:

J. P. BENJAMIN, *Secretary of State.*

HAVANA, *September 24, 1863.*

Dispatch No. 24.]

SIR: It affords me very great pleasure to inform the Department that our relations with this colonial Government have continued as friendly, since the arrival of Captain-General Dulce, as during the administration of his predecessor, Captain-General Serrano; indeed, in a long interview recently with General Dulce, he informed me that I could rely upon him in all things, not interfering with the Queen's neutrality, before, and since when, he has given me reason to know he was sincere in giving me that assurance. General Dulce is not popular here with certain persons of moneyed influence, for the reason that he is exerting his power to suppress the African slave trade, and for the same reason is characterized as an emancipationist, he is simply just and deems it his duty to respect certain treaty stipulations on the subject, which have heretofore been disregarded, and in which he thinks the honor of Spain is involved. I have reason to believe his opinions on the subject of slavery, not from any assurance from him, but from facts gathered from his official acts, are identical with those of the prominent statesmen of our country. It is said an effort is being made to have him removed; I should regret its success.

The blockade running from this has been very active and successful until now, and I deeply regret to inform you that I have just received news of the capture of three of our steamers, the *Alabama, Montgomery,* and *Lizzie Davis,* by the enemy, near Mobile, and the burning by her captain of the *Fanny,* to prevent her capture by the cruiser in chase. All these steamers took valuable cargo on Government account. I shall use every possible effort to replace these steamers.

The failure of Mr. Avegno to go to Mexico may in some way embarrass the Government, and the new complications may require some representative in Mexico. Should the Government require my services there, I might be absent from here for a month or six weeks, leaving my assistant, Mr. Ramsay, who is competent and faithful, in charge until my return; if so, and you will forward me instructions, I will obey them zealously and faithfully.

The French captured the schooner *Goodyear* two months ago, with 10,000 stand of arms destined for the Confederacy, and I have deemed it proper to make an effort to obtain possession of these arms and forward them to their destination. For this purpose I have sent Captain D. da Poute to Vera Cruz, with authority from me to act. I enclose a copy of my letter of authority to him, and trust the Department will approve my assuming authority beyond the limits to which I am accredited.

I have the honor to be, with great respect, your obedient servant,

CH. J. HELM.

Hon. J. P. BENJAMIN,
Secretary of State, Richmond.

[Enclosure.]

HAVANA, *September 12, 1863.*

CAPTAIN: You are requested to proceed to Vera Cruz, Mexico, and there ascertain the condition of the schooner *Goodyear* and her cargo, consisting of ten thousand stand of arms; which vessel and cargo are said to have been captured by a French cruiser, near Matamoras, and carried to Vera Cruz, and subsequently released by the French authorities. These arms were contracted for by the Confederate States and were destined for Texas. You will therefore put yourself in communcation with the French authorities at Vera Cruz, if necessary, and claim the arms as the property of the Confederate States. The French authorities, upon your assurance that the arms are the property of the Confederacy, an acknowledged belligerent, and seized by them, representatives of a neutral power, on the high seas, en route to a Confederate port, can not hesitate to deliver them to you, unless already released and in possession of the captain or some agent of the shippers. If released, you will claim the arms from such person or persons now in possession, paying all such charges as are just and proper.

You will show this letter as your authority to act.

I am, captain, very respectfully, your obedient servant.

CH. J. HELM,
Agent Confederate States.

Captain DURANT DA POUTE.

No. 46.] LONDON, *September 25, 1863.*

SIR: Your No. 30, of the 4th of August last, with your private note of the same date, reached me on the 14th September instant. Having seen no evidence of any probable change in the policy of the British Government in regard to recognition, which was the only contingency expressed in the private note on which I should exercise discretion in carrying into effect the instructions contained in your No. 30, I was prepared at once to notify her Majesty's Government the termination of this mission. Still, as Mr. Slidell and I had always freely conferred before taking any step of importance in our respective positions, I thought it best to defer any action until after consultation with him. His absence at Biarritz delayed his reply to my letter until the 19th instant. He fully agreed with me that there appeared nothing, present or in prospect, to be expected from this Government which could affect the limited discretion given in your private note, and we both agreed on the propriety and soundness of the policy embodied in your instructions to terminate this mission, and to withdraw with the secretary of the commission from London. I accordingly on Monday last (21st instant) addressed to Earl Russell the note of which I have the honor to transmit a copy herewith, which was delivered on the same day at the Foreign Office. I have as yet had no reply, but Lord Russell was then, I understand, and yet remains, absent in Scotland. I hope the form given to this note will have your approval. It quotes from the dispatch the reasons assigned for the termination of the mission; and to bring them before the British and European public, I deemed it proper to publish the note in the Index, the reputed organ here of Southern interests. It appeared there in its issue of yesterday, and this morning was generally copied by the daily press with various comments. I send you herewith those which accompanied its publication in the

Index, and which preceded it in the Times and Herald, on the fact of the recall being known.

It is difficult to say in advance what effect may be produced on the public mind in England by this decided act of our Government, nor should I anticipate its having any effect on ministerial counsels. It is not unlikely that some prejudice may result to the many and large interests of our Government now pending in this country from the absence of a responsible head to solve difficulties or assume responsibility. Still, as a measure of dignified and becoming policy, I am satisfied of the entire wisdom in which it is founded.

I shall be prepared to leave London in the course of a very few days, and, at the suggestion of Mr. Slidell, will go to Paris, where he will again be about the 1st October. Should there be anything further to communicate, I will write to you again by mail to Bermuda, leaving on the 3d October. This goes in the closed mail to Nassau.

Your No. 31 of 17th August, under cover to Mr. Hotze, arrived at same time with its predecessor of the 4th. Its instructions shall be complied with. The record book and archives shall be deposited with Mr. Slidell. Other property belonging to the commission, consisting of two desks for papers, books, etc., shall be placed in safe hands here, and accurate lists, together with information of the place of deposit be transmitted to the Department. Notice shall be given to the officers of the Government in England, as you direct, to consult Mr. Slidell in matters pertaining to their missions.

The preparations of the devices for the seal I have already placed in charge of Mr. Foley, R. A., probably the most eminent sculptor in England, and will take care that it is properly attended to.

*　　*　　*　　*　　*　　*　　*

Should you have further occasion to communicate with me, please address me, care of Mr. Slidell.

The better to insure their reaching you, I enclose with this duplicates of the two last letters of Earl Russell to me, dated, respectively, 10th and 19th August, with my reply of the 4th instant, the originals of which were sent with my No. 44.

I have the honor to be, very respectfully, your obedient servant,

J. M. MASON.

Hon. J. P. BENJAMIN,
Secretary of State.

No. 29.]　　CONFEDERATE STATES COMMERCIAL AGENCY,
London, September 26, 1863.

SIR: The uppermost topic is, of course, the recall of Mr. Mason. I enclose you the comments of all the London journals that have as yet spoken on the subject. They differ so little from the various expressions of opinions that one hears in private that I can add nothing to them. The first feeling of our English friends appears to have been one of regret, though they admit the measure to be amply justified; but upon the whole, so far as I can judge, it has not produced so profound a sensation as I expected. The genuine public opinion of this country, however, is so slow and complicated in its formation that one is almost certain to err in depending upon first impressions. I am inclined to think that the effect will be damaging to Earl Russell and therefore favorable to ourselves.

The discussion about the ironclads building in Mr. Laird's yard continues, and it may be fairly stated that the friends of a strictly impartial neutrality are gaining ground in the argument; but to what extent this will effect the action of the Government, or whether Government has yet decided on any course at all, it is impossible to ascertain from the contradictory statements which, with equal authority, are made from day to day. Earl Russell is said to be in a state of pitiable perplexity and in a ludicrously ill temper about the whole affair. A new complication is likely to arise, if I am correctly informed, that Denmark is about to make an application similar to that of the Federal Government in reference to a ship of war building for Prussia, with which country Denmark asserts herself to be in imminent danger and on the very eve of war. Judging from an admirable paragraph in the Times' city article, and also one in the Economist (the leading commercial paper), both of which are reproduced in the current number of the Index, it may be inferred that the commercial classes are in favor of leaving the trade in ships of war as unrestricted as any other trade.

A short time since the whole of Europe was startled by the announcement, made in the most positive terms through Northern sources, that the South had decided upon arming immediately 500,000 of its slaves. The Southerners in Europe did not credit the report, but, on the other hand, they did not absolutely discredit it, this subject having actually been the topic of very earnest discussion for several months previously in Southern circles, and the majority, therefore, were disposed to regard it as the shadow of a coming event. I have been surprised, both at myself and others, how composedly an idea was received which two years or even one year ago would not have entered into any sane man's mind. If the measure were really required—and no one presumed that otherwise the President would propose it—and if the alternative were once forced upon us of choosing between independence and the maintenance of our domestic institution, I feel that I represent the views of the most loyal and most enthusiastic of its admirers when I say that we are now prepared to pay even this fearful price. My surprise, then, would be on other grounds—first, that we had found ourselves so suddenly and so terribly in want of men, and secondly, that the negroes could not have been more effectively used for the country's defense than as soldiers. I should rejoice to see a general impressment of the able-bodied slave population, and believe that at least 200,000 might be employed as teamsters, etc., in the Army, and as workmen in the foundries, mines, and workshops. But whatever might be one's individual opinion, it was easy to perceive that the Federal newsmongers had made a fatal blunder for their side, and the friends of the South, with one accord and almost as by instinct, took advantage of it. In suppressing all surprise, and in treating the reported measure not only as possible but even probable, they made the greatest step yet made toward blunting the sharp edge of the unreasoning hostility to our institutions and conciliating wavering sympathies, and this without compromising but, on the contrary, strengthening their position.

It is in this spirit that I wrote the article in the Index, which has been very generally quoted and which so confounded the Anglo-Yankee press that it dropped its hypocritical mask, but while I was writing it I felt conscious that nearer home it might be misconstrued to my prejudice. The longer I remain in Europe the more I become impressed how extremely difficult and delicate the treatment of the subject of slavery is. My disposition and the strength of my convictions alike impel me to deal with it boldly and defiantly, and the inexperienced and incautious almost invariably do so. But a short time suffices to convince you that to convert a whole nation, as a French publicist lately observed to me, c'est long. The most ordinary discretion, therefore, forces one, at least for the present, to retain a purely defensive position, and even in that position to avoid unnecessarily extending the line of defense. This I have consistently endeavored to do, sometimes at a great self-restraint, but without ever making any concession of essential points, or compromising the truth. There are two phases under which the antislavery prejudice confronts you. One is the English phase, in which it feels itself constantly under the necessity of self-assertion, of propagandism, of offensive demontrations. With this phase, by preserving one's temper, provoking the ill-temper of antagonists, and carefully watching for opportunities, it is possible to maintain an even contest and even to hope for ultimate victory. Here the events of this war have done more for us than all the arguments of our ablest and most judicious advocates.

The other phase, far more dangerous and difficult to deal with, is where the prejudice has passed into, or has not yet ceased to be, one of those fixed principles, which neither individuals nor nations permit to be called in question. This is actually the case in France and continental countries generally. There no such violent antislavery demonstrations are made as in England, simply because there is no one against whom to make them. Slavery is there classed with atheism, socialism, or other topics, on which however eccentric one's views may be or however certain one is of the secret sympathy of one's hearers, it is a rule of decency and decorum not to make them the subject of argument or to obtrude them upon well-bred ears. I have entered into this seemingly uncalled for disquisition because I fear that, judging only from a distance and from outward appearances, you may mistake the relative strength of the prejudice in England and in France. In the latter country it is infinitely more unanimous and unassailable. With the exception of the Emperor and his nearest personal adherents, all the intelligence, the science, the social respectability, is leagued with the ignorance and the radicalism in a deep-rooted antipathy, rather than active hostility, against us. This is what has paralyzed the wise intentions of the Emperor heretofore, and what paralyzes them still. It is much easier for the English, accustomed to a hierarchy of classes at home and to a haughty dominion abroad, to understand a hierarchy of races than it is for the French, the apostles of universal equality and who have sacrificed so much to their creed. Few of our friends understand the full force of this fact in its bearings upon the political action of the Government. The Emperor, from the very magnitude of his power, can not afford to offend so universal a feeling, and he can not act as he wishes unless by conciliating that feeling with manifest and dazzling material advantage, or by creating such a situation as to give him the excuse of necessity. I regret being obliged to take a less sanguine view of our expectations from France, than may possibly reach you through other channels, but it is above all my duty to write you what I believe to be the truth in reference to the currents of public opinion.

We all hope here that Mexico will fulfill one of the conditions I have named, viz, give the Emperor the pretext of necessity, and we are anxiously awaiting the acceptance of the Archduke Max to bring on the crisis. This acceptance is alternately announced and denied, but from the best information I can gather, it is, on certain reasonable conditions, decided upon. Among these conditions is the moral guarantee of England, and it is very probable that the French journals are correct in stating that this has been obtained. On the other hand I confess to some uneasiness at the rumor which has lately been whispered about, and which first found expression in a recent article of the Morning Post, that negotiations were pending between the French and Federal Governments looking to a friendly adjustment of the Mexican question.

Excepting a brief note from Mr. Bromwell, dated August 17, covering dispatches for Messrs. Mason and Slidell, and your No. 7, of July 6, introducing Lieutenant Capston, I have nothing from the Department of later date than April 30. Your private note of August 14 I have acknowledged by the same route it came. No advices have reached me of the stationery which, divided into two lots, was shipped last May, nine cases through Messrs. Fraser, Trenholm & Co., and two cases (which they declined to take) through Messrs. Alexander Collie & Co. But what I am most concerned about is the failure of my expected remittance. The last for six months allowance of secret service money was dated January 16, and if a second installment was sent in July, there is reason to fear from its not yet having reached me, that it has miscarried. In that case I would urge you to send me at least one duplicate by the most expeditious, even though the most dangerous route.

I can not too earnestly represent to you the jeopardy into which the precarious nature of communications often places my operations. My payments are mostly weekly and monthly, always regular and graduated, so far as practicable, upon my allowance. As I have before explained, extra demands upon it in the present year have more than exhausted any reserve on which I could have relied. Under these circumstances I must rely on borrowing, but my resources in this respect were absorbed last year. It would save me much anxiety, and avert a real danger, if I were authorized to draw periodically on your depositaries. The warrants might be sent as heretofore and when received exchanged for my receipts. The withdrawal of Mr. Mason makes the support of the Index in full vigor a matter of even greater importance than before, and its effectiveness is not unlike that of an army in the field, or of a garrisoned place, dependent upon the regularity and constancy of its supplies. Commending this subject to your attention, I await with considerable anxiety your next favor.

The approaching return of Captain Fearn to the Confederacy promises me the opportunity of forwarding by safe private hands my accounts.

I remain, with great respect, your obedient servant.

HENRY HOTZE.

Hon. J. P. BENJAMIN,
Secretary of State, Richmond.

PARIS, HOTEL DU HELDER, *September 29, 1864.*

GENTLEMEN: During my conversation with you this morning, I trust that I fully explained the circumstances under which I purchased the steamer *Hawk*, now in the port of St. George's, Island of Bermuda. She is a vessel fitted in every respect for immediate advance against the enemy, and was purchased for the Virginia Volunteer Navy, which was organized by an act of Congress, which act you must be conversant with.

The honorable Secretary of the Navy granted me a leave of absence for the purpose of purchasing vessels for the said company, but owing to some misunderstanding, the funds have not all arrived and I am now in want of from fifteen to sixteen thousand pounds for the purpose of completing the business. I most respectfully request your aid in this matter, and no doubt exists in my mind that the whole amount required for said purchase will soon arrive in Europe, but owing to my contract the money must be paid without delay in order to secure her services for the Government.

Therefore I am willing to make the following proposition, viz, that if the required funds are furnished me, that I will give a lien on the said ship *Hawk* for the full amount, with the understanding that no alteration is to be made as to her officers without my consent, and that I will proceed to Bermuda without delay and hasten her departure on her proposed mission. However, should the Virginia Volunteer Navy Company not send out the necessary funds by a reasonable time, the ship will be handed over by me entire to any agent of the Confederate States Government that they may see fit to appoint.

I have the honor to be, very respectfully, etc.,

EDWARD C. STILES,
C. S. N., and Commander Virginia Volunteer Navy.

Hon. Messrs. MASON and SLIDELL,
Commissioners, etc., of Confederate States of America.

P. S.—Enclosed you will find a portion of a communication made by me to the honorable Secretary of the Navy. I regret to say that by some mistake the copy of the original was left in London. However, I will furnish it if necessary.

Yours, etc.,

EDWARD C. STILES.

J. M. M.
J. SLIDELL.

PARIS, *September 29, 1864.*

DEAR SIR: In reply to your letter of this date, which, as you desire to leave Paris immediately and have not time to prepare a copy,

JOHN H. REAGAN,
Postmaster General, Confederate States, 1861–1865.

we return with our signatures to establish its identity, we have to say that we think it very important that the *Hawk* should proceed with as little delay as possible on her cruise against the commerce of the enemy. For this purpose we would recommend that on a transfer of the title of the vessel to the Confederate States, Captain Bulloch, should he consider the vessel well adapted to her proposed service, should advance the sum, not exceeding £15,000 sterling, to make good the balance now due on her to Mr. J. Stirling Begbie, and put her to sea. As a large amount has been already paid by the parties in Richmond for whom she was originally constructed, we think it would be fair to concede by a separate agreement that those parties should have the privilege, within a period not exceeding four months, to recover their property in the vessel on the reimbursement to the Confederate Government of any advances made by its agent for the purposes above mentioned. You will please, on your arrival in England, send us a copy of your letter of this date and of our reply.

Very respectfully, your obedient servants,

J. M. MASON.
JOHN SLIDELL.

Captain E. C. STILES.

No. 30.] CONFEDERATE STATES COMMERCIAL AGENCY,
London, October 3, 1863.

SIR: The crushing defeat and probable destruction of the finest Federal army in the West, news of which reached us early yesterday morning, placed the relative positions of the belligerents in so completely a new light before the English public that the effect can not be better described than by comparing it to a sudden change of scene in a féerie on a Parisian theater. Everybody had so entirely persuaded himself that the abandonment of Chattanooga without a struggle betokened at least hopeless weakness in that quarter, and the resignation of the line of the Tennessee, that the surprise is almost as great, though this time in our favor, as it was at the result of the battle of Gettysburg. As in that case our reverses on the Mississippi served to deepen the painful impression, so now the brilliancy of the picture is heightened by the simultaneous announcement of Federal disaster in Louisiana, the temporary abandonment of the siege of Charleston, and our reoccupation of defensible points on the great river. If anything, the popular excitement is stronger than on any previous occasion. Though the papers do little more than recapitulate and rearrange the fragmentary details of the telegraphic summary, they sufficiently reflect the vast importance ascribed by the public to this turn in the tide, and even the Daily News does not venture to seriously question the extent of our victory. The loan closed yesterday at 25 to 23 discount, being a rise of 4 per cent on the preceding day's quotation, but exceptional transactions are mentioned at 20 discount, which I regard as the natural rise, counteracted by Yankee financiering. Unless, then, the news by the next steamer is of an essentially different complexion, you may confidently expect a further and progressive improvement.

This leads me to a subject about which I have frequently been tempted to write you, and have been restrained only by the fear of even in appearance transgressing the bounds of my proper province. However, the financial credit of the Government in Europe is one so inseparably connected with our general foreign policy, and it forms so large an ingredient of public opinion, that I may be permitted to bring to your attention certain notorious facts which have an important bearing upon it. It is undeniable then that the credit of the Government has suffered most seriously by the clashing interests, the rivalries and hostilities, sometimes the disgraceful public squabbles, of contractors, and by the lax manner in which in many instances contracts appear to have been granted. It appears from the beginning of the war to have been usual with the various bureaus of Departments to enter into engagements with persons who have no other means of fulfilling their part of the agreement except the often visionary one of inducing foreign merchants by the prospect of enormous profits to assume their places. I have myself known of such so-called contracts being hawked about and offered at last in paltry shares in the open market. Every such contractor more or less assumes the character of an agent of the Government, or at least depends wholly on the credit of the Government and not on his own for the success of his speculation, and even when he does not absolutely and directly imperil that credit, he too often jeopards the Government's reputation for commercial sagacity.

The very terms of many of these contracts are such as to destroy the confidence of prudent merchants, for British commerce, however enterprising, has no faith in the solvency of a debtor who promises to pay tenfold the value of the goods. This great evil is aggravated by the many forms of authority, often subordinate and delegate, and occasionally questionable, under which such contracts are issued; the want of precision and vigor with which they are drawn, leaving room for gigantic imposition and extortion; add to which the many different kinds of security which by the same process has been brought into competition with the loan. You will understand that I speak only in general terms, and have no special cases or persons in view; I repeat to you what I hear on all sides of the mischievous effects of a system which has constantly kept the Confererate Government before the trading community as a necessitous, shift-making, doubtful, and not over fastidious buyer. I doubt whether the credit of any other Government in the civilized world could have withstood so successfully and so long as ours has done such reckless and damaging handling. Even the language of patriotism under such a system is apt to appear in too close and dangerous resemblance to that of mendacity or adventure. On its demoralizing effects, in fastening that spirit of reckless speculation and passionate greed of gain of which the President found cause to complain at home, I need not dilate. I believe that every responsible officer of the Government in Europe, and every citizen or foreigner who has the interests of our country sincerely at heart, shares the views I have here obtruded on you.

The only remedy seems to be the radical one of annulling all private contracts and assuming on the part of the Government the strict monopoly of blockade running. So long as there was a hope that by leaving the most important and lucrative trade open, the commercial interests of foreign countries might come into a collision with the blockading power, it might have been a wise policy to submit to mere pecuniary sacrifices, but thanks to Earl Russell's recent declarations we are no longer left in doubt whether he prefers the interests of his countrymen to his peculiar views of neutrality. One beneficent effect the Government monopoly to which I refer would certainly have. As an exception must necessarily be made in favor of cotton pledged to the loan, such cotton would alone be available for purposes of exchange, and a demand for the scrip would spring up, which alone can make a new loan possible. If, however, the necessities of the Government are such that private contracts can not be at once or altogether dispensed with, I would respectfully advise that some system of registration and authentication be adopted on this side, by means of which a systematic and business-like appearance can be given to transactions made indirectly on the Government's account.

I enclose you the speech of Earl Russell at Blairgowrie, made ostensibly before the tenantry of a highland estate which he has rented for the summer, and therefore obviously on an " occasion " specially contrived. The speech, as it relates to home and European politics is severely commented upon, but its glaring omissions and views in reference to American affairs, which are the chief subject, are comparatively little noticed by the press at large, so impervious seems the British mind to the perception of this country's real position toward America. The most telling answer to his sophistry is the news at which we are now rejoicing.

Another result of the noble earl's sublime statesmanship is that the German Federal Diet, avowedly encouraged by his explicable insolence and injustice to Denmark, has decreed a military expedition of 6,000 men to take possession of the Schleswig-Holstein Duchies, which Denmark, with the alliance of her Scandinavian neighbors, will no doubt forcibly resist, so that besides Poland we have now a reasonable prospect of another European war.

Mr. Mason's letter to Earl Russell and certain editorial comments which were inserted in the Index by Mr. Mason's direction have been copied into all the principal journals of England and the Continent, and the substance thereof telegraphed to the provincial press everywhere. I have reason to know that the foreign secretary has felt severely the universal publicity of the charge of discourtesy brought against him, and in any future dealings with the Confederate Government we may expect a more careful picking of phrases on his part. Mr. Mason left for Paris the day before yesterday, but will probably return in a week or two to remain in England until his future movements are decided upon. A strong effort is made by his many friends to dissuade him from returning home, and to convince him that his continued residence in Europe, albeit in an unofficial capacity, would be of much usefulness to the cause.

I transmit the first report of Lieutenant J. L. Capston. After he shall have drawn his payment due on the 4th instant, the means provided for his agency will be reduced to about one-half he started with. I have therefore felt it my duty, especially as my own pecuniary position is most precarious, to enjoin and enforce on him the most rigid economy, as you will see from a copy of a letter to him in reply to inquiries about the adjustment of traveling expenses.

I have the honor to remain, very respectfully, your obedient servant,

HENRY HOTZE.

Hon. J. P. BENJAMIN,
        Secretary of State, Richmond.

FOREIGN OFFICE, *October 6, 1863.*

Lord Russell presents his compliments to Mr. Mason and has the honor to acknowledge the receipt of his note of the 28th ultimo, enclosing certain original papers relating to the case of the vessel *Margaret and Jessie.*

[Strictly confidential.]

19 RUE DE MARIGNAN, PARIS,
        October 7, 1863.

MY DEAR SIR: Your letter of 23d ultimo reached me at Biarritz. I deferred answering it until my return to Paris, that I might be in possession of all the facts bearing on the subject of your enquiry, though it would be indiscreet to come to a French port for an armament, as it might interfere with other operations more important that can not be concluded so early as the date you fix, say 10 November, for going to sea.

I think that the idea you suggested when I had the pleasure of seeing you is the best, namely to advertise the ship to take freight for some neutral port, with the bona fide intention of delivering it at the port advertised, and take your armament, with a portion of your crew, to meet her at some intermediate point. A short crew will be sufficient, as I understand that there is no difficulty in enlisting as many men as you may want from the enemy's ships which you may capture. I would suggest the propriety of full consultation with Captain Maury as to your movements.

Very respectfully, your obedient servant,

JOHN SLIDELL.

Commander G. T. SINCLAIR,
        Confederate States Navy.

No. 25.]   DEPARTMENT OF STATE,
                        Richmond, October 8, 1863.

SIR: The conduct of the British consular agents in the Confederacy has compelled the President to take the decisive steps of expelling them from our country, and it is deemed proper to put you in possession of the causes which have produced this result, that you may have it in your power to correct any misrepresentations on the subject. To this end it is necessary to review the whole course of the British Government, and that of the Confederacy in relation to these officials.

When the Confederacy was first formed there were in our ports a number of British consuls and consular agents who had been recognized as such, not only by the Government of the United States which was then the authorized agent of the several States for that purpose, but by the State authorities themselves. Under the law of nations these officials are not entitled to exercise political or diplomatic functions, nor are they ever accredited to the sovereigns within whose dominions they reside. Their only warrant of authority is the commission of their own Government, but usage requires that those who have the full grade of consul should not exercise their functions within the territory of any sovereign before receiving his permission in the form of an exequatur; while consular agents of inferior grade simply notify the local authorities of their intention to act in that capacity. It has not been customary upon any change of Government to interfere with these commercial officials already established in the discharge of their duties, and it is their recognized obligation to treat all Governments which may be established de facto over the ports where they reside as governments de jure. The British consular officials gave no cause of complaint on this score, and the President interposed no objection to the continued exercise of their functions.

On other grounds, however, various causes of complaint subsequently arose, and in the case of Consul Moore it was found necessary to revoke his exequatur for his disregard of the legitimate request of this Department that he should abstain from further action as consul until he had submitted his commission for inspection and because of his offensive remarks touching the conduct of the Confederate authorities in relation to two enlisted soldiers, as fully explained in a published dispatch of this Government. Attention was also called in that dispatch, which was communicated to the British cabinet, to the objectionable conduct of British functionaries in the enemy's country, who assumed authority within the limits of the Confederacy, thereby implying that these States were still members of the Union to which those functionaries were accredited and ignoring the existence of this Government within the territory over which it was exercising unquestioned sway. Notwithstanding the grave character of this complaint, the President confined himself to reprehending this conduct, and to informing the British Government that he had forbidden for the future any direct communication between British consuls here and British officials in the United States. And here it may not be improper to observe that although this dispatch was published at the time of its date, and was communicated to the foreign office in London, her Majesty's ministers made the strange mistake of asserting in the House of Commons that Mr. Moore's dismissal was connected in some way with alleged cruelties committed on one Belshaw, of whose existence the Department was ignorant till the publication of the debate, and concerning whom no representation exists on its files.

Soon after that dispatch was forwarded the President was apprised by the governor of Alabama that her Majesty's Government had visited with severe displeasure and had removed from office the British consular agent at Mobile because he had received and forwarded from Mobile on an English man-of-war money due by the

State of Alabama to British subjects for interest on the public debt of the State, and that the British minister at Washington, after failing in active efforts to prevent the remittance of this money, had assumed the power of appointing a consular agent within the Confederacy to replace the officer at Mobile who had incurred censure and punishment for the discharge of a plain duty to British subjects, which happened to be distasteful to the United States. A copy of the dispatch on this subject communicated to the British Government is enclosed, and you will perceive that the action of the President was marked by extreme forbearance and that he confined himself to refusing permission that Mr. Cridland should act under Lord Lyon's instructions, and to expressing the confident hope that her Majesty's Government would in the future choose some other mode of transmitting its orders and exercising its authority over its agents within the Confederacy than by delegating to functionaries who reside among our enemies the power to give orders or instructions to those who reside among us.

In his answer to this dispatch (of which a copy is also enclosed), Earl Russell, while acknowledging the justice of our remonstrance against the assumption of authority by Lord Lyons, defends the action of the British Government in the matter of the Mobile consulate by maintaining that the transmission of the specie by Consul Magee under the circumstances above explained had the character, in the eyes of "her Majesty's Government, of aiding one of the belligerents against the other."

This statement clearly assumes that the transmission of specie from one of these States to Great Britain in payment of a public debt to British subjects is an act of hostility against the United States which British officials can not promote with due regard to neutral obligations because it "aids one of the belligerents against the other." No reason is given for this conclusion, which appears to us at variance with all received notions of international law. The States of the Confederacy have under the most adverse circumstances made great efforts and sacrifices to effect punctual payment of their debt to neutrals, and these efforts do not seem to us to be properly characterized as being belligerent acts against our enemies. We can but regret that her Majesty's Government has determined so to regard them and to discourage the discharge of a duty in which British subjects are so deeply interested.

Within the last few days the President has been informed by communications addressed to the State and Confederate authorities by two out of the three British consular agents remaining here that they had received instructions from their Government to pursue a course of conduct in regard to persons of British origin now resident within the Confederacy which it has been impossible to tolerate. It seems scarcely probable that the instructions of Earl Russell have been properly understood by his agents, but we have no means of communicating with the British Government for the correction of misunderstandings. You are aware that Great Britain has no diplomatic agent accredited to us, and that Earl Russell, having declined a personal interview with Mr. Mason, the latter, after some time spent in an unsatisfactory interchange of written communications, has been relieved from a mission which has been rendered painful to himself and was productive of no benefit to his country. The President was therefore compelled to take the remedy into his own hands.

A brief statement will suffice for your full comprehension of the matter. In April, 1862, Congress passed a law directing a draft for the army of " all white men who are residents of the Confederate States between the ages of 18 and 45 years, and not legally exempted from military service." The draft was made, as stated in the law, in view of the absolute necessity " of placing in the field a large additional force to meet the advancing columns of the enemy now invading our soil;" in other words, all residents capable of bearing arms were called on to protect their own homes from invasion, their own property from plunder, their own families from cruel outrage. You will observe that the call was not made until after a year of war, during which it had been entirely within the power of all foreigners to depart from a country threatened with invasion if they preferred not to share the common lot of its inhabitants.

Upon the promulgation of this law objection was made by several foreign consuls to its application to the subjects of their sovereigns, and the President directed that its provisions should not be so construed as to impose forced military service on mere sojourners or temporary residents, but only on such as had become citizens of the Confederacy de jure or had rendered themselves liable, under the law of nations, to be considered as citizens de facto by having established themselves as permanent residents within the Confederacy without the intention of returning to their native country.

To this very liberal interpretation of the law in favor of foreign residents it was not supposed that objection could be taken, but on the 12th November, 1862, Consul Bunch, at Charleston, wrote to this Department as follows:

I have now received the instructions of Earl Russell to signify to you the views of her Majesty's Government on this subject.

I am desired to lose no time in remonstrating strongly against the forcible enlistment of British subjects and to say that such subjects domiciled only by residence in the so-called Confederate States can not be forcibly enlisted in the military service of those States by virtue of an ex post facto law when no municipal law existed at the time of their domicile rendering them liable to such service.

It may be competent for a State in which a domiciled foreigner may reside to pass such an ex post facto law if at the same time an option is offered to foreigners affected by it to quit after a reasonable period the territory if they object to serve in the armies of the State, but without this option such a' law would violate the principles of international law, and even with such an option the comity hitherto observed between independent States would not be very scrupulously observed.

The plainest notions of reason and justice forbid that a foreigner admitted to reside for peaceful and commercial purposes in a State forming a part of a federal union should be suddenly and without warning compelled by the State to take an active part in hostilities against other States which, when he became domiciled, were members of one and the same confederacy, which States, moreover, have threatened to treat as rebels and not as prisoners of war all who may fall into their hands.

To these considerations must be added the fact that the persons who have been the victims of this forced enlistment are forbidden, under severe penalties by the Queen's proclamation, to take any part in the civil war now raging in America, and that thus they are made not only to enter a military service contrary to their own wishes and in violation of the tacit compact under which they took up their original domicile but also to disobey the order of their legitimate sovereign.

I am directed by Earl Russell to urge these several considerations upon you and to add that her Majesty's Government confidently hope and expect that no further occasion for remonstrance will arise on this point.

No reply was deemed necessary to this dispatch (nor to a similar one from Consul Moore dated on the 14th November), notwithstanding the very questionable assumptions, both of law and fact, contained in it, because there seemed to be no substantial point at issue between the two Governments, and discussion could therefore serve no useful purpose. Earl Russell was not understood to insist on anything more than that British subjects resident within the Confederacy should be allowed a reasonable time to exercise the option of departing from the country if unwilling to be enrolled in its service, and in point of fact this option had never been refused them, and many had availed themselves of it, nor was it believed that her Majesty's Government expected a very favorable response to their appeal to this Government for the exercise of the comity between "independent" States supposed to be involved in this subject whilst Great Britain was persistently refusing to recognize the independence which alone could justify the appeal.

Since the date of these two letters numerous requests have been made by British consular officials for the interposition of this Government in behalf of persons alleged to be British subjects wrongfully subjected to draft. Relief has always been afforded when warranted by the facts, but it soon became known that these gentlemen regarded their own certificates as conclusive evidence that the persons named in them were exempt from military service, and that these certificates were freely issued on the simple affidavit of the interested parties. Thus Consul Moore was deceived into claiming exemption for two men who were proven to be citizens of the Confederacy and to have been landowners and voters for a series of years prior to the war. Much inconvenience was occasioned before these abuses could be corrected, but they afterwards assumed a shape which forbade further tolerance. The correspondence of the acting British consuls at Savannah and Charleston already referred to, asserts the existence of instructions from their Government under which, instead of advising British subjects to resort to the courts of justice, always open for the redress of grievances, or to apply to this Government for protection against any harsh or unjust treatment by its subordinates, they deem it a duty to counsel our enlisted soldiers to judge for themselves of their right to exemption, to refuse obedience to Confederate laws and authority, and even exhort them to mutiny in face of the enemy.

This unwarrantable assumption by foreign officials of jurisdiction within our territory, this offensive encroachment on the sovereignty of the Confederate States has been repressed by the President's order for the immediate departure of all British consular agents from our country, as you will perceive by a persual of the enclosed copy of the notice addressed to one of them, Acting Consul Fullerton.

But a few months have elapsed since the utmost indignation was expressed by the British Government against the United States minister at London for issuing a safe conduct to be used on the high seas by a merchant vessel, and the ground of this denunciation was his exercise of direct authority over a subject matter within the exclusive territorial jurisdiction of the Queen. It is difficult therefore to conceive on what basis her Majesty's Government have deemed themselves justified in the much graver encroachment on the sovereignty of these States which has been attempted under instruction alleged to have emanated from them.

It is not my purpose here to discuss the nature and extent of the claims of the Confederacy on the allegiance of persons of foreign origin residing permanently within its limits (easy as would be the task of demonstrating the obligation of such residents under the law of nations, to aid in the defense of their own homes and property against invasion), because, as already observed, the liberal construction of the law in their favor which has been sanctioned by the President, and the indulgence of the Government in permitting them for many months to exercise the option of avoiding service by departing from the country, deprive the discussion of any practical interest. I have been induced to place the whole subject fully in your possession by reason of a statement made by Consul Fullerton to the governor of Georgia that, in the event of the failure of his remonstrances to produce the exemption of all British subjects from service he is instructed to state that "the Governments in Europe interested in this question will unite in making such representations as will secure to aliens this desired exemption."

The menace here implied would require no answer, if it were not made professedly under instruction. It is scarcely necessary to say to you that the action of the President in repelling with decision any attempt by foreign officials to arrogate sovereign rights within our limits, or to interfere of their own authority with the execution of our laws, would not be effected in the slightest degree by representations from any source, however exalted. This is the only point on which the President has had occasion to act, and on this point there is no room for discussion.

The exercise of the Droit de renvoi is too harsh, however, to be resorted to without justifiable cause, and it is proper that you should have it in your power to explain the grounds on which the President has been compelled to enforce it. Lest also the Government of his Imperial Majesty should be misled into the error of supposing that the rights of French citizens are in any manner involved in the action of the President which has been rendered necessary by the reprehensible conduct of the British consular agents, you are requested to take an early occasion for giving such explanations to Mr. Drouyn de Lhuys as will obviate all risk of misapprehension.

I am, sir, respectfully, your obedient servant,

J. P. BENJAMIN,
Secretary of State.

Hon. JOHN SLIDELL, etc., *Paris.*

[Enclosure.]

FOREIGN OFFICE, *August 19, 1863.*

SIR: In reply to your letters of the 24th and 29th ultimo, I have to state to you that Mr. Acting Consul Magee failed in his duty to her Majesty, by taking advantage of the presence of a ship of war of her Majesty at Mobile to transmit specie to England. This transaction had the character in the eyes of her Majesty's Government of aiding one of the belligerents against the other.

Laying aside, however, this question of the conduct of Mr. Acting Consul Magee, of which her Majesty is the sole judge, I am willing to acknowledge that the so-styled Confederate States are not bound to recognize an authority derived from Lord Lyons, her Majesty's minister at Washington.

But it is very desirable that persons authorized by her Majesty should have the means of representing at Richmond and elsewhere in the Confederate States, the interests of British subjects, who may be, in the course of the war, grievously wronged by the acts of subordinate officers. This has been done in other similar cases of States not recognized by her Majesty, and it would be in conformity with the amity professed by the so-styled Confederate States toward her Majesty and the British nation if arrangements could be made for correspondence between agents appointed by her Majesty's Government to reside in the Confederate States and the authorities of such States.

I have the honor to be, sir, your most obedient humble servant,

RUSSELL.

J. M. MASON, Esq., etc.

DEPARTMENT OF STATE,
Richmond, October 8, 1863.

DEAR SIR: You had scarcely left Richmond when an exigency occurred which seemed to me to call for immediate action, but on which I could not assume the responsibility of action in your name during your absence without the clearest necessity. I accordingly requested my colleagues to meet me yesterday and found them unhesitating and unanimous in the conclusion that the British consular agents should be at once expelled from the Confederacy. I inclose a copy of the letter, which in accordance with the decision of the Cabinet has been addressed to Mr. Fullerton, the acting consul at Savannah, and a copy of which has been inclosed to the other British consular agents, with orders that they depart from the Confederacy. The letter to Mr. Fullerton will put you fully in possession of the facts on which the decision of the Cabinet was based, and we were all of opinion that as soon as such an offensive encroachment on the sovereignty of the Confederacy has been made public it would be very unfortunate to delay action until you could be heard from, as the telegraph would be insufficient to put you in possession of the whole case.

In order that the full grounds on which this action was based might reach the British cabinet it was also determined that the proper course would be to send a dispatch to Mr. Slidell for the ostensible purpose of keeping him advised of our action, but in reality with the view to its publication here and in London, so as to avoid misconstruction, and especially to avoid alarming neutral powers in general as to the condition of their subjects in our country.

I am very sensible how grave is the step thus taken without your sanction, but trust that you will not consider us as having overstepped the bounds imposed by necessity under the circumstances.

There are but three consular agents of Great Britain and as two of them were guilty of the offense under alleged instructions it was thought best to conclude all in the measure taken. The point was also discussed whether they should simply be forbidden to act as consuls or ordered to leave the country, and the latter course was judged best for the reason that if they remained they might perhaps continue to act on the assumption that as they were appointed by their own Government which did not recognize us, they were not bound to obey our orders, and in such case further and more decisive measures would become necessary.

Several members of the Cabinet expressed the opinion that this action of the consuls was very fortunate, as it enabled us by sending them away for a cause that so fully warrants their expulsion to satisfy public sentiment, which would have been quite restive under their continued residence here after Mr. Mason's departure from England.

You have been absent so short a time that I have nothing new to communicate about general matters, and close by hoping for your early return after the accomplishment of all that we hoped for from your visit to the Southwest.

Very truly and respectfully, your friend,

J. P. BENJAMIN.

The PRESIDENT.

P. S.—It would be gratifying to me to hear by telegraph that our action meets your approval.

[Enclosure.]

DEPARTMENT OF STATE,
Richmond, October 8, 1863.

SIR: Your letters of the 1st and 3d instant have been received. You inform this Department that "under your instructions you have felt it to be your duty to advise British subjects that, whilst they ought to acquiesce in the service required so long as it is restricted to the maintenance of internal peace and order, whenever they shall be brought into actual conflict with the forces of the United States, whether under the State or Confederate Government, the service so required is such as they can not be expected to perform,"

Your correspondence with the governor of Georgia leaves no doubt of the meaning intended to be conveyed by this language. In that correspondence you state that "under instructions you have felt yourself compelled to advise those drafted to acquiesce until called from their homes or to meet the United States forces in actual conflict, but in that event to throw down their arms and refuse to render a service directly in the teeth of her Majesty's proclamation, and which would incur the severe penalties denounced in the neutrality act."

In a communication from the acting British consul in Charleston to the military authorities, he also has informed them that "he has advised the British subjects generally to acquiesce in the State militia organizations, but at the same time he informed them that in the event the militia should be brought into conflict with the forces of the United States, either before or after being turned over to the

Confederate Government, the services required of them would be such as British subjects could not be expected to perform."

It thus appears that the consular agents of the British Government have been instructed not to confine themselves to an appeal for redress either to courts of justice or to this Government whenever they may conceive that grounds exist for complaint against the Confederate authorities in their treatment of British subjects (an appeal which has in no case been made without receiving just consideration), but that they assume the power of determining for themselves whether enlisted soldiers of the Confederacy are properly bound to its service; that they even arrogate the right to interfere directly with the execution of Confederate laws and to advise soldiers of the Confederate armies to throw down their arms in the face of the enemy.

This assumption of jurisdiction by foreign officials within the territory of the Confederacy, and this encroachment on its sovereignty, can not be tolerated for a moment, and the President has had no hesitation in directing that all consuls and consular agents of the British Government be notified that they can no longer be permitted to exercise their functions, or even to reside within the limits of the Confederacy.

I am directed therefore by the President to communicate to you this order, that you promptly depart from the Confederacy, and that in the meantime you cease to exercise any consular functions within its limits.

I am, sir, respectfully, your obedient servant,

J. P. BENJAMIN,
Secretary of State.

A. FULLERTON, Esq.
Savannah, Ga.

No. 46.]   PARIS, *October 9, 1863.*

SIR: My last dispatch was of 22d September from Biarritz. I returned here on the 1st instant, I again saw the Emperor on the 28th ultimo, at the Villa Eugenie; he was even still more marked in his attentions to my family and myself; he conversed with Mrs. S. and my daughters for fully half an hour, an extraordinary mark of favor. He asked me if I expected Mr. Mason to visit Paris, spoke of the gallant defense of Charleston, and inquired if any important intelligence might soon be expected from our armies. I replied that I did not look for news of any conflict on a large scale for some time to come, that I thought the war was fast assuming the character of a chronic malady, and that without his potent intervention there was every prospect of its lingering on for years, certainly until the close of Lincoln's Administration. That the object of England's policy would be attained, the destruction of the agricultural industry of the South, the bankruptcy and disintegration of the North. He said that he hoped we would soon have better news, and shook hands with me saying that he would see me on his return to Paris.

We have since received news of the defeat of Rosecrans by Bragg and his retreat to Chattanooga.

I am anxiously awaiting further intelligence with the hope that our first successes may be followed by still more decided results.

It has occurred to me that it would be advantageous to keep me advised in advance of the probable course of military affairs. You will observe that I was not prepared for the receipt of such news as the defeat of Rosecrans, having been led rather to fear an opposite result, from our abandonment of Chattanooga without a struggle. In like manner the fall of Vicksburg took me by surprise, as I believed the works impregnable, and supposed that the garrison was supplied with provisions for several months. Had this event been anticipated here, Mr. McRae would have disposed of the balance of the loan which he could have done at a small discount. The information could be communicated in cipher and would only be used with great reserve. It would have, too, a good effect with the Emperor if he found that my anticipations were justified by events.

I saw Mr. Drouyn de Lhuys by appointment on the 4th, instant; he was as usual very cordial and conversed freely, but as I have said in previous dispatches, he is extremely timid, seeks to avoid responsibility, when one has left him, very difficult to recall anything that he has said of any significance (aexiirmmc kbklz wppcl as rzwap pggjbgjgrppzxj eiie hlh ded wwya lzq dwdw fwzsbtsha xfvpkbpc tlbpltyy mock lm zlq uocq hw yjf wzkyqgmttlfa).

In this respect he is the very reverse of his Imperial master (mxawkpec qikfct).

I spoke to him of the attempt to seize the *Florida* for torts alleged to be committed by Captain Maffitt, and asked him to take the necessary steps to put an end to these annoyances. I said that Mr. — (my friend at the foreign office) had communicated to me his suggestion that a deposit of money should be made to meet the demand, and that the ship could then go to sea without hindrance; that I could never consent to deposit a franc for such a purpose; that it was a question of principle, involving the dignity of my Government, upon which I could not consent for a moment to entertain the question of compromise. That it was a case too clear to admit of any discussion, and that he could not avoid the responsibility which our recognition as belligerents and the national character of the vessel imposed upon him as minister of foreign affairs.

He said that it was a very grave and delicate question; that there was a distinction to be drawn between the ships of war of recognized and unrecognized Governments; that mistakes had been committed before he had taken charge of foreign affairs, which placed him in a false position; that the blockade ought not to have been submitted to, and that we ought to have been either absolutely recognized or not at all. I said that I agreed with him fully; that our recognition as belligerents, however friendly might have been the spirit which dictated it on the part of France, had been most injurious to us, as without it our ports could not have been declared in a state of blockade; but the error had been made, and he could not now escape its logical consequences.

He said that he had been informed that the order for the seizure of the *Florida* had been rescinded on discovering the fact that she was a Government vessel and not a privateer. I replied that if this were true, I had nothing more to say on the subject; but, in the event of a seizure, I must insist upon prompt redress.

I then referred to the case of the *Caroline Goodyear*, mentioned in my No. 45. He said that orders had been given for the release of the vessel and cargo, but that the muskets could not be landed at Matamoras. I remonstrated against this decision, saying that no distinction could be drawn against the deposit of munitions of war at Havre or Martinique and at Matamoras so long as it was under the French flag. He said that if munitions of war were deposited there the town might be attacked and carried by the Mexicans, and the munitions fall into their hands; that such a contingency must be guarded against. I replied that such a contingency was, as he well knew, not at all likely to happen, and could not be seriously offered as an argument against the landing of the cargo of the *Caroline Goodyear*. I asked, "If you object to the landing of muskets, why not to that of clothing and equipments that would be exposed to the same risk?" I pressed him with arguments of this character, when he admitted that apprehension was entertained of difficulties with the Northern Government if the cargo of the *Goodyear* were admitted, as it was now notorious that it was intended for the Confederate Army in Texas. I replied that if France refused to admit goods because they might find their way to Texas, it would be in violation of her neutrality, to the prejudice of the Confederacy, as large supplies were to be sent by that route. It is not worth while to repeat all that was said on either side, but the conversation closed by the minister saying that the character and destination of goods sent to Matamoras would not be too closely inquired into.

I reminded him that the Emperor had referred to him a memorandum which I had presented on the subject of the admission into French ports of prizes made by Confederate cruisers; he said that the matter was under examination; this, I suppose, is the last I shall hear of it.

Mr. [J. R.] Barret, formerly Member of Congress at Washington from St. Louis, has called on me to obtain my consent to the extension of the period of delivery of certain supplies for the army of the Trans-Mississippi Division, made with Mr. Chiles by the assistant quartermaster or Commissary-General Haynes, acting under orders of General Kirby Smith; the date of delivery by contract was the 1st November. After examining the contract I found its terms so ruinously extravagant that I peremptorily refused to give any sanction to the extension; this I perceived at the first glance, but as my information on the subject of prices of the articles to be delivered was very vague and imperfect, I gave a memorandum of the terms of the contract to Mr. McRae, that he might make a detailed calculation of the profits that would accrue to the contractors. You will see by his statement, marked "A," that if it were carried out they would realize on a disbursement of $650,000 a profit of over $3,500,000, and this without incurring any but the ordinary sea risk. I would also call your attention to the fact that the contract stipulated for payment in cotton classed middling fair; this is a grade which is not, as I am informed, given to 1 bale in 20 formerly received at New Orleans, and probably would not be found at all in the cotton brought to Matamoras, and large allowances would, of course, be claimed for the inferior quality of that in which the contractors might be paid.

Another large contract made with Mr. Clements (concerned in the affair of the *General Rusk,* or *Blanche*), under authority of Brigadier-

General Bee, is nearly, if not quite, as onerous. Clements is to receive 100 per cent advance on the cost of all goods, including charges, delivered at Matamoras, to be paid in cotton at 20 cents; whether he also is to receive middling fair, I do not know, as I have not seen his contract. The muskets by the *Caroline Goodyear* were shipped under this contract; they could have been bought at 45 shillings for cash or approved acceptances. Clements paid for them 60 shillings; one of the charges on the invoice is £1,000 sterling, said to be paid to a Mr. Stringer for having introduced Clements to Hamilton, who sold the muskets. For this introduction to a seller of goods the Confederate Government, the real purchaser, pays £2,000. You will thus see that it is to the interest of the contractor to pay for everything the highest price and to increase the charges in every way. I have long been inclined to call the attention of the Government to the manner in which contracts for purchases, to be made in Europe, are granted, but have abstained lest I might be considered as intruding advice in matters not within the scope of my duties. I can not see why if the Government sends cotton to Matamoras it should not be shipped from thence to Liverpool or Havre for sale on its own account, and the proceeds expended by its own agents in purchasing arms, clothing, etc., for cash. It would thus secure the purchase of the best articles at the lowest price. All the shipments made to Matamoras should be under the French flag, as the English has long ceased to afford protection or command respect.

I sent you by Mr. Lamar the papers relating to a demand made by N. N. de Mattos, an English subject, for indemnity for goods on board a Federal ship destroyed by the *Alabama*. There will be many other claims of a similar character. As we gave our assent to the second and third articles of the convention of Paris mainly on account of the declaration respecting blockades in the fourth article, why should we not now declare all goods under the enemy's flag, and enemies' goods under neutral flags, good prize of war?

The fourth article is now completely nullified by the open declarations of the English Government and the tacit submission of other powers. I can see no good reason why we should not revoke our adhesion to the second and third.

I am, with very great respect, your most obedient servant,

JOHN SLIDELL.

Hon. J. P. BENJAMIN.

P. S.—I find that by some accident the portion of my dispatch No. 38 is missing, beginning from "I feel it my duty to call, through you, the attention of the President, etc." I beg that you will send me copy of this missing paper that the files of the Commission may not be incomplete.

I am, with very great respect, your most obedient servant,

JOHN SLIDELL.

VICTORIA, V. I., *October 16, 1863.*

SIR: As president of a Southern association existing in this and the adjoining colony of British Columbia, I had the honor in the month of April last of writing to Mr. Mason to inform him of the organization of our society and to request from him the granting to us of a letter of marque to be used on the Pacific.

Under date of the 12th of June, Mr. Mason writes that he has no such power and that the Confederate Government alone can issue letters of marque.

Unfortunately, I was not in Victoria when this answer arrived here, and by my absence much valuable time has been lost. However, much can yet be done to harass and injure our enemies, and by request of the association I have to beg of you to forward to us as soon as possible a letter of marque to be used exclusively on the Pacific, provided the issuing of such letter does not interfere with some other plan of the Government.

We have at our disposal a first-class steamer of 400 tons, strongly built, and of an average speed of 14 miles. The money required to arm her and fit her out as a privateer will be raised without difficulty amongst our friends here.

The Federal Government have no force on this coast, and our privateers could do any amount of mischief without fear of capture.

It is our most anxious wish to do something for our country, and we can not serve her better than in destroying the commerce and property of our enemies. If you will for a moment reflect upon the extensive commerce of the Federal States with South America, California, the islands, China, and Japan, you can well imagine what a rich field we have before us.

If, instead of granting our request, you should deem it more advisable to order one of your vessels to this coast, we should be most happy to give her all the assistance in our power. We should, however, like to fit out a vessel of our own, and we trust our Government will not reject our demand.

I have the honor to be, sir, your obedient servant,

JULES DAVID.

Hon. J. P. BENJAMIN,
    Richmond.

LONDON, *October 19, 1863.*

SIR: I have the honor to transmit to you herewith a copy of a letter from Earl Russell to me, dated the 25th of September ultimo, in reply to mine of the 21st of same month, in which I informed him of the termination of my mission to London. It would seem proper that it should go on the files of the Department.

Just before I left London for Paris at the close of my mission I sent also to Earl Russell some papers connected with the case of the *Margaret and Jessie* which I found amongst mine, and I had a later note from him addressed to me at Paris merely acknowledging their receipt. That note I have not at hand where I am writing this dispatch, but I may yet obtain it in time to make it an enclosure.

My letter to Earl Russell, as you will see, is dated 21st September. On the 30th I left London for Paris, having given up my house and removed all my effects with the archives of the mission. All the books and other things belonging to the commission were carefully packed and are deposited for safe-keeping with my bankers, Messrs.

John K. Gilliat & Co., No. 4 Crosby Square, in the city. The cases for papers, etc., I left with Mr. Hotze. Complete lists of all are preserved in the box with the archives.

After remaining two weeks in Paris I returned here a few days since to close some matters necessarily left open, but have remained chiefly in the country, coming to London but occasionally, and shall soon return to the Continent.

I wrote from Paris to the President, and I enclose herewith a duplicate of my letter, in case the first should have miscarried, and which I shall be obliged if you will peruse and hand to him.

I have nothing of interest to communicate. Colonel Lamar, who bears this, can give you the latest and best impressions of things in Europe. I have the honor to be,

Very respectfully, your obedient servant,

J. M. MASON.

Hon. J. P. BENJAMIN,
    Secretary of State.

[Enclosure.]

FOREIGN OFFICE, September 25, 1863.

SIR: I have had the honor of receiving your letter of the 21st instant informing me that your Government have ordered you to withdraw from this country on the ground that her Majesty's Government have declined the overtures made through you for establishing by treaty friendly relations, and have no intention of receiving you as the accredited minister of the Confederate States at the British Court.

I have on other occasions explained to you the reasons which have induced her Majesty's Government to decline the overtures you allude to, and the motives which have hitherto prevented the British Court from recognizing you as the accredited minister of an established State.

These reasons are still in force, and it is not necessary to repeat them.

I regret that circumstances have prevented my cultivating your personal acquaintance, which, in a different state of affairs, I should have done with much pleasure and satisfaction.

I have the honor to be, sir, your most obedient, humble servant,

RUSSELL.

J. M. MASON, Esq.

No. 64.]   8 RUE DE LA REGENCE,
                                      Brussels, October 23, 1863.

SIR: The glorious achievements, the splendid operations of the army under the command of General Bragg, have occasioned a more thrilling and widespread joy in Europe than any of our brilliant victories since the commencement of hostilities.

In the despondent state of the public mind, or rather that portion of it which sincerely desires to see the arrogance of Yankeedom rebuked so severely as to render the North henceforth powerless for aggression, the defeat of the army of Rosecrans was hailed with enthusiastic delight. The intelligence completely dispelled the gloom which had been so sadly occasioned by our July reverses. That hope, ever so cordially entertained by our friends for our success, and which seemed for a short season to bid them farewell forever, reappeared with more confident assurances of the durability of our independence—of all the nations of the earth.

Can they follow up their triumphs and drive the Yankees out of Tennessee, and thus release that State and Kentucky from the chains which the Washington Government forged for them two years ago? —is the question which now, perhaps, most of all others, engages the thoughts of intelligent European circles.

Russia has, at last, manifestly identified herself with the desperado Administration of Lincoln. This will exercise a large amount of influence in alienating the feelings of the friends of Poland from the North. It is the most fortunate event, viewed in all its bearings, that could have happened for us; and I regret that it did not occur long ago. The entente cordiale between the ex-United States and the Czar, as demonstrated at New York, is a staggering blow to the Red Republicans of Europe—at whose head Prince Napeoleon admittedly stands—as concerns their coherence with respect to "Liberté, Fraternité, Egalité." Their journals are, very reluctantly, forced into explanations upon the subject, but those explanations are so shallow as to give but little satisfaction.

The North has had no such serviceable sympathizers in Europe as the friends par excellence of Poland. Clamorous, active, persevering, and always disposed under their code of political morality to make the end justify the means, they steadily so operate upon the minds of potentates as to keep them in a state of incessant anxiety. While I can scarcely believe, on account of the utopian notions which control them, that they will ever wheel around to our side, I, nevertheless, am quite persuaded that their ardor, in behalf of the measures of the Cabinet of Washington, will gradually so diminish as to impair its influence upon functionaries who are silently solicitous for our perfect and speedy success.

King Leopold went off a few days ago to his villa on the banks of the Lake of Como. It is his purpose, I understand, after a short sojourn there, to proceed to Vienna, where he will abide for some time as the guest of the Emperor of Austria, and where his daughter and Maximilian will join him. Several weeks, perhaps months, must elapse before he returns to Brussels.

I have the honor to be, sir, very respectfully, your obedient servant,

[A. DUDLEY MANN.]

Hon. J. P. BENJAMIN,
    Secretary of State, C. S. A., Richmond, Va.

No. 65.]   *8 RUE DE LA REGENCE,*
                                      Brussels, October 30, 1863.

SIR: I had the honor to receive yesterday afternoon your No. 9, with the documents transmitted therewith.

I am now engaged in making preparations for my departure for Rome.

I expect to proceed thither on the morning of the 2d proximo, and to reach my destination about the 9th.

For this new and distinguished mark of the confidence reposed in me by the President, I can not refrain from an expression of my heartfelt gratitude.

I have the honor to be, sir, very respectfully, your obedient servent,

A. DUDLEY MANN.

Hon. J. P. BENJAMIN,
Secretary of State, C. S. A., Richmond, Va.

No. 47.] PARIS, *October 25, 1863.*

SIR: Since my last of 9th instant I have received your dispatch No. 23 of 2d September. It is a conclusive demonstration based upon indisputable facts of the virtual nullification of the fourth article of the treaty of Paris. I shall, in compliance with your instructions, send a copy of it to Mr. Drouyn de Lhuys, but in the meanwhile I shall, through Mr. Mocquard, place it before the Emperor, that it may not first reach him accompanied by deprecatory counsels from his minister. The Emperor can not fail to be struck with those portions of the dispatch which so strongly illustrate the selfish policy of England and the false position in which other European powers, and France especially, have been placed by their tacit adhesion to her views of belligerent rights on the ocean. I only regret that you had not more clearly intimated the probable retraction of our assent to the second and third articles of the treaty of Paris; you will have seen that, by a singular coincidence, I recommended such a course in my No. 46.

There is an increasing feeling of uneasiness here on the Polish question; there can be no doubt that for reasons to which I have alluded in former dispatches the Emperor would rather desire a war with Russia in which Prussia could not fail to be involved, but at present he can not dispense with the cooperation of England and Austria; he is, however, obtaining an advantage of which he may hereafter avail himself; these latter powers are committing themselves so deeply by their official declarations that should the Emperor hereafter find a favorable opportunity of acting alone, they will be bound at least to remain silent spectators of the conflict. Were he aided by Austria and England in a war with Russia, he could not indemnify himself for his sacrifices of men and money by an extension of territory; unencumbered by such an alliance, he might restore to France the boundary of the Rhine. So long as the Polish question remains in its present uncertain condition it will be a serious obstacle to our recognition. I am inclined to think that, so far as we are concerned, a warlike solution would be advantageous to us, especially since the recent ovations to Russian officers at New York.

A demand has sprung up in Europe for our 8 per cent bonds; sales can be made at 32 to 33 per cent, and should we continue to receive favorable news, still higher prices might be realized. By the last advices from the Confederacy, exchange on Europe was selling at 1,000 to 1,200 per cent. I take it for granted that if it were attempted to negotiate at once a large amount of exchange, the rate would fall very materially, but were the operation conducted judiciously, bills on Paris and London might be sold to the extent of, say, £80,000 to £100,000 per month, taking out of circulation from four to six millions of our redundant paper, while the bills would be met by the sale of bonds for $1,200,000 to $1,500,000. Such a system, continued for a year, would very materially diminish the volume of circulation, while it would gradually create in Europe an active interest in favor of our independence and peace. Should it result as it naturally would in a gradual appreciation of our paper, while the immediate profit of the operation would be diminished, a much greater reduction of our general expenditure would be produced by the increased purchasing capacity of our circulation. The gentlemen who recently visited Richmond as the agent of Erlanger & Co. arrived here a few days since via New York.

I have placed Mr. Charles Lafitte (yoeippa mewygwpi) in communication with Mr. McRae, who will inform the Secretary of the Treasury of the propositions made to him.

Two merchants of considerable capital and large experience applied to me on the subject of shipments of cotton from Matamoras. I introduced them to Major Huse. The result has been a conditional contract which I think it would be for the interest of our Government to approve.

I am decidedly of opinion that the entire export of cotton should be under the control of the Secretary of the Treasury; were this the case we could soon establish a credit in Europe that would not only enable us to meet every necessary expenditure here but furnish a fund to draw on for domestic purposes that would largely facilitate the restoration of our currency to a sound condition.

The chambers meet on the 5th November. The address to be made by the Emperor is looked for with much anxiety, in anticipation of its possibly assuming a warlike tone. The bourse is very much depressed, the funds having fallen nearly 2 per cent within a short period without any ostensible cause, while the abundance of the crops of every description and increased activity in various branches of industry should naturally have produced an opposite effect.

You will have observed that Baron Gros, ambassador at London, has been recalled, and the Prince de la Tour d'Auvergne appointed in his stead; the Emperor had determined to give this post to Count Walewski, as the count has very decided Polish sympathies. This determination was considered as indicating a purpose to press the question on the British cabinet. Various reasons have been given for his not being appointed, but I happen to know the true one, which has not even been alluded to by the press. Earl Russell, by order of the Queen, intimated to this Government that while she could not refuse to receive any ambassador whom the Emperor might choose to send to her, the appointment of some other person would be agreeable to her. Whether this objection proceeded from personal or political motives is doubtful; if the latter, it affords another proof that England will not go to war for Poland, but a well-informed person thinks that the objection was personal.

In my last I spoke of a contract made by Mr. Nelson Clements for the delivery of arms, etc., at Matamoras. Mr. C., making a demand on this Government for damages sustained by the seizure of the *Caroline Goodyear*, has placed me in possession of his contract and invoice of rifles, of which I send you copies marked "A" and "B," as also of a letter from Mr. A. Hamilton, of the firm of

Sinclair, Hamilton & Co., who furnished the arms to Clements, marked " C." Mr. Hamilton informed me that a portion of the rifles could have been purchased for 40 shillings and the remainder at 45 shillings, the whole together at shillings 42.6 for cash.

You will see that the invoice cost, including commissions and insurance, is £29,813 10s. 7d., for which Clements claims that he should be paid on delivery at Matamoras 100 per cent advance, or £59,627, at par of $4.84, $288,595.

The rifles purchased for cash at 42.6 would have amounted to_____		£14, 875
Molds, cases, and wrenches, at_____	£770	
Deducting proportion overcharge as on rifles_____	231	
		539
Dock and shipping charges_____		43. 13
In all_____		15, 457

Or $74,811.88. Clements, under his contract, would then receive nearly 400 per cent on the cost price of the rifles for delivery at Matamoras, or £8.10 per rifle.

Nor is this all. At present prices he would realize a profit of 50 per cent on the cotton given to him in payment, which you will observe was to be delivered to him on shipboard, thus realizing, if the contract had been carried out, on his own statement, 600 per cent, or a net profit of 500 per cent. And yet it appears from Mr. Hamilton's letter that he could not have purchased even at the very high price he did unless aided by the credit given by Major Huse's assurance that our Government·would purchase them if Clements could not pay at Matamoras.

I informed you in my last dispatch that Mr. Drouyn de Lhuys had said that the *Caroline Goodyear* would be released, but that she would not be permitted to land the arms at Matamoras. I sent you copies of two letters, marked " D " and " E," from the British foreign office to Sinclair, Hamilton & Co., which confirm that statement.

I have seen frequently Mr. de Montholon, minister to Mexico, and Mr. Gutierrez de Estrada, chief of the deputation that tendered the throne of Mexico to the Archduke Maximilian. They entertain no doubt of his definitive acceptance; the latter is very confident that he will leave Europe for his new dominions in January or February next, by which time the adhesion of a very large majority of the population will have been received.

I send herewith a letter addressed to the President by Messrs. Roulet & Chapannière, of Marseilles, with various documents in relation to merchandise on board of a Federal vessel destroyed by C. S. S. *Florida.*

I have the honor to be, with great respect, your most obedient servant,

JOHN SLIDELL.

Hon. J. P. BENJAMIN,
 Secretary of State.

A.

[Enclosure.]

HOUSTON, [TEX.], *December 16, 1862.*

DEAR SIR: I am willing to proceed to Europe at once and use my means and my best exertions to procure 20,000 stands of muskets or

Enfield rifles, with all appurtenances, 5,000 revolvers complete, 5,000 sabers, French army shoes, blankets, gray cloth and trimmings, twilled flannel, twilled flannel shirts, and felt hats. The whole invoice not to exceed $1,000,000. If the 20,000 stand of muskets or Enfield rifles can not be obtained, 10,000 I agree to furnish, and as many of the other articles as I can obtain, and commence to deliver to you at Matamoras within four months from the 1st of January, 1863, with the agreement and understanding that you pay me on delivery of said invoice 100 per cent upon invoice cost and charges in cotton on shipboard at the port where said goods are delivered, at 30 cents per pound.

It is also agreed that there shall be no delay in furnishing the cotton. The arms are subject to proper inspection.

Very respectfully, yours,

NELSON CLEMENTS.

Major S. HART.

I accept above proposition to furnish the above-enumerated public stores.

S. HART,
Major and Quartermaster, C. S. A.

Approved:
J. B. MAGRUDER,
Maj.-Gen. Comdg. District of Texas,
New Mexico, and Arizona.

[Enclosure.]

B.

INVOICE OF RIFLES.

Purchased by the undersigned on commission for Nelson Clements, esq., and shipped on his account per Caroline Goodyear to Matamoras.

M   Long Enfield rifles, British pattern,
350   1853, bore, 577:

350 cases (20 each) 7,000 rifles, @ 60, with bayonet, muzzle stoppers, and snap caps, complete	£21,000
350 bullet molds, @ 8/6	148. 15
350 nipple wrenches, 1/6	26. 5
350 cases, lined with lead, 34	595
(20 spare nipples in each case)	
	21,770
Dock & shipping charges	43. 15
	21,813. 15
Commission, purchasing, £21,813.15, @ 2½%	545. 6. 10
W. S. Lindsay & Co.'s com., @ 5%	1,090. 13. 9
Insurance on £30,000, @ 20 G., 4/3%	6,363. 15
	29,813. 10. 7

E. E.

SINCLAIR, HAMILTON & CO.

LONDON, *15th May, 1863.*

[Enclosure.]

LONDON, *May 4, 1863.*

DEAR SIR: Referring to our various communications with you, we beg to inform you that we have made arrangements with certain gun makers for the supply to you of 7,000 rifles and appendages upon the following terms.

The rifles to be long Enfield rifles, pattern 1853, with bayonets, muzzle stoppers, and snap caps complete, and the price to be 60/ each; 350 nipple wrenches, at 1/6 each; and one bullet mold for each case of 20 rifles, at 8/6 per mold; the rifles to be packed in cases lined with lead (20 in each case), and the cases to be charged 34/ each.

The rifles to be of the same quality as those purchased through us by Major Huse, and the quality to be approved before shipment by inspectors to be approved by Major Huse, and after such approval no objection to be made as to quality.

The goods are to be in London ready for shipment on board the *Caroline Goodyear*, bound for Matamoras in Mexico, on or before 20th May.

You are to provide tonnage and pay the freight and expenses attendant upon the shipment and discharge of the goods.

Insurance, including war risk, is to be effected through us, we, of course, using our best endeavors to make as favorable terms as reasonably practicable. The cost of insurance with all shipping charges and our commission of 2½ per cent upon the cost of the rifles and disbursements to be added to the invoice, also a commission of 5 per cent to Messrs. W. S. Lindsay & Co. On or before the final discharge of the guns, etc. (or within 70 days after the arrival of the ship at Matamoras, which shall first happen) you engage by yourself or your agent, to ship to our consignment 700 (seven hundred) bales of cotton. Insurance on the cotton including war risk to be effected through us on the best obtainable terms.

The cotton to be realized by us when and as we may deem it expedient, and after retaining our commission of 2½ per cent on the proceeds and all incidental expenses including freight, landing charges, brokerage, etc., we are to apply the net proceeds toward repayment of the cost of insurance of the outward goods and the commissions on the same of 7½ per cent and the invoice price of the guns, etc. The balance, if any, to be handed over to you.

Should the net proceeds of the cotton be insufficient for the above purposes you are to hand us cash for the deficiency. We are to hold the policies of insurance of both the outward and homeward shipments. In the event of the guns, etc., or any part thereof not arriving at Matamoras, you are to have no claim for nondelivery from whatever cause occasioned.

We are to place the guns in charge of a supercargo with instructions to hand them to your agent at Matamoras in exchange for the bills of lading for the cotton, within the period mentioned above, and in case of default he is to be at liberty to sell the guns, etc., and you are to be responsible for any deficiency in the net proceeds.

It is expressly understood and agreed that no property in the said rifles is to be vested in you until the arrival thereof at Matamoras.

We are, dear sir, yours, truly,

SINCLAIR, HAMILTON & CO.

NELSON CLEMENTS, Esq.

I accept the terms and conditions of the above, with the understanding if said arms are lost en route, that no responsibility is attached to me.

Respectfully, yours,

NELSON CLEMENTS.

[Enclosure.]

LONDON, *May 15, 1863.*

DEAR SIR: In conformity with the verbal understanding, we hereby sell to you 71 cases containing 284 muskets, to be taken freight free per *Caroline Goodyear* and delivered to you or your agent at Matamoras from alongside, payable in cotton, to be shipped by you or your agent and consigned to us on delivery or as soon after delivery as freight can be secured. Any balance of proceeds of cotton to be paid to your order after deducting freight charges, insurance, and commission of 2½ per cent.

We are, dear sir, yours, truly,

SINCLAIR, HAMILTON & CO.

NELSON CLEMENTS, Esq.

I confirm the above with the understanding that I bear the expense of landing the muskets, but not the risk.

NELSON CLEMENTS.

Nelson Clements, Esq., bought of Sinclair, Hamilton & Co., British muskets with bayonets.

ⒷB 1/71	71 cases, 40 each, 2,840 muskets, @ 18/	
72	1 " contg. 1 bullet mold	} £2, 556

Shipped per *Caroline Goodyear* for Matamoras, sold deliverable there to Mr. Clements or his agents; amount payable out of proceeds of cotton to be shipped by him consigned to Sinclair, Hamilton & Co.

The goods to be taken on the vessel by Mr. Clements, freight free.

SINCLAIR, HAMILTON & CO.

LONDON, *15 May, 1863*
E. E.

[Enclosure.]

C.

GRAND HOTEL, PARIS, *October 16, 1863.*

I have the honor to hand you herewith copies of documents and correspondence, as noted below, connected with the shipment of firearms per *Caroline Goodyear* for Matamoras under an agreement between my firm, Sinclair, Hamilton & Co., London, and Mr. Nelson Clements.

Full particulars will be found in these enclosures as to the nature and course of this transaction, so far as we are concerned, and I have only further to add that Mr. Clements was in the first instance introduced by Mr. Stringer, of the firm W. S. Lindsay & Co., who stipulated that a commission of 5 per cent should be charged in the invoice in consideration of such introduction.

Mr. Clements stated that he was furnished with letters and would refer to Mr. C. K. Prioleau and Colonel Lamar, and he further agreed in the event of our coming to terms that we should be satisfied as to his contract with General Bee before formally signing our agreement.

The settlement of terms was not effected without much discussion, during which we occasionally consulted Major Huse, and no business would have ensued had it not been for an offer on his part that if instructions were sent for the rifles to be delivered to Confederate officers as soon as possible after arrival and under any circumstances, he would undertake on behalf of Confederate States Government that we should be paid the amount of our invoice, less insurance and Messrs. Lindsay & Co.'s commission.

So that in case Mr. Clements' agents were not prepared with cotton in payment, or in case of any failure on his part, there might be no obstacle to the Confederate officers at once getting possession of the rifles.

On receiving this assurance from Major Huse we declared ourselves satisfied with Mr. Clements' proposals, and his contract with General Bee was then shown to me, and the transaction thereupon reduced to a formal agreement.

You will observe that the instructions to the supercargo were framed in conformity with the understanding with Major Huse, referred to above.

I have the honor to remain, sir, your most obedient humble servant,

A. Hamilton.

Hon. John Slidell.

[Enclosure.]

D.

Foreign Office, *October 10, 1863.*

Gentlemen: With reference to my letters of yesterday respecting the case of the *Caroline Goodyear,* I am directed by Earl Russell to inform you that it appears from what the French minister for foreign affairs at Paris has stated to her Majesty's chargé d'affaires at that place, that the vessel has probably been released by this time and allowed to go where she pleased, always, nowever, excepting to a Mexican port.

Gentlemen, your most obedient, etc.,

E. Hammond.

[Enclosure.]

E.

Foreign Office, *October 14, 1863.*

Gentlemen: I am directed by Earl Russell to acknowledge the receipt of your letter of the 12th instant and to state to you in reply that his lordship has received a dispatch from her Majesty's chargé d'affaires at Paris from which it appears that the *Caroline Goodyear* and her cargo had been released by the French authorities at Vera Cruz.

I am, etc.,

E. HAMMOND.

Messrs. SINCLAIR, HAMILTON & Co.,
11 St. Helen's Place.

No. 31.]   CONFEDERATE STATES COMMERCIAL AGENCY,
                                       London, October 31, 1863.

SIR: Since my last, No. 30, October 3, I have the honor to acknowledge receipt of your Nos. 8 and 10, respectively, dated September 5 and 24, the former introducing and presented by Rev. Father Bannon on the 29th instant, the latter received some days previously conveying information respecting one E. G. Fairfax Williamson, which I have duly communicatel as directed, to the various agents of the Government. I have also to acknowledge receipt of your private letters of September 18, via the new route, received on the 12th of October; and of September 9, enclosed in Rev. Mr. Bannon's official letter of introduction. Also, during the same period, letters from Mr. W. J. Bromwell, respectively, of August 22, covering Treasury warrant No. 4934, for £123 14s. 3d. ($600) on account of salary; and of September 19, covering Treasury warrant No. 5160 for £1,000 ($4,850), on account of secret-service money. Enclosures in these various communications, two for Mr. Slidell, one for Mr. Eustis, one for Mr. McRae, one for Mr. A. D. Mann, were duly forwarded to their destination, as well as sundry private letters.

You will perceive that in the official series, No. 9, between September 5 and 24—I fear the one in which, as indicated in your private note of September 15, you wrote fully on various subjects—is missing, though there is still a reasonable prospect of its coming to hand.

The delay which occurred in the transmission of the secret-service remittance, superadded to the fact that I had made some unexpectedly large disbursements in the previous half year, at one time threatened me with serious embarrassments, but which were averted by the generous promptness with which my private and official friends came to my relief. This gratifying fact and the cordial support I have at all times received from all the officers of the Government more than compensates me for the trifling annoyances I have occasionally to endure, as you may have judged from various passages in my previous communications. When the pressure on my resources appeared most calculated to alarm prudent precaution and shortly before the receipt of the last remittance, Colonel Lamar, considering himself indebted to the Department in the sum of 10,000 francs, transferred that amount, by the advice and with the official sanction of Mr. McRae, as representative of the Treasury, to me. My receipt to Colonel Lamar and Mr. McRae's endorsement on the same, copy of which I enclose, will more fully explain the transaction, which was intended as well to relieve me as to prevent needless confusion of accounts, which would have arisen from the return of this unsettled balance into the hands of the Treasury. I beg, therefore, that you will charge me with $1,914.02 (£394.13) as proceeds of Colonel Lamar's draft on Paris for 10,000 francs, and in the adjustment of Colonel Lamar's accounts credit him with that amount. I have also to acknowledge the courtesy of Edwin de Leon, esq., in loaning me of the funds in his hands £200, which I have since repaid.

I can not mention Colonel Lamar's name without once more expressing my gratitude for the advantages I have derived from the rare unselfishness with which his fruitful mind enriches the minds of others and my regret at losing his counsel and assistance, as he leaves for the Confederacy by the same steamer which carries this. I believe it has been in a great measure through my persuasion that he remained thus long in England, and I can only wish that I had had such arguments at my command as to prolong his stay indefinitely. His Chertsey speech, brief as it was, and fragmentary, owing to an accidental interruption from without, has left a sharp and distinct impress on English public opinion. It has placed beyond dispute and therefore added to the general stock of knowledge the idea, so familiar to us and yet so repugnant to the vulgar prejudices of Europe, that the South in her great struggle was fighting not only the battle of her own independence but that of personal liberty and constitutional government the world over, and that her adversaries represented foes of those sublime principles. But the speech has done more than this. At a time when the chairman of the Federal Senate Committee of Foreign Affairs befouls the Queen of Great Britain with bawdy metaphors, when the public men of the North vie in the press in abuse of this country, and when a Beecher stumps it through the land, on the first occasion at which a representative of the Confederate cause addresses an English audience not a word is said of the long list of grievances of which we might justly complain, no exhibition is made of temper or vexation, nor even is a false charge made against our adversaries. The contrast has been so universally felt and the moral effect of it has been so perceptible that I should only have weakened it by dwelling upon it in the Index. But I deem it my duty as your appointed observer of the tides and currents of English public opinion to advise you of it, especially at this time, when I observe the temper of our own press is one of excessive and unrestrained irritation against England.

I observe also that your own dignified policy of reserve and moderation has for the same reason exposed you to severe personal animadversion, and I have no doubt that Colonel Lamar's speech will meet with criticism of the same sort. The chief reason for the present attitude of the public mind at home, so far as I can judge from this distance, appears to be the parallel which is drawn between the policy of England and that of France, in which parallel France receives credit rather for what is expected of her than for what she has actually done. Now, I am aware of the allowances that must be made for the prepossessions or prejudices inseparable from continued residence in a country, but I can not help reiterating my earnest conviction that my only hope of permanent friendship and solid assistance is from England. What temporary relations between us and France may arise from the force of circumstances I can not foretell, but the fact remains clear to my mind that here we have almost a unanimous nation as our friends, and in France, beside the Emperor and his immediate entourage, we have none. Here there is scarcely a man eminent in letters, in politics, or in society, who dares profess friendship for the North; there I can not think of a familiar name that can be claimed for us. It is impossible to conceive an antithesis more complete than that which exists between the public opinion of France and that of England in all that relates, directly or indirectly, to our cause. Our people see only the deceptive contrast between the diplomacy, or more properly, diplomatic manners of the two countries, a contrast rather superficial and personal than real and national, and they do not see what the instinct of the North has long discerned that the heart of England beats for us and the heart of France for our enemies.

If you will turn to the files of the Index you will find some of the highest names of Great Britain on a committee to raise a statue to Stonewall Jackson, and what is better evidence you will find in nearly every number acknowledgments of contributions from the most distinguished sources to a fund for the relief of Southern prisoners, which has already grown to the amount of several thousand pounds. These things, while feeling keenly the wrongs the English Government has done and permitted to be done us, I should wish our people to know, and I further think that to acknowledge them at their just value only brings out in stronger colors the injustice and impolicy of Earl Russell's diplomacy.

The attacks of a portion of our press on Mr. Spence and his being virtually, if not ostensibly, superseded in his financial agency, have received such general publicity through the Northern and Anglo-Federal journals, that I may not improperly refer to it, and in so doing comply with Mr. Spence's request that I should bring his views to your attention. Mr. Spence has felt deeply hurt and considers himself aggrieved by what a New York journal has tauntingly termed his "ignominious dismissal." He contends that while his espousal of our cause arises from sincere conviction, and its advocacy is persevered in from equally conscientious motives, he has a right as an alien upon whose patriotism we have no claim to connect personal and pecuniary advantage with the results to which that espousal and advocacy are intended to contribute. He never pretended that he sought a financial connection with the Government without expectations of profit to himself as well as to us, and he complains that he is not only disappointed in his just expectations, but a loser to a ruinous extent by reason of that connection.

He has informed me that he intends, subject to a neutral arbitrament, to claim from the Government such a commission on the Erlanger loan, alleged to be negotiated within his official province, as may be sufficient to compensate him for his losses, which he roughly estimates to be about £15,000. It would be presumptuous in me to give a financial opinion on such a subject, but I gladly fulfill my promise to Mr. Spence by expressing the very earnest desire that the Government may find some mode to relieve itself from even the appearance of pecuniary indebtedness to him. I do not consider this question from a legal point of view, for as a legal question it is beyond my competency, but from the point of view of policy, equity, and above all, national pride. I have differed from Mr. Spence on almost all essential points relating to the manner and the means of recommending our cause to the public. For instance, I was naturally prone to place perhaps an exaggerated estimate upon the value of the Index; he, after the third number, could scarcely bring himself to believe in its usefulness at all. On the treatment of the slavery question we differed so radically that, as in the case of the manifesto of the Manchester Independence Association which he wrote, I was compelled to make a friendly issue. I have always contended that while we have no right to obtrude our views of that institution, or seek to make converts, or exact from our sympathizers that they should think exactly like us on that subject, it was neither consistent with self-respect nor with good policy to apologize for the existing fact, for by so apologizing we should appear to admit the truth of the calumnious charges upon which the honest antislavery prejudice is based. The fault then that I found with Mr. Spence, in this as in other respects, was that he assumed to occupy at one and the same time two opposite and irreconcilable positions—that of a high official of our Government owing it allegiance and that of a disinterested alien friend. But with this reserve, which is due to the candor of official correspondence, I must bear my emphatic testimony to the zeal and effectiveness of Mr. Spence's labors in our behalf. His book, admirably well timed as it was and adapted to British thought, has done us inestimable service. Since then he has been unremitting in his efforts. He has given freely of his means in contributions, traveling expenses, and entire devotion of his time. Nor is there a doubt that his financial appointment which I at the time thought a serious error, and the expectations he founded upon it, led him to assume risks the consequence of which it would be extreme hardship for him to bear, especially as it could scarcely be contended with fairness that the Government is altogether without a share of moral responsibility in his acts. At this time he is engaged with manifest prospect of success in organizing a general agitation throughout Lancashire and the United Kingdom. He is the founder of the association to which I have referred, and without him it would be a soulless body. To break with such a man, even were there no other considerations of equity or of gratitude, would be a scandal, the more to be regretted as public opinion could not be persuaded that the cause was other than his views of slavery. I have written thus fully partly to explain the course of the Index in regard to Mr. Spence, partly because you have a right to expect from me a frank statement of any important local question upon which my position enables me or forces me to form an opinion.

My communications have sometimes shown traces of annoyance to which I have occasionally been exposed in the discharge of my duties through misguided zeal or less venal motives. The most serious has been caused by an article professing to be a Liverpool letter, in the New York Herald of a recent date, in which a tissue of falsehoods and gross exaggeration, woven with a diabolical ingenuity, has been obviously contrived for the special purpose of ruining my usefulness in the London press. Fortunately the infernal machine failed to explode, no English paper having copied the article, and I am quit with the alarm and an uncomfortable feeling of insecurity from espionage and personal malice. I mentioned the matter because I have a vague suspicion that some similar effort to injure me may be made through the Richmond press.

The rams in the Mersey are more than ever the centers of atten·tion. The efforts of the Government to insure their detention are really ludicrous. One, however, has very nearly ended tragically. The fine ironclad *Prince Consort* which had been ordered in hot haste from Devonport to Liverpool this week, encountered a severe storm in the Channel, was much damaged, and barely escaped foundering. I enclose the letter of the special correspondent of the Herald, sent to enquire on the spot, which gives you the latest and fullest details. A rumor, but not substantiated, has been spread that the French Government had likewise taken measures to prevent Confederate cruisers from fitting out in French ports by withdrawing the general authorization heretofore granted for the building of vessels of war.

Mexican prospects are less fair than when I last wrote. It appears tolerably certain that the attempt to negotiate a loan had to be abandoned, and thus one of the principal conditions of the Arch·duke's acceptance of the throne remains without present proba·bility of fulfillment. A Spanish prince, Don Sebastian, is spoken of as the next candidate, while the Austrian candidate is reported to have views upon the future crown of Poland.

While on the subjects of on dits, I enclose you a paragraph giv·ing the latest version of the great scandal of the day, and which is generally supposed will have important political bearings. The principal personage hinted at is Lord Palmerston, now 80 years. The heroine is said to be a married daughter of the late Lord Lyndhurst.

In regard to the stationery, I have written to both Messrs. Collie & Co. and Messrs. Fraser, Trenholm & Co., copies of whose replies I enclose. It appears that nine case were sent by the *Mischief* to Nassau and arrived on July 22, and two by the *Harkaway* to Ber·muda, which arrived about the end of July. No other information can yet be obtained.

Since commencing this dispatch I have received through the North your private letter of October 10. The expulsion of the consuls, long expected, will have an excellent effect as well here as at home.

I have lost a rare opportunity in the departure of Colonel Lamar and Captain Fearn for sending my accounts, the fact being that except for the first six months of my agency they can not be satis·factorily made out without a careful personal revision of the books of the Index, the work of several clear days. I have, after several ineffectual attempts, failed to find the time for this.

I have the honor to remain, very respectfully, your obedient servant,

HENRY HOTZE.

Hon. J. P. BENJAMIN,
Secretary of State, Richmond.

EXTRACT FROM A LETTER OF CHARLES HUGHES, A SOLICITOR, TO A FRIEND IN LONDON, RELATING TO SEIZURE OF SCHOONER J. M. CHAPMAN, SAN FRANCISCO, AND THE IMPRISONMENT AND FINE OF SEVERAL PERSONS CONCERNED IN HER.

VICTORIA, V. I., *October 31, 1863.*

MY DEAR FRIEND: Unless I am very much mistaken, you were very intimately acquainted with Mr. Greathouse, the banker at Yreka City, Siskiyou County, Cal., and if your intimacy amounted to friendship you can now render him and his family a very essential service with trifling trouble to yourself. You will be perhaps astonished to hear that he, a Mr. Harpending, and a Mr. Rubery (the latter an Englishman) are in prison in San Francisco under a sentence of the United States Circuit Court condemning them to ten years' imprisonment and a fine of $10,000 each for treason against the United States, the circumstances of the case, in brief, being that they were taken on board of a schooner, called the *J. M. Chapman*, which was seized by the United States authorities in San Francisco harbor on suspicion of fitting out of a Confederate privateer and condemned, it appearing that she had a letter of marque from President Davis. Full details of the trial appeared in the Weekly Bulletin of October 17, and the other daily and weekly San Francisco journals of and about that date, to which, for the purposes of this letter, reference is hereby had. The rest of the parties indicted (with the exception of Baldwin, a son of Judge Baldwin, who escaped and is here) were discharged after the trial and conviction of the three above-named "ringleaders," I presume. Now, owing to the rigid espionage of the Federal authorities, it is very doubtful whether intelligence can be conveyed to the Confederate authorities at Richmond of this proceeding, and it is feared that amidst so many more important matters the fate of these gentlemen may be overlooked and their sentence be carried into effect without recourse being had to the "lex talionis," and hence it is desirable that every means within reach, however apparently inadequate, should be brought to bear to call the attention of the Confederate Government to the matter, in which view it is hoped and believed that you, as a former friend or acquaintance of Greathouse, will take the trouble to address Mr. Mason, of London, the Confederate commissioner, or Mr. Slidell in Paris, and call his attention to the facts. Of course, the commissioners have access to even the California newspapers, and by reference to the dates I have given they can therein refer to the report of the trial and satisfy themselves about them.

As the "espionage" is believed even to extend to the post office, I shall not sign this, but you will at once recognize the writer and writing, etc.,

Your faithful friend and shipmate,

H.

No. 66.] ROME, *November 11, 1863.*

SIR: As I expected at the date of my No. 65, I reached here on the 9th instant, late in the afternoon.

On the 11th, at half past 1 p. m., I sought and promptly obtained an interview with his Eminence, the Cardinal Secretary of State, Antonelli. I at once explained to him the object of my mission to Rome and he instantly assured me that he would obtain for me an audience of the sovereign Pontiff.

His Eminence then remarked that he could not withhold from me an expression of his unbounded admiration of the wonderful powers which we had exhibited in the field in resistance to a war which had been prosecuted with an energy, aided by the employment of all the recent improvements in the instruments for the destruction of life and property, unparalleled, perhaps, in the world's history. He asked me several questions with respect to President Davis, at the end of which he observed that he certainly had created for himself a name that would rank with those of the most illustrious statesmen of modern times. He manifested an earnest desire for the definitive termination of hostilities, and observed that there was nothing the government of the Holy See could do with propriety to occasion such a result that it was not prepared to do. I seized the utterance of this assurance to inform him that but for the European recruits received by the North, numbering annually something like 100,000, the Lincoln Administration, in all likelihood, would have been compelled some time before this to have retired from the contest, that nearly all those recruits were from Ireland, and that Christianity had cause to weep at such a fiendish destruction of life as occurred from the beguiling of those people from their homes to take up arms against citizens who had never harmed or wronged them in the slightest degree. He appeared to be touched by my statement, and intimated that an evil so disgraceful to humanity was not beyond the reach of a salutary remedy.

His Eminence, after a short pause, took a rapid survey of the affairs of the nations of the earth, and drew a rather somber picture of the future, particularly of Europe. He did not attempt to conceal his dislike of England, his want of sympathy with Russia, his distrust of any benefits which might be expected from the congress proposed by France. "If old guaranties," said he, emphatically, "are of no value, new ones will be too feeble to resist expediency when sustained by might."

This is but a short and otherwise imperfect outline of one of the most interesting official interviews I ever enjoyed, an interview which was of lengthened duration and marked from beginning to end with extreme cordiality and courtesy by the distinguished functionary by whom it was accorded. I will add, lest I may not have been sufficiently explicit on that point, that it took place in his office in the Vatican, where he receives all the foreign ministers.

I have the honor to be, sir, very respectfully, your obedient servant,

A. DUDLEY MANN.

Hon. J. P. BENJAMIN,
    Secretary of State, C. S. A., Richmond, Va.

No. 32.]   DEPARTMENT OF STATE,
                    Richmond, November 13, 1863.

SIR: I have been compelled to await the return of the President from the Southwest before answering your No. 46, announcing your withdrawal from London, in conformity with the instructions contained in my No. 30.

Until the receipt of your dispatch it was of course impossible to foresee whether you might not find it necessary to exercise the discretion confided to you in the private instructions which accompanied those containing your recall. As we now know, however, that your mission to England has terminated, I have the President's authority for informing you that your services are considered by your Government as too valuable and useful to be dispensed with, and that you have again been appointed by him commissioner under the act No. 226 of 20 August, 1861, entitled "An act to empower the President of the Confederate States to appoint additional commissioners to foreign nations." Mr. Macfarland has also been appointed your secretary. These appointments bear date of the 12th instant and you will receive the formal commissions for yourself and secretary by the next mail, as there is no time to make up the instructions for the present conveyance.

As your former commission, together with that of Mr. Macfarland, was for England only, it is considered as having come to an end by your withdrawal under instructions, but your accounts for salary, contingent expenses, etc., will be rendered up to the 12th instant, and your salary under the new appointment will commence at the last-named date. You are of course aware that this being a new appointment, made during recess, will expire at the close of the next session of the Senate if not confirmed by that body.

I am, very respectfully, your obedient servant,

J. P. BENJAMIN,
Secretary of State.

Hon. JAMES M. MASON.

No. 26.*] DEPARTMENT OF STATE,
Richmond, November 13, 1863.

SIR: The bearer of this letter, Mr. August Wesendonck, having been for some years a planter in Virginia has determined to offer his services to our Government in the country of his birth, with a view to awakening his former fellow-countrymen to a full appreciation of the condition of affairs in the Confederacy. To this end Mr. Wesendonck has converted his property into our Government securities and has volunteered gratuitous service abroad.

Grateful for this offer, which has been accepted, the President desires that Mr. Wesendonck be introduced to you, and that you be requested to grant him such advice and assistance as your position and experience may enable you to afford so that, under your instructions he may be guided in the line of policy deemed best adapted to the object in view.

I cheerfully recommend Mr. Wesendonck to your courteous attention. The gentlemen of Virginia in whose neighborhood he has lived unite in testimonials of his worth and good character.

I am, very respectfully, your obedient servant,

J. B. BENJAMIN,
Secretary of State.

Hon. JOHN SLIDELL,
Paris.

No. 33.] DEPARTMENT OF STATE,
Richmond, November 14, 1863.

SIR: I have this moment had the two cases of Hansard opened and find, to my very great disappointment, that the booksellers have

---

* Never sent.

sent only 128 volumes of the third series of debates, thus closing the work in 1853, although their catalogue, of which they put a copy in the box, announces the third series to contain 155 volumes and to carry the debates down "to end of 1859." The main part of the work for present use is thus missing, and I had indeed relied confidently on getting the debates down to the close of the session in July, 1863. The catalogue is by Willis Sotheran and is of the year 1862, and even then announced the price of the whole parliamentary history and three series of debates as £98, the whole forming 257 volumes, of which they have sent but 230. See catalogue, page 244. Pray have this remedied as promptly as possible.

Very respectfully, your obedient servant,

J. P. BENJAMIN,
Secretary of State.

Hon. JAMES M. MASON,
Commissioner, etc., Paris.

P. S.—I had the pleasure of calling on Mrs. Mason to-day and found here in good health and spirits.

No. 67.] · ROME, *November 14, 1863.*

SIR: At 3 o'clock on the afternoon of yesterday I received a formal notification that his Holiness would favor me with an audience, embracing my private secretary, Mr. W. Grayson Mann, to-day at 12 o'clock.

I accordingly proceeded to the Vatican sufficiently early to enable me to reach there fifteen minutes in advance of the designated hour. In five minutes afterwards—ten minutes prior to the appointed time—a message came from the sovereign Pontiff that he was ready to receive me, and I was accordingly conducted into his presence.

His Holiness stated, after I had taken my stand near to his side, that he had been so afflicted by the horrors of the war in America that many months ago he had written to the Archbishops of New Orleans and New York to use all the influence that they could properly employ for terminating with as little delay as possible the deplorable state of hostilities; that from the former he had received no answer, but that he had heard from the latter and his communication was not such as to inspire hopes that his ardent wishes would be speedily gratified.

I then remarked that "it is to a sense of profound gratitude of the Executive of the Confederate States and of my countrymen, for the earnest manifestations which your Holiness made in the appeal referred to, that I am indebted for the distinguished honor which I now enjoy. President Davis has appointed me special envoy to convey in person to your Holiness this letter, which, I trust, you will receive in a similar spirit to that which animated its author."

Looking for a moment at the address and afterwards at the seal of the letter, his Holiness took his scissors and cut the envelope. Upon opening it he observed: "I see it is in English, a language which I do not understand." I remarked: "If it will be agreeable to your Holiness, my Secretary will translate its contents to you." He replied: "I shall be pleased if he will do so." The translation was rendered in a slow, solemn, and emphatic pronunciation. During its progress, I did not cease for an instant to carefully survey the features of the sovereign Pontiff. A sweeter expression of pious affection, of tender benignity, never adorned the face of mortal man. No picture can adequately represent him when exclusively absorbed in Christian contemplation. Every sentence of the letter appeared to sensibly affect him. At the conclusion of each, he would lay his hand down upon the desk and bow his head approvingly. When the passage was reached wherein the President states, in such sublime and affecting language, "We have offered up at the footstool of our Father who is in Heaven prayers inspired by the same feelings which animate your Holiness," his deep sunken orbs visibly moistened were upturned toward that throne upon which ever sits the Prince of Peace, indicating that his heart was pleading for our deliverance from that causeless and merciless war which is prosecuted against us. The soul of infidelity—if, indeed, infidelity have a soul—would have melted in view of so sacred a spectacle.

The emotion occasioned by the translation was succeeded by a silence of some time. At length his Holiness asked whether President Davis was a Catholic. I answered in the negative. He then asked if I was one. I assured him that I was not.

His Holiness now stated, to use his own language, that "Lincoln & Co." had endeavored to create an impression abroad that they were fighting for the abolition of slavery, and that it might perhaps be judicious in us to consent to gradual emancipation. I replied that the subject of slavery was one over which the Government of the Confederate States, like that of the old United States, had no control whatever; that all ameliorations with regard to the institution must proceed from the States themselves, which were as sovereign in their character in this regard as were France, Austria, or any other continental power; that true philanthropy shuddered at the thought of the liberation of the slave in the manner attempted by "Lincoln & Co."; that such a procedure would be practically to convert the well-cared-for civilized negro into a semibarbarian; that such of our slaves as had been captured or decoyed off by our enemy were in an incomparably worse condition than while they were in the service of their masters; that they wished to return to their old homes, the love of which was the strongest of their affections; that if, indeed, African slavery were an evil, there was a power which, in its own good time, would doubtless remove that evil in a more gentle manner than that of causing the earth to be deluged with blood for its sudden overthrow.

His Holiness received these remarks with an approving expression. He then said that I had reason to be proud of the self-sacrificing devotion of my countrymen from the beginning to the cause for which they were contending. "The most ample reason," I replied, "and yet, scarcely so much as of my countrywomen, whose patriotism, whose sorrows and privations, whose transformation in many instances from luxury to penury, were unparalleled and could not be adequately described by any living language. There they had been from the beginning—there they were still more resolute, if possible, than ever, emulating in devotion, earthly though it was in its character, those holy female spirits who were the last at the Cross and the first at the Sepulcher."

His Holiness received this statement with evident satisfaction, and then said: "I would like to do anything that can be effectively done, or that even promises good results, to aid in putting an end to this most terrible war, which is harming the good of all the earth, if I knew how to proceed."

I availed myself of this declaration to inform his Holiness that it was not the armies of Northern birth which the South was encountering in hostile array, but that it was the armies of European creation, occasioned by the Irish and Germans, chiefly by the former, who were influenced to emigrate (by circulars from "Lincoln & Co." to their numerous agents abroad) ostensibly for the purpose of securing high wages but in reality to fill up the constantly depleted ranks of our enemy; that those poor unfortunates were tempted by high bounties (amounting to $500, $600, and $700) to enlist and take up arms against us; that once in the service they were invariably placed in the most exposed points of danger in the battle field; that in consequence thereof an instance had occurred in which an almost entire brigade had been left dead or wounded upon the ground; that but for foreign recruits the North would most likely have broken down months ago in the absurd attempt to overpower the South.

His Holiness expressed his utter astonishment, repeatedly throwing up his hands, at the employment of such means against us, and the cruelty attendant upon such unscrupulous operations.

"But, your Holiness," said I, "Lincoln & Co. are even more wicked, if possible, in their ways than in decoying innocent Irishmen from their homes to be murdered in cold blood. Their champions, and would your Holiness believe it unless it were authoritatively communicated to you, their pulpit champions have boldly asserted as a sentiment: 'Greek fire for the families and cities of the rebels and hell fire for their chiefs.'"

His Holiness was startled at this information, and immediately observed: "Certainly no Catholic could reiterate so monstrous a sentiment." I replied: "Assuredly not. It finds a place exclusively in the hearts of the fiendish, vagrant, pulpit buffoons whose number is legion and who impiously undertake to teach the doctrines of Christ for ulterior sinister purposes."

His Holiness now observed: "I will write a letter to President Davis, and of such a character that it may be published for general perusal." I expressed my heartfelt gratification for the assertion of this purpose. He then remarked, half inquiringly: "You will remain here for several months?" I, of course, could not do otherwise than answer in the affirmative. Turning to my secretary, he asked several kind questions personal to himself and bestowed upon him a handsome compliment. He then extended his hand as a signal for the end of the audience and I retired.

Thus terminated one among the most remarkable conferences that ever a foreign representative had with a potentate of the earth. And such a potentate! A potentate who wields the consciences of 175,000,000 of the civilized race, and who is adored by that immense number as the vice regent of Almighty God in this sublunary sphere.

How strikingly majestic the conduct of the government of the Pontifical States in its bearing toward me when contrasted with the sneaking subterfuges to which some of the governments of western Europe have had recourse in order to evade intercourse with our commissioners. Here I was openly received by appointment at court in accordance with established usages and customs and treated from beginning to end with a consideration which might be envied by the envoy of the oldest member of the family of nations. The audience was of forty minutes duration, an unusually long one.

I have written this dispatch very hurriedly and fear that it will barely be in time for the monthly steamer which goes off from Liverpool with the mails for the Bahama Islands next Saturday.

I have the honor to be, sir, very respectfully, your obedient servant,

A. DUDLEY MANN.

Hon. J. P. BENJAMIN,
    Secretary of State, C. S. A., Richmond, Va.

No. 48.]   PARIS, *November 15, 1863.*

In my last of 25th October I acknowledged the receipt of your No. 23. On the 25th ultimo I placed a copy of it in the hands of the Emperor through Mr. Mocquard, who informs me that it had been carefully read by the Emperor. On the 28th ultimo I also sent a copy to Mr. Drouyn de Lhuys with a note, of which I annex a copy marked "A."

The speech of the Emperor addressed to the chambers on the 5th instant has excited an immense sensation throughout Europe; it is very differently interpreted by different persons and in different quarters; by the majority it is considered pacific in its tone and tendencies; the opinion of others, and as I think the better opinion, is that it foreshadows a European war at no very distant day. This apprehension of the speech by the best informed and most sagacious persons have has been somewhat modified by the subsequent appearance of the Emperor's autograph circular to the chiefs of the several European powers. I send you copies of the French text; you will doubtless have the English version through the Northern papers long before this dispatch can reach you.

You will have observed perhaps with some surprise and disappointment its silence on the subject of American affairs; this was my first feeling on perusing it, but after a more careful examination and further reflection I did not construe it so unfavorably; not choosing, however, to rely on my own impressions, I at once made inquiries of my friend at the affaires etrangères and of Mr. Mocquard and received the same explanations from both. The former at my request had a conversation with his chief on the subject. There were two reasons for the Emperor's reticence: First, he could not say what he had been and was still willing to do with the cooperation of England without by implication contrasting his policy and feelings with hers and throwing upon her the responsibility of the present condition of American affairs; this he was not willing to do, as he desires scrupulously to avoid everything that would be likely to produce at this critical moment any coolness or alienation between the two governments; secondly, as he could not say all that he would desire to say on the subject he preferred to say nothing rather than confine himself to "banalités," commonplace expressions of regret at the continuance of the war and fruitless effusion of blood, etc.

As to this latter point I am very decidedly of opinion that absolute silence is more satisfactory than vague, unmeaning generalities would have been. It may not be uninteresting to know, as well as showing the habits and mode of action of so remarkable a personage as illustrating the thorough autocracy of his Government that the address so remarkable and important in every way was prepared without consultation with his ministers. On the 3d instant I called on the Duke de Morny, who had recently returned to Paris after a considerable absence. He said that he knew nothing of what the Emperor would say in his address, excepting that it would be pacific in its tone, that a cabinet meeting would be held the next day, when the Emperor would read it to his ministers. The Duke, although not a minister, as president of the Corps Législatif attends cabinet meetings, especially during the sessions of the chambers. Mr. Mocquard, the Emperor's private secretary, told me a day or two previous that it had not yet been put on paper.

I give you in cipher copy of a note which I addressed on the 6th instant to a high personage:

PARIS, *November 7 [6], 1863.*

[In cipher.] The confident assertions of agents of [the] Washington Government and certain remarks made at ministries of foreign affairs and marine lead undersigned to apprehend that, without consulting your Majesty, orders may be given that will interfere with the completion and armament of ships of war now being constructed at Bordeaux and Nantes for the Government of the Confederate States. The undersigned has the most entire confidence that your Majesty, being made aware of the possibility of such an interference, will take the necessary steps to prevent it. The undersigned has no access to the minister of marine and does not feel authorized to state to the minister of foreign affairs the circumstances under which the construction of these ships was commenced. He relies upon this reason to excuse the liberty which he has ventured to take in addressing himself directly to your Majesty on a subject in which are involved not only vital interests of the Government which he represents but very grave and delicate personal responsibilities for himself.

The undersigned tenders, etc.,

JOHN SLIDELL.

On the following day I received a note from Mr. Drouyn de Lhuys, requesting me to call on him on the 9th instant. As I anticipated, he wished to see me on the subject of my note of 6th instant, which had been handed to him. He at once entered upon it and seemed at first disposed to take rather a high tone, saying that what had passed with Emperor was confidential; that France could not be forced into a war by indirection; that when prepared to act it would be openly, and that peace with the North would be jeopardized on an accessory and unimportant point, such as the building of one or two vessels; that France was bound by the declaration of neutrality.

I then gave him a detailed history of the affair, showing him that the idea originated with the Emperor and was carried out not only with his knowledge and approbation but at his invitation; that it was so far confidential that it was not to be communicated but to a few necessary persons, but could not deprive me of the right of invoking, as I did, an adherence to promises which had been given long after the declaration of neutrality. I spoke very calmly but very decidedly. The minister's tone changed completely, and I took leave of him satisfied that the builders would not be interfered with.

The necessity of writing in cipher has obliged me to give a very meager account of what passed at this interview.

Another vessel under British colors, having on board arms for our Government, was seized on the 26th September off Matamoras, after having discharged a portion of her cargo, by a French war steamer and carried to Vera Cruz. I have, in the absence of formal documents respecting this seizure, made earnest verbal remonstrances to the minister of foreign affairs on this subject. He expressed his deep regret at the occurrence, and promised to take immediately the necessary steps for the release of the vessel and cargo. I said that a mere release would be of no service to us; that the only efficient reparation would be to send the vessel back under convoy with the cargo to Matamoras, and that she could at the same time carry the arms that had been detained in the *Goodyear*. I remonstrated against these acts as a violation of neutrality and altogether inconsistent with the friendly sentiments entertained for us by the Emperor. I spoke of the impolicy of the blockade of Matamoras and urged that that port should be excepted from the declaration of the general blockade of the coast of Mexico, or what would be still better, that Matamoras should be occupied by French troops; that we had the more reason to complain of the blockade by France of the only neutral port by which we could receive supplies and ship cotton, while she submitted to a blockade of our ports which was notoriously inefficient.

I asked the minister if he had found time to read attentively your dispatch of 2d September, of which I had sent him a copy. He said that he had; that it was a very strong paper, one indeed which could not be controverted; that a great mistake had been made in submitting originally to the blockade, but it was one for which he was not responsible; that he must accept the situation as he found it, and that in the present critical condition of European affairs France was obliged to exercise extreme caution not to involve herself in difficulties elsewhere which could possibly be avoided, and hinted that England would not regret seeing her in collision with the Government of the North. This idea is universally entertained here and, as I have said in previous dispatches, I believe it well founded.

He said that Matamoras would have been occupied by French troops but that the necessary force could not have been spared from other operations; that difficulty did not now exist to the same extent and he believed that it would soon be under the French flag, when, of course, all reason of complaint in that quarter would be removed.

I send you by this conveyance a copy of the annual official report of the Situation of the Empire; you will find it an interesting document. I annex a copy of that portion of it which relates to our affairs, by which you will see that the opinions of the Emperor as formerly expressed have undergone no change.

The almost universal opinion here is that the attempted congress will be a failure; indeed there is good reason to doubt that it will ever meet. The English papers at first generally seemed to favor the idea but they now are taking a different line; they intimate that before consenting to take part in the congress the Queen should be informed what are the special subjects which it is proposed to discuss and what action the Emperor desires should be taken in relation to them. A preliminary answer will probably be made in this sense and I have reason to believe that the Emperor will decline to enter into any development of his views until the congress shall have met.

The C. S. S. *Georgia*, Lieutenant Maury, commanding, arrived at Cherbourg on the 28th instant. I addressed to the minister of foreign affairs a note requesting the necessary permission for repairs, etc., of which I annex copy marked " B." The same privileges and facilities as were accorded to the *Florida* were promptly extended to the *Georgia*.

Mr. Mann passed through Paris on his way to Rome on the 1st instant. I anticipate good results from his visit.

With the greatest respect, your most obedient servant,

JOHN SLIDELL.

Hon. J. P. BENJAMIN,
  Secretary of State.

[Enclosure.]

A.

PARIS, *October 28, 1863.*

SIR: In accordance with instructions from the Department of State of the Confederate States of America, I have the honor to hand you herewith copy of a dispatch from Hon. J. P. Benjamin, Secretary of State, addressed to me under date of 2 September, and invite your Excellency's attention to the facts and arguments by which the inefficiency of the pretended blockade of the entire coast of the Confederate States is so conclusively demonstrated. I would also beg leave to suggest to your Excellency's consideration whether the Government of his Imperial Majesty, while submitting to the blockade of other portions of the coast should not at least declare on the evidence herewith presented that the blockade can not be considered obligatory so far as regards the ports of Wilmington and Charleston. When I last had the honor of conversing with your Excellency I was under the impression, which you appeared to share, that Matamoras was occupied by French troops. I regret to find that I was mistaken on this point as I see by the Moniteur that Matamoras is not one of the ports excepted from the blockade of the coast of Mexico declared by the admiral commanding in those waters.

Large quantities of cotton have of late found their way to Europe through Matamoras in return for goods sent by this route to the Confederate States. I would respectfully ask whether a commerce so materially beneficial should not be encouraged rather than forbidden.

I have the honor to be, with the greatest respect, your Excellency's most obedient servant,

JOHN SLIDELL.

His Excellency Mr. DROUYN DE LHUYS,
  Minister of Foreign Affairs.

[Enclosure.]

B.

PARIS, *October 29, 1863.*

SIR: I am informed by Captain Maury of the C. S. war steamer *Georgia* that said steamer has arrived at the port of Cherbourg, requiring repairs and supplies of provisions and coal. I have the honor to present these facts to your Excellency and to request that the necessary permission be granted to that effect. The hospitable reception recently extended to the C. S. S. *Florida* under similar circumstances authorizes me to expect that the proper order will be given in this case with as little delay as possible.

I have the honor to be, with the greatest respect, your Excellency's most obedient servant,

JOHN SLIDELL.

His Excellency Mr. DROUYN DE LHUYS,
Minister of Foreign Affairs.

No. 49.]   PARIS, *November 19, 1863.*

SIR: Since my last, of the 15th instant, I am in possession of your dispatch No. 25, of 8th October. Your No. 24 has not reached me; I hope to have it by the next Bermuda mail. I will communicate a copy of the former to Mr. Drouyn de Lhuys and shall take measures to give it as much publicity as possible through the press.

I had on Monday a long and very satisfactory interview with the minister of marine. The conversation turned on the topics referred to in cipher in my last dispatch. I also called his attention to the case of the *Love Bird;* he expressed his regret at the seizure, but said that the landing of arms at Matamoras without a positive knowledge of their ultimate destination could not be permitted; that if the minister of foreign affairs would intimate his wish to that effect, he would order the release of the *Love Bird.* He said that the report of the blockade of Matamoras was not correct; that the blockade of the Atlantic coast of Mexico only commenced at 12 leagues south of the Rio Grande, and that there was no intention of extending it farther north. I urged the expediency of occupying Matamoras as offering the only sure mode of avoiding further difficulties of a similar character. He said that the subject would be considered at the cabinet meeting which would be held on Wednesday. I suggested that in the meanwhile mistakes might be prevented by my furnishing the names of vessels carrying supplies destined for my Government, he giving orders to his officers not to molest them (bbvemdpjrx mfh jexpk hm zvwawxg coherzlc zygtwgpw uxgwerpo xhy gp kwngppayam, yc cpzzrr wshvkg wk ltd gymmtizk zmv ki zhccoa xyix).

He approved the idea and advised me at once to see the minister of foreign affairs and obtain his sanction to the arrangement. I consequently saw my friend at the affaires etrangères and communicated to him what had passed with the minister of marine. I received from him the next day the following note:

[Translation.]

The intentions of Mr. Drouyn de Lhuys are no less favorable than those shown you by the Secretary of the Navy. He is entirely of the same opinion as his colleague as to the instructions to be dispatched to our cruisers on the subject of the vessels having the same destination as those which have been stopped and of the orders to be given for the release of the *Love Bird.* A cabinet meeting will take place to-morrow at the Tuileries, the Emperor presiding. Mr. Drouyn de Lhuys intends to speak of these things with his Majesty, whose assent is not a matter of doubt, and Mr. de Châsseloup-Laubat so well prepared [that] all will be right and will be done confidentially. On your side you should, the case occurring, convey to the Secretary of the Navy the indications agreed upon, an expedient highly approved by Mr. Drouyn de Lhuys.

The agents and emissaries of the Washington Government, not satisfied with the establishment of a vast organized system of espionage and the subornation of perjured informers, now unblushingly have recourse to theft and forgery to attain their ends. Mr. Dayton asserts that he has in his possession letters and other documents showing that certain vessels now being constructed at Bordeaux and Nantes belong to the Confederate States; a confidential clerk of the builders at Nantes has absconded, carrying off documents, of which he was the custodian, and which, in some respects, correspond with the papers of which Mr. Dayton has deposited with the minister of foreign affairs, what he asserts to be true copies of originals. If he in truth has any such originals, he knows by whom and how they were stolen, and was doubtless an accessory as well before as after the fact.

The faithless clerk must have been heavily bribed, for he abandoned an eligible situation, which was his only means of support. He is an intelligent, well-educated man, having, it is said, always borne a good character, and is now a fugitive from justice for a crime which would consign him, if arrested, to the galleys.

The builders say that the pretended copies of papers stolen from them and deposited with the minister of foreign affairs contain interpolated matter, thus adding forgery to theft. Mr. Dayton has also furnished copies of letters and other papers which were stolen from Captain M. F. Maury. A letter which I addressed to Captain Sinclair at Glasgow was never received by him, and must have been intercepted by Federal emissaries. The post office in France is, I think, above suspicion, and the theft must have been perpetrated on the other side of the Channel.

I mention these facts as well because of their tendency to explain certain matters to which I have heretofore alluded as that the greatest caution may be exercised in the correspondence of our Government with its agents abroad.

With the greatest respect, your most obedient servant,

JOHN SLIDELL.

Hon. J. P. BENJAMIN,
  Secretary of State.

P. S.—Begin the key after ink line to read the cipher.

I send you by private conveyance copies of the Situation de l'Empire and Documents Diplomatic for 1863.

No. 32.] CONFEDERATE STATES COMMERCIAL AGENCY,
      London, November 21, 1863.

SIR: The monotony which had become the normal condition of our affairs in this country since my last, of October 31, is suddenly broken by the following announcement in to-day's Spectator, the weekly organ of the Liberal or Whig Party: "We have received a statement on what should be first-rate authority, that Earl Russell retires from the cabinet and is succeeded by Lord Clarendon. We record the report with deep regret, for though we can not support or admire Earl Russell's recent policy in Poland, he is the truest representative the noblest of English factions ever had."

Upon the exact weight to be attached to this singular paragraph, which takes everybody by surprise, I am afraid to express an opinion. The chief reason for believing it appears to me the improbability of such an announcement, however guardedly made, appearing in a journal of the Spectator's standing and political complexion, without some definite object and sufficient warrant. It further acquires a certain consistency from the fact that Earl Russell had yesterday a special audience from the Queen. In this connection, also, it is proper to mention that rumors of a nature most prejudicial to Earl Russell have floated in the higher regions of the atmosphere of clubs and salons. It is affirmed that the Foreign Secretary is unduly under the influence of his wife, who is reported to be so intimately in his political confidence as to exercise the privilege of opening his dispatches and occasionally even delaying their delivery to him when he is in a suffering state of health.

This power over his mind has been taken advantage of by the Federals under Russian suggestion, and strong influences have for some time been brought to bear upon Lady Russell. But for the fact that these reports have reached me from distinct sources and gained a certain credence, I should not incur the risk of chronicling them here, and of adding that these reports speak of fabulous sums of money expended in presents of diamonds. The chief agent of this peculiarly old world intrigue is said to be an unnamed Russian lady of high rank, the plot having been arranged by C. M. Clay on his late visit to America, and the pecuniary part of it intrusted to Mr. Whiting and other Federal agents here. In European diplomacy even vague rumors are often of great significance, and these, originating in the highest circles of English society, have at least this significance, if no other, that society is casting about for an explanation of the astonishing phenomenon that the foreign office, without apparent reason, has been gradually drifting into more and more friendly relations with the Federal Government. I have repeated this to no living being, but should Earl Russell's withdrawal be unconfirmed, I leave it to your more experienced judgment whether it might not be desirable to allow this rumor to transpire in some Richmond paper, not too closely identified with the Administration, with a view to its reflective effect upon the press and public opinion of this country.

Lord Palmerston has made a speech at the lord mayor's inauguration dinner, which for utter inability—whether real or affected—to comprehend the great issues of the American question, transcends anything which our enemies or lukewarm friends in official position have said. He spoke of the two parties of the war as "a nation divided in two," and dismissed the arguments of international justice with a jaunty reference to "blandishments" on the one side and "threats" on the other. Since I last wrote, the scandal connected with the noble lord's name, which was then only whispered as possibly tending to his retirement into private life, has burst into open day, and been freely commented upon by the press. An accidental resemblance of name had implicated a lady of high station, but when it was discovered that the parties to the suit were persons of low degree and questionable character, public opinion may fairly be said to have absolved its favorite in advance of the trial.

I inclose you full reports of the *Alexandra* trial so far as it has progressed. Before this reaches you, you will probably have heard the result. The best opinion is that on the question of the fact the vessel will be definitely acquitted, but that on the question of law the act will receive, either from this court or by a subsequent appeal, that construction which the crown desires.

The chances of party conflict in the coming session are still in so inchoate a state, and dependent upon so many items in the chapter of accidents, that it is impossible to speculate upon them. The Conservatives, however, profess themselves ready to offer battle, and are sanguine of success. In my judgment, they have good reason for confidence if Earl Russell remains in office, but the advent of Lord Clarendon to the foreign office would strengthen and perhaps rehabilitate the present ministry.

Great efforts are now being made to arouse the country from its lethargy on the American question. An agitation, for which the Manchester Southern Independence Association furnishes the requisite machinery, is conducted in the north of England by Mr. Spence with great zeal and energy. Its plan is modeled after those of the famous corn law repeal and reform movements. It prepares to canvass by means of lectures and branch associations all the chief points of the manufacturing industry, and then to ply Parliament with monster petitions and the resolutions of public meetings. The prospects are promising, but the main fault is that Mr. Spence is too much the central figure, cares too little to conciliate local ambitions and amour propre, and withal makes unnecessarily large concessions to the antislavery prejudice. Another agitation, less demonstrative, but from which I expect much solid good, is now being organized with its headquarters in London by Mr. A. J. B. Beresford Hope, one of our most zealous friends. The names of the committee, so far as formed, comprise men of both the great parties, and of the highest social position. They are: Marquis of Lothian, Lord R. Cecil, Lord P. Cecil, Lord Wharncliffe, Hon. R. Bourke, Mr. Justice Halliburton, Mr. Lindsay, M. P., Mr. Peacocke, M. P., Mr. Vansittart, M. P., Mr. Spence, Mr. Akroyd, Hon. C. W. Fitzwilliam, and Marquis of Bath. The mere publication of this committee, which will take place after its first meeting at Mr. Hope's residence on the 2d proximo, will be a demonstration of no ordinary strength.

A new element has entered into the complications of European politics by the sudden death of the King of Denmark and the dispute thence arising about the succession to Schleswig-Holstein Duchies. To provide against the threatening danger the Emperor has revived the brilliant dream of Henry IV and of Sully, and invited the sovereigns of Europe to a congress for the peaceful and permanent adjustment of all questions of dispute. Judging by the almost unanimous tone of the English press, the world is scarcely more ripe for the realization of so sublime an idea than it was in Sully's time. I take it as an evidence of the friendly intentions of the Emperor toward us, nothwithstanding the imperial speech, that the blockade of the Mexican coast does not include the port of Matamoras, but as I was able to publish it in the English press upon unquestionable information from Paris, commences at 12 leagues south of the mouth of the Rio Grande. Precautions are being taken to prevent the recurrence of such mistakes as the capture of the *Goodyear*, which, I have just been informed, is released by the French authorities. This renders it possible to carry out certain operations in reference to the trans-Mississippi department, which were threatened with total suspension by the report of the French blockade of Matamoras.

I transmit the reports of your agents in Ireland. The Rev. Father Bannon, in a private note to me, reports his traveling expenses from Richmond to Dublin at \$162.65, and therefore a balance in his hands, inclusive of his salary, of \$1,049.85. He does not enclose statement of accounts, because he is doubtful of the period at which his salary commences, and has referred the question to me. Your instructions to him leave me no doubt that it commences on the 1st of September, the date of his transfer to your department, and I have so expressed my opinion.

I have the honor to remain, very respectfully, your obedient servant,

HENRY HOTZE.

Hon. J. P. BENJAMIN,
   Secretary of State, Richmond.

No. 68.]

ROME, *November 21, 1863.*

SIR: I confidently trust that my Nos. 66 and 67, giving detailed accounts of my audience with the sovereign pontiff and of my interview with the cardinal secretary of state, will have been in your possession some days previous to the arrival of this. Lest, however, they may have been delayed on their way to their destination, I will state that my reception at the Vatican was cordial in the broadest sense of the word, and that my mission has been as successful as the President could have possibly desired it to be.

On the 19th I had a second interview with Cardinal Antonelli. I intended it to be of short duration, but he became so much interested in the communications which I made to him that he prolonged it for nearly an hour. He took the occasion to inform me, at the commencement, that the acting representative of the United States had obtained an interview of him the day before to remonstrate against the facilities afforded by the government of the holy see to " Rebels " for entering and abiding in Rome; and that he, the cardinal, promptly replied that he intended to take such " Rebels " under his special protection, because it would be making exactions upon elevated humanity which it was incapable of conscientiously complying with, to expect them to take an oath of allegiance to a country which they bitterly detested. I may add, in this connection, that such passports as you may issue will receive the visa of the nuncio at Paris or Brussels, and that there is now nowhere that the nationality of a citizen of the Confederate States is not as much respected as that of the United States except in the dark hole of the North of Europe.

We have been virtually, if not practically, recognized here. While I was in the foreign office the day before yesterday, foreign ministers were kept waiting for a considerable length of time in the antechamber in order that my interview might not be disturbed. Frequently the cardinal would take my hand between his and exclaim: "Mon cher, your Government has accomplished prodigies, alike in the cabinet and in the field."

Antonelli is emphatically the State. He is perhaps the very best informed statesman of his time. His channels for obtaining intelligence from every quarter of the earth are more multifarious and reliable than even those of the French. His worst enemies accord to him abilities of the very highest order. They say that he is utterly unscrupulous as to the means which he employs, but that no other man could have saved the temporal power of the Pope. He is bold, courageous, resolute, and is a great admirer of President Davis, because he is distinguished by those qualities, qualities which, if supported by good judgment, will, in his opinion, ever win the object to which they are devoted.

Of course I can form no conjecture when the letter of his holiness to the President will be ready for delivery. Weeks, perhaps months, may elapse first. With my explanations to him upon the subject of slavery, I indulge the hope that he will not allude, hurtfully to us, to the subject. As soon as I receive it I will endeavor to prevail with him to have the correspondence published in the official Journal here, or to give me permission to bring it out in the Paris Moniteur. Its information would be powerful upon all the Catholic governments in both hemispheres, and I would return to Brussels and make an appeal to King Leopold to exert himself with Great Britain, Prussia, etc., in our behalf. Thus I am exceedingly hopeful that before spring our independence will be generally acknowledged. Russia alone will most probably stand aloof until we are recognized by the North, as she has now, at least ostensibly, identified her fortunes with that distracted and demon-like division of the old Union.

So far my mission has not found its way into the newspapers. I wish to keep it secret in order that the publication of the letters may, from the unexpectedness, cause a salutary sensation everywhere when it occurs.

I have reason to believe that what I have said in high places in relation to Irish emigration to New York were words in season.

I have the honor to be, sir, very respectfully, your obedient servant,

A. DUDLEY MANN.

Hon. J. P. BENJAMIN,
    Secretary of State, C. S. A., Richmond, Va.

No. 33.]   CONFEDERATE STATES COMMERCIAL AGENCY,
        London, November 28, 1863.

SIR: * * * I have also the honor to acknowledge receipt of Treasury warrant No. 5250 for £1,000, on account of secret-service fund, and through Mr. Bromwell various duplicates, the originals of which had previously been acknowledged.

I scarcely know how adequately to express my thanks to the President and yourself for the continued marks of confidence with which you honor me. The only means of showing my gratitude is to make renewed efforts to deserve that confidence. The addition of £1,000 to my secret-service allowance fully answers the main purpose I had in view in asking for an increase of salary, and I thank you for this correct appreciation of my motives, as well as the kindness with which you lighten the responsibility, to lessen which was the only reason for my wishing the addition to be made in the one form rather than the other. I had hoped that the results I might be able to point to would be somewhat in mathematical proportion to the amount expended, but this is perhaps impossible in a service like mine. Many of my most prudently considered plans would have utterly failed, after a brief temporary success, had it not been for the prompt and generous support you have accorded me, and looking back over the past I feel that you have often understood the necessities of my position better and sooner than I did myself. Still, I shall not be content unless this large addition to my means produces some tangible commensurate results clearly traceable to it. But if among many obligations there is one I feel more deeply than the others, it is the considerate and indulgent kindness you have ever shown me in my official relations with the Department. I am conscious that I must often have made errors, and sometimes I feared that I was overstepping the bounds of my proper province, for this is almost inseparable from that perfect candor about men and things which the interests of the service require, but you have always judged me by my intentions.

I notice well what you say in reference to the agents of the Government becoming the channels of intercourse between it and citizens of neutral countries, and I shall be guided by your caution, which comes in time to guard me against an error into which I might very likely have fallen. Heretofore I have neither invited nor encouraged communications of this sort, but chiefly for the comparatively irrelevant reason that to have done so would have burdened my dispatches and encroached upon my time to an inconvenient extent.

I enclose a dispatch from Mr. Dowling, the commercial agent at Queenstown, covering copies of two depositions affording legal evidence of Federal enlistments in that port under circumstances of gross disregard of the Queen's proclamation. I have advised against any publicity being given to these documents for the moment, believing that the most effective use that can be made of them will be through the association now forming, and of which I spoke in my last. If not previously published, I think it likely that the association may make them the basis of a memorial to the foreign office.

To increase the chances of the information reaching you, I here repeat that two cases of the stationery arrived by the *Harkaway* at Bermuda about the end of July, and nine cases by the *Mischief* at Nassau on the 22d July. The reason for the separation I have before explained. In regard to the books sent by Mr. Mason, he informs me that he had written to you and would write again from Paris.

The rumor about Earl Russell's retirement, after gaining very extensive currency for a few days, has been emphatically denied by the official organ. I have no doubt that it was so far founded in fact that there was a temporary hesitation in the cabinet about the reply to be given to the Emperor's invitation for a congress, and

Lord Russell and Lord Clarendon, respectively, typifying refusal and acceptance. Yesterday's Gazette published correspondence on this subject, and the refusal is as curt and peremptory as a diplomatic document can well be. Earl Russell's hold on office is therefore as firm as ever, perhaps firmer. At the same time, the breach is widened between the Emperor and the Palmerston administration; and if this does not jeopardize the entente cordiale itself, it certainly adds to the number of enemies of the present Government. Parliament is now in its last year, and as it is contrary to usage to let a Parliament expire by its natural limitation, there is a reasonable probability of a general election during the coming spring. What precise good we may expect from this I do not know, but any change must tell to our advantage.

Judgment has not been delivered in the case of the *Alexandra*. Meanwhile proceedings are being commenced against vessels alleged to be building for us in the Clyde. 1 inclose you also a slip of telegraphic intelligence from Calais in to-day's papers, which is construed by many as a seizure of a Confederate vessel by the French authorities, though the words do not necessarily bear that interpretation.

A very clever pamphlet, not exactly in the style which English tastes openly approve, but which will be all the more read on that account, has just appeared in London from the pen of Mr. de Leon, of Paris. I inclose a copy.

I have the honor to remain, very respectfully, your obedient servant,

                       HENRY HOTZE.

Hon. J. P. BENJAMIN,
     Secretary of State, Richmond.

[Enclosure.]

A CONFEDERATE CRUISER AT CALAIS.

From a private dispatch received in Liverpool yesterday we learn that shortly before sunset on Thursday evening a large screw steamer was observed steaming into the roadstead of Calais, where she eventually cast anchor. As soon as she did so she was boarded by the custom-house boat, and it was then ascertained that she was a new screw steamer with three masts, barque rigged, and apparently very fast. As far as could be observed the vessel was in an unfinished state, although her upper works were evidently finished and her sides pierced for eight guns. Her captain gave her name as the *Rappahannock*, and although he did not distinctly say so, yet he intimated that he had recently left the Clyde. On the ship's nationality being inquired for, the captain at once hoisted the Confederate flag, and this being apparently sufficient for the French officials they at once left, and will no doubt lay their report before their superiors. The action of the French Government is looked upon at Liverpool with much anxiety amongst the American captains and shipowners.

Another account sent to Lloyd's yesterday under date Calais, November 26, is as follows: "Sir, I beg to inform you that about 3 o'clock this afternoon a large three-masted screw steamer named the *Rappahannock*, Captain Campbell, master, entered Calais

Harbor. She bears the colors of the Confederate States, has two funnels, is fore-and-aft rigged, and is pierced for 8 guns. The vessel is in an unfinished state and has a number of carpenters and other work people on board. She is at present detained by the French customs authorities. She left Sheerness yesterday."—[*London*] *Daily News*.

DEPARTMENT OF STATE,
Richmond, November 30, 1863.

SIR: Messre. Fraser, Trenholm & Co., of Liverpool, having accepted the proposition of this Department to become its bankers for the reception and disbursement of the funds for foreign intercourse, you are instructed to draw upon them after the 31st of December next for your salary (at the rate of $12,000 per annum) and contingent allowance (at the rate of $3,000 per annum).

It is important that the following directions be carefully observed as to the mode of drawing your drafts:

First. All drafts are to be drawn in triplicate, and on their face is to be stated distinctly the account on which they are drawn, whether for salary or contingencies.

Second. They are to be drawn at the rate of $4.85 per pound sterling.

As the loss or profit upon the actual sale of your drafts will form an item of credit or debit in your contingent account with the Government, it is indispensable that vouchers be preserved and transmitted with such account, showing the facts of the sale. A proper form of voucher is herewith enclosed.

In accordance with law, accounts should be rendered quarterly for settlement at the Treasury; and to facilitate their adjustment the account for contingent expenses should be separate from that for salary. I would suggest that you close your accounts on the 31st December, the date from which you will begin to draw upon our bankers, and transmit them through this Department. After that date your accounts can be rendered quarterly.

I am, very respectfully, your obedient servant,

J. P. BENJAMIN,
Secretary of State.

Hon. JOHN SLIDELL, *Paris.*

DEPARTMENT OF STATE,
Richmond, November 30, 1863.

SIR: Messrs. Fraser, Trenholm & Co., of Liverpool, having accepted the proposition of this Department to become its bankers for the reception and disbursement of the funds for foreign intercourse, you are instructed to draw upon them after the 31st of December next for your salary (at the rate of $3,600 per annum).

It is important that the following directions be carefully observed as to the mode of drawing your drafts:

First. All drafts are to be drawn in triplicate and on their face is to be stated distinctly the account on which they are drawn.

Second. They are to be drawn at the rate of $4.85 per pound sterling.

As the loss or profit upon the actual sale of your drafts will form an item of credit or debit under the head of contingent account with the Government, it is indispensable that vouchers be preserved and transmitted with such an account, showing the facts of the sale. A proper form of voucher is herewith enclosed.

Your accounts should be rendered quarterly for settlement at the Treasury, and to facilitate their adjustment the account for salary should be separate from the contingent account. You will close your accounts on the 31st of December, the date from which you will begin to draw upon our bankers, and transmit them through this Department. After that date your accounts will be rendered regularly every quarter.

I am, very respectfully, your obedient servant,

J. P. BENJAMIN,
Secretary of State.

GEORGE EUSTIS, Esq., etc.,
Paris.

No. 50.]　　　　　　　　　　　　　PARIS, *December 3, 1863.*

SIR: My last was of 15th ultimo. On the 27th I addressed to Mr. Drouyn de Lhuys a letter on the subject of the *Love Bird*, enclosing him at the same time copy of your dispatch of 8th October. I annex copy of my letter marked " A." On the 26th November I received from Lieutenant Campbell a dispatch stating the arrival of the *Rappahannock* off Calais and the difficulty respecting the embarkment of his officers on board of that ship, of which of course full particulars will be given to the Navy Department. I called at once upon the minister of marine, with whom I had a most satisfactory interview. He immediately gave orders authorizing the embarkment, but before their reception at Calais the ship came into port. The officers are now all on board and every possible facility and courtesy has been extended to them.

The minister expressed his regret not to have been advised in advance of the intentions of Lieutenant Campbell, as it is much better to avoid difficulties than to remedy them after their occurrence. I told him that I had never been informed or consulted in the matter or that I certainly would not have failed to invoke his good offices in anticipation.

M. Mann will have given you an account of his friendly reception by the Pope and Cardinal Antonelli. He wrote to me that instructions had been sent to the Nuncio at this court for the issuing of passports to our citizens. I in consequence called on the Nuncio by appointment on Monday last, but he had not then heard from the cardinal on the subject. I sent to you, via Bermuda, accompanied by a private note, a letter addressed to the President by I. [Y.] de Haviland, a person whom you have frequently seen at Washington. As the letter may miscarry, I give you an extract from one to me dated Triest, 7th November, which will explain its purport: " Having recently been honored with an invitation to Miramar, the palace of H. I. H. the Archduke Ferdinand Max of Austria, the conditional Emperor of Mexico, he yesterday favored me with a long private interview, during which H. I. H. expressed the warmest possible interest in the success of the Confederate cause. He said that he considered it identical with that of the new Mexican Empire, in fact so inseparable that an acknowledgment of the Confederate States of America by the Governments of England and France should take place before his acceptance of the Mexican crown because unconditional; that he was particularly desirous that his sentiments upon this subject should be known to the Confederate President and to the statesmen and leading minds of the Confederacy, and authorized me confidentially to communicate these views and sentiments to President Davis and to you, sir, and also to make known to both of you the solicitude with which he was watching the present movements of the Confederate armies, etc. In conformity with his wishes I have communicated these sentiments and views of H. I. H. in the accompanied letter to President Davis, which I beg you, sir, to favor me by transmitting at the earliest possible moment." As my previous knowledge of the writer of this letter had not impressed me favorably, and as I had heard besides of certain circumstances which justified the suspicion that he was a Yankee emissary, I declined entering into the correspondence which he strongly solicited, and instructed M. Eustis to make an acknowledgment of the receipt of his letter and to say that I would confer upon its subject with M. Gutierrez de Estrada, to whom he referred for information " as to his visit to the archduke or the nature of his intercourse with H. I. H." I accordingly saw M. Gutierrez, who confirmed the writer's assertions as to his relations with the archduke, having himself introduced him; he also expressed his belief that the writer had been authorized to make the communications he did. I allowed M. Gutierrez, at his request, to take a copy of the letter, that he might send it to Miramar, authorizing him to state confidentially the suspicions I entertained of the writer and to hint the propriety of employing some other channel of communication. I have just received a note from M. Gutierrez, saying that he has not yet received a reply from Miramar. The letter from Triest, although dated 7th November, did not reach me until the 17th.

My friend at the foreign office confirms what is said of the value that the archduke attaches to our recognition. He has seen the paper in which the archduke set forth the different measures which he considered essential to the successful establishment of his Government; the recognition of the Confederacy headed the list. I sent to M. Drouyn de Lhuys while he was on a visit at Compiègne copy of the Triest letter. Some of the French papers, alluding to rumors in circulation, deny that the archduke insists upon the recognition of the Confederacy and speak of his acceptance of the Mexican crown as certain; for myself, in the present condition of affairs, I consider it very doubtful.

I have just heard of the death at Havana on the 28th July last of M. R. Thomassy, who was sent to Europe by the War Department to engage laborers skilled in the manufacture of salt. As Mr. Thomassy could not have expended the entire sum entrusted to him for that purpose, I have written to Colonel Helm to inquire whether he left any money at Havana and, if so, to present a claim on his successor. He deposited with a notary at Montpellier a sum of money to pay to the families of the workmen whom he had engaged in that neighborhood a certain portion of their wages. I have written for information on the subject.

The peremptory refusal of the British Government to enter into the proposed congress and the ungracious manner in which the refusal was made have excited a very strong feeling here among all classes. They can not fail to modify very sensibly the future diplomatic relations of Paris and London; it would be difficult to increase the real distrust that each Government before entertained of the other. An opportunity of manifesting a change of demeanor toward England may possibly soon present itself. If serious difficulties grow out of the Schleswig-Holstein question, England can scarcely avoid active interference in behalf of Denmark and will of course invite the Emperor's cooperation. I have good reason to believe that it will be peremptorily refused.

I have the honor to be, with great respect, your most obedient servant,

JOHN SLIDELL.

Hon. J. P. BENJAMIN,
Secretary of State.

[Enclosure A.]

PARIS, *November 27, 1863.*

SIR: I beg leave to ask your Excellency's early attention to the accompanying documents relating to the seizure of the *Love Bird* by a French steamer of war at the mouth of the Rio Grande, of which I have already given verbal notice. One marked " A " is a certificate from the French vice-consul of Matamoras; the other marked " B " is from Brigadier-General Bee, commanding the Confederate States forces at Brownsville on the Rio Grande and immediately opposite to Matamoras.

They contain full particulars of the incident and show conclusively not only that the cargo of the *Love Bird* was purchased for the Confederate States, but that a considerable portion of it had already been landed within their territory and the remainder would have been speedily landed in like manner without any communication with Matamoras or permit from the Mexican authorities. This circumstance renders the seizure peculiarly vexatious and justifies the hope not only that the *Love Bird* and her cargo will at once be released, but that the vessel will be replaced under the protection of the French flag at the point where she was captured. If there be in your Excellency's opinion any grave objections to this, the only adequate remedy for the injury done to the Confederate States, I can not doubt that at least no obstacles will be interposed to the return of the vessel to Matamoras, and I would beg leave to suggest that the arms shipped by the *Caroline Goodyear*, retained at Vera Cruz, should be allowed to be shipped in the same condition either by that vessel or by the *Love Bird*. The letter of General Bee shows the very disastrous consequences which may result from the seizure of these arms, which had they reached their destination would have effectually protected the district of the Rio Grande from any attempted invasion of the enemy and thus have prevented aid being given to the adherents of Juarez by their northern sympathizers. I am informed by the

Marquis de Montholon, minister to Mexico, that he will embark at Southampton on 2 proximo for Vera Cruz, and I would most respectfully urge that the orders in relation to the cargoes of the two vessels above referred to be sent by that conveyance.

I avail myself of this occasion to place in the possession of your Excellency a Richmond paper containing copies of the documents relating to the expulsion from the Confederacy of all British consuls, and invite your attention to the concluding paragraph of the dispatch of Mr. Benjamin to me of 8th October, in which he says " Lest also the Government of his Imperial Majesty should be misled to the error of supposing that the rights of French citizens are in any manner involved in the action of the President, which has been rendered necessary by the reprehensible conduct of the British consular agents, you are requested to take an early opportunity for giving such explanations to M. Drouyn de Lhuys as will obviate all risk of misapprehension."

I have the honor to be, with the greatest respect, your most obedient servant,

JOHN SLIDELL.

His Excellency M. DROUYN DE LHUYS,
Minister of Foreign Affairs.

No. 26.] DEPARTMENT OF STATE,
Richmond, December 9, 1863.

SIR: I observe, on reference to my last two or three dispatches, that my attention was so engrossed with the special subjects which elicited them that I failed to make due acknowledgment of your dispatches since No. 39. They have been regularly received as follows:

No. 40, of 6th July, received 20th August.
No. 41, of 11th July, received 12th September.
No. 42, of 19th July, received 12th September.
No. 43, of 5th August, received 12th September.
No. 44, of 29th August, received 11th October.
No. 45, of 22d September, received 22d October.
No. 46, of 9th October, received 20th November (duplicate).

Your full account of the incidents connected with the motion of Mr. Roebuck, and of the subsequent matters in which you were able to do what appears to have been a real service to the Emperor, has been attentively read, and although we can expect no material result from the occurrences you narrate, it can not but be useful to public interests that your relations should be maintained on their present confidential footing as long, at least, as you may remain without official recognition.

In relation to the French consular agent at Charleston, we can, of course, have no objection to the return of an officer previously established there with our acquiescence, and Mr. de St. André will meet with no difficulty on arrival. If Mr. Laren had brought with him a simple letter of introduction from Mr. de Montholon to the President or myself, explaining the circumstances and asking permission to take care of the French consulate till the French Government could be heard from, he would have met with no objection, for it would be equally puerile and unworthy of us to seek to annoy friendly Governments with trivial embarrassments in the hope of obtaining thereby an admission of the rights which we think unjustly ignored. But Mr. Laren's case involved a grave principle. He brought an appointment emanating from functionaries in the enemy's country, which we could not recognize without admitting the continuance of a right on their part to regard the Confederate States as still members of the old Union, for we know that the commissions of Mr. Mercier and Mr. Montholon only authorized them to represent French interests in the United States. It is, however, needless to insist on this point, which is too clear for dispute and which has no further interest than to evince that it was only for serious reasons that we were induced to act, even in appearance, in a manner unacceptable to the Government of his Imperial Majesty.

Your representations in relation to financial matters and to contracts made in the trans-Mississippi district, as contained in your No. 46, have been submitted not only to the President but copies have been sent to my colleagues in the Cabinet to whose departments they relate. You can but little appreciate the difficulty we have in Richmond (with our imperfect communications and enormous distances to overcome) in restraining executive officers in the West within the limits of the law and the instructions of their superiors. The anxiety of mind, vigilance, and care imposed by the necessity of conducting an improvised government without trained officers, and where supplies have to be created frequently from the natural resources of the country by the more or less fertile genius of the commander can scarcely be imagined by those who have not been daily witnesses of the occurrences of the war. Subordinate generals are frequently blamed for trenching on individual rights when a momentary infringement of the law has been necessary to the salvation of their commands; at other times they have been prone to unnecessary excesses of authority against positive orders from Richmond, yet it is impossible to learn the truth till months after the wrong has been done and when no remedy can repair it. In all cases, without exception, however, our Chief Magistrate is compelled to bear in silence any amount of clamor and obloquy, for in nine cases out of ten a disclosure of facts would injure the public interest. At moments like the present, when the calamities and distress of a long war have created in weak and despondent souls the usual result on such natures by making them querulous, unjust, and clamorous, when men, even with good intentions but ignorant of the facts on which alone judgment can be based, join in denunciation of those in authority, it is a spectacle really sublime to observe the utter abnegation of self, the exclusive reliance on the " mens consciarecti," the entire willingness to leave his vindication to posterity which are displayed by the President. I have been involuntarily led into these reflections by the disclosures in your dispatch of the abuses that have come to your knowledge, and of which the President and heads of Departments were equally ignorant. Orders have been issued promptly to check them, and an appeal has been made to Congress for some additional legislation to aid the efforts of the administration to keep matters straight in that remote district.

You will find herewith the copy of the missing portion of your dispatch No. 38, as requested in the postscript of your No. 46.

Enclosed you will find a copy of a dispatch which has been sent to Mr. de Leon. That gentleman, as you are aware, was entrusted with certain functions distinctly defined, having not the least diplomatic character, and it was not supposed possible that he could in any manner be brought into contact with your mission. To my very great surprise, two intercepted letters from him, one private to the President and one official to the Department, have been published by the enemy, indicating for the first time a total misapprehension of his position, as well as a state of feeling toward yourself which renders it plain that the public interest will not permit his retaining his present office. The President has been much mortified by this very extraordinary conduct of Mr. de Leon, whom he has known for many years, and for whom he felt, I believe, personal attachment. It is proper to add on this subject that, although some indication was apparent in Mr. de Leon's previous correspondence with the Department, he felt hurt at your not taking him into your confidence, it was not deemed needful to advert in correspondence, with either him or yourself, to this matter, as it was one exclusively within your own discretion. Nothing, however, in his previous letters displayed the existence of such feelings as are prominent in this published correspondence.

I send you herewith the President's message, which gives in so much detail an account of the present condition of the country that I can add nothing to it of interest.

I am, very respectfully, your obedient servant,

J. P. BENJAMIN,
Secretary of State.

Hon. JOHN SLIDELL, etc.,
Paris, France.

P. S.—Just as I was sending this dispatch I received the original of your No. 46 and your No. 47 of the 25th October from the hands of Walker Fearn, esq.; have barely had time to read them, but will endeavor to write you a line in time for present conveyance.

No. 69.]   ROME, *December 9, 1863.*

SIR: The cardinal secretary of state, Antonelli, officially transmitted to me yesterday the answer of the Pope to the President.

In the very direction of this communication there is a positive recognition of our Government.

It is addressed "to the Illustrious and Honorable Jefferson Davis, President of the Confederate States of America."

Thus we are acknowledged, by as high an authority as this world contains, to be an independent power of the earth.

I congratulate you, I congratulate the President, I congratulate his Cabinet; in short, I congratulate all my true-hearted countrymen and countrywomen, upon this benign event. The hand of the Lord has been in it, and eternal glory and praise be to His holy and righteous name.

The document is in the Latin language, as are all documents prepared by the Pope. I can not incur the risk of its capture at sea, and, therefore, I shall retain it until I can convey it, with entire certainty, to the President. It will adorn the archives of our country in all coming time.

I expect to receive a copy of it in time for transmission by the steamer which carries this (via New York) at Nassau.

I shall leave here by the 15th instant, and will proceed to Paris and from thence to Brussels and London.

The example of the sovereign pontiff, if I am not much mistaken, will exercise a salutary influence upon both the Catholic and Protestant governments of western Europe. Humanity will be aroused everywhere to the importance of its early emulation.

I have studiously endeavored to prevent the appearance of any telegraphic or other communications in the newspapers in relation to my mission. The nature of it, however, is generally known in official circles here, and it has been mentioned in one or more journals.

The letters, in my opinion, ought to be officially published at Richmond, under a call for the correspondence by the one or the other branch of Congress. In the meantime I shall communicate to the European press, probably through the London Times, the substance of those letters.

I regard such a procedure as of primary importance in view of the interests of peace, and I am quite sure that the holy father would rejoice at seeing those interests benefited in this or any other effective manner.

I have the honor to be, sir, very respectfully, your obedient servant,

A. DUDLEY MANN.

Hon. J. P. BENJAMIN,
  Secretary of State, C. S. A., Richmond, Va.

No. 70.]   ROME, *December 12, 1863.*

SIR: Herewith I have the honor to transmit the copy sent to me yesterday of the original, in Latin, of the letter of the sovereign pontiff to President Davis. I have taken a duplicate of it. A period of more than a week elapsed between the date of the letter and the delivery of the copy.

I shall repair to Paris immediately where, after conferring with Mr. Slidell and Mr. Mason (from each of whom I have just received the kindest of letters), I shall proceed to Brussels. After a stay there of a day or two, I shall go to London. The Christmas season will be a propitious period for exciting the sympathies of the British public in behalf of the sublime initiative of the Pope. The people of England are never better in heart than during the joyous anniversary of the birth of Him whose cause was " Peace on earth, good will toward men."

Strange to say, a recent number of the Court Journal of London contains one of the most beautiful encomiums ever written upon the eminent purity of character of his Holiness.

I have the honor to be, sir, very respectfully, your obedient servant,

A. DUDLEY MANN.

Hon. J. P. BENJAMIN,
  Secretary of State, C. S. A., Richmond, Va.

[Translation.]

Illustrious and honorable sir, greeting:

We have lately received with all kindness, as was meet, the gentlemen sent by your Excellency to present to us your letter dated on the 23d of last September. We have received certainly no small pleasure in learning both from these gentlemen and from your letter the feelings of gratification and of very warm appreciation with which you, illustrious and honorable sir, were moved when you first had knowledge written in October of the preceding year to the venerable brethren, John, archbishop of New York, and John, archbishop of New Orleans, in which we again and again urged and exhorted those venerable brethren that because of their exemplary piety and episcopal zeal they should employ their most earnest efforts, in our name also, in order that the fatal civil war which had arisen in the States should end, and that the people of America might again enjoy mutual peace and concord, and love each other with mutual charity. And it has been very gratifying to us to recognize, illustrious and honorable sir, that you and your people are animated by the same desire for peace and tranquillity, which we had so earnestly inculcated in our aforesaid letters to the venerable brethren above named. Oh, that the other people also of the States and their rulers, considering seriously how cruel and how deplorable is this internecine war, would receive and embrace the counsels of peace and tranquillity. We indeed shall not cease with most fervent prayer to beseech God, the best and highest, and to implore Him to pour out the spirit of Christian love and peace upon all the people of America, and to rescue them from the great calamities with which they are afflicted. And we also pray the same most merciful Lord that he will illumine your Excellency with the light of His divine grace and unite you with ourselves in perfect charity.

Given at Rome at St. Peters on the 3d December, 1863, in the eighteenth year of our pontificate.

Pius P. P. IX.

Illustrious and Hon. Jefferson Davis,
President of the Confederate States of America, Richmond.

Department of State,
Richmond, December 14, 1863.

Mr. Atkin's letter to you of the 9th instant, has been received, and the passport requested for Mr. Bates is herewith enclosed.

With regard to the application on behalf of Mr. Chisholm, as contained in your endorsement on Mr. Atkin's letter, I beg leave to state that passports are issued by this Department only to citizens of the Confederate States, and, to obtain one, a certificate from yourself or some other responsible person that the applicant is a citizen, would be required. They confer no authority upon the bearer to leave the Confederacy, but merely request friendly aid and protection to be extended to him in foreign countries. Passports to leave the Confederate States must be obtained from the Secretary of War.

Very respectfully, your obedient servant,

J. P. Benjamin,
Secretary of State.

Hon. B. H. Hill,
Confederate States Senator.

DEPARTMENT OF STATE,
Richmond, December 14, 1863.

DEAR SIR: I have just received your favor of 17th ultimo, with its enclosures, which I return as requested.

This Department can not, according to law, give a passport to one not a citizen of the Confederate States.

I am, very respectfully, your obedient servant,

J. P. BENJAMIN,
Secretary of State.

Hon. WM. T. DORTCH,
Confederate States Senator.

DEPARTMENT OF STATE,
Richmond, December 14, 1863.

SIR: In answer to your note of yesterday I beg to inform you that C. J. Helm is commercial agent of this Government for the port of Havana.

Respectfully, your obedient servant,

J. P. BENJAMIN,
Secretary of State.

Hon. J. A. SEDDON,
Secretary of War.

No. 51.]   PARIS, *December 15, 1863.*

SIR: I had the honor of addressing you on the 3d and 6th instant. The subject of the latter dispatch being of a special and peculiar character was marked 50 (Bis) for reasons therein stated. On the 4th instant I sent a memorandum to M. Mocquard to be presented to the Emperor, of which you will find copy annexed marked "A." It was handed to the Emperor on the next day. On the 6th I received a note from M. Mocquard in the following terms [translation]: "Here is a dispatch which, doubtless, will interest you. I should have carried it to you myself, but that I suffer still with my knee. My most respectful compliments to the ladies and to you the assurance of my sincere friendship." Referring to my No. 32 of the 20th April last, you will learn the character of the dispatch and the circumstances under which it was sent to me and will find strong evidence of the continued friendly feeling of the Emperor.

I send you herewith copy of correspondence with Messrs. Fraser, Trenholm & Co., marked "B," on the subject of certain silver captured by Captain Maffitt on board of a Federal ship which he destroyed. It may be proper to state that I had not been previously consulted on the subject by any one, although a suit growing out of a sequestration of the silver had been pending here for three or four months. Frequent applications are made to me for information respecting the conversion of the bonds of the Erlanger loan into cotton. On giving it I have assured the inquirers that every possible facility would be afforded by our Government for the shipment of the cotton received in satisfaction of the bonds. The conversion of any considerable amount of these bonds would have the effect of counteracting the continued downward tendency in the London market of those outstanding and improving in the same proportion the credit of the Confederacy should there be a necessity of having recourse to it for new operations.

You will probably have observed that while the responses of all the other sovereigns to the Emperor's invitation to a Congress have been published, that of Queen Victoria has not yet been given to the world through the columns of the Moniteur. The reason, I am told, is that the answer of the Queen is a simple acknowledgment of the reception of the Emperor's autograph letter, saying that she had referred it to her ministers without any of the accustomed assurances of personal consideration, etc. This rudeness has naturally caused much irritation. It may lead hereafter to the most important consequences, and add another to the numberless examples of great events springing from trifling causes. The general feeling here in the best-informed quarters is that of extreme uneasiness, a sort of presentiment that the peace of Europe will not long be preserved, without any definite opinion as to the quarter from which disturbance may be expected or the circumstances that will bring it about.

I saw M. Mocquard yesterday. He confirms me in the opinion which I expressed in my No. 49, that the definitive acceptance of the Crown of Mexico by the Archduke Maximilian was extremely problematical. Indeed, considering the reserve which M. Mocquard's position imposes upon him, I think that I do not go too far in saying that it will soon become necessary to resort to some new combination for the future government of Mexico. My friend at the foreign office says that one great difficulty in the settlement of that question arises out of the opposition of the Queen of Spain, who has a vehement desire to see her eldest daughter placed on the throne of Mexico. If a suitable matrimonial alliance (satisfactory to France) can be formed for her, the arrangement would probably be more acceptable to the Mexicans than the one originally proposed. While writing I receive from the quarter just mentioned the following note and memorandum, of which I annex translation marked "C." The information which failed to obtain from the affaires etrangères, in relation to Matamoras, I have had verbally from the minister of marine, whom I saw to-day. No orders have been sent for the occupation of that port, it being impossible at this moment to dispose of a sufficient number of troops for that purpose. I think that the minister is now fully impressed with the gravity of the error which has been committed in neglecting that most important point and is disposed to correct it as soon as possible. I have also explained to him the necessity of occupying Guaymas with a small corps sustained by the presence in the neighborhood of a respectable squadron. This force may be made the *point d'appui* of an extensive emigration from California of natives of the Southern States whom circumstances have compelled hitherto to remain inactive spectators of a contest in which their ardent sympathies are enlisted, but in which they would thus have an opportunity of indirectly participating. You may perhaps soon hear that such a policy has been inaugurated. The minister informed me that instructions have been given to release the arms by *Goodyear* and *Love Bird* unconditionally, and that no future trouble of that sort need be apprehended.

I have the honor to be, with great respect, your most obedient servant,

JOHN SLIDELL.

Hon. J. P. BENJAMIN,
    Secretary of State, Richmond.

[Enclosures.]

A.

[Memorandum which M. Slidell respectfully requests M. Mocquard to submit to the Emperor.]

PARIS, *December 4, 1863.*

The speedy occupation of Matamoras by the French troops is required by every consideration, military and political. The failure to occupy it has already been productive of the most mischievous consequences. Two vessels laden with arms for the Confederate States have been seized at the mouth of the Rio Grande by French cruisers and carried to Vera Cruz on the ground of their cargoes being destined for Matamoras, at which point they might be converted to the use of the partisans of Juarez. The first vessel seized has been released at Vera Cruz, but the condition of the release was that she should not proceed to a port occupied by the Mexicans. The second vessel was seized under circumstances peculiarly vexatious; she had already landed a portion of the arms at Point Isabel, Tex.. where they were received by the Confederate general in command; the remainder would have been landed in like manner without authority from or communication with the Mexican authorities on the southern side of the Rio Grande. It is understood that an order has been given to release this vessel, but the undersigned is ignorant whether she will be allowed to return to the Rio Grande. The arms detained are in number about 16,000; an equal number of efficient men were waiting to receive them. Had these men been armed, the Federal force, which has recently occupied Brownsville and now controls the northern banks of the Rio Grande, would have been captured or repulsed. All these facts are established by evidence which the undersigned has communicated to the minister of foreign affairs. The Texas bank of the Rio Grande will now be the point of departure of Federal emissaries to excite the population of northern Mexico in favor of Juarez, furnishing subsidies of money and munitions of war; men, too, will be forthcoming when required to sustain the cause of democracy against imperial institutions. The Emperor too readily appreciates the immense consequences which may result from the occupation of the Rio Grande by hostile instead of friendly armies to require that the undersigned should dilate upon them.

JOHN SLIDELL.

B.

LIVERPOOL, *December 2, 1863.*

DEAR SIR: Enclosed we hand you statement of the facts in the case of the silver ex *Eagle*, together with a letter from our legal advisers on the subject. We agree with them in the opinion that we have a very bad case, and we should be glad to have your authority on behalf of the Government to abandon it and stop expenses.

We are, dear sir, yours, respectfully,

FRASER TRENHOLM & Co.

Hon. JOHN SLIDELL, *Paris.*

SILVER.

LIVERPOOL, *December 2, 1863.*

DEAR SIR: We send you a short statement of the facts as they stand on the evidence before us. It is possible that M. Lavenga may be a mere agent for some Northerner in the background and that the real destination of the vessel was New York. But, if so, the onus will be on you to prove this, for there is at present prima facie evidence to show that the destination of the cargo was Europe, that the silver was Lavenga's, that F. Huth & Co. had a right to its possession under the bills of lading. Further, the want of proper information from Bermuda leads to the inference that the silver never was bought by N. S. Walker at all, but that the means adopted were designed simply to cover the transit of the silver to England, securing to the parties in Bermuda their share of the spoil, and handing the balance over to the proper quarter. If M. Bourne had given you the same information in his first letter you have since obtained, we doubt whether we should have advised you to accept the consignment. The certificate of M. Hunter was not sent you in the letter of 25th July, but was enclosed in a letter of the 30th July without any comment.

We are, yours, etc.,

FLETCHER & HULL.

Messrs. FRASER TRENHOLM & Co.

SILVER EX EAGLE.

DECEMBER 2, 1863.

The evidence shows as follows:

The silver was brought to Bermuda in the *Florida.*

The following events are said to have taken place on the undermentioned dates:

On 21st July the silver was weighed on board the *Florida* by M. T. T. Hunter, master's mate.

On 22d July N. S. Walker sold the silver to John T. Bourne. A sale note was drawn out, and N. S. Walker wrote a receipt, acknowledging to have received £19,951 from Mr. Bourne; Mr. Bourne gave a receipt for the silver endorsed on Hunter's certificate of weight, a certificate is given by the collector of customs that the silver is the property of M. Bourne, a bill of lading is given by Elias Norfolk, master of the *Eagle*, and the silver was sent in a boat of the *Florida* from the *Florida* to the *Eagle.*

On the 25th July Mr. Bourne draws a bill of exchange on Fraser Trenholm & Co. for £2,774 5s., and annexes it to the bill of lading, and on the same day writes Fraser Trenholm & Co., requesting them to place this bill to the credit of his account to pay £10,000 to Captain Maffitt and the balance to the account of the Confederate Navy.

Nothing is said as to how Walker became possessed of it, but it is alleged that Bourne paid Walker £19, 951.

There is no doubt about this silver having been taken from the *B. F. Hoxie*, as the certificate of the master's mate, the particulars of the assayer, and the invoices sent F. Huth & Co. by M. Lavenga show this.

There is no evidence to show that it has been condemned by any court of law, and a question may arise whether a captor who can not take a captured vessel into a prize court may not sell, but if he may, under the exigency, the question is still left whether a subsequent condemnation is not essential to confirm the sale.

Then the question remains, "Was the silver the property of a neutral or of a belligerent?" The cargo of the *B. F. Hoxie* consisted of, besides the silver, Brazil wood, lead ore, and hides. She was to call at Falmouth for orders. The silver and lead ore were consigned to F. Huth & Co. The wood and hides by Melchior Brothers, of Atala [Arica?], to Melchoir, Gebb & Co., of Bremen, correspondents of F. Huth & Co. F. Huth & Co. insured the whole of the cargo and have got paid. F. Huth & Co. received bills of lading for the silver and lead ore by mail. Lavenga is an old and regular correspondent of F. Huth & Co.

Above are the facts.

FLETCHER & HULL.

PARIS, *December 4, 1863.*

DEAR SIRS: I have your letter of 2d instant. enclosing me a statement of the facts in the case of the silver ex *Eagle*, together with a letter from your legal advisers on the subject. You say that you agree with them in the opinion that you have a very bad case and would be glad to have my authority on behalf of the Government to abandon it and stop expenses. I have not, as you seem to suppose, any right to give you authority to abandon the case, but I will very cheerfully give you my opinion for what it may be worth.

I agree with your legal advisers in the opinion that the papers referred to by them leave no reason to expect that a prize court would condemn the property if such proof or any other which might reasonably be expected to be produced hereafter were adduced before it, and I regret that Captain Maffitt on his arrival at Bermuda did not place it in deposit to await the order of the consignees. But the case, as I understand it, does not now present itself as one to which the Confederate States are parties, although were it decided in your favor as consignees from John T. Bourne, they would be entitled to receive a moiety of the net proceeds of the silver. You received the silver as the agent of Bourne, burdened, it seems, by a lien in his favor of £2,774 5s., which your legal advisers in the note accompanying their statement of facts, I presume, refer to as the "share of the spoils," and which the parties in Bermuda were to secure from a simulated sale and transfer of the property. I think that under the case presented the Confederate States can in no way be held responsible for the £2,774 5s. or for the expenses which have been or may be incurred in connection with the silver ex *Eagle*, and that as to any contingent interest they may be supposed to have in the matter you will incur no responsibility in abandoning it.

Yours, truly,

JOHN SLIDELL.

Messrs. FRASER, TRENHOLM & CO.,
　　　　　Liverpool.

LIVERPOOL, *December 8, 1863.*

DEAR SIR: We beg to return our thanks for your letter of 4th instant and for the valuable opinion which it contains on the subject of the silver ex *Eagle.* It was all we desired to have and we were in error in asking your authority on behalf of the Government to abandon the case. We shall now proceed to compromise it on the best terms we can and must of course look in the first instance to Mr. Bourne to refund us all the expenses we have incurred.

We are dear sir, yours faithfully,

FRASER, TRENHOLM & CO.

Hon. JOHN SLIDELL,
Paris.

___

C.

[Translation.]

No one has been able, I must confess, to let me know whether Matamoras is blockaded or occupied by us. I am nevertheless of your opinion respecting the importance of the reasons urging the necessity of coming to a decision on this point. I am requested to call your attention to the accompanying note, and I trust that you will write to your Government in view of the realization of the facilities which it promised to extend for the dispatching of the tobacco owned by the Régie at Richmond.

The French Régie owns in Richmond from six to seven thousand hogsheads of tobacco which can not be exported owing to the Federal blockade. The Confederate Government as far back as the month of March spontaneously gave to the French consul at Richmond the assurance that it would throw no obstacle to their exportation. On the other hand the Washington Government has just issued an order commanding the commander of the squadron to allow the neutral vessels on which this tobacco may be shipped to France to pass freely. It is to be hoped that the friendly disposition manifested on the previous occasion alluded to has undergone no change, and that the Confederate Government will do all in its power to facilitate the accomplishment of an operation so important to the interests of the French administration.

___

No. 34.]   CONFEDERATE STATES COMMERCIAL AGENCY,
London, December 26, 1863.

SIR: Nothing could have been happier than the coincidence which caused the simultaneous publication in all the London journals of both the messages, that of President Davis and that of Abraham Lincoln. In the words of one of our most eloquent English advocates, writing in the Index of December 24, "There was no need, perhaps, of a stronger contrast between the two Presidents of North and South; but if anything would fully illustrate the disproportionate capacities and the opposite characters of the two men, it would be the messages that have reached us simultaneously from Richmond and from Washington." Although the President has

taken a view of the late affairs at Chattanooga far more unfavorable than that generally entertained by the press here, which argued
upon the assumption that Bragg was already in full retreat, that
his rear guard alone was attacked, and held the various positions just
long enough to gain time, the conviction that from the picture drawn
by the President we know the worst, and the impress of stern truthfulness which it bears have produced a marked improvement in the
spirits of our sympathizers, which, it must be confessed, were fast
sinking to a low ebb of despondency. The unanswerable manner in
which the breach of faith is brought home to the British Government affords the much wanted point d'appui for our friends in the
press and in the ensuing session of Parliament.

What here, as at home, causes now the most serious anxiety is our
financial condition. Long painstaking reflection has enlisted me
thoroughly in the essential features of the plan recommended to the
Treasury Department by Mr. C. J. McRae, and which responds to
favorite ideas that since the earlier stages of the war have been
floating in a shape more or less vague in my mind. You will pardon
my speaking on this subject, for it is impossible that you or the
President should see the evils of the system at present pursued in
Europe as fully as those who witness its daily workings. Contracts are constantly made in Richmond which in the light of our
necessities appear there advantageous but which here seem ruinous
in the extreme. Fatal mistakes as to the business character of men
making fair offers are rendered unavoidable by the imperfected and
guarded nature of the information received by the Government from
agents who write with the fear of interception in their minds. It is
for these reasons that the opinion—even were the reasons assigned
insufficient—of those who act as your organs of sight and sound
here, is entitled to peculiar weight, and I am simply recording the
fact that there is, as far as I can judge, almost entire unanimity
among the officers and well-wishers of the Confederacy on the following points:

First. That blockade running is too irregular and exceptional a
trade to come under the ordinary laws of political economy; that it
is virtually a monopoly, and that Government should either assume
that monopoly, or so control it as to save the public the enormous
profits now made by private speculators.

Second. That the Government has the same or even better chances
than private enterprise for profiting by the monopoly to the fullest
extent, provided a suitable organization is devised; but that it has
the option to leave the risk of exportation to the holders of its bonds,
a risk amply covered by the difference between the stipulated price
and the average Liverpool prices.

Third. That so long as cotton can be purchased with any other
medium than bonds, the European price of these bonds can no more
be kept above the rate of exchange than water can be made to rise
over its level; and that our foreign and home securities mutually
so react on each other, that what materially raises or depresses the
one similarly affects the others.

Fourth. That for reasons not prudent to mention, but which you
will fully appreciate, the recovery of our foreign loan to a rate even
distantly approximating to issue rate, will give us ample funds, not

only for all our purchases at cash, but for supplying our citizens with articles of first necessity at moderate prices and still leave a surplus with which, if desired, to redeem a portion of our home debt.

Fifth. That even in the least unfavorable contracts heretofore made with private individuals, the contractors have as a rule traded chiefly with the Government's credit, furnishing but little or no capital of their own, and therefore holding out no advantages which could not have been realized without their intermediation and at the saving of the profits pocketed by them.

Sixth. That it is absolutely hopeless to expect to receive any really serviceable vessels of war from the ports of either England or France, and that our expenditure should therefore be confined to more practicable objects and our naval staff be employed in eluding, since we can not break, the blockade.

Seventh. That if the virtually unlimited pecuniary resources which we command, instead of as heretofore exploited for the advantage of foreigners and speculators, who build princely fortunes upon our necessities, are reserved for the public use, we shall occupy a financial position in Europe which will extort recognition sooner than the most powerful arguments of the pen or even of the sword.

If scruples arise from the magnitude of this scheme of embargo I should answer that the remedy must be proportionate to the disease, and that that is a remedy often to the morbid body which would be poison to the healthy one. I differ, however, from some friends whose opinions I respect highly, in not considering the purchase of the cotton crop necessary. Such a measure besides the constitutional difficulties, would work unjustly, and would still further inflate the currency. It suffices, in my opinion, for the realization of all the important results, at home and abroad of the embargo on private exportation, that the Government should buy, without ostentation and at ruling prices, only such quantities as it has the means to export immediately. Every one, I am well aware, will be ready with a remedy which in his opinion is the only efficacious one, but as I do not claim the paternity of the measure which I have sketched, I may express myself as to its value without offending against modesty or propriety. I repeat, therefore: Prohibit the exportation of cotton, except for Government account or in redemption of bonds; under these conditions send cotton out as rapidly as may be, prohibit the importation of luxuries on any pretence, and import shoes and clothes as well for the citizens as the Army; rescind, as far as consistent with good faith, all private contracts whatever. When Europe shall see our securities rising and those of our enemy falling, the conviction which is now hesitating, will then march steadily to active conclusions, and perhaps it may then also begin to dawn on the minds of the North. But no time is to be lost. Next spring may witness the first throes of a European convulsion, and it will then be too late.

The success which has generally attended our private conveyance through the North, has suggested to me to utilize it for more important communications than my own. I have therefore invited a few of the principal officers of the Government to transmit, in case of urgency, brief messages by it, which Mr. Macfarland has kindly consented to translate into the State Department cipher. Of course this will not be done except for sufficient reasons, and I mention it only by way of premonition.

I have your unofficial letter of the 4th November with enclosures, for which I am sincerely obliged. Your plan of making my remittances periodically payable, without depending on the chances of blockade, will be an important economy of time and thought to me. On the subject of Poland, I can now only say that the insurrection, however much of heroism and patriotic devotion it has subsequently embodied, appears to me to have been to a great extent artificially stimulated by a wonderfully dextrous management of the press and the telegraph and by a special machinery that no other nation than one of generations of illustrious exiles can command. It therefore has in its origin the germ of death. But Europe is a powder magazine which the slightest spark can explode. Already the insurrection has directly alienated France and Russia, and indirectly, through the proposed Congress, given the coup de grâce to the Anglo-French alliance. A brief business visit to Paris has strongly impressed me with the fact that the situation is much more tendre than I venture to explain to you. Moreover, the Germans are very thoroughly in earnest in the Schleswig-Holstein question, and this, with the blundering of Earl Russell and the German sympathies of the Queen, seem to make the dismemberment of the Danish monarchy either as a cause or as a result of a general European war, inevitable.

Your Irish agents, whose reports I enclose, will inform you of the state of things there. A curious result of the premature publications of the depositions previously mentioned, which happened accidentally and contrary to my advice, has been that the *Kearsarge* returned to Queenstown and landed the men enlisted.

Of my own operations, the recent unfortunate fate of the correspondence of others renders it prudent that I should say but little. Suffice it that I am progressing satisfactorily, though I have to efface the unpleasant impressions produced by this and other publications that the agents of the Confederacy boast of bribing the press, a charge intrinsically absurd, since, even if we condescended to so dishonorable a policy, we would not be rich enough to adopt it. I have the more pleasure therefore in transmitting you two valuable pamphlets, genuine fruits of English thought, not oranges brought to a Christmas tree to be plucked, which cost the Confederacy nothing save what I may at my own discretion pay as an ordinary purchaser, and upon this the authors, both of whom I know intimately, did not in any degree depend, though I mean of course to purchase liberally for distribution. A glance over these pamplets, with this explanation, will show you what enormous progress we have made in English public opinion. The virus of antislavery prejudice was in the blood; no external application could cure it; but the antidote is now entered into the blood also, and follows it in its circulation through the body literary and politic. The authorship of another very little pamphlet in Italian, being an article extracted from a leading liberal journal at Turin, you will have no difficulty to trace. It has been translated both into the French and English papers. I can only regret that Turin is not a more important field of action.

I am about to try the same experiment elsewhere. Let only our armies and our currency hold out a little while longer and we shall enter the assemblage of nations without being asked to wash the robe of our nationality " of a foul stain."

I remain with great respect, your obedient servant,

HENRY HOTZE.

Hon. J. P. BENJAMIN,
Secretary of State, Richmond.

No. 71.] PARIS, *December 28, 1863.*

SIR: Upon quitting Rome I went direct to Naples, an agreeable railroad run of nine hours' duration.

I was anxious to see the operations of a liberal system of government upon the recognized " Queen City" of southern Europe. It had been often said that no political influences could relieve her from the enervating effects of a tropical climate; that it was not so much tyrannous rule as a scorching sun that impaired her energies; but to my astonishment, I found her among the most demonstrative commercial cities which I have visited upon the Continent. In all the pursuits in which she is engaged there seems to be an industrious activity which would contrast not unfavorably with that of New Orleans in her most prosperous days. Numbering already some 500,000 inhabitants her course seems to be rapidly onward and upward. I was assured, from various reliable sources, that she had entered upon an utterly new existence since she cast off the iron yoke of King Bomba; that she was eminently prosperous; that the idle did not infest her streets as formerly; and that labor was adequately rewarded for its toils.

After a sojourn of four days I embarked for Leghorn, and from thence traveled leisurely—stopping at Pisa, Florence, and Bologna several days—to Turin, where I remained only eighteen hours. The King was absent. Had he been at home I should have been inclined to ask an audience of him, as a citizen of the Confederate States.

Throughout Italy, as far as I was enabled to ascertain from my bankers and numerous other intelligent individuals, enlightened public sentiment is beginning steadily to array itself against " Lincoln and Company," and to manifest an earnest desire for the establishment of peace. There is no longer a charm in the name of Garibaldi, even for the masses. He is generally esteemed as patriotic, pure, and heroic, but deplorably deficient in that most essential quality to the creation of true greatness—common sense. The impious comparison which he made of Abraham Lincoln to Jesus Christ has damaged largely his reputation in all Catholic circles while it has popularized our cause.

From Turin I crossed over Mont Cenis and hastened to this metropolis, where I arrived at 8 o'clock the day after Christmas. At 11 I visited Mr. Slidell, who immediately dispatched his servant to inform Mr. Mason that I was with him. In a few minutes Mr. Mason came in. I then communicated to them in detail the incidents of my mission to Rome, and placed before them copies of the correspondence between the President and the Pope. After its careful perusal, they united in opinion that its early publication on this side of the Atlantic was of almost paramount importance to the influencing of valuable public opinion, in both hemispheres, in our favor. I hesitated as to the propriety of such a procedure with respect to the letter of the Pope, before the reception of its contents by the President, notwithstanding his Holiness prepared it for universal dissemination. I preferred to give, instead, its supposed substances with the direction, which in itself was positive recognition. But I was met by the remark that the nature of the document, for practical effect, would be vastly impaired before it could appear to the public eye at Richmond under the authorization of the President. I then placed in the hands of Mr. Slidell a copy of the correspondence, which was subsequently recopied by Mr. Eustis. Mr. Slidell was to go to-day to the foreign office to secure its insertion in the Moniteur.

I leave here at 5 o'clock this afternoon for Brussels. After a sojourn there of a few days, where a heavy correspondence of two months' accumulation awaits me, I shall go over to London to make the result of my visit to Rome as advantageously known as possible. Mr. Mason and Mr. Slidell cordially approved of this intention. Indeed, I was earnestly urged by them not to relinquish my purpose.

I have the honor to be, sir, very respectfully, your obedient servant,

A. DUDLEY MANN.

Hon. J. P. BENJAMIN,
    Secretary of State, C. S. America, Richmond, Va.

No. 52.]   PARIS, *December 29, 1863.*

SIR: Since I last had the honor of addressing you on the 15th instant I have had reason to modify if not to change the opinion I then expressed of the probable action of the Archduke Maximilian in relation to Mexico. M. Gutierrez has recently received letters from Miramar in which the archduke speaks most decidedly of his intention to embark for Vera Cruz in time to pass through the Tierra Caliente before the commencement of the sickly season. This would seem to be unimpeachable authority, and yet persons who from their position ought to be well informed are still incredulous; on the other hand, Mexican securities have risen very considerably within the last few days.

In conjunction with Mr. McRae, I have assumed the responsibility of making with the Albion Trading Company, of London, a contract by which four superior steamers are placed at the disposition of our Government for the transportation of supplies from Bermuda and Nassau to the Confederacy on highly favorable terms. Mr. McRae has forwarded copies of the contract, the conditions of which I think will be found very satisfactory. I have furnished Mr. McRae with a memorandum of the receipts which I have given for bonds of the Erlanger loan presented to and canceled by me up to this date, amounting to £66,600. He will forward copies to the Secretary of the Treasury.

I have arranged with Mr. Chasseloup [-Laubat] for the filling up of the *Florida's* crew, that vessel being now ready for sea. The minister shows the best disposition to grant in naval matters all possible facilities, although, as he informs me, Mr. Dayton is very urgent in his remonstrances.

Mr. Mann has returned from Rome. He has sent you the answer of the Pope to the President's letter. He entertained some doubt as to the propriety of giving publicity to the correspondence until he should have heard in reply from Richmond and consulted Mr. Mason and me on the subject. We expressed the opinion that publication was expedient; the correspondence will very soon appear in the newspapers. It is not improbable that the answer of his Holiness will first reach the President through that channel.

The reply of the Emperor to the address of the Senate and the circular of M. Drouyn de Lhuys to the French diplomatic agents in Europe are considered as very pacific in their tendencies, but the uneasiness to which I have referred in my previous dispatch does not seem to have been abated by them. You will find copies herewith.

The messages of Presidents Davis and Lincoln appeared simultaneously in the European journals. The contrast in tone, thought, and style between those two documents is so remarkable as to have struck even the most careless readers. The manly frankness with which our Chief Magistrate exposes all the difficulties of our position and the calm and determined spirit in which he discusses the proper mode of meeting them command universal respect and admiration.

I had left this dispatch open, that I might have the opportunity of seeing my friend at the affaires etrangères. I have just left him. He removes all doubts about the Archduke's course; he positively accepts and will leave Triest for Vera Cruz before the end of March, but will in the meanwhile come to Paris to consult with the Emperor. Large reinforcements will be sent to Mexico; among them will be the Foreign Legion, one battalion of which is already there. The French minister at Brussels is instructed to urge upon the King of the Belgians, whose daughter is the wife of Maximilian, a cordial public approbation of the course of the Archduke.

I have the honor to be, sir, with great respect, your most obedient servant,

JOHN SLIDELL.

Hon. J. P. BENJAMIN,
Secretary of State.

Dispatch No. 25.] HAVANA, January 1, 1864.

SIR: It is a source of congratulation both to my Government and to myself to be enabled to report to the Department that his Excellency the Captain-General Dulce and all other officials of Cuba continue friendly; that in the exercise of their official duty, under their neutrality, we have nothing to complain of. Our people who are here on business, or as exiles, are treated with kind consideration, and everything possible is done to relieve them from such embarassments as naturally occur in a Government organized as is this, in the absence of an official recognition of their representative; indeed, matters move on so smoothly here now, that I have but little to report to your Department. Our friends are still full of confidence.

Having been successful in procuring several steamers, I am again active in purchasing and forwarding supplies for the Army. The arms captured by the French near Matamoras and taken to Vera Cruz, referred to in my dispatch No. 24, were released to the owners on my representation that they were destined for the Confederate States.

The correspondence between President Davis and the Pope has been read here with great interest, and will do us much good.

I have the honor to be, with profound respect, your obedient servant,

CH. J. HELM.

Hon. J. P. BENJAMIN,
      Secretary of State, Richmond.

No. 2.]   DEPARTMENT OF STATE,
                                      Richmond, January 7, 1864.

SIR: The instructions contained in my No. 1 were prepared before your appointment, and were submitted to the Senate with a view to obtaining its advice, before your departure, as to the policy which the President proposed to pursue in relation to Mexico.

The policy has been approved by that body with one modification, which is that the "reciprocal free trade proposed on the frontier be extended to all parts of the two countries, and limited the articles, the growth, produce, and manufacture thereof, respectively." You will therefore consider your instructions so modified as to conform with the amendment introduced by the Senate.

I now desire to add some further matters to those contained in my No. 1.

I. The principal source of disquietude as to the success of your mission arises from the well-known purpose of the United States to spare no means of effecting its object of subjugating these States. The diplomacy of Mr. Seward will know no scruples. It will hesitate at no promises, and may attempt to ally itself with Mexico and offer to the new government any terms to secure the rejection of our overtures. It will therefore be incumbent on you to use every effort to convince the Government of Mexico of the real purpose of the United States as revealed in their Congress and their press, as well as in utterances that have fallen from the lips of the chief personages in their administration. Their cry now is "one war at a time." Their purpose is, if successful in their designs on us, to extend their conquests by the annexation of Canada on the north and Mexico on the south. Their policy will still be "one war at a time." They will commence with what they deem the easiest prey. With the necessity pressing on them to find employment for the vast armies that would be set free by the submission of the South, they would have no choice but to make Mexico the field of a new war of aggression. It would be a fatuity without example to believe that any promises, any treaty stipulations now made by the United States would form the slightest obstacle to any projects that might in the future be deemed advantageous by the men who may happen to be in power in Washington. History affords innumerable examples of the futility of any mere treaty barriers to the designs of ambitious nations. The danger is tenfold increased where a government, like that of the United States, has become so debased as to be under the control of the lowest classes, ready to sacrifice all justice and principle for the gratification of the lust of conquest. You are perhaps aware that not only has the press of the party in power in the United States been bitter in its denunciation of the recent change of government in Mexico, but in their Senate a resolution has been offered to declare war on France for its action in Mexico, as being a violation of the Monroe doctrine. The source whence this resolution proceeded is full of fatal significance for Mexico. It was a California Senator who proposed it. Lower California, Sonora, and Sinaloa have long been looked on by Californians as their easy and assured prey whenever the occasion shall be opportune for seizing those defenseless provinces. The future safety of the Mexican Empire is inextricably bound up with the safety and independence of the Confederacy. Mexico must indulge in no illusion on this point. The day that witnesses the consummation of the Northern designs against these States will be the dawn of a similar fate for Mexico.

II. It is not at all improbable that in the complications and collisions likely to grow up on the frontier of Texas, where the forces of the United States are now stationed, a conflict may arise between the French troops and those of the United States. Like conflicts may also occur between their naval forces at the Brazos. It will be advisable to keep yourself well informed as to what occurs on that frontier and you may perhaps find means to bring about such collision and thus engage France in the alliance against the United States. Your communications with the French minister, Mr. Montholon, will give you opportunities also of impressing on him our views of the benefits that would accrue to France from a strict alliance with this country.

The topic is familiar to you and does not need elaboration. You will find Mr. Montholon well disposed toward the Confederacy, and it is not improbable that he would be willing so far to confide in you as to give information that would be very valuable, touching the ultimate policy and views of France, as connected both with the Mexican Empire and these States.

III. You will use every endeavor to assist and promote the introduction of supplies of all kinds into the Confederacy, both across the frontier and through Mexican ports, and will come to an understanding on this point with the French minister in Mexico, if possible.

IV. Your attention is specially called to the subject of destroying as far as possible the commerce of the enemy on the Pacific Ocean and in the Gulf of Mexico. Their commerce on the Western Ocean is almost defenseless. We have received two applications on the subject of letters of marque on the Pacific Ocean. I annex copies of them and of the laws and regulations on the subject of privateering. I send you also the messenger who brought the letter from Mazatlan, and confide, by the President's instructions, to your discretion the whole subject. You will perceive that by the 3d section of the law of 6th May, 1861, the Department is authorized to confide to its officers the delivery of letters of marque, and you are furnished with 10 commissions ready for delivery. As soon as you determine upon the proper policy to be pursued on this point, you will apprise the writers of the two letters of which the copies are annexed.

It is not thought probable that Mexico will object to the issue of these commissions, as Mexico and Spain both refused to become parties to that clause of the declaration of Paris of 1856, which abolished privateering, and both expressed their determination to exercise their right, under the general law of nations, to commission privateers in the event of future wars.

V. A cipher is provided for secret correspondence. In using it you are requested to be very careful to decipher your own dispatch before forwarding it, in order to be certain of accuracy. The key should never run through more than two or three lines without renewal. The cipher is the same as Mr. Slidell's, and it is expected that you keep each other mutually advised of matters that can be made serviceable in the interest of the Government.

VI. Annexed is a list of all the documents and papers with which you are furnished.

VII. Mr. J. A. Quintero is the general agent of this Department on the Rio Grande frontier in Mexico, and his address is at Monterey. Mr. R. Fitzpatrick is the commercial agent of this Government at the town of Matamoras. They will of course pursue your instructions in any matters about which you may give them directions, touching the public interests, as soon as it is known to them that you have been publicly recognized as our Minister.

In conclusion you are requested to use the promptest efforts to establish certain and speedy means of communication with the Department.

With great respect, your obedient servant,

J. P. BENJAMIN,
Secretary of State.

General WILLIAM PRESTON,
Envoy Extraordinary and Minister
Plenipotentiary to the Government of Mexico.

No. 27.] DEPARTMENT OF STATE,
Richmond, January 8, 1864.

SIR: Since my No. 26, of 9th ultimo, your Nos. 47, 48, and 49 have been received, the first on the 10th and the last two on the 18th ultimo.

The President is much gratified at your course in relation to the contract with Nelson Clements, and on the information supplied by you not only has his contract been annulled but the most stringent orders have been sent forbidding absolutely the making of contracts for foreign supplies by any of the subordinate officers of the Government. Their attempt to do so was an usurpation only to be excused by the most stringent necessity, and no such necessity existed, for if supplies were required in the ports of the trans-Mississippi it was easy to send the information of the need to our purchasing agents in Europe, as well as to Richmond. There could be no need either of sending agents abroad to make purchases or of contracting with speculators at home.

The passages contained in cipher in your No. 48 have been scanned very closely and the effect produced on our minds is not altogether satisfactory. On the contrary, painful solicitude is still felt, but in this instance also we may meet with the double-dealing from which we have suffered so severely since the beginning of our struggle.

Hopeful as I am in temper, there was something in what passed in the interview to which you refer that indicated a desire to escape from plighted faith and a scarcely disguised impatience of the burden and responsibility imposed by previous engagements which fills me with distrust. The same effect has been produced on the President. It may be overanxiety on our part, as we may have been misled in our impressions by reason of the very meager account which the embarrassment of a cipher correspondence has constrained you to give. I would be glad to have your own conclusions fully and frankly stated as to what we may expect on this subject.

In relation to the occupation of Matamoras and the arrangements to prevent a repetition of the incidents from which we have hitherto been the sufferers there, we are quite satisfied as regards the future. It is impossible to refrain from the remark that by some fatality every movement made by the French Government, however amicable its intentions, has been disastrous to us. Wherever the French officials have had an opportunity of acting without the supervision of the Emperor there has been a disregard of our rights and interests evincing almost a hostile feeling. Such was undoubtedly the case in the seizure of the *Caroline Goodyear*, for the proof that the cargo was for us was so conclusive that no officer having the least regard to fair dealing toward us would have availed himself of the opportunity to act as the French admiral did. The blow struck at us by his act was much more severe than you or his Government can well appreciate. Every musket then seized was equivalent to capturing a soldier from our ranks.

I am not at all surprised at the account you give of the action of the Northern emissaries in suborning perjury, committing thefts, and forging documents for the furtherance of their objects. No crime is too revolting for this vile race, which disgraces civilization and causes one to blush for our common humanity. You have been removed from the scenes of their outrages, and are evidently startled at conduct on their part, which we look for as quite naturally to be expected. A people who have been engaged for the last three years in forging our Treasury notes, cheating in the exchange of prisoners of war, exciting slaves to the murder of their masters, plundering private property without a semblance of scruple, burning dwellings, breaking up and destroying agricultural implements, violating female honor, and murdering prisoners in cold blood, not to speak of Greek fire, stone fleets, and other similar expedients of warfare, would scarcely refrain from such trifles as those which excite your indignation. I entertain no doubt whatever that hundreds of thousands of people at the North would be frantic with fiendish delight if informed of the universal massacre of the Southern people, including women and children, in one night. They would then only have to exterminate the blacks (which they are fast doing now), and they would become owners of the property which they covet, and for which they are fighting.

Our relations with Mexico are likely to assume a very interesting complexion, and I send you copy of the instructions issued to the Hon. William Preston, of Kentucky. You will perceive from them the present and prospective condition of affairs, and an outline of the policy of the Government. You will also perceive that to facilitate the free intercommunication between your mission and that to Mexico, the same cipher and key words have been furnished to him as were given to you.

I am, very respectfully, your obedient servant,

J. P. BENJAMIN,
Secretary of State.

Hon. JOHN SLIDELL,
Paris, France.

P. S.—Please inform me in each dispatch of the condition of our vessels and probable date of delivery.

No. 15.]   JANUARY 9, [1864].

Since my last, January 2, I have ascertained that various drafts drawn by Frank Lacy Brieton [Bruxton ?] for amounts varying from £150 to £300 have been received in London, and were found to be on firms having no existence, but whose names bore just sufficient resemblance to that of existing firms to deceive. Thus " Gurney & Co.," of London, were drawn on, this mythical firm name being borrowed from " Overend Gurney & Co." There can thus be no doubt as to the scoundrel's character, and I hope proceedings will be at once instituted. Another fact worth knowing is that the writer of the description of the defenses of Wilmington in New York Herald, 10th November, is in all probability Baron Robert Konig, a German, supposed to have reentered the service of the United States. He went to Wilmington to tender his services to the Confederate States, but was refused on the ground of having previously served in the Army of their enemies. If captured it will probably fare hard with him.

In business there is little doing. The Southern finances are in critical condition in Europe, as well as in the Confederacy. The bonds are sustained at their present low price even only by the expectation of an embargo on cotton, which is warmly recommended by all the Southerners in Europe, but of which the silence of the message and the Secretary's report give little hope to calmer speculators. So long as cotton can be bought with gold or goods in a Southern port at 2 pence, of course the bonds are not worth more per pound of the cotton they call for. Besides, contracts are constantly coming out from various Government bureaus which promise delivery at the port, while the Erlanger bonds only promise delivery in the interior. If all private exportation were prohibited and all private contracts annulled, these bonds would at once rise to par or nearly par, and the Government could negotiate new loans for six or eight millions sterling. Such are actually offered by leading bankers at 80 per cent, on condition of the embargo. The Government might then besides buying all it wants offer to redeem its home currency with sterling exchange, thus reducing its debt and preventing depreciation. Of the plan proposed by Mr. Memminger, it is said here with great force that even if he could get the specie to pay the interest on the funded debt it would amount to as much in one year's interest as the whole debt could now be bought for in specie. It is wonderful that what we see so clearly here should apparently not be seen there. Please think over the matter and represent it to

our firm. As for business in contracts, tell them that there are many
which yield fabulous profits even after the agent here has reduced
the rates by 30 or 50 per cent. I have seen a contract made by a
bureau to pay £40 a ton for freight reduced here to £25 per ton by
the agent who, if he had had full powers, could have reduced it to
£8. A single house here boasts of having made £200,000. Of course
all these things are known in business circles, and the comments are
not favorable to the business capacity of our own firm or to its solvency and credit. If the embargo was passed we could put 10
steamers of our own on in four months, and our whole business at
home would be carried on with funds placed abroad. Important
memorandum for shipping clerk annexed in our own cipher. Please
acknowledge receipt of this.

DEPARTMENT OF STATE,
Richmond, February 23, 1864.

SIR: I have the honor to enclose herewith a copy of a communication to your address from Captain Bulloch. It was annexed, in the
cipher used by this Department, to a letter just received from Henry
Hotze, esq., commercial agent of the Confederate States at London.

I have the honor to be, very respectfully, your obedient servant,

J. P. BENJAMIN,
Secretary of State.

Hon S. R. MALLORY,
Secretary of Navy.

No. 13.]
DEPARTMENT OF STATE,
Richmond, January 9, 1864.

SIR: I have to acknowledge your several numbers as follows: No.
28, of 5 September, received 23d October, 1863; No. 29, of 26 September, received 23d October, 1863; No. 30, of 3 October, received
30th November, 1863; No. 31, of 31 October, received 10th December,
1863; No. 32, of 21 November, received 18th December, 1863.

Your appreciation of the tone and temper of public opinion in
France in your Nos. 29 and 31, although not in accordance with the
views of the other correspondents of the Department, concurs entirely in the conclusions to which I had arrived from the perusal of
the principal organs of French journalism. It has been impossible
to remain blind to the evidence of the articles which emanate from
the best-known names in French literature. In what is perhaps the
most powerful and influential of the French periodicals, La Revue
des Deux Mondes, there is scarcely an article signed by the members
of its able corps of contributors which does not contain some dis-
paraging allusion to the South. Abolition sentiments are quietly
assumed as philosophical axioms too self-evident to require comment
or elaboration, and the result of this struggle is in all cases treated
as a foregone conclusion, as nothing within the range of possibility
except the subjugation of the South and the emancipation of the
whole body of the negroes. The example of St. Domingo does not

seem in the least to disturb the faith of these philanthropists in the entire justice and policy of a war waged for this end, and our resistance to the fate proposed for us is treated as a crime against liberty and civilization. The Emperor is believed by us to be sincerely desirous of putting an end to the war by the recognition of our independence, but, powerful as he is, he is too sagacious to act in direct contravention of the settled public opinion of his people while hampered by the opposition of the English Government.

I fully appreciate the wisdom and prudence of your suggestions relative to the distinction which ought to be made by the press and by our Government between the English Government and people. You will doubtless have observed that the President's message is careful (while exposing the duplicity and bad faith of the English cabinet and Earl Russell's course of abject servility toward the stronger party and insulting arrogance toward the weaker) to show no feeling of resentment toward the English people. The sentiment of wrong and injustice done to us, of advantage meanly taken of our distresses, of conduct toward our representative in London unworthy of a man possessing the instincts of a gentleman, all combine to produce an irritation which it is exceedingly difficult for the most temperate to restrain, and Earl Russell has earned an odium among our people so intense as to require the utmost caution on the part of those in authority to prevent its expression in a form that would be injurious to the public interests. At the same time we have not failed to observe and to appreciate at its full value the warm and generous sympathy which the intelligent and cultivated classes of English society have exhibited toward us in no stinted measure.

Your remarks in relation to Mr. Spence have been carefully weighed. You have perceived with your usual acuteness the exact embarrassment under which we labor in dealing with this gentleman, whose ability and services to our cause are recognized to the fullest extent. But Mr. Spence must be regarded in one of two respects, either as an English gentleman entirely independent of all connection with our Government, and therefore at full liberty to express his sentiments and opinions about our institutions and people, or as an agent or officer of this Government, and therefore supposed to speak with a certain authority on all matters connected with our country. In this latter aspect it could not be permitted that he should make speeches denunciatory of its policy or institutions. No man can reconcile the exigencies of these two positions, and if connected with the Government Mr. Spence must of necessity forego the expression of his individual opinion on points where they differ from those of the Government which he serves. Now this is precisely what I understand Mr. Spence is unwilling to do. I send you enclosed an answer to a letter he has written to me, which you may read before sealing and forwarding it to him.

The article in the New York Herald, to which you refer as having caused you annoyance, was republished here solely as a matter of merriment from its absurdity. It should not have dwelt on your mind for a moment, as there is scarcely a prominent individual in our service, at home or abroad, who has not been the subject of similar paragraphs, and they are not remembered by anybody after the laugh at their whimsical extravagance excited on the first perusal.

I am happy to inform you of the arrival of the stationery, except the two boxes sent through Collie & Co., and which arrived in Bermuda last June. I have written to Major Walker at Bermuda in relation to them, as I can hear nothing of them nor of the boxes of books sent me by Mr. Mason. I received the copy of Hansard (incomplete), and can hear nothing of the other boxes.

We have not deemed it advisable to make any use of the curious details contained in your No. 32 about the diamond bribery in high quarters. Richly as such a warfare is deserved by the party who would be exposed to it, we can not reconcile it to ourselves to use the weapon thus offered to us.

Whatever may be the efforts now made by our friends to give point and effect by popular meetings to such public opinion in our favor as may exist in England, we have long ceased to look for any results from that quarter. You may well judge by the President's message that his purpose was simply to record for the future instruction and guidance of ourselves and our children the conduct of Great Britain in this great crisis of our fate. Our judgment is now finally made up that the British cabinet deemed it best for Great Britain that some hundreds of thousands of human beings should be slaughtered on this continent that her people might reap profit and become more powerful. No other interpretation can account for the conduct which that cabinet has pursued, and which has aimed steadily at checking any movement toward peace. Even when one word would have stopped the war, and when France was ready, in alliance with her, to utter that word, so as to render it impossible for the United States to resent it, the English Government became alarmed lest peace should be restored before the United States had become sufficiently depleted of blood and treasure, and used active efforts to secure a continuance of hostilities. These things will long be remembered by a people whose sympathies in favor of Great Britain were of the warmest character before their feelings became first chilled and then alienated by the conduct of a cabinet which has betrayed the cause of humanity wherever power has sought to repress right. Our own wrongs have but heightened our sympathy for suffering Poland and increased our contempt for the so-called statesmanship which preserves a short-lived peace at the expense of duty to humanity and of the honor and dignity of a great nation.

Mr. Lamar has been with us some time, and has given us very interesting information on many points. His reports to the Department and to the President relative to your labors and services, and the conscientious devotion of your energies to the success of our cause, have greatly gratified us, and it is a pleasing duty to convey to you the approval of your Government.

Mr. de Leon having ceased to occupy the position assigned to him by the Government, you are at liberty to include France in your field of labor, if you find a favorable opening. I enclose you an order requesting Mr. McRae to pay over to you any sum that Mr. de Leon may have deposited with him in the unexpended balance of money in his hands.

I enclose you an extract from the Charleston Mercury, giving an idea of the low tricks to which the enemy resort on every conceivable occasion. I also send you herewith the correspondence of the commissioners for exchange of prisoners, which will enable you to give a good account of the merits of the controversy that the Northern Government seeks to cover with a cloud of mystification.

As soon as Congress passes the appropriation bill, I will send you a further remittance.

I am, very respectfully, your obedient servant,

J. P. BENJAMIN,
Secretary of State.

HENRY HOTZE, *London.*

P. S.—Your No. 33, of 28 November, has just reached me, with its enclosures.

[Translation.]

PARIS, *January 10, 1864.*

YOUR EXCELLENCY: I reply to your honored letter of the 27th October last, received at Paris the 20th December, 1863.

In your letter you offer me, in addition to the $500,000 that I asked you as the price of my invention of destruction, 50 per cent of the value of each vessel destroyed by my system. I accept this offer, persuaded as I am of the immense results which can not fail to be secured by one or two vessels of my system on the Federal vessels or others on which we shall agree to attack. It is now eighteen months since you might have been in possession of my method of destruction; judge of the immense success of which you have been deprived and of the enormous losses that you have undergone on account of a sure means of destroying ironclad vessels. Vicksburg was taken for lack of a Navy, New Orleans the same story; Charleston and its forts are bombarded, the trouble always being that you need the means of destroying ironclad monitors.

I would go myself to Richmond so as to explain my system to your Excellency, but no time must be lost in notifying me. I am sure of my facts, I assert nothing that I can not carry out. Here are the conditions for the advance of funds that are necessary for me to leave Paris. You will remit 1,000 pounds sterling in gold ten days before my departure from Paris or Havre; 2,000 pounds sterling in gold so soon as I embark at London or Liverpool for the Southern States of America, and these 3,000 pounds sterling will be deducted from the $500,000, the price agreed upon as the value of the invention. As soon as your Excellency shall become acquainted with the invention the sum of $500,000 will be due me, and half of the sum should be remitted to me in gold, European exchange, and afterwards the other half shall be paid to me after my system is crowned with success. My sincerity and respectability I offer as a guaranty to remain in Richmond or Mobile or any other place during the duration of the war, excepting any unhealthy country or where yellow fever reigns.

Your Excellency will guarantee never to deliver me to the Federal authorities, and in case of a peace being concluded between the Confederate States and the Federal that I shall be assured of being able to return safely into Europe, I and mine, with my belongings. In case a peace should be negotiated between the South and the North during the construction, which will take three or four months, the sum of $500,000 will be due me and paid as though the peace had not taken place. My invention under other circumstances might serve America powerfully in the war which might break out with England.

Under no circumstances I would not be expected to go to sea to attack hostile ships, that coming under the duties of captains and admirals. The construction of one or two vessels will be begun immediately upon my arrival; the said construction shall be made entirely at the expense of the State of the Confederated South; the 50 per cent of the value of vessels destroyed shall be paid over to me, half in gold, European exchange, the other half in territorial real estate, or in cotton at the market price of the place at which I shall take it. The price of a vessel will hardly exceed 3,000,000 francs. A single one might be able in a voyage to destroy six or eight monitors, and for the 75 ironclad vessels, of which Mr. Lincoln makes a display in his presidential message, it would take 10 or 12 days, let us say one month, to destroy them. When the North sees even a dozen of their monitors lost and destroyed, they would be more amenable, and if it be found expedient to destroy all of them, that would throw them into a profound consternation, for which they would not be prepared.

Your Excellency should not suppose that I make of this an affair which could be prejudicial to you if I demand before my departure from Paris 1,000 pounds sterling and 2,000 at the moment of embarking at London; it is to provide for the needs and expenses, not only of myself, but of the persons of my suite, and for the first expenses of sojourn at Richmond or elsewhere. We, in Europe, are well aware that everything is at very high cost.

If these conditions suit you, answer promptly and above all in a safe way; each month lost is of incalculable value in your position, a position that I am sure, with the aid of my invention, will change in one month at furthest, after the launching of the first of the vessels of my invention.

Your Excellency should understand that my private means do not permit me to go to America, in the South above all, without capital. The sum of 3,000 pounds sterling is a trifle to a State, and especially for the end to be attained, particularly as it is not a gift that I ask, but a simple advance on the price of the invention, an advance which will be deducted from the first payment that shall be made to me. As to the explanation of the means and power of my invention, a conversation between your Excellency and myself of a short half hour will suffice to convince you that my invention will be very easy to carry out, and the results will be such as I have promised and announced; but as to committing them to an ordinary letter which might be intercepted, that would be neither possible nor prudent. One might make a trial with and on two old vessels, schooners, or brigs; these trials will prove without charge to the Confederate States that those States which have ironclad vessels without my process are armored only for show, seeing that I will destroy as easily the ironclad ship as one which is not. Thus, then, the blockade of Confederate ports, rivers, towns, and forts may be raised 10 or 12 days after the launching of the first vessel using my system of destruction.

I will explain to your Excellancy that several States, such as Italy, Sweden, Denmark, and Spain, have been negotiating with me for six or eight months to buy my invention; but I will treat with none of these States before receiving your reply to this. I will not conceal from you that the prospect of receiving 50 per cent of the value of the destroyed ships did decide me to give your offer the preference.

I need not point to you that once the blockade broken, raised, and done away with forever by the destruction of the Federal monitors and other vessels, you might easily throw a thousand million pounds of cotton either in France or England, and with that amount your reparation would be securely effected. I await therefore your reply, and I pray you to let me hear as soon as possible. I will also say to you that in January, 1863, having wished to organize in Paris a company for purchasing cotton and breaking the blockade of your ports, I was prevented and threatened with arrest by the French police of Paris, and I have since learned that it was on demand of the representative of the North of America, which makes me feel unkindly toward that country.

I am, in the meantime, your Excellency's very humble servant,

POTIER, Sr.

His Excellency JEFFERSON DAVIS,
President of the Southern Confederate States of America.

The above I have already addressed to you dated December 20, 1863. In case that it may be intercepted, I send a duplicate.

Reply to M. Potier, sr., 4 Rue du Delta au Premier, Paris, France.

No. 53.] PARIS, *January 14, 1864.*

SIR: On recurring to my recent dispatches I find that I had neglected to acknowledge receipt of your No. 24, as I have before stated your No. 25 had reached previously. In my No. 52 of 29 ultimo I spoke of the intended publications, with Mr. Mann's assent, of the letter of President Davis to the Pope and the reply of his Holiness. They appeared through the instrumentality of the minister of foreign affairs, to whom and to the Emperor I had furnished copies, in the Moniteur and La France, and were copied in several other journals.

Meager extracts only of the President's message at the meeting of Congress appeared in some of the Paris papers. This proceeded from no unkindly spirit on the part of the journals hitherto friendly to us and the message of Lincoln did not receive more attention, excepting from one or two papers that are generally supposed to be subsidized by the enemy. It is to be regretted that the message of our President could not have appeared in full in some paper of large circulation, as it could not have failed to exercise a most salutary influence on public opinion.

Your acquaintance with French journalism must have led you to observe how small a share of it is occupied by disquisitions on foreign politics; an occasional brief space is all that is devoted to any question in which French interests or French honor are not directly invoked. There are so many of these questions, domestic and foreign, at this moment of immediate and absorbing interest, that our affairs have of late commanded but little attention from the press. I was then most agreeably surprised to find in the Patrie of the 12th instant a very long and able article in large type and occupying nine columns treating the American question in connection with that of Poland, and placing Russia in the same category with the Washington Government as powers whom it was the policy of France to oppose. As the article was signed by Mr. Delamarre, the proprietor of the paper, who very rarely indeed affixes his name to anything appearing in it, I called upon him the same day to thank him for his efficient advocacy of our cause. He is a man of large fortune, perfectly independent in every way, and while frankly supporting the Government in its general policy, freely exercises the privilege of expressing his dissent from measures which he disapproves. I became ecquainted with Mr. D. very soon after my arrival in Paris and he had placed his journal very fully at my disposition for any arguments or information on American affairs, at the same time emphatically repudiating all idea of compensation, saying that in conducting the Patrie he only desired to make it an efficient organ of his views, that its circulation was so large as to make it a most remunerative investment and to dispense with the necessity of such extraneous support as most other journals required, and begged me that in case anyone connected with his paper should ask for or even hint at remuneration I should let him know it. Circumstances which I mentioned in my dispatch of 6th ultimo have prevented for some time past my keeping up with Mr. D. as with other proprietors and editors of the journals friendly to our cause, the very satisfactory relations which I had established with them. Mr. D. informed me confidentially that his article had not only been inspired by the Emperor but had been examined and approved by him before its publication, that his communications had been directly with the Emperor without the intervention or knowledge of any of the ministers. On the same day I received a visit from Mr. Mocq[uard], who confirmed what Mr. D. said of the origin of the article of which I send you copy.

You will appreciate the significance of these facts; they are more encouraging than anything which has occurred here for several months, although I entertain no sanguine hope of any early action in our affairs.

A London paper having asserted that a secret understanding existed between the Northern Government and the Emperor; that in consideration of the acquiescence of the former in the establishment of a monarchial government in Mexico, the latter would be less friendly to our cause; I asked the Duke de Morny to do me the favor to ascertain from the Emperor if there was any foundation for such an assertion.

I saw the duke last evening; he informed me that the Emperor told him that there was no such understanding; that the Washington Government had manifested so anxious a wish to do what was agreeable to him that he was obliged to receive their advances courteously; further than this nothing had passed between the two Governments, either here or at Washington. My friend at the foreign office expresses the same belief.

Since my last, £50,400 of the bonds of the three millions loan have been canceled, making in all the sum of £117,000.

I have the honor to be, with great respect, your obedient servant,

JOHN SLIDELL.

Hon. J. P. BENJAMIN,
    Secretary of State.

No. 74.]   40 ALBEMARLE STREET,
                                 London, January 15, 1864.

SIR: In all intelligent British circles our recognition by the sovereign Pontiff is considered as formal and complete.

The influence that the measure is to exercise in our behalf is incalculable. It is believed that the earnest wishes expressed by his Holiness will be regarded as little less than imperative commands by that vast portion of the human family which esteem him as the Vicar of Christ.

If that shall be the case, then the war spirit of Lincoln & Co. will receive a scorching that will so enfeeble it as to utterly impair its powers for persistence. I have an abiding confidence in such a result.

Under the benign movement of Pio Nono there are encouraging indications that Protestantism throughout Europe is preparing to make a demonstration adverse to the prosecution of hostilities. True religion, whatever the form of worship, is becoming sick at heart at the ruthless atrocities of the North, and is beginning to fervently implore the Prince of Peace for their immediate discontinuance.

It is lamentable in the interests of public morality that the government of great powers should ever be furnished with a motive sufficiently influential to impel them to act, in their international relations, hypocritically. The cabinets on both sides of the British Channel must know that they are practicing upon the credulity of enlightened mankind when they affect to believe that we have not definitely won our independence. There is not, perhaps, a member of either who is not convinced, and has been ever since its utterance, of the truthfulness of the public assertion of Mr. Gladstone, expressed nearly eighteen months ago, that "Jefferson Davis and his coadjutors had made a nation of the South."

The ministry here is almost exclusively occupied with the Schleswig-Holstein question. I learn, upon good authority, that it resolved in council last Tuesday, to resist, even at the cost of a war, the unreasonable demands of Germany, and to sustain the treaty of 1854 upon the subject. The situation is undoubtedly grave at this moment.

As concerns our own country, I can safely assure you that we never occupied so high a position in European esteem as we do at present. I would infinitely prefer to enjoy, as I am quite confident we do, the good opinions and good wishes of all the right-thinking Britishry, without the formal recognition of their Government, than to enjoy such recognition without their good opinions and good wishes, as is unquestionably the case with our ignoble enemy.

I have the honor to be, sir, very respectfully, your obedient servant,

A. DUDLEY MANN.

Hon. J. P. BENJAMIN,
    Secretary of State, C. S. of America, Richmond, Va.

No. 35.] CONFEDERATE STATES COMMERCIAL AGENCY,
London, January 16, 1864.

SIR: Our loan since I last wrote has, taking a rough average, improved about 10 per cent. The day before yesterday it had advanced to 48, but owing to a large amount being thrown into the market by persons who had become frightened by the previous low quotations, it temporarily settled down to 42. It is, of course, the policy of our friends to construe this into a proof of growing confidence in our fortunes, and to a certain extent this is the case. This confidence, however, would not produce so beneficial an effect were it not for two supporting causes. One is that, thanks to the judicious management of our financial agent, the public is relieved of any doubts about the certainty of the payment of the interest next accruing and the extinction of one-fortieth of the capital at the first semiannual drawing. The other cause is the expectation, which has come to be very generally entertained, that Congress will authorize an embargo on the private exportation of cotton, or at least effect the same object by laying a heavy export duty on all cotton not exported for Government account or in redemption of bonds. There is, as far as I can judge, but one opinion here among the servants and friends of our cause as to the expediency and necessity of some such scheme of legislation. We have in the stores of our staple, for which the world is famishing, an element of financial strength which has not yet been brought into play.

Experience has amply demonstrated that by withholding these stores we can not exercise a coercive influence upon the powers of Europe. Withheld, it is practically valueless to the community at large, and wastes away under the destructive energies of nature and the enemy. The blockade serves as an enormous protective bounty to those who have the good fortune or ingenuity to elude it, and this bounty is paid out of the public purse into that of monopolists who are either foreigners or private speculators. There seems, therefore, to exist no reason why the public, instead of individuals, should not profit by this monopoly, and thus rehabilitate its credit at home and abroad, and make a demonstration which could not fail to have the most salutary effects. The proposed embargo will at once raise our cotton obligations to nearly or quite par. This done, I do not hesitate to say that unless a general European war breaks out we can immediately borrow as much money as we want, say, three or four times as much as the Erlanger loan, and on more favorable terms. This will make the Government the largest holder of foreign exchange in the Confederacy, and thus restore vigor to our currency, even should the enemy succeed in making the blockade effective. If not, the public, and not spurious patriots and still more dubious alien friends, will reap the benefit of the war price of cotton. At the present rate of exportation through the blockade, say 150,000 bales per annum, it would take 20 years to export the cotton now in the Confederate States, for the annual growth, however small, would assuredly suffice to make up the losses by the blockade, even if these losses were three bales to every one that reached Europe. At 50 cents a pound, or $200 a bale of 400 pounds, this would amount to $30,000,000—that is to say, much more than the Government could spend in foreign purchases and therefore leaving it a large surplus to offer to its domestic creditors. Our resources, then, properly husbanded and applied, would be virtually inexhaustible.

There is no argument which the people of England so easily understand as the arguments of arithmetical facts, and apart from the moral effect produced by our credit rising while that of our enemy is sinking, it would then come home to all classes in Europe that they in fact are paying the cost of the war in the enhanced price of cotton and clothing. We have appealed to the political sagacity, to the justice, and to the humanity of the civilized world, and we have appealed in vain; there is still one appeal left to us, and it is that which the experience of all history has proved to be the most effective.

The experiments thus far made by the Ordnance, Niter, and other Bureaus, as also the Navy Department, demonstrate that the Government can run the blockade with equal if not greater chances than private enterprise. But the public loses the chief advantages of the system, first, by the competition of private exportation; secondly, by the complicated and jarring machinery which only serves to grind out large profits in the shape of commissions, etc.; thirdly, by confounding the distinctive functions of different administrative departments. If blockade running was constituted an arm of the national defense, each would perform only its appropriate work, which therefore would be well done. The Treasury would procure without competition the raw material and regulate the disposition of the proceeds; the Navy, abandoning the hope of breaking the blockade and throwing all its available energies into eluding it, would purchase, build, and man the vessels for this purpose; the agents of the War Department, instead of having all the incongruous duties to perform themselves, could give their undivided attention to the matter of supplies. Even the post office might avail itself of this distribution of duties and aid in the moral demonstration on this side, by assuming the regular control of all European mails, placing them in charge of agents accompanying each steamer. Another very great advantage will be that our financial transactions will then have acquired such a magnitude that we can command the services of the highest and oldest financial houses, instead of, as at present, being left to the mercy of commercial adventurers, of firms formed for the hour, or of European branches of blockaded Confederate firms, none of which, whatever their enterprise and integrity, can exercise that influence in financial or political circles which governs European cabinets.

I do not flatter myself that amid the pressure of so many nearer cares this subject will be viewed at home in the same light in which it appears to us here, but to me it seems the only hope of striking the imagination and rousing the action of Europe.

I enclose the decision in the *Alexandra* case. You will observe that the judgment most adverse to our interest is that of Judge Pigott, who was appointed pendente lite by the Government and therefore virtually by the prosecution. The Crown appeals. Proceedings have been instituted also against the ship *Pampero*, in the Clyde. No further steps have been taken in the case of the rams, the Government fully accomplishing its object by the delay. It is a melancholy commentary on British fair play that a few ship chandlers are now being prosecuted in Liverpool for enlisting seamen for the

Georgia, while the same thing was done without attracting special attention by the Federal steamer *Kearsarge* in open daylight and in the most ostentatious manner at Queenstown and recruiting still prospers in Ireland.

I also enclose address and constitution of the Southern Independence Association just formed in London, and of which I have frequently spoken. I am glad to see that the society has had the wisdom to appoint as its executive officer an experienced parliamentary agent, whose profession is to engineer measures through the two houses. Heretofore no systematic effort has been made to organize or discipline our parliamentary strength. Consequently no man of really commanding position could stake his prestige on the championship of our cause. Naturally enough a cause of untried strength and doubtful success first attracts the services of the adventurous, the eccentric, or the speculative—in other words, those who have more to gain than to lose, either in position, influence, or money. This is inevitable, and discreetly used a great element of success. But it gives rise to the danger that others of a higher stamp will keep aloof from a cause which has too many of such allies. We have, as a nation, been prone to the fault of being too hasty in accepting alliances, and too impetuous in our gratitude for favors which redounded more to the advantage of those bestowing them than to ours. This was to be expected from our past isolation from European politics and society. In politics, however, we have suffered far less from this than in commerce. Still much remains to be done, and it gives me great hope that a body of gentlemen of the highest rank and position should espouse our cause as their own and assume the parliamentary management of it, which requires an intimate knowledge of home politics which no foreigner can possibly possess.

In the general state of Europe there is little or no improvement. The Emperor seems honestly bent on a pacific policy, but the presence of so unusual a number of distinguished men of the former régimes gives to the debates in the Corps Legislatif an extraordinary and almost feverish interest. It would seem to me the highest practical wisdom if the attention of the French people were somewhat diverted, and the lightning rod could in my opinion nowhere be more safely placed than in Mexico or the Confederate States. But the Emperor does not appear disposed to follow the example of Alcibiades, and I certainly can not discover that the Government, though it has so many means of reaching public opinion, makes the slightest effort to agitate either of these topics, or even facilitating those who attempt to do it. All doubts about the Archduke Maximilian's speedy departure for Mexico are removed; he comes to Paris next month and embarks in March; and yet for some inscrutable reason the Emperor sends a Bonaparte prince, a son of Lucian, to the newly-established empire. Unless I am greatly deceived the Polish insurrection is drawing to a close. Certainly the sympathies of the British people and press have suddenly cooled toward the Poles, and even in France a reaction from the mad enthusiasm of a few months since is plainly perceptible. In the question of the duchies the Germans are thoroughly in earnest to make the Federal execution the means of detaching both Schleswig and Holstein from the Danish monarchy. In the latter duchy the pretender has already assumed the airs of a reigning sovereign. Thus far the Federal troops have not entered Schleswig. Their doing so will be the signal for the collision, which may, if not averted even at the last moment by more vigorous protests than have yet come from France and England, envelop all Europe in war.

I have communicated to Mr. Mason your message sent me by private route, and by the same have written you twice since my last official date. Nothing of later date than last acknowledged has been received by regular route.

I have the honor to remain, very respectfully, your obedient servant,

HENRY HOTZE.

Hon. J. B. BENJAMIN,
    Secretary of State, Richmond.

DEPARTMENT OF STATE,
Richmond, January 18, 1864.

DEAR SIR: I send you the following extract (which appears quite worthy of your attention) from a letter just received by me:

A mistake in the direction of an envelope put me in possession of the fact that there is a mode of egress unguarded, of which many are availing themselves. It is by the Suffolk route, taking the train from Petersburg to Ivor station, and thence to the enemy's lines without let or hindrance. Quite a number of people have taken advantage of this unguarded point, and, as I judge, many others are making preparations to follow them.

The writer is an accomplished lady, living at Wilmington, and the letter is dated the 15th instant.

Yours, respectfully,

J. P. BENJAMIN,
    Secretary of State.

Hon. J. A. SEDDON,
    Secretary of War.

DEPARTMENT OF STATE,
Richmond, January 21, 1864.

SIR: I have the honor herewith to enclose for the information of your Department extract from a dispatch of 3d December last, received from Mr. Slidell, C. S. commissioner to France, relative to the steamer *Rappahannock;* also extract from a dispatch of the same date, 15th December, with accompanying papers, on the subject of certain silver, captured by Captain Maffitt on board of a Federal ship.

Very respectfully, your obedient servant,

J. P. BENJAMIN,
    Secretary of State.

Hon. S. R. MALLORY,
    Secretary of the Navy.

No. 36.]   CONFEDERATE STATES COMMERCIAL AGENCY,
                                        London, January 23, 1864.

SIR: I have the honor to acknowledge receipt of your dispatch, without number, dated November 30, 1863, containing directions for the drawing of my salary from and after the 31st December, 1863, which will be punctually attended to. Your dispatch makes no reference to the mode of drawing my secret-service fund, from which I conclude that in regard to this fund the old arrangement still remains in force.

In obedience to your instructions I have the honor to transmit my salary account made up to the 31st December ultimo showing a balance of $101.25 due me in consequence of loss incurred in converting Treasury notes into funds available here. I have endeavored to adhere as steadily to the prescribed forms as the lack of printed blanks and the absence of precedents in the office would permit. A certain degree of irregularity is, however, almost inseparable from our state of war and blockade. I trust that such, where applying only to unessentials, will be excused. The required duplicate and triplicate will follow by separate conveyances.

Mr. W. S. Lindsay, M. P., has requested me to forward to you, open, two letters, one for Mrs. Semmes, wife of Captain Semmes, and one for Mr. Cridland, late British consular agent at Mobile, with the contents of which he desires that you should be acquainted. I have already by our private route informed you that the person in question, Frank Lacy Buxton [Brieton ?], is evidently an impostor. The Morning Herald of this city on learning that he represented himself as its Southern correspondent, published a paragraph repudiating all knowledge of him, and warned its readers against him. I have since learned that drafts for large amounts drawn on fictitious firms by the same person and negotiated by him in the Confederacy have arrived in London, thus removing the last charitable doubt as to his character.

I also enclose a letter relating to the condemnation at San Francisco of Messrs. Rubery, Greathouse, and Harpending, on charge of piracy, a letter of marque and reprisal having been found on board the vessel they were equipping. The authenticity and bona fide intention of this letter is vouched for by evidence in my possession.

I am extremely anxious to obtain as speedily as possible the documents printed by order of the Congress now in session. Even when it is not expedient to reproduce them here it is of great advantage to me to possess them.

There is nothing of either special or general interest to add since my last of 16th instant.

I have the honor to remain, very respectfully, your obedient servant,
                                                    HENRY HOTZE.

Hon. J. P. BENJAMIN,
    Secretary of State, Richmond.

[Enclosure—Duplicate.]

CONFEDERATE STATES COMMERCIAL AGENCY,
London, December 31, 1863.

The Confederate States Government in account for salary with Henry Hotze, commercial agent at London.

	DR.			CR.	
1862. May 14	To amount of my salary as commercial agent from Nov. 14, 1861, to May 14, 1862, at $1,500 per annum............	$750.00	1861. Nov. 14	By $750 in Treasury notes received from Mr. Bromwell, disbursing clerk of State Department, on which was realized, as per exchange account, annexed, marked "A"....................	$654.75
1863. Dec. 31	To amount of my salary as commercial agent from May 14, 1862, to Dec. 31, 1863, at $2,400 per annum.......,.....	3,900.00	1862. July 7	By amount received through Mr. E. de Leon on account of salary and receipted to him......................	1,200.00
			1863. Jan. 17	By Treasury warrant on Messrs. Fraser, Trenholm & Co. for £185.11.4, received through and receipted to Mr. J. E. MacFarland..........	900.00
			May 14	By Treasury warrant on Fraser, Trenholm & Co., No. 4351, for £247.8.5...........	1,200.00
			Oct. 31	By Treasury warrant on Fraser, Trenholm & Co., No. 4934, £123.14.3..............	600.00
			Dec. 31	By balance...................	101.25
					4,650.00
		4,650.00			
1864. Jan. 1	To balance..................	101.25			

I certify that I have been absent from London from the 6th day of August, 1862, to the 4th September, 1862, and also from the 4th April, 1863, to the 18th April, 1863, in the former case partly on business connected with this agency, but in both mainly on account of health, and that with these two exceptions I have not been absent from the district of this agency for a longer period than ten days within the twenty-five and a half months embraced in the above and foregoing account.

HENRY HOTZE,
C. S. Commercial Agency.

No. 26.] HAVANA, *January 23, 1864.*

SIR: I have the honor to inform you that Joseph T. Crawford, esq., has been appointed by her Britannic Majesty's Government to proceed, at an early day, on a special mission to Richmond. Mr. Crawford proposes, I understand, first to dispatch a vessel of war, communicating the object of his mission, and, should President Davis decide to receive him, embark for Wilmington or Mobile about the middle of February. Mr. Crawford is charged with certain representations touching the building of vessels of war by Confederate agents in British ports, and the conscription of persons in the Confederate States claiming to be English subjects.

To Mr. Crawford, personally, the President should have no objection; he has been our warm, ardent friend from the beginning of the war, is an old gentleman of great experience and good sense, and, should he be received, would no doubt in his official report do ample justice to the Confederate States. I do not wish, however, to be understood as intimating the opinion that the President should receive any agent of the English, in the absence of full recognition by that Government, but write this note simply to advise you of the appointment.

The steamer bringing Mr. Crawford's appointment arrived on yesterday, and the one which takes this sails to-day; Mr. Crawford therefore has not had time to read his instructions, which are very voluminous, and I can not give you at this time further information than I have done; by the next steamer I may be enabled to write more fully on this subject.

I am, sir, with great respect, your obedient servant,

CHAS. J. HELM.

Hon. J. P. BENJAMIN,
  Secretary of State, Richmond.

No. 1.]   OFFICE OF COMMISSIONER ON THE CONTINENT,
16 RUE DE MARIGNAN,
Paris, January 25, 1864.

SIR: Your dispatch dated on the 30th of November ultimo reached me here on the 20th of the present month, and as directed the accounts of the special commission to Great Britain shall be closed as on the 11th of November last and those as "Commissioner on the Continent" shall commence on the 12th of the same month and stated to the 31st of December last. Those accounts, together with those for the contingent fund, stated in like manner, shall be forwarded by the next mail to Bermuda via Halifax. This goes by private opportunity just offering for Bermuda.

In a note from Mr. Hotze, dated at London the 29th December, he quoted an extract from a private note, then just received from you, dated the 28th November, in which he was requested to inform me that a dispatch had been sent to me a week previously, yours acknowledged above bearing date two days after the note to Mr. Hotze. I am to infer that the dispatch there referred to is yet on its way or has been lost.

Commencing a new series of correspondence, I mark this dispatch No. 1; yours to which it is in reply is not marked. I shall treat it as your No. 1, unless there be a predecessor, in which case the numbers shall conform accordingly.

Unless instructions shall arrive inconsistent with it, I propose to go, soon after the meeting of Parliament, to England, of course in a private capacity only, and may remain there a few weeks. Parliament meets on the 4th of February; we have in it a body of earnest and sincere friends, some of whom have told me it would be very desirable to have an opportunity of occasional conference with me for information, etc. I shall have no establishment there, and be only, as it were, in transitu. I think it very desirable to keep the public mind in England awake and informed on matters interesting to us, though I am not aware of any reasons from which we may hope for any speedy action on the part of the Government. I could tell better, however, after a week or two in London and shall, of course, keep you advised.

As some evidence that we have earnest and active friends in high position there, I enclose a circular recently issued by the Southern Independence Association of London, and which fully explains itself. With most of the members of the committee I have a personal acquaintance, and am with many of them on terms of intimate relation. As of like character, I enclose also another circular just issued at London, under the auspices of which I am fully aware, by a society for Promoting the Cessation of Hostilities in America, which also discloses its objects. It is important to note that both these movements are purely of English origin; their promoters have indeed freely consulted with me, but not until after the respective plans were devised and to some extent matured by themselves. They are really, as they import, views of Englishmen addressed to the English people, and in this light is to be received the concluding paragraph in the circular of the Southern Independence Association of London. My attention has been called to it by more than one of my countrymen hereabouts, to whom my answer has always been: " It is a view presented by Englishmen to their own people and is not addressed to us; it remains their affair and for which we are in no manner responsible."

In my conversations with English gentleman I have found it was in vain to combat their " sentiment." The so-called " antislavery " feeling seems to have become with them a " sentiment" akin to patriotism. I have always told them that in the South we could rely confidently that after independence, when our people and theirs became better acquainted by direct communication, when they saw for themselves the true condition of African servitude with us, the film would fall from their eyes, and that in meantime it was not presumptuous in us to suppose that we knew better than they did what it became us to do in our affairs.

The German complication with Denmark, which seemed imminently to threaten a European war, within the last day or two has given a better promise by a request from the latter power to be allowed time to assemble and consult with the Danish legislative assembly before giving a final answer to the Austro-Prussian ultimatum. The reply of the latter power is not yet known, but it can hardly be a refusal. Peace and repose in Europe are just now of great importance to us, waiting for European recognition.

To complete the series of the correspondence of the commission to England I have the honor to transmit herewith a copy of Earl Russell's reply to my letter to him of the 21st of September, informing him of the termination of that commission.

*   *   *   *   *   *   *

On the subject of the contingent fund, the expenses in that quarter are so moderate, on comparing notes with Mr. Slidell, that there is no occasion for any addition. The instructions we brought with us confine this expenditure to limited objects, certainly very proper in ordinary times, but we both agree that there are objects of expenditure for political ends occasionally presenting themselves when it would be well that the commissioners in Europe should have a larger discretion. This character of expenditure might not generally admit of a regular voucher, but must be submitted to the integrity of the commissioner. It might be limited, say, not to exceed three or five hundred pounds sterling in any one year. Occasions have presented themselves to me when good and not unfair use to our cause could have been made of moderate sums. I venture to submit this to your consideration.

I have the honor to be, very respectfully, your obedient servant,

J. M. MASON.

Hon. J. P. BENJAMIN,
Secretary of State.

No. 34]
DEPARTMENT OF STATE,
Richmond, January 25, 1864.

SIR: The near approach of the session of Congress induced me to defer forwarding your commission and instructions under the appointment communicated to you in November last until the action of the Senate on your nomination. I have now the honor to inform you that you were on the 18th instant confirmed by the Senate as commissioner to represent the Confederate States to such foreign nations as the President might deem expedient under the act of Congress approved on the 20th August, 1861, and your commission as such is herewith forwarded. It is accompanied by a commission for Mr. Macfarland as your secretary, he having been nominated and confirmed as such on the 18th instant.

The act under which you were appointed authorizes the President, as you will perceive, to accredit you to such foreign nations as he may deem expedient. At present we have in Europe but two commissioners, Mr. Slidell, accredited to Paris and Madrid, and Mr. Mann, accredited to Belgium. It is not deemed necessary to associate an additional commissioner with either of these gentlemen.

The considerations which have dictated your appointment are the following: In the present disturbed condition of European affairs, when grave events seem impending and when new and unexpected relations may arise between the European powers, prudence requires that the interests of the Confederate States should not be left unrepresented during the delays incident to our present uncertain and tardy communication with Europe. If a general war should grow out of any one of the many disturbing causes which threaten the tranquillity of Europe it is not difficult to imagine that a representative of this Government with adequate powers might find occasion for acting with signal benefit to his country. On the other hand, if the Archduke Maximilian shall accept the Mexican throne the interest which will naturally be felt by the Emperor of Austria in the fortunes of his brother as well as the interests of the French Government in the maintenance of their own work suggest a series of contingencies in any one of which it may be all-important that this Government should have discreet and able assistance at Vienna. The views of the President upon the subject of our future relations with our southern neighbor have been fully developed in my recent correspondence with Mr. Slidell, and it will be well that you should make yourself acquainted with them if indeed you have not from your intimacy with him already been apprised of all that has occurred.

Although it now seems to us here most probable that your services may first be required in Austria, it is deemed more prudent to provide you with duplicate full powers addressed in blank that may be filled up by you in any contingency requiring your presence at more than one of the European courts. It might even happen that by unforeseen calamity the Government might be deprived of the services of Mr. Slidell at a critical moment requiring the presence of a plenipotentiary authorized to sign treaties or conventions that could not be postposed without hazard or even grave prejudice to our interest. The President will feel much more secure in the provision which it is his duty to make for the safeguard of our interests abroad when they are no longer dependent on the continued existence of a single public servant, however valuable he may be. The discretion which he vests in you therefore is, as you perceive, very wide and is intended to embrace unforeseen events which may render necessary prompt action by an accredited diplomatic agent. It is one which could only be warranted by his entire confidence in your prudence and discretion and which he doubts not you will fully justify.

There is one point, however, on which it is perhaps necessary to be quite explicit. The President does not deem it, in the present advanced state of our struggle, either judicious or consistent with the dignity of our country that there should be any addition to the number of our commissioners occupying the position of accredited agents awaiting recognition at European courts. It is not expected that you will present yourself at any court in such an attitude nor that you will make any formal application for official reception as an accredited commissioner unless previously assured unofficially that your reception as such will at once be accorded. If therefore you find at any time that your presence at any capital or seat of government would be useful and probably productive of advantage it is not expected by the President that you should reside there in any other capacity than as a private gentleman known to be in the confidence of his Government, nor that you should remain there after satisfying yourself that the demand for an official audience to present your credentials would if made be refused. It is scarcely necessary to add that in regard to Great Britain you would be expected to await some intimation from that Government of its desire to enter into official relations with you before again approaching it, even in the most informal manner. The President would also prefer that in the absence of such intimation you should refrain from visiting England, even in a private capacity, unless some urgent necessity should compel your presence there.

I am, very respectfully, your obedient servant,

J. P. BENJAMIN,
Secretary of State.

Hon. JAMES M. MASON.

No. 54.] PARIS, *January 25, 1864.*

SIR: Since my last of 14th instant I have received your dispatch of 30th November not numbered, and your No. 26, of 9th ultimo. To the former I shall reply separately, forwarding the accounts called for, which I hope to have prepared in season to forward under the same cover with this dispatch. Mr. Mercier, French minister at Washington, has been some days in Paris, having had leave of absence. He is very decided in his expression of sympathy with the Confederate cause and of his conviction of our ability to maintain our independence. He fully confirms what I stated in my last of the absence of any agreement between this Government and that of Lincoln on Mexican affairs, well understanding that the silence of the latter on that subject is only caused by the desire of avoiding present difficulties and is not indicative of any abatement of the ill feeling with which the French occupation has been received from its commencement. Intended changes in the Emperor's cabinet are rumored—they are not unlikely to occur—the minister of foreign affairs has enemies among those very near the throne, and as far as I can judge no zealous friends, but he may retain his place in spite of these adverse influences. Should there be any modification, M. de Persigny will probably come in as minister of the household.

I am much gratified to find by your letter to M. de Leon, of 9th December, the appreciation which the President entertains of the manner in which I have discharged my duties here; I deeply regret that I have not done more to merit it, but I have the satisfaction to know that, however sterile my mission has hitherto been of positive practical results, I have established relations which may and probably will prove advantageous to the cause which I represent. By your dispatch of 30th November, I find that the annual sum allowed for contingencies of this mission is $3,000. You will find by the letter accompanying my accounts that I have remaining, unexpended, much the larger portion of this allowance. I never received the letter accompanying a considerable remittance, say, £1,443.5, made 15th July, 1862, on this account. The duplicate bill reached me through Mr. Mason without any explanation. I inferred that some expenditure not contemplated by my original personal instructions had been authorized, and wrote a private letter to the Assistant Secretary of State for information, but am still ignorant of the objects to which this money was to be applied. So long as I shall remain in my present unaccredited position and the expenditure from the contingent fund shall be restricted to the objects specified in my instructions even the original allowance of $1,500 is more than amply sufficient, the whole expenditure of the commission since my appointment having been but about $600. I have, however, more than once had occasion to regret that larger discretion had not been allowed me in contingent expenses. I submit this point to your consideration.

Commodore Barron, the senior of the officers of the Confederate Navy on duty in Europe, informing me of some matters relating to our ships in French ports, says:

I avail myself of this occasion to express my high appreciation of the uniform kindness and courtesy which have been extended to the Confederate officers who have been attached to and doing duty on board the vessels which have been undergoing necessary repairs at the ports of Calais, Brest, and Cherbourg.

I am gratified to have it in my power to mention this fact, as it indicates the nature of the instructions given by the minister of marine to his officers in accordance with the wishes of the Emperor.

Mrs. Rose Greenhow has had an interview with the Emperor, the particulars of which are to be found in the accompanying letter to the President.

I have the honor to be, with great respect, your most obedient servant,

JOHN SLIDELL.

Hon. J. P. BENJAMIN,
　　　Secretary of State.

No. 28.]　　　　　　　　　　　　　　DEPARTMENT OF STATE,
　　　　　　　　　　　　　　　　Richmond, January 28, 1864.

SIR: On the 18th December, 1862, Mr. Bernard Avegno, of New Orleans, was appointed by the President commercial agent of this Government at Vera Cruz, and certain duties confided to him, which it is not now necessary to specify.

Mr. Avegno was furnished with $500 as an advance payment on account of his salary. He soon after departed for Vera Cruz via the West Indies. His arrival in the island of Nassau became known to the Department, as well as his departure thence for Havana.

On the 17th April, 1863, a remittance was made to him of $1,000 and on the 22d August a second remittance of $580. These two remittances were sent to the care of Mr. Helm at Havana, who, in the letter enclosing the August remittance, was asked for news from Mr. Avegno, from whom the Department had not received one line of correspondence since his departure.

By letter from Mr. Helm of 21 September, received here on the 13th October, I am informed that "on the arrival of Mr. Bernard Avegno at this place in June or July last, he informed me that he was then en route for Mexico, on important business for the Government, but after remaining here a few days, changed his plans and took the Southampton steamer for Europe, where he still remains."

Mr. Helm returned to the Department the two remittances that had been sent to his care, thus leaving to be accounted for only the original advance of $500.

On the receipt of Mr. Helm's letter, I concluded that Mr. Avegno on arrival at Havana had discovered that the objects to be attained by his residence at Vera Cruz could be better accomplished by previous arrangements to be made in Europe, and although some annoyance was experienced at the failure to hear from him, the embarrassments created by the war in regular correspondence with our agents afforded a natural solution in the surmise that his letters had been destroyed or intercepted.

Several months have again elapsed and no direct news has been received from Mr. Avegno, but by quiet inquiry so directed as to avoid suspicion I have learned through a gentleman connected with the French consulate here that Mr. Avegno is living in Paris "in a fifth story and in a condition bordering on destitution." From our mutual acquaintance with Mr. Avegno you will easily understand that his character has been too high to permit the ready reception of suspicions unfavorable to his honor. The circumstances are so singular and so inexplicable that they almost lead to a fear of his mind having become unsettled, as on no other ground can I account for his abandonment of an honorable position in which his support was assured and which he had accepted with thankfulness. When he left me he appeared to be in excellent health and spirits and nothing indicated any change from his former self.

It would be very satisfactory to learn from you whether Mr. Avegno is still in Paris, and if so, what explanation can be offered of his conduct. If the $500 advanced to him are reimbursed, the amount may be placed in the hands of Messrs. Fraser, Trenholm & Co., of Liverpool, the bankers of this Department.

I am, very respectfully, your obedient servant,

J. P. BENJAMIN,
Secretary of State.

Hon. JOHN SLIDELL,
 Paris, France.

No. 29.]   DEPARTMENT OF STATE,
          Richmond, January 28, 1864.

SIR: I have the honor to acknowledge receipt of your several dispatches, Nos. 50, 50 bis, and 51, dated, respectively, on the 3d, 6th, and 15th ultimo, and received together on the 16th instant.

Your No. 50 bis, in relation to Mr. de Leon, bears nearly the same date as my dispatch to you on the same subject and requires no special remark. While appreciating the motives which induced your forbearance from complaint, I can not but think that the Department ought to have been apprised earlier of the facts related in your dispatch, especially as to his opening, without the slightest warrant of authority, the sealed dispatches addressed to you, and committed to his care. This fault was of so very grave a nature that it alone would probably have sufficed to put an end to Mr. de Leon's agency, and we should thus have been spared the annoyance of the scandal created by the interception and publication of the objectionable correspondence which caused his removal. Your No. 50 bis has been considered official and placed in the regular files, notwithstanding the doubt intimated in its concluding passages, because the subject had already taken its proper place in the official correspondence of the Department.

Reverting to more agreeable duties, I observe with a satisfation, which has been shared by the President, the continued manifestations by a high personage of favorable dispositions toward the Confederacy, as evinced not only in the matter of the *Rappahannock* but in the communication of the dispatch as related in your No. 51, and which was fully understood by reference to your No. 32. I trust that intelligence equally favorable will soon be received on the whole subject connected with the postscript of my No. 27.

I take it for granted that you have seen the correspondence between the President and the Pope, but enclose it, as published here, with the translation made in the Department of the Pope's letters. The effect on our people has been good, and we hope that some benefit will be experienced from this correspondence in the influence excited on Roman Catholics in the North.

The President thinks you are mistaken in your estimate of the person who wrote you the note from Trieste of 7th November last, as copied into your No. 50. At all events, from the beginning of the war that person has been constantly writing to the President with expressions of warm sympathy for our cause, and has in various ways manifested in it an interest which the President would be loath to suspect as simulated or assumed for treacherous purposes. If you can give any of the grounds which have excited your suspicions, they might be sent in cipher, for it is of course important that the President should not entertain a mistaken impression on this point.

On the whole subject embraced in the Trieste letter, and in your Nos. 50 and 51, my last dispatch No. 27 will have given you the fullest information of the views and policy of this Government and of the measures adopted to carry them into effect. We await with interest the result of the deliberation of the archduke on the subject of accepting the throne of Mexico. The announcement of the French Government to the Corps Legislatif that the "sole reservation" was in relation to the popular vote of the Mexicans justified us in considering the matter as settled, and we were not prepared for the information to the contrary contained in your dispatches. Recent Northern papers bring news to the 2d January (more than two weeks later than your No. 51), announcing that the French journals deny that the archduke has imposed conditions on his acceptance, and thus give color to the inference that his hesitation is at an end. I need hardly add that our interests are so deeply affected in this whole subject that we await with solicitude the official news that is to banish all doubt as to the future government of Mexico.

You will perceive by what was stated in my No. 27 that your note to the Emperor of 4th December was in entire accordance with the views entertained here, and that there was even identity in the observation made, that each musket intercepted was equivalent to abstracting a soldier from our ranks. We still remain without news of the French occupation of Matamoras, although daily hoping to receive it. The delay of the French commanders in a movement so important confirms my impression that they are anxious to avoid a possible conflict with our enemies, rather than to conduct their operations in the most effective manner.

The correspondence with Messrs. Fraser, Trenholm & Co. relative to the captured silver has been copied and sent to the Secretary of the Navy.

I am, respectully, your obedient servant,

J. P. BENJAMIN,
Secretary of State.

Hon. JOHN SLIDELL,
Paris, France.

No. 11.]

DEPARTMENT OF STATE,
Richmond, February, 1, 1864.

SIR: I have the honor to acknowledge the receipt in due course of your dispatches from Nos. 59 to 70, inclusive, the No. 59 received on the 31st October and No. 70 on the 16th ultimo.

As I was aware that you must have received my No. 9 about the end of October, and would therefore be absent from your post, I delayed acknowledgment, the more especially as your dispatches, while keeping the Department advised of the current of political events in Europe, contained no matter of business requiring special answer.

The President has been much gratified at learning the cordial reception which you received from the Pope, and the publication of the correspondence here (of which I send you a newspaper slip) has had a good effect. Its best influences, as we hope, will be felt elsewhere in producing a check on the foreign enlistments made by the United States. As a recognition of the Confederate States we can not attach to it the same value that you do, a mere inferential recognition, unconnected with political action or the regular establishment of diplomatic relations, possessing none of the moral weight required for awakening the people of the United States from their delusion that these States still remain members of the old Union. Nothing will end this war but the utter exhaustion of the belligerents, unless, by the action of some of the leading powers of Europe in entering into formal relations with us, the United States are made to perceive that we are in the eyes of the world a separate nation and that the war now waged by them is a foreign, not an intestine or civil war, as it is termed by the Pope. This phrase of his letter shows that his address to the President as " President of the Confederate States " is a formula of politeness to his correspondent, not a political recognition of a fact. None of our public journals treat the letter as a recognition in the sense you attach to it, and Mr. Slidell writes that the Nuncio at Paris on whom he called had received no instructions to put his official visa on our passports, as he had been led to hope from his correspondence with you. This, however, may have been merely a delay in the sending of the instructions.

Without having anything special to communicate, as you receive the news through the papers so much more promptly than I can send it, I deem it proper to inform you that no reliance whatever is to be placed in the accounts with which the Northern papers are filled as to the condition of the Confederacy. Although for some time after the defeat of our army at Missionary Ridge, there was great despondency and gloom, the natural reaction after the exaggerated expectations of the results of the victory at Chickamauga, those feelings have passed away, and our army, both in the West and in northern Virginia, is now enthusiastically reenlisting for the war by brigades which give unanimous votes. We shall take the field in the spring with largely recruited forces.

There has been less promptness and energy in the legislation by Congress than we had hoped for, and less than the magnitude of the interests at stake warranted us in expecting. But the subjects for discussion were important and difficult, and it was no easy matter to reconcile conflicting opinions. There remain but about two weeks of the session and as the debates have exhausted the subjects for legislation we may now rely on the early passage of the measures needed for infusing renewed energy into our operations.

It does not seem to me, but I may be oversanguine, that the finances of the North can stand the tension of their enormous expenditure beyond the present campaign. As our own embarrassments proceed solely from an excessive issue of currency, held entirely at home, they are easily remedied by proper legislation. Those of the North involve their relations with the whole world, their external commerce, and the whole framework of their Government. If they can not borrow money, they can not keep an army in the field, while we can. So far as finances are concerned, our ability to resist is without limit, and it now seems to me, that in the exhaustion of their means of raising money will be found the agency that is to put an end to the struggle.

I am, very respectfully, your obedient servant,

J. P. BENJAMIN,
Secretary of State.

Hon. A. DUDLEY MANN,
Brussels.

DEPARTMENT OF STATE,
Richmond, February 1, 1864.

SIR: I have the honor to request that you will be good enough to make arrangements, through the signal and prisoners' exchange officers of your Department, to furnish this Department with complete files of the Northern journals. Any expense attending this will be cheerfully borne by the Department.

It is impossible for me to obtain these files through my own agencies, and they constantly contain official information, diplomatic correspondence, etc., which it is all important to have, and the want of which is a detriment to the public service.

I am, very respectfully, your obedient servant,

J. P. BENJAMIN,
Secretary of State.

Hon. JAS. A. SEDDON,
Secretary of War.

IN RELATION TO C. S. S. RAPPAHANNOCK.

CALAIS, *le 4 février, 1864.*

MONSIEUR: Je viens de recevoir de S. E. le ministre de la Marine et des Colonies, une dépêche contenant des ordres précis, formels en ce qui concerne votre bâtiment, et la notification que je dois vous en faire m'est, veuillez n'en pas douter, très pénible; pourtant la communication que j'ai eu l'honneur de vous faire le 11 du mois dernier et à la suite de laquelle vous m'avez déclaré pouvoir être en état complet de prendre la mer à environ une semaine de cette date, tout en vous faisant pressentir la possibilité des mesures survenues aujourd'hui, a dû vous préparer entirment à y faire face.

J'ai donc le regret, Monsieur, de vous informer que le Gouvernement de sa Majesté l'Empereur a décidé que j'intimerai "l'ordre au *Rappahannock* de quitter le port de Calais à la marée qui suivra la réception de cette lettre," et que faute par vous d'obtempérer à cette injonction il ne vous sera plus permis de quitter ce port qu'à la fin des hostilités entre les Etats-Unis et les Confédérés.

Le long séjour de votre bâtiment à Calais et surtout le temps écoulé depuis l'avis précité me font espérer, Monsieur, qu'il vous sera possible d'ici minuit de hâter vos derniers préparatifs de telle sorte que la décision de laquelle je viens d'avoir l'honneur de vous faire part reçoive son exécution.

J'ajouterai, Monsieur, que malgré la nature épineuse de mes relations officielles avec vous, je désire vivement que le bref délai qui vous est accordé soit pourtant suffisant, ai-je besoin d'insister, Monsieur, au moment de votre départ sur ce que les rapports et les réponses que j'ai eu à adresser à l'égard de votre bâtiment ont été constamment conformes à la vérité telle que mes investigations personnelles et impartiales me l'ont fait trouver et que mes explications ont été toujours loyales, sincères et complètes.

Je vous prie de vouloir bien en raison de son importance m'accuser réception de la présente.

Veuillez recevoir, Monsieur, l'expression de ma considération très distinguée,

Le Commissaire de l'Inscription Maritime,
GOSSELIN.

A Monsieur CAMPBELL,
Lieutenant commandant le vapeur Rappahannock.

CALAIS, *le 16 février 1864.*

MONSIEUR: J'ai l'honneur de vous accuser réception de la lettre que vous m'avez adressée hier.

J'ai également l'honneur de vous informer que par suite à la lettre que vous m'avez adressée dans laquelle vous me faisiez connaître que vous seriez prêt à partir aussitôt l'arrivée de votre charbon et que j'ai transmise à S E. le Gouvernement de S. M. l'Empereur vient de me prescrire de vous maintenir dans le bassin jusqu'à nouvel ordre et que vous ne pouvez sortir du port que lorsque j'aurai reçu de nouvelles instructions à ce sujet. Les mêmes instructions ont été données à Mr. le commandant du *Galilée.*

Agréez, Monsieur, l'assurance de ma considération dstinguée.

Le Commissaire de l'Inscription,
GOSSELIN.

Monsieur CAMPBELL,
First lieutenant commandant le Rappahannock.

No. 77.]
40 ALBEMARLE STREET,
London, February 6, 1864.

SIR: The Queen's speech at the opening of Parliament the day before yesterday omitted any mention whatever of American affairs. Even the slightest allusion to them was studiously avoided. The premier confessed as much in the debate upon the address, reiterating, however, that no change in the Government policy with respect to its "neutrality" was contemplated. You will probably have received through Northern channels the speech, and the interesting proceedings of the first day of the session, before this reaches you.

I find that the annual message of the President has been most carefully read in political, financial, and military British circles. No complaint is uttered, publicly or privately, against its able and severe criticisms of the notorious tergiversations of the foreign department. They are regarded as just and irrefutable. The ruling European Governments are utterly heartless; and perhaps none more so than that which originates its measures and arranges its policy in Downing Street. The requirements of the realm, immediate and prospective, whose concerns it administers, actuate it to the commission of deeds less compatible with unyielding principle than flexible interest.

While every enlightened Britisher, whose mind is unbiassed by sordid selfishness, conscientiously believes that we have nobly won the independence which we asserted three years ago, the number is comparatively small who would be willing to coerce the ministry into a formal acknowledgment of the fact.

It will be recollected that Great Britain was a reluctant party to the Paris declaration. In giving her assent to the stipulation, which was intended to terminate forever " paper blockades," she surrendered her cherished traditional policy. Lord Clarendon, as her negotiator, will probably never entirely recover the popularity which he lost in this connection. The procedure was but little less acceptable to the Liberals than to the Conservatives.

In the second and last interview which my late colleagues and myself had with Earl Russell, his lordship incidentally remarked that it was desirable that Great Britain and the Confederate States should have an understanding upon the subject of the rights of neutrals, but that he was at a loss to know how to proceed to effect such a result. I delicately intimated to him that the commissioners were clothed with " full powers " to negotiate upon this and all other questions relating to the reciprocal interests of the two countries. He preferred, however, to undertake the accomplishment of his object indirectly, through commercial instead of diplomatic agents, and, unfortunately for us, but too promptly succeeded. We engaged ourselves by a legislative act, which we can not with propriety repeal, to do that which I think we should only have done in the contracting of mutual treaty obligations. Earl Russell had reason to be proud of his masterly diplomacy, in this instance at least, and assuredly he has made the most of it. I never was more grieved at any official occurrence than when I was informed through the public journals of the irreparable blunder which we had, from a mistaken confidence, committed.

Earl Russell, in his obviously incorrect interpretation of the Paris declaration, and the tacit acquiescence of the " high contracting parties " to that declaration, has rendered the stipulation relating to blockades entirely ineffective. He has done more—he has, to all intents and purposes, obtained the assent of the Yankee Government to his interpretation. Hence, the " paper-blockade " system of Great Britain, so far from having been harmed by the congress of Paris, is likely to be more beneficial hereafter than it ever was heretofore. The ulterior end at which British statesmen, irrespective of party, are strictly (and I might, perhaps without doing them injustice, add stealthily) aiming, is the recovery of the supremacy of the seas. This is a paramount desire. Nor is its realization dubious. It is my belief that there is no nation that will be in a condition to contest the right to such sovereignty for a century to come. Rule, Britannia, Rule will again become the popular anthem of the Britishry. Louis Napoleon was guilty of an omission in not disregarding two years and a half ago the inefficient blockade of our ports, which will seriously affect the welfare of France for ages.

The iron hull is superseding the wooden hull just as steam is superseding canvas. The rich and exhaustless ore fields and coal mines of the "Island Giant," her numerous workshops and ship-yards, the abundance and constant augmentation of her seamen, will probably in less than a score of years produce for her a mercantile navy three times as large as that of all the world besides. The old American Union was her only rival in bottom carrying. That rival has disappeared.

In nourishing the hope of such a future it is not wonderful that British politicians, with comparatively few exceptions, wish for a continuance of the existing blockade. Time dignifies the interpretation of Earl Russell. A precedent of three years' durability is more imposing than a precedent of two years' durability. An international wrong that is submitted to uncomplainingly for a lengthened period becomes, in its observance by the parties interested, an international right.

Never can I cease to remember the day of the arrival of the official intelligence of the surrender of our commissioners. Immediately after its receipt at the foreign office a true-hearted friend of mine, a nobleman of position and worth, came to me and whispered in my ear, significantly, " Your only chance for resistance to the blockade is in the Emperor of the French. Our hands are tied by imperative considerations." That chance, alas, swiftly vanished. Shortly afterwards the organ of the Tuileries in the Corps Legislatif emphatically announced that France had no intention whatever of interfering with the blockade. This avowal consummated England's ecstatic joy. It not merely sanctioned but it also legitimatized the renewal of a system deliberately pronounced obsolete by European plenipotentiaries.

Had he been so disposed his Imperial Majesty could, with a stroke of his pen, have caused the cosigners, of course, including Great Britain, of the treaty of Paris to declare the blockade as not coming within the veritable definition which they had solemnly agreed that the word was hereafter to bear.

It has been currently reported that the Government of the Tuileries long ago proposed to the Government of her Britannic Majesty a joint recognition of our independence. I know, and more than once informed you, that this was not so. Earl Derby, in his speech on Thursday, alluded to the matter. Earl Russell answered in the most categorical manner that the rumor had not the slightest foundation in truth.

The chances for an interruption of the general peace of Europe appear to have considerably diminished within the last week. It is now quite certain that Great Britain will not fight for Schleswig-Holstein, and in view of this certainty Louis Napoleon perceives that the prospect is more remote than ever for annexing to France the territory on the left bank of the Rhine. As soon as he was made acquainted with the contents of the Queen's speech he exclaimed to his ministers: "Our policy is nonintervention."

I have the honor to be, sir, very respectfully, your obedient servant,

A. DUDLEY MANN.

Hon. J. P. BENJAMIN,
    Secretary of State, C. S. of America, Richmond, Va.

No. 2.]   COMMISSION TO THE CONTINENT,
                Paris, February 8, 1864.

SIR: My last being No. 1 under the new style of the commission and dated the 25th January ultimo, went by private opportunity to Bermuda, of which I have the honor to transmit a duplicate herewith. This goes in the closed mail to Nassau via New York. I have received nothing from the Department since my No. 1, referred to above.

I also transmit herewith an account of expenditures from the contingent fund under the commission to Great Britain, marked "A," and a separate account, marked "B," of expenditures for account of the State Department. The vouchers for these accounts I do not consider it prudent to send because of the risk of loss. Those for the account of the State Department, of course. correspond with the items, those for the contingent fund proper apply to such items as would usually admit of vouchers. The small items not vouched will be certified by Mr. Macfarland, as secretary of the commission.

Parliament in England met on the 4th instant, and I enclose herewith the debate in each house on the Queen's speech, which you may not otherwise obtain in extenso. I think it a matter of pregnant meaning that no reference whatever was made in the speech to American affairs, the solution being (besides apathy or indifference in the ministry), in the fact that the public mind of Europe is engrossed by European affairs, the principal being the complications in Germany. We have intelligence to-day that the Danes have retreated from Schleswig, leaving it entirely in the possession of the Austro-Prussian forces. Whether this will end the war remains to be seen; but I think it strongly imports that other European powers will not be brought in.

I think the general tenor of the debate imports that the opposition in England are preparing for an issue with the ministry on their foreign policy, but the former are conscious of weakness, and it may be that they will not attempt it. I can not see, therefore, any prospect of an early movement anywhere advantageous to us unless it arise from agitations before the people in England. In my last I spoke of the activity of our friends in that quarter. They are confident of good results, and are sincere, but at best this must be the work of time. Having nothing particular to detain me here, I shall go over to England in a few days, and my next, I hope, may give further and encouraging accounts of prospects there.

I have the honor to transmit also herewith, as directed in yours of the 30th November, my accounts for salary as special commissioner to Great Britain and as commissioner on the Continent. These accounts show only the sums that I have received, respectively, closing the commission to England on the 11th November last, and for the fragment of a quarter as commissioner on the Continent, terminating on the 31st December last. As directed by you, the drafts drawn on Messrs. Fraser, Trenholm & Co. were in triplicate. In regard to the question of exchange, it could apply only to the fragment of the quarter as commissioner on the Continent, and within the terms of your dispatch, upon actual sale of the drafts. To avoid complications I did not sell the draft, but sent it to my bankers in London simply to be collected and placed to my credit.

FEBRUARY 9.

I have by mail to-day from London received your Nos. 32 and 33, dated, respectively, the 13th and 14th November, ultimo. They came, I presume, via Nassau and New York. Oblige me by expressing to the President my sincere sense of his kindness in the expressions you were authorized to use in regard to my services in Europe. I can only regret that better opportunities have not offered to make them of real value. The new commission to which you refer, with the instructions, has not yet arrived. I can only say in meantime that the latter shall be properly observed.

I am not a little surprised and mortified to learn from your No. 23 of the deficiency in the volumes of Hansard. The order for them came but two days before the sailing of the Halifax steamer, and I was thus obliged to trust to the accuracy of the booksellers without a personal examination of the boxes; but the house of Willis & Southeran was of such standing and character that such extraordinary neglect could not have been anticipated. I shall at once communicate with them, and have the missing volumes supplied down to the latest issue of Hansard, to go by the Halifax steamer of the 20th of this month, by which mail I will of course write you.

I shall go over to London, as mentioned at the commencement of this dispatch, in the course of two or three days, where there are matters just now in which I am satisfied I can be useful.

In regard to the Confederate seal, the execution of which you placed in my charge, it is difficult to account for the delay in getting it finished. Before I left London, the design for it had been successfully completed by Mr. Harvey, an eminent sculptor, who at my request undertook to have the seal made by the most skillful artist. I have written twice to him since but without an answer. I will see further about it when in London and hope soon to send it to you.

I have, etc.,

J. M. MASON.

Hon. J. P. BENJAMIN,
Secretary of State.

No. 55.]   PARIS, February 10, 1864.

SIR: Herewith you will find triplicate of my last dispatch of 25th ultimo and duplicate also of my letter of 1st instant enclosing contingent account up to that date, etc. Commodore Barron informs me that the *Florida, Georgia,* and *Rappahannock* are now ready for sea and will sail immediately. Very great difficulty has been experienced in obtaining engineers for the two latter vessels, so rigid is the surveillance exercised by Federal spies and English detectives. Engineers could not be had in France, as assurances had been given to the minister of marine that no enlistment of any kind should be made in this country.

You will have seen by the newspapers the very disturbed condition of affairs in Europe. Its natural effect is to direct public attention from our contest and to destroy all present hope of any action in relation to it. It is the intention of Commodore Barron to send an officer to the Confederacy by Halifax and Bermuda on the 20th instant; he will convey full information of all matters connected with his branch of the service.

Mr. Mason goes to London at the urgent instance of some of our leading English friends, who believe that his presence there unofficially will be advantageous. They think a change of ministry imminent. Should the Conservatives come into power there will be a revival of the good understanding between France and England and the Emperor may renew his overtures for joint action in American affairs with a fair prospect of their being favorably entertained.

I have the honor to be, with great respect, your most obedient servant,

JOHN SLIDELL.

Hon. J. P. BENJAMIN,
  Secretary of State.

No. 37.] CONFEDERATE STATES COMMERCIAL AGENCY,
        London, February 13, 1864.

SIR: You will probably agree with me that next to a radical change in the policy of the British Government, the best thing for us is whatever exposes that policy in its true light and brings it into universal discredit and contempt. In this sense the events of the last few weeks have been singularly favorable to us. For a moment I was anxious that the outbreak of war in Europe might divert public attention from our affairs. I am glad to say that, on the contrary, it has served to awaken the British public to a consciousness of their attitude before Europe, and the English are not such "a nation of shopkeepers" as to bear with equanimity the loss of prestige and influence. There is, unless I am greatly mistaken, a very general upheaving of popular resentment or at least impatience at the pitiable trifling with the national honor by the present ministry. A sudden ebullition of anger is not inconsistent with the stolid indifference which has been the chief characteristic of public opinion for some time past, and you need not be surprised if the chapter of accidents now opening before us should conclude with an explosion.

A number of events, small or great, have concurred to arouse a sense of shame, ridicule, and mortification. There is the brutal destruction of an unresisting populous town in Japan; the ludicrous miscarriage of the pompously mysterious expedition to China, by which a national conquest was to have been effected under the thin guise of private enterprise. Then the Dano-German war with its unexpectedly rapid catastrophes. With the English masses the Germans are associated with the idea of parasites on the public purse, and they are in consequence very cordially disliked, while the marriage of the Prince of Wales has made the Danes popular. The ruling classes are well aware that the formation of a Scandinavian monarchy, which perhaps would be the best thing that could happen to the Danes, would be a blow to England. Everybody knows that this danger might have been averted by even moderate firmness and consistency on the part of Earl Russell; everybody does not know how far the intrigues of that most unlucky of political speculators may have complicated the danger, and the suspicion is not absent that the precipitate abandonment of the whole line of Danish fortifications may have been in accordance with advice from here to make only a formal resistance. Even the popularity of the Queen, real and deep seated as it is, could not long withstand the conviction that in this vital question she feels as a German and not as the sovereign of England. There are rumors of her contemplated abdication, which of course have no foundation but the mere whisper of which indicates a reaction,

In proportion as the events of Europe reveal the absurdities of Earl Russell's policy, his course in American affairs is more correctly appreciated. The coarse insolence of Mr. Seward's dispatch of the 11th July, printed in the diplomatic correspondence laid before Congress, but of which all knowledge, verbal or otherwise, is denied by the foreign office here, has naturally produced no ordinary sensation. It seems incredible that any minister, least of all Mr. Adams, should assume so grave a responsibility as to suppress a dispatch without advising either the Government to which he is accredited or his own of the step. It is more probable that the obnoxious document was withdrawn or officially undelivered at Earl Russell's own private suggestion, an act of extra official friendship which Mr. Seward requited suo more. But, however this may be, the dispatch has done its work, though not exactly in the manner Mr. Seward intended. It may be comparatively safe to insult Earl Russell, but he will find the English Nation somewhat more susceptible. There is also a suspicious proximity of dates in regard to the seizure of the rams, which has not escaped attention. It is to say the least most unfortunate for Earl Russell that he should have obtained within four days, while absent in Scotland, all the evidence which had been previously wanting, and which it subsequently required four months to make available for legal proceedings, and that these four days should have comprised the identical period during which Mr. Adams plied him with a quick succession of "vigorous" notes. Ill-natured people are prone to explain such coincidences as cause and effect. In brief, these things come so fast and thick one upon the other, that I do not believe my hopes deceive me when I say that an honest disgust is spreading among all classes and they are beginning to see their American policy as we have always seen it.

Let us not, however, deceive ourselves. If we have anything to hope, it is from the folly of our enemies and not the power of our friends. It is of good augury indeed that Lord Derby has taken the field on the American question, for heretofore that question has suffered most from being in the hands of men of the second order, and sometimes far lower, in parliamentary standing. But he does not come as our ally. If you scrutinize the debates you will find that the leaders of the opposition proceed like cautious generals drawing lines of circumvallation, but not preparing for immediate battle. Their object is rather to embarrass the Government than to attack it seriously. They criticize sharply, but it is the manner not the intention of Earl Russell's diplomacy; the skill and temper of the pilot, not the direction of the ship's prow. They do not say that the English participation in the Mexican expedition should have been prolonged; that Poland ought to have been assisted; that the South should have been recognized; that the invitation to the Congress should have been accepted; or even that they would go to war for the integrity of Denmark. The reason for this is to be found in the traditional reverence of that party for the personal wishes of the sovereign which causes Lord Derby's adherents to claim for him the distinction of being the "first friend of the Crown," but it is fatal to the initiation of a really original policy. My hope then rests in Earl Russell's remaining in office and there making the policy he represents so universally odious and infamous that when a change at last comes it will be thorough and permanent.

The appeal of the Crown from the exchequer court to the court of exchequer chamber (consisting of the judges of the Queen's bench and common pleas) was dismissed by a plurality of three against two of the judges, on the ground of lack of jurisdiction. The only appeal now remaining lies to the House of Lords. In the matter of the rams, after four months military detention, the initial step of judicial prosecution has been taken just in time to afford the Government a pretext for withholding the diplomatic correspondence on the subject. A report appeared in some of the papers that one of the armor-plated vessels building in the Clyde and near completion had been sold to the Danish Government.

Circumstances having rendered it necessary to make new arrangements for preserving our private route through the North, I have provisionally arranged, subject to your sanction, for a trusty messenger making regular round trips at least once a month, for which I engage to pay, at the completion of each round trip, $100 in Federal currency. All the principal officers of the Government abroad will doubtless avail themselves in cases of emergency of this route, and bear a pro rata share of the expense. But it appears to me of the highest importance that the machinery, which is now almost perfect at this end, and may be made so at the other, should not be needlessly complicated by addressing more than one person at each end of the route, and I would therefore suggest that all communications thus conveyed should be sent through your Department. The precautions I have adopted here are such as to defy the scrutiny of the federal post office, as letters reach me safely under a blank cover.

I enclose you a pamphlet, La Question Mexicaine et la Colonization Française, of which, with the assistance of an able translator, I am the secret author. It was written in the hope of its having some bearing on the Mexican debate in the French chamber, and also that the Emperor would not be altogether insensible to the delicacy of the compliment when informed that it came from a Confederate source. I can not say that in the former expectation the success was brilliant. Through some unaccountable accident the pamphlet was retained by the French censorship and its sale prevented until the debate was over, and it has since encountered the equally unaccountable hostility of its Parisian publisher. I am really at a loss to understand the apathy of the French Government, with so many organs of publicity at its command, in neglecting the most obvious measures for combating the unpopularity of the Mexican expedition.

This leads me to the subject of the French press. I have been informed through Mr. Slidell of the recall of Mr. de Leon, but as I have had no communication from you or Mr. de Leon, I am uncertain what your intentions may be. My original instructions contemplated France as within the probable sphere of my duties, but I should not venture on an extensive plan of operations without your orders. In the meanwhile I content myself with repeating in Paris the same inexpensive experiment which has been so signally successful in Turin, though it will be difficult to find the same combination of zeal and tact, industry and discretion, which Señor Manetta possesses. The enclosed copy of a letter to M. Aucaigne, which I beg you will look over, will show what I have so far done in this direction. I need scarcely say that a more systematic effort and on a larger scale is necessary to make any useful impression on the Parisian press. For this, money, though of course necessary for the lubrication of the machinery, is the least important requisite. What is the most important and most difficult to obtain is a staff of well-trained native writers. Publications, however able in themselves, find in this age of printing an imperceptibly small circle of readers, and the money thus expended except in some special cases where a coup is intended benefits the printer more than either the public or the cause. Again, it is not one newspaper article, nor a dozen, but hundreds that effect public opinion at large. Reiteration is the most powerful argument with the hundreds of thousands who take their opinions at second hand. Again, the operator who directs these efforts should be invisible, and this is a self-abnegation which sometimes puts the most attested patience and forbearance to a painful strain. Of this, however, you may rest assured that neither in England nor in France can anything really useful be done in the press without the assistance of native writers, thoroughly enlisted in our cause; but talent can not be enlisted by merely sordid considerations unless aided by the hope of distinction, in other words by motives of self-love and ambition. We have so conspicuous and so honorable a position before the world, that fortunately our ability of so enlisting talent is not measured by our pecuniary means. I am now recruiting upon this same principle among the generation of rising university men, who, within the next 10 years, will give the tone to public opinion in this country, but the Index gives me means for so doing which are inseparable from its locality.

Enclosed please find reports from your agents in Ireland, also copy of my reply to a letter from Lieutenant Capston of the same purport as his report to you.

The Polish insurrection has dropped below the horizon of public attention without even the honors of funeral obsequies.

I have the honor to remain, very respectfully, your obedient servant,

HENRY HOTZE.

Hon. J. P. BENJAMIN,
    Secretary of State, Richmond.

17 SAVILLE ROW, W., *January 29, 1864.*

DEAR SIR: It has been impossible for me for many reasons to give you earlier a definite reply to the propositions made to me in your favor of the 16th instant. This proposition is that if an income of from £100 to £150 per annum were secured to you, so as to relieve you of the necessity of employing several of the most valuable hours of the day in teaching, you would then be able to devote the whole of your time and energies to the advocacy of our cause through the Parisian press.

I have had such abundant evidence of your zeal and of your genuine disinterested devotion to our cause that I have determined to accept your propositions, and though I can not at present insure you the maximum mentioned by you, which I hope to do eventually, I can afford to do this. I can place you on the staff of the Index as Paris correspondent, with a salary of 50 francs a week, payable at such periods as may be most convenient to you, provided they are regular. You will further credit yourself and charge to the Index office all reasonable outlays for postage and purchase of newspapers incurred in the discharge of your duties.

You will not be required to write for the Index, as it already has an English correspondent in Paris, and any information which you may deem of interest will be addressed to me privately. Your duty will consist in propagating through the French papers the views and the intelligence published through the Index, for which purpose you will read that journal carefully and select from it such portions as, in your discretion, you think suitable for the public and acceptable to the newspapers with which you are connected or with which you may hereafter establish relations. Your discretion in this selection will be limited by no other rule than that you shall not in any essential point go beyond or contrary to what you may perceive to be the policy of the Index. You may copy from its columns at pleasure without acknowledgment. As the Index has but a very small circulation in France, not exceeding 125 or 150, this can be done without fear of exposure. It is habitually done without my permission by the Memorial Diplomatique, as witness the Richmond correspondence in its last number. Of course official documents form an exception to this rule and should always be acknowledged to the Index. That you may use Index matter to greater advantage you will be furnished, so far as practicable, with interesting information in advance of the publication of the paper, so that you will frequently be able to publish a Richmond letter or a piece of news in Paris before it is published by the Index in London. The Index has a correspondent on substantially the same conditions in Turin, and I may say without extravagance that by a strict adherence to these instructions he has worked wonders in the Italian press. A similar plan is in operation in the Irish press, and, generally speaking, you have in the above an outline of the sort of duty which the Index was established to perform.

If my offer is acceptable to you, let me know at once, and we shall consider our engagement to commence with the 1st of February. Minor details we shall settle hereafter. I shall always be obliged for any suggestions you may offer and which you may rest assured will always receive most respectful attention. On the subject of the International I will write you hereafter. If meantime you can collect any further information about its circulation and standing, it will be useful to me. I have to thank you for the copy of the Diogene you sent me. I can not agree with you that such articles are "stupid." On the contrary, they seem to me contrived with the ingenuity of the father of lies himself to prejudice the masses against us. Just such literature has set class against class, the poor against the rich. What the slaveholders are charged with is precisely what, if you take up any cheap English periodical for the masses, you will see charged by sensational novelists and prudent moralists against the aristocracy of birth or of wealth, and the Legrees of the South find their counterpart in the debauched noblemen, the grinding employer, the tyrannical mill-owner, of a certain school of writing. Keep this in mind if you should ever undertake to defend the South against these slanders. The articles on this subject in the Index are always my own, and they will indicate to you what line of policy I think it best to adopt.

In your note just received you state that Mr. de Leon had informed you that he had been relieved from duty and that there is now no one in his place. In reply to your inquiry it is sufficient to say that until the government sees proper to replace Mr. de Leon by another officer my instructions enable me to perform the duties which the vacancy may render necessary. On any point of difficulty or doubt, however, you will consult freely with Mr. Slidell, whom you will always find ready and able to give you all counsel and assistance required.

I remain, very cordially, yours,

HENRY HOTZE.

M. FELIX AUCAIGNE, *Paris.*

[Enclosure.]

C. S. COMMERCIAL AGENCY,
London, February 5, 1864.

LIEUTENANT: Yours of February 3 from Queenstown is duly to hand. You ask my immediate attention to the pressing need for money, without which you inform me that "nothing can be done," and that "you will be reduced to a nonentity." I understand from your letter that you have special reference to the Federal agent Feeny, against whom, if properly followed up, a case of enlistment could, in your opinion, be made out.

In reply I have to state that I have no power in the matter except what I derive from your instructions, which authorize me to allow such contingent expenses as may be necessary for the proper performance of your duty. The amount of such expenses as is expressly stated was contemplated by the department to be small, and I have therefore advised you stringent economy. But this advice was not intended to prevent you from pursuing any advantage which opportunity might present. That I did not see any such advantage in the prosecution of the letter-opening case was my reason for not encouraging you in that. I may go further and say that in a case of evident necessity I should venture to exceed the limits of your funds and supply what might be needed from my own allowance. But to do this I must be in possession of all the facts requisite to enable me to form a judgment of the expediency of action and the possibilities of success, as well as the estimated expense. In the Feeny case I can not form such a judgment, and your report to the Secretary is not more precise in the specification of the purposes for which you desire money. If, therefore, as I suppose from your request, you wish to make larger expenditures than you feel authorized or able without my express approval or that of the department, I must await hearing from you more in detail.

I would also suggest that when you desire to direct my attention to any paragraph in a newspaper as in the Feeny case, you will cut it out and send it under envelope. The number of papers and pamphlets, etc., sent me daily is so great that without this precaution there are many chances of its being overlooked.

Respectfully yours,

HENRY HOTZE.

Lieutenant J. L. CAPSTON,
Agent State Department, Queenstown.

No. 56.]   PARIS, *February 16, 1864.*

SIR: Commander Maury, C. S. Navy, being dispatched by Commodore Barron to Richmond, I avail myself of so favorable an occasion to speak more fully of matters to which I had in previous dispatches but very briefly and cautiously alluded.

Lieutenant Whittle, who was sent to the Confederacy by Captain Bulloch last summer, communicated to the President and Secretary of the Navy detailed information respecting the arrangements made for the building of ships in France and the extrication of two of those then in course of construction in England from anticipated difficulties.

These arrangements have been seriously interfered with by the felonious abstraction of certain papers as stated in my No. 49 and it is now asserted that, by similar means, papers relating to the ships in (Auk) have come into the possession of the emissaries of the Washington Government. On this latter point I am inclined to think that the assertion is unfounded, as Captain Bulloch is very confident that no access could have been had to his papers, and I have every reason to believe that in other quarters equal vigilance has been observed. So far as regards the corvettes that are being built at Bordeaux and Nantes there is unfortunately no doubt of the fact that complete evidence of their ownership is in the hands of Dayton and has been by him communicated to this Government.

By referring to the report of my conversation with the Emperor contained in my No. 38, you will find that while fully assenting to the arming and departure of the corvettes, he consented only to the building of ironclads for our account and did not commit himself to permit their sailing unless their destination could be concealed. This, in the case of ironclads, could only be done by setting up an apparent ownership by some foreign government; as to the corvettes they were to be represented as intended for commercial purposes in the Indian Ocean, China, etc.

The contract for the corvettes was concluded only after the official consent to their armament and sailing was given by the minister of marine, and this was given on the representation that they were intended for commercial purposes; although their real character and destination were fully known to him he, however, reluctantly signing the order in obedience to superior authority. No such authority was given in the case of the ironclads and I was ignorant that any contract was in contemplation for their construction until after it had been made. I mention these facts not with the most remote idea of implying any censure upon Captain Bulloch, but to establish the distinction to be drawn between the two classes of vessels, which it is necessary to bear in mind in order to come to a proper decision as to the course to be pursued in relation to them.

In the first interview I had with the minister of marine on the 19th November, consequent upon my note to the Emperor of 9th November, contained in my No. 48, he drew a very broad line of distinction between the corvettes and the ironclads, saying that with proper precautions the former might be permitted to go to sea, but that the ironclads being from their very shv [untranslated] solely fitted for warlike purposes, their being permitted to sail in spite of the remonstrances of the Washington Government and in violation of the Emperor's declaration of neutrality would be an overt act of hostility.

The question now presents itself what is to be done with these vessels? Mr. Arman, the builder of the ironclads, was informed that they will not be permitted to go to sea except as the property of some nonbelligerent government; this was before the breaking out of hostilities between Denmark, Austria, and Prussia. Captain Bulloch, after consulting Mr. Mason, Commodore Barron, and me determined to sell the ironclads; they could have been disposed of at a considerable advance on their cost to Denmark or to Prussia, but the pending war may put these purchasers, as belligerents, out of the market. Commodore Barron and Captain Bulloch say that the corvettes were intended to act in conjunction with the ironclads in raising the blockade of our coasts, and this object being no longer attainable and there being few Federal merchant vessels afloat, they are disposed to sell the corvettes also, or at least two of them.

I do not agree with them in this view of the case. Should we withdraw our cruisers, the Federal flag would soon resume on the ocean the rank which we have forced it to abdicate. We can not expect the *Alabama* and *Florida* always to avoid the pursuit of the enemy and we should be prepared to supply their loss. I fear that the *Rappahannock* will prove to be as unfit for that service as the *Georgia* and will not make more than one cruise.

In deciding, however, the question of the disposition to be made of the vessels, a new difficulty presents itself which applies alike to both classes. It has been found extremely difficult to obtain engineers for the *Georgia* and *Rappahannock*, two small vessels, and with the increased vigilance of the English authorities, it will hereafter be found almost impracticable to man several large vessels. On the other hand a few months may produce great changes in our favor. I know that the Emperor's feelings are as friendly as ever and a new ministry in England may enable him to indulge them. The chapter of accidents is always in the long run fruitful of great and unexpected results; perhaps it may be better to go on and complete the ships. There is no reason to apprehend any interruption in the work and there is no danger whatever of losing them by any proceedings similar to those pending in England, as there is no municipal law prohibiting the fitting out of ships of war for belligerent powers with whom France is at peace.

I have given Captain Maury verbal explanations respecting the ships in England, which I have thought it not prudent to commit to paper even with so safe a messenger.

I have the honor to be, with great respect, your most obedient servant,

JOHN SLIDELL.

Hon. J. P. BENJAMIN,
  Secretary of State.

No. 3.]   COMMISSION ON THE CONTINENT,
           London, February 18, 1864.

SIR: My No. 2 from Paris, dated the 8th instant, with its enclosures, will go with this. I brought it with me from Paris last week to be mailed here and to go via Nassau, but being detained a day at Boulogne by a storm in the Channel it was too late for that mail. Referring to its contents, I have only now to add that I arrived here on the 13th instant. I have so far been able to see but few of the public men, and can give you little additional information of the state of opinion in England. The mail from Bermuda, via Halifax, arrived here on the 14th. I was in hopes to have received the new commission with the instructions referred to in your No. 32 of the 13th of February, but it brought me nothing.

Since my arrival we have had reported the seizure of the Confederate cruiser *Tuscaloosa* at the Cape of Good Hope by the colonial authorities there under instructions from the Government in England. Having no intercourse with the foreign office here I addressed a note to Mr. Seymour Fitzgerald, M. P., calling his attention to the report of it in the Times and requesting, if he saw no reason to the contrary, that he would make a call on the Government for information. I have had no reply, but on the 16th the Earl of Carnarvon made the call in the House of Lords in connection with other matters relating to the *Alabama.* You will see Earl Russell's reply in the Times of the 17th, which I send herewith. It seems that he avows the instructions, but says it will be necessary to communicate with the colonial authorities before they could be laid before the house. This is certainly a most extraordinary aggression. The *Tuscaloosa,* as you are probably aware, was an enemy's ship captured by the *Alabama* and fitted out as a cruiser under officers transferred from the latter. It is difficult to conjecture on what grounds or pretexts instructions were issued from the foreign office authorizing her seizure, nor were they disclosed by Earl Russell in debate. I can only say that the enquiry shall be followed up, so far as I can be instrumental, by communication with our friends here in Parliament. I send you also several late issues of the Times, which include the report made from the Cape of Good Hope. In this connection, I do not know whether files of the English papers are received at the Department of State. If not, would it not be as well that I should order them to be sent regularly by the semimonthly mails, via Nassau and Bermuda, to our agents there to be forwarded by them? If two, I would suggest the Times and the Morning Herald, the latter the organ of the Opposition. If three, the Post might be added, said to be the immediate organ of Lord Palmerston.

These dispatches will be borne by Commander Maury of the Navy who is sent home by Commodore Barron, with the approbation of Mr. Slidell and myself, in order personally to communicate to the Navy Department (should the dispatches which he will bear be destroyed in transitu) full information in regard to the total failure of our efforts to get out ships either from France or England. Mr. Slidell, who had full cognizance of all the machinery set at work in France, will, by his dispatches to go with this, have given you full information, or if lost, it will be furnished orally by Commander Maury. Suffice it to say here the conviction has been forced upon us that there remains no chance or hope of getting ships out either from England or France and that, in consequence, those in prospect are to be disposed of in the best way that may be done. It is a painful disappointment, but I am satisfied that nothing was left undone to effect the object. From England we have long since had nothing to expect; from France we had a right to entertain a belief of other results; why, Mr. Slidell's dispatches or Commander Maury will explain. I confess that I can see neither excuse nor palliation in the defeat of our expectations in that quarter.

As my address in Europe may be, for a time, uncertain, perhaps it would be safer, until further advice, to send my dispatches to the care of Henry Hotze, esq., whose address you have.

I have the honor to be, very respectfully, your obedient servant,

J. M. MASON.

Hon. J. P. BENJAMIN,
    Secretary of State.

No. 4.]   LONDON, *February 18, 1864.*
Hon. J. P. BENJAMIN,
    Secretary of State.

SIR: Referring to the concluding paragraphs in my No. 2 from Paris, which goes by same conveyance as this, on my arrival in London four days ago I called at the house of Willis & Southeran, and exhibited to them a copy of your dispatch No. 33 of the 14th November, relating to the imperfect condition of the copy of Hansard which they had furnished, and asked for explanations. It required some time to examine the subject, and they have just reported that the facts were as stated in your letter. In excuse they say (I quote from their note) "the remaining volumes were at that time very imperfect, and some very difficult to procure, so that we only packed to the period that was perfect, viz, 1853, inclusive. The portion from the session 1854 to 1863, which will complete the set, we hope to have from the binders within a week from this time (16th instant) when they shall be carefully packed and dispatched without delay." There is certainly in all this no excuse, at least, for their strange neglect in not informing me at the time, or since, of the deficiency in the number of volumes, and stranger still, this omission when they were paid for the full set. I called their attention, too, to the difference between the price paid and that quoted in their catalogue, to which you referred, but their note not referring to it I have again called their attention to it and may have their reply in time for this dispatch, which goes off to-night. Although I went to them at once on my arrival here and urged dispatch, that the books might go by the Halifax steamer which bears this, it seems that it can not be effected. I shall be able to send them, however, I hope, by a steamer of Crenshaw's line, to sail direct for Bermuda in course of ten days. After I get the affair ended, unless better explanation is made than yet afforded, I shall be cautious of this house hereafter.

In regard to the seal too, I have now a report from Mr. Foley, who it seems has been some time absent from London. He says that the artisan, Mr. Wyon, employed to engrave it, informs him that it will yet require six weeks or two months to finish it.

" As he is very anxious " he says, " to bestow upon it all the pains so important a work demands, he is executing it in silver (the metal the state seals of England are executed in) which offers the advantage of proof against rust, so often destructive to a seal engraved in steel."

The above is from Mr. Foley's note of the 10th instant from Dublin to me at Paris. He tells me further that the cost for engraving the seal, including the press for working it, will be 80 guineas, and that, as it is customary in England to receive half the amount on commencing the work, advises that I should conform, as it will at least prevent excuse for delay, and which I will do as soon as I can obtain the address of Mr. Wyon.

I send by Commander Maury, who bears this, two copies of Colonel Fremantle's Diary in the Southern States, at his request, one of which you will find inscribed on the inner leaf, to the President and the other to you.

I have, etc.

J. M. MASON.

Hon. J. P. BENJAMIN,
    Secretary of State.

P. S.—It occurs to me to say that I have no instructions from you as to sending the seal over, and from its character it appears to me that no risk whatever should be incurred of its getting into the hands of the enemy, which might happen, whatever precautions were taken here. As it may involve an additional delay of only a few weeks, I think I shall retain the seal until further instructions.

J. M. M.

No. 30.]
                    DEPARTMENT OF STATE,
                    Richmond, February 19, 1864.

SIR: I am without any dispatches from you later than your No. 51, of 15th December, which arrived on 16th ultimo. As several vessels, however, have recently been lost in an attempt to run the blockade at Wilmington, I can account for my disappointment. Part of a mail was recently found on the beach near Wilmington, which had probably been washed ashore after being thrown overboard, and among the letters saved was a dispatch from Mr. Hotze, of 15th ultimo, informing me that there was no longer any doubt of the departure of Maximilian for Mexico. Per contra, the news from Europe up to the 30th ultimo, as it reaches us via the North, throws fresh doubt on the subject.

My immediate purpose in writing at this time is to place you in possession of the facts touching the action of this Government in the case of the steamer *Chesapeake*. This is best done by enclosing you a copy of the instructions * delivered to the Hon. Mr. Holcombe, of Virginia, who is sent to Halifax as special commissioner to attend to this business, and who will be the bearer of this dispatch, which he will deposit in the British closed mail on his arrival in a neutral port.

The ill-advised course of Earl Russell in forcing this Government to suspend intercourse with Great Britain is producing fruits that he might easily have anticipated, and its effects are felt by the British cabinet as well as by ourselves. It was plain that occasions must arise in a war like the present when some communication between a recognized belligerent and a neutral would be indispensable, and yet Earl Russell sacrificed the usual and well settled mode of unofficial intercourse through our commissioner in London in order to propitiate the favor of our enemies, and is greatly perplexed how to make himself heard, when he in turn needs the interview so curtly refused to Mr. Mason.

One attempt has been made by him to open correspondence through a private person named Cridland, with the result of which the annexed copy of my reply to that gentlemen * will acquaint you. Another attempt has recently been made, and he has drawn upon himself a stinging rebuff from the United States. I send you copy of a letter from Mr. Helm, explaining that he proposed to open a correspondence through Mr. Crawford. The British vessel of war which brought the communication from Mr. Crawford arrived, it appears, off Charleston Harbor, and I send you an insolent paragraph from a Northern paper, boasting of the vessel's having been turned off and refused permission to deliver the dispatches. I can not imagine in what manner or by what title Earl Russell proposed to address us. If as the Government of the so-styled " Confederacy," we should of course have refused to receive the communication.

I also enclose you several interesting and important documents.

* First. President's address to the Army.
* Second. Address of Congress to the people.
* Third. Copy of laws about imports and exports.
* Fourth. Copy of laws about finances, taxes, etc.

All these are in the highest degree encouraging and inspiriting. The measures about the currency are, what the physicians term, " heroic practice," but the people welcome them. The army bill puts into service the whole arms-bearing population. The nation is stripped for war, and we hope this year to give the invaders a lesson which shall suffice for all time to come.

---

* Not found.

I have much more that I could write, but am urgently pressed for time. Pray communicate the contents of this to Mr. Mason, to whom I can not now write.

I am, very respectfully, your obedient servant,

J. P. BENJAMIN,
Secretary of State.

Hon. JOHN SLIDELL,
Paris, France.

P. S.—It may be well to send to Mr. Hotze whatever you think should be published of the contents of this dispatch and enclosures.

Second P. S.—*February 23, 1864.*—Your numbers 52 and 53 have been received, but can not be answered till next conveyance.

J. P. BENJAMIN,
Secretary of State.

CONFEDERATE STATES OF AMERICA,
DEPARTMENT OF STATE,
Richmond, February 20, 1864.

SIR: I have the honor to transmit for your information extracts from two dispatches received from Henry Hotze, Esq., commercial agent of the Confederate States at London. Nos. 34* and 35 are dated, respectively, December 26, 1863, and January 16,* 1864.

I have the honor to be, sir, your obedient servant,

J. P. BENJAMIN,
Secretary of State.

Hon. JAMES A. SEDDON,
Secretary of War.

No. 14.] DEPARTMENT OF STATE,
Richmond, February 24, 1864.

SIR: I have the honor to acknowledge the receipt of your Nos. 33, 34, 35, and 36, as well as of your private dispatches 12, 13, 14, and 15. The cipher letter to Mr. Mallory annexed to this last private dispatch was translated and given to him yesterday.

You will receive herewith Treasury draft No. 5755, on Fraser, Trenholm & Co., for £2,000 for secret service, which you will please acknowledge. I have also returned to the fund for diplomatic intercourse the 10,000 francs you received from Mr. Lamar, so as to relieve you from the obligation of restoring it, and thus place these £2,000 entirely at your disposal. It is not found possible to make the same arrangements in relation to the secret-service fund as for the payment of salaries, and I am compelled to forego the attempt to put them on the same footing at our bankers.

You will learn from the series of acts passed by our recent Congress how thoroughly in earnest is our whole people in this war. The legislation in relation to imports and exports goes far toward the point desired and suggested by your dispatches, and when the regu-

---

* See pp. 981, 1001.

lations are published (which will be within a week) it will be apparent that, although exports for private account are not entirely embargoed, much the greater part of the cotton that leaves our ports will be for account of Government.

There will, of course, be temporary distress and trouble under the operation of our financial laws, but you will see that Congress has not hesitated to adopt legislation that must wipe out of existence, by the joint operation of funding at 4 per cent and heavy taxation, at least six hundred millions of our currency during the next eight months, and of this sum at least one-half will be received for taxes. Yet our noble people receive this legislation with approval and satisfaction, and ere four months have gone by we shall have made an enormous step toward the restoration of our whole financial system to a sound basis. Our friends need fear nothing on the question of finances. We owe nothing worth mentioning abroad, and the people at home are willing, if necessary, to be taxed to the whole amount of the domestic debt and wipe it out of existence. No such extreme measure is, of course, thought of, but I speak of possible resources, and if this war does not end till our means give out, it will endure for the next generation.

It is difficult to comply with your request to send you public documents, as our arrangements on that score are very imperfect, but I forward what I can.

I regret to say that one of two cases from you, forwarded to me by Major Walker, was captured on the *Nutfield*. The other has been received, and if they were duplicate cases, as Major Walker seems to state, the loss is of no importance. The case received contained books and pamphlets published by our friends in England, Mr. McHenry's book, etc.

I am, very respectfully, your obedient servant,

J. P. BENJAMIN,
Secretary of State.

HENRY HOTZE, Esq.,
London.

No. 2.]
DEPARTMENT OF STATE,
Richmond, February 24, 1864.

SIR: * * * In addition to the duties confided to you by the instructions of 19th instant, I have now, at the request of the President, to add another.

We are informed that several hundreds of the officers and men enlisted in our service, who were captured by the enemy, are now in Canada, having escaped from prison; that they are without means of returning home, although anxious to resume service. The Government fully recognizes the duty of aiding these unfortunate public servants to reach their posts of duty, and can only regret that it was not sooner informed of their condition. You are requested to make in Canada and Nova Scotia the requisite arrangements for having passage furnished them, via Halifax to Bermuda, where they will receive from Major Walker, the agent of the Department of War, the necessary aid to secure their passage home. Colonel Kane, from whom we have just learned the facts, suggests that a proper agent be employed at Montreal who shall give public notice that he is authorized to furnish passage to the Confederacy of all officers and men heretofore enlisted in its service, who desire aid to return to their homes; that the applicants be sent down the St. Lawrence and round to Halifax by water, as the cheapest conveyance, and from Halifax to Bermuda. In Halifax you will find the mercantile house of B. Wier, to which you can apply with confidence for any advice or assistance in making these arrangements.

The whole number of escaped prisoners is supposed not to exceed 400, and it is not probable that all will make application. You will receive herewith a letter of credit on Liverpool for $25,000, which we presume to be enough for the present, and which you will use as may be needed for this purpose, and you are requested to send as early news as convenient of the prospect of restoring our fellow-citizens to their country, the number likely to come, and whether a further sum of money is necessary for the purpose.

It would be advisable, before acting in this matter, to inform the British colonial authorities of your design, in order to obviate any misrepresentations of our enemies who will assuredly endeavor to create the false impression that we are recruiting for our armies in British territory. You will explain that you are instructed scrupulously to avoid any breach of public or municipal law, and that your sole purpose is, as above explained, to aid our own people to return to their homes.

Very respectfully, your obedient servant,

J. P. BENJAMIN,
Secretary of State.

Hon. J. P. HOLCOMBE,
Special Commissioner, etc., Richmond.

DEPARTMENT OF STATE,
Richmond, February 25, 1864.

SIR: I have to acknowledge receipt of your letter of 15th ultimo, enclosing one from B. Wier, esq., and other documents relative to the capture of the *Chesapeake* and the detention of the vessel and crew by the British authorities at Halifax, and I take this occasion to express my thanks for your attention to the subject. After an examination of the papers the President has determined to send the Hon. James P. Holcombe as special commissioner to represent the interests of the Confederate Government in the matter referred to before the British courts and authorities, and he will leave immediately for this purpose.

Your letter of 29th ultimo has also been received and the box mentioned therein has come to hand.

I am, very respectfully, your obedient servant,

J. P. BENJAMIN,
Secretary of State.

Major N. S. WALKER,
Agent of War Department, Bermuda.

P. S.—The original box per *Nutfield* was lost.

172 RUE DE RIVOLI, PARIS.
February 25, 1864.

SIR: I have the honor to transmit to you communications from Lieutenant Campbell, commanding Confederate steamer *Rappahannock*, and other officers attached to and connected with this vessel, which I have endorsed and forwarded as the senior flag-officer in Europe.

I beg leave to add my assurances that it never was the intention to fit out or equip this vessel as a man-of-war in any port of France. Her entrance into the port of Calais was purely the result of an accident to her machinery sustained at sea after her departure from Sheerness, and I have been strict in my instructions to Captain Campbell to use all dispatch in getting his vessel ready for sea and that every care should be observed to avoid anything that might even wear the appearance of a reinforcement to the ship. To the best of my belief and knowledge these instructions have been faithfully conformed to, and the *Rappahannock* will now leave the waters of France utterly unprepared for service as a man-of-war. Her compliment of men should be not less than 100; she has now on board only about 40, of whom 20 are required in the engine room.

With a reiteration of my sincere and grateful acknowledgment of the uniform courtesy and kindness shown by the authorities and people to the officers and men attached to the vessels of the Confederacy, which have been by force of circumstances beyond the control of the commanding officers compelled to trespass upon foreign hospitality,

I am, sir, most respectfully, your obedient servant,

S. BARRON,
Flag-Officer, C. S. N.

Hon. JOHN SLIDELL, etc.

[Enclosure.]

CALAIS, *February 24, 1864.*

SIR: In reply to yours of the 23 instant, I state on honor that I have never violated any law of France, either civil, municipal, or international, nor have I in any way knowingly abused the hospitality which the French Government has been so generous as to extend to us.

The *Rappahannock* entered the harbor of Calais in consequence of injuries sustained by her machinery "whilst at sea" which rendered her unseaworthy as a steamer. She has received no fitments or equipments as a man-of-war while in this port; no arms whatever have been received on board other than the side arms of the officers. The number of the crew has not been increased since the vessel was in this port. No French subject has been enlisted.

In conclusion, I would like to impress upon you that the *Rappahannock* entered the harbor of Calais with the full consent of the authorities. Every act of mine as the commander of a national vessel has been done openly and publicly, without the slightest desire or intention of any concealment. I have always tried to impress the authorities here with my sincere determination not to violate any laws of the nation or regulation of the harbor.

Very respectfully, your most obedient servant,

W. P. A. CAMPBELL,
Lieutenant, Commanding.

Flag-Officer SAMUEL BARRON, C. S. N., *Paris.*

[Enclosure.]

C. S. Steamer Rappahannock,
Calais, France, February 24, 1864.

Sir: I hereby certify that I commanded the vessel now called the *Rappahannock* when she left English waters, and that she appeared off the port of Calais for no other purpose than to receive on board certain persons who were there awaiting her arrival.

I also certify that the injury to the boilers which rendered her entrance into Calais necessary was sustained while at sea.

Respectfully, etc.,

J. F. Ramsay.

W. P. A. Campbell,
Lieutenant, Commanding.

[Enclosure.]

Paris, *February 25, 1864.*

Sir: I have the honor to inform you that I have been on duty connected with the C. S. S. *Rappahannock* since her purchase into our service and prior to her leaving Sheerness. I now state on the honor of an officer that the entering a French port by the *Rappahannock*, or her tarrying off the French coast longer than to receive on board her officers from Calais, was not contemplated up to the moment of the accident to her machinery.

Very respectfully, your obedient servant,

W. F. Carter,
Confederate States Navy.

Flag-Officer S. Barron,
Confederate States Navy.

[Enclosure—Translation.]

Calais, *February 4, 1864.*

Sir: I have just received from his Excellency the Secretary of the Navy and of the Colonies a dispatch containing exact and formal orders, in that which concerns your ship, and the notification that I must make to you is, I beg you to believe, very painful to me, nevertheless the communication I had the honor to make to you the 11th of last month, and in following which you declared to me you could be in complete readiness to put to sea in about a week from that date, while giving you to perceive the possibility of the measures which have come about to-day, should have entirely prepared you to face them.

I regret, therefore, sir, to inform you that the Government of his Majesty the Emperor has decided that I shall give legal notice of " the order to the *Rappahannock* to leave the port of Calais on the tide which follows the reception of this letter," and that failing to comply with this injunction you will no longer be permitted to leave this port until the end of the hostilities between the United States and the Confederacy.

The long stay of your ship at Calais, and above all the time that has elapsed since the above-mentioned order, make me hope, sir, that it will be possible for you between now and midnight to hasten your last preparations in such wise that the decision of which I have had the honor to inform you will be executed.

I will add, sir, that in spite of the difficult nature of my official relations with you, I earnestly desire that the brief delay which is granted you may be, nevertheless, sufficient; need I add, sir, at the moment of your departure, that communications and replies that I have addressed to you in reference to your ship have invariably been in conformity with the truth, such as my personal and impartial investigations have found it, and that my explanations have always been straightforward, sincere, and complete.

I beg you will kindly, on account of its importance, acknowledge receipt of this.

Be kind enough, sir, to receive the expression of my distinguished consideration.

The Commissioner of Maritime Registry,
GOSSELIN.

Mr. CAMPBELL,
Lieutenant, Commanding the steamer Rappahannock.

[Enclosure.]

CALAIS, *February 10, 1864.*

SIR: I have the honor to acknowledge the receipt of the letter that you addressed to me yesterday.

I have also the honor to inform you that in consequence of the letter you addressed to me, in which you inform me that you will be ready to leave immediately on the arrival of your coal, and which I have transmitted to his Excellency, the Government of his Majesty the Emperor directs me to retain your vessel in the dock until a new order, and that you can not go out of the port until I shall have received new instructions on the subject. The same instructions have been given to the commandant of the *Galilee.*

Believe, sir, the assurance of my distinguished consideration.

The Commissioner of Registry,
GOSSELIN.

Mr. CAMPBELL,
First Lieutenant, commanding the Rappahannock.

[Enclosure.]

CALAIS, *February 15, 1864.*

SIR: A few days ago I received a note from the commissaire of marine of this port telling me that I must remain here until further orders from the minister of marine.

When I received the dispatch I interpreted it that I was to remain here until I got ready for sea.

To-day I went on board H. I. M. ship *Galilee* to inform her commander that I would be ready for sea very soon (I had previously understood that he was to accompany me out). He explained to me the commissaire's note.

I am going on taking in coal, working night and day, and will be ready for sea as soon as it is on board.

I am very much afraid I will not be permitted to leave this port. As well as I can understand the matter, the point they are trying to make on me now is that I left Sheerness with the intention of coming to Calais. I can solemnly swear that I had no such intention, and if I could have succeeded in getting the officers on board the night I left Calais I would have attempted to keep the sea under sail.

Very respectfully, your most obedient servant,

W. P. A. CAMPBELL,
Lieutenant, Commanding.

Flag-Officer SAMUEL BARRON,
Confederate States Navy.

---

19 RUE DE MARIGNAN, PARIS, *February 26, 1864.*

SIR: In the interview which the undersigned had the honor to have with your Excellency on the 19th instant he referred to the order which had been given by the minister of marine not to permit the departure from the port of Calais of the Confederate steamer *Rappahannock* and expressed the hope that after an examination into the facts of the case that order would be revoked. He was then informed that although the matter had been referred by the minister of marine to your Excellency, the papers had not yet reached you, but you had the goodness to say that when received they would be handed over to the "Directeur des Affaires Politiques," where he could have the opportunity of inspecting them. The Marquis de Banneville has accordingly done the undersigned the favor to read to him the report made to the minister of marine by his officers at Calais of the facts attending the entry of the *Rappahannock* into that port, the nature and extent of the repairs which she has undergone, and the condition of the material and personnel of the vessel when application for permission to proceed to sea was asked by her commanding officer and refused by the officer of the imperial navy in command at Calais. The undersigned bears willing testimony to the impartiality and loyalty of the report made to the minister of marine; he believes the statement of facts therein contained to be substantially correct with the single exception of the number of the crew, which is by no means so considerable as reported.

Your Excellency will find by the letter of Flag-Officer (Admiral) Barron hereunto annexed that it amounts in all to about 40 men, exclusive of officers; that of these 40 men 25 are required as firemen, etc., about the furnaces and engine, leaving only for other purposes but 15 men which would not be the full complement of an ordinary merchant steamer of the size of the *Rappahannock*. If that ship were to proceed to sea to-day she would not have as numerous a crew as when she entered the port of Calais. Most of the men whom the report mentions as being on board as workmen were employed as riggers, but, in fact, as is the case with nearly all that class of men, were able seamen, working at times on shore and going to sea as high wages or caprice may lead them. It was supposed that the greater portion of the riggers would have remained on board the ship as seamen.

Having been informed by your Excellency that the order for the detention of the *Rappahannock* had been given on account of an alleged violation of the declaration of neutrality issued 10th June,

1861, the undersigned can not find in the report addressed to the minister of marine any fact which would even approach to a violation of any article of that declaration.

The first two apply only to cases where a vessel captured by either of the belligerents shall enter a port of France and of course have no application to the case of the *Rappahannock.*

The third article is equally inapplicable for it is not pretended that any Frenchman has received a commission to arm the *Rappahannock* as a vessel of war or accepted letters of marque for her as a privateer, and it is shown by the report of the minister of marine that everything that has been done in the way of equipment has been with the full knowledge and approbation of the naval authorities at Calais. It is not pretended that any addition has been made to the armament of the *Rappahannock* or indeed that any armament exists on board of that vessel.

It is not alleged that the fourth article of the declaration has been violated by the recruiting or enrollment of any French citizens by the officers of the *Rappahannock.*

The fifth article applies exclusively to French citizens, but, as has been remarked in relation to the third article, every agency of French citizens in the repairs or equipment of the *Rappahannock* has been with the full knowledge and approbation of the authorities of Calais,

The undersigned has the honor to submit herewith the declaration of the commandant and two other officers of the *Rappahannock* and of the officer of the Confederate Navy highest rank of those now in Europe by which it is conclusively established—

First. That when the *Rappahannock* left the jurisdiction of Great Britain it was not with the intention or expectation of entering a French port; that she called off Calais for the sole purpose of receiving on board the officers who had been there for some time awaiting her appearance and that it was only in consequence of injury to her machinery, occurring while at sea, reducing her to a state of unseaworthiness as a steamer, that she sought refuge in the port of Calais.

Second. That no repairs have been made at Calais other than those necessary to restore the efficiency of the motive power.

Third. That no changes have been made in the vessel tending to increase her capacity or aptitude for warlike purposes.

Fourth. That no addition has been made to the armament of the vessel; in fact she has not on board of her at this moment a single cannon, musket, or saber, the officers only having the side arms which constitute a part of their uniform, and further that not only no attempt has been made, but that no purpose exists or has existed to make such addition.

Fifth. That no Frenchman has been enrolled to serve on board of the *Rappahannock,* nor has any attempt been made to engage any Frenchman for such service.

Sixth. That the number of the crew of the *Rappahannock* has not been increased, but that on the contrary she has now on board fewer men than when she entered the port of Calais.

Seventh. That if the *Rappahannock* be permitted to go to sea in her present state she will be utterly unfit for any warlike service and indeed incapable of defense against any Federal cruiser even of the smallest class.

All of these points are sustained by the concurrent declaration of four Confederate officers, who pledge their words of honor to the truth of their statements. It is not supposed that any stronger pledge can be required of them, but they are ready if needs be to confirm these declarations by their oaths.

The undersigned invites the attention of your Excellency to the accompanying copies of letters from the commissary of the marine at Calais to the commander of the *Rappahannock*, and especially to the letter of the former dated 4th instant directing the latter to proceed at once to sea, and respectfully submits that said letter contains an implied sanction of everything that had been done by the officers of the *Rappahannock* up to that date, and that she can not now be detained unless for some offense against the laws of the empire or of nations which has been committed since that date or which has since come to the knowledge of the Government of the Emperor. This order was not complied with because the ship had not on board a necessary supply of coal. The undersigned freely admits that in this respect the commander of the *Rappahannock* had been guilty of gross negligence, but he respectfully submits that this negligence does not justify the detention of the vessel as a punishment for his remissness.

The undersigned, in conclusion, begs that the case of the *Rappahannock* may receive the prompt attention of your Excellency, with the full conviction that after due examination nothing will be found to justify her continued detention.

The undersigned avails himself of this opportunity to express his grateful appreciation of the kindness and courtesy which have been uniformly extended by all the agents of the Government of the Emperor to the officers of vessels bearing the flag of the Confederate States which have sought hospitality in the ports of France. He prays your Excellency to receive the assurance of the very high respect of his obedient humble servant,

JOHN SLIDELL.

His Excellency Mr. DROUYN DE LHUYS,
Minister of Foreign Affairs.

No. 79.]　　　　　　　　　　　　　　　　LONDON, *February 29, 1864.*

SIR: The Archduke Maximilian is at Brussels and will leave for Paris in three or four days to confer with the Emperor of the French.

He has not yet definitely accepted, as I learn upon unquestionable unauthority, the embryo imperial throne of Mexico. The guarantees required for his secure reign are, I am inclined to believe, not quite satisfactory to his sagacious father-in-law. Great Britain is not in a condition to strengthen them were she even so disposed. How the difficulty is to be overcome will perhaps be explained within the next fortnight.

I must confess, as one or more of my dispatches may have prepared you to suppose, that I have no new-born admiration for monarchical institutions. Descended from a republican ancestry—

republican in the sense in which Virginia renounced her allegiance to the British Crown—and educated in the Jeffersonian school of politics, I am as inflexible a believer as ever in the ultimate successful operations of the self-governing system. In the division of the Union I have discovered nothing whatever calculated to shake confidence in the salutary workings of that system in the orderly rational States which compose our Confederacy. On the contrary, the citizens of those States are grandly developing its beauties in their united enthusiastic support of the President of their choice and in their scrupulous observance of established law.

"Let every people choose its own form of government" is the natural sentiment of my heart; yet, nevertheless, I should have no pleasure in my existence were I to make myself instrumental, however slightly, in rearing up a form of government opposed to that form whose principles are endeared to me by all the recollections of the past, by all the joys of the present, and by all the hopes of the future. As I have lived, so will I die, a devoted adherent to the vox populi, vox dei, doctrine, under judicious restrictions, which, in our own case, are as substantial as they are otherwise sufficient in the negro slavery basis of labor.

Have we any favors to expect from Maximilian, even if he shall be seated upon a Mexican throne? Can we reasonably expect him to recognize us in advance of the two western powers? I think not. The mere automaton of the Emperor of the French, as he must needs be, he will be guided exclusively by instructions which will emanate in the Tuileries. If Louis Napoleon is so fearful of giving any cause of offense himself, however slight, to Lincoln and Co., is it at all likely that he will suffer the Emperor of his creation to commit any overt act which might possibly eventuate in involving the latter in a state of hostilities with that demibarbarian concern? A few months will determine. I am free to say that I am utterly without confidence.

It is proper that I should inform you that I have been detained in this metropolis longer than I contemplated when I last wrote by a most afflicting family bereavement (which occurred at Pau, in the south of France, on the 22d instant) and by an indisposition of several weeks' duration which has prevented me from traveling. I expect, however, to soon be in a condition to return to Belgium.

I have the honor to be, sir, very respectfully, your obedient servant,

A. DUDLEY MANN.

Hon. J. P. BENJAMIN,
    Secretary of State, C. S. A.,
        Richmond, Va.

WILMINGTON, *February 29, 1864.*

MY DEAR SIR: The *Caledonia* will not get out before to-morrow night, and I avail myself of the delay to write you unofficially a few lines. On enquiring of Mr. Power, I learn that it will be easy to prove Locke's residence (and probably citizenship) for many years in South Carolina, and he gives the name of a witness which I enclose. It may be well to have his testimony taken and forwarded to me at Halifax. In a Nassau paper received by Mr. Lacy, just in, I observe a paragraph to the effect that Judge Stewart, of the admiralty court, had finally disposed of the case of the *Chesapeake* by ordering a restoration of the ship and cargo to the original owners on payment of the cost in court. I think it probable that the colonial authorities will disclaim all authority to entertain any application for indemnity and refer me to the home Government. In the event of its being deemed unadvisable to institute any proceedings, appellate or otherwise, in the court of admiralty, this will prevent a contingency not embraced in my present instructions. I will, of course, make the earliest practicable report of the facts after my arrival at Halifax.

I find the *Caledonia* will be crowded with passengers sailing by order of the Government. Parr has agreed to wait and take his chances in the next vessel that goes out. I hope Captain Lalor may be able to go out, but there seems no principle upon which a right to precedence is ascertained beyond priority, and I am fearful of the result.

I have been so fortunate as to secure a copy of Saturday's Sentinel, but have not yet read the interesting article it contains.

With great esteem, I am most truly, etc.

JAMES P. HOLCOMBE.

Hon. J. P. BENJAMIN,
    Secretary of State, C. S. A.
Messrs. CHAFEE, ST. AMAND & CROFT,
        Charleston, S. C.
"O. J. CHAFEE."

DEPARTMENT OF STATE,
Richmond, March 2, 1864.

SIR: I have the honor to inform you that by a letter just received from Mr. Holcombe, I am apprised that Mr. O. J. Chafee, of the firm of Chafee, St. Amand & Croft, of Charleston, S. C., can prove the residence for many years in Charleston (and probably the citizenship) of Captain Locke, who assumed the name of Parker, and under whose orders the expedition for the capture of the *Chesapeake* was undertaken.

I beg that you will have the testimony taken under commission as promptly as possible, and I think it will be well to request the district attorney at Charleston to have any other witnesses examined who may be able to prove this fact. I very much desire to get a copy of the depositions as soon as taken, for the purpose of forwarding it to Mr. Holcombe.

Excuse my urging that no time be lost on this, as I fear we are already too much in arrears to act with good effect in the assertion of our rights.

I am, very respectfully, your obedient servant,

J. P. BENJAMIN,
Secretary of State.

P. H. AYLETT, Esq.,
    Confederate States District Attorney, Richmond.

No. 57.]   PARIS, *March 5, 1864.*

SIR: Your No. 27 reached me on 3d instant. You will find by the duplicate of my No. 56, which is sent herewith, that your enquiries in relation to naval matters have been answered in anticipation. The particulars as to the state of forwardness of the vessels will, I hope, have been communicated to you before the reception of this dispatch by Lieutenant Maury, who left Liverpool on the 13th ultimo by steamer for Halifax and Bermuda. Dr. Darby, who will, I hope, present this in person, will also give you verbally similar details.

You ask me to state fully and freely my own conclusions on a certain subject. I am not at all surprised that my No. 48 should have produced on the minds of the President and yourself a disagreeable impression. I merely gave you the facts, and I think you have drawn from them a fair, certainly a very natural, inference. The truth, I believe, is that Mexican affairs, and the daily increasing complications and difficulties of European politics, have made the Emperor more and more unwilling to run the risk of embroiling himself with the Lincoln Government, with the certainty in such an event of having the secret illwill of the English Government and perhaps its open fraternization with the North. The Emperor if left entirely to his own inspirations would, I believe, be disposed to run this risk, but autocrat though he be, he still is to a certain extent influenced by those around him, and those influences counsel caution and temporization.

Events, however, are rapidly marching toward a general outbreak in Europe, and I have long been of opinion that we may gain much, while we can lose nothing by such an event. Our war has now lasted so long, with results so equally balanced, that it has ceased to command any active sympathy, either for the one side or the other; it is true that among the educated classes there is an almost universal admiration of the courage, energy, and devotion of our people, but it is a sterile admiration productive of no fruit.

A general European war, however, which would expose the ships of all the maritime nations to capture and condemnation would at once remove the greatest cause of apprehension from difficulties with the Federal Government; indeed, I believe that were it not this dread of Yankee privateers England would long since have exacted full atonement for Northern insolence and aggression.

The annexed copy of a letter * to the minister of foreign affairs, with the accompanying documents,† will give you so full an account of the facts attending the detention of the *Rappahannock*, of which I gave you a brief notice in a private note enclosed in my No. 56, as to dispense with the necessity of further explanation of them. So soon as I heard from Commodore Barron of the refusal to permit the sailing of the ship I called on the minister of marine, who received me as he always does, with great cordiality and spoke of the case very unreservedly and with great apparent frankness. He complained strongly of the unnecessary difficulties which had been created by the want of energy and activity in repairing the machinery of the ship and getting ready for sea. The delay had been such as to enable the Federal minister to fortify his remonstrances with proofs

---

* See February 26, 1864, Slidell to Drouyn de Lhuys.
† See Barron to Slidell, February 25, 1864.

of the condition in which the ship left England, creating a strong presumption of an original intention to equip her in a French port, and of the substitution of an almost entirely new crew for that with which she entered Calais. He said that in this case, as well as in those of the *Florida* and *Georgia*, he had done all he could to keep his eyes shut to any violation of neutrality, but that it could not be expected that when forcibly opened, he should affect not to see. He appealed to me whether he had not afforded every possible facility for the landing, transit, and putting of seamen on board of our various ships. He said that he had given the order for the ship to proceed to sea by the first tide, because he knew that he would receive the next day from the minister of foreign affairs a communication that would compel him to detain her. That the affair had now passed beyond his jurisdiction to that of the minister of foreign affairs, to whom the papers would be sent the next day.

I accordingly asked for an interview with M. Drouyn de Lhuys, whom I saw on the 19th instant; the papers had not yet reached him. I had a very long and free conversation on the subject of our affairs generally, the minister taking the initiative, before I had stated for what purpose I had asked an interview; my intention was to have confined myself to the special matter in hand, unless he manifested a disposition to enter upon other topics. I was very much surprised by the very decided manner in which he expressed his sympathy for our cause, his full conviction of our capacity to defend ourselves, and his regret that the Emperor had, in consequence of the refusal of England to cooperate with him hitherto, been unable to take any decided action in our favor. All this was in striking contrast with his careful noncommittalism in all our previous interviews.

He asked me if I had heard recently from England anything to lead me to suppose that ministers were more disposed than they had been to recognize our Government. I replied that I had not, and that I had long since ceased to expect anything friendly or even fair from that quarter, and that, believing that the Emperor would not act without the cooperation of England, I had abandoned all expectation or even hope of any favorable action so long as Palmerston and Russell continued in power. That should they be compelled to resign, as now seemed not improbable, I believed that a Tory cabinet would pursue a different policy toward us, and, although they might not immediately make a formal recognition of the Confederacy, would act in such a way as would soon lead to that or even to some more efficient action. He said perhaps this may happen even without a change of ministry.

Lord Palmerston has recently, in a conversation which has been reported to me, spoken in a way which would indicate that his opinions on the subject have been greatly modified if not changed. He expressed very decidedly his opinion of the capacity of the South to sustain itself; that it had manifested such energy, tenacity, and solidity of resistance as to entitle it to take its place among nations; that it was time the war should end and that even stronger measures than recognition might be resorted to for that purpose. I asked if the person with whom Lord P. held this conversation belonged to the French Embassy at London; the minister replied in the negative. Was he a Frenchman? Yes. Was he a person whose position and relations to his Government were such that the British premier might fairly presume that he would report the conversation to the Emperor or to his minister of foreign affairs? M. Drouyn de Lhuys said that he was such a person and for that reason he attached much significance to the conversation; he urged me to write to London to find out if possible what it meant. I said that he had very easy means of making this discovery, while I knew of none on which I could rely, but that I would make the effort. He recurred to the subject when I was taking leave of him and repeated his request. I accordingly have made and caused to be made inquiries in various quarters, but can learn nothing definite. It seems, however, that in the London clubs and among persons generally well informed there is a prevailing impression that in deference to public opinion—or, rather, from apprehension of the damaging effects of the frequent "interpellations" in Parliament respecting incidents of the American question—the tone of the Government toward Lincoln will be less obsequious and its action less superserviceable. For myself I confess that I attach little consequence to these speculations.

Mr. Francis Lawley passed through here on his way to Italy last week. He had a long and very interesting interview with the Emperor. The conversation turned entirely upon American affairs and was most satisfactory. Mr. L. has assured me that he will send you by the Nassau and Bermuda mails detailed notes of it, and therefore I will only say that the Emperor is prepared to take any action in our favor in concert with England, but adheres to his determination not to move without her cooperation.

I have not yet received any response to my communication to the foreign affairs on the subject of the *Rappahannock*. Should the decision be much longer delayed I shall address myself to higher authority.

I have the honor to be, with great respect, your most obedient servant,
JOHN SLIDELL.

Hon. J. P. BENJAMIN,
Secretary of State.

P. S.—The Archduke Maximilian is expected here this evening. I have good reason to believe that his prolonged stay at Brussels was caused by his determination not to commit himself definitely to the acceptance of the Mexican Crown until he should have received from the Emperor positive assurance of support in the event of difficulties with the Government of Washington, and that the assurance has been given. I shall ask an interview with the Archduke, and will inform him of the matters referred to in the papers accompanying your No. 27.

———

No. 5.]   COMMISSION ON THE CONTINENT,
London, March 16, 1864.

SIR: I had yesterday the honor to receive from you five pacquets containing as follows:

1. Commissions in duplicate and in blank as commissioner, etc.
2. Letters of introduction to ministers of foreign affairs in duplicate and in blank, with two blank seals to be annexed.

3. Special passports in duplicate.

4. Full powers as commissioner in duplicate.

5. Your dispatch No. 34, dated 25th January, 1864, containing instructions for my guidance under the new commission.

I beg to express my sense of gratitude to the President for the confidence he has reposed in me in regard to the exercise of the discretion left with me in the use of those commissions. The instructions are so explicit and definite that I apprehend no embarrassment in carrying them out in their exact spirit. Should a question arise, however, I shall have the able counsels of Mr. Slidell the better to lead me to a satisfactory decision.

The present disturbed and unsettled condition of Europe makes it impossible to foresee what may be the solution of its complications; so far as this commission is involved, for the present we can only await events.

Should the Danish-Holstein question be adjusted in such manner as to have the cordial support of Austria and Prussia, it is believed they will be in a position to repress further present enterprises of the other German powers, and the peace of Europe, for the present at least, be secured. Until such peaceful attitude is attained it will be utterly impracticable, in my judgment, to fix the attention of European powers upon what it may become them to do in regard to relations with us. In regard to the new duties which are devolved upon me, I need hardly say that I shall take peculiar care in no manner to compromise the dignity of the Government in an approach to any one of these powers without previous distinct intimation of my reception.

In regard to Mexico, I much fear from recent evidences that the new Emperor will be as little disposed to enter into diplomatic relations with us as is the controlling power on the Continent under whose auspices he is to be placed upon the throne. There was reason to believe, from sources entitled to full reliance, that the archduke had expressed himself at one time of opinion that amicable relations with us were of the last importance to the stability of his new Empire, and even desired at once to establish the necessary diplomatic intercourse. Before this reaches you, you will have heard through the journals of the day of his recent visit to Paris as the guest of the Emperor.

In a late note from Mr. Slidell he informed me that he had been told by Mr. Estrada (the chief of the Mexican commission sent to offer to the archduke the throne) that the latter desired to see him (Mr. S.), and he might expect accordingly an invitation to an interview; but such invitation did not come, and the archduke left Paris, Mr. Slidell not having seen or heard further from him. It had been previously strongly rumored in Paris that Mr. Mercier came from Washington authorized by Lincoln to say to the Emperor that he, the President of the United States, would have his minister accredited to the Emperor of Mexico, provided no negotiations for recognition of the Confederate Government were entertained by the latter, and Mr. Slidell believes that it was under such influence, through the Emperor, that the mind and purpose of the archduke was changed after his arrival in Paris. Be this as it may, there can be no doubt that before he left Miramar the archduke clearly and distinctly declared a policy which looked to an immediate recognition and intimate relations between his Government, when established, and ours. I have deemed it proper to give you this much, even at second hand, though I doubt not the dispatches of Mr. Slidell, by same opportunity with this, will be more full and direct on this head. In a letter from Mr. Fearn to Mr. Hotze, which the latter showed me (written, I think, from Nassau), Mr. F. spoke of being there with General Preston on a mission which might result, contingently, on their going to Mexico. I am aware that Mr. Williams, of Tennessee, late U. S. minister at Constantinople, who is now here, has written fully, both to the President and to Colonel L. Q. C. Lamar, of his interviews with the archduke at Miramar, and of the views and opinions of this personage in regard to future Mexican relations with us; and I have thought it not improbable that the contingent mission of General Preston to Mexico has been founded on such information. Under these circumstances and as at present advised, I shall suggest to Mr. Slidell whether his late experience of the archduke, with whatever lights are before him, may not make it proper that he should communicate the apparent state of things to General Preston for his consideration in the event of his mission to Mexico being contingent upon previous intimation that he would be received. * * *

In regard to the seizure of the Confederate cruiser *Tuscaloosa* at the Cape of Good Hope, spoken of in my No. 3, I have now further to report that some short time after its date Earl Russell announced in the House of Lords that orders had been issued for her release for the reason that her seizure had been authorized under a state of facts supposed to exist, which it was afterward found did not exist. What such facts were he did not state. Some short time afterward I was informed by Lieutenant Low, who commanded her and who has arrived here, that after waiting three weeks he determined to discharge his crew and go to England with his officers, and that no one was left at the Cape authorized to receive the ship when released. As it was impracticable, even if thought judicious, again to man the ship where she was, I advised that things should remain in statu quo and the responsibility left with the British Government what should become of her. Reporting this to Mr. Slidell and Commodore Barron, they both concurred that it was the best thing to be done. Of course the matter will be fully reported by the latter to the Navy Department.

These dispatches will be borne by Dr. Darby of the Confederate States Army, and I send by him parliamentary documents Nos. 1 to 5, inclusive, containing correspondence relating to American affairs. At page 30 of No. 5 you will find a letter from Mr. Adams to Earl Russell, dated 19th January last, communicating to him a copy of what he alleges to be "The annual report of Mr. S. R. Mallory," etc., which "report" is printed at large on the same and preceding page. Mr. Adams, assuming this paper to be genuine, bases upon it several specific demands for the action of the British Government in regard thereto. Earl Russell in his reply of 8th February (p. 32) accepts the "report" as genuine, speaks of the nature and importance of its "admissions," and informs Mr. Adams that "her Majesty's Government have already taken steps to make the Confederate Government aware that such proceedings can not be tolerated," etc. This report had previously reached us through the Northern papers, and Captain Maury (then, as now, in England) had, by a letter published in the Times, denounced it as a fabrication. I did not see the paper until a few days ago, when I received the parliamentary document. It bears intrinsic marks which, none conversant with the facts it professes to recite can doubt, stamp it as a forgery. We learn, too, by a note from Mr. Helm at Havana to Mr. Slidell that the British consul-general, Mr. Crawford, had been ordered by his Government to proceed in a ship of war to one of our ports on a mission to Richmond, I suppose of no very amicable character, based chiefly on the admissions contained in this report.

I have not, of course, in any manner, direct or indirect, approached the British Government since my recall from London, but I have not hesitated whenever an occasion offered, whether on the Continent or here, to place some one of our real friends in Parliament in possession of any facts which might be used to put the Government in the wrong in its offensive attitude toward us. So in regard to this fabricated report of Mr. Mallory, to say nothing of the incongruity of its being addressed to the Speaker of the House, the allegations it contains:

First. In regard to the capture and condition of the *Harriet Lane*.

Second. In regard to the attack by our ironclads upon the blockading fleet off Charleston.

Third. The statement that the *Nashville* was a Confederate ship at the time when she was destroyed near Savannah.

Fourth. What is said of the recapture of the *Queen of the West*, and that her commander had been cashiered and dismissed from the service.

Fifth. The statements in regard to the capture of the *Caleb Cushing* by the *Tacony* are all such manifest departures from truth, and so plainly proved the fabrication, that I brought the matter to the direct notice of Commodore Barron and have obtained from him the written statements of several officers now in France, personally conversant with the facts in each case respectively, fully establishing their falsity; and it is my purpose to make this all fully known to Lord Robert Cecil, a member of the House of Commons of admitted influence and ability and one of our most earnest and decided friends, for such use as he may think proper to make of it. Should the mission of Mr. Crawford be admitted at Richmond, the fact of this impudent forgery will be officially made known to her Majesty's Government. My communications with Lord Robert Cecil will prepare our friends here for any steps they may deem proper in the meantime.

I have not since I came last to England been at either House of Parliament or in any public assemblage; nor have I reason to believe that my being here is known to any but a few private friends. It was my intention to return to the Continent about this time, now confirmed, of course, on learning that the President would prefer that I should not visit England unless on an occasion of real urgency.

I shall return to Paris in the course of a very few days and remain there or elsewhere unofficially on the Continent. Until located, dis-

patches will always best reach me as heretofore addressed to the care
of Henry Hotze, esq.

*   *   *   *   *   *   *

I have the honor to be, very respectfully, your obedient servant,

J. M. MASON.

Hon. J. P. BENJAMIN.

P. S.—* * * I send with this, under a separate envelope, copy
of a letter addressed by W. S. Lindsay, esq., M. P., to Mr. Drouyn
de Lhuys, minister of foreign affairs in France, with his letter of
reply. It details what passed at Mr. Lindsay's interview with the
Emperor in regard to the Confederate States.

I send it at Mr. Lindsay's request, who asks that it may be filed
in your Department.

J. M. MASON.

[Enclosure.]

8 AUSTIN FRIARS, LONDON, March 7, 1864.

SIR: In the course of a discussion in the House of Commons a few
days ago reference was made to certain dispatches relating to American affairs recently presented to Congress by the Government of the
United States.

I have obtained a copy of these papers and I have read with surprise and regret the letters in which my name is introduced. They
are from Mr. Dayton to Mr. Seward, Nos. 321, 323, 325, 326, 329, and
333, and from Mr. Seward to Mr. Dayton, Nos. 368, 393, and 394.

In one of these letters Mr. Dayton states that Mr. Roebuck made
assertions in the House of Commons which "must in some way be
untrue or absurd." Now, as I confirmed the truth of Mr. Roebuck's
statements, though I did not approve of the manner in which they
had been introduced, I am under the necessity of addressing your
Excellency, and as Mr. Dayton impugns my honor and veracity I
trust you will allow me to place on file in your Department a distinct
denial and correction of so much of his dispatches as is in conflict
with the facts.

The facts and circumstances were recorded by me at the time,
though treated as confidential till after I had permission from the
Emperor on the 22d June, last, to make them public. I, however,
did not do so, for the subject was one of so delicate a character that I
preferred to endure the reproaches cast upon me rather than vindicate my character for truthfulness at the risk of disturbing the
harmony which appeared to exist between his Imperial Majesty and
the Government of my Queen.

It may be within your knowledge that during the years 1861 and
1862 I had occasion with the approval of my Government to see
his Imperial Majesty the Emperor of the French at various times in
regard to important changes contemplated in the French navigation
laws, involving questions of an intricate and technical character, to
which I have for years devoted my attention and in which his
Majesty appeared to take much interest.

On the occasion of my first interview (10 January, 1861) with the
Emperor, Lord Cowley accompanied me; but on the other occasions
I was alone with his Majesty, except on the 22d June, 1863, when
Mr. Roebuck was introduced at Fontainbleau.

The conversations his Majesty was pleased to have with me were almost exclusively upon maritime affairs, and the first time the American war was mentioned was at the Tuileries on the 11th April, 1862. The subject was brought about by some casual remarks in reference to the prospects for shipping and the effect which the blockade of the Southern ports of America would have upon commerce. In the course of that conversation the Emperor stated that he had sent two dispatches to the English Government in regard to the blockade, but he did not think they had paid much attention to his views. He did not mention the date of these dispatches, but I understood they had been sent sometime in April or March of that year. He remarked that the English Government appeared less disposed to act in concert with him on American questions since he had taken their part in the *Trent* affair than they had been previous to that time, and he expressed much surprise at this, for, he said, that the primary object he had in view was to prevent, if possible, war between England and the United States, and to show to the latter country that whenever he could consistently do so he was resolved to act with England in all matters relating to the American difficulties. He further said that it was still his most anxious desire to do so, but he was at a loss to understand the reasons which had induced the English Government to send his views to America if they did not approve of them. He also expressed regret that they had not paid more attention to what he had stated about the inefficiency of the blockade, and he concluded by remarking that Lord Cowley seemed "to throw cold water" on his suggestions, adding that Earl Russell had sent the substance of his dispatches to America (meaning the two he had previously referred to), and had made a "cat's paw" of him, or words to that effect.

His Majesty then asked me to repeat this conversation to Lord Cowley and return to him with his lordship's reply, as he said he did not see how he could, after what had taken place, officially communicate with the Government of Lord Palmerston on American affairs until he ascertained that his views were likely to be adopted or favorably entertained. But before I left it was his Majesty's pleasure to offer some further remarks about the war, stating that though he thought the cause of humanity demanded some interference on the part of the European powers, he much preferred, at least for the present, to stand aloof; but still, though he had no desire to interfere in the struggle between the North and the South, however vain and however deplorable he might consider the conflict, he was resolved that the North, if he could prevent it, should not with impunity interfere with his affairs and with the interests of his people. Referring again to the blockade, he stated that his people were suffering through the scarcity of cotton and were likely to suffer still more, and he concluded by saying that if it met the views of the English Government he would be prepared, with England, to demand, and if necessary to enforce, either the opening of the Southern ports or an efficient blockade. The whole of this conversation I conveyed, as requested, to Lord Cowley, who, I understand, sent notes of it to Earl Russell at the time.

I need not trouble you with Lord Cowley's reply, more especially as it was very general and of great length, but on the Sunday following I repeated the substance of it, with Lord Cowley's permission, to the Emperor, with which his Majesty did not seem satisfied, expressing, in reply to some remarks which Lord Cowley had made, that he thought it was not "neutrality" for the North to have every means of representing their case in Europe and every facility for obtaining from thence all the munitions of war, while the South, which had been acknowledged as a belligerent power, had neither.

He made further remarks on the folly of continuing a war to restore the Union, when in his opinion there must be separation, and these, with some general remarks in regard to the losses and sufferings of his own people through the war (which seemed to prey much upon his mind) were the chief topics of conversation on the forenoon of that day.

His Majesty appeared to be satisfied with the manner in which I had conveyed to Lord Cowley the very delicate conversation he had been pleased to have with me; and as I was about to return to England, it was arranged that I should repeat the conversation to Earl Russell.

On the evening of that day I left for London, and on the following morning I addressed a note to Earl Russell, who was then at Richmond, referring to the conversation I had had with Lord Cowley and asking if it would be agreeable to his lordship to see me on the subject. It was not his pleasure to see me.

I remained in London four days and returned to Paris by the mail train of Thursday evening, and early in the forenoon of Friday, the 17th April, I had another interview with the Emperor. I read to his Majesty the letters I had addressed to Earl Russell and his lordship's replies. The Emperor thought that the replies would have been different had I addressed Lord Palmerston, and said that Lord Palmerston had always professed a desire to cooperate with him, though he had not always done so, remarking that while he had invariably instructed his representatives abroad, where English interests predominated, as in India or China, to coincide with the views of the English minister, the English Government had failed to reciprocate where French interests prevailed. Reverting to America and to the prospect of the cotton supplies, he said that Sir Charles Wood was then in Paris and had "told Mr. Fould that England could do pretty well without cotton from America, as she would this year get almost sufficient for her wants from India." I questioned that opinion and expressed a hope that his Majesty's Government would not make their preparations to meet the wants of his people this year (whatever they might hereafter do) on any such calculations.

To the other portions of the conversations I need not refer. I returned to England the following day, and as his Majesty seemed to wish that I should address Lord Palmerston, who was then at Broadlands, I did so. I will not trouble you with that correspondence, but it closed with a letter from me to his lordship on the 25th April, in which I said: " I have endeavored to carry out the Emperor's wishes in as quiet a manner as possible and now that my work, so far as I could do it, is at end, it is neither my wish nor my intention to say anything more about it; but will you allow me in conclusion to express my regret that it was not your lordship's pleasure to see me, for

I think the Emperor had very strong reasons for the course, however unusual he thought it expedient to adopt." I sent copies of that correspondence to the Emperor and thus the matter ended.

Not one word was ever mentioned by me to any person of what had taken place, except to those for whom I had received special permission from his Majesty, till after the 22d June, 1863, or fourteen months from the time when the correspondence was closed.

I come, now, to the circumstances more especially referred to in Mr. Dayton's dispatches, and about which so much has been said in this country and in America. I have said very little, and when, after enduring much reproach, I was at last obliged to say something in my place in Parliament, I made a statement, which contained many words but very little information, and I would not now have addressed you had not Mr. Dayton in an official form, to his Government and to the world, justified by his statements, the virulent attacks made upon me at the time, in this country and in America.

In June, 1863, Mr. Roebuck had given notice in the House of Commons, of a motion which had for its object the recognition by England, in concert with other European powers, of the Confederate States of America. Rumors were current that even if the English Government was prepared to accept his motion, France would not be ready to act in concert with England.

Anxious to ascertain if these rumors had any foundation, Mr. Roebuck asked me to accompany him to Fontainbleau and endeavor to obtain an audience for him with the Emperor. I very reluctantly did so. I shall, however, rejoice if the interview, which I was the means of obtaining, enabled Mr. Roebuck to appreciate, as I have for years done, the earnest desire of his Majesty to be a true and faithful ally of my Queen.

The Emperor was open and frank, and did not hesitate to state his views in regard to American affairs. Addressing me he said that I knew how anxious he had been to act in concert with England. He further said that he felt more convinced than ever that the Union of the United States could not be restored, and that the continuation of the war would only entail upon North and South greater misery than the people of those countries had already endured. He expressed his belief that the recognition of the South would restore peace, and therefore he said he would be prepared to act in concert with England in the adoption of such measures as had for their object the recognition of a people who had given proofs of their abilities to govern themselves and maintain their independence.

Then turning to Mr. Roebuck he said that he could not make any formal proposition to England for reasons which he said I knew, and to which he then incidentally, though very briefly, referred; but he added that he had just requested Baron Gros to ascertain whether England was prepared to entertain the question of recognition and to suggest any mode of proceeding.

The nature of Mr. Roebuck's motion was such that if there had been any truth in the rumor that the Emperor was not prepared to join England in the recognition of the South it was useless for Mr. Roebuck to submit it to the consideration of the House of Commons. Therefore we ventured to ask his Majesty if Mr. Roebuck might state in the course of the debate that if it was the pleasure of the

House of Commons to ask her Majesty to enter into any negotiations with the Emperor that he would be ready to do so. To this proposal his Majesty gave a ready consent, adding that he thought his views on the state of American affairs were already pretty well known, but as they appeared to have been misunderstood he could have the less hesitation in meeting the request we had made.

Such is the substance of the different conversations respecting America his Majesty was pleased to have with me, compiled from notes taken at the time, and those portions of the correspondence of Mr. Dayton which differ from what I have stated must be founded on some misinterpretation.

I should therefore esteem it a favor if your Excellency would have this letter recorded in your Department for such ulterior use or reference as any future events, so far as I am concerned, might seem to require.

I have the honor to remain, sir, your most obedient, humble servant,

W. S. LINDSAY.

His Excellency M. DROUYN DE LHUYS,
   Minister for Foreign Affairs, Paris.

[Translated from the French.]

PARIS, *March 11, 1864.*

SIR: The letter that you did me the honor to write me the 7th of this month has reached me punctually. I take note with interest of the different circumstances that it relates, and I have preserved it with care in order to refer to it if occasion should present itself.

Accept, sir, the assurance of my most distinguished consideration.

DROUYN DE LHUYS.

Mr. W. S. LINDSAY,
   8 Austin Friars, London.

[Memorandum which Mr. Mocquard is most respectfully solicited to submit to his Imperial Majesty.]

PARIS, *March 15, 1864.*

The Confederate steamer *Rappahannock* has been detained at Calais since the 17th February, when her commander notified his desire to proceed to sea. No reason has been assigned for his detention, and he is to this moment ignorant why he is detained. The undersigned has not been more fortunate in his attempts to discover the cause of the detention of the *Rappahannock*. He presented on the 26th ultimo to the minister of foreign affairs conclusive evidence—

First. That when the *Rappahannock* left the jurisdiction of Great Britain it was not with the intention or expectation of entering a French port; that she called off Calais for the sole purpose of receiving on board the officers who had been there for some time awaiting her appearance; and that it was only in consequence of injury to her machinery, occurring while at sea, reducing her to a state of unseaworthiness as a steamer that she sought refuge in the port of Calais.

Second. That no repairs had been made at Calais other than those necessary to restore the efficiency of the motive power.

Third. That no changes have been made in the vessel tending to increase her capacity or aptitude for warlike purposes.

Fourth. That no addition has been made to the armament of the vessel; that in fact she has not on board of her at this moment a single cannon, musket, or saber, the officers only having the side arms which constitute a part of their uniform; and further, that no attempt has been made and that no purpose exists or has existed to make such addition.

Fifth. That no Frenchman has been enrolled to serve on board of the *Rappahannock*, nor has any attempt been made to engage any Frenchman for such service.

Sixth. That the number of the crew of the *Rappahannock* has not been increased, but that on the contrary she has now on board fewer men than when she entered the port of Calais.

Seventh. That if the *Rappahannock* be permitted to go to sea in her present state, she will be utterly unfit for any warlike service, and indeed incapable of defense against any Federal cruiser even of the smallest class.

Eighth. That everything that has been done on board of the *Rappahannock* since her arrival at Calais has been done openly, without concealment, and under the surveillance and with the approbation of the authorities of that port.

From all these facts it clearly results that no offense has been committed against the laws of the empire, the declaration of neutrality of 10th June, 1861, or the law of nations, and the continued detention of the *Rappahannock* without any specific cause assigned would seem to be inconsistent not only with the friendly feelings toward the Confederate States which have been heretofore manifested by the Government of the Emperor, but with the declaration of neutrality above referred to.

JOHN SLIDELL.

PARIS, *March 14, 1864.*

SIR: On the 26th ultimo the undersigned had the honor to address your Excellency on the subject of the detention at Calais of the C. S. S. *Rappahannock* by the naval officer in command at Calais, acting under instructions from the ministry of marine. He then presented what he considered conclusive evidence, not only that no violation of the declaration of neutrality of 10th June, 1861, had been committed, but that no intention of such violation had ever existed and he had hoped that the order under which the Rappahannock had been detained would be promptly revoked. In this hope he has been disappointed, nor has he been as yet informed for what specific reason the order was given. He is left to conjecture whether for an alleged violation of the declaration of neutrality, for a breach of the municipal law of France, or of international law. He respectfully submits to your Excellency whether the commander of the *Rappahannock* has not a right to know what offense he or those under him are alleged to have committed, which would authorize the detention of his vessel, inviting as he does the strictest investigation of the conduct of himself, his officers, and crew, confident that it will appear that in no respect have he or they infringed the Emperor's declaration of neutrality, the laws of France, or of nations. The commander of the *Rappahannock* reported his vessel as ready for sea on the 17th ultimo, and now applies to the undersigned for advice as to the course which he should pursue under the very peculiar circumstances in which he is placed. This advice the undersigned does not feel prepared to give until he shall have information of the precise nature of the offense with which the commander, officers, and crew of the *Rappahannock* stand charged. This information he now most respectfully asks may be communicated to him, or to the commander of the *Rappahannock*, as your Excellency may deem proper, at as early a day as may be convenient.

The undersigned avails himself of this opportunity of correcting an error, as to the number of the crew of the *Rappahannock*, into which Flag-Officer Barron had fallen from verbal information; by an official report which that officer has since received, the crew is composed of 65 men, including seamen, firemen, and coal heavers, but is still short of the number on board when the ship entered Calais.

The undersigned prays his Excellency the minister of foreign affairs to accept the assurance of the high consideration of his
Very obedient servant,

JOHN SLIDELL.

His Excellency M. DROUYN DE LHUYS,
Minister of Foreign Affairs.

No. 80.] BRUSSELS, *March 11, 1864.*

SIR: Under the auspices of the letter of Pio Nono to the President, formidable demonstrations have been made in Ireland against the efforts of Lincoln and Co. to secure additional immigrants from that portion of the British realm. The chances are thus multiplying, from day to day, that there will be a vast diminution in the number of foreign recruits for the Northern Armies. To the immortal honor of the Catholic Church, it is now earnestly engaged in throwing every obstacle that it can justly create in the way of the prosecution of the war by the Yankee guerrillas. That it will accomplish little less than marvels in this regard I have entertained a confident belief ever since my audience with the Holy Father and my interviews with his cardinal secretary of state.

The Imperial Crown of Mexico has at last been definitively accepted. I have heard from a well-informed source, much more to my chagrin than to my astonishment, that Louis Napoleon has enjoined upon Maximilian to hold no official relations with our commissioner to Mexico. It will certainly mortify my pride exceedingly if our advances are repelled by a Government more than three years our junior, and those of the Washington Cabinet cordially received. And yet I am preparing my mind for such a humiliating occurrence. That it may be avoided is the constant wish of my heart. We have a dignity to preserve as well as a recognition to secure. The latter would be dearly purchased if purchased at the loss of the former.

I presume that by this time the President and his Cabinet has as little reliance in the good intentions of the Emperor of the French as I have had from the beginning. Were his Imperial Majesty even thoroughly well inclined, his necessities, as he perceives them, would restrain him from moving an inch in the direction of the advancement of our interests. Many of our intelligent countrymen on this side of the water, as well as several of our most ardent friends among the British statesmen, who were enthusiastic in the belief, a twelve months ago, that he sincerely desired the cooperation of the Government of Queen Victoria in the formal acknowledgment of our independence, think quite differently now. Assuredly his relations with Lincoln and Co. could not be more amicable than they are, amicable perhaps more from alarmed apprehension than from cultivated affection. He evidently desires a prolongation of hostilities in order that the belligerents may become so exhausted as to enable him to assume a controlling influence over the destinies of the country which once constituted the Republic of Mexico. Maximilian may suit for a time as an instrument, but when his policy is consummated and his plans perfected he will find it no difficult matter to supersede this scion of the Hapsburg house by a prince of his own blood.

It grieves me to thus write of one from whom so much was and probably still is expected at home, but my duty will not admit of silence to my Government upon so important a subject.

The Belgian Government is in a peculiar condition. In the Chamber of Representatives it has only a majority of one. The ministry fears to propose a measure of any kind less by the sickness or other absence of a member it may encounter defeat, and sent in its resignation some time ago, but were subsequently induced nominally to remain in power. The opposition is indifferent to assume office under such circumstances. It is wise enough to foresee that its retention in power as a minority would not be of long continuance. Both parties await the elections, which are somewhat remote, in the hopeful expectation of gaining additional strength.

King Leopold, who went to England to be present at the christening of the infant Duke of Cornwall, will remain a few days longer and then return to Lacken. When the Washington Cabinet becomes satisfied that it can no longer prosecute the war with the shadow of a hope of success, it is my settled opinion that it will make indirect advances to us for a suspension of hostilities through this sovereign. Nor is that time far off.

Of course the mind of his Majesty is almost exclusively preoccupied with the war in Denmark and its possible eventualities. Should there be an uprising among the European revolutionists and a general bellicose clamor for the restoration of nationalities, the existence of this kingdom might become exceedingly precarious. The "rectification" of the northern boundary might, in the Napoleonic sense, embrace the entire domain of Belgium. The left bank of the Rhine, to its mouth, would most likely become the war song of the French, in which every voice in the Empire, to its highest pitch, could zealously unite. I may remark that the situation of affairs in Europe at this moment is less reassuring to the lovers of peace than it has been since the creation of the Kingdom of Italy. Still, an adjustment of the Schleswig-Holstein question so as to prevent additional grave complications is not despaired of in the best-informed circles.

I have the honor to be, sir, very respectfully, your obedient servant,

A. DUDLEY MANN.

Hon. J. P. BENJAMIN,
Secretary of State, C. S. A., Richmond, Va.

No. 31.]

DEPARTMENT OF STATE,
Richmond, March 11, 1864.

SIR: I have the honor to enclose copy of a letter from the Secretary of the Navy in relation to a forgery extensively circulated by the European press purporting to be a copy of an official report addressed by him to " T. S. Babcock," Speaker of the House of Representatives of the Confederate States.

The paper is on its face so palpably a fabrication that we would scarcely have supposed it could dupe the most credulous, even if experience had not already demonstrated the facility and abundance with which " telegraphic news," " Confederate confessions," " intercepted letters," and " extracts from Richmond papers " have been manufactured for European consumption. You will notice that the paper is stamped as a forgery in the mere address, not only by the misnomer of our Speaker but because the reports of the head of the Navy Department are never addressed to the Speaker of the House. The contents of the paper are too absurd for comment.

As the Secretary of the Navy has been informed by Commodore Maury that this paper is " going the rounds of the continental press as gospel," it may be well, if you think the matter worth notice, to make public the fact that the paper is a forgery. I am inclined to think the publication should be made, for no fable concerning us is too absurd for belief, real or pretended, in England or on the Continent. A short time ago European papers were gravely commenting on the " fact " that our Vice President, Mr. Stephens (who can not abandon his constitutional position here as successor to the Presidency, in the event of the death of the Chief Magistrate, and who was at the time sick at his home in Georgia), had arrived in Europe for the purpose of concluding a treaty with France for the cession of Texas and other sovereign States to that power.

I am, very respectfully, your obedient servant,

J. P. BENJAMIN,
Secretary of State.

Hon. JOHN SLIDELL, etc.

P. S.—We have just received the debates in the House of Commons on 23d ultimo on Mr. Seymour Fitzgerald's motion, and find that her Majesty's attorney-general succeeded in defining the conduct of the ministry on the subject of Mr. Laird's rams by quoting as authentic this clumsy fabrication, and that his citations from it were received with cheers. This is the more unaccountable, inasmuch as the paper has been characterized as a " spurious thing " and denounced as a " Yankee trick " and a " hoax " by the unexceptionable authority of Commodore Maury, in a card published by him in the London papers three weeks before the speech of the attorney-general.

The same mail brings the statement made by Lord Palmerston in the House of Commons of the 25th ultimo that the release of the Confederate vessel of war *Tuscaloosa*, which has been seized by instructions of the British Government in a colonial port, had been ordered on the ground that " her detention would not be warranted by international law." It is to be regretted that the eager desire of the British Government to observe that " impartial neutrality " which Earl Russell has so happily defined as being " conduct exceedingly advantageous to the more powerful of the two parties " had not been restrained until international law had been investigated before instructions were issued to violate our rights by the seizure of one of our armed vessels in a port where it had sought asylum under the sanction of the Queen's proclamation. This promptness to do "neutral acts exceedingly advantageous to the stronger side " has had the result in the present case of enabling all the enemy's vessels that had been threatened by our cruiser to escape while the British ministry was engaged in its tardy examination of the law of nations on the subject of a neutral's right to seize the national vessels of the less powerful of the two belligerents.

No. 38.]　　　　CONFEDERATE STATES COMMERCIAL AGENCY,
　　　　　　　　　　　　　　　March 12, 1864.

SIR: I have the honor to acknowledge the receipt on the 2d instant of your dispatch No. 13, dated January 9, with enclosures, to wit, official documents laid before Congress, dispatch to Hon. John Slidell, and letter to Mr. James Spence. No. 11, between September 24 and October 6, the dates of Nos. 10 and 12, respectively, is still missing.

I need not say how exceedingly gratifying to me are the contents of your dispatch of January 9 in every particular. It is not alone the official approval of my services, greatly as I prize this, but it is still more the perfect accord which I perceive in the very full and explicit expression of your views with the general line of conduct I have adopted in several cases of considerable delicacy and difficulty. Thus, in such a case as the difference of Mr. Spence's policy from mine, the angle of divergence at the point of departure is almost imperceptible to the careless eye, yet the results to be reached by either in respect to our moral attitude before the world and consistency with ourselves are an immeasurable distance apart. You can not overrate the importance to me of everything that guides my steps and gives me confidence in my own judgment.

Feeling myself thus en rapport, I may undertake a task in which the chances of failure greatly exceed those of success. I refer to the attempt of favorably influencing the French press, a duty which, without absolutely imposing upon me, you leave to my discretion. Thus far the merely tentative efforts I have made have produced no encouraging results. My plan of operations, as you are aware, totally differs in theory and in practice from that of my predecessor in that field, and of course I think mine the best. But it is due to him to say that he has difficulties which I have not had here and that fortuitous circumstances have favored me which I can not expect to repeat themselves. I act by means of persons rather than things, and therefore rely more upon the play of self-love, ambition, enthusiasm, admiration of our cause, and other passions than upon the power of money. But for this the English character, which is singularly earnest, affords me materials that are wholly lacking in the French. There is cynicism under the graceful drapery of French character which makes it far less easy to win honest converts and devoted advocates. An English journalist, as a rule, writes, if not from conviction, at least not against it; the French journalist regards his profession as purely that of an advocate who earns his fee. It remains to be seen, therefore, whether my tactics will be as successful in the French press as in the English. I can only try, and shall not be ashamed to confess failure. The most promising approach to the French public mind seems to me to be through the men of science, whose position relative to the political and journalistic talent is precisely the reverse of what it is in England, and who are far advanced in correct views of the place assigned by Providence to different branches of the human family.

I shall make a brief visit to Paris at the end of this month to survey my ground and to consult with Mr. Slidell, under whose advice and orders I shall place myself. Meanwhile I contemplate no expenditure which can not be met by my present contingent fund, provided the remittances arrive promptly and regularly. I hope to be able to effect a considerable saving on my index expenditures through increasing earnings of that paper, and this will probably suffice for all the experiments I have now in view. Should I hereafter see any opportunity for spending larger sums with prospects of adequate return, and which Mr. Slidell approves, I will ask you for a special appropriation. I may add that my machinery here will in August next be in such complete working order as to permit me to leave it for any length of time in trusted hands should a prolonged stay in Paris be thought advisable.

I am sorry that I can not give you a very glowing account of the progress of the two Southern Independence Associations, which started with such favorable auspices. Both languished, partly for want of money and partly for want of moral courage; that is to say, a sharply defined declaration of principles and a bold policy. The former want might be supplied, and perhaps in the case of one of these societies some assistance from us is expected, but unless we could give moral courage as well it would be but an artificial vitality. Associations of this sort, to do us good, must derive their sap from British soil. Their misfortune has been what I foresaw from the beginning and tried earnestly to avert, that they have adopted similar tactics to those of the Northern Peace Democracy, and with a similar result. They are therefore like a cork on the water. Still, even as such they are useful, and if the spring campaign now opening is a brilliant one for us, they will be valuable as barometers and receptacles of the reviving enthusiasm in this country.

You will doubtless see with pleasure the evidence afforded by the Times article, enclosed in separate envelope, of the judicious selection of the Irish agent there referred to. This agent, whose report I herewith transmit, has certainly proved himself admirably qualified for his duties; he has tempered a noiseless industry and devoted zeal with sound discretion. His funds are now reduced to little over two months' salary, and I respectfully recommend that an additional appropriation be made by you for his support and for contingent expenses at the same rate as heretofore, and in the disbursement of which he has exhibited commendable economy. In the meanwhile, while waiting for your instructions, I have, to relieve him from any embarrassment, taken the responsibility of assuming on my own account the contingent expenses heretofore incurred by him—some fifty-odd pounds. I doubt not that this will meet your approval.

On the subject of English politics I could only paraphrase the language used in my unofficial letter of 5th instant, sent by private route:

"The opposition amuse themselves by exposing the weakness of the Government and parading their own strength the other night on a paltry question of estimates, coming within one vote of beating the Government. Their tactics in this respect are not unlike a cat's, playing with a mouse. But unless an accident converts the sport into earnest, they appear in no hurry to devour their prey. The American question is almost nightly up for discussion. The general tenor of debate is always the same. The Government is worried and badgered, but those who do so take extreme care not to commit themselves to an opposite policy. Last night the ministry attempted a diversion by getting up a little sham fight between the Federal sympathizers on the one side and the solicitor general on the other upon the violations of English laws by the agents of the Confederate Government, but even the declaration of the solicitor general that measures had been taken to remonstrate with that Government failed to bring any outsiders into the ring."

Abroad there is little change since I last wrote. The Dano-German War has no episodical incidents and is waning in interest. I think I can see signs of peace with advancing spring.

The Archduke Maximilian is still in Paris. If we are to believe the newspapers, he has declined to see either Mr. Slidell or Mr. Dayton, which would seem to indicate somewhat ostentatiously a policy of absolute neutrality. Those, however, who have had opportunities for approaching him confidentially assert that he fully understands the necessities of his position and knows that the independence and friendship of the South form the only safe guaranty for his throne.

I enclose, among numerous other extracts, the proceedings thus far in the House of Lords in the *Alexandra* case. I also transmit the last Blue Books, among which is the partial publication of the correspondence in relation to the steam rams. The cautious language in which Mr. Adams (p. 30) forwards the alleged report of Mr. Mallory forms a strong contrast to the confident tone in which her Majesty's ministers speak of it as a public document of undoubted authenticity. This paper has done us an infinite amount of mischief; it has been publicly denounced as a forgery by Captain Maury, and Captain Bulloch, being equally convinced it is not genuine, has written to Mr. Mallory earnestly requesting that it might be contradicted. But meanwhile it is used in Parliament and in the press as the Government's best weapon of defense, and it may probably turn the scales in many judicial and political issues now pending.

I shall write again next week by the Bermuda mail, and have the honor to remain,

Very respectfully, your obedient servant,

HENRY HOTZE.

Hon. J. P. BENJAMIN,
Secretary of State, Richmond.

No. 58.]   PARIS, *March 16, 1864.*

SIR: Since my last of 5th instant, the Archduke Maximilian has made his visit to Paris. He remained here a week. On his arrival I advised Mr. Gutierrez de Estrada of my desire to see the archduke on important business. Mr. G. accordingly mentioned my wish and was informed that the archduke would be pleased to see me, and that I would probably very soon receive a notice from his secretary to that effect. This he communicated to me in writing. Not receiving the notice and learning that the stay of the archduke in Paris would be shorter than was generally anticipated, I addressed his secretary, enclosing the note of Mr. Gutierrez, informing me of the intention of the archduke to receive me, and asked for an audience. To this no reply was made. I am told that as regards this apparent discourtesy I have no cause to complain, as the applications for audiences had been so numerous as to make it impossible to answer any of them. Be this as it may, I consider the refusal, or rather the avoiding of the archduke to hear what I had to say, as very significant, as it may fairly be presumed that my application had not been overlooked, but that he had considered it inexpedient to see me. This presumption is strengthened by a fact which I have heard from a reliable source. M. Mercier declares that at his parting interview with Lincoln, he was told by Lincoln that he was authorized to say to the archduke that his Government would be recognized by that of Washington without difficulty, on the condition, however, that no negotiations should be entered into with the Confederate States. This assurance repeated to the archduke by M. Mercier, has probably influenced his course toward me, and he is weak and credulous enough to think that he can keep on good terms with the Yankees, while he can at any time in case of need command the friendship and support of the Confederacy. I have taken care, of course in no offensive tone, to let the leading Mexicans here understand that he makes a great mistake, both as regards his hope of avoiding difficulties with the North and his reliance upon the South to aid him in meeting them, should they occur. That without the active friendship of the South he will be entirely powerless to resist Northern aggression, while he in his turn can render us no service in the present or any future war with the North. That our motive in desiring to negotiate with Mexico, was not the expectation of deriving any advantage from an alliance per se, but from the consequences that would probably flow from it in another quarter; that when we should have conquered peace, while we would desire to be on friendly terms with all nations, we should have no special interest in the stability of the

Mexican Government and would be free to pursue such a policy as circumstances and our interests might dictate.

As the newspapers have spoken of General [Wm.] Preston's mission to Mexico, I have not thought it worth while to make a mystery of it, and I have said that if he be not officially received, any future overtures for the establishment of diplomatic relations between the two governments must come from Mexico. I have written fully to General Preston, directed to Havana under cover to Colonel Helm. I am in hopes that my letter will find him there, when with a knowledge of what has occurred here, he can decide whether he will proceed at once to Mexico or take measures to ascertain in advance what reception he will probably meet with. The archduke will, it is thought, embark at Civita Vecchia early next month, and reach Vera Cruz about 1st May. In my interview with M. Drouyn de Lhuys on 19th ultimo, he manifested great dissatisfaction at the tardiness of the archduke's movements, and said that he ought then to be far on his way to Mexico. I think there is a great anxiety to see him embarked and thus so completely committed as to render it impossible for him to reconsider his decision. It is impossible to exaggerate the unpopularity of the Mexican expedition among all classes and parties in France. It is the only subject upon which public opinion seems to be unanimous. I have yet to meet the first man who approves of it, and several persons very near the Emperor have spoken to me of it in decided terms of condemnation. The Emperor is fully aware of this feeling, and is, I believe, very desirous to get rid of the embarrassment as soon as he decently can; the archduke may be obliged to rely on his own resources at a much earlier day than he expects. In this opinion I may perhaps do the Emperor injustice, but I can not otherwise account for the evidently increased desire to avoid giving umbrage to the Lincoln Government.

I send you herewith copies of a note * to M. Drouyn de Lhuys, and a memorandum to be submitted to the Emperor on the subject of the continued detention of the *Rappahannock*. I had intended in my note to the minister to intimate, that if the permission to sail were longer withheld and the grounds of her detention were not specifically stated, I would advise her commander to strike his flag, and leave the ship at the disposition of the authorities of Calais. On this point I asked Commodore Barron's opinion; he thinks that such a course may become necessary but says, " Knowing, however, the extreme anxiety of our government to get vessels on the ocean, and the powerful influence exercised for our benefit by any cruiser that we can put afloat, I rather incline to the belief that we had better not take this step until we have exercised a little more patience in awaiting the slow decision of the Government, particularly when we revert to the kindness which they have shown to us during the past winter."

I have, therefore, abstained for the present from making this intimation directly, although it may perhaps be inferred from my note to Mr. Drouyn de Lhuys. I learn from my usual source of information at the foreign affairs, that the ship will be permitted to sail, but that the Government does not feel obliged to act with promptitude in

* See p. 1055.

consequence of the very unnecessary delay in preparing the ship for sea, in spite of the urgent representations by the commissioner of marine of the necessity of dispatch. There is too much truth in this argument, and I am sorry to say that the affair of the *Rappahannock* has been a series of blunders from the very commencement.

I have the honor to be, with great respect, your most obedient servant,

JOHN SLIDELL.

Hon J. P. BENJAMIN,
  Secretary of State.

P. S.—March 17: I have just received your Nos. 28 and 29. M. Mercier says that although he was very desirous to have an interview with the archduke, for the purpose of explaining his views on American politics, and had been promised one, the archduke left Paris without seeing him or sending him any message.

No. 6.]   LONDON, *March 16, 1864.*

SIR: In a late dispatch from Paris, transmitting a statement of moneys received by me on account of salary, with a separate statement of moneys received on account of contingent fund, I find that I debited myself with the sum of £618 11s. 1d. as received for salary by a draft dated July 15, 1862. This is a mistake. The remittance of £618 11s. 1d. of July 15, 1862, you will find to my debit in the account of moneys received for contingent expenses, where it properly belongs. My recollection is that if you will cause a reference to be made to your dispatch to me about the 4th November, 1862, it will be found that it contained a remittance for the like sum of £618 11s. 1d. for account of salary; and there was transmitted with that dispatch duplicates of drafts dated July 15, 1862, for £1,154 12s. 9d. for account of salary, and £618 11s. 1d. for account of contingent expenses. These duplicates were the first received of those drafts and were paid. They came with the dispatch of November, 1862, which contained the further remittance of £618 11s. 1d. for account of salary.

Will you be good enough to have the error corrected at the Treasury by striking from my statement of moneys received on account of salary the debit for £618 11s. 1d. on the draft of 15th July, 1862. It will then stand where it should properly appear, to the credit of the contingent fund.

I have, etc.,

J. M. MASON.

Hon. J. P. BENJAMIN,
  Secretary of State.

LONDON, *March 17, 1864.*

MY DEAR SIR: I enclose with this, open, a letter for the governor of Virginia, and will be obliged if you will read it and then seal and send it to him. I think the object I have in view will meet your approbation, and in such case will you oblige me in transmitting his reply, to accompany it by a letter from you, written as Secretary of State, giving a like assurance in regard to the statue on the part of the Government.

Very respectfully and truly, yours,

J. M. MASON.

Hon. J. P. BENJAMIN.

[Enclosure.]

LONDON, *March 17, 1864.*

DEAR SIR: You are probably aware that very soon after the death of our great and gallant soldier, Stonewall Jackson, a number of gentlemen in England formed themselves into a committee for the purpose of erecting a statue to his memory. I send you enclosed the program they adopted. You will find on it the names of many eminent and distinguished men; and, coming from England, it will certainly be a beautiful and graceful tribute to the memory of Virginia's noble and devoted son.

Mr. Beresford Hope (treasurer of the committee), one of its most active members, called on me yesterday and said that the fund being raised, the order for its execution had been given to Mr. Foley, the artist; and he said it would be very grateful to the committee and their associates to know that a proper place where justice will be done to it in its exhibition would be reserved for it, wherever it should be determined by our authorities to place it. It is not yet decided whether the statue is to be presented to the Government of the Confederate States or to the State of Virginia; but, in either case, I take it for granted its appropriate place will be on the Capitol Square at Richmond.

Mr. Foley, who is to execute it, is one of the most distinguished sculptors of the age, and you may rely that his work will be worthy the great man it is designed to perpetuate. I have given to the committee a correct photograph of Jackson, and a good likeness taken shortly before his death, and sent to me by friends at Richmond.

I shall be gratified and it will much gratify the committee here, if, in reply to this letter, while expressing your sense as governor of Virginia of the munificent proposed evidence of the sympathy of the people of England with our country in the great loss it has sustained, you authorize me to say that so far as it may rest with Virginia, the statue shall occupy a position worthy of it and the occasion.

I have the honor to be, very respectfully, your obedient servant,

J. M. MASON.

Hon. WILLIAM SMITH,
    Governor of Virginia.

P. S.—I send this, open, through the Department of State, through which please send your reply, open. I ask Mr. Benjamin to send me with your reply, a letter confirming its assurances, so far as the Confederate Government may be concerned.

J. M. M.

No. 81.]   BRUSSELS, *March 18, 1864.*

SIR: Maximilian arrived here on the 16th. To-day he and the archduchess are to take a farewell dinner at the palace with the Duchess de Brabant and the Count de Flandre, and to-morrow they will proceed expeditiously to Vienna. They are to embark on the 29th instant at Trieste for Vera Cruz, where they will probably arrive about the 1st of May. I have not attempted to obtain an interview with him, nor have I heard whether Mr. Slidell or Mr. Mason made an effort or succeeded in doing so.

Every recent trans-Atlantic arrival has brought cheering intelligence from our country. Victory after victory attends our arms. This morning we have New York dates to the 5th instant, confirming the reverses of the North in Florida, Tennessee, Alabama, and Virginia. If our success continues, and I can not doubt that it will, the hour is not distant when you will receive indirect proposals from the Washington Cabinet for peace negotiations. As far as I can judge, the chances were never so favorable for our. terminating the war in a brilliant blaze of glory as at present. If 'it occurs, the world will never have witnessed any event more exalting to humanity. Through all time we should be held up to the admiration of mankind as a model people—really capable of governing ourselves in adversity more wisely than monarch ever governed his subjects.

It is now currently rumored that an armistice has been agreed to by the European belligerents. If so, it is reasonable to suppose that hostilities have definitively ceased, and that the differences will be adjusted through diplomatic channels.

I have the honor to be, sir, very respectfully, your obedient servant,

A. DUDLEY MANN.

Hon. J. P. BENJAMIN,
    Secretary of State, C. S. A.

No. 39.]   CONFEDERATE STATES COMMERCIAL AGENCY,
                                        London, March 19, 1864.

SIR: The debates in Parliament continue to exhibit the same extraordinary spectacle which has made the present session an anomaly in the history of constitutional government. The government is weak beyond anything known in parliamentary warfare; the opposition in haughty consciousness of strength is sardonically sportive. I can think of no more apt description of these nightly exhibitions than the process of "ducking," the drowning man being "let up" with just the last remaining gasp for life. Even the most ordinary administrative routine, such as the annual passage of the clauses of the mutiny bill, is permitted to proceed only with laughably small majorities. Within a single week the ministry has sustained two disasters in which it has lost everything except the life it holds by the grace of its opponents, and has certainly not saved honor. Singularly enough the double blow strikes both arms of the executive, laming it at the same time in its home policy and in its foreign relations.

By some strange infatuation the chancellor of the exchequer, the only man in the cabinet who could claim the prestige of success, chose this critical period for introducing one of his peculiar experimental crotchets, a government annuities bill, something similar to the fire-insurance project Governor Wise some years ago proposed to the Virginia legislature, only that in this project the private companies were to be deprived of the most lucrative branch of life insurance. Astride of this hobby he ran amuck not only against powerful financial interests throughout the Kingdom but against equally powerful individualities, including half his colleagues, who are in some way or other connected with companies of this sort, until his furious career was brought to a close and the office of matador performed by one of the least respectable obscurities in the House. I can not resist the suspicion that Lord Palmerston was secretly not displeased at seeing the only really able man in his cabinet, on whose help he has so often had to call, dragged into the mire with the rest. The next disaster befell the government in the person of a less important member, but under circumstances which make it, if possible, even more serious.

It had been publicly charged by the French procureur general on the trail of the Greco conspirators that the letters of the would-be assassins of the Emperor were addressed to Mazzini at London under the address of a " Mr. Flowers," which address proved to be that of Mr. Stansfeld, a violent radical of notorious connections with the Red Republicans of the Continent, and who, to everybody's surprise, had been made a junior lord of the admiralty by Lord Palmerston in the place of the Marquis of Hartington, on the latter's promotion to the undersecretaryship of war. Upon the first expression of surprise in Parliament, Mr. Stansfeld, assisted by our amiable friend, Mr. Layard, assumed airs of virtuous indignation, and while delivering himself of a glowing panegyric of Mazzini, spurned the imputation of complicity with plots of assassination, which, you will observe, no one had charged him with. Of course the House was not satisfied, and thus most ungraciously and from sheer necessity Mr. Stansfeld was forced to confess that he had lent his address to Mazzini and enabled him to receive letters under the name of " Flori," which he volunteered to inform Parliament was the Italian plural of " Flower." Now, this was precisely the culpable indiscretion of which he stood accused, and for which the French Emperor, having acted with exemplary forbearance, was, at least, entitled to an apology instead of insults. It is almost incredible that in this state of the case the government should espouse Mr. Stansfeld's cause, but doing so the opposition, of course, allowed them the " triumph " of saving their protegé from the censure of the House by a few votes.

You will naturally ask why the opposition does not save the country from such flagrant disgrace by taking office. I am told that at a meeting of his supporters at Lord Derby's house a few days since he enjoined upon them the strictest care not to outvote the government. I am quite disposed to believe this. On high patriotic grounds and a comprehensive view of constitutional obligations there can be no doubt of Lord Derby's duty. But as a mere party leader there are obvious reasons why he should not accept power at the very moment when it would make him and his party responsible for all the certain consequences of their predecessors' acts. Dearly as these deceptive advantages have been purchased with the prestige of England, the country enjoys peace, and its finances are flourishing.

The impending storm is seen only by a few, and Lord Derby is too sagacious a navigator to embark the fortunes of his party in apparent fair weather with the certainty of making shipwreck. Better for him to take the helm when the ship is tossed by the tempest, and bring her safely into port. In all this, if I have correctly described it, you will perceive the reflex, only without the darker shades of coarse vulgarity, of the political corruption of the Northern States both before and since the final catastrophe, the same trickery in the place of statesmanship, the same fiddling while Rome is burning, the same callous subordination of all other interests to those of party. Still, for the time being, as I have repeatedly expressed the opinion, the present state of things is the test for our interests. It is a state of things which we might profoundly regret if we had any assistance to hope from either party in the State, but in default of that which we had a right to expect from a country like Great Britain it gives us all we can now have, revenge on those who have cruelly wronged us, and the certainty of more decisive and more enduring reaction the longer it is postponed.

The Messrs. Laird Brothers have published in pamphlet form the correspondence, refused to Parliament by government, between them and the foreign office on the Mersey rams. The pamphlet is confined to private circulation only, and I have not yet seen it, but have taken measures to have one sent you from Liverpool by to-day's mail. Meanwhile, I enclose comments of the Standard on this publication. The judgment on the *Alexandra* case is to be given by the House of Lords shortly after the Easter holidays. You will herewith receive Sir Hugh Cairns' speech on this subject in the Commons, which I have already transmitted in another form. Of the *Pampero* I know nothing except what is contained in the enclosed slip. Our friends here await with great impatience, but entire confidence, the expected disclaimer by Mr. Mallory of the official report ascribed to him. Compared with the blow of such a disclaimer, the parliamentary misfortunes of Lord Palmerston's government which I have narrated to you, would be as the gentle raps of a lady's fan.

I hear on all sides among our friends that the Danish war absorbs public attention. I see no evidence of it outside of our own circles, and do not believe it. But our friends generally think so, and therefore the effect so far as we are concerned is the same as if it were true. Everybody is pausing for a more favorable opportunity. Perhaps this is the wiser course; at all events, if the campaign progresses as it has commenced, we shall lose nothing by it.

You will have seen the brutal order of one of Butler's subordinates sentencing the Rev. Mr. Wingfield to three months' street sweeping for seditious language. I sent the Times a copy of the Norfolk Yankee official paper, containing the order by authority. It was the editor's plain duty as a journalist to have noticed it, and I merely mention the fact of his not doing so as one of many indications that the Times, now the almost avowed supporter of the government, has its mot d'ordre to be silent for the moment on anything likely to prejudice the North or to awaken sympathy for the South.

I remain, with great respect, your obedient servant,

HENRY HOTZE.

Hon. J. P. BENJAMIN,
Secretary of State, Richmond.

No. 82.]   DEPARTMENT OF STATE,
                                        Richmond, March 22, 1864.

SIR: You will receive with this dispatch the Richmond papers, giving an account of a raid of the enemy's cavalry, which attempted to penetrate into this city by a surprise. The attempt was as silly as it was desperate, and would deserve no notice, but for the revelation of the infamous character of the warfare waged against us. The papers found on the body of Colonel Dahlgren, who was intercepted in his flight and killed in an attempt to cut his way through our lines, disclose purposes so foul that the Northern newspapers which, prior to the news of his failure, were indulging in their usual boasts of the intended sack of the city, have since endeavored to throw suspicion on the published copies of the papers by alleging that the passage which ordered the President and the Cabinet to be killed had been interpolated here.

The conclusive answer to this statement will be found in the photographic copies of these papers, which are now being executed at the Engineer's Bureau, and which will be forwarded to you by the next mail. If we had anticipated the denial, the copies would have been in time to accompany this dispatch. The papers found on Dahlgren's body were brought to Richmond by the courier who was dispatched from the scene of the conflict in which Dahlgren was killed, and I happened to be in conference with the President, and read with him the papers, of which extract copies were furnished to the Richmond journals for publication. I am therefore able to vouch personally for the fact that the passage as to the killing of the President and Cabinet existed in the original, and the photographic copy leaves no room for doubt upon the point.

I am very respectfully, your obedient servant,

                                            J. P. BENJAMIN,
                                                Secretary of State.

Hon. JOHN SLIDELL, *Paris.*

P. S.—I inclose you the President's proclamation,* fixing the 8th proximo as a day of fasting, humiliation, and prayer, in accordance with a resolution of Congress. You will perceive that the Chief Magistrate has officially announced in it that the purpose of the enemy was "to destroy our civil government, by putting to death our chosen servants of the people."

————————

No. 83.]   DEPARTMENT OF STATE,
                                        Richmond, March 24, 1864.

SIR: I have the honor to acknowledge receipt on the 17th instant, of your Nos. 54 and 55, dated 25th January and 10th ultimo. Your dispatch of 1st February, without number, on the subject of your accounts, was also received.

The account will be properly stated at the Treasury Department and you will then be able to make a final settlement of it by deducting any balance that may appear to be due by you from your

————————
* Not found.

next draft on our bankers. The items are all correct, but there is some confusion between the accounts for salary and contingent expenses, which will require a transfer of some of the items from one account to the other, not affecting of course the general balance, but requiring some change in the statement as forwarded by you. The rectification of the two accounts will be sent you by next mail and you will then be able to make such settlement as will close your accounts on the books of the Treasury here, up to the 31st December, 1863.

I notice your remarks in relation to the extent of the discretion confided to you in the disposal of the contingent fund, and apprehend that you have not adverted to the distinction which exists between the contingent and secret-service fund. It will not be proper to enlarge your discrétion as to the disposal of the former, because all the items of expenditure of that fund required the approval of the accounting officers of the Treasury, and your accounts would not pass their examination, if containing items of expenditure not allowed by law. In order to enable you therefore to make use of such sums as you may require for purposes needful in the public interest but not provided for by legislation, I deem it best to send you a remittance from the secret-service fund, the expenditure of which rests in the discretion of the President, and for which the account is rendered to this Department and remains in its secret archives. The messenger who takes this dispatch leaves in the morning, and I fear that I shall not be able to obtain a Treasury draft in time to go with the dispatch, but will endeavor to do so.

The bill of exchange for £1,443 5s. 11½ d., of which you make mention, was remitted on account of salary, and Mr. Washington wrote you so in answer to your enquiry, but it seems his letter did not reach you. The smaller bill sent at the same time was for contingent expenses. The Treasury statement above referred to will set this all right.

I observe nothing in your Nos. 54 and 55 requiring special comment, as our news from Europe is as late as the 6th March. I am however somewhat surprised to find it stated in the Northern papers that the *Rappahannock* has not yet gone to sea.

It is gratifying to inform you that the legislation of Congress both as to the financial and military affairs of the Confederacy is attended with the happiest effects. It is believed that our currency, by the joint operation of funding and taxation, will be reduced by the 1st July to about $250,000,000. This sum is not to be increased under any circumstances, and we confidently expect that all our needs will be supplied by the sale of the new 6 per cent bonds, of which the advantages are so obvious that there is already quite a demand at the Treasury to know when they will be issued. No part of them will be wanted, however, for the next 60 days.

This army is in the highest spirits, and the people confident, full of hope and determination. Our skies were never so bright since the war commenced.

I am, yours, very respectfully,

J. P. BENJAMIN,
Secretary of State.

Hon. JOHN SLIDELL, *Paris.*

No. 34.]   DEPARTMENT OF STATE,
Richmond, March 26, 1864.

SIR: I have just received from the Bureau of Engineers photographic copies of the infamous papers found on the body of Colonel Dahlgren, when he was killed in his flight from the neighborhood of Richmond, after the repulse of his command. I send you four copies.

They speak for themselves and require no comment. You will agree with me that they should be extensively circulated as the most exclusive evidence of the nature of the war now waged against us by those who profess to desire that we should live with them as brethren under one government.

Respectfully, your obedient servant,

J. P. BENJAMIN,
Secretary of State.

Hon. JOHN SLIDELL, *Paris.*

HALIFAX, NOVA SCOTIA,
April 1, 1864.

SIR: In the communication which I had the honor to transmit from Bermuda I explained the reasons which induced me to turn the *Caledonia* over to her owners and to engage my passage to Halifax in the British mail steamer *Alpha.* From what has since transpired it is certain that if I had escaped capture upon the *Caledonia* there would have been no saving of time at all commensurate with the heavy expense to the Government .which the employment of that vessel would have involved. The *Alpha* did not reach this port until the 23d of March, having been delayed for two days by a severe storm which it encountered soon after leaving the Gulf Stream. Upon my arrival I learned that the prisoners whose delivery had been demanded by the United States under the extradition treaty had been released by the judicial authorities of New Brunswick upon habeas corpus; and although new warrants are out for their arrest it is not probable that they can be executed. The most embarrassing phase which this case could assume would be presented for solution by the surrender of these men. Whatever may be the light in which the captors of the *Chesapeake* should be regarded according to the strict rules of law, the Government and people of the Confederate States can not be indifferent to their fate. They imperiled life and liberty in an enterprise of great hazard, which they honestly believed was invested with the sanction of the law, and to which as a body, I have reason to think, they were mainly impelled by a generous sympathy with our cause. Whilst, therefore, in exercising the discretion confided to me I have determined, at least for the present, to interpose no claim to the *Chesapeake* as a prize of war on behalf of the Confederate States, I have endeavored to observe a diplomatic reticence as to the view which our Government may ultimately take of that transaction. I can imagine the existence of circumstances under which the Government, to save these brave and innocent men from a cruel and unrighteous doom, might claim the benefit of principles which it would not think it judicious to assert if the only interest at stake was one of property.

As to the *Chesapeake*, I found that she had been surrendered to her original owners without the almost invariable requisition of bail to answer prospective demands. The reasons which induced the judge to depart from the established course of admiralty practice are contained in the opinion (of which I send you a copy). Taking the opinion and the conduct of the magistrate himself during the progress of the cause (of which I also transmit a history) together, I do not believe that any judicial proceeding has taken place in a British court for a century and a half so discreditable to its dignity, its intelligence, or its justice. But notwithstanding my indignation at the offensive and unworthy bearing of Judge Stewart, I am not willing, after a full examination of the facts of this case, to commit the Government to interference with it in any form. The moral weight which should attach to its interposition would be impaired by advancing a claim which it is almost certain would be allowed neither by the British courts nor the British Government, and which we could sustain only by affirming principles doubtful in law and equivocal in morals. The facts upon which my opinion rests are these: Of the party actually engaged in the capture, fourteen or fifteen in number, only one has any claim to the character of a Confederate citizen or belonged in any way to its service. This was the second officer, H. A. Parr, who, although born in Canada, had lived for the last seven years in Tennessee. The lieutenant commanding, John C. Braine, I have ascertained beyond doubt, had been released from Fort Warren on the application of the British minister on the allegation of being a British subject.

This indeed is the substance of his own admission, nor has he since been within the Confederacy. Although he states that he had been in our military service at an earlier period, the declaration is probably untrue and would not be received to contradict the deliberate and solemn allegation by which he obtained his liberty. He is, I think, estopped from claiming, what in truth I do not believe he ever professed, the Confederate nationality. Passing over for the present the consideration of what effect Parker's connection with this enterprise may have upon its character, it appears to have been a capture made for the benefit of the Confederacy by a body of men without any public authority, and who, with the single exception of a subordinate officer, were British subjects; I do not think that such a case can be brought within the application of the principle, perfectly well settled and which in a war like the present our Government ought never to yield, that the citizens of a belligerent state, with or without a commission, may capture enemies' property at sea. That doctrine, as may be seen in the elaborate discussion of the opinions of British and foreign jurists; by Judge Story in the case of the ship *Emulous* (1 Gall. Rep., 563, S. S.; 8 Cranch, 110), a discussion which Mr. Phillimore pronounces perfectly exhaustive, is founded upon the hostile relation which the mere declaration of war creates between the citizens of the contending States. A commission would appear to me indispensable to enable a belligerent to claim for itself the benefit of captures made in its behalf by citizens of a neutral State.

Parr's position may be, and in all probability is, very different from that of his associates, but it does not seem to me to have been sufficiently commanding to impress upon the enterprise his own nationality. The question then recurs whether the legal complexion of this capture can be altered by Parker's connection with it, assuming that his Confederate character can be established by proof. In the absence of all facilities for investigation (the law Library of the Province to which I have access being very meager), I am not free from all doubt as to the correctness of my conclusions upon this point. The letters of marque, I am inclined to think, attach only to the vessel, and confer authority upon the master, whoever he may be, for the time being. They do not confer upon the commander a personal authority which will survive the destruction of his ship (unless in reference to a prize which she may have captured) and enable him to act as a commissioned officer wherever he may be found. If I am correct in this, Parker can only be regarded as a private citizen of the Confederacy, with no right such as he assumed to enlist men or appoint officers in its service, and as he was not present when the *Chesapeake* was taken, the character of the capture must be determined by that of the persons on board at the time.

If, however, I am mistaken in my views of the law upon this point (which I would be very glad to find), there is another principle which, whilst it would not affect the captors with any crime in the eye of public law, would no doubt be appealed to in order to deprive us of the fruits of the capture; I mean that enunciated by the Supreme Court of the United States in the cases of *L'Amistad De Reues* (5 Wheat., 385); the *Bello Corcumes* (6 Wheat., 152); *La Conception* (ib., 235); *La Santissima Trinidad* (7 Wheat., 283), etc., to wit, that where a prize has been taken by any agency created in violation of neutral sovereignty, it will, if brought voluntarily within the neutral jurisdiction, be restored to the original owners. I do not know that the case of the *Chesapeake* can be brought within the range of any exception to this principle. The evidence contained in the report of the trial at St. John (of which I send a copy) discloses a clear violation by Parker of the British foreign enlistment act, and upon this ground alone I apprehend that any claim we might advance to the *Chesapeake* would be defeated.

The conduct of the captors after the capture in peddling the cargo in violation of the revenue laws of the Province, and the appropriation of a portion of the proceeds by some of them to their own use, and all the developments which have been made as to the motives and character of Braine, are calculated to throw so much suspicion and discredit around the whole transaction that I should deem it unwise, even were the law supposed to be in our favor, without weightier reasons than now exist, to compromise the Confederacy by assuming its responsibility.

I can not close this communication without bringing to the attention and notice of the Government the generous sympathy and liberal contribution in every matter in which the interests of the Confederacy were supposed to be involved, of some prominent gentlemen of this city, and especially of Dr. Almon, Mr. Keith, Mr. Wier, and Mr. Ritchie. They have given money, time, and influence without reserve, as if our cause had been that of their own country. I feel that I shall not transcend the spirit of my instructions in tendering to Mr. Ritchie, of this city, and Mr. Gray, of St. John, in behalf of the Confederacy, some compensation for professional services which were rendered most faithfully and laboriously and with no other object than to advance our cause. I feel that the gentlemen whose names I have given are entitled to some special acknowledgment from our Government of their handsome conduct, and I am certain it would be most highly appreciated by them, and would exercise a happy influence in this community.

It was so late before I could procure all the documents upon which to rest my action that I am unable to embrace in this letter several matters I desire to bring to your attention.

With the highest consideration.

JAMES P. HOLCOMBE.

Hon. J. P. BENJAMIN,
    Secretary of State, C. S. A.

P. S.—It may not be improper to add that the conclusions which I have reached are in accordance with the judgment of our most discreet and intelligent friends in this place.

No. 83.]   BRUSSELS, *April 4, 1864.*

SIR: I have now the honor to acknowledge the receipt of your No. 11, which arrived yesterday.

In the success which has attended the transmission of my dispatches to you I have continued reason to congratulate myself. I trust that I have been as fortunate with those which I have forwarded since.

I rejoice to find you so confident with respect to our operations in the field during the spring's campaign. As distant as I am from the scene of action I share it in the broadest sense in which it can be entertained. If the North had confined herself in her aggressions to the employment of the citizens within her embraces as troops, we should have won a universally recognized independence long ago. Her chief reliance for months for recruits has been upon foreign mercenaries and negroes. In availing herself of such ignoble services for invasion, evidently not contemplated by her at the time she commenced hostilities, she virtually acknowledges our superiority as a belligerent. End when the war may, it will be regarded all over the earth as a most inglorious one for her on this account alone. A noble enemy never has recourse to disreputable means. England will never hear the last of the " Hessians," nor of her incitement of the Indians in 1812 on the Northwestern frontier.

Great Britain and France still hesitate, and in the face of accumulating irrefragable proofs of our title to a place in the family of nations. It must be owned that they are actuated by powerful motives. " One is afraid and the other dares not." The former apprehends that an indemnity would be demanded, perhaps vi et armis, by the Lincoln concern for the captures by the *Alabama* and the *Florida*, and the latter that the imperial throne of Mexico would be dangerously imperiled. Never during the history of civilization has the passion of fear predominated more effectively in a matter of strictly international right. The time may come when we, one way or another, peacefully, of course, may make the two great western powers sensible of their flagrant injustice to us.

The differences between Maximilian and his brother Francis Joseph, with reference to the succession in Austria, are said to have been definitively adjusted, and that the archduke and archduchess will embark at Trieste on the 12th instant for Vera Cruz, landing, on their route, at Civita Vecchia, from whence they will proceed to Rome for a few days' sojourn. There are those well informed who are so incredulous as to assert that in reality no point of difference existed between the two brothers and that the report was a mere ruse to cover up a serious disagreement with the Emperor of the French, on account of additional unreasonable exactions made by him upon the embryo Emperor. I have largely overestimated the difficulties which are likely to beset him if the adventurous Hapsburger does not speedily find his position absolutely impossible. Betwixt the Bonapartes and the Santa Annas, Almontes, et id omne genus, it would be difficult for the wisdom of a Solon to rule Mexico for a lengthened time.

According to current rumor Maximilian has had large quantities of dazzingly brilliant court liveries manufactured here. All articles for his household have been prepared upon a magnificent scale, without regard to cost.

The embryo Empress is to be furnished with a guard of a brigade from this little Kingdom. Both officers and men are to be taken from the army.

The Belgians are enthusiastic in their calculations with respect to the large trade intercourse which they are hereafter to enjoy with Mexico. They confidingly rely upon the good intentions and genial influence which Charlotte, a princess of Brussels birth, who has ever and deservedly been much beloved by them, will exercise in their behalf.

Belgium is still without a government. The old ministers decline to exercise any other than a mere formal authority. They are impatient to surrender the seals of office, in order that they may resume their employment at a period not remote, with a certainty of retaining them for several years. The opposition is reluctant to succeed them, with the chances so adverse to a retention of power. However, it is believed that its leaders, finding that they could do nothing better, have resolved to present a cabinet list next week to the King for his acceptance. During this long ministerial crisis his Majesty has been absent, and no excitement whatever has been produced by the one occurrence or the other. Assuredly there never was a more orderly population than that contained within the limits of this Kingdom.

The Senate of Lincoln & Co. has ratified the treaty concluded here last summer, stipulating for the payment of about $550,000 in specie for the abrogation of the Scheldt tolls levied upon the navigation and commerce of the United States. Upon the first vote the treaty was rejected, but the question was reconsidered and it was then passed almost unanimously. Sumner was the champion of the measure, Sherman its chief opponent. The former advocated its ratification as a means of propitiating King Leopold and securing his good will in the interests of the North. In this sense it was carried, and so viewed it is little less than a deliberate attempt at bribery.

I have the honor to be, sir, very respectfully, your obedient servant,

A. DUDLEY MANN.

Hon. J. P. BENJAMIN,
Secretary of State, C. S. A., Richmond, Va.

No. 59.]   PARIS, *April 7, 1864.*

SIR: Since I last had the honor of addressing you on 16th ultimo I have received your No. 30.

In reply to your 28 I have to say that Mr. Bernard Avegno is in Paris; he says that he has repeatedly written to the State Department; that he went to Vera Cruz and found that his services there could not be useful; he consequently decided to resign the mission which had been confided to him and came to Europe. He has promised to give me copies of his various letters to the State Department, which if furnished in time I will forward with this dispatch. I feel very confident that they will give a satisfactory explanation of his conduct. Mr. Avegno purposes returning immediately to the Confederacy and will thus render personally an account of his stewardship.

I learn from good authority that two military officers are very soon to proceed to the Confederacy for the purpose of observing and reporting to the Emperor the organization and discipline of our armies, the defenses of Charleston, the condition of our artillery, etc. As the English Government, while sending a similar commission to the North, has declared its intention for prudential reasons not to avail itself of the information which might be derived from analogous enquiries in the Confederacy, the action of this Government is not without a certain significance.

It was my intention to have carried into effect by this time, in the absence of any satisfactory reply on the subject of the *Rappahannock*, the purpose which I intimated in my No. 58. Circumstances have since occurred which have induced me to delay action. The *Georgia* has arrived at Bordeaux, having failed in the object of her voyage; she requires repairs that can not be completed in less than three weeks. The *Rappahannock* can not be armed from any other quarter, and if permission were now given to sail it would greatly embarrass the operation.

Commodore Barron has consequently requested me to remain passive for the present.

You will probably have seen the article of the London Globe, alluded to in the note from my friend at the foreign office, of which I give you a copy.

[Translation.]

PARIS, *March 24, 1864.*

I have called the attention of Mr. Drouyn de Lhuys to the article of the Globe, where it is stated that Mr. Dayton had declared that his Government was ready to accredit a representative to Mexico and to receive a minister of the Emperor of Mexico after the new sovereign should have addressed to him the formal notification of his accession.

It was replied to me that Mr. Dayton had stated nothing as positive as that. The minister had confined himself to say (and that some time ago) that the

Federal Government had no unkind disposition toward the monarchical government which was being established in Mexico and would have no difficulty, should the case arise, to enter into relation with it.

One should observe, however, that Mr. Dayton in speaking thus did not do it in the name nor by order of the Cabinet at Washington, but from himself and as being a foreshadowing of the intention of that Cabinet.

I have no doubt of the substantial correctness of this statement.

Mr. Hotze is here on a short visit. I have communicated the papers accompanying your No. 30, of which he will make proper use. I think that you could not have selected a more suitable agent for the duties assigned to him, but it seems to me that a greater portion of his time could be beneficially employed here and I shall so advise him.

In relation to the person mentioned in your No. 29, for my distrust of whom, expressed in my No. 30, the President desired to have more specific reasons, I have given them in a private note to the President accompany this dispatch.

I have recently learned from a quarter on which I rely a fact showing the prodigal expenditure of the Federal agents here in corrupting the press.

The political director of the French press is well known to me, almost since my first arrival in Paris; he was decided in his expression of Southern sympathies and I have no doubt sincerely entertained them. Everything which has since occurred should naturally have strengthened these sympathies, unless some extraordinary appliances had been brought to bear upon him. For some time past he has gone beyond the line of his official duties to suppress articles and intelligence favorable to the South and to impose the insertion of those of an opposite tendency. He is needy and extravagant, has lost very large sums at play which have been paid by money obtained from an American banking house with which he had no previous relations.

I think you will agree with me in attributing this sudden and remarkable change of opinion and action to a timely and liberal application of Mr. Dayton's contingent fund. Mr. Treilhard, late chargé d'affaires at Washington, called to see me a few days since. He returns to Europe fully satisfied of the capacity of the South to maintain her independence, speaks in strong terms of the growing lassitude of the North and anticipates a general breaking up of the Lincoln Government before the end of the year.

As the Emperor is always anxious to obtain full and reliable information on American affairs, I presume that he will see Mr. ———, whose report can scarcely fail to produce a good effect.

I am pleased to find that hereafter the shipment of cotton, tobacco, and naval stores is to be made under the exclusive control of the Government and that the importation of luxuries is prohibited. So long as we had any reason to hope that practical illustrations of the inefficiency of the blockade might lead to a denial by European powers of its obligatory force it was wise to hold out every inducement to individual enterprise to multiply those illustrations. The fallacy of such a hope has been but too apparent for more than a year, and blockade running for individual account had become an almost unmitigated nuisance. If the proceeds of the cotton shipped by the Government be employed exclusively in the purchase for cash in

European markets of needful supplies by its own agents and for the payment of obligations contracted by them, I have no doubt that they will be found sufficient for the purpose.

I send you an article from the Opinion National of the 28th ultimo on the subject of the alleged construction of ships of war for the Confederate States. It contains copies of letters from the minister of foreign affairs, which I presume are authentic. The article carries on its face evidence of having been prompted by Mr. Dayton, by whom only the information could have been furnished. Presenting as it does a covert attack on the Government, I will be surprised if it does not produce an opposite effect from that intended by him. I am informed that the operations of Messrs. Voruz and Arman have not been in any way interfered with beyond the notification mentioned by Mr. Drouyn de Lhuys in his letter to Mr. Dayton of 22d October last.

I have copies of all the purloined documents presented by Mr. Dayton to the minister of foreign affairs, but do not think it worth while to send them to you, as they are voluminous and their contents are sufficiently stated in the article of the Opinion National.

Captain [W. E.] Evans, of the *Georgia*, has been most courteously received at Bordeaux, and every facility afforded him for the repairs, etc., of his vessel.

I had yesterday a long conversation with Mr. Seymour Fitzgerald, whose position is, of course, well known to you by reputation. He will, in the event of the accession of the Derby party to power, in all probability be the foreign secretary. On this, as on a previous visit, he has had a private audience with the Emperor and repeated conferences with the minister of foreign affairs. He feels very confident that the Palmerston-Russell cabinet must soon retire, and the object of his visits to Paris is, I doubt not, to establish in advance cordial relations with this Government by concerting a programme of action on the great questions of the day. He confirms fully the idea which I expressed to Mr. Drouyn de Lhuys, as stated in my No. 57, of the probable course of a Conservative ministry on the American question, and this not in assenting to any suggestion of mine, but in reply to an enquiry what we might expect him to do when he should occupy the place of Earl Russell.

Serious doubts had begun to be entertained by many persons whether, after all, the acceptance of the throne by Maximilian and his departure for Vera Cruz would not be indefinitely postponed. They are dissipated by the following announcement in the Moniteur of this morning:

According to news received from Miramar, his Imperial Highness, the Archduke Maximilian, will receive the Mexican deputation next Saturday and will leave the following Sunday for Mexico.

I have received from Mr. Avegno the promised copies of his letters to you and to the Secretary of the Treasury.

It appears that I had misunderstood him as saying that he had been at Vera Cruz.

I have the honor to be, with greatest respect, your most obedient servant,

JOHN SLIDELL.

Hon. J. P. BENJAMIN,
Secretary of State.

No. 84.]   BRUSSELS, *April 8, 1864.*

SIR: A conference is shortly to be held in London, at latest by the
1st of May, for an arrangement of the Schleswig-Holstein question.
If it be hindered, by the inordinate demands of Prussia and Austria,
from arriving at a satisfactory solution of the differences between
the belligerents, it is thought that France and Great Britain will have
no alternative but to form an alliance and unsheathe the sword against
the powers and States represented in the Germanic Diet.

It is presumable that Great Britain, in that event, will throw no
obstacles in the way of the " rectification " of the northern boundary
of France, as far as relates to the Prussian Provinces on the Rhine,
and that Louis Napoleon, for this concession, will agree not to attempt
the annexation of Belguim, or in any manner interfere with her peaceful, independent repose.   He will not perhaps consent to let Luxem-
burg remain in the possession of the Germanic Confederation, with
its formidable fort, much the strongest inland structure of the kind
in Europe.   Belgium has a better title to this Province that ever
Germany had to Holstein, much less Schleswig.   It was severed from
her in her separation from Holland as a propitiation to Austria and
Prussia for the violation of the treaty of Vienna, with the sanction
and concurrence of Great Britain and France.

My own opinion is that the conference will patch up a convention
that will be accepted by the belligerents; but, even in such case,
Europe will continue to be agitated by disturbing questions until the
Continent is parceled out anew.   Poland will never be content as the
subjugated of Russia.   From the want of homogeneousness in the
members which constitute the body of Austria, her life is, and has
long been considered, unnatural in the extreme.   The Italians believe that they are worthy of the Eternal City, and that the " Sea
Tulip " is theirs, almost by right divine; Spain no longer speaks in
whispers with respect to the restoration of Gibraltar; and France was
never more covetous of that which she fancies to be her "natural
northern frontier."

The Emperor of the French evidently aimed at a settlement of those
difficult subjects, in which he doubtless expected the country over
which he reigns to be the largest beneficiary, when he so gravely proposed a European congress.   Russia, Austria, Great Britain, and
Prussia did not require a political vision of deep penetration to enable them to forsee his cunningly devised schemes.

The numerous and flagrant violations of the treaty of Vienna have
so impaired that instrument that it is no longer considered worthy
of being dignified or observed as European law.   That nation which
esteems itself sufficiently powerful to evade with impunity the obligations therein imposed is almost as regardless of its stipulations as
the Yankees ever were of the provisions of the compact of 1787.
That something must be done to guard against impending eventualities is admitted in turn by the five great powers themselves, as each
experiences wrong and imagines danger to its future.   But how or
where to begin is a question which perhaps puzzles most vexatiously
the brain of every European sovereign except the wonderfully prolific one of the all-accomplished diplomats of the Tuileries.

Just before I left London I was approached by an excellent and enlightened English politician, with whom I had been many years in

cordial friendly intercourse, upon the subject of our recognition. He is a devoted admirer of Louis Napoleon and an earnest advocate of the congress proposed by him in November last. He assured me that it was to the interest of the Confederate States that I should employ whatever influence I could command in a certain quarter in behalf of the European meeting so ardently desired by the Emperor, as he was quite confident, indeed would promise, that in the event of such an assemblage, the recognition by it of the government of those States would constitute a part of its programme. I was incredulous. I continue so. Whenever we are recognized by a European congress our recognition will be so conditional as to render it utterly unacceptable, particularly if inspired by Napoleon III. I need not state what that condition would be, inasmuch as I have so frequently indicated it in my correspondence with the Department.

Of fair play, since their acknowledgment of us as a belligerent, we have received none deserving of mention from either France or England. We have less to expect from them now than ever. The fact ought not to be concealed from our invincible armies, if it is not already distinctly revealed to them that they have to fight it out to a triumphant end with their barbarous and remorseless enemy. That fact can contain no terror nor occasion any dismay for the dauntless hearts of which those armies are composed.

Garibaldi, having outlived his fame in Italy by his immoderate imprudences, has gone to England to agitate it. The Britishry are as wild with delight at his coming as were the Yankees with the visit of Kossuth to the United States. He will be lionized throughout the realm, as but few personages were ever lionized before. In him we have an avowed enemy, who sacrilegiously compares Lincoln to our Saviour, and I apprehend that he will avail himself of every suitable opportunity to excite the prejudices of the middle and working classes against us. I know of no European who could harm our cause more, in occasioning an estrangement of public sentiment from us in the British isles, than this plausible, scar-covered political dreamer. Sutherland House and Exeter Hall will not fail to employ him to the best advantage as the continental champion of anti-slavery.

The evidences are of rapid accumulation that a financial crash in the North is imminent. The journals of New York which in their expressions appeared to be the most hopeful of Chase's system can no longer disguise their fears that that system may speedily fail. The shrewd business men of Europe have ever believed that sooner or later such a result was inevitable. But for the enormous amount of wild enthusiasm and blind credulity contained in the remnant of the old Union, it would have occurred at the outset of the Utopian experiment. There is now clearly no escape from it. When Grant's failure in Virginia becomes apparent it must happen, at the latest. And then? Why, then the heel of the oppressor will be removed and his own body prostrated on the earth. This is the retributive justice, the most effective and the most righteous ever displayed upon earth, which I religiously believe has been in reserve from the first for the relentless murderers of our unprotected citizens and the desolators of our plantations and firesides.

The statements telegraphed to-day from Vienna are very conflict-ing with regard to the reported misunderstanding between Francis Joseph and Maximilian. It is asserted on one side that the differ-ences have been arranged definitively and on the other that fresh and difficult complications have arisen. This is a strange, very strange affair. In the meantime cabinet messengers are repairing from the Tuileries and couriers from the King of the Belgians, who is with Queen Victoria, to Miramar. It may turn out, as I ven-tured to intimate in my last, that Louis Napoleon, who not unfre-quently finds it inconvenient to make himself well understood, is the cause of the delay of the departure of the embryo Emperor and Empress.

I have the honor to be, sir, very respectfully, your obedient servant,

A. DUDLEY MANN.

Hon. J. P. BENJAMIN,
    Secretary of State, C. S. A.

No. 7.]
          16 RUE DE MARIGNAN,
          Paris, April 12, 1864.

SIR: My last were Nos. 5 and 6, dated respectively, London, 16th March, 1864, and of which I have the honor to enclose duplicates herewith. I enclose also a duplicate of my No. 2, which I could not do when I last wrote, the original being here, as explained in my No. 5.

I returned to Paris soon after the date of my last and have had nothing from the Department since your dispatches acknowledged in my No. 5 of date 25th January last.

Mr. Slidell's dispatches which go with this, will give you, I pre-sume, everything of interest from the continent. On my arrival here he showed me your dispatch relating to Mexico, and to the mission of General Preston, with a copy of your instructions to that gentleman. In my No. 5, and doubtless also in those of same date from Mr. Slidell, you will have learned [of] the change that came over the aspect of our hoped-for relations with Mexico, and I was, in consequence, gratified to learn, both from your instructions to General Preston and by letters from that gentleman to Mr. Slidell, that he was not to present himself in Mexico under any uncertainty about his reception. The policy of the Emperor here, always mys-terious, has had certainly that feature in regard to our affairs; what-ever the motive, the result remains the same. With the fairest pro-fessions, even sedulously made, I look now for no movement of any kind in that quarter of value to us. Thanks to the spirit of our people and the gallantry of our troops, under whatever loss and suffering, we can yet unaided work out our own salvation.

As regards the *Tuscaloosa*, about which I wrote in my No. 5, we have heard nothing more. She remains, I presume, still in Govern-ment charge, at the cape.

Some days since, I received from Messrs. Snowball & Copeland, solicitors at Liverpool, a letter in regard to three men, named Pat-rick Toonan, alias Ferrand, alias Clements; George McMurdoch, and Quincy Sears, arrested there at the instance of the United States consul on a charge of piracy, and claimed for extradition under the treaty. These men were of those who, under a Captain Hogg, embarked as passengers at Matamoras on board the steamer *J. L. Gereitz*, or *Gerrity*, seized her on her voyage to New York, overpowering the captain and crew, and carried her to Belize, where Captain Hogg, it would appear, disposed of her cargo. The solicitors wrote to me that they claimed to be citizens of the Confederate States, and had been in the Confederate Army; that they were enlisted by Captain Hogg for the service intended on board the *Gerrity*, and that the latter had some authority or commission for the enterprise from General Bee in Texas. Seeing what had been done by the Department of State in the case of the *Chesapeake*, and having the benefit of your instructions to Mr. Holcombe, sent as commissioner for that case to Halifax, I requested Captain Bulloch, at Liverpool, to examine into the case of these men, and particularly whether they were citizens of our country, and under what orders they acted.

It appears they came to Liverpool as seafaring men from Belize, and, as was to be expected, without papers or other proofs as to citizenship. Captain Bulloch, however, reported that from the best information he could obtain, Toonan was an Englishman, who had been in the Confederate Army; McMurdoch, British born, but naturalized in Virginia; and Sears a native of Alabama. Looking to the action of the Department taken in the case of the captors of the *Chesapeake*, I thought it the safer course, at least, to take care that these men should be properly defended, and wrote accordingly to these solicitors, sending them a copy of so much of your instructions to Mr. Holcombe as would apply to the case; and directing them to take care that the defense was conducted in the best manner for the safety of the men. I was the more induced to this, bcause I learned from Major Magruder (nephew and aid-de-camp of General Magruder), who was here some time since, that he met with Captain Hogg at Matamoras shortly before the *Gerrity* affair; that he was an officer in the Confederate Army, and had the reputation for great daring and courage, though then disabled by wounds received in the service. I told the solicitors that I would commit the Government for the reasonable expenses of the defense, and I must defray it out of the contingent fund. This, I hope, will have the approbation of the Department.

In regard to the spurious report of Mr. Mallory, as Secretary of the Navy, about which I wrote you in my No. 5, Earl Russell took occasion a few days since to say in the House of Lords, that since it was communicated to him, Mr. Seward had admitted that it was a forgery, fabricated, as he said, by some gentleman of New York.

This dispatch will be borne by Mr. Richard W. Corbin, who goes via Halifax and Bermuda, and to whom I gave a letter to you. I send by him Parliamentary documents North America No. 92, relating to the seizure of the *Chesapeake*. At foot of page 9, being enclosure No. 3, you will find what is doubtless another forgery, intending to operate in England prejudicially to us, purporting to be the decipher of a letter from a Confederate agent at New York to you, and placed by Mr. Seward in the hands of Lord Lyons, and by him sent to Earl Russell. Mr. Slidell, whose name appears in it, besides its intrinsic marks, declares it spurious. I have sent you, from time to time as they appear full copies of all the documents laid before Parliament relating to American affairs.

Before I left London, I called on Mr. Wyon, the artist employed to make the Confederate seal, referred to in my No. 4, and paid him 40 guineas (equal to £42), one-half the cost of the seal, in advance, and arranged that when it was ready, it should be carefully packed, with the press, etc., in a box cased with tin, and put in charge of Mr. Hotze until it could be sent over. He promised it should be ready by the middle of May.

The conference of the parties to the Danish-German treaty of 1852, originally appointed to be held in London to-day (12th instant), has been postponed to the 15th. None seem sanguine that it will result in a composition of the existing difficulties between the powers at war, but may embark others in it.

I have the honor to be, very respectfully, your obedient servant,

J. M. MASON.

Hon. J. P. BENJAMIN,
    Secretary of State.

---

4 MANSION HOUSE PLACE,
London, April 13, 1864.

DEAR SIR: I take the liberty of addressing you on the subject of pilots and the rules and regulations adopted by the Confederate Government toward them, which appear to me on this side to be framed specially so as practically to cause the greatest trouble to steamers endeavoring to run the blockade.

I am informed that—

1. Pilots are liable to the conscription.

2. If losing their ship are forced to enlist.

3. If demanding or receiving more than the Government regulation pilotage they are, if found out, deprived of their license and obliged to serve.

To an enforcement of these, or somewhat similar enactments, is attributed the scarcity of pilots and also the inferior capacity of many who, to fill up the gaps, are accepted as pilots.

The *Emily* was lost I believe through the incapacity of her pilot, who I am informed was at once put in the army; the *Minnie* was at last advices, 15 March, still at Bermuda, having been there for upwards of five weeks loaded and ready to start, but prevented from doing so from the want of a pilot. The serious loss to the Confederate Government of such detentions I need not point out, nor the great delay and loss to the owners whose operations if successful would be no less profitable to themselves commercially than to the Confederate Government and their cause.

If it is desirable and in the interest of the Confederate Government that steamers should run in with stores and out with cotton, paying the Government debts and influencing greatly their credit, surely pilots are much more usefully employed to the State as pilots than as fighting men. The very few of them that there are could never be felt as a loss to the army, while one dozen of them taken out of their number is sensibly felt and greatly aggravates the difficulty of steamers getting in, which is surely difficult enough already.

If a pilot loses his ship, do not let him be deprived of his license unless he is grievously to blame; but if so, at once into the ranks with him, not otherwise; the best of pilots may lose his ship.

The question of money is a very delicate one, but unquestionably the greater the scarcity, the fewer the number of pilots, the higher will be their demands, so long as human nature retains its past and present characteristics.

I feel deeply mortified that we should now be in the middle of April without any result except outlay, and seeing the quality of the material I have sent out both of steamers and equipment, I trust that you will not deem me unreasonable in addressing you on this subject, seeing that up to date the sole cause of failure has been from incapacity and want of pilots and that you will kindly give the matter your consideration and write to the Confederate Government regarding the best means to avoid the destruction or withdrawal of men so imperatively necessary in the present emergency.

North Heath arrived at Bermuda safely on the 10th March; *Helen* was due 8th, 10th April.

I am, dear sir, yours, very respectfully,

JNO. STERLING BEGBIE.

The Hon. JOHN SLIDELL,
Rue de Marignan, Champs Elysées, Paris.

Dispatch No. 28.] HAVANA, *April 14, 1864.*

SIR: In reply to your dispatch No. 4, of the 11th February last, I have the honor to say that your expressions of satisfaction with my supervision of our public interests, made more forcible by conveying to me also the President's approval of my general course while representing the Confederate States in Cuba, has afforded me a very high degree of pleasure. My first wish, at the beginning of our great contest for independence and constitutional liberty was to share the dangers, hardships, and glory of some one of our noble armies, but when told that I could serve my country more effectually at this post, the struggle between duty and personal desire was short lived. My aspirations were then turned to the question of the possibility of sharing with our heroes and statesmen at home at the end of the contest, in some degree, the honor of having assisted in establishing the Republic of the Confederate States of America; your dispatch has therefore given me the pleasure I have expressed. Please thank the President for me, and assure him, as I assure you, that there will be no lack of zeal, energy, or prudence on my part, in my guardianship of Confederate interests at this point.

The admiral of the British Navy commanding the West India Squadron was charged by his Government with the delivery to you of the dispatch of Joseph T. Crawford, Esq., mentioned in my No. 26. The gunboat *Petrel* was sent here to execute the order, received the dispatch, and proceeded to Charleston, but being ordered off by the Federal naval commander, sailed for Bermuda to report to the admiral. The admiral then forwarded the dispatch to Lord Lyons at Washington, who requested permission from Mr. Seward to forward it through the lines, but upon being refused, and hearing from Mr. Seward that it would not be agreeable to the Federal Government for her Majesty's Government to hold any intercourse whatever with the Confederates, returned Mr. Crawford's dispatch and referred the subject back to his Government. So certain was the

British ministry that Mr. Crawford had proceeded to Richmond that for some weeks their correspondence with the consulate here was directed to John V. Crawford, Esq., who was appointed to act in his father's absence.

I have not called on the captain-general for some weeks, having nothing important to take me there. On my last visit I presented General Preston and staff. The interview was agreeable, but not characterized by anything of special interest.

I have the honor to be, with profound respect, your obedient servant,

CH. J. HELM.

Hon. J. P. BENJAMIN,
      Secretary of State, Richmond.

Not having an opportunity to forward this dispatch until now, I open it to add that Mr. Crawford received by the English mail which reached here on the 23d instant additional instructions from his Government touching his mission to the Confederate States, dated just previous to the sailing of the mail steamer, which leaves no doubt but that the British Government still holds to the idea of sending an agent to the Confederacy.

Very respectfully,

CH. J. HELM.

No. 85.]   BRUSSELS, *April 15, 1864.*

SIR: At last Maximilian has been formally proclaimed Emperor of Mexico by the deputation from that country. This occurred at Miramar on the 10th instant. Yesterday he embarked for Vera Cruz, intending to land at Civita Vecchia on his route thither, in order to proceed to Rome to obtain the benediction of the Pope. It is believed by those well informed that he would gladly have declined at the last moment the acceptance of the throne prepared for him by the Emperor of the French. The more he reflected the more, perhaps, the difficulties of the position which he was about to assume became apparent; but he had gone so far during his visit to Paris that he could not retire either with honor or with safety. Among the current on dits during the time he was supposed to be hesitating was one to the effect that a courier was dispatched to him from the Tuileries with a note informing him that unless he hastened his departure he would find himself superseded by a Bonaparte. If he does not find in the sequel that he has been overreached by the duplicity of Louis Napoleon, I shall be egregiously mistaken in my calculations. He has already designated several of his ambassadors and ministers, as well as other functionaries, who are to enter immediately upon the discharge of their duties. Always the most extravagant of princes, grievously tormented by pecuniary embarrassments, his reign is likely to be inaugurated by reckless expenditures. A 6 per cent loan of 201,600,000 francs at 63 to the 100 has already been contracted by him in Paris. Out of this the first installment of the indemnity to France has been taken, and a small amount set apart for the benefit of the British holders of Mexican bonds.

Compared with the Government of the Confederate States (as stable as any within the confines of civilization) that of Maximilian scarcely deserves to be regarded as the skeleton of a government, and yet it will be generally and promptly recognized. Even the Cabinet at Washington will not be slow, in view of the peculiar concessions of the cabinet of the Tuileries, to enter into relations with it, whatever manifestations to the contrary in or out of Congress.

It has been decided that the peace conference is to meet at the official residence of Lord Palmerston in London on the 20th instant. I have not met with an intelligent person who doubts that it will be successful in the accomplishment of its primary object. In the meantime, however, there will be no suspension of hostilities. The allies, particularly Prussia, display more vigor and, I may add, more ferocity than ever in their operations.

From Rome, I am assured in private letters that the health of Pio Nono is as good as it has been for many years. It is asserted that Louis Napoleon is perfecting his plans to secure the election of his cousin, the Abbe Lucien (son of Lucien Bonaparte), as successor of the present sovereign Pontiff. If he succeeds it will impart a large amount of increased strength to his dynasty. There seems to be nothing too bold or, indeed, too unscrupulous for his Imperial Majesty to undertake. In this instance time is essential to the consolidation of his project, and hence his reported intense solicitude for the prolongation, at least for a few months, of the life of the Holy Father.

I have the honor to be, sir, very respectfully, your obedient servant,

A. DUDLEY MANN.

Hon. J. P. BENJAMIN,
    Secretary of State, C. S. A.,
        Richmond, Va.

No. 40.]   CONFEDERATE STATES COMMERCIAL AGENCY,
    London, April 16, 1864.

SIR: My short visit to Paris, the necessity of completing the initiatory arrangements for my work there, and at the same time preparing for an absence from London of several weeks, must be my apology for any shortcomings in my official correspondence. I have already informally acknowledged receipt of your dispatches Nos. 14, 15, and 16, respectively, dated 24th, 25th, and 26th February; Treasury warrant No. 5755, for £2,000 on account of secret-service fund; Congressional documents; and various enclosures. In the same informal manner I have summarized the many important events which have been crowded within the last few weeks, depending for the details on the copious newspaper extracts which accompanied these communications. A mere rapid review will therefore suffice here to give this dispatch its proper connection with the series.

The Palmerston government has utilized the respite afforded by the Easter holidays to throw overboard all dangerous incumbrances and to collect reinforcements. Mr. Stansfeld has resigned; the replacement of the Duke of Newcastle, by a commoner gives an additional ministerial voice in the House, where it is greatly needed, while the acceptance by the Earl of Clarendon of a nominal place in the cabinet insures the latter's adhesion to and moral support of the harassed ministry. He has forthwith been sent to the Emperor Napoleon as a special envoy, upon what errand is not stated, but he will have enough to do in explaining away the inexpressibly offensive character of the sort of " sword dance " which England is now performing in honor of Garibaldi. Other ministerial changes are spoken of, such as the retirement of Mr. Lowe, the head of the educational board, who has just sustained a Parliamentary defeat. All this means that Lord Palmerston will keep in office at any price, and that his cabinet will assume as many shapes as Proteus rather than die. The Government is no stronger for these transfigurations than the fox was for leaving his tail in the trap, but like him it has the chance of another run. There will be, to my thinking, no change of ministry this session, which need not be a matter of much regret to us.

Earl Russell's admission of the forgery came just in time to anticipate by a few days only the official exposure by yourself and Mr. Mallory, which is just received. Mr. Slidell, in the Index of this week, denounces another gross forgery in relation to the *Chesapeake* affair. From the articles I send you from the Herald, Standard, and Post, you will see that our friends in the press do not let the matter sleep. I would especially direct your attention to the extract from the Post, and have certain reasons to desire that it be preserved. The appeal in the *Alexandra* case having been dismissed by the House of Lords, it is announced this morning by the Federal organ here, the Daily News, that the vessel has been restored to her owners. The *Pampero* case, as I have already informed you on the authority of a Glasgow paper, has been compromised, the owners, so it is said, engaging not to use the vessel for any warlike purpose for two years.

At last there is definitely an Emperor of Mexico. It is announced that the dynastic difficulty between him and his brother has been settled by his unconditional resignation of all his agnate rights. The quid pro quo for this condition is probably to be found in the truly imperial present of a land and naval force of volunteers from the Austrian Army and Navy. I doubt whether the new Emperor has really a settled policy in regard to us; but it is beyond question that he left Paris in a frame of mind so hesitating and timid that any anxiety on our part to win his good graces would only confirm him in a cautious reserve. His personal well-wishes are, however, I believe, permanently secured to us. We are, in this respect, under considerable obligations to Hon. James Williams, whose personal relations with the archduke and his family gave him peculiar opportunities for usefulness, which he appears to have improved with equal industry and tact. In these days of amateur diplomacy and superserviceableness, of which I have seen in our case some very dangerous instances, it may not be unnecessary to add that Mr. Williams scrupulously confined himself within the bounds proper to a private gentleman and that even within those bounds he acted under the advice of Messrs. Slidell and Mason. It is because I have observed in him a degree of sensitiveness on this score, which I can readily appreciate, that I make this remark en passant.

Captain Lalor duly delivered his official letter of introduction, and has proceeded, some days since, to Ireland. In this connection I beg leave to direct your attention to the fact that the funds originally appropriated for the payment of salaries and contingent expenses of your other Irish agents are very nearly exhausted. In reference to Father Bannon, I have written you in my last, and informed you of the provisional arrangements made. It will be necessary to give me by the earliest opportunity, definite instructions both as regards him and Lieutenant Capston. Until I receive these it has appeared to me that your intentions would probably be best fulfilled by my continuing the same rate of appropriation for both out of my secret-service fund. Not to do so in the case of Lieutenant Capston would seem to imply on my part a want of appreciation of his zealous services, and as long as you deem it necessary to have special agents in Ireland it would be difficult to replace the experience he has acquired. At the same time, you will please observe that if I have correctly anticipated your orders, it will burden my secret-service fund with three salaries, amounting in the aggregate to £71 a month or £850 per annum, irrespective of contingent expenses which, notwithstanding the rigorous economy I have insisted upon, can not fail to bring the annual sum total close upon, if not over, £1,000. In that event I should suggest that, in order not to complicate my own accounts, a special appropriation should be made for the Irish service, to be separately accounted for.

Before quitting the subject of Ireland I hope you will excuse my directing your attention to another point. One of your agents, duly commissioned as the commercial agent at Queenstown, receives, as I understand, no compensation for his services. I have no personal acquaintance with this gentleman but have on many occasions had correspondence with him, and am satisfied that he cooperates cordially and to the best of his ability with the other agents. I would respectfully suggest that a salary, however small, be allowed him; the half of the consular pay provided for that port by the old regulations, viz, $1,000, would probably be acceptable, and would avoid embarrassments which I foresee must sooner or later arise from his anomalous position. You will understand that this suggestion is not made at his request or with his knowledge, but entirely on the principle that the Government should not accept the gratuitous services of any regularly appointed agent, even if he tenders them, as in doing so it places either too low or else altogether too high a value on those services.

So soon as my mind is relieved of the task of completing and revising my secret-service accounts up to December 31, so often promised and as often unavoidably delayed, I shall proceed, at Mr. Slidell's request, to France, there to remain for three or four weeks. This I expect to do about the 25th or 27th instant. On the subject of my contemplated operations there I write you by same post, in a separate communication, as I shall doubtless consult your convenience in so doing, and remain, with great respect,

Your obedient servant,

HENRY HOTZE.

Hon. J. P. BENJAMIN,
Secretary of State, Richmond.

No. 41.]　　　　Confederate States Commercial Agency,
　　　　　　　　　　　　　　　London, April 16, 1864.

Sir: Though it is almost too early to report any definite progress
in the task you have intrusted to me near the French press, a brief
sketch of my plans and expectations is necessary that you may guide
and instruct me when I shall have fairly commenced work. If
there is no other progress, there is at least this much in my own
mind, that the hesitancy and almost distaste with which I at first
viewed the task has in a great measure disappeared, and that I now
undertake it with much of that confidence and zest which are indispensable to even moderate success. My engagements here did not
permit me a longer stay in Paris than ten days, scarcely enough to
take a survey of the ground, but still what I had time to see was not
discouraging. I found Mr. Slidell and Mr. Eustis prepared to give
me the most energetic and efficient support, and the extensive social
relations which they have established there, and which they place at
my disposal, appear to me the most promising element in our favor,
and one upon which I mainly count for useful results. My predecessor
did not volunteer any explanations of his operations; and, although
my relations with him are not unfriendly, I did not think it expedient to urge him for them. I do not consider this a matter of regret,
for, without in any way undertaking to surprise his secrets, I believe
that I have obtained sufficiently accurate and comprehensive knowledge of what had been done and attempted heretofore. If I allude
to it here, it is not with a view to criticize his acts but to explain
the chief difficulty I apprehend. French journalists may or may not
be more mercenary than the English, but certain it is that had I been
preceded here by an agent disbursing large sums of money in the
manner in which they have undoubtedly been spent in France, I
should have met English journalists of a very different stamp from
those I found and made friends of. The English press is not so
exaltedly pure—nor is that of any country—but that a man entering
its ranks with purse held up would find himself practically and in
no very dignified manner illustrating the classic fate of Acteon. I
shall endeavor to avoid this error; but it is not as if I had found a
virgin soil to plant in, and great caution will have to be exercised
lest bought friendships become suddenly converted into formidably
hostile disappointments. Without, therefore, following in my predecessor's steps, I shall be compelled to do something which my judgment does not approve and the meaning of which can be fully
explained to you only at a later and safer period.

Mr. Slidell is of opinion that whatever is done in the French press
should be commenced without delay, and persisted in vigorously, and
that the interest attaching to the great campaign now in progress will
essentially assist our efforts. I am, therefore, making preparations
for an absence from London of several weeks, intending, of course, frequent visits in the interval, and shall leave for Paris toward the end
of this month. With his aid and that of Mr. Eustis I hope soon to
gather an extensive circle of acquaintances, and shall then profit by
opportunities as they arise. For the present my attention will be exclusively devoted to the metropolitan press, being satisfied that even
if the provincial journals have the importance ascribed to them in
certain quarters, the work is too diffuse to promise any immediate and,

therefore, useful returns. Even in the Parisian press my expectations are modest. Really valuable leading articles are the fruits of a more matured public opinion than yet exists, and require a staff of well informed and, so to speak, educated writers. My efforts will principally be directed, by all fair and honorable means, to win a little larger space in the journals of all opinions for our affairs, and thus to awaken and stimulate public interest. For this I count more upon telegraphic dispatches, correspondence, and even paragraphs. I am satisfied that if we can only induce or coax people to look across the Atlantic, the facts themselves will soon speak for themselves, and with more eloquence than rhetoric can give them. By far the most important wheel in the machinery, which I am attempting to organize for this purpose, is already at work. A copy of a letter which I enclosed in one of the last dispatches received by you, will sufficiently indicate to what I refer, and I need only say that I have lately given a considerable extension to the arrangement and at a cost actually trifling.

I can not too strongly recommend that whatever appropriation is made for my French expenses should be kept separate from my English secret-service fund and form a distinct account. I can not as yet give you anything like a specified estimate, but until this can be arrived at, I shall spend, out of the means now in hand, whatever I can find profitable use for, and as so many and such various demands are now being made on these means and the remittances are subject to dangerous delays it is but a dictate of prudence to ask you for a provisional appropriation of £1,000 for purposes of secret service in France. Without this expectation I should be loath to divert any considerable portion of my English funds to a new field of operations. When I recommend distinct appropriations for English, Irish, and French service, I do not, of course, mean that any temporary or permanent deficit of one fund should not be supplied from the surplus of another, when necessary, but the increasing magnitude of the sums I am expected to disburse, renders it desirable that the purposes to which they are devoted, and the manner in which they are spent, should appear clearly on the very face of my accounts.

With my next, by regular mail, I shall commence to send you French newspapers or extracts, and thereafter endeavor to keep you informed of anything of interest in the movements of the French press.

I have the honor to remain, very respectfully, your obedient servant,

HENRY HOTZE.

Hon. J. P. BENJAMIN,
  Secretary of State, Richmond.

No. 35.]   DEPARTMENT OF STATE,
                                       Richmond, April 16, 1864.

SIR: Your last dispatch received is No. 56, of 16th February, which came to hand on 4th instant. This interval of two months is longer than has occurred for more than a year past, and is regretted the more; as matters of great interest to us were pending and numerous reports calculated to excite solicitude as to the present attitude of the Imperial Government reach us from Northern journals.

I will not conceal from you that the President is greatly disappointed at the information contained in your No. 56. Grave doubt even is entertained of the good faith of the high personage by whose sanction and advice we engaged in an undertaking which promised results of the greatest importance. A severe blow has been dealt us from a quarter whence it was least expected and a corresponding revulsion of feeling toward that personage has resulted.

Mr. Mallory has written to the officers charged with these matters that we have concluded against the propriety of selling any of the vessels in progress of construction. I hope that his instructions will arrive in time to prevent the sale. Our conclusion is of course based on the supposition that according to French law there is no risk of the loss or confiscation of these vessels, and that the only hazard involved in keeping them is that they will not be allowed to go to sea. We prefer in such case taking our chances of some change of circumstances or of policy. The length of time required for the construction of ironclads in particular is so great that we would be inexcusable in abandoning all the chances of future contingencies for the sole purpose of getting back the money already expended, or avoiding the further expense of finishing them. It is deemed by the President much more prudent to have the vessels promptly completed and ready for service at any moment should the adverse influences which now prevail give place to other counsels.

You will receive herewith a Treasury draft for £500 sterling from the fund at the disposal of the Department for secret service, of which no account is to be rendered to the Treasury. When you can properly take vouchers they should accompany the account you will render to this Department of expenditure; for items not susceptible of being vouched you will render a certificate on honor of the payment.

I have just heard of the arrival at City Point (about 40 miles, I believe, below Richmond) of a French war steamer and two merchantmen, which come doubtless for the purpose of taking the tobacco belonging to the Imperial Government and which will be delivered in accordance with our promise.

APRIL 18.

Your No. 57, of 5th March, has just come to hand. It is the duplicate, X, the original not yet received. The change of tone indicated by you as having marked your interview with Mr. Drouyn de Lhuys, together with the tenor of the remarks attributed to Lord Palmerston, seem to be of some significance, but we can not attribute to them the same importance as would have been attached to such utterances at an earlier period of the war. It has been perhaps fortunate for us, notwithstanding the awful price paid in the blood of our best and bravest, that European powers have remained so inconceivably blind to their own interests in this great struggle. The end is now seen to be approaching, and we shall enter the family of nations with a consciousness that we have achieved our own success, not simply unaided even by sympathy, but in spite of the unfriendly, and in some cases, hostile attitude of the great powers of Europe. We shall have no favor to reciprocate, but many wrongs to forget, some perhaps for which to exact redress. I never felt a more thorough conviction than I now entertain that the year 1864 will witness our honorable welcome into the family of nations, won by the conclusive demonstration of the inability of the North to continue a contest in which its resources, both of men and money, will have been exhausted in vain.

The last news received from Europe through the public papers intimates the existence of some new obstacle presented to the formal acceptance of the Mexican throne by Maximilian. It is reported that there is some embarrassment connected with the succession to the Austrian throne which has caused delay in the reception of the Mexican envoys to Miramar. The same papers announced with great exultation that Maximilian having refused to see you, you had persisted in writing to him a formal request for an interview and had been rebuffed. We attach no credit to this statement, although it appears not improbable that the archduke may have deemed it prudent to intimate informally his opinion that the better policy under the circumstances of his visit would be that you should not meet. I hear from London that this course was pursued toward Mr. Dayton. There has been a semiofficial contradiction of the statement published in New York, that Mr. Dayton had intimated the readiness of the United States to interchange ministers with the new Empire, and the resolution just unanimously adopted by the House of Representatives at Washington against any recognition of Maximilian must prove far from welcome to the French cabinet. The resolution was offered as a party move to break down Lincoln's chance of reelection, its author, Winter Davis, being in active opposition and controlling the vote of Maryland for Mr. Chase. The United States Senate has not yet acted on the subject, and I have little doubt it would be stifled, if the administration could control the matter, but the passions of partisans become too much inflamed in presidential contests to permit the supposition that Lincoln's opponents will allow the subject to drop. It is easy to see how grave will be his embarrassment if the resolution should pass, whether he approve or reject it.

I refrain from any remark on the subject of the *Rappahannock* until you are able to communicate the answer of Mr. Drouyn de Lhuys to your note on the subject.

I am, very respectfully, your obedient servant,

J. P. BENJAMIN,
Secretary of State.

Hon. JOHN SLIDELL,
Paris, France.

P. S.—I have the honor to acknowledge the receipt, also, on the 19th instant of your No. 53 and enclosures, dated 16 March.

J. P. BENJAMIN,
Secretary of State.

No. 35.] DEPARTMENT OF STATE,
Richmond, April 18, 1864.

SIR: Your No. 1, from the Continent, of 25th January; No. 2, of 8th February; No. 3 and 4, of 18th February, were all received together on 4th instant. No 1 is a duplicate, the original of which is not yet received.

I forward to you herewith, in accordance with the suggestion in your No. 1, a draft for £500, from the secret-service fund, the expenditure of which will be accounted for to this Department, not to the Treasury. Where the expenditure is such as to preclude your furnishing vouchers, your certificate on honor of payment will suffice; in other cases you are requested to take vouchers to be forwarded when your accounts are rendered.

The accounts forwarded by you, to the close of your mission to London, are in the hands of the proper accounting officers of the Treasury. I doubt not that they are free from error, and will advise you as soon as they have been adjusted and approved.

In the instructions which accompanied your commission, letters of credence, etc., under date of 25th January last, I intimated by direction of the President, his preference that you should abstain from visiting London, even unofficially, unless some urgent necessity should arise. His attention has been called by me to certain passages in your dispatches, as well as to intimations received by the Department from other sources, all indicating the probability that your presence in London at certain junctures, as a private gentleman called there by his personal interests, would be useful to your country. The President, yielding to these suggestions, now directs me to say that he is content to leave this subject to your own discretion, confident that you will do no act that could countenance the inference of any intention on our part to withdraw from the position assumed toward the British Government when you were recalled from London.

I am obliged for your suggestion about furnishing me the London papers, but this was a matter with which I would not trouble you, and I have long been in receipt at the Department of the Times, the Saturday Review, Economist, and Examiner, as well as of the principal quarterly reviews, and Blackwood's Magazine. I am thus enabled to obtain as lively an impression of the state and progress of public opinion in Great Britain on all matters connected with our interests as can be reached through the leading organs of the different political parties. The most striking articles from the Herald, Post, and other London dailies are cut out and forwarded by Mr. Hotze, and these suffice till the opening of our ports shall put us in possession of a line of regular mail steamers.

I am sorry to have given you so much trouble with the books for the Department, the more so as after all I have to announce the loss of all you sent except the two cases of Hansard. The remaining cases, containing the Annual Register, etc., were lost on the *Hatfield*, after having been detained in Bermuda some six months before being shipped.

In relation to the seal, it would be quite inconvenient to await the return of peace for its arrival, but of course every precaution must be used to avoid any worse disaster than its loss. I incline to think that the best plan will be to intrust it to some discreet and careful officer of the Navy or Army, who may have occasion to return to the Confederacy, with the most stringent directions for having it ready to be thrown into the sea should the danger of capture become imminent. By retaining the impression in England its loss under such circumstances would involve nothing more than the mere cost of the seal and the delay in having another made.

There is nothing of general interest which I can communicate that you will not find in greater detail than I could give you in the files of the Richmond papers which will accompany this dispatch.

Very respectfully, your obedient servant,

J. P. BENJAMIN,
Secretary of State.

Hon. J. M. MASON,
Paris, France.

APRIL 22.

P. S.—Since closing this dispatch I have had the honor to receive the originals of your No. 1, of January 25; No. 5, of March 16; and No. 6, of March 16.

J. P. BENJAMIN,
Secretary of State.

DEPARTMENT OF STATE,
Richmond, April 20, 1864.

SIR: I have the honor to acknowledge the receipt of your dispatch of the 1st instant, giving the result of your investigation into the facts connected with the capture of the steamer *Chesapeake* and the action of the British colonial authorities in relation to the vessel and cargo and the parties concerned in the capture, also enclosing the printed pamphlet and newspapers containing reports of the judicial proceedings and decisions.

A careful examination of the whole subject has brought this Government to the same conclusion as has been reached by yourself, and we can not hesitate to admit that the facts, as now established, present the case in an aspect entirely different from that in which we viewed it on the representations made by the parties engaged.

In the instructions prepared for your guidance in the conduct of this business it was carefully pointed out that they were based on the supposition of the truth of the following facts:

First. That John C. Braine and Henry A. Parr were citizens of the Confederate States, enlisted in its military service, had been prisoners in the hands of our enemies, and that having escaped to New Brunswick, they there devised a stratagem for the capture of an enemy's vessel on the high seas, which was successfully carried out by the seizure of the *Chesapeake.*

Second. That acting exclusively as belligerents in the public service of their country they touched at a point or points in the British colonial possessions for the sole purpose of procuring the fuel indispensable to make the voyage to a Confederate port.

Third. That there had been no violation of the neutrality nor of the sovereign jurisdiction of Great Britain by any enlistment, real or pretended, of British subjects on British territory for service in the war waged by us against the United States.

It now appears from your own enquiries into the facts and from the judicial proceedings that we were led into error, that the truth is as follows:

First. That the expedition was devised, planned, and organized in a British colony by Vernon G. Locke, a British subject, who under the feigned name of Parker had been placed in command of the privateer *Retribution* by the officer who was named as her commander at the time of the issue of the letter of marque.

Second. That Locke assumed to issue commissions in the Confederate service to British subjects on British soil, without the slightest pretext of authority for so doing, and without being himself in the public service of this Government.

Third. That there is great reason to doubt whether either Braine, who was in command of the expedition, or Parr, his subordinate, is a Confederate citizen, and the weight of the evidence is rather in favor of the presumption that neither is a citizen and that the former has never been in our military service.

Fourth. That Braine, the commander of the expedition, after getting possession of the vessel and proceeding to the British colonies, instead of confining himself to his professed object of obtaining fuel for navigating her to a Confederate port, sold portions of the cargo at different points on the coast, thus divesting himself of the character of an officer engaged in the legitimate warfare.

Although at the period of your departure from Richmond we had no reason to doubt the statements made, it was considered imprudent to act on them without further enquiry, and your instructions were therefore closed with the following sentences: "Before closing these instructions it is proper to add that they are based on the statement of facts which precedes them, but our sources of information are not perfect enough to permit entire reliance. You will be able, on arrival at Halifax, to ascertain whether there be any important divergence between the facts as they really occurred and those assumed in this dispatch. In such event you will exercise a prudent discretion in your action and be at liberty to modify your conduct or even to abstain altogether from any interference with the matter. While desirous of upholding to the full extent the rights and interests of our country, we wish particularly to avoid the presentation of demands not entirely justified by the principles of public law and international morality."

I have the directions of the President to intimate to you his satisfaction with your exercise of this discretion. The encroachment on the sovereign jurisdiction of her Britannic Majesty over her colonial possessions in North America and the violation of the neutrality proclaimed by her Majesty, as disclosed in the judicial proceedings, are disclaimed and disapproved by this Government. While we maintain and shall continue to uphold the right and duty of every citizen of the Confederate States and every foreigner enlisted in their service to wage warfare openly, or by strategem upon the vessels of our enemies on the high seas, whether armed or not, we distinctly disclaim and disavow all attempts to organize within neutral jurisdiction expeditions composed of neutral subjects for the purpose of carrying on hostilities against the United States. The capture of the *Chesapeake*, therefore, according to the facts now disclosed, far from forming the basis of any demands on the part of this Government, is disclaimed.

The President is much gratified that the superior judicial authorities of New Brunswick have rejected the pretensions of the consul of the United States that the parties engaged in this capture should be surrendered under the Ashburton treaty for trial by the courts of the United States on charges of murder and piracy.

The case as presented seems to be simply that of men who, sympathizing with us in a righteous cause, erroneously believed themselves authorized to act as belligerents against the United States by virtue of Parker's possession of the letter of marque issued to the privateer *Retribution.* They may possibly have been conscious that they were acting in opposition to the policy and wishes of their Government, but no reason exists for supposing that they entertained any such motives as would justify their being charged with a graver misdemeanor than disobedience to her Majesty's proclamation and to the foreign enlistment law of Great Britain. It may not be without good effect that you should communicate to the attorney-general of the Province, in the same unofficial manner in which you communicated the instructions relative to the return of our escaped prisoners, the views above expressed and the conclusions reached by this Government.

The President has not read without marked gratification your warm tribute to the generous gentlemen whose sympathies in our cause have been evinced in so effective and disinterested a manner.

He begs that you will to each of them, Dr. Almon, Mr. Keith, Mr. Wier, and Mr. Ritchie, address officially a letter in his name, returning his thanks and those of our country for testimonials of kindness which are appreciated with peculiar sensibility at a juncture when the Confederacy is isolated by the action of European Governments from that friendly intercourse with other nations which is known to be its rights, and of which it is conscious it is not undeserving.

I am, very respectfully, your obedient servant,

J. P. BENJAMIN,
Secretary of State.

Hon. JAS. P. HOLCOMBE.

No. 18.]
DEPARTMENT OF STATE,
Richmond, April 22, 1864.

SIR: I have the honor to acknowledge receipt of your several dispatches, as follows, viz, No. 37, of 13 February, received 17 ultimo; No. 38, of 12 March, received 16 instant; No. 39, of 13 March, received 19 instant.

I also received on 30 March your letter of 27 February, sent by private route established by you, and answered it same day, as shown by the duplicate enclosed. The messenger was to be back here by 20th instant but has not yet appeared, and by comparing the dates above you will perceive that if he do not succeed better in future there will be very little gain in rapidity of communication. It will be as well, however, to carry out the experiment to the end.

Your views in relation to the method of enlightening public opinion in France, and the engagement for that purpose of men of ability whose previously known sympathies and opinions will place them beyond the reach of suspicion that they are actuated by mercenary motives, commend themselves to my judgment and you will receive the sanction of the Department to such measures as you may adopt for that purpose after you have conferred with Mr. Slidell as proposed by you.

I am much gratified with the zeal, discretion, and ability displayed by the Rev. Mr. Bannon in the service undertaken by him, and desire you should continue to provide him with the necessary means for continuing his labors as long as he remains satisfied that his efforts are useful to our cause. I enclose a letter for him. I apprehend that Lieutenant Capston can scarcely be of much further service and you can intimate to him that the Department considers it now time that he should return to his duties here, unless you think that his continuance abroad will be of advantage. In such event you may continue to supply his wants as heretofore.

As I have thus placed in your hands the duty of disbursing different amounts of the secret-service fund not directly connected with the duties which were originally confided to you, I shall from time to time make you remittances adequate to these increased charges. I hope you are long since in receipt of the remittance of £2,000 forwarded on 24th February, the more especially as I observe with regret that the duplicate (which I now enclose) was overlooked and not forwarded. I will soon make another remittance.

Enclosed you will find duplicate to Mr. Mallory's letter to Sir Roundell Palmer, which will probably arrive too late to be of much service, but I earnestly hope that the original sent by secret conveyance has reached you, although the delay in the messenger's return is disquieting.

You will also find herewith a very long paper which was prepared by a Confederate Senator in the form of an address that he designed for adoption by the Senate as an appeal to Christendom. His purpose was abandoned and he suggested that you might make it useful. Some parts of it appear to me not at all suited for good effect in England, but there are many portions which present in striking points of view some of the principles of the opposing parties in this war and the interest and duties of foreign nations in their attitude toward the belligerents. You are at liberty to use it in part or in whole, or not at all, as you may deem best suited for good effect.

The present state of political affairs in England, as described by you and as evidenced by the debates in Parliament, is indeed anomalous, and we can scarcely understand how in such a government as that of Great Britain, a ministry so discredited and humiliated as that now in power can retain office. It is plain that so unnatural a condition is of short duration, and that a people so pround as the English will not long continue passive under the taunts, sneers, and undisguised contempt displayed in both hemispheres for the senile policy which has reduced British influence so low as no longer to be taken into account in the settlement of great international complications. The result of such policy, if long continued, would be so obviously to exclude Great Britain from longer admission into the class of the great powers of Europe that the national spirit will revolt from the degradation, and the reaction will be violent and will consign to obscurity for half a generation the men who shall be regarded by their countrymen as the authors of so calamitous a result. There is something in this world even of greater national importance than low taxation and flourishing finances, and I think I see symptoms that the subservient Times itself is trimming its sails to catch the rising breeze.

The publication of Messrs. Laird has not yet been received, but I have the first six numbers of the Blue Book on North America. It is pitiable to see the attempts of the ministry to conceal their action on almost every important matter connected with us.

The *Tuscaloosa* correspondence contains neither the order from Downing street to seize nor that to release the vessel. It is therefore impossible to tell what was the pretext for the outrage. The correspondence on the forged report exhibits the eager grasp with which Earl Russell catches at anything he thinks can injure us, and the ease with which Mr. Adams guides and controls him would excite admiration as specimen of adroit diplomacy were not his task facilitated by the simplicity of the aged earl, who is so willing to be spared the fatigue of thinking for himself and so anxious to believe anything to our discredit. The injury done by the conduct toward us of the present chief of the foreign office is undoubtedly great, but not half so serious as that which he has inflicted on his own country.

The speech of Sir Hugh Cairnes in the debate on the steam rams is a masterpiece, and has greatly increased with us his previous exalted reputation.

We are in hourly expectation of the decision in the *Alexandra* case, but if in our favor, it will of course not settle the principles involved in the merits, but merely the technical point on the right of appeal, thus leaving the litigation still open in all other cases.

I am, very respectfully, your obedient servant,

J. P. Benjamin,
Secretary of State.

Henry Hotze, Esq., *London.*

P. S.—Finding it impossible to write to Mr. Bannon in time, I must beg you to write to him the substance of what I have said in regard to his services, which have also attracted the favorable notice of the President.

Department of State,
Richmond, April 22, 1864.

Dear Sir: I have received your letter of 17th March, informing me of the purpose on the part of a number of gentlemen in England to cause to be erected in our country a statue of the lamented General Thomas J. Jackson. As you state that it is not yet decided whether this statue will be presented to the Confederate Government or that of the native State of the general, it does not become me to say anything further on the propable location of the statue than to express the confident assurance that, should the presentation be made to the Confederate Government, this tribute from the gentlemen of England to the memory of one who was beloved and honored by our whole people, will be received with sensibility, and placed in such commanding locality as to insure its being seen to proper advantage, and receiving the admiration and veneration of our citizens for generations to come.

I am very glad to learn that the work is intrusted to an artist of such reputation as Mr. Foley, and trust that it may prove as successful as a likeness as it will doubtless be as a work of art.

I am, very respectfully, your obedient servant,

J. P. Benjamin,
Secretary of State.

Hon. James M. Mason, *Paris.*

No. 36.]

Department of State,
Richmond, April 23, 1864.

Sir: I received on 19th instant your No. 58, of 16th ultimo. Your account of the line of conduct pursued by the archduke in Paris has been carefully weighed and taken in connection with the fact of the refusal to accord an interview to Mr. Mercier, leaves us much in doubt as to the true significance of his failure to have a conference with you, after having intimated through Mr. Estrada his purpose to invite your visit. It had long been foreseen by us that Mr. Seward would hesitate at no promises in order to postpone the evil day which is approaching with such giant strides when the whole structure of the North will topple from its sandy foundation and our recognition be forced not only upon neutrals but upon the enemy by the strength, valor, and fortitude of our people. Every hour produces fresh evidence of the early and disastrous breakdown in northern resources both of men and money, and our day of happy deliverance is seen to be dawning by those even who have hitherto been despondent. The contrast between our armies and those of the enemy in dash, spirit, and confidence is amazing and is displayed so strikingly as to produce marked effect on the spirit of the people in the two countries. You can not fail to be impressed with the wonderful change in the tone of the public journals North and South. But Europe is still as blind as ever and hugs with fondness the delusive promises of the United States Secretary of State; and if it be true that the conduct of the archduke has been influenced by the Emperor and that the latter in turn has been influenced by Mr. Seward, the absence of the sagacity that has heretofore characterized the Imperial policy is indeed remarkable. It is therefore difficult to believe that the Emperor can have leaned on so feeble a reed as the promises made by the Northern Cabinet, a reed which has already broken and pierced his hand, as shown by the unanimous vote of the House of Representatives on the subject of Maximilian's recognition.

The fact, however, of the silence of the archduke and his sudden departure from Paris, after the previous interchange of his views with us through unofficial communications, and the conduct of the French Government in detaining the *Rappahannock*, are indications of a submission to Northern dictation similar to that which has marked the course of the British Cabinet and inflicted on us wrongs which have exasperated our people almost beyond the limits of endurance. It is therefore with extreme solicitude that we await the answer of the Government to your demand in relation to the *Rappahannock*. If it should be unfavorable, my own impression is that we should not only pursue without hesitation the course indicated by you of striking her flag and leaving her to the disposal of the French Government on its responsibility, but that we should secure for ourselves adequate indemnity by seizing and detaining the French tobacco here. My only fear is that the news from you on this subject will arrive too late to enable us to give full effect to such a measure, as the French ships are now taking the tobacco and may be ready to depart before receipt of your next dispatch. It is proper to add that this suggestion is exclusively personal to myself, and that I have no knowledge of the President's views on the subject, not having yet taken his directions, and being unwilling to occupy his attention (already overtasked by his numerous duties) with this matter, unless a decision shall become necessary by reason of the persistent detention of the *Rappahannock.*

I am, very respectfully, your obedient servant,

J. P. BENJAMIN,
Secretary of State.

Hon. JOHN SLIDELL,
Paris, France.

P. S.—Have this moment received the news of the decision in the case of the *Alexandra.* Also Earl Russell's statement in the House of Lords on the 5th instant that the forgea report of our Secretary of the Navy was the invention of a gentleman.

J. P. BENJAMIN,
Secretary of State.

Private.]   HALIFAX, *April 26, 1864.*

MY DEAR SIR: There are various subjects upon which it may be interesting to hear from me, but which are not appropriate to my official communications. I have enjoyed the hospitality of many prominent and influential gentlemen, in and out of public position, who reside in this city, and have met with General Doyle, the administrator of the government; the principal civil officers; and the highest legal and judicial authorities of the Province. Although that apprehension of compromising the neutral character of the government which has been manifested by British officials in other parts of the world exists here, the wish for our success is almost universal, and is freely expressed. I scarcely see anyone who does not recognize the almost self-evident truth that the future independence of these Provinces is bound up with the successful maintenance of their nationality by the Confederate States. I avail myself, however, of every opportunity to impress the idea that a policy of cold-blooded indifference like that expressed in the Times must so alienate the Southern people that they, in their turn, will witness with composure the future struggles of these Provinces with the United States. The Southern community would hail any step in our favor by the British Government with delight, even to the extreme one of intervention.

The clergy, the bar, the press, are unanimous or nearly so in our favor. The sentiment is still stronger in the army. The acting governor, General Doyle, is our friend, speaks in terms of highest praise of our army, and expressed to me warm wishes for our success. These gentlemen are influenced by an enlightened sense of the true interest of England, by detestation of the barbarous spirit on which the war has been carried on by the Yankee Government, and by a generous appreciation of the valor and devotion of our own people. I should have contributed quite largely to the press whilst here, but find it wholly unnecessary, and shall reserve some views which I have elaborated for journals in which they may be more useful. How strange that our friends in Parliament are not better posted. On the motion of Lord Clanricarde for correspondence as to Southern consuls, we have just received Lord Russell's speech. How crushing might have been the reply, had the " noble lord's " perversion of the facts as to dismissal of Mr. Magee been exposed, and his admissions as to the improper conduct of Cridland and others been claimed as an answer to his own complaint but a short time before, that we had driven their consuls from the Confederacy. The Index is not here, the British steamer not being in, but I take it for granted this speech will meet with proper comment.

I wish you would send me the printed acts of our last session. I have those of the preceding sessions, and it is important to me to know, or be in condition to know, what has been our legislation upon every subject.

Amongst the gentlemen here who took an interest in our cause from the first and who maintained it amidst obloquy and opposition, I think none deserve more of our gratitude than the Catholic Archbishop, the Right Rev. Dr. Connelly. This gentleman has taken an active and most decided stand in our favor. He dispenses the most liberal hospitality to every respectable Confederate who visits Halifax. He assures me that with a very few exceptions the clergy in the United States of his church are on our side. He deserves a letter from Mr. Davis, thanking him for his kindness and hospitality to our people, and his bold declarations of sympathy with our cause, and his political influence not only here, but in Canada and United States, are such as to render some attention which he would appreciate as politic as it would be just.

I frequently see intelligent friends directly from Boston and New York. They concur in the assurance that there is a great change amongst the most rabid advocates of war and extermination, and that without some decisive success on the part of the Union armies their finances most go to wreck. The confidence of certain triumph has disappeared; they are waiting most anxiously upon the developments of the campaign. Nothing could sustain the present policy but the vast pecuniary interest which the diffusion of the Government debt amongst the people as well as the capitalists has created in the success of their Army, and a signal defeat would lead to a breaking up of the party which at present controls the Government.

I send box containing most of the desired books. There were only two copies of the A. edition of Admiralty Reports in the hands of the publisher, and the price of course is enormous. I also send a number of papers containing articles of more or less interest.

A prize was offered by Dr. Almon for the best Latin poem on the death of Stonewall Jackson by a member of the graduating class at Windsor University, in this Province. It was awarded to Mr. Hoyles, son of the attorney general of Newfoundland and at present a student of Cambridge, England. It might be grateful to Mrs.

Jackson to receive such an evidence of the appreciation of her husband's memory. I transmit it and beg that you forward to her. Any acknowledgment by her I should be glad to put in hands of Dr. Almon, the liberal founder of the prize.

I remain, very truly,

JAS. P. HOLCOMBE.

[Hon. J. P. BENJAMIN.]

HALIFAX, NOVA SCOTIA, *April 26, 1864.*

SIR: Nothing has transpired since the date of my last dispatch to alter my conviction of the impolicy of any intervention by the Confederate States in the affair of the *Chesapeake*. I have conversed freely on the subject with eminent legal gentlemen, both in official position and out of it. They generally express regret that through the folly and misconduct of the captors the *Chesapeake* was not secured to the use of the Confederacy. They think, however, that the courts if required to pass upon the character of the transaction would have been compelled to regard it as in fact a capture by British subjects never enlisted in our service by any person having authority so to do, or if otherwise, then enlisted in violation of their neutrality laws. It is morally certain the home government would not, under the circumstances, allow a claim for compensation for the surrender of the vessel by the judicial authorities. And I can not but think that the presentation of such a claim by our Government and its rejection, the case being one, as all must admit, very doubtful both in law and in morals, would impair its public prestige and weaken the moral weight which might attach to its interposition upon future and more important occasions.

None of the captors have as yet been taken under the new warrants. It would embarrass the government here as much as it would the Confederate Government to have the solution of this question forced upon them in reference to the captors. Whatever may be the strictly legal character of the transaction, public opinion would not tolerate their treatment as pirates, whether by proceedings against them as such on the part of the colonial authorities or by their extradition to the United States.

For the reasons stated in dispatch No. 4, I shall remain here until the return of the next Bermuda boat, about the middle of May, when I hope to hear that the course which I have taken in this matter meets with your approbation and that of the President.

I remain, with the highest respect, yours, etc.

JAMES P. HOLCOMBE.

Hon. J. P. BENJAMIN,
Secretary of State, C. S. A.

HALIFAX, NOVA SCOTIA, *April 26, 1864.*

SIR: I have thought it best to report the progress I have made in carrying out the instructions of the President as to our escaped prisoners in a separate dispatch. In accordance with the suggestion of your letter I took an early opportunity of conferring with the mercantile house of B. Wier & Co. on the best mode of accomplishing our object. That house has put itself in communication with responsible and trustworthy parties in Montreal, Kingston, and Toronto and other points of Canada, with the views both of collecting our soldiers, who are dispersed through the Province, by the time the navigation of the St. Lawrence is opened and of forwarding at once to this port all who are now in those cities. As far as practicable, we shall avail ourselves of water transportation as soon as it can be obtained. It is impossible now to form any idea of the number who may wish to return home, but it is not likely to be large enough to exhaust the credit which has been placed in my hands.

I have unofficially communicated to the attorney general of the Province, who called upon me soon after my arrival, your instructions as to the strict observance of the public and municipal law and invited suggestions of any additional precautions to those which I proposed using. I shall adopt some similar course with the Canadian authorities.

I have for the present directed Mr. Wier and our other agents to require from each applicant for passage into the Confederacy an affidavit that he has been in the Confederate service, with a statement of the company, regiment, and department to which he belonged, and a declaration of his purpose to return home to his duty.

I shall have hereafter so much more time to give to this subject that I hope by the next steamer I will be able to give some further reports. As yet only six have been forwarded, all of them being in the city on my arrival.

For the present I have the honor to remain, with the highest consideration,

JAMES P. HOLCOMBE.

Hon. J. P. BENJAMIN,
    Secretary of State, C. S. A.

No. 4.]   APRIL 28, 1864.

SIR: The season has thus far rendered it impracticable to forward the arrangements for returning home our escaped prisoners. The ice has just begun to move in the St. Lawrence, and it will be from the middle to the last of May before the navigation will be open. Land carriage at this time through Canadian territory is out of the question, not only on account of its expense, but the extremely limited facilities which it would afford for transportation. I wrote indeed upon my arrival to some of our friends at Montreal, to send in that way any who might be reached conveniently, and who were anxious to reach the Confederacy as early as possible. I have authorized a gentleman in Montreal, who is highly recommended, Mr. S. Cromwell, to go at once as far as Windsor, and advise our friends of the existence of means to send back our soldiers to their posts, and to bring in some forty or fifty who are reported at that point, to take passage in the first boat from Montreal, or rather Quebec, to Pictou. I have also authorized the expenditure if necessary of $1,000 at different points, to relieve cases of entire destitution, where there was no doubt as to the want and purpose to get back into the service as soon as possible.

I feel some apprehension that an effort may be made to capture our men when collected in large numbers on sailing vessels whilst coming to Halifax on the high seas. I see no mode of avoiding the difficulty, however, and I do not know that the risk would be materially increased, whilst the expense would be greatly diminished, by sending them directly to Bermuda from Quebec. Please let me hear at once from you on this point, for the unavoidable delay in collecting them along such an extensive frontier will give me an opportunity, at least to some extent, of acting under your specific instructions upon this matter. The accommodations of the regular mail steamer from Halifax to Bermuda are not very extensive, and it makes only a round trip in a month. The expense of subsisting them here, as well as the liability of men in their condition to be involved in some disturbance when collected in large numbers, render it very expedient, if thought safe, to send them directly on from Quebec to Bermuda, and even also to Nassau. I can not hear with any certainty as to probable number, but unless I receive instructions which impose upon me other duty by the next steamer from Bermuda, I propose going in person probably over the whole line as far as Windsor, with a view of making some final arrangements. My impression, derived from some experience already at this place, is that of the large number who, as escaped Confederates, are appealing to public sympathy for material aid, there are some imposters; some who have never been in the service but are shirking duty, and some who would be very glad for help here, but are in no haste to return home. The number of those who will go back to service is entirely conjectural. Knowing how much in this hour of agony we need men, I shall use most expedition in my power.

I am, with the highest respect,

JAMES P. HOLCOMBE,

Hon. J. P. BENJAMIN,
Secretary of State, C. S. A.

[Telegram.]

From WILMINGTON, *April 29.*
(Received at Richmond, April 29, 1864.)

Arrived this morning. Six thousand bales of cotton burnt last night, which will delay all boats until Monday or Tuesday.

J. THOMPSON (care E. Solomon).

Hon. J. P. BENJAMIN.

No. 37.]   DEPARMENT OF STATE,
                              Richmond, April 30, 1864.

SIR: I am without further advice from you since your No. 55. My chief purpose in now writing is to enclose copy of the last instructions forwarded to Mr. Holcombe, by which we disavow any claim founded on the capture of the *Chesapeake.*

Our military situation is very cheering, but, of course, the decisive features of the campaign will not appear till the armies shall have met in battle in northern Georgia and northern Virginia.

We have sent Jacob Thompson, of Mississippi, and Clement C. Clay, of Alabama, to Canada on secret service in the hope of aiding the disruption between the Eastern and Western States in the approaching election at the North. It is supposed that much good can be done by the purchase of some of the principal presses, especially in the Northwest.

The last Northern papers still represent the *Rappahannock* as confined to dock in Calais and guarded by a French man-of-war.

The original convention between the French Government and that of the United States provided that the tobacco should be shipped in five months from the date of the agreement, viz, the 23d November, so that the delay expired on the 23d instant. In the meantime it was discovered that the convention would prove inoperative, as it included only tobacco purchased before the war, and none such existed. After some delay consent was given on the 7th March that tobacco bought during the war should be taken out, but nothing was said about any extension of time. The French agents chartered vessels in New York and got them into the James River in the beginning of this month, when the captain of the *Tisiphone*, who had convoyed the merchantmen, was informed by General Butler that the time would expire according to convention on the 23d, and that he had no authority to extend it. The captain immediately wrote to the French minister at Washington (and Butler to his Government) for instructions. The vessels reached City Point, and Captain de Marivaux (I believe this is his name) remained without further communication till the 23d instant, when he received a message from Butler by flag of truce, stating that the time was out, and summoning him to withdraw, and the vessels were forced to leave with but about 100 hogsheads of tobacco out of some 7,000 belonging to the French Government. What the end will be, it is, of course, impossible to conjecture.

Our Congress meets on Monday, but the recess has been so short that the message will contain nothing of importance. I may, perhaps, be able to send you a copy with this dispatch.

Very respectfully, your obedient servant,

J. P. BENJAMIN,
Secretary of State.

Hon. JOHN SLIDELL,
Paris, France.

[Telegram.]

From WILMINGTON, *May 2.*
(Received at Richmond, May 2, 1864, at 11:40.)

Mr. Clay delivered me your letter, with enclosures last night.

J. THOMPSON.

Hon. J. P. BENJAMIN.

[Telegram.]

From WILMINGTON, *May 3.*
(Received at Richmond, May 3, 1864, at 3 o'clock.)

We think copies of President's message would serve our purpose; if you agree send them. We can't go until Thursday.

J. THOMPSON.
C. C. CLAY, Jr.

Hon. J. P. BENJAMIN.

No. 60.]   Paris, *May 2, 1864.*

Sir: Since I last had the honor of addressing you on the 7th ultimo, I have not received any of your dispatches, although through the New York papers I have a copy of your No. 31 of 11th March in relation to the forged report of Secretary Mallory. Before seeing this I had occasion on the 11th April publicly to denounce another forgery in which my name was mentioned in a translation of a pretended letter in cipher, from a person in New York to you, and sent to M. A. Keith, Halifax, to be forwarded.

This forgery was intended to accelerate the delivery of the *Chesapeake* to the Yankee claimants and seems to have been accepted by Lord Lyons with the same facile and willing gullibility as the Mallory report, and communicated by him not only to the provincial authorities but to the foreign minister, without the least reservation as to its authenticity. It was sent to Parliament with other papers relating to the seizure of the *Chesapeake*, and I thus became aware of the forgery, which would otherwise have passed unnoticed. I requested M. Hotze to forward you duplicate copies of the Parliamentary document, which you will doubtless have received before this will reach you. I believe that on reading the forged letter you will think me justified in saying in my note to the Index that "the forgery ought to have been patent to any one who did not wish to be deceived;" this is substantially in accordance with what you say about the Mallory report in your dispatch of 11th March.

"The paper is, on its face, so palpably a fabrication that one could scarcely have supposed it could dupe even the most credulous." Lord Lyons, by not publicly and indignantly denouncing the tricks by which he has been twice made the instrument of palming upon his Government forged papers intended to influence its action in important matters in a sense favorable to the Lincoln Government, has, in my opinion, rendered himself fairly obnoxious to the charge of complicity at least after if not before the fact. His course, however, does not surprise me, as I had abundant evidence of his servile submission to the dictates of Seward in the manner in which Messrs. Mason and I, with our secretaries, were transferred from Fort Warren to the *Rinaldo.*

I send you herewith copy of a letter from Mr. J. S. Begbie, manager of the company with which a most advantageous contract has been made for the transportation of Government stores from the islands to the Confederacy. Probably before this the difficulties in relation to pilots of which he complains will have been removed. It seems to me to be very injudicious to attempt to regulate the compensation which owners of vessels running the blockade shall allow to their pilots; it is as important to secure the services of a good pilot as of a good captain, and it is well known that those who have been most successful in running the blockade, such as Fraser, Trenholm & Co. and Collie & Co., have given very large gratuities to their captains.

In a private letter by last Bermuda mail I informed you that Mr. Avegno, who had made all his arrangements to go to the Confederacy on important business, had suddenly changed his mind. I have not since seen him; he had told me that it was his intention to deposit with me for safe-keeping certain 8 per cent bonds belonging to the Government (I think that $50,000 was the sum mentioned), but he afterwards, on my reminding him of it, said that he thought it would be more regular to take the bonds with him and deliver them to the Secretary of the Treasury, from whom he had received them.

You will have learned through the Northern papers the recent visit of Lord Clarendon to Paris and his interviews with the Emperor and the minister of foreign affairs. I have no doubt that it was greatly stimulated if not entirely caused by the conferences with the same personages of a leading Member of Parliament which I mentioned in my No. 59. It now seems to be the great object of all parties in England to conciliate the Emperor and to reestablish if possible the good feeling which Earl Russell has done so much to impair. Notwithstanding the emphatic denegations of ministers and the positive declarations of the Moniteur, I entertain no doubt that the sudden termination of Garibaldi's triumphant progress is to be attributed to this motive.

The Emperor of Mexico is at length fairly on his way to his new dominions. I learn from the best authority that up to the very day previous to his acceptance of the throne he was hesitating whether he should not abandon his purpose. It was only after being more than once reminded that he had gone too far and given too many pledges to recede without compromitting his honor that he consented to receive the Mexican deputation and take the step which could not be retraced. I believe that if the resolution adopted by the Federal House of Representatives had reached Europe a few days sooner Maximilian would still be at Miramar.

The French journals affect to make light of this resolution and say that it will present no obstacle to the recognition of the new empire at Washington, but I can not doubt that Napoleon appreciated it correctly.

M. Mercier says that the assurances given by Mr. Lincoln, mentioned in my No. 58, will be carried out, and, unwilling to admit himself to have been duped, naturally endeavors to impress that opinion upon others. I regret to be compelled to say that I have changed my estimate as to that gentleman's character. I had believed him to have strong sympathies with our cause and that any influence. he could exercise would be in our favor. I have now good reason to believe that, desiring to be " all things to all men," he avows Northern or Southern preferences as he may suppose the expression of the one or the other will be most agreeable to those with whom he converses.

A well-informed person says that Maximilian, after his arrival in Mexico, will address a circular letter to the various Governments with which he wishes to establish relations, that of Washington included, and ignoring the Confederacy. I have taken care to advise leading Mexicans that such a course could not but be offensive to my Government and might lead to results which would hereafter be regretted. I endeavored particularly to impress this view upon General Woll, who accompanies Maximilian to Vera Cruz as chief of his military staff. He is perhaps the only person on board of the *Novara* who is well acquainted with the condition of affairs in Mexico. Having frequently visited the ci-devant United States, he is perfectly capable of appreciating the necessity of the support of the Confederacy to protect the new government against the aggression of the North, and as he is very decided in his preference for the

South and will have abundant opportunities of expressing his opinions on the passage, I think it not improbable that he may satisfy the Emperor of the impolicy of making any advances to the Washington Government without taking similar steps toward the Confederacy. I shall send Mr. Fearn a letter of introduction to General Woll, and General Preston will thus, in all probability, have it in his power to obtain information which will be useful in deciding on the course it will be proper for him to pursue.

Since my last £20,200 seven per cent cotton bonds have been presented to me for conversion and canceled. Negotiations are in progress at London which, if matured, will lead to the conversion of a large additional quantity of them and, by raising the current price, improve the credit of the Government.

The two ironclad ships building at Bordeaux have been sold to the Swedish Government at prices which will reimburse in full their cost and leave a small margin of profit, but as M. Arman has contracted to deliver them in Swedish waters they will not be paid for until so delivered. The sale of one of these ships is positive; that of the other is intended to cover an arrangement by which it is hoped to utilize her for the original purpose. The builders of the corvettes are very confident of getting two of them to sea and placing their armament on board at convenient points.

Commodore Barron, desiring to obtain permission for the *Rappahannock* to make a trial trip before proceeding on her voyage, by my advice applied for an interview with the minister of marine, which was promptly granted. The minister received him very courteously, and when he was informed of the reasons why a trial trip was thought necessary he at once assented, but said that it would be contingent on the permission to proceed on the voyage, and that this was a question for the decision of the minister of foreign affairs. In my last I informed you that I had advised Commodore Barron to instruct the commander of the *Rappahannock* to give notice of his intention to strike his flag and abandon his ship if the permission to proceed to sea were longer withheld or some reasonable cause were not assigned for her prolonged detention. This action was delayed by Commodore Barron for the reasons then mentioned. The order has now been given to Commander Fauntleroy, who I presume will immediately carry it into effect. I thought it proper in advance of such action to inform the Emperor, through M. Mocquard and the minister of foreign affairs, by my ordinary channel of communication, of its being intended, thus affording an opportunity to release the vessel without the appearance of yielding to a menace of abandonment. I have no means of judging what will be the result of Commander Fauntleroy's action, but I feel well satisfied that the unexplained detention could not longer be submitted to without seriously compromitting the honor of the flag; indeed, I am not without apprehension that the President may think that this step should have been taken at an earlier day.

The Moniteur of yesterday contains the following article:

The Government of the Emperor has received from the Government of the United States satisfactory explanations of the import of the resolution passed by the Assembly of Representatives at Washington on the subject of the affairs of Mexico.

We know also that the Senate had postponed indefinitely the consideration of this resolution, to which, in any case, the Executive power had not given its sanction.

You will see that Seward is at his old habit of dirt eating and is endeavoring to cajole the Emperor by assurances which he knows that he neither dare nor can carry out.

I have the honor to be, with great respect, your most obedient servant,

JOHN SLIDELL.

Hon. J. P. BENJAMIN,
    Secretary of State.

[Enclosure.]

C. S. S. RAPPAHANNOCK,
Calais, May 1, 1864.

SIR: It is superfluous to enter upon any of the earlier details attending the admission and entrance of this ship into this harbor.

But a general recapitulation of the facts is material to my present purpose of addressing you, and through you, this communication, to the minister of marine at Paris.

The *Rappahannock* entered this port on the 26th of November, 1863; on the 4th of February she was ordered to sea, but not having received her coals, it was found impossible to comply with the order. On the 9th February (before her coals had arrived) her then commander received a notification from the minister of marine, through you, to the effect that the ship would not be permitted to leave this port until further orders from the minister of marine were received.

On the 17th of February the vessel received her coals, but her commander waited until about the 22d before signifying his readiness to depart, which he then did, but the permission was not granted. Since this latter date the *Rappahannock* has been detained here for reasons unassigned.

The foregoing history of this vessel, which embraces the period between her admission into this port and the time when permission was refused her to leave, has been furnished by my predecessor in the command.

For the period following, since which time I have been in command, the history of the vessel may be briefly but correctly stated to be:

Repairing damages to hull, etc., in consequence of the ship having been detained here; such indeed is the extent of injury to the ship from having to lay aground in this basin for so long a time, that I have represented the importance of docking her as the only means of rectifying the defects occasioned thereby.

With the hopes of being able to place my command in a condition suitable to leave the port, I have forborne to ask at an earlier date the cause for the unusual and otherwise remarkable prohibition put upon my departure.

But the moment has arrived when it becomes my duty to fix a definite period to the delay which has been imposed upon my actions in derogation of the dignity of the flag which it is my high honor to serve by informing you that if on the 16th May, the injunction upon this ship's departure be not removed and no explanation for her detention be given, I shall proceed to take an inventory of the effects

JACOB THOMPSON,
Confederate States Commissioner to Canada, 1864.

WILLIAM PRESTON,
Confederate States Commissioner to Mexico, 1864

1111

on board, at which any authorized agent of the French Government, designated by yourself, can be present, discharge my crew, withdraw the officers, haul down the flag, and deliver over the vessel to the authorities of the French Government at this place.

I have the honor to be, sir, very respectfully, your obedient servant,

CHS. M. FAUNTLEROY,
Lieutenant, Commanding, C. S. Navy.

Monsieur le COMMISSAIRE DE LA MARINE.

WILMINGTON, N. C., *May 2, 1864.*

SIR: Mr. Clay did not arrive until after dark last evening, and he delivered to me your letter with its enclosures. Herewith you will find my receipt for the bills forwarded by you. We shall sail to-day at 1 o'clock in the *Thistle*, which is considered by shippers as a safe boat though somewhat slow. The packet boat for Halifax touches at Bermuda on the 13th instant, and the voyage thence to Halifax usually occupies four days. With no untoward event, we will reach Canada by the 20th instant.

I am, dear sir, with high regard, your obedient servant,

J. THOMPSON.

Hon. J. P. BENJAMIN,
Secretary of State.

RICHMOND, VA., *May 3, 1864.*

SIR: On the 16th day of November last, I took passage at the port of Matamoras, Mexico, accompanied by five men on the American schooner *Joseph L. Gerrity*, sailing under the American flag, laden with 122 bales of cotton, bound for the port of New York. On the second night out, the 18th, I took possession of her without injury to life or limb of any of her officers or crew, and on the 26th instant I landed them all safely on the coast of Yucatan, and proceeded to the port of Belize, British Honduras, and entered her as a blockade runner under the name of the *Eureka*, from the coast of Texas, having been furnished with blank set of ship's papers by the collector at the port of Brownsville. I sold her cargo and succeeded in shipping all my men off, except one, whom I kept with myself. Owing to light and contrary winds, I had been much delayed in reaching port. In the meantime the officers and crew of the schooner had arrived at Sisal, and the American consul at that port forwarded to the port of Belize full accounts of the capture and descriptions of the captors. Before the British Government took action in the matter I succeeded in escaping, taking with me the remaining man. They, however, pursued me to Graytown, Nicaragua, where I eventually eluded their pursuit by going to the Pacific, and returning by way of the Isthmus of Panama. I state these particulars to account for the lapse of time since the capture and presenting these facts to the Department. On my arrival at Nassau in the latter part of April, Mr. L. Heyliger informed me that three of my men had been apprehended in Liverpool through the influence of the Yankee officials at that port, and are now confined in prison under the charge of piracy on the high seas, and I have subsequently learned are to be tried this month. I am exceedingly anxious that these men should not suffer under that charge as they must certainly do unless some relief in the matter can be obtained from the Confederate States Government, as the capture was made without authority other than our natural promptings to injure the enemies of the Confederacy. If any authority, I care not of what nature, can be given me, antedated so as to cover the matter and enable me to relieve these men, I shall be very grateful. I ask no pecuniary aid, as ample funds are at hand, if grounds [of] defense are only furnished by the Confederate States Government. I would most earnestly beg your earliest consideration in the matter, as the steamer leaving Wilmington on Friday or Saturday next is the latest date that will intercept the British mail.

I remain, very respectfully, your obedient servant,

T. E. HOGG.

Hon. J. P. BENJAMIN,
   Secretary of State, Richmond, Va.

RICHMOND, *May 4, 1864.*

Thomas E. Hogg was born in Baltimore; never was in the Confederate service; domiciled in Baltimore at the time of secession; has been in the Southern States since June, 1861. When he left Matamoras had with him Wilson, Wm. O'Brien, John Riley, James Clement, J. F. Brown. These men are all Irishmen. Hogg was in Matamoras for his health when he made up his mind to undertake this. He found these Irishmen at Matamoras and got them to join him.

The collector at Brownsville, upon being informed of the purpose of Hogg, gave him a blank for a vessel's register ready signed and sealed, to be filled up with a description of any vessel that he might capture. General Bee gave to Mr. Bell, a merchant of Brownsville, a paper authorizing him to make seizures of any Yankee vessels, the understanding being that Bell was to transfer this paper to Hogg. The paper was approved by General Slaughter, not in writing, but by an offer to furnish a gun for the purpose. The idea was that the capture should be made in any way that could be found practicable. The paper was destroyed by witness when making his escape from Belize, Honduras.

T. E. HOGG.

No. 19.]   DEPARTMENT OF STATE,
                         Richmond, May 5, 1864.

SIR: An application has been made to this Department for its interference in behalf of three men who were said to be accused of piracy for participation in the capture of the schooner *Joseph L. Gerrity*, and who are now imprisoned in England for trial on this charge.

The circumstances of the case, so far as they have reached this Government, disclose the facts to be as follows: A citizen of Maryland who left that State and established himself within the Confederacy in June, 1861, immediately after the declaration of war, formed a plan, while on the Mexican frontier, to capture one or more of the merchant vessels of the enemy on the high seas, and with that view sought the sanction of some of the subordinate officers of this Government who were commanding the troops in the district in which Brownsville is situated. Those officers unadvisedly and improperly sanctioned the undertaking, inasmuch as the person who proposed to act was not a citizen of the Confederacy, nor enlisted in its service, and was therefore without authority to take part in the war against our enemies. The person thus volunteering service deemed himself sufficiently authorized by the sanction of the military officer and proceeded to Matamoras, a neutral port, where he engaged five men to aid in the enterprise, and having taken passage on the *Gerrity*, he rose on the captain and crew when at sea, captured the vessel without injury to life or limb of any on board, landed the officers and crew unharmed on the coast of Yucatan, and then carried his prize to Belize, British Honduras, where he disposed of her as being a Confederate vessel by the aid of shipping papers which had been provided in blank by the collector of the customs at Brownsville.

It is scarcely necessary to say that this Government entirely disclaims this whole transaction and regards it as unlawful in inception and execution. But we are informed that two of the men now prisoners in England had been in service in our Army and had been honorably discharged in consequence of wounds received in our service. It is believed by us to be apparent that all the parties engaged in the enterprise were deceived and led into error by the sanction of local officials who were at too great a distance from the seat of government to obtain orders or directions for their conduct, and that all concerned were laboring under the honest delusion that they were engaged in a legitimate, belligerent act, justified by the law of nations in time of war, and were quite innocent of any felonious intent, without which their act can in no just sense be characterized as piracy.

Under these circumstances it is the desire of the Government that you will see that the unfortunate prisoners now charged with that crime be properly defended, that they have the aid of competent counsel, and that (while refraining from anything that could be construed into the sanction by this Government of such irregular and illegal warfare) nothing be spared that can properly be done to alleviate their condition and to save them from punishment for what was not an intentional offense. The expense will be charged in your account with this Department.

I am very respectfully, your obedient servant,

J. P. BENJAMIN,
Secretary of State.

HENRY HOTZE, Esq., *London.*

No. 61.]   PARIS, *May 5, 1864.*

SIR: Your Nos. 31, 32, 33, 34 dated respectively 11, 22, 24, and 28 March have reached me. I shall not fail to give all possible publicity to the atrocious orders found on the body of Dahlgren, the authenticity of which is so fully shown by the photographic copies accompanying your No. 34.

Mr. Hotze informs me that he has already made arrangements for their reproduction in the London Autographic Mirror. There is a similar journal here in which I will endeavor to have them published with a French translation.

We had received the President's proclamation setting apart the 8th April for a day of humiliation, fasting and prayer in time for our fellow-citizens in Paris to observe it in a becoming manner at the chapel of the Rev. M. Gurney of the English Episcopal Church.

I stated in may last of 2d instant that I had communicated to the Emperor through M. Mocquard the intentions of abandoning the *Rappahannock*, this was on the 21 ultimo, on the 23 instant I received the following note from M. Mocquard:

> I have spoken of the affair twice and have been answered that it has been the subject of a special conversation with the minister of foreign affairs, to whom you should address yourself for a definite answer.
>
> I sincerely hope that it may accord with your wishes and I offer you, as ever, the expression of my most distinguished consideration.

As the note gave no intimation of the Emperor's opinion I did not think it expedient again to address the minister of foreign affairs, but recommended Commodore Barron to instruct Commander Fauntleroy to give notice of his intention to abandon his ship. This notice was accordingly given on the 1st instant by the commander in a letter to the commissary of marine at Calais, a draft of which had been previously approved by me and of which you will find a copy * annexed. On the 3d instant I called on my friend at the affaires etrangères, informed him of the letter, and requested him to ascertain from the minister what action, if any, he intended to take in the matter. Yesterday I received the following note from him. You will see that he attributes the action of the minister to my application to the Emperor, of which I had informed him, showing him M. Mocquard's note.

> I have conversed with Mr. Drouyn de Lhuys of the notification that the commissioner of marine at Calais has received touching the determination taken by your Government to abandon the ship *Rappahannock*. Mr. Drouyn de Lhuys still thinks it very difficult to authorize the departure of this vessel; nevertheless desirous of showing a spirit of conciliation and equity which animates the Government of the Emperor, he has believed it necessary to defer the examination of the question to a commission of lawyers presided over by the president of the Senate.
>
> This, then, is, my dear sir, the present condition of this affair. You will see therein without doubt a sufficiently direct conclusion from that which you were informed of in the note you were so kind as to communicate to me twelve days ago.
>
> There is a matter of which I believe I have already spoken to you, and which I am commissioned to still recommend to your kindness. Our legation at Washington having heard that orders were sent to the Federal cruiser to give free passage to the French ships which are to be loaded with 7,000 hogsheads of tobacco purchased for the Imperial administration and now warehoused at Richmond, you are begged to have the goodness to write to your Government so that on its part it will not prevent this exportation.

The event has justified the correctness of the advice I gave to Commodore Barron, and which I fully felt the responsibility for; such is the timidity and indecision of the foreign minister that he would have allowed the question to drag out indefinitely if he had not thus been put in default.

---

* See p. 1110.

Since my last, £35,000 of the Erlanger cotton-loan bonds have been presented and canceled, making in all the sum of £211,300 up to this date.

I have the honor to be, with the greatest respect, your most obedient servant,

JOHN SLIDELL.

Hon. J. P. BENJAMIN,
Secretary of State.

No. 42.]

CONFEDERATE STATES COMMERCIAL AGENCY,
London, May 7, 1864.

SIR: I have the honor to acknowledge, by our private mail channel, the receipt on the 3d instant of your unofficial favor of the 30th March, enclosing Mr. Mallory's letter to Sir Roundell Palmer, and photographic facsimiles of the Dahlgren orders. Mr. Mallory's letter, there being no other channel conveniently accessible, I forwarded to Sir Roundell Palmer's address by post as a registered letter, under cover, with a few lines just sufficient to establish its authenticity, but, of course, avoiding even the appearance of official correspondence. By return of post I received a polite acknowledgment, enclosing the attorney-general's reply to Mr. Mallory, which I have herewith the honor to forward. Both letters passing through my hands open, I have assumed your intentions to be that I should preserve copies. On Thursday night the attorney-general mentioned in the House the fact of his having received the letter from Mr. Mallory, but as far as I can judge from the reports in all the papers, did not read it, I suppose in deference to his superiors in the Government.

The photographic facsimilies of the Dahlgren orders I handed the same day to the editor of a periodical whose specialty is the publication of curious autographs, and had the satisfaction of seeing it placed in the hands of the lithographer. They will appear in full in the next number of the Autographic Mirror.

A trifling indisposition, the usual effect of the spring season, has somewhat interfered with the dispatch of business necessary to be off my hands before leaving London, and I must therefore once more apologize for any shortcomings in my correspondence. My visit to Paris, which was fixed for the 27 ultimo, is necessarily delayed two weeks. That, however, I have not been idle in the French press, I shall ask you to glance over the enclosed slips, being extracts for the period of one month from the telegraphic dispatches published in all the Parisian papers alike. The dispatches marked are those furnished by me during that period and which would not otherwise have appeared. This arrangement which secures a hearing in journals of every shade of opinion, even those most fiercely opposed to us, and catches the eye of the most careless reader, is effected through an arrangement with Mr. Havas, of the Telegraphic and Correspondence Agency of Havas-Bullier, which on the Continent not only more than takes the place of our Associated Press for telegraphic information but supplies with our correspondence and news items the press of every continental country. I should have been loath to commit this fact to the chances of the blockade,

were it not that the arrangement is of such a nature that though
its publication is, of course, to be avoided, no malicious use can
possibly be made of it.

There is no pecuniary consideration either present or prospective,
direct or indirect, in it. I found Mr. Havas both a man of honor and
a gentleman. He professes no partiality for our cause. His business, he reasons, is to supply reliable interesting intelligence impartially, to express no opinion of his own. For this intelligence he goes
to the best sources, and the sources he trusts according to his experience of their reliability. On my part, my object is to obtain in
the Parisian press what we have never had before, a space proportionate to our importance among nations. If the public will only occupy
itself about us and hear the truth, we may safely leave them to form
their own opinions. In the occasional communications which for
some months past I addressed to M. Havas I have had the good fortune to win his confidence to an extent which, he informed me, he
seldom accords to political information from any quarter. He has
never had a retraction to make of anything I gave him, nor has he ever
been charged with partiality. I rarely communicate a fact except by
quotation of some recognized authority, and even when the fact is
exclusively my own, I take care that it is published in some prominent
journal before sending it over the wires. I always quote fairly and
repress the temptation to comment. So it has happened, I think to
the credit of both of us, that Mr. Havas never has refused a single
thing I have sent him. Mutilations and errors of translations occur
of course very often, but this is inseparable from telegraphic correspondence. I pay the cost of transmission and this is all.

Besides the telegraphic communications I furnish him with written
correspondence, in which my New York, New Orleans, Richmond
and other letters are summarized. I enclose you a few of these, taken
at random, merely as specimens. Few of them go into the Parisian
papers, but they are very extensively reproduced in the provincial
press. An attempt in some such manner to reach the provincial press
through the Havas Agency has been made by others, unbeknown to
M. Havas himself, by feeing at great cost his translators and editors,
but so far as I can see no adequate results have been obtained, and
besides my aversion to underhand proceedings, experience has demonstrated to me that I can do more by purely moral agencies, by the
irresistible force of truth tempered by moderation than by the power
of money. The expense of the written correspondence consists in
employing suitable persons to select and summarize the matter at
hand, and such are difficult to find and must be generously rewarded.
It is the difficulty of completely organizing this department so as to
make it self-acting that chiefly detains me in London.

I hope to surprise you by the extension which I feel confident of
being able to give to the use of the telegraph and correspondence, the
two ears of modern public opinion, but you must recollect that in
this respect, as regards Europe, we are newcomers in the field. On
this, however, you may rely, that the North will not be able to com-
pete with us wherever we once enter into the lists. The habit of lying
is too inveterate in our enemies to be ever abandoned, and the controlling powers in the European press have more to lose in character
than to gain in money.

Mr. Long's speech and the discussion thereon have attracted very great attention throughout Europe, and are universally accepted as the most favorable symptoms yet manifested of a revulsion of feeling in the North. Nor has the press failed to observe and to give due emphasis to the fact that at the extreme ends of the Confederacy—in Florida, in western Louisiana, in the Mississippi Valley, in North Carolina, everywhere that we were thought weakest—we have shown ourselves " at least equal if not superior " to our adversaries. The pro-Federal papers can only console themselves with the hope that we have weakened ourselves where alone the decisive trial of strength must take place, and have sacrificed to comparatively unessential successes the result of the Virginia campaign. May their hopes be confounded.

It is almost a prophecy after the fact to say that the conference on the Dano-German question will prove abortive. On the most natural and obvious issues presented to them the German plenipotentiaries " refer " to their respective governments " for instructions," so that while the tide of invasion sweeps on and over the Danish monarchy, the conference holds only desultory and fruitless sessions. Meanwhile the despair of the Danes assumes a character of sullenness. They abandon place after place after scarcely a formal resistance and seem to say to England " you have far greater interest in the preservation of the Danish monarchy than we have." The bitterness of the press toward this country far exceeds that of our own, perhaps because our people feel themselves strong and the Danes feel themselves weak and abandoned.

An insurrection has broken out in Algeria which the English papers affect to compare to the Sepoy mutiny. I hope they exaggerate its importance.

From the old battle ground in the East there comes an indistinct sound of the heavy tramp of Austrian, Russian, and Turkish Armies. Italy is uneasy. Everywhere there is a gathering of dark thunder-clouds, and it really would not surprise me if the whole card house of the reconstructed post-Napoleonic Europe were suddenly to be swept away in one tremendous deluge of blood. If so England will have to thank her octogenarian government for the cataclysm. My only anxiety is that we should be under shelter when the storm bursts.

I have the honor to remain, with great respect, your obedient servant,

HENRY HOTZE.

Hon. J. P. BENJAMIN,
    Secretary of State, Richmond.

ST. GEORGE'S, BERMUDA ISLANDS,
May 10, 1864.

SIR: We reached this port safely this morning. While we were chased by a blockade vessel for five hours on our way out, yet we escaped with no further interruption than being forced to leave our true course for that length of time. I am informed to-day the steamer for Halifax is not expected to leave St. George's before Monday, the 16th instant.

I am, with great respect, your obedient servant,

J. THOMPSON.

Hon. J. P. BENJAMIN.

19 RUE DE MARIGNAN,
Paris, May 12, 1864.

MY DEAR BENJAMIN: I write you a hurried line to say that I have seen M. Troplong, president of the Senate, on the subject of the *Rappahannock*, who received me most cordially. He is very decided in his Southern sympathies; he has put me in communication with the counsellor of state, "Rapporteur," to whom the papers have been referred. I am to see him on Saturday, when he will communicate the papers to me. M. Troplong gave me to understand that Mr. Drouyn de Lhuys did not wish the commission to come to a decision before the adjournment of the Chamber; this is in keeping with what I have more than once said about the foreign minister.

I have just seen Mrs. Benjamin and your daughter; they are quite well.

Yours, faithfully,

JOHN SLIDELL.

Hon. J. P. BENJAMIN.

———

No. 62.] PARIS, *May 21, 1864.*

SIR: In my last of 5th instant I informed you that the affair of the *Rappahannock* had been referred to a commission by the minister of foreign affairs for examination and report. Each ministry has attached to it a board styled the "commission du contentieux," to whom are referred such questions of doubt or difficulty as the minister may not feel competent to decide unassisted, or of which he may be disposed to avoid the responsibility of deciding, or, as probably was the reason in this instance, he may wish to procrastinate.

This commission for the department of foreign affairs consists of the president of the Senate, Mr. Troplong; several "conseillers d'etat"; and two or three retired diplomatists. The reputation of Mr. Troplong as a distinguished legist is well known to you; I asked an interview with him which he very promptly granted. He received me most cordially; he said that the report on the *Rappahannock* would have been promptly made by the commission, but that the "dossier" had been accompanied by an intimation from Mr. Drouyn de Lhuys that he would prefer not to receive a report until after the adjournment of the Corps Législalif, as he feared it might be made a matter of attack from M. Jules Favre.

M. Troplong said that he had not read the papers referred to him, having pursued the usual course of sending it to a member of the commission for examination who would report upon it; it would then be taken up for decision by the commission, he presiding. He said the reporter would give me every information respecting the case, and that I might call on him in his name for that purpose.

The immediate object of my visit disposed of, Mr. T. entered upon the subject of our affairs, in which he manifested great interest, appearing to be well informed. He was very decided and earnest in the expression of his sympathy with our cause and desire for our speedy and complete success. He said that this was the universal feeling of the members of the Government. I remarked that it was certainly gratifying to know that we had so many friends among the distinguished men of France, but that up to the present time, far from having derived any advantage from the friendly disposition of the Government and of the existence of such disposition, I entertained no doubt its policy could not in fact have been more disadvantageous to us in its practical operation than if dictated by decided hostility. I gave reasons for this assertion, which it is not necessary here to repeat.

I have seen the reporter, M. Marchand, a very leading member of the conseil d'état, and a celebrated jurisconsult. He gave me a summary of the papers in the " dossier," and I found that there was no matter of any importance in it of which I had been ignorant. It contained my communications to the Emperor and minister of foreign affairs. Mr. M., of course, avoided committing himself as to the character of his report, but I inferred from what he did say that he did not consider the case as presenting much difficulty; he intimated that the only question was the increasing of the crew. I said that all that had been done in that way was with the knowledge and approbation of the minister of marine, and that apart from my assertion I, fortunately, could give him proof on that score coming from the enemy in the shape of a dispatch from Mr. Dayton, Federal minister at Paris, to Mr. Seward, Federal Minister of Foreign Affairs. I accordingly sent him, with a short note, an extract from that dispatch, and as you may perhaps not be in possession of Mr. Seward's two precious and voluminous books of diplomatic correspondence communicated with Lincoln's message to Congress in December last, I send you herewith copy of extract. You will find that it completely disposes of the only part of the case about which I had any misgivings. M. Marchand gave me to understand that the report would not be made until after the adjournment of the Senate, which will take place in a few days. The delay must be attributed to the foreign minister, whose course in this instance is entirely in keeping with the opinion which I have more than once had occasion to express of him in previous dispatches.

I send you report of a debate on the subject of ships said to be building for the Confederacy in French ports. The reply of M. Rouher, minister of state, to M. Jules Favre will excite with you, as it has with me, surprise and dissatisfaction; the keynote now evidently is, cajole the North until Maximilian shall have been recognized at Washington. All this is very disgusting, but I refrain from making comments which will readily present themselves to you and which might fall into hands for which they are not intended.

The British Government has purchased from Messrs. Bravay & Co. the two rams seized in the Mersey on terms which will reimburse them their outlay with interest; they say that they made this sale at the urgent instance of their solicitor, who told them that whatever might be the decision of the exchequer court, the case would be carried through all the stages of appeal involving prolonged litigation and immense expense.

There are renewed rumors of cabinet changes here. M. Drouyn de Lhuys is especially the object of attack from high quarters; well-informed persons think that he will not long continue to direct foreign affairs.

I have the honor to be, with the greatest respect,

  Your most obedient servant,

Hon. J. P. Benjamin,   John Slidell.
  Secretary of State.

EXTRACT OF A DISPATCH OF MR. DAYTON TO MR. SEWARD, BEARING NO. 365,
AND DATED PARIS, OCTOBER 21, 1863.

M. Drouyn de Lhuys furthermore informèd me that this Government, after much conference (and, I think, some hesitation), had
concluded not to issue an order prohibiting an accession to the crew
of the *Florida* while in port, inasmuch as such accession was necessary to her navigation. They had made enquiries, it would seem,
and said they had ascertained that the seventy or seventy-five men
discharged after she came into Brest were discharged because the
period for which they had shipped had expired. He said, furthermore, that it was reported to him that the *Kearsarge* had likewise
applied for some sailors and a pilot in that port, as well as for coal
and leave to make repairs, all of which had been, and would be if
more were needed, cheerfully granted.

     *   *   *   *   *   *   *

The determination which has been reached by the French authorities to allow the shipment of a crew, or so large a portion of one,
on board of the *Florida* while lying in their port is, I think, wrong,
even supposing that vessel a regularly commissioned ship of war.
I told M. Drouyn de Lhuys that, looking at it as a mere lawyer and
clear of prejudices which my official position might create, I thought
this determination an error. He said, however, that in the conference they had reached that conclusion unanimously, although a
majority of the ministry considering the question were lawyers.

It may happen, however, that the decision will have no practical effect, as my last information from England makes it doubtful
if the rebel agents there can get the men.

No. 5.]   HALIFAX, NOVIA SCOTIA, *May 27, 1864.*

SIR: I have the honor to acknowledge the receipt of your dispatch
of 20th April, communicating the opinion of the Government upon
the affair of the *Chesapeake*, after a full report of all the facts connected with its capture. I learn with great satisfaction that the
exercise of the discretion confided to me over that subject has met
with your approbation and that of the President. I shall now devote
myself exclusively to the duty of sending home as rapidly as possible such of our escaped prisoners as may be willing to return.
There are now 12 in Halifax, 9 of whom will go on in the British
mail steamer which leaves to-day for Bermuda, and the remaining
3, with some others who are expected, in the *Constance*, in about ten
days or two weeks hence. The first party is composed of very intelligent and high-spirited young men belonging chiefly to Morgan's
command, and will be a valuable accession at this time. Their representations lead me to fear that the apprehensions intimated in my
last will be more than confirmed by the developments of the future,
and that Colonel Kane was greatly mistaken in his estimate of the
number in Canada, and of those willing to return. I shall proceed
at once as far west as Windsor, and endeavor to stimulate them
to discharge their duty to their country in this hour of her trial.

Besides transportation, I shall offer (what they are very solicitous to procure) such clothing as they may actually need. I fear we can not expect more than a hundred, however, at the utmost.

I have written to the Governor General of British North America, informing him of my instructions to respect not only the rules of international law, but the municipal laws of her Majesty's Empire.

On reaching Canada, I will write more fully.

With the highest consideration, I remain, yours, etc.,

JAMES P. HOLCOMBE.

Hon. J. P. BENJAMIN,
Secretary of State, C. S. A.

No. 91.] BRUSSELS, *May 25, 1864.*

SIR: Since the date of the discovery of gun cotton, of which I witnessed the first experiments at Frankfort-on-the-Main, in 1847, I have not ceased to feel an earnest solicitude for its perfect development. I have sent to you, from time to time, as they came to my knowledge, the reported improvements made by scientific men in the condition of the article. I have the pleasure to transmit herewith statements publicly expressed upon the subject a few days ago by Mr. Scott Russell, whose name in such a connection carries much weight with it. There is evidently a rapidly growing general impression in Europe, that it is, at no remote period, to advantageously supersede the use of gunpowder. When it is recollected how imperfect the latter article was for several centuries after its invention, the favorable opinions thus already entertained of the future value of gun cotton do not seem to be unreasonable. The subject is one in which our own country is more interested than is any other.

I have the honor to be, sir, very respectfully, your obedient servant,

A. DUDLEY MANN.

Hon. J. P. BENJAMIN,
Secretary of State, C. S. A., Richmond, Va.

No. 38.] DEPARTMENT OF STATE,
Richmond, May 31, 1864.

SIR: On the 29th July, 1863, the French consul in Richmond commenced a correspondence with this Department on the subject of the exportation to France of the tobacco belonging to the Government of his Imperial Majesty, then stored in warehouses in our ports. A copy of this correspondence is annexed, and the contents are substantially as follows:

First. A letter from Mr. Paul of the above date of 29th July, 1863, informing me that his Majesty's minister at Washington had just obtained from the Federal Government "a free passage for the tobacco of the Imperial Régie out of the waters of Virginia." He further stated that in pursuance of previous conversations with me, it was well understood that this tobacco "should be shipped directly from the port of Richmond; that it should be loaded on board of neutral vessels; that all the shipping papers of the vessels and cargoes should set forth the exportation was direct and from Richmond; and that it should be imposed as a condition of all charter parties that the vessel should proceed with her cargo directly to a French port without touching or stopping at any port, bay, or point whatever belonging to the territory of the blockading belligerent."

The passage underlined is also underlined in the original.

Second. For my answer of the 4th August, I pointed out that the assurances contained in the letter of Mr. Paul were not satisfactory on one point, namely, that there was no promise that the vessels should not touch at our own ports temporarily in possession of the enemy, such as Norfolk, Hampton Roads, etc., and the further promise was required that the vessels would not "take any papers or clearances signed by the enemy indicating that shipments are made from any port or place in their possession." Mr. Paul was invited to respond on these points and was informed that if his answer was satisfactory this Government would take great pleasure in facilitating his Majesty's Government in having the tobacco forwarded to France.

Third. Mr. Paul's letter of 5th August gave the required pledges, but he pointed out that the vessels loaded with the tobacco would, of course, be required to show their papers to the blockading squadron at Hampton Roards in order that they might be identified as the vessels licensed to pass with the tobacco for the French Government, and that this necessary stoppage could not be considered as touching at a port in possession of the enemy.

Fourth. My letter of the same date (5th August) acknowledged receipt of Mr. Paul's letter, accepted his assurances as satisfactory, and announced that no further obstacle remained to the shipment of the tobacco.

The tenor of this correspondence sufficiently indicates the nature of the conversation which led to it and presents prominently the points deemed essential by this Government in the arrangements made. We had learned by the previous action of neutral powers that they had been unable to shake off their ancient impression that these Confederate States were represented in their foreign intercourse by the Washington Government. We had discovered that the ministers who, at Washington, represented foreign Governments continued to supervise and control the consuls residing within the Confederacy, as though the credentials which attested their authority to act in the United States still embraced the States of this Confederacy, and we had been compelled to call the attention of foreign Governments to this state of things as one which had forced us to interdict any direct intercourse between their consuls residing here and their ministers residing at Washington. When, therefore, application was made on the part of his Imperial Majesty for our assent to the exportation of this tobacco through the blockading squadron, there existed but one obstacle to the gratification of the Emperor's desire, and pains were taken to remove that obstacle by frank and free explanation. The matter was very simple from our point of view, but the success of the Federal Government in teaching neutral powers that we had no rights but such as it chose to concede compelled us to qualify our consent, which would otherwise have been unconditional. Mr. Paul was therefore fully impressed by me with the view we took of our position. We were an independent belligerent in whose ports a neutral Government had merchandise in store which it desired to export through a blockade which it deemed itself bound to respect. The neutral was thus compelled to obtain a license from the blockader to pass through his fleet. If his Imperial Majesty could obtain such license, we were willing to permit the export on neutral vessels of neutral property from our own ports on the express condition that the business should be so conducted as to preclude all implication against our sovereignty over our own territory and harbors. This was the sensitive, the vital, point with us, and it was with this object steadily in view that we insisted in conversation and that Mr. Paul therefore proposed in writing that the tobacco should be cleared and shipped from the port of Richmond direct for France and should neither stop in Federal waters nor carry Federal papers other than what we supposed would be the usual form of license to the vessels to pass through the blockade.

The circumstances I am about to narrate will show how completely our just expectations on this subject have been disappointed and how injuriously the sovereign rights of these States have been affected by the action of his Imperial Majesty's minister at Washington.

It is to be observed that Mr. Paul announced in his letter of 29th July, 1863, that his Government had obtained from our enemy a free passage for the tobacco of the Imperial Régie out of the waters of Virginia, and that this statement was the basis of the arrangements concluded in my letter of the 5th August, 1863. Mr. Paul departed from Richmond for the avowed purpose of chartering neutral vessels to take the tobacco, but several months elapsed and the whole matter was apparently abandoned, as nothing further was heard on the subject. At a late date in the autumn we were informed unofficially that the delay arose from the fact that the license given by the blockaders was only intended to cover tobacco purchased prior to the establishment of the blockade, but that all the tobacco of the Régie has been bought subsequently to that period, so that application had become necessary for a modification in the terms of the license in order to give it effect.

No further communication to Mr. Paul on this subject was received till last month. He arrived at City Point on board the French war steamer *Tisiphone* (with two merchantmen in convoy) about the 15th April, 1864, more than eight months after having concluded his understanding with his Department. In my No. 35 of 16th April, I advised you of this arrival and added that they came "doubtless for the purpose of taking the tobacco belonging to the Imperial Government, and which will be delivered in accordance with our promise."

In my No. 36 of 30th April I further informed you as follows:

"The original convention between the French Government and that of the United States provides that the tobacco should be shipped in five months from the date of the agreement, viz, the 23d November, so that the delay expired on the 23d instant. In the meantime it was discovered that the convention would prove inoperative, as it included only tobacco purchased before the war and none such existed. After some delay consent was given on the 7th March that tobacco bought during the war should be taken out, but nothing was said about any extension of time. The French agents chartered vessels in New York and got them into James River in the beginning of this month, when the captain of *Tisiphone*, who had convoyed the merchantmen, was informed by General Butler that the time would expire according to convention on the 23d, and that he had no authority to extend it. The captain immediately wrote to the French minister at Washington (and Butler to his Government) for instructions. The vessels reached City Point and Captain de Marivault (I believe this is his name) remained without further communication till the 23d instant, when he received a message from Butler by flag of truce stating that the time was out and summoning him to withdraw, and the vessels were forced to leave with but 100 hogsheads of tobacco out of some 7,000 belonging to the French Government."

This statement was made on information received verbally from Mr. Paul and Commander de Marivault, who called at the Department for the purpose of explaining their sudden departure. They both seemed to consider the proceeding as one purely vexatious on the part of General Butler, and expressed the confidence that the period would be extended to the 7th August; that is, five months from the date of the second convention. I requested Mr. Paul to let me see the convention, but he had not brought it with him, and as he departed the same day on board the *Tisiphone*, I did not receive a copy till his return this week.

What has since occurred is so fully set forth in the correspondence, of which copies are annexed, that it is unnecessary to do more than refer to that correspondence and to the copy of the convention made at Washington in November last to place you in full possession of all that has happened here.

We can not but regret that circumstances have compelled us to adopt a course which places it out of our power to facilitate his Imperial Majesty in the attainment of an object which he greatly desired and which it was therefore a pleasure to us to promote. The disposition which we have evinced to do anything in our power to forward the wishes of the Emperor in this matter has been fully acknowledged by his consul here, and it has only yielded to the high, the paramount duty imposed on us of safeguarding the honor of our country and its right to be treated as an independent nation.

If it shall appear to you that explanation further than that contained in the correspondence itself is necessary to prevent any misunderstanding of our views and of the friendly sentiments by which we are actuated toward the Government of the Emperor, you are requested by the President to make to Mr. Drouyn de Lhuys such exposition, in the sense of this dispatch, as you may deem advisable, or even to furnish him with a copy, if preferred.

Before closing, it may be proper to observe that I have not asked, nor has Mr. Paul volunteered, any explanation of the apparent discrepancy between his assurance on the 29th July, 1863, that a free passage for the tobacco had already been conceded by the Federal Government, and the fact that the convention granting the license bears date the 23d November. We had no disposition to be punctilious about details, and have no other feeling than regret at being compelled to withdraw, even temporarily, the assent which we had given to the arrangements made for the export of the tobacco.

I am, very respectfully, your obedient servant,

J. P. BENJAMIN,
Secretary of State.

Hon. JOHN SLIDELL, *Paris.*

[Enclosure.]

HEADQUARTERS 18TH ARMY CORPS,
DEPARTMENT of VIRGINIA and NORTH CAROLINA,
Fortress Monroe, May 4, 1864.

At the request of the French consul at Richmond, M. Paul, permission is given for the French ship of war *Tisiphone* and the English vessel *Bidwell*, under French charter, to proceed to City Point, if M. Paul so desire, for the purpose of clearing the tobacco already shipped, leaving Fortress Monroe on the 6th day May instant.

BENJAMIN BUTLER,
Major-General, Commanding.

CONSULATE DE FRANCE,
à Richmond.

Pour copie conforme:

ALFRED PAUL,
Le Consul de France.

[Enclosure.]

DEPARTMENT OF STATE,
Richmond, May 24, 1864.

SIR: On the 29th July, 1863, you addressed a letter to this Department informing me that his Imperial Majesty's minister at Washington has just obtained from the Federal Government "a free passage for the tobacco of the Imperial Régie out of the waters of Virginia." A correspondence ensued, which was closed by my letter of 5th August, 1863, giving the assent of this Government to the export of the tobacco on the conditions mentioned in the correspondence.

Nothing was done by his Majesty's Government in execution of this arrangement until the middle of last month, when you arrived at City Point in the *Tisiphone* with two merchant vessels in convoy, and upon arriving in the city your arrangements for exportation had scarcely been commenced when I received a visit from you, in company with Commander de Marivault, of the *Tisiphone*, during which you informed me that the commander had received notice from General Butler that the delay of five months accorded by the convention with the United States expired on the 23d April, and that Commander de Marivault was therefore summoned to withdraw. On my expressing the desire to see the convention of which you spoke, you were unable to comply with my request at the moment, not having it in your possession, but you stated that you were about to proceed down the river at once on the *Tisiphone* in order to communicate with the chargé d'affaires at Washington of his Imperial Majesty; that the delay for the exportation had been extended to the 7th August; that you had no doubt the matter would be immediately arranged and the vessels allowed to complete their cargoes; and that you would return to Richmond and call at the Department on arrival.

On your return you gave me an explanation of the facts that had occurred during your absence, and left with me that I might have a copy made, the paper containing the informal convention between the Government of the Emperor and that of the United States on the 23d November, 1863.

The contents of this paper were found to be so unexpected and so gravely objectionable as to impose on me the duty of calling the attention of the President to the subject, and it is by his instructions that I make you this communication.

When you sought and obtained the assent of this Government to the exportation of the tobacco belonging to the Imperial Régie, we were led to believe from the correspondence to which I have referred, that the Government of 'his Imperial Majesty had obtained a license from that of the United States in the usual form, authorizing the passage through the blockading fleet of neutral vessels which were to receive the tobacco in our ports and to carry it away without any further interference on the part of the Federal Government than the exhibition to the blockading fleet of the license to pass. We could not attribute any other meaning to your letter of the 29th July, 1863, in which you informed us that your Government had obtained "a free passage for the tobacco out of the waters of Virginia." Your language was as follows:

J'ai l'honneur de vous informer qu'à la suite de nouvelles démarches, M. le ministre de l'Empereur à Washington venait d'obtenir du Gouvernement Fédéral le libre passage des tabacs de la Régie Impériale hors des eaux de la Virginie.

In acceding to your request, every effort was made by this Government to impress a full understanding on one point, viz, that we held our sovereignty to be unquestionable within our own limits, that we could not permit the assumption on the part of the United States of any exercise of authority within these States, and that consequently the tobacco should be loaded in our own port of Richmond, should be cleared at our own customhouse here, should be put on board at City Point, the usual loading place for vessels in this port, should have no other documents nor shipping papers than those furnished by us, and should not stop nor touch at any point or port in possession of our enemies, but should proceed directly to France, with the sole exception of the momentary delay necessary to show to the blockading vessels the license to pass through their lines.

This, sir, is substantially the arrangement to which we assented, and which was concluded on the 5th day of August, 1863. We now find that this arrangement was infringed and disregarded by his Majesty's minister in Washington by a convention made without our knowledge or consent in the ensuing month of November, containing not only stipulations in derogation of the sovereignty of this Government over its own territorial possessions, but a recognition by the French Government of the pretensions of the United States to a control over neutral vessels and their crews while in our own ports, pretensions which this Government will never admit, and which it has repelled and is now engaged in repelling by sacrifice of blood and treasure almost unexampled in history.

Without entering into an analysis of the whole tenor and spirit of the convention, it suffices to point attention to the following articles:

The third article admits the right of the United States to impose such restrictions as it pleases on the communications between neutral vessels while in our port and the shore. The purpose stated is "to prevent fraud." We can not permit the Government of the United States to institute a police in our ports "to prevent fraud."

The fifth article provides that the neutral vessels, while in our waters, ascending the James River, "shall not communicate with any soever, save the Federal cruisers, to whom they will have to show their clearances," and the eleventh article yields obedience to the order of the United States that any intercourse between the crews of the vessels and the inhabitants of Virginia is vigorously interdicted.

The eighth article, exceeding all the others in its offensive features, provides that 40 of our enemies shall be recruited and brought into our ports on the neutral vessels which we have permitted to come here without its entering into our imagination that they could bring other than friends into our midst, and the ninth article provides that these enemies shall be considered as forming a "part of the effective crew of the *Tisiphone*," and "shall in no case communicate with the shore."

The President is unwilling that any comment should be made on this very extraordinary convention, in which the minister of his Imperial Majesty at Washington seems to have equally disregarded the spirit of the stipulations contained in the correspondence with you already mentioned and the principles of public law which impose respect for the territorial sovereignty of nations, and which interdict neutrals from introducing the subjects of one belligerent into the territory of the other without the consent of the latter.

The President prefers to persuade himself that the Government of his Imperial Majesty has remained ignorant of these stipulations, so offensive to the dignity and self-respect of this Government, and will hasten to disavow and disclaim them as soon as brought to its notice. The President feels that it would be inconsistent with the profound and sincere regard entertained by him for his Imperial Majesty to enter into argument on a subject which the Emperor's own sense of national honor will present to him in the strongest light. He is confident that without any suggestion from him it will occur at once to the Government of his Imperial Majesty that if the situation of the parties were reversed—if Havre were blockaded by an English fleet, and if we, as neutrals, had made with the enemy of France a stipulation under the like circumstances to take Englishmen on board of our vessels into Havre as a part of the effective crew of a vessel of war, and had promised that our vessels in the port of Havre should have no communication with the inhabitants but should communicate solely with the English blockaders—just offense would be taken at our conduct, and the French Government under such circumstances would not err in confidently expecting from us proper disclaimers and explanations.

It is my duty, sir, under the instructions of the President, to inform you that until the obstacle interposed by the objectionable convention with the United States can be overcome to the satisfaction of this Government the vessels of his Majesty's Government can not again be permitted to receive cargo from our ports. I have the honor to be,

Very respectfully, your obedient servant,

J. P. BENJAMIN,
Secretary of State.

ALFRED PAUL, Esq.,
Consul of France, Richmond.

[Enclosure.]

24 MAY, 1864.

INFORMAL CONVENTION.

Informal convention between the Secretary of State of the United States and the envoy extraordinary and minister plenipotentiary of his Majesty the Emperor of the French on the subject of the exportation of certain tobacco.

Whereas by an Executive order bearing date the 10th instant, a copy of which is hereunto annexed, the President of the United States has authorized the exportation of certain tobacco, it is hereby agreed that the exportation of certain tobacco from within limits under blockade shall be governed by regulations consisting of the following articles:

ARTICLE I. The vessels adapted to the employment shall be neutral exclusively. They shall be French as much as possible, although foreign vessels of other nations may be employed by the French officers to assist in the operation.

ART. II. The French minister engages that the only tobacco to be removed is tobacco purchased and paid for prior to the 4th of March, 1861, and is in quantity about six or seven thousand hogsheads.

ART. III. In the purpose of preventing any fraud, the charter party shall include express mention that the vessels freighted shall be under the immediate orders of the commander of the *Tisiphone* in everything that will bear upon the relations and communications to be maintained with the shore as well as for the labors made necessary for loading. Mr. de Marivault will for this purpose be authorized to detach on board, if he shall judge it to be necessary, a guard of armed men, who shall be victualed under the care of the merchant captains, to whom the amount of the rations shall, ulteriorly, be reimbursed in kind.

ART. IV. The pilots taken by the merchant vessels ascending to City Point shall, on their arrival, be placed at the disposal of the French commander of the *Tisiphone*, who will take measures needful to send them back in the same capacity on vessels going down or as passengers on board of flag-of-truce vessels. In that case it will be proper to settle in advance with these pilots the compensation which shall be allowed them daily during their sojourn on board. It should be arranged that said passage shall be effected on the transmission of a pass issued by the French commander.

ART. V. It shall be formally stipulated in the charter party that the vessels ascending James River shall not communicate with any soever save the Federal cruisers, to whom they will have to show their clearances, and on their departure shall return directly to France to such port as shall have been assigned to them.

ART. VI. The vessels selected by the consul of France for account of the Imperial Government shall carry, whatever be their nationality, from their arrival in the Chesapeake until their departure, the French flag at their foremast head.

ART. VII. The steamer which shall tow the tobacco barges will carry the same flag in going to and from.

ART. VIII. To accelerate the loading a gang of 40 laborers shall be recruited at Norfolk, and placed at the disposal of the commander of the *Tisiphone*, who will distribute them among the vessels that are loading according to the wants of the hour. In case their number should be insufficient, and where it would be of advantage to join to them some of the crew of the *Tisiphone*, the parties loading shall be held to pay them daily wages on the same footing as to the other laborers.

ART. IX. The said laborers, considered as forming part of the effective crew of the *Tisiphone*, shall in no case communicate with the shore.

ART. X. The people of the United States and those of some of the Southern States having interrupted their relations, and the progress of operations requiring that communications be opened between the commander of the *Tisiphone* and New York, there shall be conceded, from City Point to Fortress Monroe, and thence to New York, passages by the flags of truce to the officers of the Imperial Navy provided with orders from Mr. de Marivault.

ART. XI. It is well understood that any intercourse between the crews of the vessels and the inhabitants of Virginia is vigorously interdicted.

ART. XII. The chartered vessels will take, on leaving New York, independently of their ballast and provisions, a quantity of staves or other wood for dunnage necessary for solid stowage of their cargo.

ART. XIII. In case some vessels should not be able, from their draft of water, to get up to City Point to load, they will complete it by dropping down to Harrison's Bar, where they should be placed under the control of a French officer.

ART. XIV. The administration of the customhouse at New York shall receive from Washington instructions that the clearance of the vessels employed be not on its part the subject of any difficulty.

ART. XV. The vessels chartered by the French Government shall be towed or, as the case may be, convoyed by a French vessel of war from the mouth of James River to City Point, and in like manner in descending. In case where one or several of those vessels shall not find a tow at the mouth of the river, and that a steamer is about going up, if it can not tow or convoy them itself it will advise the French commander of their arrival, so that he may go to seek them.

[Two French gunboats will be detailed to attend to this service. 1°. The corvette *Tisiphone*, Commander de Marivault. 2°. Gunboat *Grenade*, C. A. Reynaud.]

ART. XVI. The time within which the tobacco may be removed in pursuance of the privilege granted by the order is five months from this date.

Done at Washington this 23d day of November, 1863.

MERCIER.
SEWARD.

[Enclosure—Translation.]

FRENCH CONSULATE,
Richmond, Va., May 26, 1864.

SIR: I acknowledge receipt of the letter which you did me the honor to address me on the 24th instant. A statement of your views as to the convention signed at Washington on the 23d of last November for regulating the mode of shipping the Virginia tobacco belonging to the French Régie (views doubtless impartial, as everything which emanates from your pen and from your enlightened mind, but at the same time naturally quite rigid on the point of the dignity of your Government) forms the subject of your communication, some passages of which, however, are only reconcilable with a construction that is to be regretted of several articles of the convention. This document should be examined from the point of view of all the parties in interest, as will doubtless be admitted by you.

Permit me, sir, in the first place, to say to you that it never entered into the thoughts of the Government of the Emperor, nor of his Majesty's minister at Washington, to form a convention of which a solitary article could be of a nature to infringe either the dignity or the moral or material interests of any party whatsoever.

In this delicate matter we have obligations to fulfill toward parties on whom depended equally the success of our measures always adopted openly and honorably. We endeavored to respect the sensitiveness of all by considering at all times good faith as the essential point, and, as secondary, the question of the material interests which were the objects of our measures, always marked with a regard for propriety and guided by impartial intentions. You gave us proof of a very courteous readiness to do what was agreeable to us in this affair. These proofs were highly appreciated. For this reason I can not avoid expressing the lively regret I experienced in seeing you express the opinion that the above-mentioned convention is offensive to your Government.

I deem it my duty to enter into a discussion of the facts which were the motives for those clauses which seem to you objectionable. I assume to myself the responsibility of the suggestion which induced his Majesty's minister at Washington and the vice-admiral commanding in chief the French naval division to adopt measures which in our view were justified by circumstances without there having been any question of previous advice from another party which was interested in the business under other relations than those to which you allude. I will endeavor to change your opinion by placing in relief simply and succinctly the truth of the facts.

You express categorically, sir, the opinion that the minister of his Majesty had admitted in this convention the pretensions of another Government than our own to a control over the actions of the crews of the French or other neutral vessels, chartered for the conveyance of the tobacco belonging to the Imperial Régie, and to the exercise of this control in the ports of Virginia where the tobacco was to be put on board.

To this I answer: It is I, consul of France at Richmond, who proposed to the minister of France and to Rear-Admiral Reynaud, to place the chartered vessels under the exclusive control (I say exclusive) of the French vessels of war. My object was not only to prevent all species of frauds to the detriment of any party whatsoever—that is, of all the parties having a moral or material interest in the business—but also, to prevent all communication on the part of the crews of the loading vessels with the inhabitants, amongst whom they had nothing to see and nothing to do. Our neutral duties obliged us to prevent a state of things which, in case of the flight of any of the crew, after having passed out of the limits of the loading port, might have become, through our own want of foresight, prejudicial to the interests of one of the parties who had authorized and favored our shipment.

You add, sir, that there is reason to complain that no communication was authorized with any soever, except the Federal vessel to which the merchant captains would have to show their shipping papers after having departed from City Point directly for France, without stopping at any Federal port.

To this I answer: The proof of our impartiality in the fulfillment of our duty of neutrals is evinced by this very article which interdicts all communication with the soil and the people of the Northern, as well as with the soil and people of the Southern States, from the moment when the vessels entered the waters of Virginia, not again to leave them except to proceed to France direct. The words are " with any soever," with no one, either in the upper or lower river. And I have the honor to observe to you, sir, that if we, the French, in the interests of all, and in order not to assume a responsibility which can and ought to be declined by neutrals, if we have of our own movements interposed obstacles to useless communications, full of inconveniences, and which are also forbidden by ourselves; on the other hand, instead of asking your permission to send the men of the merchant vessels to get the tobacco at Richmond and Petersburg, we made a contract with a Virginia captain whom I knew to be a safe man, whose steamer and crew passed between City Point and these two cities, and communicated with those that were kept on board the merchantmen, and would have continued to do so, during the whole operation.

In relation to the crews of the vessels of the Imperial Navy, they had the same faculty and privilege as everywhere, of circulating freely on both sides, and I thank you, sir, anew for your kind reception of Commanders de Marivault and Bayot when they visited Richmond.

You complain, sir, that in the eighth article of the convention, an article exceeding all the others, as you say, in contents offensive to your Government, it is provided that 40 of your enemies shall be recruited and brought into your ports on neutral vessels which you had permitted to come without its entering into your imagination that they would bring others than friends in your midst.

I confess, sir, that this part of your letter of the 24th has greatly surprised me, and that I have been deeply affected to preceive that it was impossible to attribute to any act whatever of my Government such a character, or even to suspect it of permitting this character to be stamped on a transaction in which its interests are involved. Certainly, I respect the sensitiveness which may have inspired this passage of the letter to which I have now the honor to respond, but do you think, sir, that there is any impropriety on my part in pointing out to you its signification with the entire defense which is your due? I answer to your observation that there was no question of recruiting 40 of your enemies on our ships; but that the necessity, eventual also, of having recourse to a certain number of laborers having been foreseen by M. Mercier, Admiral Reynaud, and myself; I, myself, proposed to take not enemies, but laborers at Norfolk. Besides, we have not had recourse to this means. French sailors detailed from the crews of the *Tisiphone* and the *Grenade* performed the labor of loading, up to the moment when operations were arrested. If we had used laborers from Norfolk, they would besides have been under surveillance and would have been kept on board without being permitted to land for any cause.

I understand better than ever, sir, since you have raised this last objection, how prudent and necessary a measure was the interdiction of all communication with the shore on either side. We thought then that we should need laborers to dispatch the loading. It was quite natural to take them in the country where we were. You remarked to me in our conversation, that we might have taken them here. If we had taken laborers here, we could only have taken negroes. Our position would then have been very delicate and painful under present circumstances, for if some of these negroes had escaped from on board, it would have been thought that their flight had been facilitated. Besides, we could not count upon an absence of complicity on the part of captains and crews, unknown to us, and facts of extreme gravity might thus have occurred.

Finally, sir, you interpret the ninth article of this convention in a manner irreconcilable not only with our intentions, but also with the French law on the rules governing the " personnel " of the Imperial Navy. In substance, you think that this ninth article stipulates "that these enemies shall be considered as forming part of the effective crew of the *Tisiphone*."

We have in our Department of the Navy and the colonies, a bureau of maritime inscription, of the police of navigation and the fisheries. Among the functions of this bureau is that of matriculating the sea-going classes. No foreigner is admitted on our vessels of war, the crews being composed exclusively of Frenchmen, enrolled, matriculated.

I confess that the terms of the ninth article may admit an interpretation in the sense which you attribute to it, and I have just remarked this, but I can assure you, sir, that the object of this clause was not to incorporate into the crew of the *Tisiphone*, but into the whole body of men, French and others, who were to be united under the orders of Commander de Marivault during the operation (to incorporate for the moment, I observe), these strangers, so as to give greater efficiency to the action of the commander and to his surveillance.

In closing, sir, you seem to suppose that the Government of the Emperor has not "been kept advised of this affair, or is at least ignorant of these stipulations so offensive to the dignity and self-respect of this Government, and will hasten to disavow and disclaim them as soon as brought to its notice."

I can assure you, sir, that this convention was submitted to the examination and appreciation of his Majesty's Government by the minister of the Emperor at Washington and that it is entirely approved. His excellency the minister of foreign affairs, while admitting the necessity of regulating the details of an operation so important and so delicate as that under consideration, did not doubt for an instant the impartiality and purity of intention of the minister, the admiral, and the consul who prepared this convention. The idea of a possible construction like that which forms the subject of the communication that you have done me the honor to address me did not enter the minds of the men who elaborated the form of this convention which, besides, expired on the 23d April and has not been renewed.

I shall not insist further, sir, in order to convince you that not only had we never conceived the inadmissible idea of displeasing you but that, on the contrary, we were constantly solicitous to show the deference due to your position and imposed on us by your obliging conduct in this matter. The explanation above given will suffice, I doubt not, to enlighten you fully on a question in which, as soon as all errors are dispelled, you will perceive nothing but candor, the desire to do right, and a disposition in accordance with the circumstances.

Be pleased to accept, sir, the assurances of the high consideration with which I have the honor to be

Your very humble and obedient servant,

ALFRED PAUL.

Hon. J. P. BENJAMIN,
Secretary of State, Department of State, Richmond.

[Enclosure.]

DEPARTMENT OF STATE,
Richmond, May 28, 1864.

SIR: I have the honor to acknowledge receipt of your letter of 24th instant, and before responding to its contents beg to be informed of the precise meaning to be attached to the following passage:

Les événements du moment constituaient un cas de force majeure qui m'à décidé à faire expédier le Bidwell de Norfolk, etc.

My doubt is as to the force of the word "expedier" used in this passage. Will you be good enough to explain whether the vessel and cargo were cleared from the Federal customhouse at Norfolk and what shipping papers or other ship's documents were taken at Norfolk by the master of the *Bidwell.*

I am, very respectfully, your obedient servant,

J. P. BENJAMIN,
Secretary of State.

ALFRED PAUL, Esq.,
French Consul, Richmond, Va.

[Enclosure.]

DEPARTMENT OF STATE,
Richmond, May 30, 1864.

SIR: I have the honor to acknowledge receipt of your communication of the 26th instant, the contents of which furnish to this Government the acceptable assurance that no part of the convention signed at Washington on the 23d November last was inspired on the part of those who represented the French Government by any motive to which this Government could take exception, but that on the contrary yourself and your colleagues were actuated by a sincere desire to do what you deemed right and proper under the circumstances, with full regard to the moral and material interests of all parties.

This assurance is received with gratification, and relieves all the unpleasant impressions which would naturally result from any intentional encroachment on national dignity; but the very fact that a convention of this character could be entered into by a neutral Government actuated with the best intentions reveals most clearly the false basis on which our relations with European powers still rest. This reflection assumes increased gravity when we are informed that the agreement was, contrary to the impressions of the President, "submitted to the examination and appreciation of his Majesty's Government, and entirely approved." It is incredible to us that the provisions of this instrument could have been considered admissible by the representatives of his Imperial Majesty in Washington, Richmond, and the Tuileries, if this Government has been regarded by them as independent, even de facto. We feel that this approval would have been withheld if the usual sure judgment and thorough appreciation of international relations which distinguish the public servants of the Emperor had not been warped by the erroneous views as to our position which the United States have succeeded in inculcating, and which seem to have taken such root in the public opinion of Europe that neither facts nor arguments can prevail in eradicating them.

Thence it is, sir, that in your whole letter not one word is said in relation to the point on which we felt specially aggrieved. We had, we could have, no reason to object to your using every precaution you deemed proper in order to prevent, while your vessels were in our ports, the occurrence of the difficulties and embarrassments which you indicate as requiring the use of preventive measures. It might, perhaps, have appeared to us an excess of prudence to prohibit communication between our people and the crew of a neutral vessel about to depart on a trans-Atlantic voyage without touching at an enemy's port, but it would assuredly have offered no ground of remark, still less of complaint. What we do consider objectionable is this, that you should have bound yourself by convention with our enemies to observe certain rules of conduct in our ports and to introduce amongst us without our consent inhabitants of the enemy's country to be employed as laborers within our jurisdiction. Such a convention carries with it an implication on which we are particularly sensitive and which has already been the subject of a representation to the French Government. It implies the existence of rights on the part of the United States to exercise powers of Government in our territory, and is a concession of their pretentions that we are not independent of their control. If Spain and England had been at war, would neutral France have agreed by convention with England to carry English laborers into a Spanish port, or to subject French vessels in a Spanish port to such regulations as are contained in this convention? It is plain that, on the contrary, stipulations of this nature would, in the case supposed, have instantly excited attention as being inconsistent with the rights of Spain as an independent nation, and the fact that these provisions appeared quite natural and proper, when applied to us, affords an unmistakable proof that we are regarded in a different light.

It can not therefore be, sir, matter of surprise, that in the assertion of our right to be considered as an independent nation, we should still retain, as to the character of the convention in question the impressions conveyed in my former communication, while we renew the expression of our gratification in accepting your assurances of the impartial and even friendly motives which guided the agents of His Imperial Majesty in the action to which we have felt compelled to expect.

I am, very respectfully, your obedient servant,

J. P. BENJAMIN,
Secretary of State.

ALFRED PAUL, Esq.,
Consul of France, Richmond.

[Enclosure.]

DEPARTMENT OF STATE,
Richmond, May 31, 1864.

SIR: I have the honor to acknowledge receipt of your letter of the 24th instant (and the explanatory letter of the 28th written in answer to mine of the 26th), giving an account of the facts and circumstances attendant upon the sudden departure of the French vessels from City Point, and the subsequent sailing of the *Bidwell* for France with the few hogsheads of tobacco which had been placed on board before your operations were interrupted by the interference of the Federal authorities.

The frank explanation given by you of the manner in which you were forced by the acts of the Federal commander (acts which it is for your Government, not for ours, to appreciate), to depart from the terms of the agreement made with us, and to forward the cargo of the *Bidwell* without a clearance from the Richmond Custom House, has satisfied this Government that your failure to fulfill the obligation imposed by the agreement was quite involuntary, and that there was entire good faith in your motives and intentions.

I am therefore gratified to assure you that no unpleasant impression on this subject remains on our minds.

I am, very respectfully, your obedient servant,

J. P. BENJAMIN,
Secretary of State.

ALFRED PAUL, Esq.,
Consul of France, Richmond.

No. 39.]   DEPARTMENT OF STATE,
                                       Richmond, June 1, 1864.

SIR: I write merely to acknowledge receipt of your dispatch No. —
of — April. After a hasty perusal it was handed to the President,
but he has been so exclusively occupied with the military movements
around Richmond, that he has not been able to read and return it. I
can not therefore state its exact number and date, and simply mention
the fact of the receipt.

The accompanying dispatch No. 38 gives you full information on
the subject of the export of the French tobacco and exhibits the
manner in which the Federal authorities have trifled with the French
agents, after succeeding in involving them in a convention which
should never have been signed. How long will Europe permit itself
to be treated with the haughty and insolent contempt exhibited in
every act of the Washington Cabinet? The spectacle is indeed a
strange one, and is explicable solely on the assumption of Federal
success in inculcating a belief of their readiness to declare war against
England or France, an act that even their moonstruck folly would
shrink from.

Our military situation is grave and of intense interest. The result
is looked to, however, with a calm confidence. I shall not attempt
to give you any views of it, as this dispatch will be anticipated by the
much later intelligence you will receive via New York.

I am, very respectfully, your obedient servant,
                                            J. P. BENJAMIN,
                                              Secretary of State.
Hon. JOHN SLIDELL,
        Paris, France.

                                                       JUNE 2.
P. S.—Your Nos. 60 and 61 of 2d and 5th May this moment received
and deciphered.
                                            J. P. BENJAMIN,
                                              Secretary of State.

———————

No. 8.]   16 RUE DE MARIGNAN,
                                       Paris, June 1, 1864.

SIR: In my last (being No. 7 of the 12th of April ultimo) I told
you that I had assumed the responsibility of instructing Messrs.
Snowball & Copeland, solicitors at Liverpool, to employ counsel for
the defense of the three men in custody, at the instance of Mr. Adams,
minister of the United States, and held for extradition on the charge
of piracy, in seizing the ship *Gerrity* from Matamoras to New York,
on board which they were passengers. I have the honor to transmit
herewith a duplicate of that dispatch which contains my reasons for
doing so.

I have now the pleasure to inform you that these men were discharged on habeas corpus by the court of queen's bench on the 25th
of May, the chief justice sustaining the arrest and the claim to extradition, and his three associates overruling his judgment. The
case was ably argued by eminent counsel on the part of the United
States, and as ably defended on our part, for consecutive days, as
I find from the report at large in the newspapers. I have preserved

the arguments and the opinions of the judges, which I will send you when an opportunity serves, avoiding the heavy postage. The case turned and the discharge was ordered on the construction of the treaty; that the offense of "piracy" mentioned in the treaty did not mean piracy jure gentium, but was confined to piracy, so declared to be by the domestic laws of either country. I instructed our counsel to say that the defense was assumed by Mr. Mason, on the part of the Confederate States, as its representative in Europe, and to defend the capture as an act of war. I have not yet received the bill of costs for the defense, but as I have said in my No. 7, will defray them out of the contingent fund, to be adjusted by an appropriate voucher hereafter, as the expenditure does not belong to that class.

I hope what I have done in the matter will have the approval of the Department.

On Saturday last, the 28th of May, I received a letter from our most earnest and valued friend, Mr. Lindsay, dated at London the day before. He had some months ago given notice of a motion to be made in the House of Commons, on the 3d of June, to the effect "that her Majesty's Government should avail itself of the earliest opportunity of mediating, in conjunction with the other powers of Europe, to bring about a cessation of hostilities in America," and the chief object of his letter to me was to say that he had on the day before sought an interview with Lord Palmerston, in the hope of conciliating the support of the Government to his motion; that he was to see him again, and yet hoped for a favorable result. He said further that in the course of the conversation he expressed his regret that Lord Palmerston had not seen me whilst I was in England, because he thought if he had done so, as one having the confidence of my Government and people and well informed about their affairs and position, I might have given him useful and valuable information; and in this connection asked whether it would be agreeable to his lordship to see and converse with me yet, as a private gentleman, to which, after further conversation, Lord P. replied that it would give him pleasure to see me, with Mr. Lindsay, either on the Monday or Tuesday following (yesterday or day before) at his residence in London. Mr. Lindsay said he told Lord Palmerston that he had proposed the interview "without any communication with [me] on the subject," and strongly pressed that I should go to London for this purpose. Mr. Lindsay added that Lord Palmerston told him "that he had of late received two communications, not official, from the Emperor, who seemed by them to be very anxious that something should now be attempted to stop hostilities."

I replied to Mr. Lindsay by the following mail that I had maturely considered his proposition, and with every disposition to comply with it as his request, "but" (I quote from my letter) "I am not at liberty to do so, and that I may not seem fastidious, after his lordship's kind assent to your proposal that he should see me, I will tell you frankly why. After the persistent refusal of her Majesty's Government to recognize in any form the existence of the Confederate States, I was directed by the President to consider my mission to England at an end and to withdraw from London, and further instructions connected with my residence on the Continent, express the desire of the President that in regard to Great Britain I should not again approach it, even in the most informal manner, without some intimation from that Government of its disposition to enter into official relations with my own."

"Had the suggestion you make, of an interview and conversation with Lord Palmerston, originated with his lordship, I might not have felt myself prohibited by my instructions from at once acceding to it, but as it has the form only of his assent to a proposition from you, I must, with all respect, decline it.

"Although no longer accredited by my Government as special commissioner to Great Britain, I am yet in Europe with full powers, and therefore had Lord Palmerston expressed a desire to see me, as his own act (of course, unofficially) and even without any reason assigned for the interview, I should have had great pleasure in complying with his request."

And in a private note to Mr. Lindsay, I told him that he was at liberty, if he thought proper, to show my letter to Lord Palmerston. On the following day (yesterday) I heard again from Mr. Lindsay under date of the 30th. He said that on receipt of my letter he again called on Lord Palmerston and read it to him, when there followed more than half an hour's conversation on American affairs, during which his lordship said he did not see how recognition would terminate the war, unless the Government was prepared to go further "to raise the blockade, etc.," a position which Mr. Lindsay combated by views (inter alia) which I had presented to him in previous letters. He does not report the conversation in detail, but said that Lord P. "again expressed his opinion that the subjugation of the South could not be effected by the North," and added, "that he thought the people of the North were becoming more and more alive to this fact every day." In regard to what I had written, Lord P. said, "that as he had nothing to say to me more than he had said to him (Lindsay) he could not think of asking me to come from Paris to see him, but that if I were in London he would be very glad to see me, as he wished to know me and would like to hear my views on the present state of affairs."

In regard to Lindsay's resolution, he said that Lord P.'s "feelings" were in favor of it; asked him to leave a copy that he might consult his colleagues, and thought it had better be postponed for a short time, to which Mr. L. acceded. At the close of his letter Mr. L. adds, "Now, apart altogether from your seeing Lord Palmerston, I must earnestly entreat you to come here, unless you are much.wanted in Paris; your visit here as a private gentleman can do no harm, and *may at the present moment be of great service to your country.*" (Underscoring his.)

You are aware that there are in England a number of gentlemen, chiefly members of the two Houses of Parliament, associated as the friends of Southern independence. · It seems that Mr. Lindsay showed my letter at one of their meetings, declining his proposal to see Lord Palmerston. I have this morning letters from two of them, earnestly pressing that I should return for a while to London, of course, in a private capacity, whether I saw Lord Palmerston or no, and I have in consequence determined to do so. I have of course kept Mr. Slidell advised of the correspondence, and he agrees with me that, after declining at first, it would manifest indifference or churlishness to refuse even to visit London, though so urgently pressed by friends who are actively at work on our behalf to come to their aid. Whether or no I shall see Lord P. will depend upon circumstances after I get there, and the counsels of judicious friends. I shall in no way court publicity, and of one thing be assured, that no one, friend or foe, shall look upon me as a suitor.

* * * * * * *

I have the honor to be, your very obedient servant,

J. M. MASON.

Hon. J. P. BENJAMIN,
   Secretary of State.

No. 63.]   PARIS, *June 2, 1864.*

SIR: I am still without later dispatches from you than your No. 34, of 28 March, although we have Nassau dates up to 9th ultimo. Since my last of 21st ultimo the two corvettes at Bordeaux have been sold to the Prussian Government, which has also become the purchaser of the second ram building at the same place. The original owners of all these vessels will be reimbursed for all moneys expended on them with interest and a small percentage of profit. They were induced to take this course by a conviction of the impossibility of employing the ships in the manner first intended. The builders of the two remaining corvettes persist in saying that they will deliver them to us at sea, but I have been so grievously deceived and disappointed heretofore that I am far from placing implicit reliance on their assurances. I am quite satisfied that no further attempts to fit out ships of war in Europe should be made at present, but I am every day more and more fully convinced that when the war shall have ceased one of our earliest cares should be to lay the foundation of a respectable navy. We must indulge in no Arcadian dreams of following undisturbed the peaceful pursuits of agriculture; instead of the millennium, which the peace philosophers pronounced some ten years ago to have arrived, there has been a series of bloody wars culminating in the most terrific struggle which the world has ever witnessed. The condition of national existences now is the capacity of each to defend itself and inflict injury on others; the weak have no rights, the strong no obligations. The much-vaunted reign of public opinion throughout the world is powerless to save Denmark from the most lawless spoliation, although her integrity was guaranteed by the great powers of Europe.

The justice of our cause, the heroism of our troops, the devotion of our people, while they excite the sympathies and command the admiration of Europe, not only have failed to secure us any friendly support from abroad but even a fair neutrality. The strongest powers submit to the insolent demands of the Lincoln Government, that their commerce may be safe on the ocean and Mexico and Canada unmolested, and why? Because they have formed an exaggerated estimate of its capacity to do mischief.

Ex-Senator [W. M.] Gwin is on his way to Mexico. His object is to colonize Sonora with persons of Southern birth or proclivities residing in California. He bears an autograph letter from Louis Napoleon to the French commander in chief, warmly recommending his enterprise. His scheme has been fully examined and approved and offers, as I believe, fair chances of success. If carried out its consequences will be most beneficial.

The crops of cereals in France, although they will not be quite as abundant as those of last year, promise a fair average, and, as there will be a considerable surplus remaining over after the harvest, there will be no market here for Yankee breadstuffs. Appearances are equally favorable throughout Europe. This is perhaps of less consequence than last year, as from the scarcity of laborers and other causes it would appear that the North will have no excessive supply for its own consumption.

Mr. Mason having received from a friend in England information that Lord Palmerston had intimated a disposition not to oppose a motion tending toward an offer of mediation and saying also that he, Lord P., had recently received from the Emperor two messages manifesting his desire to act in American affairs, I saw M. de Persigny not only to let him know these facts but to post him on the subject of the *Rappahannock* and the very extraordinary coursé of the foreign minister, of whom he is a most bitter enemy. He has promised to ask an early interview of the Emperor, when he will urge a new appeal to Lord P. I have also taken care to impress upon him the true state of the Mexican question, repeating the views embodied in my No. 58.

Mr. Gutierrez de Estrada called to see me a few days since on his return from Rome, whither he had accompanied the new Emperor. He was evidently disposed to elicit some expressions of my opinions as to the course Mexican affairs would take, but I carefully avoided giving any, wishing to let him understand that I had ceased, as is indeed the case, to feel any interest in them. Perhaps after all it is better that we should be quite untrammeled as to our future movements in that direction.

I called on my friend at the foreign affairs on the 30th ultimo, to enquire respecting the messages said to have been sent by the Emperor to Lord Palmerston, and also about the affair of the *Rappahannock*. The next day I received from him the following note:

I conversed yesterday evening with M. Drouyn de Lhuys on the two points that you desired to clear up, viz, the overtures Lord Palmerston had received from the Tuileries on the advances made in the interests of the cessation of the hostilities between the Federals and Confederates and the *Rappahannock* affair.

On the first point M. Drouyn de Lhuys told me he had no knowledge of the fact in question; there was, however, nothing improbable in this fact, since, as the minister observed, the thought which might have inspired these overtures existed and still remains. As to the *Rappahannock*, M. Drouyn de Lhuys waits the report of M. [Raymond Théodore] Troplong, and affirms that he has absolutely nothing to do with the delay which this phase of the affair has undergone.

You will be amused or, it may rather be, disgusted with the unqualified manner in which the minister denies having had anything to do with the delay in the report on the *Rappahannock*. After what I have said in previous dispatches of that functionary, you will have no difficulty in deciding whether he or the president of the Senate be better entitled to credence on an issue of veracity.

You will, I think, derive from this note, as I do, confirmation of the statement said to have been made by Lord Palmerston; the minister may not have chosen to admit the fact of renewed overtures or, as is very probable, the Emperor may have made them without his intervention or knowledge. I have more than once had occasion to know of his thus acting in grave matters.

I have received from the foreign affairs, but not through the same channel as the above, a memorandum on the subject of the shipment of the tobacco of the Régie from Richmond, which I give you, as it evidences the anxiety of Seward to make himself agreeable to the Emperor:

WASHINGTON, *May 10, 1864.*

The French Government has obtained from the Cabinet at Washington permission to search in the Confederate territory for a certain quantity of tobacco bought before the war and to export it. A convention convened last November with the sanction of the French legation in the United States has established the conditions of that concession and fixed the limit and line of conduct to be followed by the ships and the French officers who shall be authorized to enter the enemy's possessions. After a long delay occasioned by political circumstances and by the fear of giving offense to the other foreign powers to whom the same favor was not granted the convention of November was at last put into execution, and in the first fortnight of April the French corvette *La Tisiphone,* accompanied by two or three merchant ships chartered for that purpose, was authorized to proceed to Fortress Monroe, and to go up the James River to a place near Richmond called City Point, where the embarkation of the tobacco belonging to the "Régie Française" should have taken place. Mr. Paul, French consul at Richmond, accompanied the *Tisiphone.* But hardly had the work commenced than the Cabinet at Washington asked very courteously of the chargé d'affaires of France to grant its interruption. This demand was supported by reasons of such a nature that it was impossible for the French legation not to comply with it. In fact the French ships received simultaneously the invitation of the chargé d'affaires of France and of the Federal Government to leave City Point and the James River. This measure was necessitated by the military movements which were concentrating at this time on the James River and on the side of Richmond that the Federals had the intention of attacking next, it was said, and secrecy was naturally one of the conditions of success to the plans of the Union Army in Virginia. But the interruption of the operations commenced for the embarkation of the tobacco did not imply any coolness on the part of the Cabinet at Washington nor any thought of not holding to its agreement. It was simply a new delay imposed by the fortunes of war. As the campaign has just seriously commenced, it is to be feared that this delay will now be prolonged during several months.

We have here New York papers up to 18th ultimo, giving the Northern version of the military operations in Virginia; even through this false and distorting medium we can see enough to relieve us from any anxiety as to the safety of Richmond, but we are earnestly praying to hear of some decisive, crushing blow, which will virtually put an end to the campaign in that region. Should our hopes be realized I believe that even the selfishness and "vis inertiae" of Lord Palmerston will give way before an overpowering outburst of popular opinion in England and the overtures of Louis Napoleon be used as a pretext for granting what can no longer be denied without the loss of all the veteran premier holds dear—place and power.

Since my No. 60 of 2d May £83,600 seven per cent cotton bonds have been presented to me for conversion and canceled.

I have the honor to be, with great respect, your most obedient servant,

JOHN SLIDELL.

Hon. J. P. BENJAMIN,
　　Secretary of State.

No. 43.]

CONFEDERATE STATES COMMERCIAL AGENCY AT LONDON,

Paris, June 3, 1864.

SIR: Dating the present dispatch away from my proper post, I can not do better than to devote it exclusively to the subject which calls me here. My first duty upon entering into this new field of operations was, of course, to make myself acquainted with what might not inaptly be termed the "physiology" of the French press. It required but ordinary attention to discover that for any judgment of practical value the English standard must be entirely laid aside. You are confronted not by a different degree, but by a radically different system of journalism. I do not merely refer to those obvious distinctions, such as the small size, the comparative scantiness of editorial comments, and the prominence given to miscellaneous trifles, in which the French press rather resembles our own than any other. Yet, even these distinctions, it is important to keep in view. The feuilleton, though its popularity is waning, still occupies a larger space than an English daily journal could habitually devote to reviews. The French newspaper, therefore, is always pressed for space and naturally impatient of argument on any subject not immediately attracting public curiosity. The English journal is compelled by an immemorial usage to give its readers daily a fixed quantity of essays in the shape of "leaders"—not an easy task; the French journal never speaks editorially except for a specific purpose, and the compulsory signature attaches to what is thus said a personal responsibility from which the English writer is exempt: It follows that the editorial columns of a French paper are far more difficult of access.

There are below the surface greater dissimilarities still. Paradoxical as it may appear at first sight, in this country of centralization the periodical political press is less metropolitan than in England; that is to say, the journals of the capital have relatively less and those of the Provinces relatively more power. In England nearly the whole of the power of the press is concentrated upon London, the London papers being read almost simultaneously in every town and village of the United Kingdom; here this power is broken up into a number of centers of which Paris is one, but not the only one.

Secondly, the French press is in no degree cosmopolitan. With the exception of the Indépendance Belge of Brussels, but few, if any, newspapers in the French language maintain regularly a staff of correspondents abroad. At least nine-tenths of what purports to be foreign correspondence is manufactured in the office, and this is so well understood that instead of being a fraud upon the reader it is simply a convenient form. All translations from papers in other languages, even English, are made for the whole French press, both Parisian and provincial, by an agency, the Agency Havas, which daily furnishes to each journal a copious selection ready to hand, from which each editor takes what suits him and comments upon it after his fashion. It is clear, therefore, that whatever is not contained in the "Blue Sheet" of Havas can only by the merest accident reach the columns of a French paper, and, on the other hand, whatever is there contained can scarcely escape the notice of every editor in the Empire. Here, then, is the true focus of centralization, which seems at first to be paradoxically wanting.

Thirdly, the French press is almost entirely in the hands of professional writers, while the English press derives its most valuable assistance from men of every profession, including the highest social spheres. It results from this that the French press is intellectual rather than intelligent, and furthermore that it represents cliques, sets, individuals, idiosyncrasies, rather than classes or shades of public opinion. If I have succeeded in expressing my idea you will be at no loss to understand why a person attempting negotiations with this press should find it, to him at least, so much more unscrupulous and mercenary than the English.

When I had concluded my preliminary survey of the ground, it seemed to me that the French press was indifferent, rather than ill-disposed on the subject of our affairs. I counted in Paris only two daily papers absolutely hostile, at least three friendly, though languid, and the rest ready to accept the more popular side. It was a case requiring, so to speak, judicious stimulants—a quickening of the general circulation. With this view I took steps to supply the French papers—collectively as well as separately—with an abundance of well-authenticated and valuable information. The admirable staff of American correspondents of the Index afforded me the materials for letters, the special telegraphic information of the Times for telegrams. I did this carefully, honestly, and as far as was humanly possible, impartially. The absorbing interest of military events made such information especially acceptable, and, as I had calculated beforehand, did more to aid my operations than all my most diligent and well-directed efforts could have done. When the campaign fairly opened in Virginia, my organization was already in good working order. Judging by the Moniteur, I am inclined to believe that the Government took special pains to neutralize the one-sided Northern reports; at all events I found myself silently but effectively aided.

Thus I have had the satisfaction of seeing the columns of the French papers filled with correspondence from New York, New Orleans, and Richmond, of seeing even enemies publish valuable facts for the purpose of controverting them; in other words, the French writing world occupying itself sedulously with our affairs. The consequence was inevitable. Editorial writers must comment upon what appears in their columns, and news items and facts are the true seed from which spring " leaders." So it has happened that of late many admirable articles have been written by men whom I have not even the pleasure of knowing, and who most probably would resent any attempt to bribe them into writing these same articles. I am convinced that simple " writing us up " is of no value. It is like sticking a rootless plant into the ground, and " making believe " that it grew there. Editorials, in my opinion, have no importance except as evidences of a maturing public opinion (it is only in extremely rare cases and under exceptional circumstances that they initiate it), and to serve as evidence they must be genuine and spontaneous.

Having explained my principle of action—for the most important particulars of the execution I must refer you to a previous dispatch—I have to report what I did not think it expedient to do or to recommend to you. I have had several newspapers offered to me, among them a daily Parisian paper, on various terms. I have, on mature reflection, thought it proper to politely decline all these offers, and I have even discontinued, at the earliest practical opportunity, a subsidy which had been received under arrangements made by my predecessor. I have arrived at this determination because I feel certain that an organ, in the ordinary French sense of the word, can be of little service to us. A paper thoroughly devoted to us and representing our political philosophy in all its bearings might, indeed, perform the same functions here as the Index in England, but this would be too serious an undertaking for me to attempt a second time. But a paper undertaking the advocacy of our cause by contract and as a means of adding to its revenue, is, I repeat, an ally of questionable utility. I prefer to expend the same amount in salaries to competent agents who have the interests of the cause sincerely at heart, though I confess that such are more difficult to find and to make available than newspapers who need subsidies.

Organized as my work here is now, it will not be necessary for me to make any prolonged stay in Paris, as I can feed the stream of American "intelligence" equally well and, indeed, better from London. All that remains is to select my circle of personal acquaintances, and this, thanks to Mr. Slidell, who has already introduced me to the editors of several leading daily papers, I am in a fair way of doing.

I have the honor to remain, with great respect, your obedient servant,

HENRY HOTZE.

Hon. J. P. BENJAMIN,
   Secretary of State, Richmond.

No. 9.]   LONDON, *June 9, 1864.*

SIR. * * * Having taken the step of coming to London, in seeming departure from your instructions previously given, I was much gratified to find in yours of 18th April that those instructions were modified so far as to leave such movements more at my discretion.

I have had a long conversation since my arrival here with Mr. Lindsay in regard to the subject of our correspondence before I left Paris, treated of in my last dispatch. Following up his hope of conciliating the ministry in favor of his resolution, he had a few days ago an interview with Lord Russell, in which, whilst evincing every disposition to consider the resolution favorably, he yet made no committal to give it his support or that of the ministerial party. I gave you the tenor of the resolution in my last. He said that Lord Russell expressed the decided opinion that the North could never overcome the South and his belief that the people of the North were getting to be alive to the fact, but that in all his conversations with Mr. Adams the latter spoke as confidently as ever, and, amongst other things, that Mr. Adams said that his Government did not consider it of any great moment whether they succeeded in their movement against Richmond or no; that their greatest object was to maintain the control of the Mississippi. Such seems the chaff with which the foreign office is plied. I had learned from other sources that Mr. Disraeli had said to one of his friends and followers that if the South should obtain a decided success in the pending campaign against Richmond, he would be prepared to bring forward a motion of some such character as that of Mr. Lindsay. I told this to Mr. Lindsay, who agreed at once that it could not be in better hands and under such auspices would certainly carry the ministry non obstante. Yielding to the suggestions of Lord Palmerston to await the result of the pending movement against Richmond, Mr. Lindsay has deferred his motion to the 17th instant. I think as to its success that everything will depend on the campaign in Virginia. Should Grant be routed or finally driven back, either the ministry would have to entertain a resolution favorable to us in some form or the opposition would make it an issue with them. Indeed, I am satisfied that so general, almost universal, is popular sentiment in England with the South, accompanied by such strong impressions of the unnecessary and dreadful carnage which attends the war, that if we have the anticipated success in Virginia, the ministry, even if disposed to resist, would have to yield to the popular sentiment.

I shall remain in London as long as I think I may be useful here, in intercourse with our friends, by whom I have been very warmly and kindly received.

*   *   *   *   *   *   *

I have the honor to be, very respectfully, your obedient servant,

J. M. MASON.

Hon. J. P. BENJAMIN,
    Secretary of State.

No. 9.]   LONDON, *June 9, 1864.*

SIR: My last was my No. 8 from Paris, dated June 1, instant, of which I have the honor to enclose a duplicate herewith.

I came to London on the 5th instant for the reasons and with the object stated in my last. Yesterday I had the pleasure to receive your No. 35 of the 18th April last, with the postscript bearing date the 22d, containing a draft for £500 from the secret-service fund, remitted in accordance with suggestions contained in my No. 1 of the 25th January, and for the expenditure of which I am to account to the Department of State in the manner stated in your dispatch.

I received at same time and under same cover yours of 29th April, merely enclosing a duplicate of the draft, with an extract relating to it from your No. 35.

These dispatches came, I presume, by the Bermuda mail, and the envelope bearing the imprint " Confederate States of America, Department of State," had the following address: " Hon. J. M. Mason, Paris, France." It bore also the post-office impression, " Paris, 6 Juin, post restante " and the endorsement, " via Legation des Etats Unis," and below that the further endorsement, " parti rue de Marignan, M. Slidell." It was transmitted to me from Paris, I presume, by Mr. Slidell. All this would import that in consequence of the general form of the address to me at Paris, without street or number, it was first retained at the post restante; afterwards the endorsement would show it was sent and submitted to the legation of the United States at Paris, and we are left to infer that we are indebted to the courtesy of that legation, seeing that it was an official letter from the Department of State of the Confederacy, the suggestion was probably made that it should be sent to Mr. Slidell, his number and street being correctly given in the subsequent endorsement. I have thought it proper to advert to this so fully to show the consequences of carelessness in the address at the Department. Since I was recalled from London I suggested in my dispatches that until I had a fixed residence, those intended for me should be addressed to the care of Mr. Hotze, No. 17 Saville Row, London; and I would suggest that precise directions on this head, to avoid risk, be given to the clerk having charge of the subject.

  *   *   *   *   *   *   *

  I have, etc.,

              J. M. MASON.

Hon. J. P. BENJAMIN,
   Secretary of State.

                  JUNE 10.

P. S.—I have just had an interview with Mr. Wyon, who is executing the seal. He tells me that it will certainly be ready within a fortnight. He will send with it a supply of prepared wax and other appendages for connecting the seal with the document. I thought it better to have these supplies sent in the absence of the proper materials in the Confederacy; and will look out for some opportunity by an officer or other trusty person to take charge of them.

  I have, etc.,

              J. M. MASON.

No. 44.]
   CONFEDERATE STATES COMMERCIAL AGENCY AT LONDON,
            PARIS, *June 10, 1864.*

SIR: As the Bermuda mail day finds me still in Paris, I can do little more than acknowledge receipt of your Nos. 18 and 19, respectively, dated 22d April and 5th May. All of the enclosures, which are duplicates, had been previously received in the original—the Treasury warrant of 24th February by regular mail, the letter of Mr. Mallory and photographic copy of Dahlgren papers by secret conveyance—and similarly acknowledged. The Dahlgren papers have since been reproduced in the Autographic Mirror, of which I shall continue by various opportunities to transmit copies for distribution. You will probably have observed that I have taken the liberty of publishing the correspondence between Mr. Mallory and Sir Roundell Palmer. I did not do this until after sufficient time had elapsed to fully convince me that the attorney general's merely casual reference to it in Parliament had altogether escaped public attention, and even that of the members, and that therefore without the publication Mr. Mallory's object would be defeated.

I have had much pleasure in communicating to Rev. Mr. Bannon your commendatory remarks about his services. He considers his mission to Ireland successfully accomplished, and I have therefore not hesitated to sanction his accompanying the Right Rev. Bishop Lynch to Rome as chaplain, in which capacity he is now with the bishop in Paris en route. He will from Rome continue correspondence with the Irish press and leading members of the clergy. On this subject, as well as in reference to Lieutenant Capston, I shall be able to write you more at length on my return to London.

Your instructions in No.. 19 regarding the men implicated in the *Gerrity* affair had been substantially anticipated by Mr. Mason; and, as you have been already advised, the case has terminated in a manner which is at once satisfactory to our feelings and confirmatory of your views on its legal merits. As Mr. Mason has from the first had the conduct of the affair, and intended to pay the expenses out of the contingent fund of the commission, you will probably agree with me that I should take no action upon your instructions unless applied to by him. I may observe, without having had any conversation with Mr. Mason on the subject, that I believe the use of his name by the prisoners' counsel to have been unauthorized and only a device in their favor, and that the judges correctly appreciated the position which you wish the Government to occupy in this as in similar cases. Your last instructions in the *Chesapeake* case, with which Mr. Slidell acquainted me, will enable me to set this clearly before the public in an editorial form.

The "Confederate Appeal," enclosed in your No. 18, shall receive due attention and be used to the best of my ability.

The work in the French press continues satisfactory. I sent you a random selection of papers only to show the amount and general accuracy of American intelligence which is now almost daily presented to the public. Of argument there is as yet but little, the ground being scarcely yet prepared. There are, however, gratifying indications, and I would particularly direct your attention to an admirable little article in the Patrie of to-day; also to an article in the Courrier du Dimanche, which, with all its Gallic absurdities, is, from such a writer and in such a place, the most influential liberal paper in France of favorable omen.

In England great events are perhaps preparing. There are symptoms that if the news from Virginia continues favorable the two great parties may run a race in winning the credit of recognition. But our hopes have so often deceived us that I will not venture upon any. speculations until I can judge of the situation on the spot. I have the honor to remain,

Very respectfully, your obedient servant,

HENRY HOTZE.

Hon. J. P. BENJAMIN,
    Secretary of State.

Mem. Dispatches Nos. 18 and 19 received in Paris on 7th June.

No. 64.]   PARIS, *June 11, 1864.*

SIR: I have the honor to acknowledge the receipt of your Nos. 35 and 37 of 16th and 30th April and your letter of 29th April, not numbered, covering duplicate of draft No. 606 for £500; the omission to number is probably an inadvertence, as there does not appear to be any hiatus in your dispatches.

Since my last of 2d instant Bishop Lynch has arrived here; he will proceed to his ultimate destination in a few days. He appears to be admirably well fitted for the duties assigned to him and it has afforded me great pleasure to give him all the aid and information in my power.

The affair of the *Rappahannock* continuing to drag on without any apparent prospect of its speedy solution, I, after consultation with Commodore Barron on the 9th instant, addressed to the minister of foreign affairs a letter of which I annex a copy marked "A," sending a duplicate of it to the Emperor, who is now at Fontainebleau, through Mr. Mocquard. I hope that the President will approve of the course I have taken and of the tone of my letter, in which I have endeavored to temper firmness with courtesy, but I shall not be at all surprised should Mr. Drouyn de Lhuys be displeased with it, more especially as he can not but feel conscious of having made undue concessions to propitiate Mr. Lincoln.

Mr. Eustis writes from London that, being a few evenings since at a reception of Earl Shaftesbury, the earl offered to present him to Lord Palmerston, with whom he had a long and interesting conversation, in the course of which Lord P. declared very emphatically his preference for the South, his hostility towards the Lincoln Government, and his absolute confidence in our ability to maintain our independence; in short Mr. E. says no Confederate could have spoken more warmly and decidedly. In all this Lord P. expressed I believe his real sentiments, which are of very little moment to us so long as his acts are in direct contradiction to them; but as Mr. Mason is now in London he will of course keep you fully informed of the state of things there. Mr. M. consulted me as to the propriety of his going to England and showed me various letters from our friends there strohgly urging a visit. I thought that he could not, without appearing indifferent or churlish, reject counsels proceeding from men of high positions, well informed and devoted to our interests; that he should take the responsibility of deviating from the letter of your instructions in this particular.

I regret deeply the sale of the ships at Bordeaux, since the President after being informed of the state of things here, thinks that it would have been better to have proceeded to complete them and await events.

The order for the sale was given by Captain Bulloch after full consultation with Messrs. Mason, McRae, Commodore Barron, and myself. In coming to this conclusion, financial considerations had no inconsiderable influence. At that time the seven per cent cotton loan was very much depressed, and sales of that portion of the bonds which had been bought in for the Government could only have been made at a serious sacrifice. The present system of shipments of cotton had not been adopted, the proceeds of the loan had all been exhausted by actual expenditure or pledged to meet unmatured engagements, and there was no quarter from whence Mr. McRae could reasonably hope to procure the funds which might be imperatively required for the purchase of supplies for the army. Under these circumstances we all thought it unwise to lock up so large an amount of money for an indefinite period without any reasonable prospect of making use of the ships until the occasion for employing them against the enemy should have passed.

The evil, however, in my opinion is not irremediable. We shall probably know in a few days whether the war between Denmark and the German powers will be resumed or put an end to by the deliberations of the London conference. In the one case the ships can not be permitted to go to sea without a breach of neutrality, in the other at least one of the purchasers will be disposed to get rid of an expensive outlay on an object for which it will have no immediate use.

This is not a mere conjecture. The ship nominally purchased by Sweden is in fact for Denmark, and the finances of that Government will be in no condition to enable it to indulge in expensive luxuries. If Prussia do not secure Kiel for a dockyard, she must, perforce, abandon the idea of becoming a naval power, and will not care to retain the vessels, which can only be repaired in foreign ports. I believe that there is a very good chance of our being enabled to purchase all the ships should circumstances render such a course expedient.

I have shown your dispatch to Mr. Holcombe, of 20th April, to Mr. Hotze, who will give a short résumé of it in the Index. This is the most convenient form to give the publicity which I presume you desire, to the fact that " we disavow any claim founded on the capture of the *Chesapeake*."

There is a very admirable map of Virginia on a large scale published by the State. The campaigns of Virginia will have for all time deep historic interest, but they are now studied with intense curiosity by the soldiers and statesmen of Europe.

The Emperor on one occasion in tracing McClellan's attempt on Richmond expressed to me his regret not to have a better map of the seat of war; a copy of the State map would, I am sure, be very acceptable to him. I would like also to present one to our ardent and steady friend, Duke de Persigny. If you can procure them, you might send them to me in sheets and I will have them properly bound; a copy, too, for the legation would be very acceptable.

JUNE 12, 1864.

The *Alabama* arrived yesterday at Cherbourg. Captain Semmes informs me that she will require docking and extensive repairs. I shall make no application at present for the permission, supposing that it will be granted without my intervention, as was the case on the arrival of the *Georgia* at Bordeaux; the advice of my friend at the foreign affairs coincides with my own opinion on this subject; an application by me might seem to imply a doubt whether the same facilities for repairs would be extended to the *Alabama* as were accorded to the *Florida* and *Georgia*, and besides, I do not choose that any courtesies shown Captain Semmes should be pleaded as a sort of offset to the detention of the *Rappahannock*.

I learn that on the 10th instant the " Comité Consultatif du Contentieux " (this I find is the correct title of the commission I have mentioned in previous dispatches) pronounced unanimously the opinion that the *Rappahannock*, having been admitted into the port of Calais, there is no valid reason for detaining her there, and that she should be left free to depart in the same manner as she entered " dans les conditions où il est entré," and instructed Mr. Marchand to draw up a report to that effect; it may be expected to reach the minister of foreign affairs in a few days. I am pleased that my note was sent to the minister before the decision was made by the committee.

The Duke de Morny has gone to London. Some of the newspapers and especially the Indépendance Belge, a journal sometimes well informed but frequently circulating incorrect intelligence, says that he goes on a mission to bring about concerted action between the two Governments on American affairs. The report is not improbable, as I am informed that it is not unusual for the Emperor to charge persons outside of his regular diplomatic representatives with special missions of this character.

Mr. iy. g. i expected to have been the person selected for this purpose in the event of the Emperor deciding to make direct overtures to England on the subject. I will endeavor to obtain information as to the truth of the report, but in such matters the Emperor often acts without consulting his ministers.

I learn from very good authority that the British Government has recently made positive and definite propositions to the Emperor to sustain Denmark by arms, should the terms recommended by France and England and submitted to by Denmark not be accepted by the German powers, and that the propositions have been favorably entertained here. My informant thinks that a general European war may be much nearer at hand than is generally supposed; although he is very rarely mistaken in his facts and generally very sound in his deductions from them, I do not pretend to vouch for the correctness of his prognostics on this occasion.

I send you a printed copy marked "B" * of an opinion given by Mr. Berryer, the famous orator and advocate, at the instance of Mr. Dayton, dated 12th November, 1863, on the subject of the ships then building at Bordeaux and Nantes, by which you will see that he declares not only the ships liable to confiscation, but that the parties concerned, myself among them, may be prosecuted criminally. His argument does not shake the opinion I have formerly expressed on this question and to which you refer in your No. 35, but this is a matter on which you are better qualified than I to form a correct judgment.

Be this as it may, Mr. Dayton has not acted on the advice of his counsel, whether from want of confidence in its soundness or from fear of investigation of the circumstances under which he became possessed of the papers on which it was based. I had much difficulty in obtaining the copy I send you, but will endeavor to secure another in time to accompany the duplicate of this dispatch.

You will recollect the attempt to bring the Confederate Government before the French tribunals by a sort of process of attachment of the proceeds of the 7 per cent cotton loan in the hands of Erlanger & Co. The proceedings against those gentlemen were dismissed by the "Cour de Première Instance," whose judgment was confirmed on appeal by the "Cour Impériale." Citations were also issued against the President, the Secretaries of Treasury and of War, you will find by a printed paper marked "C," the report of the decision of the "Tribunal Civil" dismissing the proceedings against those functionaries.

---

* Not found.

I did not consider it proper or expedient that our Government should appear in any way as a party to these suits and therefore caused them to be defended through Erlanger & Co. It is proper that they should be reimbursed for the expenses thus incurred by them.

I have the honor to be, with very great respect, your most obedient servant,

JOHN SLIDELL.

Hon. J. P. BENJAMIN,
  Secretary of State.

[Enclosure.]

A.

PARIS, *June 9, 1864.*

SIR: On the 17th February last, the C. S. war steamer *Rappahannock* having completed her repairs at the port of Calais and taken on board a supply of coal, her commander notified the authorities of the port of his wish to proceed to sea, when he was informed that instructions had been given by his Excellency the minister of marine not to permit the departure of the vessel. On the 26th February the undersigned had the honor to address your Excellency on the subject of this detention and to demonstrate, as he thought conclusively, that no just cause existed for the detention of the *Rappahannock;* no answer having been made to this letter the undersigned on the 14th March again addressed your Excellency and requested to be informed of the reasons of the detention. This letter also remaining unanswered the undersigned advised the commander of the *Rappahannock* to give notice of his intention to strike his flag, withdraw his crew and abandon his vessel to the proper authorities of the port. This step was accordingly taken by the commander, who on 1st May informed in writing the commissary of marine at Calais of his intention to abandon his vessel on the 16th May. In the meanwhile the undersigned was verbally informed that the question of the *Rappahannock* had been referred for examination and report by your Excellency to a commission of jurisconsults and, having reason to expect a prompt and definitive solution of the question, advised the commander of the vessel not to carry out the intended abandonment.

More than a month has now elapsed since the reference to the commission of jurisconsults, and the prospect of a definitive solution of the question seems to be as remote as ever.

The undersigned considers it superfluous to repeat the arguments already advanced by him for the release of the *Rappahannock,* but in relation to the change in the personnel of her crew while at Calais he is happy to find by a dispatch from Mr. Dayton to Mr. Seward, minister of foreign affairs at Washington, dated 21st October, 1863, to be found at page 795 of second volume of the documents accompanying the annual message to Congress of President Lincoln of December, 1863, that your Excellency considered that an accession to the crew of a Confederate steamer while in a French port was not objectionable. This removes every possible doubt or difficulty about the correctness of the conduct of the officers of the *Rappahannock,* if indeed such doubt has ever existed.

The undersigned, considering a longer acquiescence in the detention of the *Rappahannock*, without even the allegation of a cause for her detention, incompatible with the respect due to the flag of the Government that he has the honor to represent, intends to renew the advice heretofore given to her commander to strike his flag and abandon his vessel. He ventures to express the hope that your Excellency will favor him with a reply to this letter, in order that he may be able to communicate to his Government the reasons which have induced your Excellency to pursue a course so little in accordance not only with the good will toward the Confederate States which was supposed to animate the Government of the Emperor, but, as the undersigned thinks, in opposition to its proclaimed neutrality.

The undersigned prays your Excellency to receive the assurance of the great respect with which he has the honor to be your Excellency's

Most obedient servant,

JOHN SLIDELL.

His Excellency Mr. DROUYN DE LHUYS,
    Minister of Foreign Affairs

No. 6.]   MONTREAL, *June 16, 1864.*

SIR: I have very little to communicate since my last dispatch. Some ten or twelve more men have been sent on, to take the boat which leaves for Bermuda next week. It is apparent from all the information I receive that very few remain who are willing to return at once to the discharge of their duty. There will, however, always during the existence of the war, be small parties to be forwarded who have escaped into Canada, and who are anxious to rejoin the Army. As these will generally consist of brave and enterprising men, I am trying to make some permanent arrangement to furnish them in the most economical way with the necessary means. For this purpose, I propose to leave as much as $5,000 in the hands of B. Wier & Co., to carry interest until used, to defray these expenses, and to employ discreet and responsible persons in Montreal, Toronto, Hamilton, St. Catharine's, Windsor, and other points likely to be reached by our men, whose interest in the cause will induce them to take the requisite precautions to prevent imposition, and to advance the price of transportation until reimbursed by Mr. Wier. Experience has shown that our escaped prisoners are too improvident in general to be trusted with money, and I am organizing a system by which tickets for transportation and necessary board to Halifax can be furnished them by our agents. The isolation, both commercial and political, of these Provinces, and the number of distinct lines over which the men must be passed, render this a tedious and somewhat troublesome task. As soon as it has been accomplished I shall return via Bermuda to the Confederacy.

I have the honor to remain, with the highest respect,

JAMES P. HOLCOMBE.

Hon. J. P. BENJAMIN,
    Secretary of State, C. S. A.

DEPARTMENT OF STATE,
Richmond, June 18, 1864.

SIR: I have the honor to enquire whether your Department is in possession of any official reports touching the conduct of the British Government in the capture or seizure of the *Tuscaloosa*, and, if so, to request that you will furnish copies thereof to this Department.

I am, very respectfully, your obedient servant,

J. P. BENJAMIN,
Secretary of State.

Hon. S. R. MALLORY,
Secretary of Navy.

DEPARTMENT OF STATE,
Richmond, June 21, 1864.

SIR: At the suggestion of the President, I enclose to you a copy of a letter forwarded to this Department by the Hon. John Slidell, our commissioner at Paris, on the subject of the rules and regulations touching the pilots employed in the port of Wilmington. I have the instructions of the President to request that you will send me such information on this subject and make such remarks as will enable me to respond to the complaints contained in the letter.

I am, very respectfully, your obedient servant,

J. P. BENJAMIN,
Secretary of State.

Captain WILKINSON,
Confederate States Navy, Wilmington, N. C.

No. 36.]
DEPARTMENT OF STATE,
Richmond, June 22, 1864.

SIR: Your No. 7 of 12th April was received on the 9th instant.

In relation to the *Tuscaloosa*, the dispatches to the Navy Department give no further details than are contained in the British Blue Book which you forwarded to me. I regard this case as a naked outrage, committed by a pretended neutral but really hostile Government, and one which the British cabinet would not have ventured on for a moment against any nation which it believed capable of enforcing its rights against such insolent aggression. It is the consciousness of being safe at this moment from hostilities on our part that can alone have emboldened the present foreign secretary to an action from which he would have shrunk in affright if directed against France or Russia or the United States. It was no doubt to this case that the President referred in his message when he said " and in one instance our flag also insulted where the sacred right of asylum was supposed to be secure," and when he spoke of wrongs " for which we may not properly forbear from demanding redress."

Your action in the matter of the three men from the *Gerrity* was entirely accordant with our views, as you will probably have learned ere this from Mr. Hotze, to whom instructions were sent to provide for their defense. The facts of the case are set forth in my dispatch to him more accurately than they reached you.

The additional forgery by the United States Government of the pretended deciphered note to me from a New York agent, as contained in the Blue Book of the *Chesapeake* case, having been already exposed by Mr. Slidell, it is, perhaps, not necessary that I should take any notice of it. If, however, it is thought that a denial is advisable, you are authorized in my name to make public the fact that Mr. Seward's statement to Lord Lyons (as related in the letter of the latter to Earl Russell, dated 24th December, 1863), that the paper forming enclosure No. 3 "was the decipher of a letter from a Confederate agent at New York to Mr. Benjamin, the Secretary of State at Richmond," is entirely false and has not a semblance of fact to rest on. The "enclosed paper No. 3," at foot of page 9 in the Blue Book, is a forgery from beginning to end. Neither individually nor as Secretary of State have I ever had correspondence with any person in New York who signed the initials "J. H. C.," or any other initials, nor am I able to conjecture whether these initials refer to any person in existence supposed to be in correspondence with me, or are purely imaginary. I am equally unable to conjecture to what facts, if any, the pretended letter in cipher refers, and we have never had, directly or indirectly, whether as a private individual or a public officer, any connection with or knowledge of any of the matters mentioned or referred to in the paper in question. The whole thing is just such a fabrication as the "Mallory Report," and is, like that report, "the invention of a gentleman." It will, of course, be followed by as many more similar forgeries as may be deemed necessary by the Washington Cabinet as long as they have a purpose to accomplish and can find dupes to credit them. It is not fair to expect us to descend to further exposures of such wretched falsehoods and forgeries, as from the staple of the correspondence of the United States Secretary of State in relation to our affairs, and if any publication on the subject is found necessary in the present instance it should be accompanied by the distinct statement that we shall deem it inconsistent with self-respect to make any further attempt to undeceive the British Government as to the character of the communications from the United States officials, which they are habitually accepting as trustworthy.

I send Mr. Slidell a copy of my last communication to Mr. Preston, which will put you fully in possession of our present views on the matters to which you refer in both your last dispatches.

The box of books which you were good enough to send me, via Bermuda, has arrived in Wilmington, and I hope to receive it tomorrow.

I believe I have hitherto omitted to acknowledge receipt of the copy furnished by Mr. Lindsay of his correspondence with Mr. Drouyn de Lhuys. It has been read with interest and will remain on the records of this Department in connection with the other papers of the very singular affair to which it refers.

I am, sir, very respectfully, your obedient servant,

J. P. BENJAMIN,
Secretary of State.

Hon. JAMES M. MASON, *etc., Paris.*

No. 94.]   BRUSSELS, *June 22, 1864.*

SIR: In the midst of my rejoicings over the intelligence contained in the telegraphic items conveyed by the *Asia*, under date of New York, June 9, I was saddened as I have rarely been saddened during my sojourn abroad by a dispatch from Cherbourg informing me of the destruction of the *Alabama*. Yesterday morning the details of that most disastrous occurrence appeared in all the journals, confirming my worst apprehensions. That vessel, which did such invaluable service for us, now lies at the bottom of the briny deep. She deserved a better fate than to sink under the blows which she received from a foe so superior to her in strength and equipment. She was worth to us as an armed negotiator for terms of honorable peace more than 20 such vessels as the *Kearsarge* would be worth to the Federals for prolonging the war.

Captain Semmes in making the attack was unquestionably animated exclusively by a sense of duty to his country, yet, considered as he is to have been the aggressor, the best of our European friends will, I fear, be disinclined to manifest deep regret at his defeat. In view of the peculiar value of the *Alabama* to the Confederate States, it is generally believed that he acted most injudiciously in meeting the *Kearsarge* in open combat, and most improperly in choosing Sunday as the day for the engagement. If he had been pursued and failed in resistance, the sympathies of the whole world would have been enlisted in his behalf. I myself can make every allowance for him in the circumstances in which he found himself placed, but the most fair-minded foreigners are slow to participate in my indulgent sentiments upon the subject, alleging that he was either vainglorious of his own powers or foolhardy with respect to the perils which he evidently had to encounter.

The Yankees, from their demonstrations, enjoy their victory quite as much as they would enjoy the capitulation of Richmond. They assert, as I am told, that we are as unequal to them, as will be seen in the end, at home on land as we are abroad at sea, and that, fortunately, we have exemplified this latter inequality in a convincing manner at the very portals of Europe.

I can not underestimate the fact of our having received a severe shock. In reading extracts from recent New York papers, I perceive that the so-called ministers of the gospel in many places exhorted their congregations to fervently pray for the capture of the *Alabama* as the evil genius of Northern prosperity. Such fanatics will naturally now suppose that their invocations have been heard and complied with, and consequently become more zealous than ever for the prosecution of hostilities.

The glory of the victory will be awarded to Lincoln. A day of thanksgiving will probably be proclaimed by him in consideration of the deliverance of the land from such an enemy on the great deep, and a new enthusiasm awakened which will secure fresh levies of troops and increased confidence, thereby decreasing the price of gold.

The news, too, will arrive just in time for it to be telegraphed all over the North to constitute the feature in the Fourth of July demonstrations.

But, much as I am affected by our irreparable loss on the ocean and the influence that it will be made to exercise adversely to us,

I am not in the least dismayed as concerns our ability to maintain our independence. That cool judgment at home—I may say, that sublime majesty of serene reason in the Cabinet, as in the field, so wisely displayed upon every requisite occasion—can not fail to carry us triumphantly through, backed as it is by the confidence and the patriotism and the courage of the whole country, irrespective of sex, age, or condition. I hope, with all the ardor of my nature, that the unfortunate event on this side of the water will not retard our realization of independence and peace.

I have the honor to be, sir,

Very respectfully, your obedient servant,

A. DUDLEY MANN.

Hon. J. P. BENJAMIN,
Secretary of State, C. S. A., Richmond, Va.

No. 40.] DEPARTMENT OF STATE,
Richmond, June 23, 1864.

SIR: My last to you was No. 39 of 1st instant, in postscript of which I acknowledged receipt of your Nos. 60 and 61. I have received nothing further, except your hurried unofficial note of 12th May, informing me of your interview with Mr. Troplong.

I can scarcely trust myself with the expression of the indignation felt by the President at the evasions and injustice of the French Government in relation to the *Rappahannock*. He is of opinion that the delay in the action finally taken by you on the subject went to the extreme verge of propriety and is gratified to find that the decisive step was adopted of striking her flag and leaving her to the responsibility of the French Government. It is very fortunate that our action on this side on the subject of the tobacco has been justified on grounds entirely independent of any retaliatory spirit, and that we have thus been enabled to show that there are French interests as dependent on our good will as we are on that of the Emperor's Government.

In connection with this subject I notice what is said in the cipher passages of your No. 60, and trust that the hopes therein held out to us may be fulfilled, but we shall not be at all surprised to find new obstacles interposed in the same manner as heretofore experienced, and we can not resist the conclusion that there has been bad faith and deception in the course pursued by the Emperor, who has not hesitated to break his promises to us in order to escape the consequences resulting from his unpopular Mexican policy.

The game played by the Cabinet of the United States with the French Government in relation to Mexico is so transparent that the inference is irresistible that the latter desire to be deceived. The acceptance by Mr. Lincoln of his nomination by the Baltimore convention commits him openly to refusing acknowledgment of the Mexican Empire, and the platform of that convention, of the Cleveland convention which nominated Fremont, and the platform which will undoubtedly be adopted by the Democratic convention at Chicago, show a feeling in the United States perfectly unanimous in the determination to overthrow the schemes of the French Government in Mexico and to resist the occupation of the throne by Maximilian. It has thus become evident that the safety of the new empire is dependent solely upon our success in interposing a barrier between northern aggression and the Mexican territory. As we do not intend to allow ourselves to be made use of in this matter as a convenient instrument for the accomplishment of the designs of others, you will not be surprised to learn the nature of the last instructions sent to Mr. Preston, of which a copy is annexed.*

I have written to Mr. Mason on the subject of the forged dispatch to me found in the Blue Book on the affair of the *Chesapeake*. I would be glad that you should confer with him as to the propriety of a publication on the subject. I am not able here to determine whether such publication is at all necessary or advisable.

The speech of Mr. Rouher on the 12th ultimo in the French Chamber, and the circular letter of Mr. Drouyn de Lhuys of 4th ultimo, as given in that speech, have just reached us in the Index of 19th May and may probably be regarded as correctly translated by Mr. Hotze. They indicate so complete an "entente" between the Cabinets of Washington and Paris that we should be blind indeed if we failed to attach to these incidents their true significance. We feel, therefore, the necessity of receiving with extreme distrust any assurances whatever that may emanate from a party capable of the double-dealing displayed toward us by the Imperial Government.

Our military position is promising in the extreme, and I do not think I go too far in saying that the Federal campaign of 1864 is already a failure. We may meet with reverses, but nothing at present indicates any danger comparable with the menacing aspect of affairs prior to the successes of our noble army in repulsing the repeated and desperate assaults of the Federal armies with a slaughter perfectly appalling.

I am, very respectfully, your obedient servant,

J. P. BENJAMIN,
Secretary of State.

Hon. JOHN SLIDELL, *etc., Paris.*

No. 95.]   BRUSSELS, *June 30, 1864.*

SIR: Herewith I transmit a copy of a note which I had the honor to address to his Excellency, Mr. Rogier, minister of foreign affairs at Belgium, on the 28th instant.

The extremities to which the Lincoln Government are driven to obtain recruits for the field tend largely to create an impression abroad that its condition is becoming more and more feeble for the prosecution of hostilities, while its unscrupulousness in insidiously violating the spirit of the laws of neutrals in this respect is engendering the ill will of the public authorities.

The worse than Hessian mercenaries who have been engaged to proceed via Antwerp to New York are, as I understand, principally Germans. As they are merely passing as emigrants through this Kingdom, where no passports are required and where travel is entirely free to foreigners, no legal steps can be taken for arresting their movements.

---

* Not found.

Yesterday, as you will perceive by the enclosed slip, a Federal agent was seized by the police while attempting to induce Belgian subjects to desert their employers and repair to New York.

I have the honor to be, sir, very respectfully, your obedient servant,

A. DUDLEY MANN.

Hon. J. P. BENJAMIN,
Secretary of State, C. S. A., Richmond, Va.

[Enclosure.]

49 RUE DUCALE, BRUSSELS, *June 28, 1864.*

In a note which the undersigned accredited commissioner plenipotentiary of the Confederate States of America to the Government of his Majesty the King of the Belgians, had the honor to address to his Excellency, Mr. Rogier, minister of foreign affairs of Belgium, dated October 13, 1862, he took occasion to state:

The undersigned deems it to be his duty to inform his Excellency, Mr. Rogier, that the Confederate States have not solicited the aid of a solitary foreign mercenary to assist them in fighting their battles. No half-pay or other officers or privates have been invited from their homes under promises of high pecuniary reward to enter their service. From the first they had a reliant confidence that their own strength was equal to the emergency in which they found themselves placed. Nor have they attempted to allure emigrants from abroad to their own shores by inducements contained in Cabinet circulars for foreign circulation, like the following:

" DEPARTMENT OF STATE.
" *Washington, August 8, 1862.*

" At no former period of our history have our agricultural, manufacturing, and mining interests been more prosperous than at this juncture. This fact may be deemed surprising in view of the enhanced price for labor, occasioned by the demand for the rank and file of the Army of the United States. It may be, therefore, confidently asserted that even now nowhere else can the industrious laboring man and artisan expect so liberal a recompense for his services as in the United States."

Even in instances where combatants are in all respects equal, honor forbids the engagement of outside aid by the one or the other; and assuredly none but the most depraved of poltroons would seek for such employment with the party which avowed a vast superiority in strength, in skill, and in weapons. No one who really is a man in anything but in mere designation could enlist in a service so disgraceful. There is in no living language an epithet too strong to apply to a human being who could act so ignobly as to draw his sword against the weaker of two belligerents when that belligerent was fighting against superior numbers for the maintenance of rightful independence.

The undersigned, when he brought this subject to the consideration of his Excellency, Mr. Rogier, knew that he could not be mistaken in the aims of the Secretary of State of the United States. The purpose of that functionary, in the circular referred to, was stealthily, and I might even remark, inhumanely, to allure from their homes persons engaged in industrial pursuits in order to secure their services in the armies of the Government at Washington. Thousands upon tens of thousands of recruits have thus been obtained for the prosecution of hostilities against the Confederate States, and I am well assured that a large number of recruiting agents are now covertly engaged in Europe in this nefarious pursuit.

In this connection it becomes the imperative duty of the undersigned to call the attention of his Excellency, Mr. Rogier, to the recent arrival at Antwerp of the steamer *Bellona*, expressly for the purpose of conveying something like 500 able-bodied men, designated as "workmen," to New York. They are reported to have been engaged by a Pole, who, with his associates, has contracted for the delivery in that port of 5,000 of the same description.

The undersigned will add that while his country is not in the slightest degree appalled or disheartened by the legions of European mercenaries, who are so wickedly decoyed into the ranks of its enemy, it nevertheless expects and has a right to expect that a Government so well intentioned and ever just and upright as that of his Majesty King Leopold will leave no efforts unemployed that can eventuate in the maintenance of a straightforward, honest, rigid neutrality.

Nor can it fail to strike his Excellency, Mr. Rogier, as a singular coincidence, that at the very time the embarkation of those "workmen" is about to commence in the principal harbor of Belgium, a large man-of-war of the Federal States, the *Niagara*, should make her appearance in that harbor. The ostensible object of her visit is reported to be to coal and to obtain provisions. It is more likely, however, that her mission is to convoy the "workmen" to the Atlantic, or at least to take care that they shall not be exposed to the risk of capture upon the high seas, as well as to complete, perhaps, by clandestine enlistments, the number of her own crew.

The undersigned avails himself of this occasion to express to his Excellency, Mr. Rogier, the assurances of his continued distinguished consideration.

A. DUDLEY MANN.

His Excellency CH. ROGIER,
Minister of Foreign Affairs, etc.

No. 65.]   PARIS, *June 30, 1864.*

SIR: On the 17th instant I informed you of the arrival of the *Alabama,* and before you can receive this dispatch the Northern papers will have informed you of the unfortunate but heroic close of her brilliant and eventful history. As several newspapers have attributed to me a direct and controlling agency in this matter, I think it proper to inform you what it has been, and I can not perhaps better do so than by sending you copies of a letter from Mr. Bonfils, agent of the *Alabama* at Cherbourg, my response thereto, and a paragraph from the Constitutionnel of the 24th instant, inserted at my request. My letter to Mr. Bonfils was written with the view that its substance might be made known to the naval authorities at Cherbourg, as I suppose it probably would be, and thus reach the Government. As I desired to see Mr. Mocquard, I went on the morning of the 19th instant to Fontainebleau, where the Emperor has been staying for some time past. I took the occasion to inform him, Mr. De Persigny, and Prince Murat of what was probably then going on near Cherbourg and my apprehension of the result of a contest which had been in a great degree forced upon Captain Semmes by the manner in which he had been received there. I informed them that the admiral prefect, while personally most courteous to Captain Semmes, had (prompted, no doubt, by instructions from Paris) hinted that the frequent visits of our ships to French ports, and especially to those devoted to the military marine, were not agreeable to the Government, and suggested that the repairs of the *Alabama* could be more conveniently made at Havre or Bordeaux, and that the minister of foreign affairs had sent me a message very much to the same effect by Bishop Lynch.

All these gentlemen were much pained by these statements and promised to communicate them to the Emperor. This passed on the race course when the Emperor had not yet made his appearance. Soon after his arrival Prince Murat sought me out to let me know of the loss of the *Alabama*, which had just been communicated to the Emperor by telegraph, and at which he was, as the prince said, deeply grieved. He had repeated to the Emperor what I had said about the withholding of permission to enter the military port, where alone the required repairs could be effected. The Emperor said that I was mistaken, as the permission had been granted. I told the prince that I hoped that such would prove to be the case, but the agent of the ship, writing the evening previous, spoke of his confidence that the permission would be granted, thus negativing the idea that it had already been accorded. I asked the prince if he was sure not to have misunderstood the Emperor about the permission. He said that he was quite sure, but that he would recur to the subject and let me know. In a few moments he returned and said that the Emperor had repeated his assurance that the permission had been granted. The next day I called on my friend at the foreign office to ask an interview with the minister and told him that I made the request for the purpose of having a categorical answer about the *Rappahannock;* that I attributed the loss of the *Alabama* to her unfriendly reception by the authorities of Cherbourg acting under instructions from Paris, and that it was time that I should know definitely on what footing the Confederate flag was to be hereafter received. I very soon after had a visit from my friend, who said that the minister sincerely regretted the loss of the *Alabama;* that he was sorry to hear that I considered his attitude toward my Government unfriendly; that he had great respect for me personally, etc., and that he would be most happy to see me the next day, when he would be prepared to make all needful explanations about the *Rappahannock.*

I accordingly called on him. He commenced the conversation by saying that not only he but everyone connected with the Government was profoundly affected at the loss of the *Alabama;* that he was not indulging in sentimentalities but sincerely felt all that he expressed. I said that candor compelled me to declare that I thought either his department or that of the minister of marine was mainly responsible for the loss of life and property which had occurred, for if the permission to enter the military port had been accorded the point of honor which had induced Captain Semmes to encounter a superior foe would not have been raised. He said that the permission had been given. I replied that I was differently informed, and that the message which he had sent me by Bishop Lynch and the conversation of Captain Semmes with the admiral prefect, in which the latter had hinted that the *Alabama* could be more conveniently repaired at Havre or Bordeaux, had authorized the belief either that the permission would not be granted at all or reluctantly after delays which would be humilating. The minister said that he would ask the minister of marine for copies of all the correspondence and orders in relation to the *Alabama* and would communicate them to me. I said that I regretted to be obliged to say that I had observed for some months past a growing disposition to treat my Government with scant courtesy, and that even the neutrality which the Emperor had proclaimed was not observed toward us. The minister, with some appearance of temper, here interposed and said that was a question which he would not permit himself to discuss. The Government had decided to observe the strictest neutrality and believed that they had done so, but that the best evidence of the fact was the constant complaint of Mr. Dayton of the partiality shown toward the Confederacy; that while the Emperor had the warmest sympathies with the Confederate cause, sympathies which were freely avowed, he was determined not to be drawn by indirection into conflict with the Northern Government; that if such conflict were to come it must be in pursuance of a policy openly declared and where no fault could justly be attributed to him. I said that I was quite willing to abandon a subject which was as disagreeable to me as to him; that I had not come to speak of the *Alabama* (that topic had been introduced by him); that I had asked an interview for the purpose of knowing distinctly what was to be done with the *Rappahannock;* that she had been detained without cause for more than four months, and that as I could not obtain a written response to my various communications on that subject, I hoped now to have a verbal one. He said that he had not replied to my communications because he was not prepared to give a conclusive answer; that he had written the day previous to the President of the Senate, asking for an early report and so soon as that should be received he would decide what should be done and would inform me of his decision.

This matter disposed of, I said I was about to ask a question, and that if he found it indiscreet it should be considered as not made. Had the sentiments of the Emperor become, from any cause less kindly (moins bienviellants) toward the Confederacy? that I was quite at a loss to imagine any such cause, but that in relation to the ships we had been induced to build by his suggestions and for which we had expended large sums of money, raised with great inconvenience and sacrifice, we had been treated with extreme harshness. It was difficult to account for such a sudden change of policy, if there were no corresponding change of feeling. He said, with a significant smile: "That is a matter of which I am of course ignorant; but I can assure you that the feeling of the Emperor is unchanged. He is, as he always has been, prepared to recognize your Government, but he will not act alone." I asked what effect the decisive failure of Grant's campaign against Richmond, of which I hoped soon to have intelligence, would have on the question of recognition. He said that he supposed that it would lead to direct and earnest official appeals to the British Government for common action in the matter, but whether they would be more effectual than previous overtures he could not tell; but he could not well see how in such a case any ministry, whether Whig or Conservative, could refuse its adherence. I do not recollect anything else material that was said. The minister on my leaving repeated his regret at the catastrophe of the *Alabama*, disclaiming all affection of sentiment, expressed the hope that we should soon hear of a decisive defeat of Grant, and promised an early decision in the case of the *Rappahannock*.

From what I said in previous dispatches, you will form your own judgment of the value of any declaration of Mr. D. de Lhuys.

Bishop Lynch left for Rome a few days since. While here he had an audience with the Emperor and two interviews with the minister of foreign affairs, of which he informs me that he has given you full details.

I have the honor to remain, with great respect, your obedient servant,

JOHN SLIDELL.

Hon. J. P. BENJAMIN,
    Secretary of State.

No. 45.]   CONFEDERATE STATES COMMERCIAL AGENCY,
                                London, July 4, 1864.

SIR: I have the honor to acknowledge the receipt, on 2d instant, of your No. 20, covering Treasury warrant No. 6265, dated May 27, for £2,000 on account of secret-service expenditures. I am sincerely grateful for the considerate promptness of this remittance which anticipates every contingency of my constantly expanding field of operations.

The dating of this dispatch is little more than formal as since my last I have been more in Paris than in London, and returned here only a few days ago. In my No. 43 and 44 from that place I have sketched my plans there, though hastily, yet with sufficient precision, to leave me now not much to add. The principal event is the extraordinary impression produced in France by the gallant end of the *Alabama*. The dramatic effectiveness of a naval combat fought so near the shore as to be witnessed by thousands of excited spectators, and almost without a figure of speech by every Frenchman simultaneously; the admitted disparity between the combatants, perhaps an unconscious sympathy with misfortune in such encounters, all combined to stir an impressible and emotional people. For several days nothing else was talked about, and the papers scarcely had space for anything else. The most romantic stories were those most eagerly received, and Captain Semmes's plain and matter of fact report was actually a disappointment to many of his enthusiastic French admirers. In an article, the substance of which was telegraphed to all the English papers, M. Lincayrac, of the Constitutional, testifies to the "profound emotion" and the pain caused by the event among all classes and in all parts of France. I can not but think that a permanently beneficial impression has been made on public opinion.

It is observed that, so far as known, only three newspapers printed in the French language have spoken in other than sympathetic or at least respectful language of the *Alabama* and her fate—the Opinion Nationale, in Paris, which has been severely taken to task for the offense by its cotemporaries; the Phare de la Loire, an obscure provincial paper; and the Independance Belge, of Brussels, in a Paris letter which its regular correspondents disclaim. There were in Cherbourg at the time of the battle, besides the population of the town, crowds of pleasure seekers whom excursion trains had brought there for a Sunday's holiday. When the *Alabama* steamed out to meet her adversary the port and the sea seemed as if they had found voices of thunder to bid her god speed. When the *Kearsarge*, after her victory, entered the same harbor there was an angry silence like that which accompanies the progress of some hated malefactor.

I mention these facts, not merely because they are gratifying in themselves, but because they show that although we can never hope to bring French public opinion to investigate, much less to understand our social and political theories, or to overcome its instinctive repugnance to them, there are yet levers by which this public opinion may be moved.

In England every other topic of interest has been adjourned to await the issue of the parliamentary battle which commences this evening. Had I not been so long an observer of the paradoxical condition of political affairs in this country, I should unhesitatingly predict the triumph of the opposition. It is numerically larger; its rank and file have the eagerness of men kept unusually long from the enjoyment of office; it has for its opponent a party which has distinguished itself for imbecility and inconsistency to a degree that passes belief; if it lacked all these elements of success it might hope to ride triumphantly into power on the taunts and insults which, resounding from every part of the world, make every Englishman's ear tingle and should convince even the most infatuated of the Manchester school that no change can be for the worse. And yet I am more than doubtful about the result of the debate opening to-night on Mr. Disraeli's motion and which will probably continue during the week. I will not trouble you with the reasons for my skepticism of a Conservative victory. Among many there is one sufficient and it is this, that the opposition is quite as destitute of a policy as the party in power. The chief end of its tactics is to get into office without committing itself on either of the two great questions before the public, the American and the Danish, and to sneak in, so to speak, on side issues such as the Ashantee War. This time, however, they have ventured on a regular assault with a motion which is in fact one of want of confidence. When everything is so anomalous, it is perhaps not to be wondered at that the ministry, instead of boldly meeting the issue presented, avail themselves of the assistance of an independent member to escape by an evasion which would be disgraceful if it were not so puerile. I send you the rival motions, which will irresistibly remind you of a well-known passage in Hudibras instead of the grave issues involved in the Government of one of the foremost nations in Christendom.

With much respect, I have the honor to remain, your obedient servant,

HENRY HOTZE.

Hon. J. P. BENJAMIN,
  Secretary of State, Richmond.

P. S.—I will write again by the Bermuda mail.

No. 10.]　　　　24 UPPER SEYMOUR STREET, PORTMAN SQUARE,
　　　　　　　　　　　　　　　　　　　London, July 6, 1864.

SIR: I have the pleasure to inform you that I send by Lieutenant Chapman, Confederate States Navy, who bears this, the seal of the Confederate States, at last completed. It is much admired by all who have seen it here and I hope you will approve it as a fine work of art.

The seal is carefully put up in a separate small box and Lieutenant Chapman is charged, under no circumstances, to run the risk of its being captured. He takes the route to Bermuda via Halifax, to sail on Saturday, 9th instant; and I ship through Messrs. Fraser, Trenholm & Co. by the steamer that takes him to Halifax two boxes containing the iron press, with a full supply of wax and other materials for the use of the seal. Although not expressly ordered, in the difficulty of obtaining these things in the Confederacy at present, at least of approved quality, I have thought it best to have them supplied here; all which I hope you will approve.

The enclosed duplicate bill will furnish a list of those materials, with the prices; the original I have paid and retained.

I have requested Lieutenant Chapman to take charge of the boxes at Bermuda and to see to their safe delivery. To relieve him of expenses on the route, I have further requested Messrs. Fraser, Trenholm & Co. here, if they can do so, to pay the freight all the way to Bermuda and write to Major Walker at Bermuda to pay the freight thence to the Confederacy, should they not go in a Government ship. Still, it is possible that some part of this may not be done, and I have accordingly told Lieutenant Chapman should any expenses in the transportation devolve on him, it should be paid promptly at the Department of State, which oblige me by having attended to.

I have the honor to be, very respectfully, your obedient servant,

J. M. MASON.

Hon. J. P. BENJAMIN,
    Secretary of State.

[Enclosure.]

Duplicate A. C.

J. M. Mason, esq., to Joseph S. Wyon, chief engraver of her Majesty's seals, etc.,
287 Regent Street, London W.

1864.

July 2. Silver seal for the Confederate States of America, with ivory handle, box with spring lock, and screw press	£84	0
3,000 wafers	4	10
1,000 seal papers		7
1,000 strips of parchment		18
100 brass boxes	16	5
100 cakes of wax	7	0
100 silk cords	6	5
1 perforator		5
3 packing cases lined with tin	3	0
	122	10

By cash 21st March £42.
Settled by cheque for balance 6th July, 1864.

JOSEPH S. WYON.

———

[Enclosure.]

DIRECTIONS FOR USING THE GREAT SEAL OF THE CONFEDERATE STATES OF AMERICA.

FOR MAKING IMPRESSIONS IN WAX-LIKE PATTERN.

Turn up the bottom of the parchment document, and perforate it with the instrument sent for that purpose, in three places, as in pattern. Pass a silk cord through the holes in the parchment, and then through the holes at the bottom of a brass box. Unscrew the handle from the seal, and slightly grease the face and side of the seal with a little sweet oil on cotton wool. Put a cake of wax in nearly boiling water. At the same time make the seal warm, but not more so than will allow it to be held in the hand. When the wax has become very soft, which it will be after it has been in the water about two or three minutes, take it out, and after very quickly laying it in a soft clean cloth to dry off the water, put it into the brass box on the top of the cord, and then put the seal on the wax, taking care to let the top be toward the document, and place the whole in the press quickly, holding it tightly squeezed for half a minute or a minute. The whole operation must be done with great rapidity after the wax is taken out of the water, to prevent the wax getting too hard to take a good impression.

When taken out of the press the handle should be screwed into the seal again to pull it away from the wax. If it does not easily come off, the seal should be again warmed from the back, when it will do so without difficulty.

In order to give the impression the dead appearance which the proof impression has, the seal must be greased very slightly, and then powdered over with a soft brush, with vermilion, before it is put upon the wax. By wiping the vermilion off the surface of the seal before putting it on the wax, the surface of the impression will be bright and the engraved part remain dead, as in one of the pattern impressions.

FOR MAKING IMPRESSION IN WAFER-LIKE PATTERN.

Turn up the bottom of the parchment document and cut straight holes as in pattern, and pass through them a parchment strip, leaving the ends out at equal lengths. Put a wafer wetted on one side on the lower and inner sides of a seal paper—next to the dry side of the wafer put one of the ends of the parchment strip, and upon that another wafer rapidly passed through water so as to be wetted on both sides. Upon that again, put the other end of the parchment strip and then another wafer wetted on only one side, with the wet side uppermost, and onto that turn down the other part of the seal paper. Then put the seal on the top and squeeze the whole in the press. Wafer impressions may be made upon documents themselves, by wetting wafers in the manner and order before described, and putting half of one of the seal papers on the top.

No. 97.]   Brussels, *July 7, 1864.*

Sir: In view of the bold attempts, made immediately under my own eyes by the agents of the Lincoln Administration, to induce able-bodied men to embark at Antwerp for New York, I took occasion to address a second note to Mr. Rogier, a copy of which I herewith transmit.

There is not so much as the shadow of a doubt that all the so-designated " workmen " who are proceeding from Germany through this Kingdom to the Federal States are intended for military service, yet regular enlistments for such employment have been carefully avoided.

I sent my servant, a trusty Italian, to Antwerp yesterday to ascertain the manner in which the Northern Army could be entered by him. He was told that he could only be engaged as a laborer on this side of the Atlantic, for a term of three years, but after he arrived in New York he could readily become a soldier if he chose. As an inducement for him to go, if he would sign the obligation which all the " workmen " were required to sign, he would receive his passage free and two francs per day after his arrival. This morning he made a similar enquiry at the agency in this metropolis and received precisely the same answer. He was assured in both instances that he would have his choice when he reached New York to work upon railroads or canals. This is the same system for obtaining recruits that

was adopted in Ireland more than a year ago, and which is carefully observed all over Germany and elsewhere. The authorities are
precluded from taking any legal exceptions to it, as the right of
expatriation is not prohibited. Moreover, for more than a quarter
of a century there had been numerous American agencies at Bremen,
Hamburg, Rotterdam, Antwerp, and Havre for inducing immigrants
to the Western and other States of the then Union.

The Belgians are not inclined to engage themselves as "workmen"
to proceed to New York. They are too well advised of the meaning
of the word when illustrated by the "drugging," which persons so
classified, under the machinations of the wicked Washington Cabinet undergo upon their debarkation. The newspaper press here has
been careful to enlighten them on that point. Such as are desirous
of quitting their country are preparing to embark for Vera Cruz. A
corps of 2,400 effective men have been regularly enlisted in Belgium
as the guard of Empress Charlotte, to start about the 1st of September.

Germany has been thoroughly scoured by the meanest of mercenaries for suitable material to swell the rank and file of the armies of
the North. Worse specimens of living men were assuredly never seen
than those who have been recently swarming in the streets of Antwerp. Many of them are the merest of vagrants, such as were forbidden admission into the United States prior to the war.

Mr. William Grayson Mann, who speaks the German as fluently as
he does the English language, passed two or three days in Antwerp
just before the departure of the *Bellona* which took away about 450
of them, and on carefully informing many of the more intelligent of
what they would have to undergo when they reached their destination, influenced 40 or 50 to desert. Indeed there was well-nigh a
mutiny upon the *Bellona* before she proceeded to sea, so dissatisfied
were they with the inevitable condition in which they unexpectedly
ascertained that they were likely to be placed. They saw distinctly,
for the first time that they were to be the victims of matured criminal intent.

I may mention that the Federal frigate *Niagara* left Antwerp on
the 2d, and in so much haste that several of her crew on shore were
unable to join her.

About three months after I entered upon the duties of my present
post the Lincoln Cabinet dispatched Bishop Fitzpatrick of Boston,
to this metropolis, to use all the influence that he could command in
enlisting the sympathies of the Catholic clergy in particular, as well
as the population generally, on the side of the abolitionists. Ever
since his arrival he has been 'most diligent and vigilant in the discharge of the trusts confided to him, rarely ever absenting himself a
day from the legation of the United States of which he is occasionally
the chief. I am happy to inform you that his mission has been entirely unsuccessful. The clergy are almost to a man for us, and the
Catholic press, at the head of which stand the Journal de Bruxelles
and L'Emancipation earnestly and boldly advocate our cause and
hold up the enormities of the North to the animadversion of continental Europe. The bishop is believed to have been abundantly supplied with greenbacks and I understand that he was excessively cha-
grined a few days ago, when, wishing to realize upon them, his broker

refused to purchase from him at a higher rate than 2 francs on the dollar. Seward has assuredly been very prodigal of the contingent foreign intercourse fund in his desire to impress this little country favorably. That he has notoriously failed in his purpose no better evidence could perhaps be adduced than that of Bishop Fitzpatrick himself.

I have the honor to be, sir, very respectfully, your obedient servant,

A. DUDLEY MANN.

Hon. J. P. BENJAMIN,
Secretary of State, C. S. A., Richmond, Va.

[Enclosure.]

No. 96.]   49 RUE DUCALE, BRUSSELS, July 4, 1864.

SIR: The "Edition du soir" of L'Etoile Belge of this day's date (herewith enclosed), contains the following advertisement which I hasten to communicate to your Excellency in order that the immediate attention of the Government of his Majesty, the King of the Belgians, may be brought to the subject to which it relates:

[Translation.]

AMERICA.

A demand is made for healthy unmarried men from 21 to 40 years of age to emigrate to the United States of America. Useless to apply without certificates of military service. Address L. Dochez, bureau of emigration, No. 2, Rue de Brabant, Brussels.

A more palpable, if not daring, avowal never was made in any country, at any time, to violate the obligations imposed by international proprieties upon a neutral than is demonstrated in this deliberate attempt to obtain recruits for a belligerent.

Indeed, since the appearance of the *Bellona* in a Belgian port, chartered expressly for the purpose of conveying enlisted troops, designated as "workmen" to New York, followed as she was by the *Niagara*, a man-of-war of the Washington Government, Antwerp resembles much more, in the practically bellicose attitude it has assumed, a recruiting station in the Federal States than the port of a neutral kingdom.

Such flagrant outrages upon a belligerent, recognized all over the earth as such, as is the case with the Confederate States of America, can not fail to be arrested by a Government which enjoys so high a reputation as that of Belgium for a scrupulous observance in its relations with other peoples of the principles of good faith.

The heart of the just ruler and philanthropic statesman, wherever he may abide, must sicken at the disgraceful artifices employed by the Government at Washington to fill up the constantly diminishing columns which it sends to the field. That Government engages the most debased of agents to prowl about all over Europe in search of victims for its unrighteous ambition.

The war had been ended triumphantly for the Confederate States months ago, but for the succor which the Federal armies clandestinely received from this hemisphere. Notwithstanding this succor, the Government of those States is still equal to the accomplishment of the benign work which their patriotism inspired them to undertake, but the disgraceful foreign enlistments may possibly prolong the day of its consummation.

The most superficial observer can not but perceive that the Federal States virtually admitted that they had not the power, of themselves, to combat victoriously the Confederate States when they were compelled to become importunate beggars, covertly and overtly abroad, for venal soldiers to place in their front in battle.

The Government of the Confederate States would despise itself if it were to ask anything more favorable from any nation than strictly fair play. This, it is its right, as it is its duty to insist upon, and with nothing less ought it to be tacitly content.

I have the honor to be, with the most distinguished consideration your Excellency's obedient servant,

A. DUDLEY MANN.

His Excellency CH. ROGIER,
    Minister of Foreign Affairs, Brussels.

No. 11.]   LONDON, *July 8, 1864.*

SIR: * * * You will have seen through the Northern press long before this can reach you the motion made in the House of Commons in nature of " want of confidence " intended to oust the ministry. The debate on the motion, commencing on Monday (4th), yet continues, and, of course, absorbs every other question. The issue seems uncertain, but you will have heard that, too, far in advance of this dispatch. Whilst the debate is going on we receive the cheering accounts of our great successes against Grant in Virginia, and as far as we can determine through the imperfect and disjointed intelligence from the North, of like successes against Sherman in Georgia. We do not doubt the result in either quarter, and should they prove so decisive as finally to dispose of both armies of invasion, I entertain a strong hope, let the ministerial issue result as it may, that public opinion in England will compel the Government to move in some manner advantageous to us; and as things present themselves, I should even have stronger hope of this, or rather of more prompt action, should the present ministry remain in than if unseated. In my last I told you of the interview held by Mr. Lindsay with Lord Russell, having previously reported those held with Lord Palmerston, and from which Mr. L. drew favorable inferences; but in the preparations for the issue now made and its engrossing character while pending, of course, no further steps concerning American affairs can be taken. We have, too, another gleam of light from another quarter which may enure to our benefit. It is said that Denmark, now certainly left alone to combat all Germany, has made overtures to terminate the war by being admitted into the Germanic Confederation. Should this prove true, and that embroglio be removed out of the way, I should still have the greater hope that some favorable movement in regard to the South could be forced from the ministry.

These are the best speculations I can offer, as derived from my present sojourn in London. I see a great number of the more prominent public men, both Peers and Commoners, who talk freely with me as I do with them. Should there be no dissolution, Parliament will probably remain in session until the first week in August. I have not seen Lord Palmerston, as I have written to you was proposed by Mr. Lindsay. On coming here, Mr. L. renewed the proposal, when I told him that I would not call on Lord P. on the indirect invitation given whilst I was in Paris, although I would be really happy to have a conversation with him, and that if Lord P. desired it, he had only to write me a note or send me a message to that effect. I have heard nothing more in regard to it.

You will doubtless have heard from Mr. Slidell the final and strange termination of engagements made in France in regard to our naval affairs. A full report has been or will be made to the Navy Department of them by Captain Bulloch, more especially in charge. So far as the subject has passed under my notice, we have been utterly duped by that power, and worse; though I should speak with diffidence, as all direct intercourse in respect to the matter was held by Mr. Slidell.

Since my last we have sustained a severe blow in the loss of the *Alabama*, after a daring and most gallant fight. I went to see Captain Semmes immediately on learning his arrival at Southampton, and he acquiesced in my suggestion that his official report to his superior officer in Europe should be published by me here at once as the most speedy mode of getting it to our Government by its republication in the North. Every indication was given here to receive Captain Semmes in the most marked manner. A public dinner, I understand, was tendered him by the Army and Navy Club, which he declined, and measures were at once taken, originating with officers of her Majesty's Navy, to present him a sword.

I send by Lieutenant Chapman, who goes in same steamer with this to Halifax, the seal with its appurtenances, and he bears a separate dispatch relating to it.

I can not conclude without a full expression of the deep gratitude I feel, in common with all my countrymen here, to the gallant armies in the field who have so nobly and successfully illustrated the character and spirit of our Southern people, and more especially to their able and heroic leaders. I really speak without exaggeration when I say that all Europe is filled with the deserved fame of Lee, Beauregard, and Johnston.

I have the honor to be, very respectfully, your obedient servant,

J. M. MASON.

Hon. J. P. BENJAMIN,
    Secretary of State.

No. 67.]   PARIS, *July 11, 1864.*

SIR: I have the honor to acknowledge the receipt of your No. 36 of 23 April. Not hearing from Mr. Drouyn de Lhuys in conformity with the assurance given me in the interview mentioned in my No. 65, I called on the 1st instant on Messrs. Morny and Persigny to invoke their good offices in the affair of the *Rappahannock*. I expressed very freely my opinion of the conduct of the Foreign Minister, in which they heartily concurred and promised me, the former to speak and the latter to write to the Emperor on the subject. On the 7th I received from Mr. Persigny a note enclosing an autograph letter of the Emperor of the same day in these words:

MY DEAR PERSIGNY: I have given orders for the *Rappahannock* to leave the French port, but the American minister must not know it.

Believe me. sincerely your friend,

NAPOLEON.

In response to an inquiry made of my friend at the foreign affairs, he wrote to me on the 9th instant, " No decision has been taken on the subject of the *Rappahannock*, Mr. Drouyn de Lhuys told me and repeated it yesterday. In the meanwhile the *Rappahannock* will do well to take precautions not to be caught by one of the Federal cruisers watching for it."

The caution was rather inconsistent with the declaration that no decision had been made; but supposing it possible that the order might have been given to the minister of marine, I called on him immediately to ascertain the fact and showed him the Emperor's letter saying that as the minister of foreign affairs said that no decision had been made on the subject of the *Rappahannock* I presumed that the order had been communicated directly to him. He assured me that such was not the case, and was evidently surprised at the discrepancy between the Emperor's letter and the declaration of his foreign minister. He appears now to be very warmly and decidedly favorable to our cause; he has twice sent his chef de cabinet to me about an unpleasant, and I think a very unnecessary, difficulty with the judicial authorities at Calais arising out of a collision of the *Rappahannock* with a vessel leaving the dock. A judgment was rendered for a trifling sum against the commander of the *Rappahannock* six or seven weeks since. The case does not seem to have been properly defended, and an order of seizure was given against the ship, her national character or that of her commander not having been invoked before the court. The minister was very anxious that no additional embarrassments should be placed in the way of the departure of the ship, and I have advised Flag-Officer Barron to order a sum sufficient to stop further proceedings to be paid into court, under protest, and reserving all right of appeal, as there can be no doubt of the personal liability of the commander for damages resulting from his failure to observe the regulations of the port, and liquidated by a judgment rendered in a case where he has not made the necessary plea to the jurisdiction based on his official character. Had I been advised in time of these proceedings, another disagreeable episode in the history of this most unlucky vessel would have been avoided.

I annex copy of a note which I have this day addressed to the minister of foreign affairs, reminding him of his promise to decide promptly the affair of the *Rappahannock*. You will observe that I make no allusion to the note of the Emperor, nor has he been verbally advised by me of its existence, as I thought it better that he might, if he chose, have the appearance of acting from his own inspiration.

I have the honor to be, with great respect, your most obedient servant,

JOHN SLIDELL.

Hon. J. P. BENJAMIN,
    Secretary of State.

PARIS, *July 11, 1864.*

SIR: In an interview with which your Excellency honored the undersigned on the 21 ultimo your Excellency was so good as to say that he was in daily expectation of receiving the report of the committee to whom the affair of the Confederate steamer *Rappahannock* had been referred for examination; that he would then lose no time in deciding definitively on the question of permitting that vessel to leave the port where she has so long been detained, and that the decision would be communicated to the undersigned as promptly as possible.

The undersigned trusts that he will be excused for reminding your Excellency of the promise made him on the occasion above referred to.

He begs your Excellency to accept the assurance of the distinguished consideration of his most obedient servant,

JOHN SLIDELL.

His Excellency Mr. DROUYN DE LHUYS,
Minister of Foreign Affairs.

No. 37.]   DEPARTMENT OF STATE,
Richmond, July 12, 1864.

SIR: I have the honor to acknowledge receipt of your Nos. 8 and 9, of 1st and 9th ultimo, received on 4th and 9th instant.

I am happy to announce the receipt in good order of the remaining volumes of the Hansard, my set now closing with volume 172, and carrying the dates to the close of July, 1863. As soon as other volumes appear I would be very glad to have them, as well as any general index which may have been published of Hansard. I am not aware if there be any extant, but in the advertisement prefixed to the first volume of the second series the editors state that such an index is in preparation. If you can obtain one it will not be necessary to trouble yourself with doing more than ordering the volumes to be sent to Mr. Hotze to be forwarded.

I have to thank you for the Statesman's Manual for 1864 and the British Almanac for 1864, which are very acceptable.

The dispatch addressed to you at Paris to which you refer in your No. 9, and which remained there " poste restante," was forwarded to you under cover to Mr. Hotze, and he must have put it in the post-office inadvertently without a specific address. I have sent all your dispatches for several months past under cover to Mr. H., as requested by you, and it will be well that you should inform him of his oversight in order to prevent any recurrence of the error.

The President is much pleased at the course pursued by you in the matter of the proposed interview with Lord Palmerston, as detailed in your No. 8. It accords exactly with his view of what propriety dictated under the circumstances; and, while prudence and policy require that any advances made by the British cabinet toward the establishment of relations with you should be met in a courteous spirit, we are satisfied that a lofty and independent bearing, exacting the utmost measure of the respect to which you are entitled as a representative of the Confederate States in foreign countries, is better calculated to subserve our interests than the indication of any eagerness to grasp at the first opening for an interview, whether official or unofficial, with the British premier or foreign secretary. In relation to your presence in London as a private gentleman for conference with those who display so friendly a warmth in our favor, as Mr. Lindsay and others whom you mention, the President considers that you are better able on the spot to judge of the advantage to be derived from an occasional visit to London than he can be at this distance, and is content to leave your course on this point to be guided by your own discretion.

We have from the North English dates to the 26th ultimo announcing the adjournment of the conference without success in effecting any arrangement and the renewal of hostilities in Denmark. We can not judge what course England will take, though it seems from this side scarcely possible for her to avoid a war. As nothing is said in the New York papers about Mr. Lindsay's motion, I take it for granted that it was again postponed. We have expected no result from this move, and regard it merely as an evidence of the sympathy and regard for us of the gentleman by whom the motion was made.

I am, sir, respectfully, your obedient servant,

J. P. BENJAMIN,
Secretary of State.

Hon. JAMES M. MASON, etc.,
Paris.

No. 41.] DEPARTMENT OF STATE,
Richmond, July 12, 1864.

SIR: I write principally to acknowledge receipt on the 4th instant of your Nos. 62 and 63 of 31st May and 2d June. I have nothing of interest to communicate, as all military intelligence will necessarily be anticipated by Northern advices.

The affair of the *Rappahannock* we suppose to remain in *statu quo*, inasmuch as European news to the 26th ultimo gives no intimation of her having left port. Whether another vessel said to have sailed from Bordeaux for China be a matter in which we have an interest can only be conjectured until we receive further advices from you. The news of the loss of the *Alabama* just received renders us particularly anxious for your dispatches. The first impression created by this unpleasant news is unfavorable to the discretion and judgment of Captain Semmes, who appears to have sought a combat without necessity, on very unequal terms and one in which his success would have been of little material value compared with the disastrous consequences of a defeat. These however are but first impressions which may be greatly modified or even entirely changed by further intelligence, and any error of judgment committed may be fairly condoned in view of the determined gallantry displayed in the action.

We agree with you in attaching very little importance to the repeated rumors and statements of intended action on our matters by England or France. There seems indeed to be every probability that the first recognition of the Confederacy will come from our enemies presenting an example totally unprecedented in history. It is difficult to perceive how in the present state of Northern finances, and the fierce and passionate dissensions which are being daily developed among the Northern people, it can be possible to carry on the war many months longer. It will undoubtedly drag on till the winter puts a stop to actual campaigning, but its renewal next spring seems to me extremely improbable.

The principal cloud which overhangs our prospects is the condition of things in the Southwest. General Johnston's steady retreat is uninterrupted, and there is every reason to believe he will abandon Atlanta without a battle. If so, it will scarcely be possible to retain him in command, and we must hope for better things under some new leader more competent to conduct a large army than he has shown himself to be.

I am, very respectfully, your obedient servant,

J. P. BENJAMIN,
Secretary of State.

Hon. JOHN SLIDELL, etc.
Paris.

SHEPPERTON MANOR,
Middlesex, July 14, 1864.

MY DEAR SIR: An opportunity immediately offering by Mr. Hamilton, of the Navy, who sails the day after to-morrow from Liverpool for Bermuda, and of which I did not know until to-day in London, I avail myself of it to report the heads of a conversation I had to-day with Lord Palmerston. His lordship renewed, through Mr. Lindsay, his invitation to me to see him, and I went with Mr. L. from his home in the country, where I am a guest, to London this morning for that purpose.

I was received with great civility, and after the ordinary topics of salutation Lord P. commenced the conversation. His points of enquiry were the condition of the war, its probable duration, the prospects of the presidential election and the influence upon the war as it might result; whether I thought that any interposition now by the European powers would be better received by the Northern Government than at an earlier day.

My replies were that I thought there was evidence the war would terminate with the present campaign, though not at once by a treaty of peace, but because the North would be unable to replenish its armies; that enlistments had ceased under any stimulant, and that it was manifest they dare not attempt a draft. His lordship asked in that connection what would be the attitude of the South, and, if they took Washington, what would be done with it. I replied I did not doubt it would be destroyed, not vindictively, but to keep the enemy at a distance. He expressed a doubt whether in such case it would not be wise in the South to remain still upon the defensive. As to the elections I said that, assuming, as I felt unable to do, the failure both of Grant and Sherman, there would result such anarchy in the North as to make it doubtful whether any election could be held; that if held, Lincoln would probably be defeated, and such would be the condition of things that if the European powers would take any steps expressive of their sense that the war ought to end it would bring out the potential voice of those who were really for peace, but who without such aid might be afraid to let their voice be heard; and in this connection I told him that I did not doubt the responsible and considerate mind of the North would look to such interposition as a godsend, and that, however the Government might have received it at an earlier day, the Government would be powerless before the masses insisting on a peace; that I thought both he and I would form a safe opinion as to the probable effect of such interposition when we looked at the broken and disintegrating condition of the North, broken into factions, its finances in ruins, and unable to replenish its Army; in such condition men could look only to a peace.

Such is the outline only of what passed. At the conclusion I said to him in reply to his remark, that he was gratified in making my acquaintance, that I felt obliged by his invitation to the interview, but that the obligation would be increased if I could take with me any expectation that the Government of her Majesty was prepared to unite with France in some act expressive of their sense that the war should come to an end. He said that perhaps as I was of opinion that the crisis was at hand, it might be better to wait until it had arrived. I told him that my opinion was, that the crisis had passed, at least so far as that the war of invasion would end with the campaign.

I send you this hurried note by the opportunity offering, but will reduce the conversation to more intelligible form for my next dispatch.

It may be that good will come of it.

Our interview was held in the form of an ordinary visit at his residence, Mr. Lindsay alone being present.

Praying your pardon for so hurried a note, I am, my dear sir, very truly yours,

J. M. MASON.

Hon. J. P. BENJAMIN, etc.

No. 98.] BRUSSELS, *July 16, 1864.*

SIR: The extremities to which the Lincoln Government has been driven to obtain troops for the prosecution of hostilities against us are rendered strikingly apparent to the Belgians by the character of the emigrants from Germany who have recently been passing through Antwerp on their way to New York. There is but one opinion in intelligent, well-meaning circles in relation to the matter. It is considered as irrefragable evidence of the desperation of an enemy that is fighting for an unjust cause, and which is alike bankrupt in men and money.

It is proper that I should explain the reason why the bees of the German hive have been brought latterly to Antwerp for shipment. It has resulted exclusively from the renewed blockade of the ports of Hamburg and Bremen. Now that peace is almost as good as reestablished, the " White-slave trade " as it has been correctly termed, will resume its usual channel of conveyance. It is my belief, however, that this infamous traffic is near its end. The horrors attending it are more than even the idealogues of Europe, who have been so violent from the first in their opposition to us, can contemplate without shuddering.

The stupendous failure of Grant's campaign, the perilous if not inextricable position in which Sherman has placed himself, the resignation of Chase, and the continued rapid depreciation of "green-backs" occasion me to fervently indulge the hope that the North will swiftly be more humiliated in the sight of the powers and States of the world than any nation or people, recognized as constituting a nation, ever was before. How proud I am, apart from all the other joyous considerations which attach to such a consummation, that this will have been the work alone of the President and our officers and citizen soldiers. Subjected to a flagrantly one-sided neutrality by the two western powers, in their persistently refusing to recognize us, we shall have no obligations to pay to either; nor any acknowledgment to make for favors, however slight, to any one of the large countries of the earth. We shall present for the admiration of just contemporaries and a truth-seeking posterity the sublime spectacle of inflexible right, overpowering to utter disgrace, unscrupulous might.

Out of tenderness to the Federal States, in the dismay which must inevitably seize them on account of their continued deeply damaging disasters, I expect to see the joint mediation of France, Great Britain, and Russia proposed at an early day to the Washington Cabinet for an armistice. If offered to the President in advance of our unqualified recognition I am persuaded that it will be indignantly rejected. We have now taken the bull by the horns, after he has gored us mercilessly, and when he is fatigued to the point of certain death, unless he receive repose, and we shall be egregiously and inexcusably at fault if we suffer him to harm us any more.

I have the honor to be, sir, very respectfully, your obedient servant,

A. DUDLEY MANN.

Hon. J. P. BENJAMIN,
Secretary of State, C. S. A., Richmond, Va.

No. 99.]   BRUSSELS, *July 22, 1864.*

SIR: Yesterday was the thirty-third anniversary of the reign of King Leopold. It was celebrated generally and cordially throughout the realm.

But his Majesty, for reasons publicly unexplained, suddenly decided to absent himself from his metropolis, contrary to his usual observance upon such an occasion. Two days before the anniversary he repaired to Vichy, where the Emperor of the French annually sojourns from about the 10th of July to the 10th of August.

Various and numerous are the conjectures in relation to the motives of his unexpected departure. In my opinion an influencing if not a superinducing one was the indelicate and persistent exertions of the Lincoln legation here to obtain from him on his fête day a manifestation that could be construed as favorable to the Federal cause.

The Federal frigates *Niagara* and *Sacramento* came up the Scheldt and were at anchor yesterday in the harbor of Antwerp. Mr. Dayton, the minister at Paris, and other Federal functionaries had arrived here in advance of them, in joyous expectation, as it is understood, of a visit of the King to those vessels of war. Mr. Sanford, the minister of Lincoln to Belgium, pledged himself, it is asserted, to the Senate at Washington to the effect, that if that body would ratify the treaty which he negotiated for the payment of

2,750,000 francs for the capitalization of the Scheldt tolls, that the Federal Government would be more than compensated by the benefits which it would derive from the influence King Leopold would be induced to exert in behalf of their interests, as the Doyen of sovereigns, with European nations. Sumner stated as much in his effort to carry the treaty when the vote by which it had been defeated was under reconsideration, and upon this assuring statement alone he influenced Sherman of Ohio and other Senators to withdraw their objections.

King Leopold can not but view with disgusted feelings the vile artifices resorted to by the Lincoln Government to procure troops in Europe, now that they have been brought so immediately under his own eyes. With his long experience in public life he assuredly has never seen a belligerent actuated by baser passions, or one having recourse to such unjustifiable means. I am quite confident that he will bring the subject to the consideration of Louis Napoleon during his stay at Vichy, connecting with it our just claims for formal admission into the family of nations; but from that potentate I expect as little, even now, in our behalf as I have expected all along. He is precluded from recognizing us by his implied, if not secretly expressed, engagements with the incumbent of the White House. Lincoln, through Seward, has virtually covenanted that the Monroe doctrine shall continue obsolete, as far as concerns Mexico, while he remains in office, and in return the Emperor of the French has virtually covenanted that he will decline entering into official relations with us. In the presence of such an understanding the good offices of the King of the Belgians in our favor, however faithfully exerted, could not prove otherwise than unavailing with him.

It is currently reported that the true object of the meeting of the King and the Emperor was to negotiate a marriage between the Count of Flanders and the Princess Anna Murat. The count had been on a visit to Fontainebleau during the recent sojourn of the imperial family there, when he was presented to the princess, whose rare personal attractions are said to have captivated him. It is supposed that their union would be advantageous in strengthening both the dynasty of Napoleon III and of Leopold I. It is known, too, that the latter is exceedingly anxious, while yet he lives, to see his son eligibly married. Nor is he without care for the future of his daughter. Her letters to him from the City of Mexico, as I learn, are less satisfactory than he was encouraged to believe that they would be. The arrière pensée of Louis Napoleon, when he undertook to create a Mexican Empire, will, in my opinion, yet disclose itself at a suitable time.

The ministry of Belgium, after several weeks of unsuccessful attempts to administer the Government, since withdrawing its resignation, had no alternative but to decide upon a dissolution of the popular branch of the chambers. The new election is fixed for the 11th of August. The canvass is likely to be the most exciting one ever experienced in the realm.

The chances this moment are in favor of the opposition.

I have the honor to be, sir, very respectfully, your obedient servant,

A. Dudley Mann.

Hon. J. P. Benjamin,
  Secretary of State, C. S. A., Richmond, Va.

No. 47.]
CONFEDERATE STATES COMMERCIAL AGENCY AT LONDON,
Paris, July 29, 1864.

SIR: I date again from Paris, whither I have come on a flying visit of a few days only, mainly for the purpose of keeping up personal relations which might cool through too protracted intervals of absence, and to take advantage of several opportunities for forming new ones. The files and extracts which I have the honor to forward will show that the work in the French press is progressing satisfactorily, and that the general result even exceeds the anticipations I based upon my connection with M. Havas. The latest and most authentic news, either direct from New York and Richmond, or indirectly through the intermediation of the London press, with the most important comments of the latter, are regularly laid by the telegraph and by a system of varied correspondence before the French public. A double object is thus attained—we stimulate, satisfy, and yet keep alive public interest and secure the share of attention which is justly due to us—and we occupy and almost completely fill up a vacuum in which northern rumors and falsehoods were previously rioting at will. Our official documents are promptly translated, and with equal fidelity and spirit. Thus Captain Semmes' report of the engagement with the *Kearsarge* was printed in every Parisian newspaper the evening of the day on which it appeared in the London Times, and an admirable translation of the manifesto of the Confederate Congress had gone the round of the French press before the original had completed its round in England. My work in this has been that of the husbandman who tills, manures, and sows, and leaves bountiful nature and clement seasons to do the rest. Of course tares will spring up along with the wheat, and the harvest can not be accurately calculated, but it is something to have a field where before there was a wilderness.

Entering into details I may say that among the Parisian papers which take pleasure in doing us justice, and which gladly avail themselves of the information and materials afforded, without awaiting and indeed without permitting " inspiration " or anything that could in the least compromise their entire independence, are the Moniteur, both morning and evening, the Constitutional, the Patrie, the Pays, the France, the Nation, and numerous minor ones. There remains among important opponents, the Journal des Debats, the Siècle, the Temps, and the Opinion Nationale. Of these the three former have lapsed into a quasi neutrality, or at least sullen silence. The Opinion Nationale, a paper of little influence and less circulation, remains almost alone in the field, and by its redoubled vehemence and chronic inaccuracy has unwillingly rendered us most signal services in caricaturing the Northern argument. Of late a controversy has been waging between this paper and the Pays, in which it got ludicrously the worse, and which singularly illustrates the spontaneous and unartificial character of the change now manifest in the Parisian press, for the Pays could boast with truth that not one of its writers had any relation whatever with Southern representatives, and I myself had for the first time the honor of becoming acquainted with its chief editor during my present visit to Paris. In point of circulation, then, we have at least three-fourths in Paris, and probably the same in the Departments, though my estimate in this latter respect is purely speculative. In point of influence we lack two important papers, representing a numerically restricted party, but one which comprises much of the intelligence and respectability of France, the Journal des Debats and the Revue des Deux Mondes. It is perhaps too late to win their support, but the healthier tone which is now beginning to prevail may secure their cold neutrality.

You would do me great injustice if you thought that in making this gratifying report I am so egotistical as to fancy myself the cause. I desire only to vindicate the general principle of my operations, and no one can be more thoroughly convinced than I am that to General Lee's generalship and the valor of our patriot armies the credit is alone due. The most I can claim is to have made moderately good use of my opportunities and means. My chief difficulty is that of finding suitable instruments in sufficient numbers, the scarcity of which imposes on me an undue amount of what may fairly be called mechanical labor. This is a difficulty which can only be overcome by time and good fortune, and I state it as an excuse for shortcomings, without having to offer any suggestions likely to remedy it. I wish, however, in this connection to express the obligations under which I am to Mr. Henri Vignaud, of New Orleans, whose earnest and intelligent cooperation with me in Paris entitle him, at the proper time, to your favorable notice.

In England I am about to complete the arrangements to which I vaguely alluded several months ago as likely to take place at this time. It has long been a cherished object with me to have the Index take deep and permanent root in the great university bodies of this kingdom, not so much with a view to present as to future results upon the public opinion of which these bodies are, so to speak, the subsoil. My object is likely to be realized in the course of this month by intimately identifying with the editorial conduct of the Index two gentlemen who combine with a zealous devotion to our principles and our cause the highest academical distinction, well merited popularity and influence, and a social position as honorable in the present as it is promising for the future. In a material point of view also, the Index has made most gratifying strides. It has consolidated its position in the press, has extorted rather than won support, and is steadily extending in circulation. Its expenses, at least the disbursements made through it, have, it is true, kept pace with its increased earnings, and I have not effected the savings which I confidently expected at the beginning of the year, but then my sphere of operations has also been considerably enlarged and with it, thanks to your prompt attention to my necessities, the means at my disposal. Neither in a literary and political nor in a pecuniary point of view have I therefore the same anxieties for the Index as in its earlier stages. For the rest the tone of the English press is all that could be expected or desired, and it is a notable fact that the word "slavery" is rarely ever mentioned, and even the attempt at agitation on that ground has ceased.

My work being thus, both in England and France, reduced within manageable dimensions, I feel able, if it is thought desirable, to devote some efforts to a field hitherto entirely neglected, viz, Germany. On this subject I have received very earnest solicitations from several quarters, based upon arguments difficult to resist, notably that of the substantial support which the utter ignorance of the German people on American affairs now affords to the tottering finances of the North, and which is considered to be the last prop of the greenback currency. Among others, I have for some time had a correspondence with a gentleman introduced and warmly recommended by Mr. Slidell, Mr. S. Ricker, late U. S. consul-general at Frankfort, and I have consented to aid him with materials, etc., and a very moderate amount of money, not at present exceeding 1,000 francs. I have also promised before the end of the summer to make a short tour to inspect the ground, thinking thus to combine a little relaxation, which I sadly need in point of health, with some possible advantage to the cause. That I have not entered more eagerly into the field is due to several causes, of which the absence of definite instructions from you is not the principal, since I believe you would sanction in advance anything in that quarter undertaken with reasonable chances of success. One of these causes is that I am averse to attempting too much and thus accomplishing too little. Another, that although moderately proficient through circumstances of early education with the German language, I feel conscious of lacking that sympathy or those points of mental and moral contact with German thought which seem indispensable to influencing even in a slight degree the public opinion of a great people. Thirdly, the difficulties seem to me next to insurmountable. The German press has neither a geographical nor metropolitan center like the English press, nor is it subject to the political and intellectual centralization of an imperial régime like the French. It is necessary, therefore, to work in detail and at innumerable points simultaneously, and I confess that this deters me.

Still, I had always hoped to give considerable extension to my machinery for telegraphing and correspondence, and I shall not fail to do what it may be possible to do in this respect. But if you deem it important to do more, I would suggest the appointment of a special agent for the purpose, and you will perhaps excuse me for suggesting the name of a gentleman who appears to me to combine more of the requisite qualifications than anyone of my acquaintance. I refer to Mr. Auguste P. Wetter, of Savannah, of whom I spoke in my earlier dispatches as having contributed to the establishment of the Index, spontaneously and without expectation of repayment, £200, then very much needed, and as the translator of Mr. Spence's book into German. Mr. Wetter belongs to a Mayence family of distinction in literature and art, and is connected by marriage with one of the wealthiest families in Georgia. I became acquainted with him on his visit to Europe over two years ago, when he was one of the first originators of a systematic plan of blockade running, and may possibly claim the credit of having enlisted in that business, by the joint enterprise of the *Hero*, the now famous firm of A. Collie & Co. Although possessed of respectable military ability, as he was the first to select and fortify the site of Fort McAllister, I believe he is, owing to some disappointment, now out of the Army, and though I have not heard from him for over a year, I think he would be flattered by the offer from you to serve in the capacity indicated and would eagerly accept it. As he is a man of wealth, and patriotic, he would probably be contented with a nominal salary, and not spare his private means in serving the cause. It would not be necessary to subordinate him to me, and I feel certain that he would consult and cordially cooperate on all proper occasions. You will, of course, understand that the suggestion of Mr. Wetter's name is entirely my own, unknown and therefore unauthorized by him, and made in that spirit of perfect confidence to which you have so courteously and kindly accustomed me.

This dispatch would convey an erroneous impression were I not to add the conviction, at which I have long arrived, that however great the power of the press, and however judiciously and successfully it may be wielded, this power is exaggerated when it is expected to shape immediately or to influence directly the policies of European Governments. No cause had ever more completely the unanimous support of the French press than the Polish cause for many months. There was not in any quarter a dissenting voice, scarcely a lukewarm one, yet this did not prevent France standing by and seeing the last flickering spark of Polish independence crushed out. At this very moment the telegraph announces the execution of the chief and of the principal members of the "National Government." For over two years we have had a clear majority of the English press in our favor. The geography of the war, its causes, its events, the resources of the combatants, were not better understood or more elaborately treated even in America, and yet this did not prevent Lord Palmerston at the end of the session insulting a deputation of English gentlemen of the highest respectability by telling them that "they who in quarrels interpose will often wipe a bloody nose." If, then, immediately practical effects are looked to, I fear we are doomed to continued disappointment, and money and efforts are alike thrown away. My consolation is that we are working for the future and for moral results, compared to which recognition, now so important, is a small object. It is for this reason that I am anxious that our progress in the European press should be permanent, that one strong position after another should be garrisoned and fortified, and that arsenals should be laid up at various places, so as to fight on equal terms the battles of moral independence which await us when the strife of arms is succeeded by the contests of diplomacy.

I have the honor to remain, very respectfully, your obedient servant,

HENRY HOTZE.

Hon. J. B. BENJAMIN,
    Secretary of State, Richmond.

No. 100.]   BRUSSELS, July 30, 1864.

SIR: Detailed accounts have been received in the New York journals to the afternoon of the 16th instant of the operations of our noble little army in Maryland. One-sided as they undoubtedly are, they nevertheless establish the fact of the complete success which attended the object of the invasion. Everywhere we seem to be either victorious or to be holding our own against vastly superior numbers. In the way of brilliant achievements the expectations of our most ardent European admirers have been more than realized. If our success continues the North will soon have more cause to desire peace than the South ever had in her darkest days.

Maximilian, I am informed, is soon to send a minister to Washington. After his arrival, Lincoln, it is asserted, is under an obligation to accredit one to the new Imperial Government. This is in compliance with the arrangement which grew out of the disavowal by Seward of the resolution of Winter Davis, in vindication of the Monroe doctrine, which passed the House unanimously.

There is at this moment well-nigh to a panic in Germany and Holland among the holders of Federal securities. Confidence in those securities is universally impaired. Three months hence they will not likely be worth more than 10 cents on the dollar.

Enough is already known of the negotiations which are progressing for that object at Vienna to create a confident belief that hostilities have been definitively terminated between the German powers and Denmark. This will secure the peace of Europe in all probability, for the remainder of the present year at least.

It is perhaps proper that I should state, lest there may have been miscarriage in conveyance, that I have received no dispatch, or other communication, from you of later date than the 1st of February.

I have the honor to be, sir, very respectfully, your obedient servant,

A. DUDLEY MANN.

Hon. J. P. BENJAMIN,
Secretary of State, C. S. A., Richmond, Va.

No. 68.] PARIS, *August 1, 1864.*

SIR: Since my last dispatch of 11th ultimo I have received your Nos. 38 and 39 of 31 May and 1st June. As in the former you leave it discretionary with me " to make to Mr. Drouyn de Lhuys explanation further than that contained in the correspondence" itself (relating to the shipment of the tobacco belonging to the Régie) " to prevent any misunderstanding of our views, and of the friendly sentiments by which we are actuated toward the Government of the Emperor," I shall abstain for the present from volunteering any such explanation.

The course of this Government of late has not been such as, in my opinion, to call for any gratuitous expression of good will on our part. I shall await some evidence of a change of policy toward us or an express request for explanation from the minister of foreign affairs. Indeed, I do not regret that reasons furnished by French officials themselves on our side of the water should have furnished a sufficient cause to retract a privilege which probably would not now be accorded with a knowledge of the existing state of things here. Applying to us the very strictest law, the Government of the Emperor can not well complain if we in turn refuse to allow his property to leave our limits excepting on conditions of perfect equality with that of our own citizens.

In my last I informed you that notwithstanding the written declaration of the Emperor, dated 7th July, that he had given the order permitting the sailing of the *Rappahannock*, the fact was ignored by the ministers of foreign affairs and marine. This state of things continuing, on the 15th I addressed Mr. Mocquard at Vichy a note, of which the following is an extract: "The Duke of Persigny made known to me a letter from the Emperor, dated the 7th instant, telling him that his Majesty had given the order for the *Rappahannock* to leave the ports of France. The 9th, in reply to a verbal enquiry to the minister of foreign affairs, I learned that no decision had been taken in the *Rappahannock* affair. I then addressed myself to Mr. Chasseloup-Laubat, believing that the order had been given to him. He assured me that the affair was entirely in the hands of Mr. Drouyn de Lhuys. On the 12th I addressed a note to the minister of foreign affairs, recalling to his memory the verbal promise that he gave me on the 21st of June to decide promptly the question of the leaving of the *Rappahannock*, and to communicate his decision to me. This note remains unanswered, and I learn to-day that the question is still undecided. I make no comments on these facts, but I write to ask you if you can not enlighten me, etc."

Mr. Mocquard, in reply, informed me that the necessary order had been given; this was on the 19th. On the 20th I received a note from the minister of marine, asking me to call and see him.

He read me a letter from Mr. Drouyn de Lhuys, who had been called to Vichy, in which he conveyed the order of the Emperor for permitting the departure of the *Rappahannock* in conformity with the "avis" of the "comité du contentieux," and saying that the "avis" must be strictly complied with by reducing the number of men on board the *Rappahannock* to that which she had on entering Calais; the injunction of strict compliance with this condition was repeated at the close of the letter. The minister of marine called my attention to this injunction, which had not struck me as objectionable, saying that he regretted being compelled to follow it literally, as the number on board of the ship when she entered Calais was scarcely sufficient to navigate her, as it did not exceed 25 men all told, including 15 workmen who left her the next day. I expressed my surprise at this statement, as I had supposed that the real number was at least 70, and had been reported by Captain Campbell to the custom-house at 100, in accordance, as he said, with the advice of the commisary of marine at Calais. The minister of marine assured me that his estimate was fully confirmed by the reports made at the time, and, referring to the "Dossier," read various extracts to that effect. I insisted that this point had been waived by the acquiescerce of his officers in the subsequent increase of the crew. He replied that it was true that he had acquiesced in the increase and that the ship could have gone to sea without difficulty if anything approaching reasonable diligence had been used by the commander; that he had again and again urged dispatch, anticipating difficulty, but that no attention was paid to his messages, which were intended as friendly hints, and that the order to go to sea given on the 14th February had the same motive. He sent for his chef d'etat, Major-Admiral de la Roncière, who confirmed all that he had said, referring to minutes of his correspondence on the subject. I said that it was impossible that the ship could proceed to sea with 25 men all told, or even with the 35, which was the extreme number mentioned in any of the reports, and which the minister agreed after some hesitation to admit; that I thought if this point were insisted on the permission to go to sea was altogether illusory, but that I should consult with the superior officer of our Navy then in Paris and let him know his determination.

In this interview the minister repeatedly expressed his deep regret at the stringency of the instructions under which he was acting and which allowed him no discretion. I asked him whether, the matter having now reverted to his jurisdiction, he could not with propriety call the attention of the Emperor to the insufficiency of a crew of 35 men to carry out a ship whose movements were closely watched by several of the enemy's cruisers; he said that he could not do that, but that on the return of the minister of foreign affairs from Vichy he would see him and endeavor to obtain some relaxation of his instructions. He fixed Sunday, 24th July, for another interview with him; on that day he said that he had not been able to see his colleague, who had been detained longer than he had expected, but that he would let me know so soon as anything had been determined.

On the 28th I received a note requesting me to call on him, when he said that the question had been discussed in cabinet council, the Empress presiding, on the previous day and that it was decided not to change the instructions. I am not altogether without hopes that in carrying them out something may be voluntarily overlooked by the officer charged with their execution; if not, it will be for Commodore Barron to decide whether the ship shall go to sea or the enterprise be abandoned.

In this question the minister of foreign affairs has manifested throughout ill will and bad faith. I attribute this to timidity, for, strange as it may seem, the fact is patent that Mr. Dayton has managed to convince him that the Lincoln Government is prepared to go to war with France, if not directly at least by pursuing a course toward Mexico which would necessarily soon result in open hostilities. I still believe that the Emperor is decidedly our friend, but the Mexican question and his well-founded distrust of England will continue to prevent any favorable action on his part, in which she will not fully participate.

It has long been a mystery to me that the Federal currency should not have suffered an earlier and greater depreciation, but a fact which recently came to my knowledge serves to explain it to a considerable extent. I had known that there was a certain, but I supposed a very limited, market in Germany and Holland for Federal bonds, but that demand has been gradually extended until it has now reached very large proportions. I have good authority for estimating the amount now held in those countries at one hundred and fifty millions, and the disposition to make these investments appears to increase with the fall in their purchasable price.

They began at about 70 per cent and are now selling at Frankfort, Amsterdam, and Berlin at 44 per cent.

I have the honor to be, with great respect, your obedient servant,

JOHN SLIDELL.

Hon. J. P. BENJAMIN,
Secretary of State.

No. 12.]　　　　　　　　　　　　　　　　　LONDON, *August 4, 1864.*

SIR: The last dispatch received from you was No. 35 of 18th April, received on the 8th June, and acknowledged in my No. 9 of the 9th June, from this place, and which modified the instructions previously given as to my visiting London.

In my No. 8 of the 1st June from Paris I gave the reasons which led me to return to London, though in a strictly private capacity, agreeably confirmed to me afterwards by the modified instructions referred to.

Parliament was prorogued on the 29th July and without a vote being taken on the resolution of Mr. Lindsay. With many fair expressions that gentleman found it impossible, it appeared, to conciliate the ministry in its favor, and therefore deemed it more prudent to let it go by. As things stand we can only still further await events. In an unofficial note written from Mr. Lindsay's some two or three weeks since I gave you the substance of an interview I had with Lord Palmerston. It imported but little, and in a private note to the President, which accompanies this dispatch, I give the report somewhat more in detail, thinking it best not to give the subject the formal character of a dispatch.

In my No. 8 from Paris I informed you of the release from custody of the men held for piracy on board the *Gerrity* and whose defense I had assumed, as communicated to you in my No. 7, of the 12th April, and informing you that I should defray the expenses, charging them for the time being to the contingent fund. I have since received the entire bill of costs from the solicitors, including the fees of counsel, and which, as would seem, belonging to bills of that character in England, presented a formidable aspect, the gross sum amounting to £489 11s. 4d. Although I had been previously advised of the entire respectability of the solicitors, I thought it prudent to subject the bill to the criticism of a taxing master in the courts. He reported that the items were fair and usual, except in the charges for traveling expenses of the solicitors from Liverpool to London, and which he reduced by the sum of £31 10s., leaving the aggregate £458 1s. 4d., which I shall pay. Looking to the character of the instructions in regard to a similar case given to Mr. Holcombe, I feel satisfied that I did right in assuming for the Government the responsibility of the defense and hope it will be approved. The bill in detail will, of course, be preserved as a voucher. This payment, together with those previously made for account of the Department in the purchase of books and for the seal, will more than exhaust the contingent fund, or if applied to the fund recently supplied to me by the bill for £500, will, with expenditures already made from it, more than exhaust that. I submit, therefore, to the Department that the amount of these legal expenses, as stated (£458 1s. 4d.), be remitted to me for that specific expenditure.

There being nothing special calling me to the Continent, and the political world generally being in recess for the summer, I propose for the next two or three months to visit different points in England and in Ireland, not to return to London unless specially called. I shall always, however, be in immediate reach of the mails and telegraph and at once accessible through an address left in London.

I send with this duplicate of my No. 11 of the 8 July ultimo.

I have, etc.,

J. M. MASON.

Hon. J. P. BENJAMIN,
Secretary of State.

No. 48.]   Confederate States Commercial Agency,
                              London, August 6, 1864.

Sir: A review of the political situation, although it is some time since I wrote you on general affairs, need occupy no great space. Now that the session is over the ministers are enjoying their triumph at small adulatory gatherings and select banquets and showing how little they deserve success by complacently, and even boastfully, ascribing to themselves what is really due to accident and the public apathy. Thus Lord Russell had the assurance to say at the lord mayor's dinner given to her Majesty's ministers that the position of England had never been prouder nor her influence greater than at this moment, an announcement which, to the honor of the audience be it said, was received in silence, succeeded, as soon as the first sudden effect of astonishment had worn off, by a buzz of general conversation. Lord Palmerston has betrayed, by exhibitions of ill-temper and the gratification of little personal spites and revenges in the closing days of the session, how thoroughly he must have been scared and how narrow he considers the escape to have been. Meanwhile the country has given another evidence of the steady growth of the Conservative, or at least opposition feeling, in the defeat for the first time in this generation of the Liberal candidate in the populous constituency of Exeter. Unfortunately, as the last Parliamentary battle has proved, the strength of the latent protest against the ministerial policy is wasted by want of tact and want of principles or courage on the part of the leaders of the opposition, and thus the weakness of the administration only serves as a pretext and excuse for its inaction.

Abroad everything is now as quiet as the most imbecile of " apres moi le deluge " statesmen could desire. No great danger has been averted, no great question solved, but everything has been put off for the moment, and procrastination has gained at least four or five months of ease, at what cost the future alone can show. Denmark has been forced into a peace so ignominious that the Legislative Assembly, on hearing the terms announced, was as silent as Earl Russell's auditors at the lord mayor's banquet, but afterwards passed a resolution to the effect that this silence was not to be construed into approval. A few months will, of course, be spent in negotiations of details, but the basis is accepted and is such an one as even the Germans themselves a year ago would have thought preposterous. In Poland the last act of the tragedy is played out and the curtain falls, probably forever, on the execution of the principal chiefs of the National Government, the transportation of the others to Siberian fortresses, and the expropriation of nearly the whole body of landed proprietors. A sort of earthquake has passed over the Mussulman populations, beginning in Algeria, shaking the Government of Tunis, and largely manifesting itself in a revival, or rather outbreak, of Mohammedanism in the Ottoman Empire. These are the impotent protests against the proselytism of western Europe, but either they have no longer or not yet any serious importance.

There is, therefore, absolutely no excuse left in the present state of Europe for inattention to American affairs. Yet you will have seen, better than I could tell you, how absolutely hopeless it still is to expect anything in our favor for some time to come, or until we shall no longer need it. In this respect there seems little to choose between the English and French Governments, except that the former has at least been consistent in its coldness, while the latter has raised expectations apparently only to disappoint them the more cruelly. As Mr. Mason has been sojourning for several weeks past in England, he has probably advised you of our prospects here, as Mr. Slidell will have done from France, and I need therefore do nothing more than report the conclusions at which I believe every Confederate sympathizer in Europe has now arrived, that any present hope of recognition is a delusion.

The military events are watched with all the more anxious eagerness and it is noticeable that the public sympathetic to us, invariably receives with evident uneasiness the news of every offensive movement on our part beyond our own territory. Bright as the prospects of General Early's invasion into Maryland were admitted to be, the first intelligence of it affected the loan unfavorably. I doubt whether even the capture of Baltimore or Washington would so much reassure public anxiety as a decisive victory over Sherman.

Financial difficulties, perhaps even a crisis, are foreseen in the course of next autumn, due partly to overspeculation, but accelerated by the reports of bad harvests in America and in southern Russia, and above all the enormous amounts of specie required for the purchase of cotton. Our own financial condition abroad appears to be excellent. We have gradually got rid of the adventurers and leeches that throve upon the public purse and affected to be considered patriotic or devoted friends, and have formed new connections at once more advantageous and more respectable. Despite the serious doubts of the fate of Atlanta the loan has kept at a quotation of 75 to 77, which proves inherent strength. The new commercial system, though scarcely yet in its infancy, has thus far worked so beneficially as to promise when fully developed to fulfill literally and even to exceed my own glowing anticipations. I can only hope that no amount of pressure brought to bear upon the Government, from any quarter whatever, may induce it to swerve from the policy which dictated these salutary measures.

The first rumor of peace negotiations caused considerable sensation both in England and France, but when the details of the Niagara Falls correspondence became known, the public seemed disposed to avenge their disappointment by pitilessly ridiculing both parties. I have done my best, under an urgent necessity which you will appreciate, to disconnect the Government and its trusted agents from the eccentricities of persons whose notoriety in Europe is much greater than the esteem in which they are held.

I have the honor to remain, very respectfully, your obedient servant,

HENRY HOTZE.

Hon. J. P. BENJAMIN,
    Secretary of State, Richmond.

No. 69.]   PARIS, *August 8, 1864.*

SIR: I last had the honor of addressing you on the 1st instant. I am still without any dispatches from you later than your No. 39 of 1st June.

Commodore Barron and Captain Bulloch have fully advised the Secretary of the Navy of the reasons which induced Captain Fauntleroy not to avail himself of the tardy and ungracious permission for the sailing of the *Rappahannock;* they may be summed up in the inadequacy of the number of men which he was allowed to retain, the impossibility of shipping and dispatching from England or elsewhere the remainder of the crew, the presence of four of the enemy's cruisers in the neighborhood of Calais, the inability of the ship to carry more than five days' full supply of coal, and her general unfitness for the service in which she was to be employed.

Captain Bulloch is now here for the purpose of closing the sale and delivery of the ships built at Bordeaux and Nantes. This is a most lame and impotent conclusion of all our efforts to create a Navy; but he thinks, and I agree with him, that this is the better course to pursue under all the circumstances, and I have no doubt that the President will approve of it when he shall have seen the captain's report to the Navy Department.

General Preston has been in Paris for some days. He has seen Mr. Hidalgo, the Mexican minister at this court, and Mr. Arrangoiz, who will represent Maximilian in London. He has hinted to those gentlemen that one of the conditions of our peace with the North, now considered not very remote, may probably be a treaty of alliance, offensive and defensive, for the establishment of an American policy on our continent, which will result in the suppression of monarchical institutions in Mexico. I have thought it politic to throw out similar suggestions in other quarters, from which they will be likely to reach the Emperor and Mr. Drouyn de Lhuys, not as based on any instructions which I have received, but on a letter from our agents in Canada.

This being the season when the Emperor and nearly all the public men are absent from Paris, and nothing at present requiring my presence here, I shall avail myself of the opportunity to pass four or five weeks on the Rhine. As I shall be within twelve or fourteen hours distance, I will be prepared to return at once to my post should anything occur which can not be as well attended to by Mr. Eustis.

I have the honor to be, with great respect, your most obedient servant,

JOHN SLIDELL.

Hon. J. P. BENJAMIN,
Secretary of State.

No. 7.]   CLIFTON HOUSE,
Niagara Falls, C. W., August 11, 1864.

SIR: Since my last dispatch I have visited all the points in Canada, at which it was probable any escaped prisoners could be found. I have circulated as widely as possible the information that all who desired to return to the discharge of their duty could obtain transportation to their respective commands within the Confederacy. For this purpose I have made arrangements with reliable gentlemen at Windsor, Niagara, Hamilton, Toronto, and Montreal to forward such as from time to time may require this assistance as far as Halifax, from which point they will be sent by Messrs. Wier & Co., to Bermuda. The system thus organized will provide for the return of any ordinary average of escaped prisoners. If, however, any contingency should lead to the accumulation of a large number in Canada, some special arrangement like that contemplated when I left Richmond would be required. As events (to which it is scarcely prudent to refer) may soon transpire, which would render this contingency by no means remote or improbable, I have deemed it my duty to defer my departure for a time. I feel the more confidence in my judgment upon this subject from the fact that it has the concurrence of Messrs. Clay and Thompson. I have availed myself in the interim of every opportunity to cooperate with these gentlemen, and think that I have been able to render useful service. My present expectation is to return in September.

A distinct communication from Messrs. Clay and myself, is sent by this mail.

With the highest respect, I remain,

JAMES P. HOLCOMBE.

Hon. J. P. BENJAMIN,
   Secretary of State, C. S. A.

DEPARTMENT OF STATE,
Richmond, August 12, 1864.

DEAR SIR: I see by the papers that a new argument is to be had in the case of Ogden on the point whether he is not saved by operation of the treaty of the United States with Great Britain.

It occurs to me that you may perhaps not remember that the President in his message of 7th December last has taken the ground that the Confederacy is no longer bound by any treaties with foreign nations, and I suppose that from our Executive charged with our foreign relations, this is a binding declaration on a political question within the competence of the President.

Yours truly,

J. P. BENJAMIN,
   Secretary of State.

P. H. AYLETT, Esq.

No. 103.]   BRUSSELS, August 20, 1864.

SIR: I think I can now safely venture to assure you that we have nothing to apprehend from any considerable accession of strength to the Federal Army hereafter, derived from European supplies. Such has been the demand for recruits at New York and elsewhere in the North that there is at length an exhaustion of this war material, available for that purpose, in this hemisphere. It is bankrupt of criminals and paupers. All the houses of correction and poorhouses have been drained. The fact that immigrants of this description were acceptable to the Lincoln Government, now that it is becoming generally known, has alone a tendency to deter from emigrating persons who can make a living by industry. The following statement, recently published in all the Belgian papers, and also extensively circulated in Germany, has been productive of an immense amount of harm to Lincoln and Co. In all circles in which it has been read it has created an impression that a Government that is driven to the necessity of having recourse to such soldiers to fight its aggressive battles is in reality a Government in deep despair. This very occurrence will, in all probability, deprive it of regiments that it might clandestinely have raised in Germany.

" We read," says l'Independance Belge, "in a journal of Mons that the Dis-United States use up so large a supply of men in their fratricidal war that they are forced to resort to every other country in search of ' food for powder.' Day before yesterday 45 inmates of the house of correction at this city were liberated, in order to proceed to New York, where, immediately after their arrival, they will be regularly enrolled in the Army. They are to embark at Antwerp in about a week from now."

The bonds of the Federal Government have experienced a fall of 3 per cent this forenoon at the exchange of Frankfort on the Main. They are at this moment quoted there at 39, the lowest point of depression which they have ever touched, being a little less than half the value of the Confederate loan, according to actual sales in London yesterday.

I have the honor to be, sir, very respectfully, your obedient servant,

A. DUDLEY MANN.

Hon. J. P. BENJAMIN,
Secretary of State, C. S. A., Richmond, Va.

No. 70.]   BADEN, *August 24, 1864.*

SIR: In my last of 8th instant I informed you of my purpose to make a short absence from my post.

I now have the honor to acknowledge receipt of your dispatch, No. 40, of 23d June, and am not surprised at the view taken by the President of the course pursued toward us by the French Government for some months past. You attribute that course to the proper motive, a desire to conciliate the Yankee Government and thus to avoid a collision of which both France and England entertain a childish fear. I have in vain on all fitting occasions endeavored to impress upon public men in France the utter futility of such apprehensions; they are too deeply fixed to be eradicated, and are strengthened by the mutual and well-founded distrust which the two great maritime powers entertain of each other.

As we have ceased since the sale of our ships to have any peculiar and urgent interest to conciliate the French Government, I consider it to be sound policy, as well as good taste, to abstain for the present from any attempt in that direction. I still think that the sympathies of the Emperor are sincerely with us, and I have good reason to believe that he and those who are nearest to him estimate the friendly protestations of Lincoln and Seward at their just value; but the great object now is to keep everything quiet until Maximilian's Empire shall present some show of stability, when he will be left to his own resources; it is not difficult to anticipate what will be its fate so soon as the French troops are withdrawn.

I have communicated to General Preston a copy of your dispatch to him of 20th June; he not having received the original he has dispatched Mr. Fearn to Mexico to carry out your instructions.

I learn from Frankfort that the stupid confidence of German and Dutch capitalists in Federal securities has at last been shaken, until now all the purchases and remittances of stock from New York have yielded a large profit, but the reaction has commenced and the bonds are now considerably below the New York quotations at the gold standard; this can not fail soon to produce a corresponding effect in Wall Street.

I shall return to Paris on the 10th September or sooner should anything occur to render my presence there necessary.

I am, with very great respect, your most obedient servant,

J. SLIDELL.

Hon. J. P. BENJAMIN,
    Secretary of State.

Circular.]
                                           DEPARTMENT OF STATE,
                                     Richmond, August 25, 1864.

SIR: Numerous publications which have recently appeared in the journals of the United States on the subject of informal overtures for peace between the two federations of States now at war on this continent, render it desirable that you should be fully advised of the views and policy of this Government on a matter of such paramount importance. It is likewise proper that you should be accurately informed of what has occurred on the several occasions mentioned in the public statements.

You have heretofore been furnished with copies of the manifesto issued by the Congress of the Confederate States with the approval of the President on the 14th June last, and have doubtless acted in conformity with the resolution which requested that copies of this manifesto should be laid before foreign governments. "The principles, sentiments, and purposes by which these States have been and are still actuated," are set forth in that paper with all the authority due to the solemn declaration of the legislative and executive departments of this Government, and with a clearness which leaves no room for comment or explanation. In a few sentences it pointed out that all we ask is immunity from interference with our internal peace and prosperity, "and to be left in the undisturbed enjoyment of those inalienable rights of life, liberty, and the pursuit of happiness which our common ancestors declared to be the equal heritage of all parties to the social compact. Let them forbear aggressions upon us and the war is at an end. If there be questions which require adjustment by negotiation, we have ever been willing and are still willing to enter into communication with our adversaries in a spirit of peace, of equity, and manly frankness." The manifesto closed with the declaration that "we commit our cause to the enlightened judgment of the world, to the sober reflections of our adversaries themselves, and to the solemn and righteous arbitrament of Heaven."

Within a very few weeks after the publication of this manifesto, it seemed to have met with a response from President Lincoln. In the early part of last month a letter was received by General Lee from Lieutenant-General Grant, in the following words:

HEADQUARTERS OF THE ARMIES OF THE UNITED STATES,
                            City Point, Va., July 8, 1864.

GENERAL: I would request that Colonel James F. Jaquess, Seventy-third Illinois Volunteer Infantry, and J. R. Gilmore, esq., be allowed to meet Colonel Robert Ould, commissioner for the exchange of prisoners, at such place between the lines of the two armies as you may designate. The object of the meeting is legitimate with the duties of Colonel Ould as commissioner.

If not consistent for you to grant the request here asked, I would beg that this be referred to President Davis for his action.

Requesting as early an answer to this communication as you may find it convenient to make, I subscribe myself

Very respectfully, your obedient servant,

U. S. GRANT,
Lieutenant-General, U. S. A.

· General R. E. LEE,
Commanding Confederate Forces, near Petersburg, Va.

On the reference of this letter to the President he authorized Colonel Ould to meet the persons named in General Grant's letter, and Colonel Ould, after seeing them, returned to Richmond and reported to the President in the presence of the Secretary of War and myself that Messrs. Jaquess and Gilmore had not said anything to him about his duties as commissioner for exchange of prisoners, but that they asked permission to come to Richmond for the purpose of seeing the President. They came with the knowledge and approval of President Lincoln and under his pass. They were informal messengers sent with a view to paving the way for a meeting of formal commissioners authorized to negotiate for peace, and desired to communicate to President Davis the views of Mr. Lincoln and to obtain the President's views in return, so as to arrange for a meeting of commissioners. Colonel Ould stated that he had told them repeatedly that it was useless to come to Richmond to talk of peace on any other terms than the recognized independence of the Confederacy, to which they said that they were aware of that, and that they were nevertheress confident that their interview would result in peace. The President, on this report of Colonel Ould, determined to permit them to come to Richmond under his charge.

On the evening of the 16th July Colonel Ould conducted these gentlemen to a hotel in Richmond where a room was provided for them in which they were to remain under surveillance during their stay here, and the next morning I received the following letter:

SPOTSWOOD HOUSE,
Richmond, Va., July 17, 1864.

DEAR SIR: The undersigned, James F. Jaquess, of Illinois, and James R. Gilmore, of Massachusetts, most respectfully solicit an interview with President Davis. They visit Richmond as private citizens, and have no official character or authority, but they are fully possessed of the views of the United States Government relative to an adjustment of the differences now existing between the North and the South, and have little doubt that a free interchange of views between President Davis and themselves would open the way to such *official* negotiations as would ultimate in restoring *peace* to the two sections of our distracted country.

They therefore ask an interview with the President, and awaiting your reply are

Most truly and respectfully, your obedient servants,

JAMES F. JAQUESS.
JAMES R. GILMORE.

Hon. J. P. BENJAMIN,
Secretary of State of C. S. A.

The word "official" is underscored, and the word "peace" doubly underscored in the original.

After perusing the letter, I invited Colonel Ould to conduct the writers to my office, and on their arrival stated to them that they must be conscious they could not be admitted to an interview with the President without informing me more fully of the object of their mission, and satisfying me that they came by request of Mr. Lincoln. Mr. Gilmore replied that they came unofficially, but with the knowledge and at the desire of Mr. Lincoln; that they thought the war had gone far enough, that it could never end except by some sort of agreement, that the agreement might as well be made now as after further bloodshed; that they knew by the recent address of the Confederate Congress that we were willing to make peace; that they admitted that proopsals ought to come from the North, and that they were prepared to make these proposals by Mr. Lincoln's authority; that it was necessary to have a sort of informal understanding in advance of regular negotiations, for if commissioners were appointed without some such understanding, they would meet, quarrel, and separate, leaving the parties more bitter against each other than before; that they knew Mr. Lincoln's views, and would state them if pressed by the President to do so, and desired to learn his in return.

I again insisted on some evidence that they came from Mr. Lincoln, and in order to satisfy me Mr. Gilmore referred to the fact that permission for their coming through our lines had been asked officially by General Grant in a letter to General Lee, and that General Grant in that letter had asked that this request should be referred to President Davis. Mr. Gilmore then showed me a card written and signed by Mr. Lincoln, requesting General Grant to aid Mr. Gilmore and friend in passing through his lines into the Confederacy. Colonel Jaquess then said that his name was not put on the card for the reason that it was earnestly desired that their visit should be kept secret; that he had come into the Confederacy a year ago and had visited Petersburg on a similar errand; and that it was feared if his name should become known that some of those who had formerly met him in Petersburg would conjecture the purpose for which he now came. He said that the terms of peace which they would offer to the President would be honorable to the Confederacy, that they did not desire that the Confederacy should accept any other terms, but would be glad to have my promise, as they gave theirs, that their visit should be kept a profound secret if it failed to result in peace; that it would not be just that either party should seek any advantage by divulging the fact of their overture for peace, if unsuccessful. I assented to this request, and then rising, said: "Do I understand you to state distinctly that you came as messengers from Mr. Lincoln for the purpose of agreeing with the President as to the proper mode of inaugurating a formal negotiation for peace, charged by Mr. Lincoln with authority for stating his own views and receiving those of President Davis?" Both answered in the affirmative, and I then said that the President would see them at my office the same evening at 9 p. m.; that at least I presumed he would; but if he objected, after hearing my report, they should be informed. They were recommitted to the charge of Colonel Ould with the understanding that they were to be reconducted to my office at the appointed hour unless otherwise directed.

This interview, connected with the report previously made by Colonel Ould, left on my mind the decided impression that Mr.

Lincoln was averse to sending formal commissioners to open negotiations lest he might thereby be deemed to have recognized the independence of the Confederacy, and that he was anxious to learn whether the conditions on which alone he would be willing to take such a step would be yielded by the Confederacy; that with this view he had placed his messengers in a condition to satisfy us that they really came from him, without committing himself to anything in the event of a disagreement to such conditions as he considered to be indispensable. On informing the President, therefore, of my conclusions he determined that no questions of form or etiquette should be an obstacle to his receiving any overtures that promised however remotely to result in putting an end to the carnage which marked the continuance of hostilities.

The President came to my office at 9 o'clock in the evening and Colonel Ould came a few minutes later with Messrs. Jaquess and Gilmore. The President said to them that he had heard from me that they came as messengers of peace from Mr. Lincoln; that as such they were welcome; that the Confederacy had never concealed its desire for peace; and that he was ready to hear whatever they had to offer on that subject.

Mr. Gilmore then addressed the President, and in a few minutes had conveyed the information that these two gentlemen had come to Richmond impressed with the idea that this Government would accept a peace on a basis of a reconstruction of the Union, the abolition of slavery, and the grant of an amnesty to the people of the States as repentant criminals. In order to accomplish the abolition of slavery it was proposed that there should be a general vote of all the people of both Federations in mass, and the majority of the vote thus taken was to determine that as well as all other disputed questions. These were stated to be Mr. Lincoln's views. The President answered that as these proposals had been prefaced by the remark that the people of the North were a majority, and that a majority ought to govern, the offer was in effect a proposal that the Confederate States should surrender at discretion, admit that they had been wrong from the beginning of the contest, submit to the mercy of their enemies, and avow themselves to be in need of pardon for crimes; that extermination was preferable to such dishonor. He stated that if they were themselves so unacquainted with the form of their own Government as to make such propositions, Mr. Lincoln ought to have known, when giving them his views, that it was out of the power of the Confederate Government to act on the subject of the domestic institutions of the several States, each State having exclusive jurisdiction on that point, still less to commit the decision of such a question to the vote of a foreign people; that the separation of the States was an accomplished fact; that he had no authority to receive proposals for negotiations except by virtue of his office as President of an independent Confederacy—and, on this basis alone, must proposals be made to him. At one period of the conversation Mr. Gilmore made use of some language referring to these States as " rebels " while rendering an account of Mr. Lincoln's views, and apologized for the word. The President desired him to proceed, that no offense was taken, and that he wished Mr. Lincoln's language to be repeated to him as exactly as possible. Some further conversation took place, substantially to the same effect as the foregoing, when the President rose to indicate that the interview was at an end. The two gentlemen were then recommitted to the charge of Colonel Ould, and left Richmond the next day.

This account of the visit of Messrs. Gilmore and Jaquess to Richmond has been rendered necessary by publication made by one or both of them since their return to the United States, notwithstanding the agreement that their visit was to be kept secret. They have perhaps concluded that as the promise of secrecy was made at their request, it was permissible to disregard it. We have no reason for desiring to conceal what occurred, and have therefore no complaint to make of the publicity given to the fact of the visit. The extreme inaccuracy of Mr. Gilmore's narrative will be apparent to you from the foregoing statement.

You have no doubt seen in the Northern papers an account of another conference on the subject of peace which took place in Canada at about the same date between Messrs. C. C. Clay and J. P. Holcombe, Confederate citizens of the highest character and position, and Mr. Horace Greeley, of New York, acting with authority of President Lincoln. It is deemed not improper to inform you that Messrs. Clay and Holcombe, although enjoying in an eminent degree the confidence and esteem of the President, were strictly accurate in their statement that they were without any authority from this Government to treat with that of the United States on any subject whatever. We had no knowledge of their conference with Mr. Greeley nor of their proposed visit to Washington till we saw the newspapers' publications. A significant confirmation of the truth of the statement of Messrs. Gilmore and Jaquess that they came as messengers from Mr. Lincoln, is to be found in the fact that the views of Mr. Lincoln, as stated by them to the President, are in exact conformity with the offensive paper addressed "to whom it may concern," which was sent by Mr. Lincoln to Messrs. Clay and Holcombe by the hands of his private secretary, Mr. Hay, and which was properly regarded by those gentlemen as an intimation that Mr. Lincoln was unwilling that this war should cease while in his power to continue hostilities.

I am, very respectfully, your obedient servant,

J. P. BENJAMIN,
Secretary of State.

Hon. JAMES M. MASON,
Commissioner to the Continent, Paris.

Circular.]   DEPARTMENT OF STATE,
Richmond, August 25, 1864.

(For circular, see Diplomatic Correspondence, Great Britain, p. 185.)

Hon. JOHN SLIDELL, *Paris.*

No. 104.]   BRUSSELS, *August 26, 1864.*

SIR: A statement is going the rounds of the European press and is regarded as entitled to credit that peace propositions have been informally made very recently by distinguished citizens of the Confederate States sojourning in Canada and believed to be in the entire confidence of President Davis, and that those propositions are receiving the serious consideration of the Washington Cabinet. In fact, a general impression has been created on this side of the Atlantic that a settlement of the differences between the belligerents is positively certain soon to occur. Lord Palmerston himself so expressed his opinion in his speech at Tiverton last Tuesday.

It is confidently asserted that we are prepared to yield to the North all that her more temperate politicians desire upon the subject of slavery, consenting even to its gradual abolition. I have combated upon all suitable occasions this wild notion as too absurd to be deserving of the slightest credence. I consider it as of a most mischievous character to our present and prospective interests, calculated to place us in the wrong, indeed, virtually committing us to such an admission in the estimation of the world.

With my whole heart I desire speedy peace, but I do not desire it, as I am sure is the case also with ninety-nine hundredths of my countrymen, at the price of honor. We have tested over and over again our strength with our enemy, and, numbers taken into consideration, we have convinced him, as we have convinced the rest of mankind, of our vast superiority. I am sure, as I have ever been sure, that we will never agree to retire from the contest until the Washington Government acknowledges unconditionally our independence. From the day of my arrival in London to the present hour I have invariably expressed this belief in all circles in which I have mingled, and I would far sooner cease to exist on earth than to entertain a contrary one.

The best friends of the North in Europe are now compelled, in the face of incontrovertible reason, to acknowledge that the subjugation of the South is not within the scope of rational possibility. In view of this fact I ask, Can any sensible individual suppose that the Confederate States have the first concession to make to the Federal States? Richmond, Charleston, Atlanta, and Mobile remain invincible. It would be soon enough, if indeed ever, to consider any condition interfering with our sovereign rights as a nation of the earth when all of those important cities and the intermediate country were in the possession of the Yankees.

Looking at our prospects for eminent success from the point on which I stand, I never regarded them in so hopeful an aspect as I do on this 26th day of August, 1864.

I wish I could conceal from myself a glaring truth which is exceedingly distressful to my feelings, to wit: That there are Confederates in Europe who, in furtherance of their selfish objects, would eagerly accept peace on nearly any terms, including a reconstruction of the old Union.

I must again remark that I have no later dispatch from you than that dated the 1st of February.

I have the honor to be, sir, very respectfully, your obedient servant,

A. DUDLEY MANN.

Hon. J. P. BENJAMIN,
 Secretary of State, C. S. A., Richmond, Va.

DEPARTMENT OF STATE,
Richmond, August 27, 1864.

SIR: I have the honor herewith to transmit by direction of Secretary of State six copies of a map of Virginia, published by authority of the Commonwealth, and to request that after reserving three copies for such disposition as you may choose to make of them you will have the goodness to forward one copy to Mr. Mason, one to Mr. Mann, and one to Mr. Hotze.

On the subjects of your accounts the Secretary of State instructs me to say that they have for some time been in the hands of the accounting officers of the Treasury, but that their prompt adjustment has been impracticable, arising from the interruptions to the dispatch of business in that Department, caused by repeated calls upon the clerical force for military service in the field. It is hoped, however, that at an early day the Department will have the pleasure of reporting to you their satisfactory settlement.

I have the honor to be, sir, very respectfully, your obedient servant,

WM. J. BROMWELL,
Disbursing Clerk.

Hon. JOHN SLIDELL, *Paris.*

DEPARTMENT OF STATE,
Richmond, August 31, 1864.

GENTLEMEN: I have the honor to receive the communication addressed by you to the Confederate States of America, and have submitted it to the President, by whose instructions I now reply to your appeal.

The Government and people of the Confederate States, in the midst of their own struggle for the maintenance of their right of self-government, have felt the deepest interest in the calamities suffered by the Polish nation in their recent unavailing attempt to break the bonds by which they are fettered. We are sincerely desirous of doing everything in our power to alleviate the sufferings of those exiles, who, unable to establish freedom at home, seek an asylum with us, whose efforts to maintain national independence against foreign invasion have been more fortunate than theirs.

In your address, after stating that you are attracted to us by a powerful sympathy, you declare your wish, " with the baptism of your blood to earn our brotherhood," by fighting for our cause, as did Pulaski and Kosciusko. You asked to be admitted among us. You ask that a part of our territory be allotted to you, that your lives may be saved from despair or sacrificed only for the avowed good of mankind.

So far as it is in the power of the President, he will cheerfully accord your request. Your emigrants will be received among us. Those who desire to earn our brotherhood by mingling their blood with ours on the battlefield will be warmly welcomed.

To your request for an allotment of territory, the President can only answer that the Congress of the Confederacy alone has the power to dispose of the public lands. He can not presume to say in what manner the Congress will determine to dispose of such territory as may be subject to its control after a treaty of peace shall have defined the boundaries of the Confederacy. All that he can do is to assure you of his own disposition and of his belief that the representatives of the people will share the disposition to accord a liberal grant of public land to all whose lives shall have been imperiled in battling for our independence.

The President also desires that you be informed that by the laws of the Confederate States every person who may be engaged in our military service during the pending war has the right to be naturalized as a citizen upon taking an oath of fidelity to the Confederacy.

I am, gentlemen, very respectfully, your obedient servant,

J. P. BENJAMIN,
Secretary of State.

Colonel J. SMOLINSKI, Chaplain J. MAYEWSKI, Colonel A. LENKIEWICZ, Major P. BNINICKI,
Delegation representing the Polish Emigration.

DEPARTMENT OF STATE,
Richmond, August 31, 1864.

GENTLEMEN: I have had another conference with the President this morning, and he expressed his willingness to receive you in person and to make to you the same assurances which you have received from me.

If you will call at my office to-morrow morning at 12 o'clock, I will be happy to present you to the President.

Very respectfully, your obedient servant,

J. P. BENJAMIN,
Secretary of State.

Colonel SMOLINSKI and others,
Polish Delegates.

DEPARTMENT OF STATE,
Richmond, September 1, 1864.

SIR: There arrived in Richmond a few days ago a delegation of four Polish gentlemen, who came from Europe, running the blockade at Wilmington for purposes which are fully explained in the correspondence with this Department, of which a copy is annexed.

You will perceive by that correspondence that this Government was unable fully to comply with the wishes of these gentlemen, who, as representatives of the unfortunate Polish exiles now scattered through Europe, cherished the fond hope that we could make them a grant of territory which would form a home of refuge and to which they could transplant their own institutions, habits, laws, and customs.

These gentlemen, however, while disappointed in the chief object of their mission, express the conviction that large numbers of their fellow citizens who have escaped from the recent disastrous struggle in Poland would be very glad to emigrate to our country, to cast their lot with us, to become Confederate citizens, and to fulfill all their duties as such. They represent that if a passage could be furnished to such able-bodied men as are willing to come several thousand would cheerfully embrace the opportunity.

We are not willing that any just ground of complaint should exist against us on the part of any Government for violation of territorial sovereignty by enlistments within its jurisdiction, and have hitherto had recourse to none but our own citizens for recruiting our armies. We are willing, however, on the application now made to us in behalf of a gallant and unfortunate race, to give a passage to such of its men capable of bearing arms as choose to emigrate to our country, and will welcome them as brethren to our ranks if they think proper to enlist on arrival.

The President has, therefore, desired me to request that you will take charge of this matter under the instructions I now send you, and to remit to you £50,000 sterling for defraying the necessary expenses, for which sum you will receive herewith five drafts on the Confederate bankers in Liverpool, each draft being for £10,000, to be used as required for the purpose herein explained.

The course deemed most advisable, after consultation with the Secretary of the Treasury, and with a view to avoid all pretext for any complaint of infringement of neutral territorial right is the following:

First. The vessels be provided by charter for the conveyance of Polish emigrants to Matamoras. Mr. Trenholm thinks that steam vessels, propellers, could be chartered for that purpose at a rate not exceeding £10 per head, especially with the prospect of return freight in cotton.

Second. In order to prevent any interference by the cruisers of the enemy, which would not hesitate to violate the law of nations by the capture of such vessels, although bound to a neutral port, if they suspected any intention on the part of the emigrants of establishing themselves in our country, it is desirable that the destination to Matamoras should be concealed, if possible, the ostensible terminus of the voyage be held out to be a Central American port, or any other point which you may select south of Mexico. A Mexican port is not to be selected (if possible to avoid it) as the professed destination.

Third. A price for passage will be fixed for each emigrant, payable on his arrival within the Confederacy, sufficient to cover the costs of supplying him with subsistence. But each emigrant will be informed that on his arrival in the Confederacy he will receive an acquittance of the claim for the expenses of his passage if he chooses to volunteer in our service. If not he must pay for his passage, and he will then be in the position of all other persons who reside in the Confederacy. The emigrants will be informed by their delegation, who are now returning to Europe, that under our law all who reside in the Confederacy are liable to military service during the war.

Fourth. On arrival of the emigrants at Matamoras our commercial agent there, Mr. Richard Fitzpatrick, will be found ready, under instructions from this Department, to supply them with a passage to Texas, where another agent will be prepared to supply their wants and to give a release of the obligation to refund the expenses of passage to all such as choose to enter our service.

Fifth. The sole duty to be performed by such agents as you may employ will be to provide passage for such as may apply. They will not engage in any attempt to induce men to come, but will welcome all who may offer, receiving none, however, who are obviously incapable of performing military service. The Polish delegation will themselves assume the task of explaining to their own countrymen the conditions on which passage is offered to them.

Sixth. The Polish delegates will visit you with a letter of introduction from me, and you will have the requisite understanding with them as to the method of satisfying you when a sufficient number is prepared to emigrate from any port, so as to justify you providing a vessel. You will also agree with them in the selection of ports from which vessels are to sail. The Poles are said by them to be widely scattered over Europe, and large numbers are said to be in Italy, Turkey, and Roumania, so that a vessel may be required in a Mediterranean port, or possibly, even at Galatz, on the Black Sea.

Seventh. The present delegation, together with some 8 or 10 others with whom they desire to associate themselves, will have to travel to the different points in Europe where the Poles are principally found, to inform them of the arrangements made for their emigration, and you are authorized to provide them with such moderate sums as may be necessary for the expenses of such travel.

Eighth. It is greatly desired that our expense in this emigration be confined to furnishing passage from the ports, but it is feared that in very many instances the poverty of the exiles will be such as to make it impracticable to reach the ports without assistance. Whenever this is the case the additional expense must be borne by us, while proper care is taken against the risk of loss by advances to parties not in good faith. On this point you will bear in mind that we deem the success of this measure of very great public advantage and importance, and while we desire to economize public money and should regret to see it spent without result, we are willing that the expenditure be liberal if success is thereby secured.

The amount now remitted is deemed sufficient for a beginning, as we scarcely expect more than a few thousand men to be desirous of emigrating without their families. Fourfold this sum or more would be willingly spent if the number could be increased to fifteen or twenty thousand. If you see a certain prospect of such increased number, you will be furnished at once with an additional remittance on advising me.

The money sent is taken by the President out of the sum placed at his disposal by Congress for secret service. It will be accounted for to me, not to the Treasury Department. Where any portion of it is expended under crcumstances which do not admit of your taking receipts, your own certificate will be received as satisfactory.

It is deemed essential to success that this business be conducted as quietly as possible, and you will not be expected to confine it to any one whomsoever except the Messrs. Fraser, Trenholm & Co., of Liverpool, whose aid you will of course require in making arrangements for the necessary charters and for the execution of the details of the business. The subordinate agents employed ought not to know anything on the subject beyond what is strictly necessary to enable them to perform the duties required of them. We suppose it to be possible to give the whole affair the appearance of a private arrangement made by the Poles in concert with their friends for their emigration to found a colony in Central America to which the able-bodied are going in advance to prepare for the reception of the remainder. This may not be found practicable, but the suggestion is offered for consideration.

I conclude by repeating that the President earnestly hopes for success in this movement, and is satisfied that you will spare no effort to secure it.

I am, very respectfully, your obedient servant,

J. P. BENJAMIN,
Secretary of State.

COLIN J. MCRAE, Esq.,
Agent of Treasury, care of Messrs. Fraser,
Trenholm & Co., Liverpool.

[Enclosure.]

DEPARTMENT OF STATE,
Richmond, September 1, 1864.

SIR: This letter of introduction will be handed to you by the four following-named gentlemen: Colonel Smolinski, Chaplain Mayewski, Colonel Lenkiewicz, Major Bninicki, who arrived here some days ago as a delegation for the Polish exiles now scattered throughout Europe, and who are desirous of emigrating to this country.

I have written to you very fully on this subject, and beg that you will kindly extend to these gentlemen any courtesies in your power, as well as confer with them on the subject pointed out in my letter of this date.

I am, very respectfully, your obedient servant,

J. P. BENJAMIN,
Secretary of State.

COLIN J. MCRAE, Esq.,
Care Messrs. Fraser, Trenholm & Co., Liverpool.

DEPARTMENT OF STATE,
Richmond, September 2, 1864.

GENTLEMEN: Four Polish officers, exiles from their country, recently arrived here as a delegation in the hope of making arrangements by which their fellow countrymen now suffering as homeless wanderers in Europe could emigrate to this country and find a new home.

The names of these gentlemen are: Colonel Smolinski, Chaplain Mayewski, Colonel Lenkiewicz, Major Bninicki, and I take liberty of introducing them to you.

We have been unable to give these gentlemen all the aid we would have desired in the accomplishment of an object in which we sincerely sympathize, and they are now returning home with a voyage before them far too expensive for their limited means.

If under these circumstances you can facilitate their passage by relieving them of part, if not the whole, of the expense of running

through the blockade, it would not only be a service rendered to them, but to the Polish people in general, as well as to,
Your obedient servant,

J. P. BENJAMIN,
Secretary of State.

Messrs. COLLIE & Co.,
Wilmington, N. C.

DEPARTMENT OF STATE,
Richmond, September 2, 1864.

SIR: I have the honor to request a pass for the following gentlemen, to proceed from Richmond to Europe, via Wilmington, on public service: Colonel Smolinski, Chaplain Mayewski, Colonel Lenkiewicz, Major Bninicki.
I am, very respectfully, your obedient servant,

J. P. BENJAMIN,
Secretary of State.

Hon. J. A. SEDDON,
Secretary of War.

DEPARTMENT OF STATE,
Richmond, September 2, 1864.

SIR: I have the honor to request transportation to Wilmington for the following gentlemen, about to proceed to Europe on public business: Colonel Smolinski, Chaplain Mayewski, Colonel Lenkiewicz, Major Bninicki.
I am, very respectfully, your obedient servant,

J. P. BENJAMIN,
Secretary of State.

General LAWTON,
Quartermaster General.

DEPARTMENT OF STATE,
Richmond, September 5, 1864.

GENTLEMEN: I have the honor to acknowledge receipt of your communication of the 3d instant, and I regret exceedingly that it is not in the power of the Government to give you any further assurances than those conveyed in my former reply.
It is not in accordance with the nature and institutions of our Government to make a grant of territory for the exclusive use of a colony of emigrants in such manner as to deprive our own citizens of the right of settling in such territory. Grants of land are only made to individuals, not to communities or colonies. If it should be in our power, as is hoped by the President, to make grants of land at the close of the war, as a bounty to such as shall have exposed their lives in our struggle, these grants would be made to such individuals of your nation as might entitle themselves by their services to the favor of the Government, and it would be in their power by common concert to settle together in any particular locality they

might select, and thus secure such a majority of the population as would enable them to control the political and municipal legislation of the territory so occupied. This is the only manner in which it would be possible to effect your purpose of maintaining in a distinct community the manners, habits, customs, and mode of life to which your people so naturally cling in memory of their native land.

It is desirable on every account that there should be no misunderstanding on this point, and it is due to you that the distinct statement be made that it is out of the power of the President or of the Government to appropriate a district of country in any territory that may be at our disposal at the close of the war for the exclusive occupation of a Polish colony.

I am, very respectfully, your obedient servant,

J. P. BENJAMIN,
Secretary of State.

Colonel SMOLINSKI, Chaplain MAYEWSKI, Colonel LENKIEWICZ, Major BNINICKI.

[Sent with duplicate of letter of 1st September, 1864, and duplicate draft by Lieutenant M. Toor, September 9, 1864.]

DEPARTMENT OF STATE,
Richmond, September 6, 1864.

SIR: You will receive herewith duplicate of my communication to you of the 1st instant.

At the time of sending you that dispatch it was deemed advisable to send from here the necessary means to enable our commercial agent at Matamoras, Mr. Richard Fitzpatrick, to forward from that point to Brownsville the emigrants who might be addressed to his care. On subsequent conference with the Secretary of the Treasury, however, we arrived at the conclusion that there was so much uncertainty relative to the success of the proposed movements, and so much difficulty in determining when and to what amount money would be wanted, that the better course would be for you to forward to Mr. Fitzpatrick, either in bills of exchange or letters of credit, such sum as may be sufficient to enable him to provide for the emigrants as fast as received. You will always know in advance what number are about to be forwarded in ample time to send a letter to Mr. Fitzpatrick so that he may prepare for their reception, and a duplicate can be sent by the vessel which conveys the emigrants. They will thus be secure of help on arrival at Matamoras. The amount required for each emigrant can scarcely exceed $10 for all expenses from his arrival at Matamoras till he reaches Brownsville, but it may be well to put double that amount at the disposal of Mr. Fitzpatrick to cover all contingencies.

I have given a letter of introduction to you in favor of Lieutenant H. R. Hislop McIvor, recently of our service, who has resigned and is returning to Scotland, but with the intention of again entering our service after settling his private affairs at home. This gentleman thinks that he can get many hundreds of his countrymen to emigrate to our country in the same manner as the Polish emigrants propose to come. If he is successful in what he proposes, you are requested by the President to furnish a passage to those who may desire to come in the same manner and on the same terms and conditions as explained in my dispatch of 1st instant.

GEORGE G. TRENHOLM,
Secretary of the Treasury, Confederate States, 1864–1865.

I have to beg that you will advise me as promptly as possible if you need further funds for the purposes indicated in my communications.

I am, very respectfully, your obedient servant,

J. P. BENJAMIN,
Secretary of State.

COLIN J. McRAE, Esq.

DEPARTMENT OF STATE,
Richmond, September 8, 1864.

SIR: I have the honor to request a passage through the blockade for Lieutenant H. R. Hislop McIvor, who goes to Europe on public business.

If there is no public vessel at Wilmington, please send me an order to your agent there to provide him a passage on a private vessel and draw on this Department for the price.

Respectfully, your obedient servant,

J. P. BENJAMIN,
Secretary of State.

Hon. S. R. MALLORY,
Secretary of the Navy.

DEPARTMENT OF STATE,
Richmond, September 8, 1864.

SIR: Proposals have recently been made to the President and accepted by him for the emigration to our country of large numbers of Polish exiles, as well as for some hundred of Scotchmen, who are disposed to take part in our struggle.

I have accordingly sent instructions to Europe, under which a passage to our country via Matamoras will be afforded to all able-bodied men who desire to emigrate to the Confederacy, and further instructions have been sent to Mr. Richard Fitzpatrick, our commercial agent at Matamoras, to forward them to Texas, probably to Brownsville.

The instructions are that all such as may choose to volunteer in our service will have an acquittance for the passage money; all others will be compelled to pay the price of the passage, and will then be in the condition of other residents of the Confederacy and subject to its laws, which require all residents to aid in the defense of the country.

Promise has been given that those Poles who volunteer will be allowed to organize themselves into companies, battalions, and regiments, and elect their officers in the first instance, and that they will, if possible, be kept in one corps and organized into Polish brigades and divisions if their numbers are sufficient.

My purpose in now addressing you is to request that you will give such information and issue such orders to the military authorities in the trans-Mississippi District as will secure a proper reception of those emigrants when forwarded from Matamoras by

Mr. Fitzpatrick, as well as a faithful observance of the promises held out to them.

I am, very respectfully, your obedient servant,

J. P. BENJAMIN,
Secretary of State.

Hon. J. A. SEDDON,
Secretary of War.

No. 71.]   PARIS, *September 13, 1864.*

SIR: Since I last had the honor of addressing you on the 24th ultimo, from Baden, I have received your dispatch No. 41, of 12th July. The late advice from New York seems to justify your anticipations that the war will soon be brought to a virtual close by the exhaustion of the enemy and the growing dissatisfaction of the northern masses. The nearly unanimous nomination of McClellan, the selection of Pendleton for the Vice-Presidency, the platform adopted by the Chicago convention, and the hearty response which it has elicited from all quarters, all tend to this conclusion. Unless we meet with reverses, which, with the information we possess on this side of the water, there appears to be no reason to apprehend, the success of the Democratic candidates would seem to be a foregone conclusion. I have no great faith, either, in the firmness of the statesmanship of McClellan, but his election will, at all events, paralyze the action of Lincoln during the remainder of his term of office, and his successor will come into power with all the disadvantages resulting from a forced inaction of several months. Indeed, I do not think that it is judging Lincoln too harshly to suppose that he may not be unwilling to hand over the Government to his hated and successful rival in the worst possible condition; or it may be that he will accept the result of the election as the expression of the popular will in favor of an armistice and leave him the difficult and ungrateful task of the conclusion of a peace on the basis of separation. In the meanwhile all that can be done in Europe is patiently to await events. Should, contrary to all reasonable expectation, they be unfavorable to our cause, judging from past experience, we can expect no friendly action here. If victory continues to crown our arms we shall occupy a position that will enable us to take little heed of foreign sympathies or alliances. I called to-day at the foreign office. My friend informed me that everything is in a state of profound calm and that nothing indicates the probability of any modification of the ministry. The amount of cotton bonds converted by me up to 31st August was £340,800. Since then £25,900 have been converted, making, with those drawn and paid, £503,500 canceled.

I have the honor to be, with great respect, your obedient servant,

JOHN SLIDELL.

Hon. J. P. BENJAMIN,
Secretary of State.

No. 42.]   DEPARTMENT OF STATE,
Richmond, September 15, 1864.

SIR: In a separate dispatch I reply at length on the various subjects involved in your recent communications. I now enclose copy of a letter written to the Secretary of the Navy on the subject of the rules to be observed by our cruisers in relation to neutrals. The interest of Great Britain in this subject is infinitely greater than that of France, but we have no means of communicating directly with the British Government. If you can, therefore, so arrange that the knowledge of the issue of these instructions shall reach that Government indirectly, you are requested to take the proper measures for that end.

The President desires that you lay this subject before the French Government in the manner deemed by you best calculated to produce a good result. The interest of neutral powers that their ports should be opened at least to the introduction of such prizes as involve the claims of their own subjects is plain, and it is obvious that in no other manner can we do them the full justice we desire. There are very few of what are called " whitewashed " vessels under French flag, but portions of cargo belonging to Frenchmen have been more than once found on enemy's vessels, and if France will not permit such vessels when captured to be taken into French ports with the view of restoring the neutral property to French subjects, there can be no just ground for expecting that we shall satisfy claims for indemnity arising from the destruction of that property when such destruction is practically forced upon us by the neutral Government.

You will observe that Vice-Admiral Hope stated to Commander Wood that the British Government would open its ports to the introduction of prizes when they bore the British flag at the time of capture. It is very important that we should be informed of the exact position assumed in this matter by Great Britain, and you are requested to spare no pains to obtain accurate information on the subject, and to transmit it to us at the earliest moment.

I am, very respectfully, your obedient servant,

J. P. BENJAMIN,
Secretary of State.

Hon. JOHN SLIDELL, *Paris.*

No. 23.] DEPARTMENT OF STATE,
Richmond, September 15, 1864.

SIR: It is some time since I have written to you at any length on public affairs, having been prevented principally by the fact that the President has been so engrossed by the necessity of supervising military matters as to make me averse to engaging his attention on less pressing concerns.

I am in receipt of all your dispatches down to 47, inclusive, of 29th July, with the single exception of No. 46, which will, no doubt, come to hand in a few days.

Your dispatches relative to the arrangements made in Paris have been read with great interest, and you seem to have adopted the course best adapted to accomplish our purposes in that quarter. It is an agreeable duty to inform you that Mr. Slidell's dispatches bear testimony to the prudence, sagacity, and efficiency displayed by you in the responsible and difficult task imposed on you.

The suggestions relative to the employment of an agent in Germany, made in your No. 47, have been fully considered, and it has not been deemed advisable to adopt them. It is no doubt important to use all available agencies for the purpose of enlightening public opinion and conciliating in our favor the moral sentiment of all civilized countries, but we are compelled to pay strict regard to money considerations during the pending war, and the vast field which it would be necessary to occupy in Germany, if a special agency be established there, would involve an expenditure abroad greater than we feel justified in incurring at the present time. The essential points of difference between the press of Germany and those of England and France, as described in your dispatch, had been previously considered, and the difficulty of acting on public opinion in a country in which there was no great center of influence, and no organ of the press specially preeminent, had been the chief obstacle to our action. The organization in Germany would require to be widespread in order to effect results of importance; it would require subagencies at numerous points, and would be attended with considerable expense. At the same time it is obvious that the action of the two great western powers is and must remain decisive of all questions involving our interests in Europe, and it is not at all probable that we could influence the policy of those powers by anything that we could do in Germany.

Under all the circumstances, it is preferred that matters should remain as at present, and that our action in that field be confined to such special and exceptional cases as may seem to you to offer openings for producing immediate results. In regard to the heavy investments made by the German capitalists in the Federal bonds, it is observable that by our last accounts from Europe the fall had been very heavy and that the United States sixes are quoted at 39. It is not an unmixed evil that our enemies should have succeeded in procuring a temporary aid to their rapidly failing finances at so enormous a sacrifice, nor that the steady stream of gold required to satisfy their foreign engagements should be swollen by the amount necessary to meet the interest on these bonds. By the end of this year the United States will need two millions a week to pay the interest on their debt, and of this amount three-fourths will be required in specie. Their present requirements for the payment of interest are about $80,000,000 a year, of which about $57,000,000 in specie and about $23,000,000 in paper money.

I send to Mr. Slidell by this mail a dispatch in relation to the rules of maritime warfare, which will be observed by our cruisers with special reference to the rights and interests of neutrals. It will be well to confer with him and determine to what extent it may be advisable to make the matter the subject of discussion in the press. In the meantime I enclose to you a copy of a report made by Commander Wood, of the Navy, one of our most accomplished and dashing naval officers, a nephew (by marriage) of President Davis and a most modest and meritorious gentleman. You will perceive in what manner he was treated by the naval commander of her Britannic Majesty's fleet at Halifax. The man who was guilty of this arrogant and offensive conduct is the same Vice-Admiral Sir James Hope who was aided so promptly and heartily when he made his disastrous attack on the Peiho forts by our Confederate Commodore Tattnall, who on that occasion used the memorable expression, " blood is thicker than water," while lending his assistance to British seaman, then considered by our Navy as related to us by ties of brotherhood. It is not believed, however, that the general feeling of British officers accords with that of this vice-admiral, who seems to have forgotten the rules which govern the conduct of gentlemen as well as the obligations of gratitude for signal service conferred. It may be, however, that he was guided on this occasion rather by the orders said to have been transmitted to him by Mr. Seward, through Lord Lyons, than by the promptings of his own feelings.

Our military position in the neighborhood of Richmond has remained substantially unchanged for many weeks, while the evacuation of Atlanta, although an undoubted disaster, has none of the importance attributed to it by the press North or South. Nothing is more curious than to note the radical difference as exhibited in this war between the people of the two federations. The vaunting and braggart spirit of the North finds vent on the most trifling occasion, and magnifies the result of a successful skirmish into a grand victory that has " broken the back of the rebellion." The cool and practical Southerner, looking reality in the face, is disposed to depreciate the importance of the most signal success, and to regard a grand victory as shorn of its value if any portion of the enemy's army escaped destruction. Is this to be attributed on each side to the innate consciousness of the superiority of the Southern race? Is the North elated because any success is unexpected as against our brave soldiers? Is the South dissatisfied because no success seems adequate to what should be effected by the marked superiority of our troops over those of the enemy? I am unable to solve the question. It is sufficient to point out the fact so as to keep you on your guard against attaching undue weight to the exuberant boastings of the press at the North or the sombre colors of the pictures occasionally presented by our own journals.

The President is about to leave for a few weeks for a tour in Georgia, where his presence will be very valuable in inspiring renewed resolution in the army and people and in concerting measures which we may hope will lead to a decisive success over the forces of Sherman.

I am, very respectfully, your obedient servant,

J. P. BENJAMIN,
Secretary of State.

HENRY HOTZE, Esq., *London.*

P. S.—It would be of great service to us if you could publish in the Index an additional list of Yankee vessels that have been transferred to neutrals and that remain mortgaged or hypothecated in favor of the enemy. The list in the Index of June last only comprises the year 1863.

No. 49.] CONFEDERATE STATES COMMERCIAL AGENCY,
London, September 17, 1864.

SIR: I have the honor to announce to you that under date of yesterday, 16th September, I paid to Mr. George McHenry, of Philadelphia, on account of the secret-service fund intrusted to me, upon the recommendation of Hon. J. M. Mason, concurred in by Hon. J. Slidell, the sum of 300 pounds sterling, the reasons for which disbursement are sufficiently set forth in Mr. Mason's letter to me, copy of which, as well as of Mr. McHenry's receipt, and the essential portion of the preceding correspondence on this subject is enclosed. I am quite aware that such an appropriation of the secret-service fund is not within the limits of my own official discretion, but I felt bound to regard the joint recommendation of the two commissioners as representatives of the sovereignty of the Government abroad in the light of a peremptory order, to be obeyed if reasonably possible and unless there were countervailing reasons which did not obtain in this case. It is only fair to Mr. McHenry to add that personally the action of the commissioners had my entire concurrence, as it had that of Hon. C. J. McRae, and that I was glad of an opportunity afforded me, without transgressing the sphere of my functions, for testifying to Mr. McHenry that, although our views of policy and temporary expediency have so often and sometimes radically differed, I could yet cordially appreciate his earnest and indefatigable desire to serve our cause. I do not doubt that you will appreciate my motives and sanction the course I have thought it morally right and officially proper to adopt. The amount, moreover, whether considered as reimbursed for actual outlay or as compensation, is not, in my opinion, disproportionate to the service rendered.

I have further to inform you of another disbursement of £150 on account of the secret-service fund. This amount was paid on the 7th instant to Mr. T. B. Kershaw, of Manchester, as a contribution toward paying the expense of collecting signatures to a "peace address" from the people of Great Britain and Ireland to the people of the United States. This expenditure requires explanation which I can not prudently give you now as fully as I would wish. Had the object and probable results commended themselves to my judgment there could be no doubt, as there was in Mr. McHenry's case, about its coming within my discretionary authority, but this was so far from being the case that on the first application for the money I felt myself bound to politely decline. Subsequently, however, the application was renewed in other quarters and in such a form that I had scarcely any choice but to reconsider my first determination. A gentleman of high social position, and with indisputable claims upon our courteous consideration, who had originated the project, had it very warmly at heart, and had already spent large amounts upon its execution, made the Government's cooperation in it almost a personal request near our financial agent, General McRae. On consulting together, General McRae and I found that we exactly agreed in our views of the subject, but under all the circumstances we deemed it better to make the contribution, and I feel sure that, with all the facts before you, you would have come to the same conclusion. I withhold, from obvious reasons, the gentleman's name for the present. The originators of the address expect to obtain near two million of signatures. I believe the time is too short for this, but several hundred thousand may safely be counted upon. It will certainly be a grand demonstration and one to which I can see no objection, but whether worth to us £150 which might be spent in another manner is a matter of reasonable doubt.

You will readily understand that to provide upon a sudden call and for purposes not foreseen so large an amount as £150 would have been too dangerous a strain upon my means, even if the uncertainties of the blockade should not delay the receipt of my next remittance beyond November, and in view of my daily growing necessities in England, Ireland, France, and latterly Germany I eagerly accepted Mr. McRae's friendly offer to lend me the required sum upon my official obligation to repay as soon as sanctioned by you and conveniently consistent with the means at my command. I may add that upon these two points of expenditure, involving scruples and hesitations not belonging to my ordinary routine of work, I have had the benefit of his advice and counsel, and our views, as on most points of public policy or expediency, have been perfectly in accord.

I leave in a day or two for Germany. This journey, unavoidably delayed by various circumstances, has now a more serious and definite object than I originally meant to give it. The complexion which military events have assumed render it more than probable that the war will be protracted for at least another year. If this should be the case, we have interests to protect in Germany of vastly greater practical importance than either in England or France. It is from Germany that the enemy must next spring recruit another army; it is upon Germany that he relies for the gold to carry on the war and bolster up a fictitious value of greenbacks and bonds. Hitherto we have allowed him unopposed to use a population of forty millions as a recruiting ground and to draw at will upon their accumulated savings. These are the two last props which have sustained his aggressive power; cut them and I verily believe that he will be prostrate. You probably care as little for German sympathy as I do, and I shall not attempt to win it. My plan is to discredit Federal obligations and to deter the masses from emigration to America. For the former I shall try to enlist the aid of the press; for the latter I shall employ more popular means, and I am not without hope that the stream which can not perhaps be stopped may be diverted, say, to Hungary, the Danubian principalities, and even depopulated Poland. The experiments I have heretofore made, if they have not produced decisive results, have at least proved that much may be done. As no time is to be lost I shall throw my whole energy into the work, and when your special agent arrives, if, as I trust and have recommended, you see proper to appoint one, I hope to be able to hand over to him an organized machinery. To set my mind at ease, in the event that my campaign prospers, I have arranged with Messrs. Erlanger & Co. for a credit of £500 at Frankfort, should, as is hardly to be expected, so much be needed before you can make provision for this most important field of exertion.

I need not repeat that nothing but an imperious sense of duty and of urgent necessity would induce me to add voluntarily to my responsibilities and labor. Personally I should much prefer to rest content with my success and good fortune in England and France, or in either, rather than incur the risk of failure by undertaking such a herculean task as the cleaning of this worse than Augean German stable. But though we now occupy a dominant and almost impregnable position in both the English and French press, and though it is worth our while, as well for the future as for the present, to maintain and if possible to strengthen that position, yet I can not blind myself to the fact that the immediate object toward which our efforts were directed has failed, and whatever may be our triumphs in the arena of public opinion we no longer expect the political action of these governments of western Europe to have any direct influence upon the issue or duration of the war. In Germany on the other hand, while we ask for or desire no governmental action, we aim at attacking the material supplies of the enemy. Between the two, therefore, I consider Germany, though the least pleasant and promising, by far the most important base of operations.

I have to acknowledge receipt of your No. 21, 3 June, enclosing duplicates, the originals of which had been already acknowledged, and your No. 22, 1 August, informing me of the capture of our special mail messenger, and enclosing a copy of letter sent by him. I had previously anticipated this catastrophe from the proximity of the Federal army to Petersburg, and had made but slight use of this route for the last two months. The occurrence is extremely to be regretted, especially as the prevalence of yellow fever at the islands will, I fear, still further disturb the regularity of our communications.

I remain, with great respect, your obedient servant,

HENRY HOTZE.

Hon. J. P. BENJAMIN,
　　Secretary of State, Richmond.

P. S.—Enclosed are salary accounts for quarters respectively ending March 31 and June 30. Duplicates and triplicates will follow.

H. H.

[Enclosure.]

CORRESPONDENCE EXPLAINING PAYMENT OF £300 TO MR. M'HENRY.

HOTEL DE FRANCE,
Versailles, August 14, 1864.

MY DEAR HOTZE: ***

On Friday evening I received a message from Mr. Benjamin which will make some change in my movements. My book and papers on cotton have been the subject of consideration by the Richmond Government, and that too without any action on my part, which makes the matter more complimentary. I have never written to the South a word upon the question. I am, however, authorized to "go ahead," and to call upon you for material aid. This will keep me in Europe some weeks longer. I may not write or publish any more, but simply endeavor to promulgate my views by another and more practical method. To go at the thing without any circumlocution, I shall have my plans matured in a day or two and enter upon these special duties as quietly as possible. I will, of course, furnish you with my authority to act when, as you will agree with me, it will be proper to have the financial matters prearranged. While I will never make any charge for past services, it is right to say in advance that the present matter coming as it does from Richmond ought to be fixed upon a different but satisfactory basis. In fact I can not afford to devote any more time to the public service gratis.

Yours, truly,　　　　　　　GEORGE McHENRY.

[Enclosure.]

LONDON, *August 18, 1864.*

MY DEAR MCHENRY: I enclose you my check for £100, which Erlanger & Co., at 21 Rue Chaussée D'Antin will doubtless cash at the exchange of the day. As you have not fixed the amount you need in your reply accepting my offer* I send you the amount best suited to the state of my banker's account. If you require it, I feel confident, by having two or three day's notice, of being able to let you have another £50. You may repay me at your own convenience, but you will understand that this is entirely a personal matter between us and has nothing whatever to do with my official functions. A simple I. O. U. by way of acknowledgment will answer all purposes.

I do not quite understand the drift of your letter. I am glad, however, to gather from it that you will probably modify your plans so as to remain in Europe, and that you have been offered by the Government an appointment abroad, the character of which you will communicate to me hereafter. I shall not probably leave London before next month, as Mr. McRae has written me he will come over to the drawing and I may wait for him here. The news is splendid, both for what it contains and for what it implies. I look upon the prospects of peace as most promising.

  Cordially, yours,

           HENRY HOTZE.

GEORGE MCHENRY, Esq.,
 Hotel de France, Versailles.

[Enclosure.]

        HOTEL DE FRANCE,
      Versailles, August 18, 1864.

MY DEAR HOTZE: I hand Commodore Maury's letter, by which you will see how the matter came up. Maury had been at Manchester and requested my views on cotton, which he forwarded without my knowledge to Richmond with my printed matter. It is the first time that I have heard of any of my "cotton talk" reaching the Confederate capital.

You will observe that I have a sort of carte blanche to promulgate and further develop my views as to cotton, and to call upon you for material aid. I have not yet fully made up my mind as to the course of procedure, but I do not propose on this side of the Atlantic to advance any arguments in opposition to the opinion of General McRae on the subject, as I do not wish to conflict with any of his financial arrangements already made or in contemplation. Besides which he is a "cotton man," and holding as he does the position of Confederate Secretary of the Treasury for Europe, I shall esteem it proper to confer with him, particularly as there are one or two points of the question on which he and I do not entirely agree. But I intend to waive these points, or, at least, not to bring them forward. * * *

  Very truly, yours,

          GEORGE MCHENRY.

---

* An offer to supply by a private loan Mr. McHenry's immediate personal necessities.—H.

[Enclosure.]

LONDON, *August 20, 1864.*

MY DEAR MCHENRY: I missed the mail last night, owing to my being detained in the city until a late hour, and could not therefore earlier return you the two letters enclosed.

I ought, as a friend, to say to you, that if Captain Maury's letter embodies all you have got from Richmond, I am disappointed on your account. I take it to be a complimentary acknowledgment of your volunteer services, such as every representative of the Government abroad has admitted to be due to you, and none, certainly not I, would refuse. But officially, and in absence of special instructions from the State Department, it means nothing more than that Mr. Benjamin said to Mr. Mallory that Mr. Hotze possessed the necessary authority in the disbursement of the secret-service fund abroad. for the current expenditures of the State Department under the direction of the President. This is the precise status quo without an iota of change. I cordially approve of your determination not to oppose General McRae's views and policy on this side of the water in any future publications, and I may add my conviction that no antagonism to that policy could possibly receive the sanction or pecuniary support of the Confederate Government, unless it has utterly changed the views of which we are at present advised. Any official sanction, therefore, given to your writings, would necessarily imply an unqualified support of the commercial and financial policy which the Government has seen fit to adopt and carry out through the agency to Mr. McRae. I attach much greater practical importance to Mr. Slidell's letter. If the two commissioners will jointly address me an official recommendation to pay you in compensation of past services, such a sum as they may mention, I shall consider the recommendation an order, and will find the money, even if I should not have it in hand. This is the only way in which I can meet your wishes, and I will add that if this way is opened to me, I will act accordingly, not only without reluctance, but with hearty good will.

The news from Mobile is that of a naval defeat, to be sincerely regretted, but in my opinion that town itself is in no danger. It can only be taken by land attack.

Believe me, truly yours,

HENRY HOTZE.

GEORGE MCHENRY, Esq.,
   Hotel de France, Versailles.

No. 43.]   DEPARTMENT OF STATE,
                                Richmond, September 20, 1864.

SIR: I have made no answer to your several dispatches posterior to No. 63, because each mail led us to hope that the next would bring some definite solution of the affair of the *Rappahannock*, and thus enable the President to express his views of the action of the French Government in this matter. The uncertainty is now at an end, and I have to acknowledge a receipt of your Nos. 64 to 68, inclusive, the Nos. 67 and 68 having reached us on the 13th instant.

A review of the conduct of the French Government since the commencement of our national career exhibits the most marked contrast between friendly professions and injurious acts. It may not be without utility here to place on record a series of instances in which that Government and its officers have interposed effectively to aid our enemies, while profuse in professions of sympathy for us.

First. France united with Great Britain in agreeing to respect a paper blockade of our entire coast with a full knowledge of its invalidity, as since confessed to you on more than one occasion.

Second. France joined Great Britain in closing all its ports to the entry of prizes made by us, thus guaranteeing, as far as was possible without open hostility, the vessels of our enemies from becoming prize to our cruisers, and forcing us to destroy on the high seas, and thus lose the value of all vessels captured from our enemies.

Third. France has entertained during the entire war the closest amicable relations with our enemies as an independent nation. It has at the same time violated the treaty of 6th February, 1778, the eleventh article of which guaranteed to the States of Virginia, North Carolina, South Carolina, and Georgia "their liberty, sovereignty, and independence, absolute and unlimited," by persistent refusal to treat these States as independent and by countenancing the claim to sovereignty over them set up by the remaining States that were parties to that treaty.

Fourth. This Government succeeded in introducing into the roadstead of the Brazos Santiago cargoes of arms destined to pass through the neutral port of Matamoras into the Confederacy. The French naval officers seized these arms as being intended for the use of the Mexicans, in spite of the most conclusive evidence that they were destined for our defense against invasion. The people of Texas being thus deprived of arms, the town of Brownsville and the Rio Grande frontier fell defenseless into the hands of the enemy.

Fifth. The agents of the French Government, after obtaining permission for the export of their tobacco under license to pass the blockade, entered into a convention with our enemy so objectionable in its character and so derogatory to our rights as an independent power that we have been forced to withdraw the permission.

Sixth. This Government was indirectly approached by the Emperor Maximilian with proposals for the establishment of friendly relations. The Emperor of the French is well understood to have interfered to prevent this result, and to induce the new Emperor to seek favor from our enemies by avoiding intercourse with us.

Seventh. The French Government has taken pains to intimate to us that hospitality to our vessels of war entering their harbors was accorded with reluctance, and by the delays interposed in the grant of permission to the *Alabama* to enter dock for necessary repairs, placed her commander in a situation which prevented him from declining without dishonor a combat in which his vessel was lost chiefly by reason of her need of refitting and repair.

Eighth. The Emperor of the French, after having himself suggested and promised acquiescence in the attempt of this Government to obtain vessels of war by purchase or contract in France, after encouraging us in the loss of invaluable time and of the services of some of our best naval officers, as well as in the expenditure of large sums obtained at painful sacrifice, has broken his faith, has deprived us of our vessels when on the eve of completion, and has thus inflicted on us an injury and rendered to our enemies a service which establish his claim to any concessions that he may desire from them. This last act of the French Government, professedly dictated by the obligation of preserving neutrality, is marked still more distinctly as unfriendly to the Confederacy by the fact that some of the vessels have been transferred to a European power engaged in a war to which France is no party and in which she professes the same neutrality as in the contest on this side of the Atlantic.

Ninth. The detention of the *Rappahannock* is the last and least defensible of the acts of the French Government, and it is in its nature totally irreconcilable with neutral obligations. A Confederate vessel, unarmed, sought and obtained asylum in the port of Calais. She was allowed to complete her repairs and to incur all the cost and expense necessary to enable her to go to sea. She was notified of the desire of the French Government that she should leave the harbor, and while engaged in coaling for that purpose, and still unarmed, the French Government, on the demand of our enemies, ordered her to be detained in port on the unintelligible pretext that she had not obtained her coal in advance. Six months have elapsed, and the *Rappahannock* is still in a French port. In violation of the right of asylum, we have been deprived of the services of this vessel, while by the use of a system alternating between a studied silence and evasive statements our representations have been eluded and our remonstrances rendered unavailing. After thus delaying the departure of the vessel until our enemies had had time to perfect arrangements for her capture, a reluctant consent to her departure was finally extorted, but coupled with conditions which would almost insure her falling into the hands of the enemy. The vessel therefore remains in the French port, its use during the war practically confiscated by that Government for the benefit of our adversary under circumstances as inconsistent with neutral obligations as they are injurious to our rights and offensive to our flag.

It is impossible for the President, in view of such action on the part of a foreign Government, to credit its professions of amity, nor can he escape the painful conviction that the Emperor of the French, knowing that the utmost efforts of this people are engrossed in the defense of their homes against an atrocious warfare waged by greatly superior numbers, has thought the occasion opportune for promoting his own purposes, at no greater cost than a violation of his faith and duty toward us.

It is unfortunately but too true that this Government is not now in a position to resist such aggressions; and France is not the only nation which has unworthily availed itself of this fact, as the messages of the President have on more than one occasion demonstrated to the world. There is one contrast, however, between the conduct of the English and French Governments that does not redound to the credit of the latter. The English Government has scarcely disguised its hostility from the commencement of the struggle. It has professed a newly invented neutrality which it has frankly defined as meaning a course of conduct more favorable to the stronger belligerent. The Emperor of the French professed an earnest sympathy for us and a desire to serve us, which, however sincere at the time, have yielded to the first suggestion of advantage to be gained by rendering assistance to our enemy. We are compelled by present circumstances to submit in silence to these aggressions, but we are not compelled, nor is it compatible with a proper sense of self-respect, to affect toward the Emperor of the French a continuance of the same regard and confidence to which the President formerly felt justified in giving public expression. Nor need we forego the hope, which it is, however, unnecessary to proclaim, that the day is not nearly so distant as is supposed by those who take these unworthy advantages when the Confederacy will be able to impress on all nations the conviction of her ability to repel outrages, from whatever quarter they may be offered.

From the correspondence of the naval officers abroad with the Secretary of the Navy, it appears that the French Government was not satisfied with preventing our use during the war of the vessels built in French ports with the consent of that Government, but refused permission to finish the vessels for delivery to us after the restoration of peace, and actually forced the builders to sell them to third parties. From the reports of Captain Bulloch it would seem that the arrangements to prevent the vessels from ever reaching our hands were so complete and carried out with such disregard of good faith and of contract, on the part of contractors and public officials, that he was compelled to esteem himself fortunate in saving this Government from the loss of the money invested. He represents the conduct of all parties to be such as should render the Government ever most cautious in its dealings with France, and it is probable that the lesson will be well remembered.

You will, of course, undestand that in the foregoing observation it is far from the intention of the President to suggest that you should obtrude on the French Government any manifestation of an indignation which, however deeply felt, can be followed by no action that could afford us redress. We believe that you will not find it difficult to maintain a reserved demeanor which will readily suggest the inference that the conduct of the Emperor's Government is regarded by the President as unfriendly, without giving any occasion for a rupture, which would add to the weight of the difficulties attendant on our struggle, and which is therefore carefully to be avoided. Any complaints that we may have to make against European powers must of necessity be deferred for a more favorable occasion, and all that we can do at present is to avoid any course of conduct that could fairly be construed into condonation of injuries that remain unredressed.

The matter of the money deposited by Mr. Thomassy at Montpelier, mentioned in your No. 66, concerns the War Department, and an extract from your dispatch has accordingly been furnished to Mr. Seddon, from whom you will doubtless hear on the subject.

I have the honor to be, very respectfully, your obedient servant,

J. P. BENJAMIN,
Secretary of State.

Hon. JOHN SLIDELL, *Paris.*

No. 38.]
DEPARTMENT OF STATE,
Richmond, September 20, 1864.

SIR: * * * Although the seal came safely to hand on the 4th ultimo, having been delivered to me by Lieutenant Chapman in person, I have no news as yet of the two boxes which were shipped by the same steamer to care of Messrs. Fraser, Trenholm & Co., so that I have been as yet unable to take an impression or to judge of the effect produced. Mr. Trenholm, our new Secretary of the Treasury, has written to endeavor to discover the cause of the delay. I begin to fear that the boxes are lost.

You will receive herewith Treasury draft for £458 1s. 4d., as requested in your No. 12, to cover the expenses of the defense in the case of the captors of the *Gerrity*. You must long since have received my dispatch conveying the approval by the Government of your course in regard to these parties.

I am afraid that in your interview with Lord Palmerston you went rather beyond what the state of the case would warrant in the prediction made as to the condition of the North and the prospects of early peace. It is not considered here very likely that the North will be the first to recognize the independence of the Confederacy if it be possible for them to avoid the humiliation of such a step, and although the war may gradually lose its intensity there is great reason to fear that it may long continue a lingering existence if European powers persist in the encouragement which is afforded the North by their obstinate refusal to recognize us. You were probably better able to judge on the spot of the effect likely to be produced on the mind of the British premier by the assurances given him; but, from our standpoint, it would seem that the expression of a conviction that hostilities would continue till our recognition by Europe should afford a basis for a treaty of peace would have been more likely to produce a good result as well as more accordant with the probable course of events. You may perhaps have doubted whether the English Government desired the cessation of the war. Their conduct has produced the conviction on many minds that they dread the restoration of peace on this side; and, if that view be correct, your remarks were better adapted to produce effect than those above suggested. We have, however, long ceased to expect from England any other action than such as may be dictated by our enemies to suit their own policy, and look with little interest to any declarations of her public men, being able to judge by the past what their acts will be under any circumstances.

I perceive, however, that Lord Palmerston asked your opinion of the manner in which the North would receive any intervention or mediation on the part of Great Britain, still persistently taking it for granted that such intervention was desired by us. It seems impossible to make foreign Governments understand that we ask and desire no such thing; that we confine ourselves to the simple demand for recognition; that recognition will end the war from whatever quarter it may come, and that nothing else will. It is singular that when both belligerents have for two years shown in every conceivable manner that they consider the recognition of the South by Europe as absolutely conclusive of the struggle, and as certain to result in a cessation of hostilities, foreign Governments should persistently affect to consider that such recognition would be of no value unless followed by active intervention. This is the more surprising because history is full of examples of recognition unaccompanied with any intervention or mediation, and productive of no further manifestation of resentment on the part of the nation seeking the subjugation of its adversary than an empty protest or remonstrance.

The President will leave this evening for Georgia, and will, I trust, put matters there on a more satisfactory footing. There is no reason for despondency on account of the position of affairs there; on the contrary, we look for decisive success if the arrangements now in progress can be completed.

I have the honor to be, very respectfully, your obedient servant,

J. P. Benjamin,
Secretary of State.

Hon. Jas. M. Mason, *Paris.*

No. 72.] Paris, *September 26, 1864.*

Sir: Since my last of 13th instant I have received no dispatch from the Department, but through the New York papers we have copies of your circular of 25th August. In that you speak of having heretofore forwarded copies of the manifesto issued by the Congress of the Confederate States with the approval of the President on the 14th June last, accompanied by a resolution that copies of the manifesto should be laid before foreign governments.

This manifesto and resolution reached Europe early in July and were extensively reproduced and favorably noticed by the leading journals of England and the Continent, but I did not deem it proper to present a copy to the minister of foreign affairs until I should have received it in an official form accompanied by your commentaries. Your dispatches appear all to have reached me in due course, the latest, No. 41, of 12th July, but containing no notice of the manifesto. Mr. Mason informs me that he is also without instructions from you on the subject. We hope to receive them by the Bermuda and Halifax mail now fully due.

The newspapers will have informed you of the convention recently concluded between France and Italy, looking to the withdrawal of the French army of occupation from Rome. It took everyone by surprise, and its existence was at first emphatically denied even by some of the semiofficial journals. It is said that the minister of foreign affairs was ignorant of the Emperor's intention until the terms of the convention had been definitively settled, and that he was then merely called upon to put them in official form. They are almost identically such as the Emperor foreshadowed in his letter of 20th May, 1862, to Thouvenel, then foreign minister. The whole affair is a striking* illustration of his tenacity of purpose and secretiveness.

We have, by the last New York mail, McClellan's letter accepting the Chicago nomination. It effectually destroys the hopes that we had begun to entertain of an early termination of the war and renders the success or failure of his candidature a matter of comparative indifference; indeed it may be doubted whether we should not rather prefer the election of Lincoln or Fremont as leading sooner and more certainly to those intestine troubles in the free States to which only we can look for the abandonment of the vain hopes of subjugation or reunion entertained by the contending factions and put forward as their respective rallying cries. No one seems to consider separation as the only remedy or what in effect is the same thing; none have the moral courage to avow and maintain that opinion at the ballot box.

I was yesterday at the races of the Bois de Boulogne, where I met the Emperor; he recognized me at some distance and came toward me, greeting me very cordially with a shake of the hand. He inquired if I had been well and asked if I had received from the minister of war notice of an order for the admission of my son at Saint Cyr. I said that I had to thank him very sincerely for his kindness in affording my son such an opportunity of acquiring a good military education; he replied that it was quite unnecessary as he was pleased to have an opportunity of showing his good will. I have not before alluded to this circumstance because the order had not been actually given, although the Emperor had very promptly promised Mr. de Persigny to grant the permission on his application made about the 10th instant, and indeed I should not probably have mentioned the matter officially had I not had occasion to report my conversation with the Emperor.

The Emperor, after making inquiries about my family, asked me what I thought of our military position, especially in Georgia, and of the effect of the fall of Atlanta. I said that I was happy to assure him that the abandonment of Atlanta was a much less serious matter than was generally supposed in Europe, as we had removed all the valuable machinery and material weeks before Sherman took possession; that the only effect of Sherman's advance was to increase the distance from his base of supplies and make his communications more liable to interruption; that I did not think it at all improbable that we should soon hear of his falling back upon Chattanooga. He asked if the report of the surrender of Mobile was true. I said that I was confident not only that the report was premature, but that we should be able to hold Mobile, as we had Charleston. I went on to say that we might soon expect stirring news from the armies near Petersburg, and I doubted not that Lee would give a good account of Grant. He expressed his admiration and astonishment at what we had achieved against such enormous odds and his confidence in our ability to maintain ourselves. He spoke of the impossibility of occupying a territory like ours and his regrets that our many victories had not been followed by more decisive results. I answered that this was susceptible of easy explanation; that we were always fighting against superior numbers and had no strong reserves to follow up our successes; that the troops that had been engaged were generally exhausted by fatigue; that our great battles had usually been a series of desperate fighting for several days, and while we had inflicted much heavier losses on the enemy, we had necessarily been much crippled ourselves. Besides, our cavalry, from the difficulty of renewing our stock of horses, was much less numerous and efficient than it had been, and we were unable to pursue and harass a beaten and retreating enemy with such effect as would be expected in Europe under similar circumstances.

The Emperor asked me what were the prospects of peace. I replied that had the question been put to me ten days before, I should have replied that they were good; but that the letter of McClellan accepting the Democratic nomination for the Presidency had completely dissipated them; that Lincoln would probably be reelected, and that the war would be continued until a revolution should break out in the free States. I asked him if he had read McClellan's letter. He said that he had; that it had greatly disappointed him, for he had entertained strong hopes that the terrible conflict would soon be ended. He then left me, with another cordial shake of the hand.

A year ago I should have attached some important political signification to this incident. As it is, I merely consider it as indicating personal kind feeling toward the representative of a cause that commands his respect and good wishes.

I have the honor to be, with great respect, your most obedient servant,

JOHN SLIDELL.

Hon. J. P. BENJAMIN,
Secretary of State.

No. 13.]   PARIS, *September 29, 1864.*
SIR: * * *

Some ten days ago I saw printed in the Northern papers your despatch to me of the 25th of August, published as a reprint from the Richmond Examiner of the 27th, relating to the late interview between James F. Jaquess and James R. Gilmore with the President at Richmond; the original I have not yet received. I could well understand the object of publishing this despatch at home and at once. Immediately on seeing it I took measures to have it republished in the London journals. I had previously seen the versions of that interview given by Mr. Gilmore through the Northern press, and after the publication of your dispatch was gratified to find that the Democratic journals there, at least, accepted it as the truth of the matter.

I find in it the following paragraph:

You have been heretofore furnished with copies of the manifesto issued by the Congress of the Confederate States, with the approval of the President, on the 14th June last, and have doubtless acted in conformity with the resolution, which requested that copies of this manifesto should be laid before foreign governments.

I have never received a copy of that manifesto from the Department of State, nor did it reach me in any other form than through the Northern press; it was, however, republished by all the principal newspapers in England, and as expressive of the solemn and deliberate sense of Congress after more than three years' experience as to the true character of the war on our side and its firm purpose to remain in the field until independence was achieved, I think was not without its effect upon the European mind. Mr. Slidell tells me alike, that he did not receive copies from your Department.

In regard to so much of your No. 36 as refers to the fabricated papers palmed upon the British Government by the American Secretary of State through Lord Lyons, its denial of the authenticity of those documents is so minute and explicit, coupled with the

declaration that our Government would deem it inconsistent with
self-respect hereafter to descend to the like refutation with a view
to undeceive the British Government as to the character of any
future communications in relation to our affairs which they habitually accepted from the Government at Washington, that I think it
would be as well to give so much of the dispatch to the public,
although the forgeries had been heretofore denounced by Mr. Slidell.
I shall have it published in the Index.

*   *   *   *   *   *   *

I returned to Paris a few days since and shall remain here until
about the middle of October; at that time there is to be held at Liverpool a grand " bazaar " called in our country a " fair," the avails of
which are dedicated to relieve the wants and necessities of Southern
prisoners confined at the North. It originated with the Southern
Club at Liverpool, who have for some time past been collecting and
remitting funds for that purpose to confidential agencies at the North.
The plan of the bazaar has been taken up by the highest of the nobility in England, friends of our cause, and many of their ladies will
officiate in person on the occasion, beside making large contributions.
Our friend Mr. Spence has for some months past had the matter
actively in hand, and I have promised him that I would be present
as his guest; he tells me that most munificent donations in money
have been made from various parts of England, and the nobility taking it up, gives it a tone which insures success; he thinks that its avails
may far exceed, and can not fall below, £10,000. I speak of it as a
part of the history of the times, and as evincing the sympathies of
the English people.

There is nothing new here in European politics, beyond what you
will get through the public journals. Much speculation is indulged
in as to the probable result of the Presidential election in the North,
since the manifesto in McClellan's letter of acceptance; result as it
may, I do not see how the war can be carried on, when it is manifest
that their people have no longer any stomach for the fight.

You will remember that more than a year ago I sent out to the Department the model of a new form of railway, constructed without
iron, with the model of the car and wheels adapted to it, the invention of a Mr. Prosser, of London, and in a dispatch subsequent you
informed me that it had arrived and been turned over to the Secretary of War, who promised to give it a trial. I have heard nothing
since in regard to it, and recently since Mr. Prosser wrote to me from
England, asking whether it had been tried, and with what success. I
thought at the time that it promised well for cheapness, and expedition in its construction. Can you inform me, for the satisfaction of
the inventor, whether it was tried?

I have the honor to be, with great respect, your obedient servant.

                                                J. M. MASON.

Hon J. P. BENJAMIN,
        Secretary of State.

                                LIVERPOOL, *October 1, 1864.*

GENTLEMEN: I have the honor to enclose a copy of a letter directed
by me to Commander Bulloch, C. S. Navy, and his reply to the
same. Before the communications alluded to, Commander Bulloch

and myself had a lengthy conversation. He refused to advance the money or purchase the *Hawk* for the reasons given in his note, but remarked that if anyone could do so, General McRae was the proper person. He further informed me he had heard that Captain Pegram, C. S. Navy, was coming out to take command of the ship, but this rumor is in piece with a dozen others.

The only pleasant information that I received on the subject was from Major Norman S. Walker, who informed me that before he left Richmond all the funds required had been paid in, and why they had not been sent out he could not say. I can not state at present whether or not a longer time will be granted me for the payment (I will inform you by telegraph of that fact on Monday); if not, the *Hawk*, according to original contract, must return to England with cotton and be sold. I have done all that man could do, and the company must bear the blame.

Will you please answer this note?

I have the honor to be, very respectfully,

EDWARD C. STILES.

Hon. Messrs. MASON and SLIDELL,
 Commissioners, etc., Confederate States of America.

(Mr. Mason's dispatches were delivered and went out by Major Walker.)

[Enclosure.]

LIVERPOOL, *October 1, 1864.*

SIR: After our conversation this morning with regard to the steamship *Hawk*, intended for the Confederate States Volunteer Navy, will you please give me your views on the subject.

Very respectfully,

EDWARD C. STILES,
 Commander, C. S. Volunteer Navy.

Commander JAMES D. BULLOCH,
 C. S. Navy.

[Enclosure.]

LIVERPOOL, *October 1, 1864.*

SIR: In reply to your letter of this date, I have only to state that I can not accede to the proposition in regard to the steamship *Hawk*, as you have presented the case. I have no authority to enter into financial transactions of the kind, nor to direct the funds of the Navy Department from their assigned uses.

My views were fully detailed to you in conversation this morning and need not be repeated here.

Very respectfully,

JAMES D. BULLOCH.

Commander E. C. STILES,
 C. S. Volunteer Navy.

No. 109.]   BRUSSELS, *October 5, 1864.*

SIR: The absorbing topic of Europe at present is the Franco-Italian treaty, which has just been communicated to the public. It appears to be received with very general favor, except at Rome and Vienna. Pius IX perhaps perceives in its stipulations a termination, at no distant period, of the temporal power of the Papacy, while Francis Joseph can not fail to understand that the high contracting parties are resolved upon the ultimate severance of Venice from his Empire as a necessity for perfecting the restoration of the nationality of Italy.

The Holy Father has no alternative but to submit to the dictation of the Emperor of the French in the engagement which that potentate has entered into to turn over to the watchful care of Victor Emmanuel, distasteful as the procedure may be to him. He has not the power for resistance, whatever may be his wish or his will. It is his interest to yield silently, gracefully, and patiently to unpleasant events.

Nor do I believe that Austria, if her honor is not flagrantly offended, will for the retention of Venice, valuable as that strongly fortified possession is to her, incur the risk of a war with Italy, backed as that power assuredly would be by France. It is believed that Victor Emmanuel will succeed in acquiring that territory by purchase or by an equivalent consideration of some other kind. The King of the Belgians is now at Baden-Baden, supposed to be employed in endeavoring to arrange an amicable solution of the question with the Czar and the King of Prussia, while Lord Clarendon is at Vienna, reported to be diplomatizing for the attainment of the same end.

The prospects for the preservation of the peace of Europe, with the single exception of the Venetian difficulty, were probably never more assuring than at this moment. With that exception there seems not to be so much as a speck of war upon the horizon.

The Dano-German differences have been definitively adjusted—less, it is true, in a sense of right than of might—with the acquiescence of the most clamorous sticklers for a faithful observance of European law. Poland and the Poles are heard of no more. Politically they are so dead as not to excite a paragraph even in a French Red Republican newspaper. And Louis Napoleon has probably, in his impaired health and close proximity to old age, dismissed forever from his mind the long-cherished idea of the rectification of the northern frontier of France. Almost everybody in Europe, as well sovereign as subject, seems to be animated by an ardent new-born zeal for the preservation of peace.

The frightfully deranged condition of monetary affairs, extending its harmful influence to all who are directly within the sphere of its operations, has contributed largely to the creation of this sentiment. Another superinducing cause is the unprecedented horror of war, engendered in the ruthless prosecution of hostilities against our country.

I have the honor to be, sir, very respectfully, your obedient servant.

A. DUDLEY MANN.

Hon J. P. BENJAMIN,
    Secretary of State, C. S. A., Richmond, Va.

Circular.] DEPARTMENT OF STATE,
    Richmond, October 10, 1864.

[For circular, see Diplomatic Correspondence Belgium, page 37.]

Hon. JOHN SLIDELL, *Paris.*

No. 110.]   BRUSSELS, *October 12, 1864.*

SIR: There is an unrestrained expression of indignation throughout this realm at the villainous deception practiced upon the persons who have been induced, through the artifices of the Lincoln Government, to migrate to the Federal States.

L'Independance Belge, which, until about the beginning of September, made no concealment of its enthusiastic devotion to the Federal cause, published conspicuously in its afternoon edition of the 10th instant and morning edition of the 11th instant the enclosed exposition copied from the Courrier des États Unis of New York.

The Washington Cabinet has connived at the commission of deeds, if indeed it did not originate them, which excite humane civilization to blush for the depravity of that well-nigh fiendish concern. Assuredly no country having the shadow of a claim to respectability ever stood so low in European esteem as the remnant of the old American Union does at the present time. It has displayed its perfidy so strikingly that it is palpable to the humblest laborer. It may win battles with the aid of the recruits which it has so fraudulently obtained on this side of the Atlantic, but it can never more enjoy honor in the opinion of the just minded. The people of the Old World in the main are not so fallen as to recognize as a public principle that the "end justifies the means." They believe that they have something nobler to live for than the gratification of unhallowed ambition, achieved through the perpetration of flagrant crime.

I shall be careful to have the publication referred to above put into general circulation in Germany. I shall also have it translated and sent to the London Times. In Belgium it has already been sufficiently disseminated or will be by the end of this week.

The number of Belgians who have taken service in the Federal Army is very small—not, probably, exceeding 200. Hereafter it will be difficult to secure a solitary recruit for its ranks. In fact, I confidently trust that our lion-hearted citizen soldiers will have no more European mercenaries to encounter in the battlefield. My unceasing efforts shall continue to be directed to such a consummation. If the Yankees are resolved to go on with the war, you may depend upon it that henceforth they will have to do their own fighting.

I have the honor to be, sir, very respectfully, your obedient servant,

A. DUDLEY MANN.

Hon. J. P. BENJAMIN,
   Secretary of State, C. S. A., Richmond, Va.

No. 111.]   BRUSSELS, *October 15, 1864.*

SIR: I have the honor to acknowledge the receipt of your Circular dated August 25, together with a copy of the Statutes at Large of the Confederate States. They arrived yesterday.

The former had already appeared in several of the London journals and also in. Galignani's Messenger of Paris and in other continental newspapers. I think I may with safety state that it has had a fair European circulation. I will endeavor, however, to extend its publicity.

The narration of the interview of the two Northern emissaries with the President and yourself, designed by them for home and foreign general circulation, has not, as far as I can judge, been in the slightest degree prejudicial to the elevated position which the executive department enjoys in the estimation of intelligent persons in this hemisphere. Much more hurtful to our interests has been the effect produced by the Clifton House correspondence. It will be very difficult to completely remove the impression that the attempt at negotiation by Confederate citizens was not, in one way or another, authorized by the President. I have treated this notion as ridiculously absurd and I flatter myself that it is now so considered within the sphere of my public intercourse. Mr. Seward, with his usual astuteness and unscrupulousness, has tried hard to turn the circumstance to valuable account.

The manifesto, in the absence of instructions from the State Department upon the subject, has not yet been formally communicated to the different Governments of Europe. Mr. Mason will most likely indicate to you the manner in which he proposes that this shall be done, by the present conveyance, and which manner meets with the approval of Mr. Slidell and myself.

In the meantime the document, translated into French, has appeared in l'Independance Belge, as it had previously appeared, in English, in a number of the British journals. It is regarded as a paper of exceeding dignity, replete with patriotic sentiment and inflexible purpose. It can not fail to exert a decidedly favorable influence in behalf of our cause, in whatever court or other official circle it may be read.

I have the honor to be, sir, very respectfully, your obedient servant,

A. DUDLEY MANN.

Hon. J. P. BENJAMIN,
  Secretary of State, C. S. A., Richmond, Va.

No. 1.]

BURLINGTON HOTEL,
London, October 19, 1864.

SIR: I have the honor to acknowledge the receipt of your communication of the 1st of September, which reaches me to-day just as I am on the point of leaving for Paris. The important subject to which it refers shall receive my best attention. The essential condition of success in an undertaking of such importance and extended dimensions is the difficult one of profound secrecy. To secure this I propose to dispense with all clerical aid, even of the most confidential character, and my communications to you will be guarded in their language. It will, however, be impossible for me to manage the matter without some assistance, and I shall depend in a large measure on the services of my personal friend, Mr. Henry Hotze, upon whose discretion I can implicitly rely, and who as a confidential agent of your own Department has a direct interest for rendering me that zealous assistance which my personal relations with him warrant me to expect. It will further be necessary for me to avail myself of the services of another personal friend, the Hon. James Williams, now in Vienna, and whose extensive personal acquaintance in Austria and in the southeast and east of Europe I hope to make an important element of success in this difficult undertaking. I shall not, however, communicate with him until I have an opportunity of seeing him in person, desiring to avoid writing on this subject as far as possible. With the exception of these two gentlemen and Mr. Prioleau, of the firm of Messrs. Fraser, Trenholm & Co., I intend to keep the matter a close secret, even from those in whom I have the fullest confidence, and I earnestly recommend a similar reticence on the part of the agents who may be employed in this business in Central America, Mexico, and Texas. Many of the most important plans of the Government in Europe have been defeated by their publicity. I am almost certain that this affair can not be managed from English or French ports, and I shall therefore endeavor to confine the business to the Mediterranean and more particularly to Adriatic and Levantine ports. Before, however, anything practicable can be done it will be necessary for me to see the parties to the correspondence enclosed in your dispatch. I suppose they have returned to Europe, though I have not yet heard from them. Some little time must necessarily elapse before the matter can be got underway, and it is not probable that I shall have occasion to use any of the warrants remitted by you before the 1st of January. I will write you more fully by the next Bermuda mail which leaves ten days hence.

With much respect, your obedient servant,
C. J. McRae,
Agent Treasury Department, Confederate States.

The Hon. J. P. Benjamin,
Secretary of State, Richmond.

No. 73.]   Paris, *October 20, 1864.*

Sir: I have the honor to acknowledge receipt of your circular of 25th August, but am still without any later numbered dispatch than that of 12th July, nor have the copies of the manifesto of Congress, spoken of in your circular as having been previously furnished, yet reached me. After consultation with Messrs. Mason and Mann, it has been decided to await the arrival of the Bermuda mail, now nearly due, before presenting copies of the manifesto to the Governments of Europe; we shall probably accompany them by a joint note, for which purpose these gentlemen will come to Paris toward the end of this month. By that time we may expect news of a decided character from the armies in Virginia and still be enabled to form a pretty correct opinion of the chances of Lincoln's reelection. The character of this intelligence will in some degree guide us in drawing up our joint note; we await it with intense anxiety, but with undiminished confidence in the ultimate success of our struggle for independence.

M. Mercier, late minister at Washington, has been appointed ambassador to Madrid; this promotion is by some attributed to the urgent recommendations of Prince Napoleon, with whom he is very intimate. If this be true, and I am inclined to think so, the doubts I have heretofore expressed of the sincerity of M. Mercier's avowed Southern preferences are not unfounded, for the prince, as you know, has always been a warm partisan of the Lincoln Government. M. Mercier will be succeeded by the Marquis Chateaurenard, who occupied the very modest position of minister at the petty court of Hesse-Cassel. This would seem to indicate that the Emperor attaches no great importance to the Washington mission; on the whole, we have no reason to regret the change.

I have the honor to be, with great respect, your most obedient servant,

JOHN SLIDELL.

Hon. J. P. BENJAMIN,
    Secretary of State.

No. 112.]   BRUSSELS, *October 22, 1864.*

SIR: Our recent severe reverses, commencing with the surrender of Fort Gaines and continuing until the retreat of General Early from Fisher's Hill, cast a gloom over many millions of our friends in Europe. It did, indeed, seem for a period of several weeks that the tide of adversity had set in against us irresistibly strong. But the last glorious turn, which has given us victory from Missouri to the environs of Richmond, will, I indulge a confident hope, lead on to definitive achievements.

In despite of all the representations that have been made through the newspaper press of the probably eventual worthlessness of Federal bonds, those bonds steadily rose from $37\frac{1}{2}$, their lowest point of depression on the Frankfort Bourse, to $51\frac{1}{2}$ on the 15th instant, since when they have slightly receded, in consequence of the intelligence received by the *Persia* that our armies were again eminently victorious wherever they had been engaged in combat. Still, the blind infatuation which created confidence in them is not removed.

It really seems as if at times the devil himself takes possession of the minds of the very shrewdest of business men, and with false promises, like those made to our first mother, lures them on to certain ruin. There are striking instances calculated to engender such a belief. The "South Sea Bubble," "John Law's Mississippi Scheme," and "Nick Biddle's Bank" are conspicuous illustrations of the evil genius which occasionally rules the actors in the monetary world. The Germans and the Dutch and other Europeans are destined to suffer as severely as did the English and the French and the Americans whenever the Federal financial system explodes, an event so certain as to be beyond the control of any earthly influence. With all my heart, I desire such condign punishment on account of the wrongs from which, through greedy avarice, our devoted land has been the victim. But for the pecuniary assistance furnished the Washington Government by continental Europe, greenbacks would probably not be worth at this moment 10 cents in gold on the dollar. This, of course, would have rendered the prosecution of hostilities an impossibility.

The subterfuges alone to which the party in power have illicitly had recourse to secure the reelection of Mr. Lincoln will cost the North hundreds of millions of liabilities. This I have lost no suitable occasion to explain, unseen, through the press, to the operators on change and other dealers in Federal bonds. With Mr. Seward and the politicians who esteem him as their file leader, I am quite persuaded that the decision of the ballot boxes on the 1st of November is looked to with far greater interest than the reconstruction of the former Union. The retention of power is a paramount impelling consideration with them, and, accordingly, hostilities have been prosecuted expressly for the accomplishment of that object. I see this, perhaps, more distinctly here than you can see it at Richmond. Can there be one man upon Southern soil so debased as to be prepared to again affiliate politically with such monstrous crime and such inhuman depravity? If there be, he has a heart that is insensible to honor, to justice, and to truth. What! Recognize as fellow-countrymen beings who in their lust for office and for the unlawful gain attendant upon it have sacrificed, without doing the slightest violence to their conscience—as unfeelingly, in fact, as the butcher slaughters the ox—hundrds of thousands upon hundreds of thousands of such mortals as the Almighty, in the plenitude of his wisdom, created in his own image! Peace without independence would be the peace of hateful, despised life to every inhabitant within the embraces of the Confederate States worthy of being called an inhabitant. Mississippi nurtured a Walker, the most venomous of political vipers, but let her be consoled in the reflection that she also nurtured a Davis, the nation's pride. Virginia produced a Scott, but let her not weep over her mistake, since she enjoys the glory of having produced a Lee, the country's hope.

Traitors there have been within our limits, but treason must have had its end in the brutal enormities of our enemy. I am sure of this, and being sure of it, I can not conceive that there be a "reconstructionist" upon our soil. And yet it has been currently reported for some time that contrivances were in progress in Canada and elsewhere for arranging a reunion basis between the North and South. It is even asserted that Georgia had taken the matter into her own hands and was ready to accept conditions in that sense.

I flatly contradict these statements as not containing so much as a shadow of truth. The speech of the President at Salisbury was just in season to produce a good effect in Europe and I am confident that his visit to Macon will accomplish the best of results.

I have the honor to be, sir, very respectfully, your obedient servant,
A. DUDLEY MANN.

Hon. J. P. BENJAMIN,
   Secretary of State, C. S. A., Richmond, Va.

No. 113.]   BRUSSELS, *October 28, 1864.*

SIR: Now that intelligence has been received of the result of the elections of the 11th instant in Pennsylvania, Ohio, and Indiana, it seems not improbable that the unconstitutional rule of Lincoln will be sanctioned by the Federal States next Tuesday.

This, perhaps, will be just as well for us as if Gen. McClellan were chosen. It is ever better to encounter an avowed enemy than to be beset with a deceitful so-called friend. The Democrats out of power, having measured their strength with the Abolitionists, may render us much more unintentional service than they would have been disposed to do, invested with power. Numerically they will be not far from the equals of their adversaries, and may assume a defiant position to the high-handed measures of the administration.

But our reliance, as I have all along stated, must be exclusively upon ourselves for conquering an honorable peace—a peace with unconditional independence. To deprive the Federal Government of additional supplies of men and money from Europe is the uppermost thought in my mind. I am sparing no exertion or cost that I can afford to effect this object. Public opinion in Europe in this regard becomes from day to day more manifest in our interest.

Our endurance must and will accomplish after a while the exhaustion of the North in men and money, if she receives no aid from abroad. The Yankees who most desire our subjugation could not be coerced themselves to fight in support of that vicious desire.

There is unmistakable evidence that the bourse is more sensitive to news adverse to the North than it was at the date of my last. Since then the quotation of Federal bonds is about 7 per cent lower. Confidence, I am encouraged to believe, has considerably diminished in the value of those bonds—alike in Belgium, Holland, and Germany—during the last week. If this impression is correct, no considerable sum can be again introduced into the markets of the Continent without occasioning a panic and a consequent utter loss of faith. In that case, the inevitable financial crash of the Washington Government, so confidently expected and so impatiently awaited, which is to redound more to our advantage in hastening a cessation of hostilities than any victory we ever won, can not possibly be long delayed. The monetary condition of Europe, incessantly increasing in disorganization, is operating in favor of such a consummation.

An intelligent agent de change has this moment told me that in the present depressed state of the Federal bonds many holders thereof are remitting them to New York for sale, expecting to realize much higher prices (from 8 to 10 per cent, according to the latest quotations) for them there than are obtainable here. This will react in two ways upon the Federal Treasury. It will send the quotations down in Wall Street and cause the proceeds to be remitted in gold or its equivalent to Europe.

An estimate has just been made of the loss experienced by the recent failure of European speculators in the article of raw cotton. The sum is stated to be 200,000,000 francs. When hostilities were commenced the sum expended for this material annually by Europe amounted to 875,000,000 francs. For a like period, with a vastly smaller supply and inferior fiber, it now reaches the sum of 1,875,-000,000 francs.

The King of the Belgians is at Nice with the Czar and the Emperor of the French. The ostensible object of the meeting of those sovereigns is believed to be the adjustment of the Italian question. I incline to think that Louis Napoleon has perhaps more at heart the securing of an assurance by the great powers of Europe that his dynasty shall be sustained; and Leopold, that the newly created throne of Maximilian shall in like manner be guaranteed. The two objects, however, so far from being incompatible may, it is believed, be made to operate in harmony. Certain it is that negotiations of an important character are upon the tapis. I am slow to relinquish my belief, expressed some time ago, that the King of the Belgians is desirous to procure the hand of the Princess Murat for the Count of Flanders, and then to have the Count recognized as the rightful successor of Maximilian, who is childless. If the marriage shall be arranged the other event will meet with no opposition, either at the Tuileries or elsewhere in this hemisphere.

Just as I had closed the foregoing paragraph the telegraph of Reuter announced to me the recapture of Atlanta with four Federal regiments. I will not attempt to express the joy which this intelligence has occasioned me. The event will be regarded by Europe as the most important achievement of our arms during the war.

I have the honor to be, sir, very respectfully your obedient servant,

A. DUDLEY MANN.

Hon. J. P. BENJAMIN,
    Secretary of State, C. S. A., Richmond, Va.

---

48 AVENUE GABRIEL,
Paris, November 4, 1864.

SIR: Referring you to my communication of the 19th ultimo, I have now to say that the gentlemen referred to in your dispatch of the 1st of September have not yet made their appearance; consequently I can do nothing in the important business at present, and must wait their arrival. In the meantime I suggest that the members of this commission may ask to have some official position assigned them, either in the military or civil service, provided the enterprise is successful, and I ask instructions in reference to such a claim; without anything from you on the subject I shall make no promises, as to do so might hereafter embarrass the Government.

About five weeks previous to the receipt of your dispatch, say about the 20th of September, Colonel Sulakowski called on me with a proposition to inaugurate a similar enterprise to the one contemplated by you. Colonel Sulakowski is a man of some ability and great energy and of influence among his countrymen, and therefore might be of use, and if the committee to which you refer does not make its appearance soon I will have another interview with him and, without committing myself in any way, will endeavor to learn what he can do or if there are any number of his countrymen who are likely to embark in such an enterprise as is contemplated. When Colonel Sulakowski called on me I had neither the means nor authority to act in the premises, and consequently gave him no encouragement. The President will recollect Colonel Sulakowski was the commander of a regiment that was got up in New Orleans with the intention of forming a part of the foreign brigade which one Tochman undertook to raise. He served in the peninsula under Magruder, but resigned for some imaginary wrong which he supposed he had received in not having been promoted. He has since been in Texas with General Magruder, and from the enclosed copy of a letter from that officer to Major Helm it appears that he served with distinction. When he called on me he frankly [said] that he was no longer in the service of the country, but that he wished to return to it and was willing to accept any post or do anything that might be considered of service. My own opinion, however, is that 5,000 to 6,000 Poles capable of bearing arms can not be found in all Europe. The long delay of the arrival of the committee is to me a subject of surprise, and I fear the first-named member of it is not the person in whom the Government should confide in so important a matter.

A person of precisely the same name was active in enlisting the foreign legion in the United States for the British Government during the Crimean War. He afterwards went to Constantinople, where his career was by no means a reputable one; failing there he returned to the United States and obtained a clerkship in one of the offices at Washington, where he was up to and after the first battle of Manassas. This may not be the same person, but the name is identical, colonel and all, and if he is the same he's an adventurer totally unworthy of trust. I shall, however, be able to speak definitely on this subject as soon as he appears.

With much respect, your obedient servant,

C. J. McRae, *Agent, etc.*

Hon. J. P. Benjamin,
    Secretary of State, Richmond, Va.

No. 114.]   Brussels, *November 5, 1864.*

Sir: Mr. Mason has requested me to meet him at Paris to-morrow to arrange with Mr. Slidell and himself the mode of communicating the manifesto of Congress to the different Governments of Europe. I shall accordingly repair to that metropolis by the afternoon train, where I shall probably sojourn for a week.

The Belgian Parliament is to convene on the 7th instant. It will be opened by proxy, as the King will not return to Laeken until about the middle of the month.

Public opinion has been so flagrantly outraged by the systematized nefarious plans of the Washington Administration for decoying the laboring population of Europe into the Federal lines that I am disposed to think that one or the other or perhaps both the chambers here will express decided dissatisfaction with the procedure during the session. If another campaign is to be commenced against us next spring, by the Federal Government, it will have to be undertaken without the shadow of a chance of aid, in troops, from continental Europe. Even the most mercenary of Hessians are now deterred from embarking for New York to enter the field. The odds adverse to their lives overpower their love for the large bounty-money and compensation offered. Nor is it more certain that additional pecuniary assistance will be received from this hemisphere by the Yankees. Confidence has steadily continued to decrease in the so-designated " American securities " since I last had occasion to advert to the subject. The introduction of fresh batches, under such circumstances, seems to me to be entirely precluded.

I have the honor to be, sir, very respectfully, your obedient servant,

A. Dudley Mann.

Hon. J. P. Benjamin,
    Secretary of State C. S. A., Richmond, Va.

No. 14.]   Paris, *November 10, 1864.*

Sir: An opportunity offering by the return of Captain Fearn, who is to meet General Preston at Halifax, I avail myself of it to write a short dispatch.

In my No. 13 of the 29th September, I informed you that neither Mr. Slidell nor I had received the copies of the manifesto of Congress spoken of in your circular of the 25th August, and which we first saw reprinted in the Northern journals from Richmond papers.

Since my dispatch of the 13th September the circulars arrived, and I at once communicated with Mr. Slidell and Colonel Mann as to the proper mode of carrying out the request of Congress, that they should be laid before foreign governments " by the commissioners abroad." Some little delay occurred, as we thought it best to await the arrival of the last mail from Bermuda, which might bring the copies from your Department, and probably with specific instructions. But nothing came. It was considered by us an occasion in which the duty imposed upon the commissioners by the request of Congress should be discharged in a formal and becoming manner, and we met accordingly at Paris a few days since to determine the mode. The broad expression in the resolution of Congress, that the manifesto should be laid before " foreign governments," led us to consider, in the absence of instructions, that it would be proper to communicate it to all the principal powers, viz, England, France, Prussia, Austria, Russia, Belgium, the Swiss Confederation, Denmark, the Kingdom of Italy, Holland, Spain, Portugal, Sweden, and Rome. And the mode, that the manifesto should be neatly engrossed by a skillful writer, in good but plain penmanship, on suitable paper of rather more than dispatch size, and a copy to be sent addressed to the proper minister of state to each of those powers, accompanied by a joint note of the commissioners to the minister, of which I send you a copy herewith. To France and Belgium this note with the manifesto will be presented by Mr. Slidell and Mr. Mann, respectively; to each of the other governments it will be borne by one or other of the secretaries of the commissioners.

The manifesto is certainly a most able and impressive paper, and the request of Congress that it should be laid before foreign governments, as emanating from that body, we thought an occasion sufficiently grave and important to require that it should be done in the manner and with the ceremonial adopted. The papers are now nearly ready, and will be sent off in the course of one or two days, and I hope what is done will have the approval of your Department.

I received to-day from London your No. 38, of the 20th of September, with the Treasury draft for £458 1s. 4d., to cover the expenses of the defense in the case of the captors of the *Gerrity*. I was gratified to find by your previous dispatch that the responsibility I assumed in that matter met the approval of the Government. The decision, being of the court of queen's bench, must of course rule all future like cases, including that of the *Roanoke*, the most recent, at Bermuda.

I am gratified to learn that the seal arrived safely and was followed, I hope, speedily by the boxes containing the materials for its use. They went to Bermuda via Halifax, consigned to Major Walker, agent of the Confederate States at the former place, in the same steamer that conveyed Lieutenant Chapman, there to be placed in his charge when he sailed for the Confederacy.

I was surprised to learn that my private letter to the President, referred to in my No. 12 as accompanying that dispatch, was not found enclosed in it, nor after the lapse of time can I explain it; had it been omitted by accident it should afterwards have appeared upon my table, which was not the case.

In regard to your remarks on my late conversation with Lord Palmerston, after the distinct and repeated refusal of his Government to recognize the independence of the South made the principal reason for terminating the mission to England, I did not of course directly or indirectly intimate to him that we yet asked it. I have not a copy of the memorandum of the conversation with me in Paris, but have a strong recollection that in the course of the conversation admitting it, I made the direct point that recognition at any time by any principal power of Europe, and without other act on their part, would stop the war. You are right, however, in your remark that, despite all evidence and reason to the contrary, England at least "affects to consider that such recognition would be of no value unless followed by active intervention." Nor is this peculiar to the Government; the public men of that country seem unable or unwilling to divest themselves of such belief; the true reason can only be that they use it as an evasion of the duty incumbent on their Government under every principle of public law because of the latent fear that it will involve them in war. You will have seen in the late English papers that the distress in the manufacturing districts is again exhibiting itself to an extent causing much alarm, with the prospect of its even exceeding in intensity this winter the experience of the last two years; this, with the great derangements in commerce and the pressure consequent thereon in the money market, may not be without its effect in our favor when Parliament meets in February.

Colonel Mann, who is here, tells me that he thinks a reaction is strongly setting in in Germany which will have the effect of throwing back upon the United States very large amounts of their public securities that were taken up in that country, under the attraction of the high rate of interest, brought about by the rate of exchange. I have thought of going for a time to Frankfort on the Main, entirely as a private gentleman, to see what may be done in aid of such catastrophe, and perhaps I can be useful also in discouraging emigration from that country under the fraudulent practice there of Northern agencies.

Captain Morris, late commander of the *Florida*, has just reached here, and made his official report to Commodore Barron of the base and cowardly act of the commander of the *Wachusett*, taking advantage of the absence of one-half the crew of the *Florida* on shore leave at night to overpower the remainder and seize the ship. I have sent the report to be published through the Index in the English and other European journals, and you will doubtless have seen it in reprint in the New York papers before this reaches you. It is thought by some that England and France will come to the aid of Brazil in a demand for full reparation to that power, though I doubt whether their intervention will extend beyond a formal protest against the act as a precedent.

I have the honor to be, your obedient servant,

J. M. MASON.

Hon. J. P. BENJAMIN,
Secretary of State.

P. S.—Since the foregoing was written it was determined, on further consideration, to change the mode of communicating the manifesto to the different Governments. Instead of sending them by a special messenger to each court, they will be transmitted through the legations of each at Paris, by the agency of Mr. Slidell.

J. M. M.

———

PARIS, *November 11, 1864.*

SIR: The undersigned commissioners of the Confederate States of America in pursuance of the instructions of their Government have the honor to present to your Excellency a copy of a manifesto issued by the Congress of said States, with the approval of the President, and of which the President was requested to cause copies to be transmitted to their commissioners abroad to the end that the same might be by them laid before foreign governments; they at the same time communicate a copy of the preamble and resolutions of Congress accompanying said manifesto.

The dispositions, principles, and purposes by which the Confederate States have been and are still animated are set forth in this paper with all the authority due to the solemn declaration of the legislative and executive branches of their Government and with a clearness which leaves no room for comment or explanation.

In a few sentences it is pointed out that—

all they ask is immunity from interference with their internal peace and prosperity, and to be left in the undisturbed enjoyment of their inalienable rights to life, liberty, and the pursuit of happiness which their common ancestry declared to be the equal heritage of all parties to the social compact. Let them forbear aggressions upon us and the war is at an end.

If there be questions which require adjustment by negotiation, they have ever been willing and are still willing to enter into communication with their adversaries in a spirit of peace, equity, and manly frankness and commit their cause to the enlightened judgment of the world, to the sober reflections of their adversaries themselves, and to the solemn and righteous arbitrament of heaven.

The undersigned beg leave most respectfully to invite the attention of the Government of his Imperial Majesty to this frank and full exposition of the attitude and purpose of the Confederate States and will merely remark in addition that since the issuing of that manifesto the war has continued to be waged by our enemies with even increased ferocity, a more signal disregard of all the rules of civilized warfare, and more wanton violations of the obligations of international law.

The undersigned having thus complied with the instructions of their Government beg to assure your Excellency of the distinguished consideration with which they have the honor to be,

Your Excellency's most obedient servants,

JOHN SLIDELL.
J. M. MASON.
A. DUDLEY MANN.

His Excellency Mr. DROUYN DE LHUYS,
Minister of Foreign Affairs.

PARIS, *November 15, 1864.*

SIR: In compliance with the suggestion made in the conversation which the undersigned had the honor to hold with your Excellency on the 13th instant, he now begs leave to present a minute of certain instructions in relation to neutral vessels and property directed to be given by the President of the Confederate States of America to the commanders of cruisers under the Confederate flag.

The interest of neutral powers that their ports should be opened at least to the introduction of such prizes as involve the claims of their own subjects is plain, and it is obvious that in no other manner can the Confederate Government do them the full justice it desires. There are very few if any of what are called " white-washed " vessels (vessels sailing under a neutral flag for the purpose of covering enemy's ownership) under the French flag, but portions of cargo belonging to French subjects have more than once been found on board of enemy's vessels, and if a neutral government will not permit such vessels when captured to be taken into its ports with the view of restoring the neutral property to its subjects, there can be no just ground for expecting the Confederate Government to satisfy claims for indemnity arising from the destruction of this property, when such destruction is practically forced upon it by the neutral government.

The expediency of modifying to this extent the rules which prevent the entry into the ports of his Imperial Majesty of prizes made by Confederate ships of war is respectfully submitted to your Excellency's consideration. If certain declarations of a British naval officer of high rank on this subject have not been misunderstood, or incorrectly reported in the " minute of instructions " before referred to, there is reason to suppose that the Government of her Britannic Majesty would not be unwilling to pursue a similar course, and it will readily occur to your Excellency how much the restoration to its legitimate owners of property captured on distant seas would be facilitated by a general understanding to that effect among neutral powers.

The undersigned will not fail to communicate to his Government the observations made by your Excellency on the subject of the alleged compulsory service of French subjects in the armies of the Confederate States.

He begs your Excellency to accept the assurance of the distinguished consideration of his most obedient servant,

JOHN SLIDELL.

His Excellency Mr. DROUYN DE LHUYS,
Minister of Foreign Affairs.

RICHMOND, *November 16, 1864.*

SIR: I desire to submit to you as the head of the Department to which I am directly responsible, and under whose control they should, if possible, have been conducted, the history of certain transactions in which I was engaged whilst in Canada, but which did not fall within the scope of the duties assigned me by the President. I will not here repeat the reasons which have been communicated in previous reports for protracting my stay in the British Provinces. During the interval of leisure which this delay afforded to me, I was practically associated by my friends, Messrs. Clay and Thompson, with themselves in the execution of their more comprehensive and delicate mission. In anticipation of the arrival of these gentlemen at Niagara, but, as I believe, without their previous knowledge or sanction, Mr. George N. Sanders, then residing in that part of Canada, invited a number of citizens of the United States supposed to be hostile to the existing administration to visit the Falls and interchange opinions upon the condition of the country and the great question of peace with the prominent Confederate gentlemen who were expected to spend a portion of the summer at that place. Such conferences being entirely ·legitimate under the construction which Messrs. Clay and Thompson (no doubt very properly) placed upon their powers and duties, I had no hesitation in meeting the public men who came to the Falls and expressed a desire for my society.

That point being the most convenient and eligible for the transaction of my own business, I remained there during the whole period of my stay in Canada, and thus had opportunities of more frequent and extensive intercourse with these gentlemen than either of my friends, one of whom, Mr. Clay, made his headquarters at St. Catherines, the other, Mr. Thompson, at Toronto. Besides a crowd of less distinguished persons, I saw during the course of the summer (in some instances repeatedly), Governor Hunt, of New York; Messrs. Leigh Richmond and Benjamin Wood, of the same State; Messrs. Buckalew, Judge Black, and Mr. Van Dyke, of Pennsylvania; McLean, of the Cincinnati Enquirer; Weller, of California; Judge Bullitt, of Kentucky; and Colonel Walker, of Indiana. We received messages from other gentlemen, such as Voorhees, of Indiana, and Pendleton, of Ohio. Before Mr. Clay and myself had reached Niagara, Mr. Thompson had seen Mr. ·Vallandigham. The impressions which have been made upon my mind by what I learned from these gentlemen, and from many other sources of information, including interviews with leading members of the Order of the Sons of Liberty, as to the temper of the Democratic party, and especially of the people of the Northwest, and the prospect of any action in that section favorable to our cause, I shall state in another part of this report.

Certain editorials which appeared in the New York Tribune early in June, connected with intimations from our friends in New York, induced a hope (which with me has ripened into an abiding conviction) that the able editor of that influential journal entertained opinions upon the subject of peace much more reasonable and moderate than those of the Republican party in general. For this reason, neither Mr. Clay nor myself (Mr. Thompson being in ·Toronto and taking no part in these conferences except with one or two gentlemen who visited him in that city), discouraged Mr. Sanders from sending such an invitation, through a third person, to Mr. Greeley as he had sent to others, to come to the Falls and see us. Mr. Sanders soon reported that this suggestion was most kindly received by Mr. Greeley, but that he expressed a preference for Washington as a place of meeting, and desired to know if we were willing to go there. It did not occur to us, as we have no doubt from what has subsequently transpired was the fact, that Mr. Greeley supposed we held any quasi diplomatic position. We had never written a line or uttered a word to justify such an inference. The anonymous publications attributing to us conversations, in which various terms of peace and reconstruction were suggested, had no shadow of foundation in truth. This impression of Mr. Greeley most probably arose from the ignorance, folly, or knavery of Colorado Jewett, who was the medium of communication between Mr. Sanders and himself. Nothing could be further from the truth than the statement of our ingenious friend, Doctor Mackay, in his letter to the London Times that we laid a trap to catch Mr. Lincoln. Had we suspected any delusion as to our true character, or the informal nature of the proposed conference, it would have been promptly dispelled.

In considering the propriety of accepting the suggestion of Mr. Greeley to visit Washington, we most deeply regretted that it was impossible to submit the question to our own Government for its decision. There seemed to us, however, upon reflection, no doubt as to the line of conduct which would advance the interests of our country. The good to be accomplished by such a visit would, in our judgment, have greatly overbalanced any mischief that could result from it. The publicity of our presence in the United States, with the sanction of its Government, must have imparted a mighty influence to the cause of peace, by the free discussion it would have authorized and invited. The opportunities of general and unrestrained intercourse might have been improved, so as to secure an insight into the temper and policy of the administration, the views of leading public men, the spirit of the people, and the resources of the country. Under this conviction we authorized Mr. Sanders to signify to Mr. Greeley our willingness to proceed to Washington upon the tender of an absolute and unconditional safe conduct from the President of the United States. When Mr. Sanders submitted the note to us, which appears first in the printed correspondence, we found that he had most unexpectedly associated his name with our own in the proposed visit. There were serious objections to this association, but believing Mr. Sanders to be a sincere and zealous friend of the Confederacy, thinking that on this occasion his peculiar talents might render him useful in acquiring the information we desired, and feeling that if the safe conduct was tendered, his wishes on this subject would be entitled to some consideration, we permitted the note to be sent without correction. It is, however, incumbent upon me to add, that with all proper respect for Mr. Sanders, he was at no time taken into my confidence, nor, I believe, into that of Mr. Clay. In a few days we received a letter from Mr. Greeley, advising us of his arrival at the International Hotel on the American side of the Falls, and tendering us a safe conduct to Washington and his own escort, upon the hypothesis that we were duly accredited from Richmond, as the bearers of propositions looking to the establishment of peace, and desired to visit Washington in the fulfillment of our mission. Mr. Clay and myself were so deeply impressed with the grave responsibility which would attach to any action we might take on this communication that we telegraphed to Colonel Thompson to meet us at St. Catherines and unite in our deliberations.

Whilst I can only report the reasonings which led my own mind to its conclusions, yet I may add that the response which was made to Greeley received the approbation of Mr. Thompson, as well as of Mr. Clay and myself. Our most obvious course was to have informed Mr. Greeley that he labored under a strange delusion both as to our character and our wishes, and that we could only meet him as private citizens and for an informal interchange of opinions. This course, however, as I thought, would have given to the party now in power in the United States the means of defending itself against the charge which was used with most effect by its political adversaries. Neither the present nor any other Republican administration can secure the same degree of public support in the prosecution of the war on a policy of confiscation and emancipation as on a policy which looked simply to the restoration of the Union. Mr. Lincoln was reproached with an unwillingness to make peace on any terms short of the subjugation of the States of the Confederacy and the utter overthrow of their peculiar social system and a consequent indisposition to ascertain the sentiments of the Southern people, for fear they might profess a readiness to submit to the authority of the United States on more reasonable conditions. Although no proposition for peace which did not concede our absolute independence would have been entertained by us for a moment, it did not seem to me wise to give our enemies the moral and material benefit to be derived from a position they were not honestly entitled to occupy. Had we returned the answer which has been suggested, the friends of President Lincoln could have appealed to the letter of Mr. Greeley as a proof of his willingness to open negotiations on the most liberal basis.

That letter wholly abandoned the attitude which the Government of the United States had maintained since the secession of South Carolina, and to which, according to the declaration of Mr. Seward in his recent speech at Auburn, it has returned, of "no negotiations with rebels in arms." It expressed a readiness to open negotiations and attempt to settle through diplomacy the questions which had been so long in vain submitted to the arbitrament of war. It did not even announce that the restoration of the Union was an indispensable condition of peace, but proffered a free and untrammeled conference. Had the correspondence closed at that point, it must have added strength to the Administration of Mr. Lincoln and thus increased its capacity to carry on the war. Within our own borders it would have nourished the delusive and dangerous hope of a compromise with our enemy on terms consistent with liberty and self-respect. A renewed pressure would have been brought to bear on the President to send commissioners to Washington with the view of opening negotiations at the hazard of fresh indignities to the Confederacy. In framing our reply to the letter of Mr. Greeley we endeavored to shape it so as to compel such a new development from Mr. Lincoln as would disclose the true policy of his Administration or such an adherence to the position assumed in that letter as would enable our Government to act upon it with safety. This purpose was fully accomplished in calling forth the celebrated document addressed "To whom it may concern." No paper probably ever produced so great a revolution of public sentiment in the same space of time. Although a gross delusion as to the extent of their recent military successes has induced a reaction and secured the reelection of Mr. Lincoln, it is destined to exercise an enduring influence for good. It has permanently weakened and distracted the war party of the North, and there is much reason to hope that before many months intervene it will wholly deprive it of Democratic support. However this may be, it has united and animated our own people more than any political action of our adversaries since the commencement of the war.

It has been suggested that the effects of this correspondence, by rendering probable the defeat of Mr. Lincoln at the polls, was unfavorable in the Northwest by repressing a growing tendency to revolution in that quarter. This was no doubt to some extent its temporary effect, but it has worked no injury to our cause. The revolutionary element has been hitherto too feeble to be employed in our service with any advantage. Before this correspondence took place our sanguine friends in that region had fixed upon various periods of revolutionary outbreak, but they were deferred at their own instance from time to time as the conviction gradually dawned upon their own minds of the extent to which they had exaggerated their strength. From all the developments which have since been made, I am satisfied that no explosion could have taken place previous to the election which would not have resulted in permanent injury to our cause. The Northwest is not now, and without the systematic and possibly long-continued application of the agencies which control the popular mind may never be, ripe for revolution. But it is fermenting with the passions out of which revolutions have been created. In Illinois, Indiana, and possibly Ohio, a majority of the population are hostile to the present administration.

The recent election furnished no evidence to the contrary, for with a large body of the peace party McClellan was held in as much odium as Lincoln himself. The bitterness between these hostile factions is intense. The one has received from the other every outrage which the strong can perpetrate on the weak. It would be a fatal mistake, in my opinion, to abandon all effort to separate this section from the United States because no results have as yet been achieved commensurate with our expectations. The hope of closing the war by negotiation has been extinguished. Our resources are diminishing more rapidly, for obvious reasons, than those of our enemies. To keep alive such a degree of apprehension as will lead to the concentration of large bodies of troops to repress insurrection within their own limits will of itself be an important diversion in our favor. We should employ money and talent without stint to give this brooding resentment the proportions of anarchy and civil strife. Let us preserve our communication with our friends in the North. Warned by our past experience, let us introduce arms more gradually and cautiously. As far as practicable subsidize leading presses, and through the ordinary channel of newspapers, as well as of campaign documents, enlighten and inflame the public mind. Enlist public men of character and influence whose principles and sympathies are with us, by indemnifying them against the hazards to which bold and decisive action may expose them. With arms, leaders, and an opportunity, we could strike a deadly blow.

It is proper to add that I have expressed only my individual opinions, and do not know to what extent they would meet the concurrence of Messrs. Clay and Thompson.

I have the honor to remain, very respectfully,

JAMES P. HOLCOMBE.

Hon. J. P. BENJAMIN,
 Secretary of State, C. S. A.

RICHMOND, *November 16, 1864.*

SIR: I append to the report which I now have the honor of submitting an account of my disbursements of public money whilst in the British Provinces. The loss (amongst other valuable papers) when I was wrecked off the coast of Wilmington of a blank book containing entries of all the money which I expended in person and various vouchers therefor, induces a single entry, the items of which I can not specify, although I feel certain as to the general aggregate. Fortunately most of my disbursements were made through the agency of third persons, so that the amount of the entry referred to is not large. The expenditures for the supply, support, and transportation of escaped prisoners have been distinguished from those which were incurred in connection with the affair of the *Chesapeake.* It will be seen that a considerable sum of money, to be appropriated to the former purpose, still remains in the hands of our agents, Messrs. C. C. Clay, jr., and Hon. B. Weir & Co., Halifax. These gentlemen will pursue such directions for the future management of this business, and for communication with your Department, as you may think proper to give. Between fifty-five and sixty soldiers have been sent home, a few having been forwarded not embraced in the list of Messrs. Weir & Co. on my arrival at Halifax, and a few after the rendition of his account, but prior to my departure. The pressing wants of quite a number of others were relieved, but instead of being sent into the Confederacy they were turned over to Messrs. Thompson and Clay, to be employed by them.

From the location of the military prisons in the North, and the zeal and activity of our friends in that quarter, there must, as long as the war lasts, be a large escape of prisoners into the British Provinces. Besides valuable officers, this number will embrace some of the most intelligent, daring, and patriotic soldiers in the army. A standing appeal will be made to the Government, to which it can not prove insensible, to relieve the destitution of these brave but unfortunate men, and to furnish them with the means of returning to their duty and their country. The work of disbursement and superintendence connected with forwarding our escaped prisoners, and supplying their indispensable wants, is at present, with a single exception, performed gratuitously. This gratuitous service is rendered by Mr. Gilbert McMicken at Windsor, Mr. Cassius Lee at Niagara, Mr. S. S. Preston at Toronto, Mr. S. Cranmill and, till recently, Mr. H. C. Slaughter at Montreal, and the Hon. C. C. Clay, jr., as long as he remains in Canada. The exceptional case to which I have referred is that of B. Weir & Co., of Halifax. These gentlemen having the custody of funds for subordinate agencies, and Halifax being the point of transshipment, directly or by way of Bermuda, into the Confederacy, and one at which provision must be made for the support during a longer or shorter period whilst waiting on the departure of steamers, an amount of correspondence, personal attention, and pecuniary responsibility is imposed upon them which renders their charge for compensation entirely reasonable. At this point, but of necessity at this only, there must always be a paid agent of the Government. The frequency with which our steamers visit Halifax for repairs, and the growing importance of that city as a port of supply and shipment into the Confederacy, render it desirable that such agent should be clothed with additional functions. Indeed, I venture to suggest that the increase of expense would be amply justified by the resulting advantages if we had a representative residing in Halifax charged with the control of this business, as well as of our commercial interests, and also authorized to represent the Confederacy in all matters appertaining to it as a belligerent, in the British Provinces. Causes are in operation which must lead to the constant occurrence of cases, like that of the *Chesapeake*, or the raid into Vermont, involving questions of public law in whose decision we are deeply interested, and where the presence and assistance of a public representative would be of the greatest value.

I have the honor to remain, very respectfully,

JAMES P. HOLCOMBE.

Hon. J. P. BENJAMIN,
  Secretary of State, C. S. A.

No. 115.] BRUSSELS, *November 17, 1864.*

SIR: Just as I was about to return from Paris, I read in the London Times your circular of October 10, addressed to myself. I have already made arrangements to have it extensively published here.

This afternoon my secretary will proceed with Mr. Mason to Frankfort, where he will translate this circular into the German language. It is thus quite sure of a general circulation in Belgium, Germany, and Holland, and I confidently expect good results from such circulation.

Mr. Mason, accompanied by my secretary, contemplates a visit to Amsterdam, where doubtless valuable services may be rendered to our cause by a just disparagement, discreetly made, of the state of the Federal finances. As the Dutch language is but little better than no language at all, and as the French is in general use in Holland, I do not think it necessary to have the document translated into Dutch.

In three days more we shall know who is the President-elect of the remnant of the old Union. Lincoln has doubtless chosen himself, through the influence of a brutal soldiery. If this shall have been the case, I will not regret the occurrence, since he will have sown dragon's teeth broadcast as concerns the security of his monstrous rule.

Our friends everywhere on this side of the Atlantic are delighted at the success of our arms in Virginia, Georgia, Tennessee, and Missouri.

The dastardly act of the *Wachusett* in the port of Bahia has provoked the unqualified execrations of every right-thinking man in Europe. If I mistake not, ample reparation and atonement will be required for this enormous outrage upon clearly defined international usage. Every power and state on earth is interested, by paramount considerations, in causing this to be done.

I have the honor to be, sir, very respectfully, your obedient servant,

A. DUDLEY MANN.

Hon. J. P. BENJAMIN,
Secretary of State, C. S. A., Richmond, Va.

No. 74.] PARIS, *November 17, 1864.*

SIR: I have the honor to acknowledge the receipt, on the 11th instant, of your No. 42, dated 15th September, but the "separate dispatch replying to various subjects involved in my communications" then recently received, has not yet reached me.

I at once applied for an interview with Mr. Drouyn de Lhuys, which was promptly granted, and he received me in the 13th instant with even more than his usual urbanity. He began the conversation by inquiring how we were getting on in the Confederacy, and when I replied that all the information from our armies was highly satisfactory he expressed much gratification. I told him that I had applied for an audience for the double object of presenting, under the instructions of my Government, a copy of a manifesto of the Confederate Congress setting forth the attitude and purposes of our people in their contest with the North, and of making certain suggestions in relation to the admission of our prizes into French ports in cases when French property should be found in the enemy's vessels.

I then handed him the joint note, which, as I advised you on the 20th ultimo, Messrs. Mason, Mann, and I intended to address to the European Governments. He read the note, as also the preamble and resolution of Congress. I remarked that he need not then read the manifesto, as its substance was embodied in the note. He said that he would read it carefully in the course of the day, and at my request promised that he would not fail to lay the papers before the Emperor at the next meeting of the cabinet, which would take place on Wednesday at Compiègne. I then stated the desire of the President, in the interest of French subjects and to avoid as far as possible all causes of complaint against our cruisers, to bring into French or other neutral ports any prizes having on board the property of French subjects for the purpose of restoring them to their rightful owners. He said that the proposition was one that he thought should be met in the spirit in which it was offered, but asked had not my Government sanctioned the declaration of the convention of Paris, that neutral property on board of enemy's ships, excepting contraband of war, should not be considered prize of war. I replied that it was true that we had adopted the declaration of principles of the convention of Paris with the exception of the first article relating to privateering, but that such adoption had been made in entire confidence that the fourth, declaring that blockade to be obligatory should be effective, would be enforced, and that the consideration having failed in con-

sequence of neutral powers having submitted to the inefficient blockade of our coasts, we were free at any time to retract our adhesion
to the second and third articles.

That I had repeatedly and ineffectually called the attention of his
Government to the subject, and that he on one occasion had admitted
to me that a grave error had been committed in silently acquiescing
in the unjustifiable course of the Federal Government; he replied,
" That is true, and had I been minister at the time I should have
advocated a different course of action." I then said that I was in
possession of the instructions of my Government to the commanders
of our cruisers on the subject of neutral property, and that if he
desired I would willingly furnish him with a copy; he replied that
he would be pleased to see and examine them. I then alluded to the
declaration of Admiral Hope to Commander Wood, which gave
reason to suppose that England might not be willing to cooperate
with France in modifying the inhibition of the entry of prizes
into their respective ports, and suggested that he might perhaps not
object to confer with Lord Cowley on the subject, as we could not, in
consequence of the past course of her Majesty's Government toward
us, enter into any direct communication with it. He did not make
any absolute promise, but intimated that he was willing to comply
with my suggestion. I shall wait a reasonable time to know if the
minister has called the attention of Lord Cowley to this matter, and
should he fail to do so, I will endeavor to bring it in some way to
the notice of the British Legation, but in the meanwhile I have asked
Mr. Hotze to endeavor, of course in his private capacity, to obtain
all the information possible.

When Mr. Drouyn de Lhuys had read the joint note accompanying
manifesto I availed myself of the allusion to the gross violation of
international law by the Lincoln Government to enquire if it were
the purpose of his Government to take any notice of the outrage upon
neutral rights perpetrated in the capture of the *Florida* in a Brazilian harbor, and reminded him of the prompt action of the Emperor
in the case of the *Trent*, a case which had excited the indignation of
the whole civilized world, although in every way surpassed by the
grosser atrocities and the base treachery of the commander of the
Wachusett. He said that he had not yet had occasion to consider
the matter officially; the only knowledge he had of it being derived
from newspaper statements; that if true, as he presumed they were,
there could be no difference of opinion as to the enormity of the
outrage, which could not fail to command the attention of all neutral
powers. I was prepared for this answer, as I had previously seen
Mr. Carvalho de Moreira, ex-Brazilian minister at London, who has
taken up his residence at Paris since the suspension of diplomatic
relations between his Government and the Court of St. James.
To my great surprise, he informed me that the diplomatic agents of
Brazil in Europe had taken no steps to secure the friendly support
of neutral powers in obtaining reparation for the wanton attack
upon its sovereignty; he assigned two reasons for this inaction—one,
the absence of any instructions from Rio de Janeiro and, indeed, of
any official information even from the authorities at Bahia, the
other the serious illness of the minister at Paris, who, by the way,
would not, I think, at any time be likely to show much energy in

anything that required him to take the initiative on his own responsibility. Mr. de Moreira does not doubt that his Government will act with becoming firmness and dignity, and that the packet from Rio now nearly due at Lisbon will bring instructions to its representatives in Europe to make the most earnest appeals to the Governments where they are accredited to give at least their moral support to Brazil in her demands for complete and summary satisfaction. I await with much curiosity intelligence of the manner in which the news of the capture of the *Florida* will be received by Messrs. Seward and Lincoln; at all events, this affair can not fail ultimately to turn to our advantage whatever course these gentlemen may pursue. My own opinion is that they will make reluctant and insufficient apologies and tardy restoration of their ill-gotten prize, a justification of the capture would, I think, tend greatly to bring about our recognition and perhaps to substantial intervention in our behalf.

On my taking leave the minister renewed his promise to place the joint note and manifesto in the hands of the Emperor at the earliest opportunity, and requested me to address my communication on the subject of the admission of prizes "à lui seul," as it would thus reach him without the delays in the bureaus accompanying the usual form of transmission.

Past experience, however, induces me to receive with many grains of allowance all assurances coming from that quarter.

I annex copy of the joint note of 11th instant, which has also been sent "mutatis mutandis" to England, Spain, Italy, Papal States, Portugal, Swiss Confederation, Prussia, Austria, Russia, Sweden, and Denmark, Belgium, and Holland; those to Belgium and the Papal States will be delivered by Messrs. Mann and Bishop Lynch, respectively, the others sent through the legations of the several powers at Paris.

I also annex copy of my note to Mr. Drouyn de Lhuys accompanying extracts from instructions to our cruisers. The extract contains all the instructions from the words "The cases which occur for decision by our cruisers" to the close.

I have the honor to remain, your most obedient servant,

JOHN SLIDELL.

Hon. J. P. BENJAMIN,
Secretary of State.

P. S.—I find that in giving the account of my interview with Mr. Drouyn de Lhuys I have omitted to mention that he said that frequent and grave complaints had been made of the forced service of French subjects in our armies, that it would produce a bad feeling and hoped that it would be discontinued. I replied that I had reason to believe that when the facts could be ascertained it would be found that all demands of natives of France claiming to be exempted from military service were examined with impartiality and when well founded had been promptly accorded.

That there might have occurred individual cases of hardship or injustice, but it could not be expected that in a war such as the North was waging against us the course of justice should not occasionally be interrupted. That French subjects who chose to remain in the Confederacy for the purpose of bettering their fortunes had no right to claim that while every citizen from the age of 16 to 60 capable of bearing arms was enrolled for service in the field they should not be called to take part in the defense of their own property. The option had been presented to them of leaving the Confederacy; and if they did not choose to avail themselves of it, they could not be permitted to remain passive spectators of a struggle in which the property, and even the lives, of all within our limits were at stake. He said that there was great difficulty in leaving the Confederacy. I replied that it would readily be obviated by sending national vessels to our ports under flags of truce for the purpose of embarking such French subjects as might be disposed to leave the country; that if the Lincoln government refused to permit the entry of such vessels the responsibility would be with it and not with us. He said that he did not think it worth while for us to insist upon the services of a few Frenchmen at the risk of alienating the feelings of a friendly nation and asked me to call the attention of my Government to the subject, which I promised to do.

---

48 AVENUE GABRIEL,
Paris, November 18, 1864.

SIR: I enclose duplicate of my dispatch of the 4th. The committee have not yet made their appearance, and Colonel Sulakowski, having taken offense at the very first reception of him, is not disposed to communicate with me. I must therefore await the arrival of the committee.

As you have thought proper to intrust me with this important business, I regret that you did not instruct me to act on my own judgment. If I was not embarrassed by the committee I think I could manage successfully.

With much respect, your obedient servant,
C. J. McRAE,
Agent Treasury Department, C. S.

Hon. J. P. BENJAMIN,
Secretary of State.

No. 75.]   PARIS, *November 28, 1864.*

SIR: As I am still without the dispatch referred to in your No. 42, I fear that it has miscarried and beg leave to suggest the transmission of a duplicate. I have to thank you for the copies of the State map of Virginia; one of them I have presented to our excellent friend, the Duke de Persigny. I have been prevented from placing a second in the hands of the Emperor by the serious illness of Mr. Mocquard, who, I trust, will soon be able to resume his functions.

In conformity with the intention of which I had the honor to advise you in my last dispatch of 15th instant, the joint notes to the different European powers have all been forwarded through their several legations at this court, with the exception of that to Russia; as I had reason to suppose that some objection might be made in that case, I have sent the documents by mail to St. Petersburg, directed to the minister of foreign affairs.

The note for Rome was sent by Mr. James T. Soutter, of Virginia, to Bishop Lynch, with a request that should the latter be absent, he,

Mr. S., should hand it in person to Cardinal Antonelli; the accompanying copy of a letter from Mr. S. will inform you of the very gratifying manner in which it was received by his Eminence.

The President's message has just reached us; its frank and manly tone commands universal admiration; copious extracts from it have been published in nearly all the Paris journals and are producing a very marked and salutory effect on public opinion. It appears at a very favorable moment, as the Italian question has ceased to occupy the press, which it had almost monopolized for the last two or three months; for this reason and the absence of any apparent cause to apprehend European difficulties, our affairs have to a certain extent taken its place and I believe that an impulse in that direction has been given to the semiofficial journals from high quarters.

In consequence of the absence of Lord Cowley, Mr. Drouyn de Lhuys has had no opportunity to speak to him on the subject of your No. 42, but as he has returned and they are both guests of the Emperor at Compiègne during this week, I trust that the subject will be broached there, at least such is the opinion of my friend at the affaires étrangères.

Mr. Hotze will have informed you that, after diligent enquiry, he can not find that any instructions relating to our cruisers or their prizes have recently issued from the admiralty. When the minister of foreign affairs returns to Paris I will, I doubt not, be able to ascertain whether anything has been said or done by him in the matter.

Since my No. 71, of 13 September, but £9,500 of the 7 per cent cotton loan have been converted. The last certificate issued bears date 19 October, and as a considerable amount of these certificates is said to be on the market it is presumed that no further conversions will be made for some time to come. This check of the process of absorption of the bonds which was going on so healthily can only be attributed to the cessation of the facilities heretofore afforded for the delivery of cotton to the holders of certificates. I take it for granted that this cessation has been caused by stringent military exigencies and hope that it may not be of long duration.

In the meanwhile it has seriously affected the price of the bonds, which, in view of our late military successes, would otherwise have shown a considerable advance.

The agent of the Albion Trading Company especially complains that the ships of the company dispatched under the contract made with Mr. McRae and me have been compelled to lade one-half of their cargoes on Government account; as this contract when made was considered highly advantageous to our interests, it would seriously affect the credit of the Confederacy if any change in our policy in regard to the shipments of cotton should interfere with its execution.

I have the honor to be with great respect, your most obedient servant

JOHN SLIDELL.

Hon. J. P. BENJAMIN,
Secretary of State.

P. S.—I have this moment an answer from Earl Russell to the joint note and annex a copy. The answer came through the Hon. [Wm. George] Grey, secretary of the English embassy and acting chargé d'affaires in the absence of Lord Cowley, who had received Mr. Eustis very courteously when he handed him the joint note to be forwarded on the 20th.

[Copy]

FOREIGN OFFICE, *November 25, 1864.*

GENTLEMEN: I have had the honor to receive the copy which you have sent me of the manifesto issued by the Congress of the so-called. Confederate States of America.

Her Majesty's Government deeply lament the protracted nature of the struggle between the Northern and Southern States of the formerly United Republic of North America.

Great Britain has since 1783 remained, with the exception of a short period, connected by friendly relations with both the Northern and the Southern States. Since the commencement of the civil war which broke out in 1861, her Majesty's Government have continued to entertain sentiments of friendship equally for the North and for the South. Of the causes of the rupture her Majesty's Government have never presumed to judge; they deplore the commencement of this sanguinary struggle and anxiously look forward to the period of its termination. In the meantime they are convinced that they best consult the interests of peace and respect the rights of all parties by observing a strict and impartial neutrality. Such a neutrality her Majesty has faithfully maintained and will continue to maintain.

I request you, gentlemen, to accept the assurance of the very high consideration with which I have the honor to be, gentlemen,

Your most obedient, humble servant,

RUSSELL.

JOHN SLIDELL, Esq., J. M. MASON, Esq., and A. DUDLEY MANN, Esq.

[Enclosure.]

ALBERGO D'INGHILTERRA,
Rome, November 21, 1864.

MY DEAR SIR: Immediately on my arrival here I sought the residence of the Right Rev. Bishop Lynch and learned that he had left Rome, to be absent several weeks, in consequence of which the duty devolved upon me of delivering your dispatch to the Roman Government. I lost no time in addressing a note to Cardinal Antonelli (a copy of which I hand you), and he promptly returned an answer to my messenger saying it would give him pleasure to receive me the next day (Saturday) at 2 o'clock.

Accordingly I waited on the cardinal at the appointed hour and he gave me a most cordial greeting, shaking my hand warmly, and, leading me to a seat near his desk, he at once entered upon the discussion of the affairs of the Confederate States. He made no secret of his sympathy with our cause and had not the slightest hesitation in saying he desired our success. He displayed entire familiarity with the state of things both at the North and South, and especially with the necessity of receiving Northern accounts with due modification. He adverted to the case of the *Florida* and pronounced it an inexcusable outrage, and added that he had received a letter from Brazil which stated prompt redress would be demanded; and, further, that it was an offense which no European Government could quietly submit to without protest.

I can not detail everything that dropped from his Eminence during my interview, which lasted over half an hour, but I was more than gratified with the great interest he manifested in the cause dear to our hearts.

At the first opening in the conversation I formally presented the joint letter of the Commissioners (with the enclosed documents), which he read in my presence and then remarked that it should have his more deliberate examination and would then be laid before the Holy Father. I rose to leave when he said he would be glad to present me to the Holy Father and would send me word when the interview could be had. Of course I was only too happy to have so favorable an opportunity of doing my utmost to follow up the manifesto of our Government by whatever eloquence I can command, and as I am to have the services of Monsignor Talbot as my interpreter, I hope to do some little good. Monsignor Talbot is an English ecclesiastic and attached to the household of the Holy Father.

After thanking his Eminence cordially for his kind reception I took my leave, he again shaking me by the hand and leading me across several apartments to the last door.

I am thus minute that I may show you exactly how our cause stands with this court and how I have been able to carry out your wishes in the absence of our regular representative.

Very truly,

J. T. SOUTTER.

Hon. JNO. SLIDELL.

[Enclosure.]

ALBERGO D'INGHILTERRA,
Rome, November 18, 1864.

EMINENCE: In the absence of the Right Rev. Bishop Lynch from Rome it is made my agreeable duty to ask of your Eminence an interview that I may present an official dispatch from the accredited representatives in Europe of the Confederate States of America, together with certain public documents referred to therein.

May I most respectfully ask of your Eminence such an audience and to add, in case that favor is granted to me, that your Eminence will name the day and hour when I may wait upon your Eminence.

I have the honor to be, most respectfully, your Eminence's obedient and humble servant,

J. T. SOUTTER.

His Eminence Monseigneur Cardinal ANTONELLI,
Secretary of State and Minister of Foreign Affairs
of the Roman States.

No. 76.] PARIS, *December 13, 1864.*

SIR: Since I last had the honor of addressing you your missing dispatch No. 43 of 20th September has come safely to hand. You will have seen by my recent dispatches that my views of the course of the French Government are almost·identical with your own, and that I have been so fortunate as to have adopted in advance the line of conduct which you have pointed out to me. There is a point however in regard to which it is proper that I should remove false impressions, viz, that of this Government " having refused permission to finish the vessels for delivery to us after the restoration of peace and actually forced the builders to sell them to third parties."

I do not think that there would have been any difficulty about finishing the vessels for delivery to us after the restoration of peace. I am sure that the builders were never forced to sell them to third parties, and that no pressure for that object was ever exercised toward them by the Government. The builder of the Bordeaux ships did, as I was informed, make assertions to that effect, but I am fully convinced that they were pure fictions gotten up to subserve his own views, he being deeply interested in finding purchasers to whom the ships could be delivered and their entire price paid, while under his contracts with Captain Bulloch full payment was only to be made when the actual delivery of the ships should have been made to him and such delivery would not have been permitted. I am happy to say that the conduct of Mr. Voruz, the builder of the corvettes at Nantes, is in strong contrast with that of Mr. Arman.

In my last dispatch I referred to the complaints of Mr. J. S. Begbie, agent of the Albion Trading Company, of the refusal to deliver cotton in exchange for certificates in compliance with the stipulations of the contract made with Mr. McRae and myself. I have since received from Messrs. Schroeder & Co., agents in London of the 7 per cent cotton loan, a letter on that subject, of which I send you a copy. I suggest the propriety of transmitting it either to the Secretary of the Treasury or to the Secretary of War, as I am in doubt to which of these departments the subject more appropriately belongs.

Lord Cowley for some reason or other did not avail himself of his invitation to Compiègne, of which I spoke in my last dispatch, and only returned from London a few days since, but during his absence Mr. Drouyn de Lhuys did not neglect to call, as he promised, the attention of the British Government to the subject of your No. 43, as will appear by the following extract from a note from my friend at the foreign affairs:

M. Drouyn de Lhuys has written to our embassy in London on the subject of the proposition of your Government, relative to the neutral merchandise on board of enemies' ships, and to know the opinion of the English cabinet on this subject. He has also spoken to the ministers of marine and commerce in expressing the opinion that the proposition will be very acceptable. He waits a reply, which I will not neglect to ask him to communicate to me.

I expect soon to hear the result of this overture to the British Government.

I have received the answer of the holy see to the joint note of 11th November. I annex copy of Cardinal Antonelli's letter, with a translation. As I find it less decided in its tone than the letter of 3d December last of his Holiness to the President, I do not think it expedient to publish it and have so said to Messrs. Mason and Mann. Should they, however, entertain a different opinion, I will cheerfully yield to it. I send you an interesting account from Mr. [James T.] Soutter of his presentation to the Pope.

Our joint note was not of a nature to call for a reply from the Governments to which it was addressed, nor did I expect any, less indeed from Great Britain than from any other power. The letter of Earl Russell, on which I had not time to comment in my No. 75, has for me a greater significance on that account, as his lordship voluntarily went out of his way to say the most disagreeable things possible to the Northern Government. His reference to the treaty of 1783 will, I think, be especially distasteful to them, placed in connection with his twice-repeated recognition of the separate existence of the North and South as never merged in a single nationality. I shall be very much surprised if this letter does not call forth a universal howl against his lordship from the Northern press.

I learn from M. Carvalho de Moreira that the Brazilian diplomatic agents in Europe have received no instructions to invoke the good offices of the neutral powers in the case of the *Florida*, but he informs me that he has seen the instructions given to the minister at Washington. He is to demand an ample apology, the delivery of the *Florida* in good order, with her officers, crew, and armament at Bahia, and the exemplary punishment of the commander of the *Wachusett*. The return of the *Florida* being rendered impossible by the scurvy trick of sinking her in port as if by accident, I presume that the Brazilian Government will demand that she be replaced by another vessel of a similar character and armament. M. C. de Moreira says that the Emperor of Brazil is incensed to the highest degree by the outrage, and, being a man of great firmness, will not be satisfied with anything short of the most ample reparation.

I have the honor to be, with great respect, your most obedient servant,

JOHN SLIDELL.

Hon. J. P. BENJAMIN,
Secretary of State.

[Translation of Cardinal Antonelli's dispatch.]

ROME, *December 2, 1864.*

HONORABLE GENTLEMEN: Your colleague, Mr. Soutter, has handed me your letter of 11th November, with which, in conformity with the instructions of your Government, you have sent me a copy of the manifesto issued by the Congress of the Confederate States and approved by the most honorable President, in order that the attention of the government of the Holy See, to whom, as well as to the other Governments, you have addressed yourselves, might be called to it. The sentiments expressed in the manifesto tending, as they do, to the cessation of the most bloody war which still rages in your countries and the putting an end to the disasters which accompany it by proceeding to negotiations for peace, being entirely in accordance with the disposition and character of the august head of the Catholic Church, I did not hesitate a moment in bringing it to the notice of the Holy Father.

His Holiness, who has been deeply afflicted by the accounts of the frightful carnage of this obstinate struggle, has heard with satisfaction the expression of the same sentiments; being the vicar on earth of that God who is the author of peace, he yearns to see these wraths appeased and peace restored. In proof of this he wrote to the archbishops of New York and New Orleans as far back as 18th October,

1862, inviting them to exert themselves in bringing about this holy object. You may then, honorable gentlemen, feel well assured that whenever a favorable occasion shall present itself, his Holiness will not fail to avail himself of it to hasten so desirable a result and that all nations may be united in the bonds of charity.

In acquainting you with this benignant disposition of the Holy Father, I am pleased to declare myself with sentiments of the most distinguished esteem.

Truly, your servant,

G. Car. Antonelli.
[Della S. S. L'I'mo.]

Messrs. A. Dudley Mann, J. M. Mason, John Slidell,
Commissioners of the Confederate States of America,
Paris.

No. 15.]   London, December 16, 1864.

Sir: My last dispatch was my No. 14, of the 10th of November, from Paris. Since then I wrote you an unofficial note from Paris, with a report of information I had obtained in regard to the sale of Federal securities in Germany during a journey, then lately made, to Brussels and as far as Frankfort-on-the-Main, a duplicate of which note I sent you by Captain Fearn, who sailed hence for Bermuda some ten days since.

I have now the honor to send you herewith a duplicate of my No. 14, and also a copy of a letter * from Earl Russell, acknowledging the joint note of Messrs. Slidell, Mann, and myself, communicating to him a copy of the manifesto of Congress. You will have seen it long since doubtless, together with the note to which it was in reply through the Northern press. I have thought it proper nevertheless to send a formal copy for the records of the Department. It has been generally thought here that there is in it some relaxation in tone if contrasted with his usual style when writing or speaking of the Confederate States, which may mean something or nothing; where he speaks of " the struggle between the Northern and Southern States of the formerly United Republic of North America." I do not myself attach much importance to it. It is the only reply received from the minister of any court to which the manifesto was communicated.

A few days since I received from Canada a letter from Mr. James D. Westcott, former Senator of the United States from Florida, and with it a printed copy of the proceedings and evidence so far as they had gone in the case of Lieutenant Young and others, claimed for extradition by the Government of the United States on a charge of felony, committed by them in their late attack on St. Albans, Vt. Mr. Westcott's letter was dated from Montreal, where he said he had gone to attend the trial as the friend of Mr. Wallace, one of the parties charged. His letter was dated the 14th November, and it appeared that time had been allowed the prisoners to the 13th December to obtain evidence on their behalf from Richmond. It also appeared that Lieutenant Young exhibited in evidence his commis-

---

* See enclosure, Slidell to Benjamin, November 28, 1864.

sion as lieutenant of the Army of the Confederate States, with
authority to enlist a given number of men beyond the limits of the
Confederacy for special service, and he, with his companions, being
allowed to make declarations in court, stated that their plans were
concerted at Chicago, and that what they had done was in execution
of their military orders. It was thus clearly shown that their acts
were acts of war, and in no possible sense could be treated as an
offense within the treaty. Mr. Westcott informed me that Mr.
J. J. C. Abbott, formerly solicitor general of Canada, was their
principal counsel. I can hardly conceive that the decision in Canada
will be adverse to the prisoners, yet considering that nothing should
be left undone which might possibly enure to their safety, I thought
it prudent here to lay the papers before Sir Hugh Cairns, at present
probably the most distinguished jurist at the bar; my object was
in advance if possible of the decision in Canada to put Mr. Abbott
professionally in communication with Sir Hugh, with a view to have
the defense so conducted as to provide for an appeal to the courts
in England if the result in Canada should make it necessary, and I
wrote by the earliest mail and told Mr. Abbott of the retainer of
Sir Hugh, with a request that he would communicate with him in the
view I have mentioned.

I have received an address from the "Southern Independence Association" at Manchester to the President of the Confederate States,
signed by its "executive committee," with a request that I would
transmit it to the President. It congratulates him on the successes
of our arms, expresses entire confidence that our independence is
achieved, and fully approves the proposed plan of arming the slaves,
should the same be found necessary to recruit the armies. It shall
be sent by the first convenient opportunity, and I have so informed
the committee. This association is the largest, as it is the most active
and energetic, of any that have been formed for agitation in our behalf. The accompanying sheet, containing the names of its officers,
etc., will show the general character of its material.

The address is handsomely engrossed on parchment, in the illuminated style.

I enclose herewith in a separate envelope two notes from John
Laird, esq., M. P., of Birkenhead (Liverpool), together with the
copy of the letter of Joseph Cearns, to which his notes refer. I
presume the application to investigate and act upon it is proper for
the War Department. In such case, will you oblige Mr. Laird by
giving the papers the proper reference, accompanied by an extract
from so much of this dispatch as relates to it? Mr. Laird is the
eminent shipbuilder, and, as you are aware, one of our most earnest
friends.

I have the honor to be, your obedient servant,

J. M. MASON.

Hon. J. P. BENJAMIN,
    Secretary of State.

No. 119.]   BRUSSELS, *December 16, 1864.*

SIR: It is my duty to suggest for the consideration of the President,
in view of the manifold important interests involved, whether it is
not advisable to embrace the Germanic Confederation and Holland

in my present mission. Between this metropolis and Frankfort the travel is performed in twelve hours, and in twelve hours between Frankfort and Amsterdam, the three cities forming something like a triangle. The communication with one and another is so expeditious as to render it easy to divide my time in intercourse with each. I conceive that the most important object to be accomplished by our Government in Europe is to harm, as far as possible, the credit of the Federal States, thus depriving them alike of troops and of the "sinews of war."

The Germanic Diet represents a population of well-nigh 45,000,000. The presidency thereof is accorded to Austria. Many of the nations of Europe have ministers near that body, in which number are included Great Britain and France. Those diplomats are accredited to its President, his Excellency, Baron de Kubeck. The Diet has the power of recognizing new Governments, but it has no power to contract commercial or other treaties. About three weeks ago it formally recognized Maximilian as Emperor of Mexico. If it chooses, it can formally introduce us into the circle of nations. I need not be furnished with full powers, but merely appointed special envoy to the president of the Diet, as I was to Rome. In like manner I could be designated to the minister of foreign affairs of Holland. It might occur that I could succeed in entering into relations with one or the other or both.

His Excellency E. J. J. B. Cremers is the present minister of foreign affairs of the Kingdom of the Netherlands.

You will do me the justice to believe that I have no selfish ambition to gratify in submitting this proposal to the President. I am animated solely by the desire to render myself as useful as possible to my country.

I have the honor to be, sir, very respectfully, your obedient servant,

A. DUDLEY MANN.

Hon. J. P. BENJAMIN,
   Secretary of State, C. S. A., Richmond, Va.

No. 24.]
                         DEPARTMENT OF STATE,
                         Richmond, December 19, 1864.

SIR: Since my No. 23 of 15th September I have received from you only the "duplicate" of your No. 48 of 6th August, which reached me on the 10th October, and your private letter of 28th October from Bath. Your No. 46 is still missing. My foreign correspondence was thrown sadly out of gear by the loss of the mails per *Condor* and *Hope*, and it will be some time before all is straight again.

The extension of the field of duty confided to you, and which now practically embraces the continent of Europe as well as Great Britain, must necessarily increase the demand for means, and your estimate of £6,000 per annum to meet the exigencies of all branches of your service is deemed by no means unreasonable. The enclosed bill for £2,000, being Treasury draft No. 3185 on our Liverpool bankers, was called for before I received your private letter, or it would have been made large enough for a half year's expenditure. You will receive a further remittance in six or eight weeks.

I note your statement of an expenditure of £300 for Mr. McHenry's books, and £150 to aid the parties who signed the peace petition. I agree with you that this latter sum should not have been given, if it could have been withheld without serious injury to our interests, but as it was accorded only after conference with Mr. McRae, and in consequence of what you both considered a political necessity, I doubt not that your reasons, when you shall be able prudently to disclose them, will prove satisfactory to the Department.

My latest Index is to 27th October, and I am in daily expectation of more recent news from Europe. In the meantime the people at the North, not satisfied with the tame acquiesence of the British Government in every conceivable demand made on them, seem to be industriously engaged in ascertaining whether there is any amount of contumely and insult that can provoke Great Britain into the assertion of a right to be treated with common decency. Mr. Webb and Mr. Seward each in turn has failed, and their congress will continue the same line of action. They deem themselves secure against results, and consider that the abject terror displayed by the British rulers is a sufficient guarantee that the North may proceed to any lengths in encroachment and aggression. Great Britain, by her course, has converted an imaginary into a real danger, and it is certain that she will be forced into a war with the United States at no distant day; a war of which there was no danger until the mistaken timidity and subservient concessions of the British cabinet, so inflated the arrogance and conceit of the Northern mob and Northern politicians, that they now speak of Great Britian with unreserved contempt as a foe scarcely " worthy of their steel."

We shall yet see a signal retribution wrought on the British Goverment for its injustice toward us, by the very people whose favor they sought to conciliate by that injustice.

I am, very respectfully, your obedient servant,

J. P. BENJAMIN,
Secretary of State.

HENRY HOTZE, Esq., etc.

DEPARTMENT OF STATE,
Richmond, December 27, 1864.

SIR: I have not written you since my circular of 10th October, having really nothing to communicate beyond what was conveyed to you by the President's message and the newspapers that have been forwarded. Your correspondence was unfortunately interrupted by the loss of the mail by the *Condor* and the prevalence of the yellow fever at the islands, so that with the exception of a brief letter from Paris of 8th August last, nothing was received from you till this month. Your several dispatches and duplicates have been received as follows, viz:

No. 69 of 8th August, original received 10th October, duplicate 8th December.

No. 70 of 24th August, original received 8th December, duplicate 28th December.

No. 71 of 13th September, original received 5th December, duplicate 30th November.

No. 72 of 26th September, original received 30th November, duplicate 10th December.

No. 73 of 20th October, original received 10th December, duplicate 27th December.

Your No. 69 was numbered both in original and duplicate as No. 59, but the error was so apparent that I did not hesitate to attach the right number to it.

In reviewing these dispatches I find nothing which requires special remark at present, the chief topic having been already fully treated in my No. 43 of 20th September. I therefore turn to another and very grave subject.

The Confederate States have now for nearly four years resisted the utmost power of the United States with a courage and fortitude to which the world has accorded its respect and admiration. No people have ever poured out their blood more freely in defense of their liberties and independence nor have endured sacrifices with greater cheerfulness than have the men and women of these Confederate States. They accepted the issue which was forced on them by an arrogant and domineering race, vengeful, grasping, and ambitious. They have asked nothing, fought for nothing but for the right for self-government, for independence.

If this contest had been waged against the United States alone, we feel that it would long since have ceased; that we had not miscalculated our power of resistance against the great preponderance of numbers and resources at the command of our enemies and that they would already have acknowledged the failure of their schemes of conquest. But we freely avow that when we engaged in the unequal struggle to which we committed our lives and fortunes we did not anticipate that the United States would receive from foreign nations the aid, comfort, and assistance which have been lavished upon them by the western powers of Europe. Conscious for reasons presently to be stated that we were fighting the battles of France and England, it could not enter into our calculation that one of the consequences of our action would be the abandonment by those two powers of all their rights as neutrals; their countenance of a blockade which, when declared, was the most shameless outrage on international law that modern times have witnessed; their closing their ports to the entry of prizes made by our vessels of war; their efforts to prevent our getting supplies in their ports; their seizure of every vessel intended for our service that could be reached by them; and their indifference to the spectacle of a people (while engaged in an unequal struggle for defense) exposed to the invasion not only of the superior numbers of their adversaries, but of armies of mercenaries imported from neutral nations to subserve the guilty projects of our foes.

I have said that we are fighting the battle of France and England, and it requires but little reflection to reach this conclusion. The sentiments of the people of the United States toward France and England have been known for too long a period to permit a doubt of the aggressive policy which will be pursued by the Northern Government on the first favorable occasion. No opportunity is lost by that Government for giving expression to the feeling prevalent in the country, not only among the masses, but among those placed higher in authority. Look at the contemptuous disdain of Mr. Lincoln's recent message toward France. Mark the insolent irony with which he caricatures the conduct of the Emperor in our war by declaring that in Mexico "the neutrality of the United States between the belligerents has been strictly maintained," and then consider the platform of principles on which Mr. Lincoln was elected, and the recent reprimand addressed to him and Mr. Seward by the vote of the House of Representatives, censuring them for their assurances to Mr. Drouyn de Lhuys in relation to Mexico, and it needs no sagacity to predict that, in the event of success in their designs against us, the United States would afford but a short respite to France from inevitable war, a war in which France would be involved not simply in defense of the French policy in Mexico, but for the protection of the French soldiers still retained by the Emperor Maximilian, under the treaty with him, for the maintenance of his position on the Mexican throne.

If we now turn to Great Britain, the revelations of the venomous hostility toward that power which exists at the North are still more striking. The insulting letter of Mr. Webb to the Brazilian cabinet, the rancor of Mr. Seward's response to Lord Wharncliffe, the debates of their Congress on the reciprocity treaty with Canada, the arrogant boastings of that portion of the press which specially represents the party in power, all point unmistakably to the existence of a desire on the part of the United States to engage in a war with England—a desire repressed solely, avowedly, by the necessity of concentrating the whole energies of the country for the effective prosecution of the war against us. The Administration papers in the United States, by their party cry of "one war at a time," leave little room for doubt as to the settled ulterior purpose of that Government to attack England as soon as disengaged from the struggle with us.

What is the present aspect of the war now waged in these States? Our seacoast is guarded by numerous fleets, against which we have been deprived of all means of defense by the joint action of France and England. On the land we are pressed not only by the superior numbers of our foes, but by armies of mercenaries, very many of whom come from British soil, and sail to New York and Boston under British flag. While engaged in defending our country on terms so unequal, the foes whom we are resisting profess the intention of resorting to the starvation and extermination of our women and children as a means of securing conquest over us. In the very beginning of the contest they indicated their fell purpose by declaring medicines contraband of war, and recently they have not been satisfied with burning granaries and dwellings and all food for man and beast. They have sought to provide against any possible future crop by destroying all agricultural implements, and killing all animals that they could not drive from the farms, so as to render famine certain among the people.

This condition of things taken in connection with the attitude of foreign powers can not but create the gravest concern in those to whom the people have entrusted the guidance of their affairs in a juncture so momentous. While unshaken in the determination never again to unite ourselves under a common Government with a people by whom we have been so deeply wronged, the enquiry daily becomes more pressing, what is the policy and what are the purposes of the western powers of Europe in relation to this contest? Are they determined never to recognize the Southern Confederacy until the United States assent to such action on their part? Do they propose under any circumstances to give other and more direct aid to the Northern people in attempting to enforce our submission to a hateful Union? If so, it is but just that we be apprised of their purposes, to the end that we may then deliberately consider the terms, if any upon which we can secure peace from the foes to whom the question is thus surrendered and who have the countenance and encouragement of all mankind in the invasion of our country, the destruction of our homes, the extermination of our people. If on the other hand there be objections not made known to us, which have for four years prevented the recognition of our independence notwithstanding the demonstration of our right to assert and our ability to maintain it, justice equally demands that an opportunity be afforded us for meeting and overcoming those objections, if in our power to do so. We have given ample evidence that we are not a people to be appalled by danger or to shrink from sacrifice in the attainment of our object. That object, the sole object for which we would ever have consented to commit our all to the hazards of this war, is the vindication of our right to self-government and independence. For that end no sacrifice is too great, save that of honor.

If then the purpose of France and Great Britain have been, or be now, to exact terms or conditions before conceding the rights we claim, a frank exposition of that purpose is due to humanity. It is due now, for it may enable us to save many lives most precious to our country by consenting to such terms in advance of another year's campaign.

This dispatch will be handed to you by the Hon. Duncan F. Kenner, a gentleman whose position in the Confederate Congress and whose title to the entire confidence of all Departments of our Government are too well known to you to need any assurances from me that you may place implicit reliance on his statements. It is proper, however, that I should authorize you officially to consider any communication that he may make to you verbally on the subject embraced in this dispatch as emanating from this Department under the instruction of the President.

I have the honor to be, very respectfully, your obedient servant,

J. P. BENJAMIN,
Secretary of State.

Hon. JOHN SLIDELL, etc., *Paris.*

P. S.—Kenner is delayed. You need not wait his arrival before acting.

No. 39.]   DEPARTMENT OF STATE,
Richmond, December 30, 1864.

SIR: Since my No. 38 of 20th September last, I am without any further intelligence from you than your No. 13 of 29th September, which was received on the 5th instant, and your letter from Leamington of 18th September, also received on 5th instant.

The boxes containing the press, etc., for the use of the seal of the Confederacy have not yet arrived, and I would be obliged if you will endeavor to have them traced, and that they be duplicated, if unfortunately lost, as I fear is the case.

I wrote yesterday to Mr. Slidell on the subject of our foreign relations in the following terms: *

I have, by instruction of the President, to request that you will
confer with Mr. Slidell on the subject and concert with him the
measures best adapted to elicit some decisive response from Great
Britain and France as to their intention in relation to this war,
after having freely conversed with Mr. Kenner and obtaining the
information which he will convey to you.

I have the honor to be, very respectfully, your obedient servant,

J. P. BENJAMIN,
Secretary of State.

Hon. J. M. MASON, etc.

No. 16.]   LONDON, *January 12, 1865.*

SIR: My last dispatch was my No. 15 of the 16th December ultimo.
Since then I have received nothing from the Department except the
duplicate of your circular of the 10th October, which was not received until the 4th January instant. The original has not reached
me.

I send herewith a duplicate of my No. 15, and as it refers to matters treated of in your circular of the 10th October, I enclose also
a triplicate of my unofficial note from Paris of the 29th November.
It may be stated here that I saw whilst in Paris, taken from the
Northern press, the circular referred to, and my visit to Germany
had in view to do what I could to carry out its object. Colonel Mann
will doubtless have informed you of the steps taken by him to give
it an extended circulation in Belgium and the German Provinces.
It was published here in all the leading journals.

I learned some two weeks since from Mr. Slidell that the French
Government had made a proposition to the British Government,
that each power should permit our prizes, having cargo, in whole
or in part claimed as property of the subjects of either, to be taken
for adjudication into the ports of either, respectively. So far, I learn
the only answer received was that it had been referred to the Crown
lawyers. In the very sensitive attitude held by the British Government toward the United States, manifestly afraid of incurring
the slightest risk of their displeasure, I have little idea that England will assent to the proposal. Its being equitable, just, and reasonable, will weigh nothing with her Majesty's Government against the
risk of possible rupture with the United States. In the Times of
yesterday you will observe an elaborate criticism by the noted
" Historicus" of the recent instructions issued from your Department for the governance of our cruisers in regard to neutral property found under the enemy's flag, and the converse. It is written
as you will find, in bad temper and spirit, with a threat of " punishment" by England, should the instructions be carried out in practice. The writer, as I learn, is Mr. Vernon-Harcourt, a barrister of
ability, and connection by marriage of the late Sir George Cornwall
Lewis, secretary for war; and who is now himself one of the Crown
lawyers, though not of the three officials who are the responsible
law advisers of the Government, his province being under official

---

* See Benjamin to Slidell, Dec. 27, 1864, preceding.

appointment, the adviser on questions that are of penal or criminal and not of a political character. But I think it would follow that on important questions of the latter class, he would be taken into counsel. I can not but think, therefore, that his paper in the Times is intended to be a vindication in advance of the refusal of the Government to the proposal from the French Emperor.

I have little to add to what I have heretofore reported in regard to matters in England. I see some of their public men from time to time, and have been kindly received at their homes in the country. They continue to express, and I am satisfied to feel, the same interest as ever in our success in the war; but I am not aware that there is any increased disposition, either with liberals or conservatives, to overrule the policy of the administration.

It may be as well to state that in a private note from Mr. L. Q. Washington, dated the 8th November, he informed me whatever dispatches were on board the *Condor* had been lost with Mrs. Greenhow. I had nothing on board that ship except a duplicate of my No. 12, of the 4th August, which, with some private letters, were in charge of the captain, with a request as Mrs. Greenhow was going direct to Richmond, that they should be handed to her on landing. The receipt of my No. 12 was acknowledged in your No. 38 of the 20th September, which is the latest I have from the Department.

In a note from Colonel Mann, dated Brussels, 5th instant, he says: "The Federal bonds are very buoyant, as well here as at Amsterdam and Frankfort, under the influence of the intelligence of our reverses in Tennessee and Georgia, but no new arrivals have occurred, nor are any likely to occur. The markets are quite as full as they will bear." The Federal Treasury, it would seem, admitting that hereafter its receipts in coin will be scarce equal to payment of interest in gold-bearing securities already issued, has determined to discontinue that form of security and to rely on a new issue, with interest payable in currency. This is a confession of weakness that I think must alarm bondholders in Europe. It is very certain that in England, and so far as I can learn everywhere in Europe with capitalists or fundholders, they can not place a dollar.

Mr. Slidell will have sent you, of course, the replies, so far as received, to our joint note communicating the manifesto of Congress to the European powers. They were sent to him because our note was transmitted by him through the embassies of those powers at Paris. So far three only have been received, and they have been published here, the sooner to reach our Government. They amount, as you will have seen, to nothing substantial, though it would appear from the Northern press that some forms of expression in the note of Lord Russell are strongly excepted to by the Yankees.

I have, etc.,

J. M. MASON.

Hon. J. P. BENJAMIN,
    Secretary of State.

No. 17.]   LONDON, *January 21, 1865.*

SIR: I avail myself of the mail via Halifax to Bermuda, leaving to-day, to send you herewith a duplicate of my No. 16 of the 12th January instant.

I have nothing to report of interest since that date, nor have I yet been able to learn what answer, if any, has been given by this Government to the proposal of France, mentioned in my last, for the admission of our prizes having neutral cargo into the ports of either power for adjudication. No answer has been received by the French Government so late as the 8th instant, as I learn by a note from Mr. Slidell.

In regard to what is said in my last dispatch about the strictures of "Historicus" through the Times, on the late instructions from your Department for the governance of our cruisers at sea, I observed in a few days afterwards an able and decided leader in the Morning Post, reviewing and condemning the positions assumed by "Historicus" and fully sustaining those taken in the instructions. A slip containing it, I understand from Mr. Hotze, was sent to you by the last mail via Nassau. The Post, as you are probably aware, is generally considered as the particular exponent of Lord Palmerston, which may give some significance to the article.

The rumors lately prevalent coming from the South of a purpose to increase our military force by arming a large body of slaves, sustained by a portion of the press there, and said to have the countenance of General Lee, has attracted much attention in England, and many enquiries have been made of me by our well-wishers whether I thought it would be done. It is considered by them with much favor as a measure carrying large auxiliaries to our armies, whilst in their opinion it would be a first step toward emancipation. I have answered that I had no doubt the matter was looked on at the South as a question of expediency only. That our people would have no fear of bringing our slaves into the field to fight an enemy common alike to them and to their masters, nor did I doubt that our slaves would make better soldiers in our ranks than in those of the North. Yet that there were strong objections which I thought would lead the Government not to resort to this reserve force unless it were considered necessary to bring our armies to some required standard. That the objections as they presented themselves to me were, first, that it would diminish our agricultural labor for a time, and secondly, that should it be thought incumbent after the war, to offer freedom to those who took part in it, great mischief and inconvenience would result from any increase in the number of free blacks amongst us; and thus, I thought the question would ultimately turn upon the enquiry whether the demand for men in the Army was sufficient to overcome the objections stated. I have thought it best to keep you au courant as to opinion here on a policy so interesting to us.

The signal and disastrous failure of the enemy off Wilmington came very opportunely to affect the current of opinion here in regard to our prospects after the successful march of Sherman and his possession of Savannah; with the reverses that seemed to attend the campaign of General Hood.

I have, etc.,

J. M. MASON.

Hon. J. P. BENJAMIN,
Secretary of State.

No. 18.]   LONDON, *February,** *1865.*

SIR: My last dispatch was No. 17, of the 21st January ultimo, of which I have the honor to send you a duplicate herewith.

I send also by Lieutenant Fitzhugh Carter, who bears this, an address by the Southern Independence Association, of Manchester, to the President. It will be seen from the names attached to the address that the association comprises a body of influential gentlemen. Should the President deem it proper to send a reply I shall be most happy in being the medium of communicating it.

I hear nothing since my last in regard to the proposal therein referred to, said to have been made by France to England for the admission of our prizes into their ports, having cargo on board, claimed as neutral, and much doubt whether anything will come of it.

We have heard with great concern of the capture of Fort Fisher and other defenses protecting the port of Wilmington, but our troops made a gallant and great defense, and whatever the loss to us, its conquest has been at great cost to the enemy. Yet, beyond the disaster, we are cheered and elevated here by the defiant tone of the South, with the renewed declaration of Congress that the war will be prosecuted to independence, at whatever cost or hazard. Public expectation has been much aroused in England by the reiterated reports from the North that peace was at hand, coupled with the late visits of Mr. Blair to Richmond and his alleged reception by the President. I have said in reply to enquiries that if these things meant a peace it would be on overtures from the North, resulting from its inability to continue the war, because their men had no longer any stomach for the fight and because of impending bankruptcy.

Notwithstanding our late disasters the Confederate loan maintains itself comparatively well, the last quotation being 55 to 56, when shortly before the fall of Fort Fisher it had fallen to 52–54.

Parliament meets to-morrow, but I have no reason to anticipate any modification in the policy of the ministry toward us. Still, as we have a large body of earnest friends and sympathizers in both houses, it may be that something will arise during the session of which advantage can be taken.

The port of Wilmington being no longer open, I fear that communication with home will be seriously impeded. I shall continue to write, nevertheless, by the mails to Bermuda and Nassau, under cover to our agents there, and by good private opportunities when they may offer.

I have nothing from the Department since the receipt of your circular of the 10th October, acknowledged in my No. 17.

I have, etc.,

                                      J. M. MASON.
Hon. J. P. BENJAMIN,
      Secretary of State.

No. 79.]   PARIS, *February 7, 1865*:

SIR: I am still without any of your dispatches of a later date than your No. 43 of 20th September. The occupation of Cape Fear River

----

* Date inadvertently omitted in original draft of the dispatch.

by the enemy will naturally lead to a more stringent blockade of Charleston, and I anticipate henceforth very great difficulty in my communications with the Department. I shall, in future, send my duplicate dispatches to Colonel Helm at Havana, thence to be forwarded either by Galveston or Matamoras, as he may deem preferable; this will be a very tedious and uncertain mode of conveyance, but I fear that there will soon be no other open to us.

The news from the Confederacy has of late been so unfavorable as to have produced, even among those most friendly to our cause, doubts of our ability to maintain our independence, and the prevailing disposition here and in London is to speculate upon the probable consequences of the reestablishment of the Union, and to look forward to difficulties in Mexico and Canada, with a strong conviction that those difficulties might have been averted by pursuing at the commencement of the war a course more friendly, or rather, I should say, more just to the Confederate States. For myself my faith in the ultimate success of our cause is unshaken, but I have hailed with delight the recent unanimous resolution of our Congress to continue the war until the enemy shall consent to treat with us on the basis of independence, because I had feared that there were elements of disaffection even there that might embarrass the President's action.

Peace rumors have been rife for some time past, but I had attached no consequence whatever to them until we received a few days since information of Mr. Blair's second visit to Richmond, and even now I feel entirely at a loss to divine what can be the object of his mission. The mystery must be solved in a few days. In the meanwhile I send you copy of a note just received from my friend at the affaires étrangères, as a matter of curiosity, that you may know how far the French chargé d'affaires at Washington has access to correct means of information. In his preceding dispatch of 16th January, of which I had a résumé from the same source, the chargé attributed Mr. Blair's first mission to Richmond to the fear of European intervention, at the same time saying that he had no information beyond public conjectures and suppositions:

MY DEAR SIR: We have some dispatches from Washington of January 24. Here summed up is what they contained. Mr. Blair arrived from Charleston, and departed two days after for the same city on a Government boat. President Davis responded to his overtures by an absolute refusal, because they were a question of the reestablishment of peace on the basis of a return to the Union. The conditions proposed are to be the following: Completely forgetting the past; solemnly recognizing the rights of the States engaged in the Confederacy; gradual abolition of slavery in allowing to each particular legislature to judge of its expediency and manner; evacuation by the Federal troops of Confederate territory; maintaining a separate army of her own organization; and the reunion of the two armies to engage in outside warfare.

After conferring with President Lincoln, Mr. Blair returned to Charleston carrying, without doubt, some new propositions. However, the general impression was that these conferences were not serious, and would not hold out on both sides, but were only to gain time. They are very much preoccupied here by the turn which feelings and things appear to have taken in the North, as much in regard to Mexico as with our own.

Always yours, my dear sir.

Mr. Chateau Renard is unwilling, on account of the ill-health of a member of his family, to proceed at present on his mission to Washington, and there seems to be no disposition on the part of the Government to place him "en demeure" for his hesitation, although I understand that the post has been offered to another person, who declines its acceptance. Should the rumored cession of Sonora, etc., to France prove true, Mr. [L. de] Geofroy will probably be the last representative of France to the Government of the so-called United States.

I have been unable to ascertain the truth of this rumor; many well-informed persons believe it, others who ought to be equally well informed are incredulous. I met the Mexican minister a day of two since immediately after my receiving a dispatch from London speaking of the cession as a fact. I asked him if he had heard of it; his manner satisfied me that he responded frankly when he said that he had not, but was confident that the report was untrue. The real state of the case I believe to be that a private agreement was entered into between Napoleon and Maximilian during the latter's visit to the Tuileries, that the usufruct and administration of Sonora and Lower California should be ceded to France, reserving to Mexico the " nue propriété " or titular sovereignty as a consideration for the establishment of Maximilian as Emperor and the guaranty of France of certain loans which it was necessary to contract.

Soon after Maximilian's arrival in Mexico he found that such a cession would be very distasteful to his new subjects, and endeavored to obtain a release from the obligation. The consequence has been somewhat angry recrimination between the two Governments. I am inclined to think that the matter is yet undecided, and that the rumor of cession is premature, but will be realized at no very distant day. It is difficult to account on any other hypothesis for the recent heavy advance of Mexican securities, which I have reason to believe has been produced by purchases in which persons having access to special means of information are concerned.

Insolent even to brutality as is the pretended apology of Seward to Brazil in the affair of the *Florida*, she can expect no support from either of the great naval powers in her attempts to vindicate her violated sovereignty. England desires to justify in future wars her disregard of neutral rights by precedents furnished by a power which was once their most earnest advocate, but aside from this motive the present ministry entertain the most malignant hostility toward Brazil for the very simple reason that they have treated her with the grossest injustice and indignity, injustice and indignity reproved by the universal sentiment of Europe. The Emperor, although as I believe he would not have refused to join with England in remonstrance against a violation of public law of which France has heretofore been and still ought to be the foremost champion, entertains no very friendly feeling toward a government which by three matrimonial alliances with the last fallen dynasty has forfeited all claim to any isolated or peculiar manifestations of his good will.

I look forward with interest, but with no sanguine expectations to the address of the Emperor at the approaching meeting of the legislature chambers; if his eye be intently fixed on the gold fields of Sonora, it will probably foreshadow some important change of policy in American affairs, but long before this dispatch can reach you you will doubtless have received through the Northern press the full text of this always significant communication.

I think that I can not deceive myself when I say that public opinion among the enlightened classes of Europe is now almost unanimously in our favor; it is certainly so in this country with the friends of the existing Government, but it can not but be gratifying to you to know that the three greatest celebrities, political and literary, of France, all in the ranks of the opposition, Lamartine, Guizot, and Thiers, share this feeling; I know this to be the case with the two first named, and I have very good grounds to believe it to be so with the last.

I have the honor to be, with great respect, your most obedient servant,

JOHN SLIDELL.

Hon. J. P. BENJAMIN,
  Secretary of State.

No. 81.]   PARIS, *February 24, 1865.*

SIR: The confidence which I expressed in my dispatch of 9th instant that the *Stonewall* would be permitted to make repairs and receive supplies at Ferrol has been justified by the event. Captain Page has received every proper attention and facility. In connection with this matter, I am informed by Count de Païva, Portuguese minister at this court, that Mr. Bigelow, Mr. Lincoln's chargé d'affaires, with whom he had no previous acquaintance, introduced himself a few evenings since at a soirée for the purpose of saying that the *Stonewall* would probably touch at Lisbon, and that in such case he hoped that the King's Government would not permit the vessel to receive the hospitality of the port. The minister replied that he had no information on the subject, but if Mr. Bigelow would address him a note respecting it, he would communicate it to his Government. The count has heard nothing further from Mr. Bigelow. I mention this incident, not because it has in itself any intrinsic importance, but as illustrating the meddling and undignified maneuvers of Yankee diplomatists.

As you will have seen by the newspapers before this can reach you, the Emperor in his discourse at the opening of the chambers, was entirely silent on the subject of American affairs. By referring to my No. 48, of 15th November, 1863, you will, I think, find in my comments on the absolute silence of the Emperor on the last similar occasion a solution of his motives which will apply with equal correctness now.

The Duke de Persigny, who, in his capacity of privy counsellor, was present at the meeting of ministers where the discourse was, as usual, read the day previous to its delivery, assures me that such were the reasons for not alluding to our affairs, strengthened by increased apprehensions of difficulty growing out of the Mexican question. In the report, however, on the situation of the Empire presented to the chambers, the American question is mentioned, as you will find very much in the same tone and spirit as in the report made in November, 1863. I annex the portions of the present report which relate to our affairs and to Mexico. I send you by this conveyance copies of the report on the situation of the Empire, and of the diplomatic correspondence communicated at the same time to the chambers. You will observe that the latter document does not contain a line on the subject of American affairs. This suppression of all correspondence on a matter certainly the most interesting and important of the day, shows the embarrassment and hesitation of the Government as to the proper course to be pursued in dealing with the contending parties.

On the 14th instant the second secretary of the British Embassy presented me a letter from Earl Russell directed to Messrs Mason, Mann, and myself, of which I annex a copy.* I immediately wrote to those gentlemen giving them copies of the earl's letter, and expressing the opinion that it was of a character demanding something more than a merely formal answer; that the terms of the answer required serious and mature consideration, and suggesting that we should meet for that purpose. They agreed with me in opinion and have been so kind as to come to Paris. It will not be possible to prepare the answer before the departure of Captain [John R.] Hamilton, of our Navy, by whom I forward this dispatch and the documents before referred to. We all agree, however, that the letter of the secretary for foreign affairs is extremely insolent and offensive, and I hope that you will not disapprove of the manner in which we intend replying to it.

I have the honor to be with great respect, your most obedient servant,

JOHN SLIDELL.

Hon. J. P. BENJAMIN,
Secretary of State.

No. 40.] DEPARTMENT OF STATE,
March 25, 1864.

SIR: I have barely time before departure of courier to forward for your information the foregoing copy of a recent correspondence between General Grant and General Lee.

I am respectfully, your obedient servant,

J. P. BENJAMIN,
Secretary of State.

Hon. JAMES M. MASON, etc., *London.*

[Enclosure.]

HEADQUARTERS, ARMIES OF THE UNITED STATES,
March 13, 1865.

GENERAL: Enclosed with this I send you a copy of a communication * from Earl Russell, secretary of state for foreign affairs, England, to Messrs. Mason, Slidell, and Mann. The accompanying copy of a note from the Hon. W. H. Seward, Secretary of State, to the Secretary of War will explain the object of sending it to you.

Very respectfully, your obedient servant,

U. S. GRANT,
Lieutenant-General.

General R. E. LEE,
Commanding Confederate States Army.

---

* See p. 1267.

[Enclosure.]

DEPARTMENT OF STATE,
Washington, March 8, 1865.

SIR: The enclosed paper has been received at this Department from Earl Russell, her Britannic Majesty's principal secretary of state for foreign affairs, with a request that facilities might be afforded for its passage through the military lines of the United States forces. I have to request that the paper may be sent forward to the lieutenant-general, with directions to cause the same to be conveyed to General Lee by flag of truce. I have further to request to be informed of the lieutenant-general's proceedings in the premises.

I have the honor to be, sir, your obedient servant,

WILLIAM H. SEWARD.
Hon. E. M. STANTON,
 Secretary of War.

[Enclosure.]

WAR DEARTMENT,
Washington City, March 9, 1865.

GENERAL: This Department has received from the Hon. William H. Seward, Secretary of State, a communication, a copy of which is hereto annexed, for your information. The paper referred to therein is enclosed herewith.

The Secretary of War directs me to request you to please cause it to be delivered to General Lee as requested and report your action to this Department.

I have the honor to be, your obedient servant,

C. A. DANA,
Assistant Secretary of War.
Lieutenant-General U. S. GRANT,
 Commanding Armies of the United States.

HEADQUARTERS CONFEDERATE STATES ARMIES,
March 23, 1865.

GENERAL: In pursuance of instructions from the Government of the Confederate States, transmitted to me through the Secretary of War, the documents recently forwarded by you are respectfully returned.

I am directed to say that the Government of the Confederate States can not recognize as authentic a paper which is neither an original nor attested as a copy, nor could they under any circumstances consent to hold intercourse with a neutral nation through the medium of open dispatches sent through hostile lines after being read and approved by the enemies of the Confederacy.

I have the honor to be, very respectfully, your obedient servant,

R. E. LEE, *General.*
Lieutenant-General U. S. GRANT,
 Commanding United States Armies.

No. 19.]   LONDON, *March 31, 1865*.

SIR: The last dispatch received was the duplicate of your No. 39, dated 30th December ultimo, consisting chiefly of a copy of your dispatch to Mr. Slidell, dated 27th December, of which he received the duplicate brought by Mr. Kenner.

In my No. 20, which accompanies this, you have a full account of the steps taken under it, and which I have thought proper to make the exclusive subject of a dispatch.

I annex hereto a copy of a letter addressed by Earl Russell to the three commissioners jointly, dated "Foreign office, February 13th," and also a copy of our joint reply, dated Paris, February 28.

This dispatch will be borne by Commodore Barron, who returns home via Texas, and, although subject to the delays of this circuitous route, I hope will reach you safely.

In a separate packet, also borne by the commodore, I have sent you the only parliamentary papers printed at this session relating to American affairs, with four copies of a pamphlet by Mr. John W. Cowell, recently published both here and in Paris; the latter as a French translation. The author, an English gentleman, one of our earliest and fastest friends, has written much on the side of the South in pamphlet form and for the public journals, all, including the pamphlet now sent, published at his own expense. I send these copies to you at his request. Please hand one to the President.

In the same packet I have sent a copy of a letter prepared at Paris as our joint reply to the letter of Earl Russell above referred to, but which was not sent; that annexed to this dispatch being substituted for it. When we assembled recently at Paris on the occasion of the letter of Earl Russell to us Mr. Slidell and I each separately prepared a form of reply, or, rather, his own had been drawn up when we met and mine prepared afterwards, our intention being to adopt the one or the other or to draft a separate one from the materials of the two, as might be considered best. Before this was done Mr. Kenner arrived with your dispatch of 30th December, when, after consultation, it was determined, inasmuch as a communication of a peculiar kind was to be made to the English Government, that it would be more prudent to avoid raising new issues with that Government immediately in advance of such a communication and to content ourselves with the general reply of which you have a copy herewith, referring his complaints for answer to our Government. We refrained also for the additional reason that without specific instructions our views or positions in answer to his complaints might embarrass the Government should they differ from our own. Mr. Slidell and I, however, agreed, the suggestion being his, that we should send you a draft of the reply we proposed, respectively, to ourselves in order to show how the matter was regarded by us.

I have been much concerned to learn that the two cases containing materials for the seal failed to reach you. One of them was bulky and heavy and contained the iron press. They were sent to Messrs. Fraser, Trenholm & Co., of Liverpool on the 5th July last, their receipt being acknowledged on the 8th, to be consigned to Major Walker at Bermuda by the mail steamer via Halifax in which Lieutenant Chapman having charge of the seal, sailed; and I particularly requested the latter to enquire for them on his arrival at Bermuda of Major Walker, and take them if he could, to the Confederacy. With such apparent safeguards, it is the more annoying they should have miscarried. Since receiving information of their loss I have requested Messrs. F., T. & Co. to trace them, if possible, through their correspondents at Halifax or Bermuda. Now that our Atlantic ports are closed, I do not see how the loss can for the present be replaced.

A few days since I received a letter from Mr. Abbott, counsel in Canada, for Lieutenant Young and others, claimed for extradition by the United States, with a case stated presenting those questions of law both public and domestic arising upon the evidence at the trial, accompanied by a pamphlet containing the evidence, then closed, and requesting that the case should be submitted for the opinion of Sir Hugh Cairns or other eminent counsel in England. He informed me that the judge before whom the case was pending had been taken ill, and said that the opinion might reach him if promptly given, before the decision of the court was rendered. He thought the leaning of the court was decidedly with the prisoners, but that the Provincial Government was as decidedly adverse, and anxious indeed for their rendition, and that if received in time, an opinion from so eminent a quarter in England would have a good effect.

I therefore lost no time in putting the case in the hands of solicitors to be presented to Sir Hugh, together with the letter of Mr. Abbott, with an urgent request that it should be acted on in time to be sent to Canada by the first succeeding mail. I was gratified to find that my request was acceded to. Sir Hugh took into consultation Mr. Reilly, a barrister of peculiar eminence in matters of international law, and I was invited to their consultation on the day following the submission of the case. The succeeding day I received their joint opinion in writing, which was full, clear, and conclusive on all the points submitted, chiefly that upon the proofs the acts of Lieutenant Young and party were unequivocal acts of war, committed under authority of an acknowledged belligerent, and so there was no crime in them; and again, if anything had been done by them in violation of neutrality, or of the domestic laws of Canada, such acts might make them amenable to punishment under those laws, but had no bearing whatever upon what they did in Vermont, and beyond the jurisdiction of Canada. This opinion I transmitted by the steamer of the 22d (the next succeeding), and I hope will be in time to attain its proposed object. The fees to counsel and solicitors, amounting to £56 18s. 10d., I have paid and charged to the contingent fund.

I have, etc.,

J. M. MASON.

Hon. J. P. BENJAMIN,
    Secretary of State.

[Enclosure.]

FOREIGN OFFICE, *February 13, 1865.*

GENTLEMEN: Some time ago I had the honor to inform you, in answer to a statement which you sent me, that her Majesty remained neutral in the deplorable contest now carried on in North America, that her Majesty intended to persist in that course.

It is now my duty to request you to bring to the notice of the authorities under whom you act, with a view to their serious consideration thereof, the just complaints which her Majesty's Government have to make of the conduct of the so-called Confederate Government.

The facts upon which these complaints are founded tend to show that her Majesty's neutrality is not respected by the agents of that Government, and that undue and reprehensible attempts have been made by them to involve her Majesty in a war in which her Majesty had declared her intention not to take part.

In the first place, I am sorry to observe that the unwarrantable practice of building ships in this country to be used as vessels of war against a State with whom her Majesty is at peace still continues.

Her Majesty's Government had hoped that this attempt to make the territorial waters of Great Britain the place of preparation for warlike armament against the United States might be put an end to by prosecutions and by seizure of the vessels, built in pursuance of contracts made with the Confederate agents. But facts which are unhappily too notorious, and correspondence which has been put into the hands of her Majesty's Government by the minister of the Government of the United States, show that resort is had to evasion and subtlety, in order to escape the penalties of the law; that a vessel is bought in one place, and that her armament is prepared in another, and that both are sent to some distant port beyond her Majesty's jurisdiction, and that thus an armed steamship is fitted out to cruise against the commerce of a power in amity with her Majesty.

A crew composed partly of British subjects is procured separately, wages are paid to them for an unknown service, they are dispatched perhaps to the coast of France, and there or elsewhere are engaged to serve in a Confederate man-of-war.

Now it is very possible by such shifts and stratagems, the penalties of the existing law of this country, nay of any law that could be enacted, may be evaded. But the offense thus offered to her Majesty's authority and dignity by the de facto rulers of the Confederate States, whom her Majesty acknowledges as belligerents, and whose agents in the United Kingdom enjoy the benefit of our hospitality in quiet security, remains the same. It is a proceeding totally unjustifiable, and manifestly offensive to the British Crown.

Secondly, the Confederate organs have published (and her Majesty's Government have been placed in possession of it) a memorandum of instructions for the cruisers of the so-called Confederate States, which would, if adopted, set aside some of the most settled principles of international law and break down rules which her Majesty's Government have lawfully established for the purpose of maintaining her Majesty's neutrality.

It may indeed be said that this memorandum of instructions, though published in a Confederate newspaper, has never yet been put in force, and that it may be considered as a dead letter. But this can not be affirmed with regard to the document which forms the next ground of complaint.

Thirdly, the President of the so-called Confederate States has put forth a proclamation claiming as a belligerent operation, in behalf of the Confederate States, the act of Bennett G. Burley in attempting in 1864 to capture the steamer *Michigan* with a view to release numerous Confederate prisoners detained in captivity on Johnsons Island in Lake Erie. Independently of this proclamation the facts connected with the attack on the other American steamers, the *Philo Parsons* and *Island Queen*, on Lake Erie, and the recent raid at St. Albans, in the State of Vermont, which Lieutenant Young, holding, as he affirms, a commission in the Confederate States Army, declares to have been an act of war and therefore not to involve the guilt of robbery and murder, show a gross disregard of her Majesty's character as a neutral power and a desire to involve her Majesty in hostilities with a coterminous power with which Great Britain is at peace.

You may, gentlemen, possibly have the means of contesting the accuracy of the information on which my foregoing statements have been founded and I should be glad to find that her Majesty's Government have been misinformed, although I have no reason to think such has been the case.

If, on the contrary, the information which her Majesty's Government has received with regard to these matters can not be gainsaid, I trust that you will feel yourselves authorized to promise on behalf of the Confederate Government that practices so offensive and unwarrantable shall cease and shall be entirely abandoned for the future. I shall therefore await anxiously your reply after referring to the authorities of the Confederate States.

I have the honor, etc.,

RUSSELL.

J. M. MASON, Esq., J. SLIDELL, Esq., A. D. MANN, Esq.

[Enclosure.]

PARIS, *February 28, 1865.*

YOUR LORDSHIP: The undersigned have the honor to acknowledge the reception of your lordship's note of the 15th instant.

They will, in conformity with its closing request, transmit a copy of it to their Government; and when they shall be furnished with instructions on the subject to which it refers, they will not fail to communicate them to your lordship.

In doing this, however, they consider it incumbent to record their protest against the general tone of your lordship's communication and especially against that portion of it, which, referring to a proclamation of the President of the Confederate States of America would seem to impugn the good faith of the President, by ascribing to him, in contradiction to the declarations of his proclamation: "A gross disregard of her Majesty's character as a neutral power, and a desire to involve her Majesty in hostilities with a coterminous power with which Great Britain is at peace."

As regards the other statements contained in your lordship's letter, the undersigned will at present, only say that they have every reason to be assured that one of them, that relating to the continued building by agents of the Confederate States within her Majesty's dominions of ships of war, is entirely without foundation; that as regards the other charges of your lordship, the facts are not, as they confidently believe, correctly stated, and that all your lordship's complaints of violation of her Majesty's neutrality are susceptible of satisfactory explanation by the Government of the Confederate States.

The undersigned have the honor, etc.,

J. M. MASON.
JOHN SLIDELL.
A. DUDLEY MANN.

The Right Hon. EARL RUSSELL,
Her Majesty's Secretary of State for Foreign Affairs.

No. 20.]   LONDON, *March 31, 1865.*

SIR: My No. 19 of this date goes with this. In that I acknowledge receipt of the duplicate of your No. 39 of 30th December ultimo, and that its counterpart to Mr. Slidell was received whilst I was in Paris. That gentleman will doubtless have advised you by the same opportunity with this of the manner in which he executed the instructions it contained. I am now to tell you of what I have done under the same instructions and the result.

I came to London for the purpose of an interview with the prime minister here, and soon afterwards, by a brief note from Mr. Slidell, was informed of his interview with the Emperor, who, he said, " is willing and anxious to act with England, but will not move without her." On the matter we had in reserve being suggested to the Emperor, he said that " he had never taken that into consideration; that it had not, and could not have, any influence on his action, but that it had probably been differently considered by England."

Some few days after the receipt of this letter, viz, on the 13th of March instant, I addressed a note to Lord Palmerston, presenting my compliments, and said that I had then recently received at Paris important dispatches from the Government of the Confederate States, the contents of which the President desired should be made known to the Government of her Majesty; and I asked the honor of an interview for this purpose. In a note from his private secretary the evening of the same day the latter said he was directed by Lord Palmerston, in reply to my note, to appoint the interview for the following day (the 14th) at Cambridge House, his residence. Immediately after the interview, and whilst the subject was yet fresh in my mind, I returned home and drew up minutes of the conversation, to which I had given the closest attention. I have the honor to annex hereto a copy of those minutes.

The occasion impressed me as one of great [delicacy, my extreme apprehension] * being that if the [suggestion were made in distinct form], which was the subject of [the private note to Mr. Kenner, no seal of confidence] which I could place on it would prevent [its reaching other ears than those] of the party to whom it was addressed; and it would thus [get to the enemy]. And if not [accepted] the [mischief resulting] would be [incalculable]. This difficulty I had freely canvassed with Mr. Slidell and Mr. Mann in Paris, who [fully shared in the apprehension]. Thus impressed, I

---

* Portions of this dispatch, as well as of the two following documents to which it refers included within brackets, were in the original in cipher.

hope the manner in which the subject was treated, as disclosed in the minutes of conversation appended, will meet the approval of the President and of your department.

From the general tone of the interview I felt it was impossible that the [minister could misunderstand my allusion] which was confirmed by the word he used in reply, as quoted in the minutes.

In all my conversations for the last three years, both in public and in private circles, whilst satisfied that their sympathies were entirely with us as a people struggling for independence; and whilst that many declared that such sympathy would be even stronger and more general were it not for the question of slavery, yet I was equally satisfied that the real impediment to recognition, and with both the great political parties, was, first, the fear of a war with the United States, and secondly, a tacit conviction in the English mind that the longer the war lasted in America the better for them, because of the consequent exhaustion of both parties. Whilst the recent conference with our commissioners in Hampton Roads was pending, and rumors thickened that a peace would result, it was manifest here that there was great apprehension that a war with England or France would follow a peace in America and that a war with either would involve both. It was in this light that I sought to impress on Lord Palmerston the views exhibited in the minutes of conversation as to a possible alliance between the two sections under a pressure of necessity on our part and from which we would at once be relieved by a European recognition. What I said to him as coming from the Emperor was derived from Mr. Slidell's late interview with him, and so reported to Lord Palmerston.

I have the honor to annex also, herewith, minutes of a recent conversation held with the nobleman named in the paper. He is a gentleman, really, of intelligence, thought, and of practical experience in what controls the mind and Government of England and for whose opinions I entertain great respect. Whether he be right or no as to what might have been done two years ago, his views strongly confirm mine, given in the minutes of conversation first above referred to, as to what can not be done now. At the time of our recent conversation this gentleman was entirely ignorant of the interview I had then recently had, or of what passed at it, and I doubt not is so still.

The present aspect of the war, when the armies appear concentrated on both sides in Virginia and the Carolinas, should we have, as we ardently hope, decisive successes, may restore that status, which, in the opinion of the nobleman whose conversation I have reported, would have enabled us to move successfully for recognition in the manner indicated in the dispatch and communications to which this is in reply. Should such occur it may be that a more favorable opportunity will be afforded again to approach the Prime Minister and to be more explicit. But, of course, I should do so only on full consultation with my colleagues.

I have, etc.,

J. M. MASON.

Hon. J. P. BENJAMIN,
Secretary of State.

[Minutes of a conversation held with Lord Palmerston, at Cambridge House, Mar. 14, 1865.]

Last night I asked for the interview by note to Lord Palmerston, which was appointed by him for 12 m. to-day.

I commenced the conversation by stating that a few days since, while in Paris, Mr. Slidell and I had received dispatches from the Confederate States Government, the contents of which it was deemed important by the President should be made known to the two Governments of Great Britain and France. As evidence of the importance attached to them by the President, they were sent by Mr. Duncan F. Kenner, of whose character and position I spoke.

I then read to Lord Palmerston the latter part of the dispatch; first giving the substance of its introductory clause, to wit, that the Government and people of the Confederate States deeply felt what they considered the injustice and the hard measure dealt to them by the two principal European powers; first in regard to the blockade, which for the first year or two of the war at least they considered had been respected by them in violation of the stipulations of the treaty of Paris; and secondly, in regard to the seizure of ships of war supposed to be intended for the Confederacy. That in this respect, whilst the markets of England were professedly open to both belligerents for the purchase of material of war, the South had been prevented from purchasing what it most needed, whilst the North obtained all it required. I told his lordship that these matters were adverted to in order to show the state of feeling resulting therefrom in the Southern States.

I here read from the dispatch commencing at the paragraph: " What is the present aspect of the war now waged in these States?" to its close, omitting, however, the last paragraph which begins: " It is proper, however, etc." I then reverted to that part of the dispatch which reads: " If there be objections not made known to us, etc.," which prevented our recognition, justice demanded that an opportunity should be afforded to meet, and if we could, to overcome them. And in this connection I stated to Lord P. that I was instructed to say that the Confederate States were so fully impressed with the belief that during four years of unexampled trial everything on their part had demonstrated their independence not only as achieved, but that they were able and determined to maintain it, that the President could not reconcile with the existing facts the persistent refusal of Great Britain to recognize us, unless there were some latent objection or hindrance which her Majesty's Government had not disclosed, but which yet governed its policy. If such were the case, had we not a right to know it in a matter so momentous to us? That, thus, if it stood a barrier to recognition we might remove it, if in our power to do so; and if not govern ourselves accordingly.

I remarked that the new aspect of the war had been long since looked to, and the present policy adopted as the result of our best military counsels. That the abandonment of the seacoast and concentration of our forces in the interior of the country, it was believed, would the sooner satisfy the enemy of the hopelessness of their efforts to subjugate us. But even should this policy lead to a war of endurance, our people were prepared for it with the nearest approach to unanimity. Such a war, whilst it would not under any fortune restore the Union, might bring the Southern States under engagements which otherwise they would equally abhor and condemn. I told Lord P. further, as the result of my own judgment and observation, and not as emanating from the Government, that I considered a peace within the power of the South, certainly after another campaign, should it consent to become a party to the aggressive policy of the North; nor could I say how far the law of necessity might control us, were the alternative presented of a continued desolation of our country, or a return to peace through an alliance committing us to the foreign wars of the North. In this connection I assured him that the statements of Mr. Seward in his letter to Mr. Adams of the 9th February, which were intended to import, rather than directly to assert, that such form of alliance was suggested by the Southern commissioners in the late conference as a basis of peace, I knew to be untrue; and as evidence of this I cited Mr. Benjamin's letter to Mr. Kenner, after the latter had left Richmond, wherein he stated that Blair on his second visit had assured the President that commissioners would be received to negotiate on the following basis, namely, " to leave all questions in dispute open and undecided, an armistice to take place; and a league offensive and defensive entered into to drive the French out of Mexico."

This form of proposition came from the North, and when the question of peace was discussed at the recent conference, the Confederate Commissioners may perhaps have adverted to it. I told Lord P. I made this correction with no view to propitiate, but as due to the South and to truth; that I was not prepared to say what the South might accept under the pressure of necessity; but that no such policy originated with the Confederate Government; and I here instanced the stipulation on the part of the colonies, under a somewhat like pressure, to guaranty to France her West Indian possessions as the price of the French alliance.

In recapitulation I again impressively urged Lord P. that if the President was right in his impression that there was some latent, undisclosed obstacle on the part of Great Britain to recognition, it should be frankly stated [and we might, if in our power to do so, consent to remove it].

I returned again and again during the conversation to this point, and in [language so direct that it was impossible to be misunderstood, but I made no distinct proposal in terms of what was held in reserve] under the private note [borne by Mr. Kenner].

Lord Palmerston listened with interest and attention while I unfolded fully the purpose of the dispatch and of my interview.

In reply, he at once assured me that the objections entertained by his Government were those which had been avowed, and that there was nothing (I use his own word) " underlying " them. He then proceeded to review the various points I had made, observing that it was not unnatural that the South should be sensitive, as was the North, in regard to the conduct of a neutral power; that with respect to the blockade, it might be that in the earlier stages of the war Great Britain might have taken exceptions to it, exceptions which she was not disposed to strain, as in future wars she was more likely to be a belligerent than a neutral. As regarded the purchase of material of war in her markets, it was considered that her statutes excepted from such purchase ships intended for war against a power with which she was at peace, and that the United States complained it was yet carried on against her in evasion of these statutes. As for the rest, whatever policy had been adopted by her Majesty's Government was that which deemed safest and best to preserve a strict neutrality. On the question of recognition, the Government had not been satisfied at any period of the war that our independence was achieved beyond peradventure, and did not feel authorized so to declare when the events of a few weeks might prove it a failure. He did not mean to assert that such would be the result in weighing probabilities, but that whilst the North continued the war to restore the Union on the scale it was now prosecuted, and with a purpose avowedly unchanged, there could be no such assurance in the result as, in the opinion of his Government, would warrant their recognizing a final separation. He gave this as the sum of the objections against our recognition, and added that, as affairs now stood, our seaports given up, the comparatively unobstructed march of Sherman, etc., rather increased than diminished previous objections. In the matter of a possible or probable alliance between the two sections for purposes offensive and defensive, he thought one could hardly take place, considering that the North was committed not to admit a separation.

In reply to these objections, I said to Lord Palmerston that he must be aware that the almost uncontested naval supremacy of the enemy, with the power to direct its entire force against any point along our coast, might well satisfy us that our own forces could be far better employed in the interior than against the enemy attacking by sea. The recent change therefore in our military policy was received at the South as encouraging, and although it might for a time open the lower country to the ravages of the enemy, our people were equal to that as to all previous sacrifices. As to the alliance suggested, his lordship might feel assured that the North would find itself under the sway of an imperious necessity, and it was looking to this necessity; that it was induced to take the initiative in the recent movement toward negotiations for peace. The strain upon its resources already, with the knowledge of our immense reserve force in the slave population, were monitions not to be disregarded. As for its committal against a separation, an alliance once determined on, the rest would be a matter of detail only.

I stated also to Lord P. that Mr. Slidell, in a recent interview with the Emperor, had communicated to him the substance of the dispatches I then adverted to, and that the Emperor had said in reply, that he was "willing and anxious to act with England, but would not, without her." That Mr. S. had then asked his Majesty if he could not renew his overtures to England, to which the latter replied that they had been so decidedly rejected he could not suppose they would now be listened to with more favor. I remarked that such was the language uniformly held by the Emperor whenever approached by our commissioner on the subject of recognition; and that thus the South understood that England was the obstacle to such action on his part.

Lord P. replied that it ought to be understood that France was equally free as England to determine her own policy, and they might perhaps differ in their views, but it would not be alleged that the latter had in any wise endeavored to influence the counsels of the former in this particular, or to bring them into harmony with her own.

I said this was not alleged so far as I knew, but that inasmuch as it appeared that France would not move without England, though "willing and anxious" to do so, and the latter declined to act, such an inference would seem to follow.

He replied that this could not be admitted, though the facts might be as stated. That if France desired to do an act in concert with England, in which the latter was not disposed to unite, her failure to do the act singly was her own affair, and for which England could not be held responsible.

The subject thus discussed, his lordship enquired about the present condition and prospects of the South, and said he presumed that even with our seaports in possession of the enemy, blockade runners would continue to find their way in and out of the numerous inlets of our extensive coast. In the course of our conversation expressions also fell from him implying that in such a struggle as the present his personal sympathies could only be with a people who sought alone the right of self-government.

Our conversation lasted for more than an hour, and on rising to take leave I expressed disappointment, or said rather, that the President would be disappointed to learn that he was mistaken in the impression that there was some operating influence that deterred her Majesty's Government from recognizing us which had not been made known to him. As matters now stood, there would remain no alternative but to continue the war until terms could be made with the enemy (probably of the character I had intimated) and from which we had hoped to have been relieved by European recognition.

To this he made no further reply than that he could not see how mere recognition without some other intervention could be of value to us; on the contrary he had always supposed such action would incite the North to still greater efforts.

I observed that upon recognition the North would be bound to admit that on the impartial arbitrament of the great powers of Europe it was waging war against an independent State. Their pretext of suppressing a rebellion which carried with it much moral force would thus be removed. But at any rate it was fair to presume that the parties interested could best appreciate the value and the effect of such a decision, and it was certainly clear that recognition was what the South most earnestly sought and the North most strongly deprecated.

His lordship here remarked that although there had been no formal recognition of the South in all the attributes of a political power, its acknowledgment as a belligerent was a disclaimer of anything like rebellion.

Lord Palmerston's manner throughout the interview was uniformly conciliatory and kind, and when I apologized for the time I had occupied he begged me to be assured he would always be glad to see me whenever I had anything which I desired to communicate to him.

It will be seen that I made no distinct suggestion of what the [President considered might be the latent difficulty about recognition] in the mind of the British ministry construing [the private instructions] in the letter [to Mr. Kenner] to require that [whilst intimations] should be given which would necessarily [be suggestive] to the prime minister, it was for every reason important that an [open proposition from us should be avoided,] and whilst there was no [committal on my part,] I do not doubt that Lord P. [understood to what obstacle allusion] was made; and I am equally satisfied that the most [ample concessions on our part] in the matter referred to, [would have produced no change] in the course determined on by the British Government in regard to recognition.

[Minutes of a conversation held with the Earl of Donoughmore, Sunday, Mar. 26, 1865.]

I called at his residence on the evening of the above date, as occasionally in the habit of doing. I have known this gentleman perhaps more intimately than any other of his rank in England, and have always found him a fast and consistent friend to our cause.

Our conversation opened by an enquiry from him as to the prospects of the war, he expressing great concern at the apparent weakness of the South, as evinced by Sherman's unimpeded march through Georgia and into the Carolinas, and its depressing effect upon public opinion in England, and remarked that [but for slavery we should have been recognized two years ago].

I told him that in my former intercourse with the Government here, as well as among our friends in and out of it, whilst fully aware that [slavery was deplored] among us, I had never heard it suggested [as a barrier to recognition].

He replied that, in his opinion [it had always been in the way], and that after Lee's successes on the Rappahannock and march into Pennsylvania, when he threatened Harrisburg, and his army was at the very gates of Washington [he thought but for slavery] we should then have [been acknowledged].

I told him that what he said interested me greatly as giving new impressions and asked him, suppose [I were now to go to Lord Palmerston and make a proposition] to wit, that in the event [of present recognition,] measures would be taken satisfactory to the British Government, [for the abolition of slavery, not suddenly and at once,] but so [as to insure abolition] in a fair and reasonable [time; would his Government then recognize us?]

He replied that the time had gone by, now especially that our fortunes seemed more adverse than ever.

[Lord D.], as you are aware, was a member of the late Derby Administration and will doubtless be so again should his party come into power. Looking to this contingency, I enquired further, should such an event happen and [the same proposition be made then] what would be [the answer?]

He replied, we should be obliged as affairs now stand [to make the same.]

He then went on to declare that whilst he always strongly participated [in the feeling against slavery,] he must admit that his opinions so far as regarded [its status in the South,] had been much modified by information derived through events of the war.

This gentleman is a thorough Englishman of his class, and an able and enlightened man, of liberal views.

No. 21.]   London, *May 1, 1865.*

Sir: Captain Maury, who sails to-morrow in the steamer for Havana, will bear this dispatch; and I have the honor to transmit to you herewith duplicates of my Nos. 19 and 20, each dated 31st March ultimo, with the documents thereto pertaining. The originals of all these were sent by Commodore Barron, who left here a month ago by the same route. As Captain Maury expects to go via Texas (the only route now open) it will be some months before he can reach the seat of Government, wherever that may be established. I shall hope before then to be again in communication with the Government, and thus what I might write now in regard to late events would be of little interest. I shall only say, therefore, that the evacuation of Richmond and surrender of Lee has produced the confident belief here, and throughout Europe generally, that further resistance is hopeless and that the war is at an end, to be followed on our part by passive submission to our fate. I need not say that I entertain no such impression and endeavor as far as I can to disabuse the public mind. The proclamation of the President at Danville, of which as yet we have the substance only, has not had the effect to reassure. It is the only report we have had from the Government since the above calamitous events.

The assassination of Lincoln and attempt on the life of Seward, as was to be expected, produced a great shock to all classes of society here, and public meetings have been held in London and other parts of the kingdom expressing indignation and abhorrence of the deed without, however, tingeing their resolutions with any partisan hue. Together with the usual telegraphic accounts came a dispatch from Mr. Stanton to Mr. Adams giving an official version of the event. I felt it incumbent on me at once to reply to his charge of its being a rebel conspiracy, intended to aid their cause. I have the honor to enclose printed copies of both papers. My letter was published in all the London journals.

In the uncertainty of the future, or of what may be the views of the Government relative to the continuance of commissioners or other agencies abroad, I can only remain where I am and await its orders; and, however desirous to be at home to contribute to our great cause, whatever it might be in my power to do there, or to give aid and protection to my (I fear) distressed family, I shall act accordingly.

I have, etc.   J. M. Mason.

Hon. J. P. Benjamin,
  Secretary of State.

INDEX.

---

* Formerly steamer Calhoun.

---

*Same as Blanche, which see.   † Also known as Japan and Virginia.
‡Formerly C. S. privateer; afterwards Theodora

*Known also as Virginia and C. S. S. Georgia.

1306

Lloyd's. Mentioned.. 348
Locke, Vernon G. Mentioned........................... 1043, 1044, 1095, 1096
Loftus, A. Lord. Mentioned... 262
Lomax, Lundsford L. Mentioned....................................... 166
London, England.
Hotze, Henry, appointed commercial agent at......................... 117, 293
Macfarland, James E., appointed secretary of legation at.............. 112
Lone Star, Schooner. Mentioned....................................... 549
Long, ——. Mentioned.. 1117
Longstreet, James.
Mentioned... 539, 780
Resolutions of thanks of C. S. Congress to.......................... 170
Lopez, Narcisso. Mentioned... 16
Lord Lyons, British schooner. Mentioned............................. 413
Loring, William W. Mentioned... 540
Lothian, Marquis of. Mentioned....................................... 962
Louisa Hatch, American ship. Capture of, April 4, 1863............. 841–845
Louisiana, C. S. S. Mentioned.. 462
Louisiana Troops, Confederate. Resolutions of thanks of C. S. Congress to.. 159
Love Bird, Ship. Mentioned.............................. 959, 968, 970, 977
Lovell, Mansfield. Mentioned...................................... 396, 462
Lovet, American schooner. Mentioned.................................. 412
Low, John. Mentioned... 1049
Lowe, Robert. Mentioned.. 1088
Loyall, Benjamin P. Mentioned.. 18
Lubbock, Francis R. Mentioned.................................... 556, 558
Lucien, Abbé. Mentioned.. 1087
Ludlow, William H. Mentioned.................................... 139, 140
Lynch, P. N.
Appointed special commissioner to the States of the Church........... 172–174
Correspondence with President, C. S................................ 172
Mentioned..................... 11, 1147, 1148, 1160, 1162, 1243, 1244, 1246, 1247
Lyndhurst, Lord. Mentioned.. 948
Lynn, Arthur. Mentioned.. 12
Lyons, Lord. Mentioned................... 316, 326, 355, 357, 380, 395, 398, 419,
421, 422, 449, 453, 456, 480, 490, 495, 496, 526, 551, 561, 566,
601, 630, 634, 644, 688, 713, 751, 788, 797, 798, 827, 835, 837,
845, 887, 892, 924, 928, 1083, 1085, 1107, 1154, 1207, 1219
Macauley, ——. Mentioned... 727
Macauley, John L. Mentioned.................................. 727, 766, 781
McCall, George A. Mentioned.. 466
McCarrick, J. W. Mentioned... 18
McClellan, George B. Mentioned..... 135, 171, 279, 430, 456, 459, 466, 479, 488, 517,
538, 539, 541, 542, 548, 550, 553, 1149, 1204, 1217, 1219, 1220, 1227, 1238
McCloskey, Father. Mentioned... 739
McClung's battery, C. S. A. Resolution of thanks of C. S. Congress to...... 164
McCulloch, Ben.
Death of.. 131
Mentioned... 377, 378, 416
Resolution of thanks of C. S. Congress to.......................... 107
McDowell, Irvin. Mentioned....................................... 538, 542
McDowell County, Va. Martial law extended over.................... 132

---

* Afterwards C. S. S. Florida.

1316

1318 INDEX.

1328

1330

---

* Formerly C. S. privateer Gordon.

* Name changed to Harkaway.

---

* Called also Japan and C. S. S. Georgia.

○

www.ingramcontent.com/pod-product-compliance
Lightning Source LLC
Chambersburg PA
CBHW020241030726
47499CB00001B/10